Eightsome Reel

Magda Sweetland was born in 1943 in Edinburgh, where she was educated and brought up. She now lives in the south of England. *Eightsome Reel* is her first novel.

Magda Sweetland
Eightsome Reel

Pan Books
in association with Macmillan London Ltd

The characters in this novel and their
actions are imaginary. Their names and experiences
have no relation to those of actual people,
living or dead.

First published 1985 by Macmillan London Ltd
This edition published 1986 by Pan Books Ltd,
Cavaye Place, London SW10 9PG
9 8 7 6 5 4 3 2 1
© Magda Sweetland 1985
ISBN 0 330 29385 0
Printed in Great Britain by
Richard Clay (The Chaucer Press) Ltd,
Bungay, Suffolk

The extract from 'The Love Song of J. Alfred Prufrock' is taken
from *Collected Poems 1906–1962* by T. S. Eliot and is reproduced
here by kind permission of Faber and Faber Limited.

The publisher acknowledges subsidy from the Scottish Arts
Council towards the original publication of this work by Macmillan London Limited.

Part one

1

It was November. November in Edinburgh meant a biting north-easterly wind cutting through the fog which blew up from the firth of Forth, so the atmosphere in the streets of the city was damp and dry in equal parts, a combination locals know as raw weather, and fear because there is no sheltering from it. Seagulls came inland. They congregated near the outlets where the many springs that rose among the Pentlands flowed into the channel of the Forth, merging fresh and salt water in one. All along the coast the birds screamed and wheeled, fighting over the effluent from tugs and barges, or small fishing vessels that lay moored on the mud flats left by the outgoing tide. It was a high-pitched sound which was cut now and then by the muffled blast of a ship's hooter somewhere down the estuary on its way to the sea.

Esme came out of the over-heated wards of the hospital and, meeting the chill blast, shivered and fastened up her coat. She'd managed to shake off the matron and the sister who kept running after her with pieces of paper to sign as next of kin, then found she was under age and couldn't. Names, dates, other next of kin she was asked to dig out of a distant past. She queried the official forms, but gave way when they insisted they must all conform to regulations. The hospital administrator was called for and it was an hour before she was able to get clear of them and be alone, to think.

She stood at the top of the steps and looked along the road that linked the quays and landing stages on the coast. She was only half a mile from home but the familiar things she saw around her had taken on a strangeness so that she felt she did not know really where she was. Something had been thrown over them, making the streets and people walking in them seem removed, remote. Or maybe something had changed in her perception, a shift in stance that angled her viewpoint. She hesitated, the way a hibernating animal must do when it has been dormant for a time and surfaces again, dazed by the differences and the intervening gap of consciousness which memory does not span; or the migrant bird so intent on making progress on the wing that it loses direction and flies off course.

She tried to relocate herself in time, adjust, veer to reality. She wondered what time of day it was, re-establishing circadian precision. She looked up at the sky but it gave back no clues. It was a form of twilight that settled in the city streets, but it could have been an early morning grey or the onset of night which made the light dim. Near her a scavenger was working, sweeping up the leaves, concrete proof that the moment fell within the range of labour and even as she watched, his hour struck. He packed up and went home. He pushed his metal trolley up the road ahead of him, ignoring the mounds he'd been collecting during the afternoon. Tomorrow was soon enough. Even the action of the trolley rolling past undid them and insidiously they broke up like cairns pelted by weather. Why did he bother? There were more leaves in the city parks than he could ever trap and every minute more fell to the ground, mocking his efforts.

The trees during her absence had turned skeletal and bare. At night in the hospital, she'd heard the first autumn storms break and knew, as the wind tore across the rooftops, catching on slates and flues, that it meant their own roof was under threat. But she hadn't connected the fact with a visual image and so the marked contrast between bare and foliated trees took her by surprise, denoting the largest alteration. Without warning, the season had started on its descent into the winter solstice. The clocks had changed. She hadn't noticed that slight shift in the constant penumbra of the hospital, but it made a difference to the appearance of the time of day, and the season overall, as it made its dejected advance to midwinter and the shortest day. It was technically, more than in actual fact, winter time. One hour. A single week undermined her chronology.

The minutes passed. She stood immobilised, wondering where to go and what to do, who to tell first. Behind her a factory siren sounded. It was going home time. In a few minutes the streets would be crowded. The queues at bus stops would lengthen as men and women after a day's work huddled their way through the early evening dark to fires, gas stoves, even a welcome from some other human being.

And on instinct she joined them, heading home.

The shopkeepers as she passed tidied away the business of the day. Some were busy with mops and cloths ready for a fresh start in the morning, dousing their windows with a bucketful of water and sweeping the splashings over the pavement and under her feet, forcing her to step aside. Others hoped for a late customer, the tardy or slack housewife running out to the shops before they closed for a bit of something for the dinner. Forced out of the natural rhythm of her day, she joined them, remembering that there was likely to be no food indoors. She looked at fish and looked at meat but could not take to either, when they were remaindered flesh.

Crossing the road, she reached the public library and with a spasm of guilt remembered all the other things she'd let slide while her mother's illness occupied them both. Mechanically, she walked in and went through the turnstile. She moved on but she didn't know what she was looking for because, for a while, she couldn't focus on where she was in relation to her studies. Words and titles came to her in a blur, like pages blown in a wind. Where had she reached, exactly? She thought there was an essay pending, a reference book overdue. She imagined that at home the hallway would be strewn with reminders from the daily visits of the post-man. She calculated the fine then dismissed it. That had been neglected, like everything else, from haste.

Above her head rows of bookshelves towered, six feet into the chamber. The top shelf was well above her reach, but rubber-topped stools spaced out the gangways and she balanced on one of these. What was she looking for? Something . . . She ransacked her brain. Some title eluded her in its furthest recesses. Something to do with Shakespeare – the problem plays? She simply couldn't remember, for it seemed unimportant. It would have to wait. She'd have to consult her notes to tell her what she was learning. Her glance slewed down the racks. So much to read and she reflected grimly that even as she dithered here, undecided, a scholar was putting the last word to yet another tome. A thousand books accused her for her indolence. Unread, they were a blank and impenetrable wall. And worse, the fact that several genera-tions of students had been here before her, and thumbed the books into fragility, worn away the lettering on the spine and made pencil jottings in the margin here and there, was reinforcing evidence of her slackness. Read, concentrate, study, the successful told her. Well, I can't, she replied. I'm tired and hungry and I must go home.

'Couldn't you find what you wanted?' the librarian asked with seeming concern, but her eyes peered into Esme's bag and wide pockets in case she'd filched a book.

She shook her head and submitted herself to the buffets of the wind, funnelled between buildings. Food, she thought, and slowed outside the dairy.

'Miss Rosowicz? It is Miss Rosowicz?'

The owner of the dairy, or rather his son who continued in business alongside his father, came outside to shift milk crates. Finding her beside him, he spoke up, not noticing that she had not noticed him. 'I heard your mother's been taken into hospital. We're all very sorry. You will give her our best wishes. Perhaps you're going down to visit her?'

Esme hesitated. He hadn't heard then. How could he have heard? She'd come from the bedside this last hour. It was idle to think that bereavement displayed itself like a visible scar, warning the onlooker. And, considering how to formulate the words, she followed him inside the shop.

At close quarters, the man was disappointed in the person of the girl. Mother and daughter were thought of as rare women in the area. The rarity was due partly to their actual appearance, but also to the legend which the large but dispersed family had created in the neighbourhood, going back a century, and their present con-fined and solitary existence in the big house hidden in its garden. No one could understand why they lived there, or indeed how. Twelve rooms for two women, and upwards of an acre of ground. Peculiar. Certainly the mother was a local landmark, an acknow-ledged beauty that men came discreetly to their doors and windows to watch in passing. She had flaming red hair that defeated her best efforts to anchor it. He'd often seen it start to fall down her back as she went about her shopping, or crossed the road to the library or the bus stop, and watched as she pegged it up with a sideways inclination of the head to the left while the right hand searched through the hair, for grips and combs. The daughter was a less gorgeous creature, and no such exuberance crowned her head. She wore her hair short, cropped like plumage to the line of her scalp and he thought her features were too bold, the eye too challenging for femininity.

'Perhaps you'd like to take her something at visiting time?' His eye roamed the shelves and his hand went forward to a box of chocolates.

Esme panicked. She didn't have enough money in her purse to pay for that, and was about to refuse it outright when it struck her that it might have been meant as a gift. But why should a stranger choose to make such a lavish gesture? Either way she would be ashamed, to show an almost empty purse, or greed. And, after all, it was taking under false pretences. She wondered how she, or anyone, could speak the words. How did one begin to give death a context in the everyday – she died; in spite of everything she died – she phrased it to herself and rehearsed the man's reaction. Shock. He would be shocked and ask for details, names, dates and next of kin. She thought she could not bear the expression of the man's dismay and sympathy, heaped on her own. She felt she could not open her mouth to say the words, not here in the middle of the petty groceries of life.

So instead she said, 'No. I don't think I will take anything today.'

He stopped in his effusions, feeling rebuffed. 'My father would have liked to give something.'

But how could she accept it now that it was demonstrably a present? That was even more grasping. She should have made it plain to begin with, but was forced to go on complicating a false position when the situation between them was irretrievable.

'What I would really like, what I came in for,' she said to extricate herself, 'is to buy half a dozen eggs, those free-range eggs that come from the farm at Dirleton.'

'Yes, very nice for someone convalescing.' He disappeared into the back shop and put six brown eggs into a paper bag for her. He was mollified at being given something to do, but still she would not allow him to make a donation and put her coins down insistently on the counter before resuming her journey home.

She took the shortest route, crossing the road and turning right at the junction. She did not need to measure the distance or look where she was going. She could have walked it blind, so that her feet fell automatically into the pattern of the pavements, anticipating a kerb or turn on reflex. She'd paced it out almost every day for twenty years, wearing her own groove in the sets.

As the shop lights died, one by one, those in the houses sprang up. Bedrooms, attics, sculleries were illuminated for a second before the curtains were drawn by unseen hands and the evening settled in. The big house where she was headed stood separate behind a screen of trees, and was shrouded in darkness. Its neighbours leaked light, life, a trail of music or the six o'clock news from behind closed doors but the house standing apart in the centre of its garden was poised on a different dimension. It had come adrift from time or space, and entered the eternal.

She walked up the driveway to the porch and under the shadow of its pillars. This was her grandfather's house and his before him, handed down as far as her, its last inhabitant. She approached it with a huge sense of responsibility. It was a building marked on ancient maps, once grand, but slipping tile by tile into desuetude. Her grandparents, Rab and Hannah, kept house in the old way. He was the eldest of his brothers and when their father died, they stayed on, importing their wives as he did, and their firstborn. Some left. Some came to take their places. This was a pattern repeated by his own children eventually, so that there grew up an enormously extended family who had had some association with the house. There was always room for someone's sick aunt or widowed mother. It was a house where every traveller was welcome, where the door was never shut. A dozen at table was routine, and double that far from exceptional.

They attracted more from outside. It was the house where neighbourhood children met by course, becoming its own playground, thronged with visitors. They came to take turns on its single swing, hooked into the horizontal branch of a beech tree, when they were given the run of grounds and greenhouses as well. The orchard with a hundred trees, pear, plum, quince and apple in a medley, was a daily adventure; climbing frame, tent, ammunition for pitched battles, the arena for a theatre – it was all of them. There was no bar to where they went. No hand stayed them.

Esme compared herself with these exterior children and discovered an important difference. They returned to one father and one mother in one house and did not live in this agglomeration of aunts, uncles, cousins, grandparents. They observed definitions and boundaries, went to visit, sent greetings cards and other such niceties which, when you lived on top of one another in layers, seemed superfluous. This family into which she had been born was novel, she observed, and her own place in it was unique. True, there was her cousin Aileen, older by some months, but she lived with her parents in an entirely normal fashion somewhere in the Highlands. She sensed that her strange position in the household was due to being tacked on between the end of one generation and the start of the next. The youngest of her uncles was her near contemporary, Rab and Hannah were more like her parents than her grandparents, her mother more a sister, and all known to her by their Christian names, so that even the basic distinctions were muted in Esme's mind by a lateral familiarity. They were people before they were relations. She paid less regard to title and seniority than she might.

This changed little by little. The district became unfashionable, inconvenience being given as the excuse. People drifted south or escalated to the fine purlieus of the New Town. The family moved on and out, buying better real estate until she and her mother Rhona were left at last, keeping up appearances in the huge place that drained their resources without a return of comfort or joy. A death or a removal emptied rooms. They let out rooms to boarders but boarders complained of cold or draughts, and left. Her mother was reclusive by nature, however flamboyant in appearance, and she could not maintain this breadth of hospitality. She shut her own doors and retreated.

Esme let herself in. She hadn't anticipated how cold it would be inside. A week without any form of heat had permeated the stone walls. It was a chill that was deep and intense compared with the almost bracing exhilaration of the wind outdoors. The air was damp and stagnant. She was inclined to throw open the windows and remove the stale, exhausted atmosphere, but common sense prevailed. That would have to wait until the morning.

She stopped to rummage through the letters. A get well card from a neighbour, superfluously sent, a gas bill she couldn't pay but only one reminder from the Reading Room.

She kept her coat on, going down a flight of stone steps to the scullery. The kitchen was like a mausoleum. It was inconveniently placed and never quite clean because it sided the garages and dust

11

filtered through the loose-fitting windows that should have been replaced years before, if anyone had thought about it. The dust was thick on ledges. She did not feel inclined to stir it. In the fluorescent glare, the room was as inhospitable as a barn. She half filled the electric kettle and took it upstairs to the front room, where she could boil it with an egg inside, and toast some of the petrified bread she had found, in front of the gas fire. She dug herself into cushions on the floor and ate. The glow from the fire was enough. The cold, the dark, the solitariness might have deterred less independent spirits than hers but for Esme the echoing house held no specific fear, when it was peopled by her ancestors.

Until, that is, she put her hand up to the tray and came across the cups. Two cups sat on the tray, and one evoked an absence. She brought her hand up to her mouth, aghast at such forget-fulness and thought, How long will I go on laying the table for two? How long will it be before my head stops accommodating more than myself? The empty space at her side suddenly became defined, the chair declared itself to be eternally vacant, although, in the corner, its cushion retained some impression as though it would not be long before she came back and sat in it again.

But even that she had not managed to ensure.

'Speak to her,' said the doctor. 'Sometimes they surface for a while.'

'What shall I talk to her about?'

'Anything. Everyday things. Sometimes the small things get through. Or the voice can comfort them.'

So her recital began, endless days and nights of it. She talked the sun up and down again. She talked about the house and all the people who had lived in it, gave her the latest news about them and what each was doing in his own successful way. She spoke about the garden getting out of hand and how they would have to hire a man to see to it, clear some of the shrubbery that had started to impinge on pathways. She described the weather, the view outside the window, or the view inside. She outlined what they would do tomorrow and even talked about the essay and the problem plays. Then when all else failed, things done, said, shared experience, read her the newspapers in despair.

But never a word got back. Nothing. Not a murmur, not a

flicker. At the end of many shapeless days, they pronounced her clinically dead and Esme was overwhelmed by the futility of speech. She wondered what form of words she should have used, convinced that there was something more she could have done to reach her. Just one, perhaps, to trigger the recall. One missing word she had not found that would have stopped her slipping away, and she would always wonder what it was.

She remembered coming out of the drive one day, and finding a group of maybe twenty rooks gathered on the road. One of them, a young bird, had been run over by a car and, though they did not know it, was already dead. The others shielded it, hovering and landing. There were so many of them, making up a dense cloud, that later cars had to slow down to avoid them. Their wings bated in the air and all the time they went on calling, calling noisily, willing it to rise. She could not bear to watch such misplaced faith and walked away. At what point would they leave it, sensing mortality? And how long would it be before they forgot, or did they never forget? The act was so powerfully wrong that they would threaten their own existence to put it right. She walked away, but heard them hoarse with crying, as she was, trying to find the utterance that could resurrect the dead.

She lay prostrate on the ground, like a penitent before an altar waiting for remission. Immobility was the expression of her grief, a still centre she tried to hold in the middle of a vortex. Others rolled, threshed, wept tears. What a relief it would have been to be so obvious, to be so clamant for oneself. She lay full length with the weight of the house pressed on her, four storeys high. Too much. It was too much to cope with on her own. It was the rapidity of the descent that struck her, the swiftness of decay that made her responsible for arresting it and accused her when she could not.

She went upstairs at last, remembering there were things to be done for the uptake of normality. On the half landing was an oriel window, facing west, and it was out of this that she saw the first rocket explode. Or rather she heard the sound and, glancing out, was in time to catch sight of a burst of sparks and follow with her eye the descent of the flare. At first she thought it was a distress signal from a ship in the Forth, coming without warning from what was by this time a blackened sky. But then another one went up overhead, showering sparks, and then a third followed the same erratic course, trailing colours behind it like the dust cone of a comet, or the ribbons on a kite, higher and higher until it exploded and collapsed back to earth. The noise and the surprise of the flare jolted her. She had forgotten it might be the fifth of November. That was the date, then. And other people celebrated still. It startled her into the present. There were things to do, weren't there? There would have to be a notice in the *Scotsman* and a visit to the minister, and phone calls to the family and some sort of reception after the funeral. All by herself. She racked her memory for some detail about funerals, but the distant burials of Rab and Hannah had left no impression on her, shielded by youth. She could not recall anything practical. She realised that at heart she wanted someone to come and help, come and remove some of the burden of arranging it all, but abandoned the idea at once. It was not anyone she knew.

She went on up from the half landing to the first floor and was on her way to the top of the house, which was her private sanctuary, when she heard the door bell ringing far below. The house was totally black. No one would know that she was here; who was there to know anyway? She waited breathlessly, wondering what unexpected visitor this was. From the front windows she could overhear the sound of children's voices in hurried consultation. They rang again. But still she did not move towards them. Emboldended by the dark interior of the house, one of them pushed open the letterbox and yelled with pent-up force. The words were meaningless, distorted by the method of their transmission through the aperture and the curling echo in the empty house. After this display of bravery they scampered away from the entrance porch until she saw in the street lamps that they were a troupe of guisers extending the legitimate period of their activity from Hallowe'en to embrace the Gunpowder Plot. They were an assortment of moving scarecrows, faces horribly daubed with red and black, while in front they pushed a battered pram in which the smallest of their number bumpily rode. Frustrated by getting no reply, they took an easy revenge. And Esme too fell into vengeance, hurling the words 'Keelies – Tinkers – Riff-raff' after them in thought.

As their laughter faded, she reached the attic which was less shadowy than the rest of the house because its openness to the air admitted the light from the houses opposite as well as the illumination of the clock face on the church tower at the corner of the street. She pulled back the inward facing windows of the coom-ceiled landing whose deep sides sheltered her from the invading wind, and breathed in the salt tang carried from the Forth. As she looked directly north, the intervening houses between this one and the water of the inlet were obliterated by the gardens and their screen of trees. She was so high, and this sensation was particularly heady when she was four or five and had to balance on the sill to see the distant Forth at all, that she might imagine herself as weight-less, as unimpaired as a bird, looking down on treetops, roofs, people with an aerial superiority. They were rooted and attached. She was free. They walked: she soared. Beyond this middle distance there was a vacant space defined by the wavering line of bright street lamps. Only foreknowledge, the lick of salt on the breeze and the occasional cabin or bridge lamp told her it was the sea itself, collected drop by drop from mountain streams, springs, burns, wide estuaries until they all merged into this one great and undammable effluent, the sound of which transported her into the remote.

Behind rose the grey shape of Fife, an outline engrained on her memory. That was her horizon, the limit of her knowledge, the scope of her travels. Further than that was conjecture, although on a clear day her grandfather, putting his glasses on his forehead, said he could see the snow-peaked Highlands and sometimes it did seem there was a gleam of white among the blue haze of the hills.

The bell rang again. She determined to ignore it again. Thirty seconds later a more shrill and piercing note sounded round the vaulted interior of the house. Goodness, couldn't they leave her alone? Guiltily, she fastened up the window and snibbed it, afraid that some aura of her presence might filter down to the ground floor and betray her. She did not want to be seen, to speak, and had nothing in her purse to give the most persistent urchin. She heard footsteps go round the back of the house, directly under the spot where she was standing, but the overhang of the building pre-vented her from seeing who it might be. Perhaps the unlit windows had attracted a burglar on a night when many families would be outdoors, at bonfires and firework displays. What could she do now? Make a noise in the hope of scaring them away? She was the more scared. Show herself after all?

She went downstairs stealthily, though her heart thumped enough to quell her breathing. What an absurd house this was. Perennially, boys invaded the garden to raid the orchard. Access was unimpeded from front to back and from no vantage point could a caller at either door be scrutinised before the door itself was opened.

She had forgotten. The bell at the back door was not working and whoever sought entry had knocked and knocked at it, abandoned the attempt and gone round to the front again. Tentatively, she drew back the bolts to release the door which admitted the person, half way between sympathy at the errand and annoyance at the reception, of her cousin Aileen; and the present started.

2

'Somewhere in the Highlands' was as near as Esme's imperfect knowledge of geography came to defining the location of her aunt's house. In truth, it bore a vague address, Inchcombe, Lochearnhead, which would not inspire confidence in an Edinburgh mail office but to the local postie the words were a signpost to a familiar destination. Never a day passed but he took the burden of his mailbag along the shore to that address, swung open the five-bar gate into the old yard, crossed past the weaving sheds and ceremoniously laid the pile in the master's office, on the exact spot of the desk which had been designated for that purpose twenty years before and retreated, backwards if the man himself were present.

Every day there was a score of outgoing envelopes, orders, bills, invoices inscribed in the sloping characters of a script-faced typewriter, and personal notes in his own hand. He knew he stepped outside his duty in transporting these letters to the post office in person. They should have been taken to the box directly. But for the man who gave the strath half its earnings and half its fame, he waived officialdom and provided a gold star service.

At about seven on the evening of the fifth of November, it was

Mairi who received the telephone call from the hospital. They were in the final stages of preparation for a grand party which had taken on the form of tradition among their acquaintances. She undertook the indoor arrangements while Alexis, dodging the end of a day's business, was busy outside with the bonfire. During the course of the afternoon she had watched it grow and swell from the concentrated effort of himself and the newest apprentice. They had been drying flotsam and driftwood for a month in the boathouse, for a hundred guests were invited and the fire was expected to burn for two or three hours and must not turn into a disappointing centre-piece. The phone message put her in a quandary. Would it be best not to tell him, to let apparent normality run its course till midnight, and face him when they had gone? No, she could not brave his wrath when he discovered the delay, and more than that her censorship of what he should and should not know. He would decide. Piecing her way down to the foreshore, it did strike her as odd that her first reaction to her sister's death was anxiety as to how her husband would take the news.

And that pointed to the equivocation of her own response.

Amazement. Rhona was thirteen months her junior, so close in age that they were often taken for twins. There was no greater perturbation than the death of a contemporary, and more so of a sibling. It cast a shadow over one's own longevity and Mairi experienced a definite chill of anticipation that her own calling might not be too far removed. True, Rhona was not robust; the few redheads of their family were less sturdy than the mainstream, but certainly she was not ill. She rehearsed Alexis' question to herself. No, she was not sick, or rather she had not told them she was sick. But she knew Rhona of old. She could be discreet to the point of secretiveness. Making no demur, she could pass out of life almost as an apology and leave them guessing eternally at her motives.

Sorrow, yes. She had been her greatest friend when they were young, before the men came into their lives and divided them. But the sorrow was complex. It operated less for a life lost than for one unfulfilled. No one could contemplate Rhona without coming up against the frustration of a riddle. Why had she not achieved happiness? But the answer to that lay with the last and meanest of her reactions, one that she had only a second to acknowledge as she

17

reached the line of fine sand that marked the endlessly reworked margin of the loch.

Relief.

A delivery van drew into the courtyard at the house, and Alexis glanced up as she approached, but looked beyond her to the gate and the winking tail lights. 'He was due back an hour ago.' He consulted his watch. 'Ian, go and check everything is in order and come back and tell me. At once.'

Mairi was dumbfounded at the way his employees submitted to his tyranny. The boy should have been away on his bicycle at five for he was due back in the evening to help with the party, a paid employment, and yet here he was putting in overtime on the bonfire, out of devotion. Devotion. Was there any other explanation for the way Alexis got twelve hours' labour in an eight hour day? He stooped again wordlessly and began to sort the twisted wood they had brought down from the boathouse in the last relay.

'Alexis, there is something I must tell you.'

He squared on to her. He was a blunt man, blunt in speech and in appearance. Or rather the civilisation he had acquired by travel, education, a cosmopolitan background and most of all by his self-made success, was an overlay on a tough and unyielding make-up. At moments of tremendous physical exertion which he sought and enjoyed as an antidote to the sedentary nature of his work, his shirt seamed to his body in three dark rivulets down his back, she was as much in awe of him as she would be of a dray horse or a bull, neatly penned at a county fair. Rosettes and reins could not disguise their force. They were brute animals. She sidled towards him tentatively as though presenting her narrowest angle would least alarm him.

'There is something I must tell you. Something you are not prepared for. I can't take it in myself. That was the matron of her local hospital on the telephone. Rhona died at four o'clock this afternoon.'

Grief and disbelief hit him at once, a fine pain that starts in the eyes and eventually saps every muscle, but if she went on talking she might avoid or not notice what he felt, that he felt more than she did. 'No, not an accident. She was in there for a week. No, Esme was with her. Well of course Esme wouldn't let us know. She doesn't think other people exist.' She diverted onto the less fraught subject of her niece, mildly accusing her for conforming to a lifestyle set by her mother and ratified by their near relations. 'Why, she's never so much as phoned.'

'Have we? I can't believe what you say. I saw her last month. She seemed well.'

Mairi managed to overlook the implications of this remark as Ian arrived back. The van had had a puncture on the way to Perth and fully loaded it was too heavy to jack up, so the driver had had to unpack the bales of cloth before changing the tyre. Alexis waved him back to the house thanklessly after this explanation.

'We'll have to change that van. It's always causing delays,' she said. He nodded. On business they agreed.

'Of course we'll have to cancel this party. We can't have all these people here.'

'Oh, I knew you'd say that, but it's too late to cancel. Some of them will be setting out by now. Everything's ready. It will be much more difficult coping with stragglers who turn up in spite of phone calls. And they would take me another hour to make. It's too late.'

'And go ahead as though everything were all right?'

'And go ahead,' she said falteringly. 'We don't need to say anything. We could pretend we heard it in the morning.'

He watched her fixedly. 'Isn't that callous? Or should we manage to put on a brave face? Keep the tears for the funeral?'

'That's unfair,' she countered, knowing through the course of past arguments that this was an accusation of her specifically. 'I've cried my fill over Rhona and her disappointments, as you well know.'

The bonfire was eight or nine feet high, too tall for him to reach the peak singlehanded. He turned, picked up a heavy log and for an instant Mairi thought he would hurl it at her. She winced, waiting for it to strike. But moving no more than ten degrees off line from her direction he launched it at the apex of the pyramid. It juddered and stuck. He hurled another after it with the ease of a hunter releasing an arrow. 'Have your party. I won't be there.'

'Oh, be reasonable.' She ground her teeth. 'That's worse than cancelling, and you know it is. How could I possibly explain your absence? We've got to go on with it and the least we can do is act with dignity.'

'Decorum first.' He stubbed his heavy working boot into the base and lifted the structure apart an inch or two to allow the fire to burn more brightly. 'They'll see this fire all the way to Perth. Where is the girl now?' he asked without warning.

'In the flat at Canonmills,' she answered simplistically.

'No, not Aileen. The girl . . .'

'Esme? The matron said she'd left. Gone back to the house, I expect.'

'Alone?'

'There's no one else there. I suppose so.'

'Then, I think one thing you could do is go and phone Aileen and tell her to go round and see her cousin. It shouldn't take ten minutes. Abominable they live so close and never see each other.'

'Oh, they move in different circles.'

'Yes, we've brought Aileen up well. But perhaps she could afford a little concern. Nothing excessive.'

Mairi forbore and plied her way meekly back to the house. Hopeless, she thought. Hopeless. Rhona always created division, eternally trouble. The relief she had admitted to herself half an hour back changed through the rapid alchemy of jealousy to something near gratitude. Thank heavens she was gone.

Left to himself, Alexis resumed his interest in the pyre. So Rhona had gone without warning. Not a word to him. She might have said something. Hadn't their friendship meant more, so that going out of a door for the last time, she might have turned and wished him farewell? Was that entirely selfish, to ask for some proof that he had not been forgotten? No, not altogether selfish. Simultaneously he would have sought an assurance that Rhona had not felt herself forgotten. What a solitary exit. Had she suffered, he wondered with a pang. But her physical anguish was less than the destructive sense of being overlooked, of not mattering, and of that neglect he was surely as responsible as anyone else.

Even a dispassionate observer could have seen if she were ill. She had been a little wan the last time they met, but her pre-Raphaelite colouring was something she did not seek to relieve with make-up or other artifice. He had been full of himself and his own concerns. Patiently listening she had smiled, looked remote. Was there a hint he should have picked up, a frown, a weariness, a lack of zest? He racked his memory but there was nothing. That meeting followed the pattern of all their encounters. Impossible to believe that such harmless diversion was at an end, although the pleasure of her company was at all times attenuated by a degree of guilt. There was the superficial guilt at being seen with a woman who was not his wife, but she was his wife's sister and their lunches, excursions to the theatre, the Usher Hall or the National Gallery wore a legitimate air. Besides he had long dismissed the opprobrium of the native Scot. He derived a kind of glee from giving them something to talk about; a raised eyebrow added an undeniable fillip. More profound and insidious was the guilt of omission, the awareness of trying to make amends for the cruelties of their youth. He should have taken more care of her, been more concerned, asked more questions. He would not make the same mistake again.

Delving this way and that, he worked until his stock of fuel was exhausted and the bonfire reached like an untidy eyrie into the sky. The lights of the house gleamed at him, signalling, in a semaphore he could interpret from afar, Mairi's sequence of preparation for their guests. Kitchen to dining room; dining room to parlour. The outhouses went dark. Lamps were lit upstairs. The porch, the perimeter hedge were in turn illuminated. He ignored their urgency, their imperative call to come and get changed, take his share of work, be present to put the front on normality. Night was his natural medium. The slow soughing of the loch at his side kept up a refrain while his feet crushing the damp scree made a rhythmic pounding. Remorse eroded him, the human loss went on gnaw, gnaw, gnawing till he thought his temples would cave in.

But by the time he came downstairs to greet the arrivals there was no hint of irregularity, for he had learned to live in snatches. His life was complex, as the variety of guests that evening could testify. Viewed from the workshops as Ian viewed it, hanging about to make himself useful, it was a baffling array. The folk from the strath he knew well, Graeme Sutherland the gamekeeper at Curriedon, the landlord from the hotel, some newcomers who had taken a house on the Melville estate, he'd done a hand's turn in their garden, overgrown with bracken and whin and bramble; they all beat a path to Alexis' door. Then there were faces that came once in a while to the weaving sheds, businessmen from Perth and Edinburgh, feeling the tweed cloth of the looms, arguing over colour and sizes of their famous knitwear. Never over quality.

There was no gainsaying that. Ian waited at the gate and opened it for the cars of the rich to pass through, the Daimlers, the Rovers, an occasional Rolls-Royce. Not so impressive were the vehicles of the teaching fraternity at the college in Perth which sent Alexis a handful of apprentices for practical experience in textile design. They tended to shuffle up in motors eccentric and antique, but the drivers were less queer in themselves than his artist friends. For he dabbled in painting. Mairi had insisted that he keep these invitations to a minimum. Was it for that very reason that he went out of his way to spend the evening with them, when he could have been doing the business some good, making ground with the right people? He would not cast himself principally in the role of husband.

All evening, Ian watched the game they played with each other. Mairi would detach him from someone she considered irrelevant, to introduce him to the wife of a celebrity, or an up-and-coming name. 'Alexis, have you heard what interesting things Brian has been doing in the States this summer?' And move on to another group, only to discover two minutes later that he had in turn introduced the wife, the up-and-comer, to someone else and was back in fervid discussion with his own group – about what?

She could hardly listen to her own interlocutors for trying to catch his conversation. Paintings, exhibitions, oil versus acrylic, indoor versus outdoor, mounts, frames and all laced with terms she could not grasp and therefore did not consider important. She fumed. He was trying to undermine her good work. He would not talk to 'her' end of the guest-list and if she protested by word or frown he could easily perpetrate some ghastly social indiscretion, call them to silence, announce Rhona's death and hold a two minute prayer; disappear into the sheds to prove an abstruse point about jacquard weaving; fall asleep in an easy chair till they had all gone home. She could have wept with vexation. She would not give a party for him again.

'Ian,' she said pleasantly, 'light the first rockets about nine, will you? Then they won't disturb the lakeside homes too much.'

'Mr Alexis told me to start at ten. He said all the neighbours in earshot were here anyway.'

'Very well. Ten. You'll be glad of a lie-in tomorrow after all this.'

'Lie-in? Oh, no. Mr Alexis and I are going over to Loch Lomond first thing. He's hired a speed boat for the day. I've to be here at six.'

She nodded. 'I'd forgotten you were going,' but she said it with such emphasis he wasn't certain if she'd known all along or if he'd split on Alexis by mentioning it and so made trouble for him. You couldn't tell which way to jump round here.

At ten the party filtered in penny numbers down to the lochside though some of the ladies took shelter in the boathouse, while a very few were content to look from the south-facing windows of the house. But the majority were carried along by Alexis' insistence. To the accusation that a bonfire was a childish pursuit for a hundred adults, Alexis would have replied that any gathering which was not orgiastic in purpose had as its centrepiece or theme some child-like notation, fancy dress, games, charades. In groups the most sophisticated people descended to the lowest common denominator, and the fifth of November had a pedigree longer than Guy Fawkes for disguise and absurdity.

But for him the bonfire signalled something else. He took the lighting of it ceremoniously into his own hands. From the storm lantern he took a single flame on a wax taper and gently probed the inner core of the pyramid at its base. He scorned the use of paper or petrol-soaked rags which some resorted to. Only by selection of dry, fine burning woods at the core could the success of a fire be guaranteed, and sure enough the twigs of larch and elder crackled, spread their flame outward to the stouter boughs and in five minutes the cone was ablaze, a perfect inferno, heat creating turbulence which in its turn drew fresh air between the spars of the tetrahedron.

He was like the chief jarl at Up-helly-a when they burned the longboats to signify the end of the old year. No, that was a modern institution by comparison. In the light of the flames, it was easy to imagine Alexis without the trappings of fine gear, helmeted with the cuspid horns of the Viking, shaggy and bearded, red-eyed from smoke and blood-hunting, easy to imagine him presiding at the ritual funeral of the old chief before his entry to Valhalla. Norse, pagan, piratical; civilisation was nothing but a membrane over raw energy.

Ian let the first rockets go up. They streaked the sky, stars in miniature, coloured constellations that were born and died in a millennium of ten seconds. The crowd below gasped in admiration. When had such fireworks been seen, or in such profusion? Hundreds of pounds' worth disappeared before their eyes, in a twinkling of red, yellow, green. Catherine Wheels, Roman Candles, fountains of dramatic size and complexity amazed them on every side, the finale a pyrotechnic in pure white that drew the ladies from the boathouse, the laggards from their windows.

The crowd swayed, caught up in the flames and transfixed by their heat and light. 'Come now,' shouted Alexis, 'we'll dance. We've no more rockets, so we must keep the bonfire high. Ian, get your pipes.'

Mairi frowned. This was not rehearsed and she put out a hand to stay the boy from his errand. But she had no power with him.

'Come, ladies, who will partner me? Who'll keep pace with me step for step?' He cast off the restricting jacket and revealed the garment he favoured most, a brocade waistcoat which was a masterpiece of flowers and ferns. Rumour put a price on it and fell short.

Ian warmed up. Over the loch a pibroch sounded as it had in the days of Bruce who hid in the enclosure of the surrounding hills, or of Charles Edward Stuart, a call to arms, a battle cry, a lament for the dead. The pitch of the organ struck along the air horizontally, so low and powerful that it could cleave the strata in rocks like a hammer blow. 'Who'll take a measure then?' Alexis held out an arm and there was no shortage of offers. The dancers made an impromptu set and in no time the ground between the shore and the house was covered with other groups of eight, keeping far from accurate time or shape in their squares. They reared and plunged by the light of the fire. It was primitive, heathen. It curdled the blood to see savages dancing round a bonfire and the music of the wailing pipes was drowned out by laughter and shrieking like that of banshees on lonely moors.

Mairi was aghast. The throng seethed and writhed around her uncontrollably. It was a lunatic fit, a seizure such as impassions dervishes. She thought of hasty solutions. A bucket of water or sand would soon douse the fire that had driven out their senses, or she might run back to the house and sound the gong, or scream. Alexis grinned and would not meet her eye. She did not object to her guests enjoying themselves, but to the fact that she could not share whatever it was they were doing. There was no calling them to order now. The lights, the fire, the frenzied dance had hypnotised them. She went indoors and let them get on with it.

Alexis slept elsewhere.

3

The telephone rang for some minutes before Aileen answered.

'Oh, it's you. What an unearthly hour to call. You know it's Saturday?'

'Yes, I suppose it is. I forgot you wouldn't be at classes. My time scale is all out. I had a patchy night after the bonfire and was up at daybreak. I said I'd go out with Ian to Loch Lomond and couldn't let him down.'

'Oh yes, the acolyte. How did the party go?'

'Quite well. Too bacchanalian for your mother's tastes.'

'Did you incite them to rowdiness?'

'Yes, I did rather. Then I fell asleep in the boathouse when I got bored with it all, and didn't even see the end of festivities. I expect they all think I sloped off with some delectable creature, which I didn't. And sleeping inside a boat on a pile of tarpaulin is not the most restful position. So you see I'm feeling raw and out of sorts.'

'I'm trying to feel sorry for you, but you sound as though you were dreadful. Not even a good host.'

'I met three people this morning who said it was the best party they'd been to. But I'm feeling a niggle of anxiety about it all. Not least because of Rhona. Did you go and see the girl?'

'That's why you're ringing. In the hope that I'll ease your conscience. You are transparent.'

'Only to you.'

'Yes, I did see Esme.'

'And?'

'Well, I don't know what to say to you. She's not like Rhona.'

'She's plain?'

'No, you'd be surprised just how unplain she is. When did you last see her?'

'Oh, it must be . . . ten years.'

'That's shameful, you know. No, she's much more volatile than I remember Rhona, more appealing. And quite unselfconscious with it.' A tremor of curiosity unsettled him at this judgment, but then he rejected his daughter's opinion. Loveliness made him look a second time, but he had become more judicious about the unwitting recipients of female attractions. A single foolish remark, a coarse response would quickly disillusion him. Beauties were seldom bright and never good.

'I found her wandering about in the dark. No lights on any- where. And everything covered in dust. Of course she'd been away a week but even so it was more than a week's dust. That place is far too much for Esme to cope with on her own.'

'It'll be sold promptly. The house was entailed in a strange way but I seem to remember it was at the disposal of Rab and Hannah's children who wished to use it during his or her lifetime, and then the proceeds of the sale were to be divided equally amongst them or their heirs. Fortunately for Esme the waiver does not extend to her.'

'It sounds as though Rhona was holding the rest of them to ransom by living there.'

'In a sense she was. Not a very popular decision in some quarters. But Rab and Hannah could foresee her need and provided for her. An old ramshackle place like that isn't worth much as real estate. Rhona wasn't pauperising anyone.'

'Is that why no one had much to do with them?'

'Partly. She wouldn't be shifted, but also Rhona didn't encourage casual visitors.'

'Esme certainly lives like a recluse. What *did* happen to her father? It suddenly struck me I'd always assumed he died when she was young, in the war, and then I realised I didn't actually know.'

'You didn't mention her father, did you? That wasn't very tactful.'

'No, I didn't mention him. She did.'

'How?'

Aileen was used to these sudden demands for every detail she could muster of a conversation or event, and thought hard. 'I was saying the conventional things about how difficult it must be for her to take it in when she said, let me see, "No, at twenty I am too old to be an orphan. Losing your mother when you have already lost your father is less shocking. I was inured to loss." `

'Oh dear. So what did you say?'

'I asked if she remembered him, and she could in a shadowy sort of way, which I thought was rather romantic because she could reconstruct him exactly the way she wanted him, tall, greying, with a moustache . . . permanently kind and doting.'

'That's most flattering.'

'And inaccurate, if I take you as standard. She thought that sounded too like a lover. She would want him more abrasive. So I offered you on loan. You're abrasive enough.'

'Not in the least. This morning I am terribly meek.'

'I hope you will be when you see her. I feel very bad that we've been so off-hand.'

'You used to see her at school, didn't you?'

'Not much. We were a year apart, and don't forget I was a boarder and she was a day girl. Then, when you bought the flat and I moved in to Canonmills, that was even more isolationist. We pass each other occasionally in the Refectory or the Reading Room, but surprisingly seldom. Anyway, I want to make amends. She's very adoptable as a worthy cause.'

'You may find she thinks differently. But we'll do what we can. The funeral is Tuesday?'

'Yes.'

'Mairi's on her way down by train later today, so if you could be on hand to pick her up at the Waverley. She'll phone with the time.'

'Oh, is she? I'd better tidy up. Thanks for the warning.'

'Yes, and you'd better shift Rejean back to his own pad for the rest of the week. I know you're engaged but your mother sees these things in a different light.'

'Yes. That's what the thanks were for. Rejean's coming to meet Esme this evening. When are you arriving?'

'Not before Tuesday. Too much exposure to relatives isn't good for me. I'll drive down and back in a day.'

He put his head back against the chair and swivelled to face the loch. An occasional wisp of grey showed the bonfire had been too grand to die overnight. It might keep heat for days. He sat in a form of contentment that accompanied most of his thoughts on Aileen. She was his only familiar, and he had yet to experience with her the disappointment of misplaced trust. There were moments, he conceded, when he found her too frugal with her emotions, her mother's child, but to counter that he was practically relieved that she was 'living in sin' as the standard phrase prescribed. The course of her engagement to the overwhelmingly likeable French Canadian had been so smooth as to give rise to doubts on whether it was a relationship between two adults at all. They were more like a couple of nursery children, engaged in play beside rather than with each other.

It had deeply impressed him that when Aileen was studying *Hamlet* for some exam, she told him her favourite line was 'Give me that man That is not passion's slave.' Why such cool phraseology should appeal to a schoolgirl he could not guess, but five years had not supplanted it as a yardstick of suitability. Aileen thought passion was a mess, was incoherence, violence, jealousy, all the unattractive emotions. She saw no reason to clutter her life with these impediments. A smooth passage, that was what she had always aimed for.

And achieved.

Not many romances could have started in the French Institute, but that was where Aileen had met Rejean Simard about eight months previously. She was on holiday from her temporary post as *assitante* in a girls' academy in Rheims which was required as part of her French degree. She'd called in at Randolph Crescent to pick up some books she could find nowhere else in town, and encountered her man. He was the son of a Montreal timber merchant who was sufficiently thriving to set up a small office in the capital, awkwardly placed at Goldenacre but with a small apartment behind where Rejean lived. Most of the time he seemed to be on the mainland of Europe, as he would infuriatingly refer to it, as though the British Isles were a postscript, researching forestry techniques in Scandinavia.

But by the end of her holiday they had seen each other every day, spent a few days at Lochearn where Rejean won the unmitigated approval of everyone, even his own grudgingly given. Rejean could outwalk, outshoot and outfish him and was in all respects a considerable advance on the effete intellectual Aileen might well have brought home.

She spent a memorable week with him in Paris at the end of May, kissed under the Eiffel Tower, kissed in the Champs-

Elysées, kissed in a *bateau-mouche* floating mindlessly down the Seine. But it was not passion; it was altogether removed from that, pleasant but manageable. In July they were engaged, and the rest of the summer Aileen spent in Montreal or in the Simards' lakeside home on the edge of Ontario, a glorious six weeks of constant movement, of laughter, of ceaseless introductions to friends and relatives and neighbours and business associates, all eager to meet Rejean's future wife. They swam and water-skied and Rejean promised that in the winter they would take to the ski slopes of the Cairngorms together, for that he liked the best.

So much she told him, because she told him everything if he asked minutely enough. But he could not help feeling it was beyond the laws of probability that things should go perfectly according to plan. Had he made it all too easy for his child, to the point where she sought solutions that were not stressful? He was not narrow-minded enough to wish that she relive his life, heaven forbid, or see things from his standpoint, but where was the grit in it? Was she content to float along on this middle level of niceness all her days? Moreover, he sometimes suspected Rejean had chosen her because she was the only girl who spoke French well enough to make him feel at home.

Then he laughed to himself. That was the jaded view of an old cynic. Time would tarnish their ideals without help from him.

4

Turning the Rover out of the slip road towards Lochearnhead, Alexis felt an undue elation at the prospect of the two hour journey ahead of him. The sun shone inappropriately bright for November. Late flocks of birds, not to be stayed a day longer, clustered on fences and overhead wires and for a while he winged with them over the Channel, through the Bay of Biscay in their wide migratory passages till they reached the Mediterranean and the warm shores of Africa.

Sun! How he longed for that dry baking heat, shimmering on the continental plain with mirages of waving cornfields against the wild dense vegetation of the forests. He remembered with envy the summers of his truncated childhood before the war, spent roaming Europe with a mother who was idle and rich enough to indulge her idleness. Then with a fishing line, a notebook and a pencil he would make off to the quiet shallows of the Loire, the Po, the Rhine (he could not recall where this reverie had its origins, or if it had existed at all in fact, for it had become emblematic of his escapism) and sketch the lazy fields, the farmboys moving in slow motion, the carts lumbering under the heavy heat until the fish bit, and he justified the six hours spent selfishly, by providing a delicacy for the table. This meagre northern sunlight was the one condition of his existence which he could not reconcile himself to. He was a warm-blooded creature and found the monochrome of his surroundings depressing. But today the filtered light gave a benison to the mellow landscape, pocketing the hills with dashes of colour, as it picked out remnants of fading heather against the grey rock and sharpened the white curl of the streams. Though there was a drawback. He cursed the nature of his calling that whenever things were looking perfect he was in too much of a hurry to record them.

He drove past the salmon runs at Callander, admired once more the rocky garrison of Stirling Castle and promised himself a more thorough exploration of Linlithgow Palace, tempting distantly from the road.

Descending by the western approaches to the city, he regretted that he had not chosen to live in the Border region. The finest views were from the Borders. From hills and hummocks along the twisting road spectacular glimpses were afforded to the watchful traveller, hints of the attendant beauty of the capital which made him alternately pause to admire, and hurry onwards to experience. By east and west, however, such dizzy possibilities were denied.

The larger landmarks were, as always, prominent on the sky-line. The Castle Rock, Arthur's Seat and Salisbury Crags dominated. To those trained in perspective the lateral map of the city presented in this oblique fashion could be set on end, like the paintings of Renaissance artists, and the confused impressions of an initial glance corrected. By such a tilting of the eye he could arrange the conglomerated spires of the city churches in order, defining as they did the central poles of its architecture. He saw in review the fine streets of the West End, the Georgian terraces and squares running off at right angles like essays in perspective, pillared, castellated, trimmed with neat black railings and balconies of wrought iron. The sobriety of its classicism was chastening, like the virtue of a wife one admires rather than yearns for. The reason he came back again and again to the city with renewed enthusiasm was not because of its strait-laced New Town, however justifiably celebrated, but for the exuberance, the sheer waywardness of its peripheries. Ann Street where the houses were indeed neo-classical but none was identical to its neighbour. Stockbridge that disguised many charming façades in its byways, and best of all the Dean Village, piles of rusticated stones, rough hewn, indigenous. That which worked for its living, arose from necessity or accident rather than planning, appealed most to his taste. He habitually took the same circuitous route in, winding and weaving to cover as many of his old and favoured haunts as he could. Auld Reekie; Athens of the North. The contrast was almost too stark. Juxtaposed, the two styles were incongruous, but it was the gardens of the inner city that grew up and softened the outlines, making the paradox plausible.

His wanderings had made him late, and he decided to avoid the house and go straight to Warriston crematorium where he arrived in time to seat himself discreetly. He wanted no limelight in a family pew and found a secluded corner where he could see without being seen. The filter of mourners was steady, the outliers of the family not already congregated at the house, a few of Rhona's colleagues from the library service, some faces he recalled from her photographs of conferences, holidays, working parties, people who felt little beyond a professional interest in a colleague who would not be at her desk on Monday and whose only remarkable act was to quit in so unusual a manner that there was no time for notice to be served. They nodded to each other, beckoned silently to empty places in the chapel, and made him groan inwardly with anguish that mourning should be so ceremonious. Public events brought out public emotions. Well, his own regret was scarcely more substantial, tinged with the relief that had afflicted Mairi at the news, relief at the end of guilt, however slight the cause. He knew that for the spreading family he had become the focus of all the ills Rhona had endured, unfairly since he had stayed, adapted, been pre-eminently the respectable father and husband, but he was nevertheless a permanent reminder of other fathers and other husbands. However much he might try to apologise, attempt to absolve the stain, there was the faint residue of recrimination in their dealings with him. He was of course foreign, and therefore suspect.

The cars came. The family foregathered in strength. Mairi bustled past him, unseeing, and the two slight figures of the cousins blended with the mourners up ahead. 'Brethren, we are gathered here today to mourn the untimely passing of Rhona Rosowicz, dearly loved younger daughter of Robert and Hannah also late of this parish, beloved mother of Esme, sister . . .' He found the pressure of people, the heady perfume of flowers, too many flowers because they assailed and overwhelmed the senses, the swelling themes of the organ and the minister's voice from the pulpit, too heavy. He felt compressed by emotion.

The homily tolled on, scant of information for Rhona had eschewed all such pastoral comfort, so it was confined merely to cataloguing her virtues as they had been recounted, and to exhorting the congregation to reflect on their own passage into the hereafter.

Mairi, he could see between a brown shoulder and a feather-trimmed hat, was fidgeting.

She was trying to count the heads without turning round directly so that she could say afterwards, 'A good turnout,' or, 'Very disappointing attendance,' as it befitted. She flicked dust from her sober black costume purchased for the day, and costed the wasteful tributes. Much better to have contributed to charity as she'd suggested. Still, the girl couldn't be expected to know everything, with the shock and her studies and the house to run, as well as herself to look after. But Rhona might have thought, instead, if as they now believed she had known about her illness for the last year. Typically Rhona, of course, to keep the disease at arm's length so long that it was past healing. She remembered seeing her hang out washing in the summer, holding the line down as low as possible with her left hand and using the right both to secure the clothes and open the pegs. It was an odd, lopsided movement evolved to put as little strain as possible on her left side, she realised belatedly, but at the time she had thought Rhona merely peculiar, lacking briskness or domestic skill. Rhona was feckless, first to last, always making the wrong choice, forever in debt. The girl seemed to have more sense, and a good leavening of stubbornness too. Her mind turned again to the inheritance Esme was to receive directly as her mother's portion, and she felt a degree of pique that the girl was to have as much as herself, and while she was still a minor. At the same time Mairi was aggrieved that her sister's child was cast off in the world, without human support, and determined that they should have charge of her at Lochearnhead sometimes since Aileen seemed to like her cousin's company.

The role of patroness pleased Mairi. There was, it must be admitted, a certain glow of smugness in her thoughts. She had done well; Rhona had done not at all well. The capital of her sister's talents, cleverness, a pretty face, an easy manner, had not been made to yield any return, except Esme, and she was something of a disaster in disguise. Without her, Rhona might have remarried. Well, it was all done now. The minister was winding up. She had sat at the end of a pew to move out quickly. The men would stay to shake hands with the guests and make sure they were going to come back to the house. She should have reminded Alexis that he was expected to stand in line and would have done so had he arrived early enough. She felt an irritation as at an item on a list not ticked, and could not even glimpse him to prescribe his role by a nod.

Alexis knew without telling that he should stand in reception, and did so for the same reason that he had consented to wear something approximating to a tie. This was not from the invisible compunction of his wife's wishes, which he was well able to withstand, or from that even more pressing definition of his duties in the eyes of a society he had accepted but not adopted. He did as he did from a desire to render a last service to Rhona and lined up beside his brothers-in-law at the door of the chapel. He shook hands but did not smile; he nodded but did not converse; he was there but was apart. Then he took himself back to the house at a leisurely pace, hoping to escape without detection after as brief an interlude as possible with his wife's family.

He was so late that the convenient parking was taken near the

33

house, and he was tempted to sneak away without putting in an appearance. Many alternative pleasures beckoned. Two paintings of his were being framed in the Frederick Street dealers. He could call in at a knitwear shop he had seen newly opened in Stockbridge to poach a few ideas. Several friends would be at home at this hour, delighted to see him, take him through passages to an aperitif, a good dinner, a lazy unwinding in front of a November fire. He measured them and relished their delights, but anticipated that in the midst of the fire and the wine he would feel that something had been neglected. Mairi might not exact it from him, but the past and friendship did. Duty was stronger and he gave in, telling himself he was dull and predictable and quite disappointing. He would not enjoy himself.

In the first place, the dark Victorian interior of the house depressed him. Its rooms were badly arranged, with furniture bought many years before at the lane sales because it was cheap and large enough to fill the spaces. Here was the hallstand with its protrusion of fist-like knobs, and the mahogany chest with drawers so heavy they tipped forwards. He supposed the runners had gone. Nothing had been updated. Nothing had changed since he and Mairi had moved from the attic flat to Lochearn. Even the paint on the main door he himself had put on during one holiday. Rab had burned the old paint off the door, popping his glasses onto the top of his forehead when he was hot, and Alexis had come after, varnishing. No, it wasn't varnish. They had used a curious paint that was in vogue at the time which separated naturally into clear and opaque, and when it was striated with a brush the effect was of normal wood grain. Why had they not left the wood natural instead of simulating a finish?

If anything, the rooms seemed more sparse. Was it an illusion? Did his memory cheat him, or had his own level of opulence made him lose sight of what was average and accepted? Had Rhona been forced to sell the few better items in the inventory to make ends meet? He thought not, since they were held in trust.

The guests poured round him. Mairi went past with a tray of drinks and hissed 'Whisky or sherry,' so he helped himself but thought afterwards he was meant to find a second tray and serve others. The whisky was unpalatable and tasted of a dusty glass. It soured him. The room was overpoweringly hot and noisy. Had he been early he would have installed himself by a window and edged it open, but fresh air was eighteen feet and forty bodies away. He would have to expire.

He turned his back and when an usher went out he slipped through behind him and escaped upstairs to the true drawing room. He was more at ease here. The downstairs room had never been more than a reception area near the hall, but he found this room on the floor above had been used of late as a bedroom. The chamber had the single distinctive feature of the house, a superb fireplace with a glass screen over the mantel. Hannah had called it an Adam fireplace. He smiled for the first time that day. It was nothing of the sort. It was an art nouveau addition, but to Hannah anything redolent of style or good taste was Adam, and his attempt to change her terms of reference failed. The angles were tiled with stylised irises, mauve on a lemon ground, and he was pleased to see the original fender and fire irons were in place.

But finest of all, mounted on brass dogs, was a gas fire shaped like two cinder covered logs of wood, the antecedent of a recurring fashion. Cold, it was merely realistic; hot, the logs leapt with blue and yellow flames, grew red and then incandescent white. Yes, there was the same trap door let into the skirting board to accommodate the taps. It was here that they had done their courting, he and Mairi, Rhona and Stefan, sprawled on mountainous sofas, laughing and teasing. He stretched out his hands instinctively for a touch of borrowed warmth.

She knew at once who he was, had seen him arrive, join the throng and depart discomfited. And being curious to see where he went and what he did, she followed him. Besides, she wanted to estimate for herself the giant of their entourage, the man who had befriended her mother, and went after him without fear.

'Am I disturbing you?'

No, of course not. How could she? She was an extension of his thoughts. In looking round at her, the nostalgia which had enveloped him all day caught him off guard again. Aileen had warned him what to expect. His own good sense and the law of probability had whispered that she might not be entirely plain, but even so he could not be wholly prepared for what he saw. Aileen did not know what he knew, or remember the faces he remembered.

He held out his hand to her, then recalled it was the foreign

35

fashion, but without a second's hesitation she grasped it. Unmoulded, she could adapt to any form.

'You admire the fireplace,' she prompted.

'Yes, I came to look at it again, but I hadn't realised it was your room. I'm sorry, I'm intruding.'

'No, Rhona used this. I still prefer the attic flat, but this has the best sun.'

How unpremeditated, he thought. Even the modulations of her voice struck chords in him.

From the room below there came a gust of laughter. It was for most of those present a social event, a chance to meet old friends, pass anecdotes, drink in the afternoon, but across Esme's face there passed a flicker of distaste as well as distress. He caught it, being prepared.

'Don't mind. They grieve differently.'

'No, no I don't mind. They don't matter. I was wishing they would all go away and let me think.' But as though to contradict this impression that she could do without anyone's company she sat down in the corner of a window seat and with a hand invited him to join her. The late sun, made intense by the window pane, beat against their backs and it felt so natural to be in this room again, although he had not seen it for a decade, and with this total stranger about whom he knew almost everything there was to know, apart from her nature, that he began to repair his spirits. 'I have so much to think about. So much work to catch up on. And then I have to see the lawyer. I suppose you know him, Mr Scott? He seems to have dealt with the family business since time began. My mother died intestate, not surprising, is it, and there are some irregularities he wants to see me about.'

'Irregularities? What kind?'

'Well, I suppose they tend to be diverse by nature. Do you know him?'

'Yes, I have had dealings with him in the past, over house purchase and suchlike.'

She did not hesitate but acted on his trustworthiness as an article of faith. Later she wondered if she had already made up her mind to ask him before he arrived, presupposing that her mother's good opinion was not misplaced.

'Would you come with me to see him? I made an appointment

for Friday. But I forgot, you probably have to go back to Lochearnhead by then. It doesn't matter.'

So readily he laid one burden to rest and took up another.

'In fact,' he drawled, to weigh his own responses and give himself time to cancel out the first impulse of flattery, almost as an honour she had bestowed on him by asking what was really a great inconvenience, 'I don't have any formal engagements for the rest of the week. None I couldn't cancel. I could drive back at the weekend.'

She did not smile in concurrence but nodded her head and said nothing as though that was exactly as she would have required.

From where he sat he could see two sets of disturbance that he had overlooked in making for the fireplace. The first was a table laden with oddments, knick-knacks he half recognised. What are these? he wondered, turning them over in his hands. There was a clock in black marble, hideous but worth something, with green pillars flanking the gilded face; some second-rate paintings, street scenes with wistful and sentimentalised portraits of barrow boys and pedlars, a few pieces of china Rab had picked up at auction. 'Are you selling these?'

'No, Mairi stopped off at Mr Scott's office yesterday and read Rab and Hannah's will again. The contents of the house go to the daughters or either survivor; that is, all the furniture and furnishings, for what they're worth. So these are Mairi's really. The Mini is full of other bits and pieces. She's made a couple of trips already to Canonmills with the smaller items.'

'You can't mean it! What kind of thing?' He fumed and Esme was in awe. Perhaps Aileen was right. In spite of his appearance here, he was abrasive.

'Linen tablecloths, old dishes. I think there were a couple of teasets.'

Pushed roughly together on the table top they were a greedy hoard. The ugliness of the individual items was heightened by being scrabbled together in this way, and so he was aghast at Mairi's rapine haste. She might have waited till the funeral day was over. What was she afraid of, that Esme might enjoy the objects of her own home for a day longer than her just apportionment?

'What do you think about this?' he asked.

She glided away from the question and studied the barren trees.

'Oh, don't ask me what I think.' Her attitudes were immaterial. The thing was done, and was not to be undone. Its offensiveness lay not in having the wretched bric-à-brac pulled from under her, but in the obvious hostility of her aunt. In Esme's eyes, there was no other interpretation of the deed, and the fact that Alexis censured it too was the best solace she could derive. It reassured her that she was not in the wrong and that her instincts were true.

Beside the table on which the offending booty rested were two chairs back to back. Round them Esme had wound wool which she had unravelled from an old sweater. A touch confirmed it was cashmere, and renewed the notion that it was a sweater of Rhona's. The various stages of its rejuvenation lay before him like a lesson. The back whole, the sleeves unpicked but not unwound, the front in process of being wound into hanks before it was washed and dried and rewound. Then it would be worked up into a new garment. He had heard of such industry in the war years when 'make-do and mend' was a national obsession, but he had never seen the labour in practice.

'Why are you doing this?' he demanded a little more gently than in his previous question.

'It's marvellous wool. Indestructible.'

'Don't you find the worn areas are weak?'

'Wear seldom occurs in the same place twice. I often double up and that strengthens the yarn.'

'Then you've done this before?'

'Yes, of course. I never throw anything away.'

'Have you ever dyed your yarn?' He fingered the twisted wool. It would take dye well and be more interesting afterwards.

'Yes, without great success.'

He was impressed. It was a task the intensity and care of which only he, or someone in the business, might estimate. The small tension, the fine yarn, what hours of labour they had given her to unravel. A book was propped open on the jardinière at eye level. Two occupations in one. Admirable creature.

But the more admirable he found her, the more he deprecated Mairi's grasping gesture. He could not have devised a painting to illustrate the contrast more effectively. The tableau was worthy of Hogarth. A companion pair. Industry and Idleness. Labour and

Capital. Prey and Parasite. He was wrung by his own sardonic twist of humour.

'Leave this with me. I'll see to it.'

And Esme breathed a sigh of relief. Had she found an ally? Had she, watching him ill at ease like herself amongst the screechers downstairs, identified a friend? How comfortable he was. On either side of the fire on two huge settees it was easy to feel drawn in, to experience the seductiveness of human warmth as the talk drifted over studies, work done and not done, the house, the past, memories of things known mutually. Easy for Esme to defer her suspicions born of twenty years' habit, her dislike of gossip, exchanges that too often ended in the abuse of reproof or correction, fear of intimacy. She felt herself loosening the hold on her own personality to absorb his.

'Esme,' a voice trilled from below. 'People are going now. Perhaps you should come and say goodbye.'

Her jaw set in a line he could correctly describe as arrogant. 'Excuse me. I am reminded of my duty.' She disappeared downstairs.

Proud, he thought, proud and disdainful. Will not tolerate correction, certainly not from Mairi. There was no avoiding the fact that the girl had made an impression on him, with her features, her voice, her stance like echoes he strained to catch. He admitted to himself that the reason he had avoided seeing Esme during the years of his clandestine meetings with her mother was that she troubled memories evocative not of pain, pain is easily borne, but of the elusive happiness that had been the token of optimism when they were young.

Moreover in half an hour he had not found her either foolish or coarse.

'The shameful thing is,' confessed Aileen when the guests had gone and the four of them set about squaring the kitchen, 'that when we were small, I was miserably jealous of Esme. I'm sorry, I really was. The reason was that you were always Rab's favourite. I could never think why. He would boast about the things I did, as if coming top of the class were any compensation for being liked less.

'Do you remember one time he brought out a huge box of chocolates to give us one each? He was such a hoarder of sweets.

Probably someone had given him this for Christmas and he'd had the odd one or two in secret. Often when he brought them out of his cubby hole, they were mildewed and stale, or tasted of developing fluid if he'd kept them by him in the dark room. But this time, worst of all, there was just one sweet left, a huge Brazil nut in maple fondant, not the sort of thing you could cut in half. So the problem was, which one of us was going to be given it. He rustled among the papers to make sure there was only one, though it was a cavernous box with drawers and trays and a fancy flip-up lid. And then he presented it to me, paper and all. I was overjoyed. The prospect of eating it was nothing compared with putting Esme's nose out of joint, and I gloated for a full ten seconds until he said, "And here's the box for you, Esme." '

They all laughed out loud, recalling how like Rab's justice this was, till Alexis distinguishing Esme's unaccustomed laughter said, 'Oh, lovely. Do it again.' And she fell silent in modesty.

'I expect he knew I didn't care for sweetmeats.'

'How fly of him. What did you do with the box? Can you remember?'

'I kept my drawing materials in it for years and years. You're right. It had about eight little sections.'

'You draw, Esme?'

Mairi clattered the dishes noisily. 'Come along. I promised the off-licence I would have the glasses back by six. They were already ordered for a party and I only had them as a concession. They admitted you can't legislate for people dying.'

Compressing her lips, Esme picked up a tea towel. 'Not any more. I came to terms with my lack of talent.'

'But you're taking Fine Art this year, aren't you?' interposed Aileen.

'The history of art. That is different.'

'You shall come with me to the National Gallery before I go back.'

'Did you manage to get something in this year's exhibition?'

'You weren't supposed to tell her that.'

'Oh, you weren't planning to stand her in front of it and allow her to damn it with faint praise? That's cruel.'

'I was planning to do just that, and still shall.'

'I'll tell you how to recognise it, Esme. It'll be the one without a red sticker.'

'You are mistaken. I have been notified that it has found a buyer.'

'I do think,' reflected Aileen with a serious air, 'it's terribly egocentric buying your own paintings, and not very good economy.'

'How much was it sold for?' asked Mairi.

'I have not, I promise you, bought this or any other painting of mine.'

Aileen made a noise that could be described as scathing, while her cousin was perturbed by the familiarity that held between father and daughter. Did one address one's father in so jocund a manner? With her mother, however equable, she had always observed a restrained politeness. This laughter was infectious. It made her wish, oh it made her wish for all sorts of things she could not have now or ever, but it made her wish, first and foremost, that she had seen more of her cousin, that the house had been more of a meeting place where these people and these ideas had been welcome. Why had the door always been shut?

'And are you contemplating staying in Edinburgh to make this proposed trip to the National Gallery? Funny, I imagined you were rushing back to Lochearnhead.' This Mairi.

'No, I'll stay here a day or two.'

'Where? Aileen and I are occupying the two rooms at Canon-mills,' she finished triumphantly.

He waved his arms wide. 'There are rooms enough here.'

Esme put her head in a cupboard to hide her joy. He was going to share her exile in the house for the next three days. She was to have a companion.

'Oh!?' was Mairi's response. She had a way of uttering this word as though it were both question and denial. Pronouncing it on an upward lift with a strong tail off, she effectively broke the back of the syllable.

'It seems there's a removal going on. You may need an extra hand to load up the car.'

The air grew still.

'Is Esme to have a stick of furniture left to sit on, or were you thinking of bringing a few orange boxes from the greengrocer's on your way back?'

Mairi flushed a little. 'I am taking no more than I am entitled to.'

'Oh, entitled. Yes, I am sure you are within your rights.'

'Some things are Rhona's and they stay with Esme, of course. But they did have the use of the furniture all these years, not to mention occupation of the house. Why, in lost interest alone that is worth a fortune to the rest of us. I don't think we should be shy of claiming our rights now. Rhona claimed hers for long enough.'

'That's a pejorative logic. It overlooks need.'

'Then, what do you suggest? It seems pointless to have a house full of furniture you can't use.'

'For Esme, that is, but not for you. I seem to have a house stuffed full of furniture as it is.'

'There are some good pieces here. The Regency drawing-room chairs and the bedroom suite.'

'Oh, yes, do let's have a new bedroom suite.'

'I don't intend to take it all.'

'No. Only the best. Leave all the awkward stuff for someone else to dispose of.'

'I will.'

'I suggest I go through it all with Esme, and sort out what she actually needs and uses as a minimum requirement. And that is a priority, at least till the house is sold. The rest you can do as you like with. Sell or keep or chop for firewood. It doesn't interest me.'

Esme, listening and wishing she could not listen to a banter that never rose to a crescendo but persisted along a steady monotone of well-worn antipathy, thought, It is all very well to admire a family from the outside, but this is a marriage close up. Two people arguing backwards and forwards about giving and not giving while the child goes between like the whipping boy. And marriage rose before her like a cliff face, unscalable, the place from which one falls. Could they not see how they compressed her till she throbbed with the anxiety of the unexpected? She was a stranger to intimacy. Equally, she did not know human anger on this scale: Enough. I want none of it.

'I have one or two phone calls to make,' said Mairi, drying her hands. 'A couple of people I should see before I go back tomorrow.

We can't both be away. So inconvenient, Esme, not having your own phone in the house.' She tidied away automatically before she left, with the expertise of one who dwells longer on systems of organisation than on patterns dictated by human behaviour, with swift efficiency. It did not matter that, traditionally, tea things were kept on a tray for convenience in this house where the living rooms were one, two flights above. Any resident, however temporary, could perceive that and respect its rationale. To Mairi, who had forgotten her own contact with the house and its mores, that was wrong, untidy, disorganised. The tray's contents were dispersed, cup, saucer, caddy to their proper place.

'Tell me, Aileen,' said the older woman when they got into the Mini, 'do you think it is quite – right for Alexis to be staying there?'

'Right? What do you mean, right? It's more right than the three of us squashing into Canonmills. I've got an essay to finish off for tomorrow and I need the time to concentrate. Goodness knows how Esme's managing. This last week's been hectic. Why, do you want to stay there? Surely not. It's morbid.'

'No, I meant, should they be there together?'

'Well, whyever not? Do you mean morally? Oh heavens, she's his niece. You wouldn't think anything about it if one of the uncles were staying there to help with moving out, shifting furniture.'

'There is a difference, my dear, between an uncle and the husband of an aunt.'

Aileen heard this with astonishment. Her mother was warped, quite definitely she had a mind that saw disorder, irregularity wherever she looked. There were times when she had suspected as much from the almost pathological attempts to restrict Alexis' movements, to make sure she was with him in the most unlikely or unnecessary circumstances. Outwardly, this might show as devotion. Aileen thought otherwise. There was too much panic in her desire to oversee his activities. She was afraid. And absurdly. They were married, weren't they? And Alexis was . . . Aileen changed gear. No, he wasn't just her father, and to be dismissed as an older or old man. He most certainly wasn't. She re-adjusted to the idea that he might be a man after all. That was the greatest surprise.

'You make these things happen by believing they could. If Esme needs help now, why shouldn't she seek it from Alexis? We wouldn't begrudge her that, surely, since she's had no father of her own.'

Mairi shrugged. 'She can't miss what she's never had.'

5

A fine drenching rain began which drove them indoors after their goodbyes were said, and Esme and Alexis performed a tour of the house, wordlessly pausing to close a casement, draw a curtain to shut off their habitation from the street. Before the house and their common past in it slipped away, they relived it and preserved it in their memory.

Unconsciously their hands touched a dresser or a washstand.

'Don't you want any of this?'

'No, apart from some of the books I use.'

'Take what you want. It's all yours.' They went upstairs. He leaned out of the top window from where she had seen the rockets firing, and jumping onto the wide sill examined the roof above his head, flicking off paint and, with it, shreds of wood. 'Time to let this place go. It's falling down. Rotting frames. Weak mortar.'

'Couldn't I buy it somehow and do it up?'

'Do it up? What a multitude of sins that covers.' He slithered back down beside her. 'Admirable impulse. Unworthy objective. It's time to move on, Esme, let go. I'd give you the money to buy it if I thought it was a useful acquisition. Anyway, you don't want property. It's a tie and the world's yours now.'

'But I want to go on living here. And I feel I owe the past something. We've been custodians of antiquity so long I can't imagine not being in charge any more. I ought to pass it on, keep it alive.'

'The past is always preserved.' He touched his temple. 'Material objects are only a reminder. They are not the past itself.'

'I'll take your word for it.'

They decided to begin at the top, and at once. She found an ancient boiler suit in a cupboard which might have been his own, abandoned in one of his earlier phases of living in the house and then forgotten, and they set to. They agreed to tackle a floor a day, that there was no hope of cleaning as they went, and that they would be ruthlessly selective. Beyond that they scarcely spoke, though they made a point of being in the same room, accepting by common understanding that it was more congenial to work if someone else was labouring alongside.

Gradually the contents of the cupboards in the attic were emptied, sorted, distributed amongst cardboard boxes and tea chests denoted 'Yes', 'No' and 'Maybe'. But in that system, however simple on the surface, lay their downfall. As recipient of the Yes box, Alexis was fairly anxious that it should be kept to a minimum. Esme, on the other hand, could bear to throw nothing away. Broken statues could be mended; books were, well, books were sacrosanct; old light fittings, picture frames, a treadle sewing machine would each find a place in someone's heart. For every item she pleaded a special case.

'But I don't care for it, and I haven't got space to store it.'

'But someone else might want it. It's been here such a long time.'

'That's no justification for keeping it even longer.'

'But it is, it is. There's no other reason for keeping things. Look at this sewing machine. Now Hannah was a wonderful cook, but she was the most abominable seamstress. And yet every year she made dozens of those ghastly aprons for the "Sale of Work". How I dreaded that Sale of Work. Was it held in support of the Women's Institute? No, of course, you wouldn't remember, but I do. I had the job of sewing on the strings. And she used to darn on this machine too, awful lumpy darning that looked like a bird's nest. It must have made everything practically unwearable.'

He was assuaged, not by the artefact, not by her recital but by the way she laughed. Only the recollection of the past, it seemed, could produce that phenomenon. 'Then, I'll find a corner for it, and when you want it back, you shall have it. But you mustn't hoard. You really mustn't load yourself up with useless junk.'

'Useless? Nothing's useless if you use it.'

'There you go again.'

So when it came to lifting the Yes box to the lower floors, they found they could barely move it. Alexis could shift it in bulk by heaving his weight against the side, but had no control over the direction it took, and it was quite likely to plummet down the well of the staircase, bruising the walls as it went. The alternative was to unpack it item by item and transport each downstairs individually. What a fag.

'No, I'll take a hand. We'll manage it between us.'

'But this work is too heavy for you.'

'Rubbish. I'm not that feeble. Goodness, how do you think I've managed all these years! Had a crane to take boxes up and down stairs?'

They bumped it down a few steps, Alexis taking the brunt of the weight, Esme guiding from above, but then it wedged against the turn in the stairs. Nothing was said. No orders were necessary. She slipped into the narrow space of the corner turn in the staircase and re-directed the box away from the wall, though for a moment it threatened to topple as the shifting weight unbalanced it. The slight manoeuvre meant that he could swivel the edges away from the wall, and past the bend they succeeded in wielding it down one flight of stairs, across the landing and down the second flight to the hall, by compensating shifts and stresses.

She didn't pause, plead backache or trapped feet which he trampled on more than once in narrow turns. And he didn't excuse himself for the offence. There was no breath spare for politeness. She didn't seem to expect special consideration for being female, didn't complain about her fragile nails or tender flesh. She wrestled with it like a man. Was that the highest compliment he had to pay her? No, she wrestled with it like a woman, to the limit of her resources, and that was just as good.

They collapsed at the bottom of the steps, exultant with self-congratulation. Her hair clung damply to her forehead and the cheeks that had seen too little sun were redly invigorated. The struggle with the tea chest was nothing compared with the effort of will power he required not to smooth back her moist hair, not to run an appraising finger from cheek to ear along the line of her jaw. He stretched and looked away.

'Do you know, you used to be able to crawl up these steps long before you were able to get down again? Once when we were living in the top flat, I came back and found you fast asleep at the top of the stairs having elbowed your way up thirty, forty steps from the hall, and not able to turn around. Hannah had no idea where you were.'

'Where was Rhona?'

'Oh, I expect Rhona was at work.'

'And we were all of us living in this house at the same time?'

'Odd, isn't it? You don't remember?'

'Not that far back, no. I wonder when memory begins.'

In the evening they sat by the gas fire in the middle room. 'Just a peep,' she said. 'It's too dear.'

He told her about his failures, batches of wool that dyed disastrously, harebell blue instead of navy, ochre instead of tan, though he added, 'I couldn't afford in the early days to jettison a hundred pounds of wool, so I had to use it somehow. That was when I found out I could redeem almost anything by mixing it with another yarn. I suppose that's where my style came from, my particular signature. People think I discovered it. But it was forced on me when things went wrong. Though it didn't always work out. Once I wrote a pamphlet about hand-loom weaving. In vainglorious moments I could see it being issued to every cottage industry in the country. It was going to be the definitive text. But I was in a hurry when I came to proof read, and I missed a mistake of the compositor's. I let the first printing go ahead, and then had to withdraw them from circulation and pay for a new printing out of my own pocket. That diminished my enthusiasm for the exercise, as well as my profit.'

'Someone else should have done that for you. You can't see your own mistakes.'

Esme listened and smiled, and went on listening to something other than what he said. She listened to the quality of the silence when neither of them spoke. It was not tense. It did not vibrate with expectancy but felt complete in itself. She discovered earlier that it was possible to share a room with him in comfortable dialogue, the give and take of communication, but underneath that she was finding out another harmony. How extraordinary for two people to agree. He made no fuss. He slipped into the life of the everyday, her routine, as naturally as if it were a progression from his own way of doing things. They did not need to discuss or come to a decision. It was taken for granted. What she chose, he would implement. That was all there was to it.

He slept in one of the back bedrooms of the middle flat. He woke in the best of tempers, knowing the rain had cleared overnight and left them a fresh and bracing day. He went to the window and saw she was already out and about feeding the birds on the back lawn, looking like a bird herself, cropped and neat. They trusted her and one or two came to her hand, while round about her the blackbirds and the fatted thrush pecked at the ground like mechanical wooden toys. He pushed the window up to draw her attention, but the noise alarmed them and they flew away. He went down to apologise and they scattered the last of the food together, old oats and scraps, and changed the water in the dish which she put out.

They strolled along the perimeter paths, once edged in box, tidily trimmed. Now the path was most conspicuous by its weeds. He foresaw the hours of work needed to straighten it.

'What a mess it's in out here. Rab would be horrified. He kept a tidy garden. No,' he caught her dejected look, 'I don't mean to blame you. Someone else should have thought about it.'

'It wasn't the same after the dove-house was sold. It left such a huge space against that wall. Nothing wanted to grow there.'

That was true. Rab chose it because it was a damp and sunless spot and going under the shade of the wall Alexis shivered and came out into the light again. He checked the delineations of the garden against his memory from where he stood. It was unrecognisable because the man who had inspired it worked in it no more. There were the espalier fruit trees, trained against a wall to catch the sun, but still there was never a plum or a pear off them in forty years of cultivation. They blossomed but would not fruit and Rab never knew why for all his efforts they frustrated him. By contrast the apple trees in the orchard were thick with fruit and some boughs dipped towards the ground.

'How have you managed to keep the pilferers away? We must pick these, you know. We can't let them rot where they hang.'

'But what about the packing?'

'Oh, we can pay people to do that. We can't pay apple pickers. Besides, this is fun. Have we got more boxes somewhere?'

She found three or four grocer's cartons and brought them out to him. He climbed up into the heart of the tree, looking like a schoolboy enjoying his truancy from the serious and the mundane, and handed the apples down to her. The morning was kind. It ruffled the leaves and showed their silver undersides. She did not know why she was illogically happy. She should have been at classes, and ignored them. She should have been reading something, anything, to minimise her colossal ignorance, but pushed it away. Next week, she said. Next week when he has gone, I will start in earnest. But for now she took each apple in her hand and wrapped it in a scrap of newspaper, and put it by the others in the box in layers. Occasionally, she was the object of a missile when one fell from his hand or pocket, or in being too ambitious to stretch to some out of easy reach he showered them in a rainfall, leaves and all.

They paused for a meal that straddled breakfast and lunch, sitting in the warm shelter of the dusty summerhouse. Its windows, like the greenhouse, sustained many breakages, cracks through which the rain seeped, mossing the inside. Everything in view was tinged with this verdigris which to the busy or the proud would have been a symptom of neglect to be brushed away, restoring all to shiny newness. For both of them, however, the present state was irrelevant apart from the fact that they shared it. The setting underwent the enhancement of memory so that today was minimal compared with yesterday. Glancing sideways at him, Esme could see that wherever he looked, he found the vacant spaces filled as she did, by bustle and activity. Moments were re-lived in his head as they were in hers and between them, if they were inclined, they could evoke the dead and the missing.

'Were you ever in on the blackcurrant picking?' she asked.

'Oh, the blackcurrants, yes, I'd forgotten those. They were in the border, weren't they? What happened to them?'

'They got leaf curl or some form of the mange and we had to root them out.'

'I'm surprised. They were such sturdy bushes. Prolific fruiters. Yes, I remember those sessions when everyone had to lend a hand. They were the most feverish pickers, that family. They ripped the lot off the branches, fruit, stalk, leaves in one. It took Hannah days to clean them. I remember her standing over the pan, boiling it up for jam. That went for ever too. Vats of the stuff she ended up with. She would run out of jam jars in a good year, but she wasn't fussy. She used to use whatever came to hand, glasses, vases. I even recall a soup tureen full of blackcurrant jam.'

Esme laughed and let him talk on about the past when he had lived among them, one in twenty. She listened in particular to his praise of Rab, the centre of this universe, and wondered if it was true when he ended, 'What a man he was. What a worker. There was nothing he couldn't turn his hand to. I never saw him sitting down outdoors.'

'You liked him?' she asked tentatively, knowing there was something else behind her question she hadn't reasoned out.

'Like him? Of course I liked him. He taught me how to live. He was a great man, and a great loss to you that you didn't know him better. What were you, ten, eleven, when he died?'

She nodded. 'Do you think he was a great man? I think he was a good one. That's enough, isn't it?'

He acknowledged the correction. Yes, he thought, I must not be bombastic in her company. She will reprove me with her moderation. Partly to regain her approval, he said, 'I've been thinking about what Aileen said yesterday about your being Rab's favourite. I hadn't thought of that before, but it was true. He doted on you. You were the absolute and undeniable favourite and it must have infuriated the others, not just Aileen. His own children were not so far removed from you in age that they were proof against jealousy. Yes, you could use the typewriter if you wanted. Taboo to anyone else. Yes, you could go into the loft where the doves and pigeons were kept though it was out of bounds to more marauding visitors. Annoying, you must admit.'

'But why? He had his own children.'

'Why? Why anything?' He mused and brushed the leaves from his sweater and out of his hair. 'There were so many of them and only one of you. A bird-alane. He fancied himself as an amateur geneticist. Did you know he bred the birds as well as racing them? He had quite an industry going out here. And he used to graft his own orchids in the greeenhouse. That sort of thing interested him, and he always looked on you as a hybrid, a cross-breed of two strains, and he was simply curious to see how you would turn out.'

'What do you mean, a cross-breed?' she probed.

'That your mother was Scots and your father Polish.'

'But the same was true of Aileen. You are . . .'

'Indefinably foreign? Yes, my mother was Swedish, so I am what you are, a mixture, but that uncertain or unstable element was diluted in Aileen. She was always more her mother's child than mine. Rab knew the pattern by heart. There were no surprises there.'

'I see.' But really she did not. It was very hard to think of herself as an on-going experiment in genetic strains.

'And he tried to make it up to you.' She queried this with an eyebrow, but it was a minute or two before he answered, and she began to think he had forgotten what he said. He was thinking back to the time he came across Rab in one of the sitting rooms of the house, watching a television play of Marghanita Laski's *Little Boy Lost*. A man goes back to France to try and find his son, gone missing in the aftermath of war. Alexis sat beside him and saw out the end. The other's tears streamed under his glasses while he patiently wiped them away without disguise. Almost forty years after his own battlefields. Alexis was moved by such humanity, such capacity to understand. They were neither of them men who could forget the unrecorded casualties of war.

But he did not know how to phrase this story for her hearing. She had not fought, and perhaps she was too young to realise the world was wide enough to lose each other in. So all he said was, 'You were fatherless. He tried to give you something back.'

She shook her head, sensing the unease of that silence. 'You give such logic to emotion. What you say does not account for everything.' But she didn't dare to ask him further questions, although she had begun to feel sometime before that he was the only person who could satisfy her curiosity about herself and what was missing, and who would tell her the absolute truth. To lighten the sadness which had settled on his expression, she said, 'This used to be my playhouse. Don't you think it's a fine house?'

'You weren't a very good housekeeper.' He created a cloud of dust by banging the seat that ran round the inside of the octagon.

'I grew afraid of spiders and didn't come in any more.' She paused.

'You're smiling and quite wickedly. What are you thinking?' he demanded.

'Something I'd forgotten. We sat here once before, one afternoon. You and I were in here watching the others play tennis on

51

the lawn. Someone hit a loose ball and it came flying across the garden and smacked me straight in the face. You were very concerned and looked for an old net to put over the doorway. Shutting the door wasn't enough because it was glazed and another ball might have broken the glass. And then Rab came back from work and he was livid because they'd churned up the grass.'

'But that doesn't explain why you were smiling.'

She blushed entirely. 'I was sitting on your knee at the time.'

'And you remembered that now, this minute, because I am sitting here with you today?'

'I think so,' she flustered, wishing she had said nothing. 'But maybe I did record it a long time ago and put the memory by till now. I didn't invent it, did I?'

'No, what you say is true, exactly as it happened.'

But a wary silence fell on them, for not dissimilar reasons, and by common consent they left the crumbling summerhouse and went back to the next round of apples.

Before dinner, they set about the middle flat, which was in less of a muddle than the rest, and they dismantled it in double time until they came to the landing, where there was a broad, bow-fronted wardrobe which stood immemorially on this spot. Between them they couldn't have circled it with their arms.

'We'll have to leave that for the removal men. It's far too heavy to budge.'

'I can't find the key for it.'

'It's open, isn't it?' He held out the door of the central mirrored section, and that on the right hung ajar revealing a selection of well-worn coats and skirts of indeterminate period. They could have been Esme's or Rhona's or Mairi's left over from the post-war era, or even Hannah's.

'It's the far end. We used to keep bedding and towels in there. I don't know why Rhona locked it or where she could have put the key.'

He remembered it had drop-fronted drawers for shirts and small items. He tapped the side panels. It wasn't empty. 'A small key. Fairly common, I would have thought. Have you tried other keys?'

'All of them. The one in the chest downstairs fits but doesn't turn. Wait. I'll get it for you.'

He examined the ward and barrel microscopically, with a

searching minuteness that reminded Esme she had heard his father was a jeweller. It made her feel ashamed of the trifling task she bothered him with, in fact of the whole time-wasting interlude. 'I can cut you another key, but it's a slow job. The trouble with this Victorian furniture is that it's built by a cabinet maker and there's no way of unscrewing it from the outside.'

'I don't want you to damage it. You could cut the key at your leisure once the wardrobe's delivered to you. I would like to have the contents, but there's no hurry.'

'If you are sure that suits you.'

She fed him splendidly on broth, speckled with the bright shapes of carrot, turnip, grean pea, potato and the pot barley that was plump and swollen. She bought four herring from the itinerant fish man and fried them in oats to serve with mashed potatoes. He thought he hadn't eaten so well in years, and afterwards they sat down with one of the apples from the garden. He sorted books and from time to time she went on with her winding and unravelling of wool.

'So you keep two homes, then. Lochearn and the flat in Canonmills.'

'Homes, no. One home is all anyone has. I run two establishments.'

'Two establishments. How wasteful. Isn't one of everything enough?'

'Yes, normally. But there are reasons. You like having a variety of tasks to occupy you. You read your book, then you turn round and do something with your hands. It's very stimulating as well as restful to think in the middle of one pursuit, I'll pause and take up the other for a while. When I'm in Lochearn for a long time, I want to hear the traffic go by on the city streets, and I want to drop in to a bar where I know I'll meet old friends. And then after a few days of amusement round the town, I want to be back in the strath and walk along the water's edge, and pick up ideas here and there, colours and designs. There is no colour in the city, but no glamour in the country. I need them both, for I was city born but country bred. Is that wasteful?'

She waited to find a reply. The fire spurted a blue flame and in its core a yellow one. She was silent. For most people, silence is dead, or a neutral experience. For Esme it involved feverish activity. He felt her explore the side issues of what he had said, as though she ran down the paths of a maze searching for an answer. Most people would say the first thing that came to mind; an approximation served as a final opinion. But she wanted something more lasting, she really wanted to come to the heart of what he was saying, and in the search would reject any comment that seemed too shallow, too obvious for utterance. What would it be like, he wondered, to know her well enough to read the movement of her thoughts and see where she was going down the long labyrinth of her mind, dodging this way and that before she came up with her considered statement? She was like one of his apprentices who handed over a polished design for his appraisal, not realising that he was more interested in the devious processes of creation which had gone into its making; idea followed by rejection; the everlasting balance of impulse and revaluation. He looked forward with unabashed excitement to being privy to the preliminary sketches.

'Don't you think sometimes that such duality makes for a nomadic existence?'

'And in that lies stimulus. I am a nomad by nature. All hybrids are because they never finally know where they belong. The strains pull them in two directions. Don't think you'll end your days in the place where you were born.'

And she flew away from him again and out of sight.

After two days of this intensive work, they felt they deserved a rest and gave themselves a day off. They had an appointment to see the lawyer at two, so they had lunch in town and preceded that by a visit to the Gallery. Esme knew the permanent collection well by this time; her tutor arranged a study trip almost every week, but she didn't know the gallery at the front so well for it was used for housing temporary and travelling exhibitions or showing the collections of the Royal Scottish Academy.

'Winter collection,' he grumbled to the catalogue. 'Sounds like a fashion show.'

She was reassured by what she saw. The paintings were of recognisable subjects in styles that did not make too great demands on her powers of invention. This was a garden with a French window swung back to reveal a cat basking, a paved walk, a wheelbarrow full of geraniums ready for potting out. This was the portrait of a man in a raincoat. Why would a man want his portrait painted in a raincoat? It assumed he was in too much of a hurry to care. Well, maybe he was. He certainly looked as though he was on his way to doing better things, for he was young and jaunty, and this was not art but an interlude in living. And so she spoke to him, every now and then saying, 'What do you think, Alexis? Do you agree?' Only he took care not to agree so that she would frown, looked puzzled, explain further to seek an explanation, all in the conspiratorial whisper which is required as a token of respect in art galleries.

He would not let her see the catalogue in case it dulled her responses. It gave him a certain authority too to say, 'How much do you think he's asking for that? No, no, treble it. You're way out. What a hopeless estimate.' Or when she condemned one painting as laboured and unoriginal, he took pleasure in replying, 'He's a very good friend of mine. Such a pleasant fellow but, I agree, a dismal artist. Paints his own frames.'

'You are cruel to trap me like that. Then I am obliged to like this. Actually I do, rather. Good use of the limited palette. Doesn't that add strength?'

He peered into it. 'If you say so.'

'Oh, you stint praise. This is good.' A mountain stream broke under a hump-back bridge, perhaps one of General Wade's. It was brackish water with a hint of spume, water going somewhere, water urgent after a spate. Everything had energy. The stones of the bridge, laid without mortar, seemed to leap out and declare their identity with the mountainside they were cut from, the cottage, the young spruce and pine all surged across the picture without an indecisive line or a muddy patch of colour. So she informed him, and when he allowed her the catalogue, that confirmed it was his, a sole but meritorious contribution to that season's showing.

'And I would like you to verify for sceptics that it has been sold.'

'Is that the estimate of its value?'

'No, indeed no. I was being facetious.'

She sat down on one of the circular settees which were provided in each chamber of the gallery, to give him a little more consideration. She weighed her opinion so long it made him uncomfortable for he too had to look at the object he created, but such a long time ago it was almost meaningless to him apart from the imperfections which were still vivid. The whites needed to be toned down and he saw himself muting them a shade.

'How very talented you are. I can't keep envy out of my admiration.'

'This is no great talent.' Though he thought there weren't many commendations he would prefer.

'No? But it's not the only one. You have other talents.'

'They're related, wouldn't you say? This is simply a different branch of design from the way I earn my daily bread. But it's all colour and pattern and shape in the end.'

'But this is what you would prefer to do, isn't it? It must be. More important than running a business or designing fabrics or knitting. Isn't it?'

He was silenced by the skill she had in perception. But he was almost annoyed she saw to the bottom at once, and implied he put his effort into the wrong things. He wanted not to be so obvious. Then he looked into her expression and realised his own was embittered. She was not criticising. She cared. Underneath the stark simplicity of what she said, she was honest. He'd lost that, and warned himself it was compounding the loss if he forgot how to esteem the truth.

'Yes, you are so right. But if I had to consider the way things are arranged at the moment it's the balance I would alter. As I said to you, being in one place all the time doesn't stimulate me. My occupations are in some ways dependent on each other. Selling two paintings a year doesn't pay the bills. But the success of the business means I personally have more time to daub canvas. And it's sociable. Painting is very lonely.'

'And you couldn't live by painting?'

'I doubt it. Meagrely, perhaps.'

'And meagreness is not enough?'

'No, not for me or my dependants. I like comfort too much to follow art to the bitter end, Esme. Besides, operating as I do on the level of a good amateur painter may be satisfying a very moderate ability, which is all I have.'

'Then, if that's your estimate of your talent, that's what you deserve.'

Yes, she was impossible. She hadn't had the raw edge of her tongue refined by polite conversation. She said what she was thinking and said it outright! 'You are a minx. You are quite awesomely outspoken.'

'I shall become a dullard then, and bore you.'

'Never. You could never do that. Come on. Let's go to Henderson's and have some lunch. Scott is still off George Street? Fine, it's on the way.'

6

The office was reached by way of one of Edinburgh's tenement stairs, which even in the finest neo-classical quarters have a dampening effect on the spirits of visitors. Stone built with wide, worn steps to higher flats, inadequately lit except by means of a cupola that could occasionally shed water as well as light over the upper storeys, they gave no external hint of the glories behind the stout, painted and brass-bedecked entry doors. Each brass plate on the way up announced a solicitor, a doctor, an architect, reminding a newcomer that this was the most professional of cities. Every plate was polished daily by a fleet of cleaning women, and shone splendidly in the dark interior of the stair well.

A secretary opened the door and ushered them into a room of which Alexis gradually recalled the significant features from earlier visits. A table with cabriole legs, the top covered with a layer of green baize. Mr Scott was not too particular with the direction of his ash for some lay like a paint spatter over the hearth, but most had evidently landed on the baize which was now perforated with a thousand singe marks. He wondered abstractedly at what intervals the cloth was considered to be too ash-eaten for public display and was replaced. A gas fire of the upright kind with curved white mantels purred in the grate, and heavy chenille curtains kept at bay whatever sunlight there was on a raw November afternoon.

But the room itself! It was a masterpiece of classical symmetry, one and a half times as long as it was wide; the proportions of wall to ceiling were perfect, stucco frieze and centre rose timeless examples of moulding. Each one in the stair would be different. But over all these splendours lay a tobacco film, a soft brown stain that curled round the mouldings and added a dimension to their intricacies the architect had not envisaged. It overlaid the paint-work with a yellow tinge, concentrating in one patch directly above his head, and had succeeded in filtering behind the glass face of the grandfather clock, obliterating the symbols of mortality on its dial while the legend 'Tempus Fugit' was itself dimmed by the ravages of time.

Mr Scott rose from behind the table, tall and ashen too. His fingers were deeply dyed with nicotine, and even his hair looked crisp and burnt. There was something etiolated and sunless about his complexion and Alexis underwent the pleasant experience that every man acknowledges at intervals in his working life, of not wanting to change places with him.

'Ah, yes, we have met before, many long years ago. You have had a good deal of success since then. Word passes. Yes, I am glad, Miss Rosowicz, that you are to have some family support. It is an odd situation that while you are strictly speaking a minor, if only by a few months, it is more satisfactory if you deal with your business personally rather than through the next of kin. So this seems the happiest compromise.' He fumbled among a hundred different files tied with vivid pink string and found Esme's.

'I was most distressed to hear of the death of your mother. I hadn't seen her since, oh, I suppose she was almost your age, but I had business with the family for many years and would like to extend my sympathy to you.' He cleared his throat after what he considered a personal declaration and began officially, 'You will probably know in general terms the contents of your grandparents' will whereby the sale of the house will follow upon the death of the last heir to quit the family home and the proceeds be divided amongst the surviving children or their heirs. That means as far as you are concerned that you are eligible to inherit a fifth of the estate.

'Now, there are two problems regarding your portion of this will. The first is that your mother died intestate. We can prove fairly easily that you are your mother's child and her only child.' He produced from among the sheaf of documents (such a small concern to justify so many pieces of paper) a slip which he passed to

Esme. 'If you would verify that this is a copy of your birth certificate.'

'I have never seen my birth certificate but I can check the details.'

He tutted in disbelief. 'Surely you have required your birth certificate for some purpose prior to this? Passport? Student matriculation?'

'I think I used other documents, or Rhona saw to it. But yes, that is my full name and my date of birth.' Esme had not expected this interview to be easy. Arguably, that was why she had asked for Alexis' help, so that he could act as a screen between her and the disinterment of the past, reducing its immediate impact. She believed his strength was such that he could hold her stable through the confusing passage of effects. But she was at once disturbed, and from a quarter she had not anticipated as troublesome: her own birth certificate. She put her finger on the date of marriage and the date of birth and calculated their discrepancy. Had she known this and forgotten it? Her emotion ran so high at that point she did not know exactly what she knew.

The two men saw the moment of shock and were surprised themselves. Alexis leaned forward and said under his breath, 'That's so,' and she accepted his word.

The lawyer hesitated while he thought. He disliked his task more and more. 'Your title is therefore irrefutable. The second problem is in a sense a related one. Your father, Stefan Rosowicz, who is named on the certificate as your father and was the spouse of your mother, must have a claim on your mother's estate since there is no divorce action registered in their names and no evidence of a death certificate for your father. He is therefore assumed for legal purposes to be alive, unless you can tell me differently.'

'You are telling me that as far as you know my father is alive?'

'As far as the evidence proves, yes.'

'But I know nothing. My father was not there and so I assumed that he was dead. I admit I didn't ask but I can't credit that all these years I've been labouring under a false assumption.' Esme remembered how her mother spoke in parables, telling a tale so slowly that a child would go on playing. She wished she'd paid attention to those missing words.

'No, you should not jump to conclusions. All I am saying is that we do not have a death ceertificate and in lieu of that piece of confirmation I must take steps to seek information relating to Stefan Rosowicz' death or possible whereabouts, since he may have a claim. Unfortunately, your mother made no will. That could have cleared up the untidy corners. I don't suppose,' he turned to Alexis, 'that there is additional information known to members of your family.'

'Nothing substantially more than you have indicated. I mean, nothing that would help you with the legal aspects.'

The receptionist came in with a tray of tea, slopping a little onto the green baize top, and pulled the curtains together. Instantly winter came.

'What I suggest, therefore,' he continued after the girl had left, 'is that an advertisement be placed in a national newspaper, seeking information. The *Scotsman* can hardly be bettered. You have seen these in the past?' Esme nodded, dumbfounded.

'An unpleasant experience,' interceded Alexis.

'Yes, I am afraid so. A great many inquisitive people find out things that don't concern them in the least and Edinburgh is not so large a city that it affords anonymity, but it is a step I must take if I have no address to write to or no line of inquiry to follow.'

'Were you thinking of inserting a notice immediately?'

'Yes, the sooner the better. I will advise you of the date of printing if you wish. Nothing will come of it, I am certain.'

Esme was more sanguine. Her spirits rose and fell alternately as she enacted to herself the possible reunion with an unknown and hitherto unsuspected father, and then dismissed the hypothesis as foolish. And at different moments each aspect of her reverie caused in her conflicting emotions. Now the thought of meeting her progenitor aroused joy, so much to say, so many details, memories, associations to re-live as she had done with Alexis, an arm flung round a neck which was a gesture she had never carried into fact; and then conversely the edifice of her dreams would dissolve and fall about her in disarray. There was nothing to say for they were strangers. Blood was not enough. Familiarity, a shared life mattered more.

'Of course, you must understand it is the sale of the house itself which is essentially my concern. Your mother did not instruct me to act on her behalf and it is an afterthought to the will of your grandparents that I am dealing in this matter. You do wish me to proceed?'

'Yes, oh yes, of course. You know the background.'

'An assessor will be visiting the property in the next few days and advising on the upset price. I shall place an advertisement in the property pages of the *Scotsman* and maybe the *Edinburgh Evening News*, if that is suitable to you. I shall be informing . . .' he flicked through the sheets again, 'let me see, the eldest son, I have his address here, of developments. You are in residence at the moment, but I should warn you that it is not a right you hold legally. It is a concession.'

'Oh, but no one would object,' said Alexis, but the assertion was tinged with hope. How Mairi would object! Complain that she was holding up the sale, make visits to see she was not damaging the fabric of the house, wasn't living on her inheritance. Take her furniture. Take the roof from over her head. Oh, Mairi would complain all right, and he wouldn't be there to shield her.

'Your occupation does touch on a few matters. Rates and feu-duty on the house must be calculated from the date of your mother's death and met from the estate. And to some buyers you might appear as a sitting tenant, and discourage offers. You don't mind my saying that. It is the law.' He began to feel sorry for her, crushed by the weight of new responsibility and knowledge.

Esme acceded with a nod to his excuse. 'But, alternatively, the house is better seen occupied than unoccupied. I need the house for only a few months more. I take my final exams in June, and the sale may take that length of time for completion. I will stay put till then and pay any dues up till the date of the sale.'

He acknowledged there was some sense in this. 'And all furnishings and furniture are the property of your aunt, your wife, I believe.'

'We have established that.'

'Then there will be no confusion. An assessor does not require to evaluate the fittings since they are not part of the whole estate.'

'I won't take anything I am not entitled to,' said Esme irritably. Already she had gone in spirit, and fretted that her body should so lag behind.

'Well and good. Then, that is the end of my business for the moment. I shall be in touch presently.' He stood and ushered them to the door.

Outside, night had fallen and with it a heavy fog rose from the estuary of the Forth, rolling over the city as thick as a dew. They paused as they reached the bottom of the steps and adjusted to the dark, muffled streets. She leaned against the bell pull and looked blankly into the dismal evening.

'Don't shiver so.' He fastened up her lapels to keep out the cold. 'Your coat isn't adequate.'

'I have no other.'

'Can't you stop your teeth chattering?'

'No, I detest the cold. I'm awful in winter, chilblains, colds, sore throats, the lot.'

'Come on, you'll be fine when we get back to the car. We parked it at the Gallery, didn't we? Would you prefer if I went for it and drove back for you?'

'No, it's colder waiting. We'll go together.'

He took her ungloved hand and, encased in his, dug it deeply into his overcoat pocket. 'I don't want to lose you, Dushka.'

They struck out along George Street in unison, step for step ringing like a refrain on the wide paving stones of the New Town. With her warmth rising along his side it was not difficult to re-enact her feelings, as though the fact of mere proximity gave him the insight he had wished for the other evening. She swayed, yes, she swayed in her mind. Sometimes words formulated themselves on her lips, what would it take to know what they said, but were not uttered. In silence, she blamed, she railed, she grew passive and regretful and in the space of ten minutes lived through more passions than most of the stolid citizens they passed would experience in a year.

'You knew, didn't you, that my father was alive? You didn't register one jot of surprise back there.'

'No, I can't say I was surprised. But equally I don't know any more than you do now. But let's get back to the house. We'll talk in a while.'

The car journey slowed to a pace below that of pedestrians in the thick blank fog. They inched their way down Hanover Street, bypassing Canonmills.

'We haven't seen much of Aileen,' he remembered.

'She hasn't seen much of us.'

'I expect Rejean is back.'

'Yes, he came to see me one evening. Very – personable – I think is the word.'

And so they descended from the urban to the suburban streets, unified behind the misted darkness, until they gained the last stretch towards home.

Home? No, home no more. It was going to strangers. The relentless processes of death and division were removing her from the person she thought she was, and her own niche in the vacancy of the universe. The familiar objects greeted her with an imperfect welcome for already they had passed into another form of ownership than hers. Can what they call civilisation be right, if people mayn't die in the room where they were born? Custom, fondness, the pattern of life imposed by hanging your coat on the same hook, burning wood in the same grate, taking the sun in a favourite chair under the window with a book and a bag of green apples from the garden; that was gone. The mutations of progress were under way.

'You sit down. Will I get you something to eat?'

'No, nothing, thank you.'

'But you should eat something.'

'A boiled egg then, nothing more.'

A boiled egg? He found the saucepans eventually, singed his fingers turning toast on an antediluvian grill, forgot how long the eggs had boiled, made strong tea after re-assembling the tray of things to take upstairs, and laughed out loud to himself. What would the good folk of Lochearn say if they could see him pottering round this bleak, ill-lit kitchen? And then his mind leapt ahead. He would be going back tomorrow. He had been away three days and he hadn't given the place a thought till now.

She ate distractedly, sitting in the chair where on the previous evenings she had been happy in his company. She waited till they had cleared their trays to one side before she asked, 'Why didn't you say something to me in the last few days? I can't help feeling that you deceived me.'

'Why didn't you ask? For the same reasons. We each assumed that we were cognisant of the same facts. I'm sorry but I must say I am baffled why Rhona didn't speak up. It was hardly my place to rectify her omissions, which I wasn't aware of in any case. Are you sure she didn't say?'

'Well, maybe she did when I was very young and it didn't matter then when there were so many others. But now they're all gone, it seems to matter more. What was my father like? I've never so much as seen a photograph of him. Tell me about him.'

'Very well. Be patient. But don't accuse me of deliberately withholding something from you. I wouldn't have denied you if you had asked. You do believe that?' He moved back in the seat and tried to recollect the sequence of events. 'Well, he looked like you. It took my breath away when I walked in on Tuesday and you were the living image of him. He was very good natured, a rather relaxed and easy going person. Not ambitious, not stressful. A drifter perhaps.'

'How did they meet?'

'That was my doing. I met him first and brought him back here. I'd been in the Navy for some time. Mairi and I were already engaged, and I was staying upstairs, renting a room I suppose. I'd been down to the docks on some business, a travel warrant I had to pick up as I remember, and as I was walking back another sailor stopped me and asked the way to the depot I had been to myself. His English was broken and I think he asked me because I was in uniform and was likely to know what he meant, without too much strain on either side. I took him there eventually and we got talking. He was a Polish émigré who'd left the country before the war. His family was in northern France, working in the Boussac textile factories in Lille. So we had that in common as well as the uniform we wore. He was fighting with the allied forces. There were big Polish contingents, you know. Polish families still all up and down the east coast.

'He had some other problem he needed help with, missing luggage or papers, and I said Rab was the man to help. He was in one of the big mercantile marine insurance offices in town and knew everyone who worked in shipping. So back he came. What was one more among all that crowd?

'Rhona was very young. They both were, but they seemed to hit it off. The four of us went everywhere together at the start. You couldn't explain to anyone now how feverish it was, the war years. It was unnatural, hectic, like being on a permanent high of excitement. He didn't go home on leave. He came here. It was the war really that threw people together, dispersal and then when it's all over, you think – Well, what was all that about? He was torpedoed in the Mediterranean and badly burned, spent months in hospital. That accounts for the delay in the wedding that you didn't know about.'

'But why did they break up? If there was enough to begin with, to marry, why wasn't there enough to keep them together?'

Alexis made up acidulous replies to this but restrained himself from saying he wished he had such a monopoly on wisdom. 'As I say, when they settled down to a full time life together, they found they had almost nothing in common. People were doing it all the time, leaping before they looked. How many thousand GI brides? It had been the classic wartime romance. I must say you were probably a hindrance. A marriage begun with a child already on the way seems to be under additional pressure. They didn't know each other. There hadn't been time to know each other. They spoke a different language, literally. And they were very different people. Rhona was articulate, maybe bookish. As long as she had a book she didn't care what was going on around her. She was a graduate, a librarian and well placed for promotion whereas he had no qualifications and very middling English. The labour market was flooded with ex-servicemen coming back and they pushed him down the order. It was hard to make a start in this country unless you had a special skill. Now Rab liked your father. He did everything he could to help him but that dependence was in itself an irk. Do you see? Stefan was living here, earning a paltry wage, being kept by his wife and his wife's family, and he didn't have it in him to strive. He complained constantly about the weather, the food, there weren't enough salads, at home they had fresh fruit every day. Things were different at home in France and they were all better, according to him. Why can't some people adapt to new conditions? I don't know. My mother hated Scotland all her life. I don't think she spent more than six months in the country at one time. She had to keep escaping, and so I could understand someone who always wanted to move on.

'And it wasn't all his fault. Rhona was the wrong person. Look, I cared about the woman, but she could be infuriatingly disconnected. She would never come to the crunch of things. She could be talking to you and looking through you at the same time. She could say, "It's failed," and will it to fail.'

Esme thought there was some truth in this. Would he be shocked if she said, She willed herself to die, she willed herself not to put up a fight. But though she did not say it, she knew that sometime she would tell him how it was.

'In the end they decided the only way out was to emigrate. You would be maybe three at the time. He applied for immigration papers into Canada and was accepted, because of his service record I think. Rhona thought it would be better if you and she waited until he had found permanent work, though I do seem to recall he had a letter of introduction to a textiles firm out there, Montreal I believe, and the plan was for Stefan to send for you when he was settled. He never did. He simply sailed and disappeared.'

'She must have heard from him. She must have tried to trace him.'

'There was a letter or two, fraught with difficulties. He had been robbed, and lost his papers. There was nowhere suitable to stay. He wasn't going to come back. She wasn't prepared to go out to nothing. It was stalemate.'

'Did you talk about it?'

'Rhona and I? Not substantially.'

'But you did see her, didn't you, from time to time?'

'Yes, I used to make a point of seeing her when I came to Edinburgh. She was one of my oldest friends. I counted myself privileged to be in her confidence, but as for discussing you or Stefan, or showing me letters, or asking my advice, no. She kept her personal life very close.'

'But there's something else. Why did you never come here, or the others? Her brothers scarcely set foot inside this house after the last funeral.'

'That was the way Rhona was. Withdrawn. She didn't encourage callers. She used to say, "You open your door to open other people's mouths." That's a fair inhibition to casual visitors.'

'And what must I do now?'

'Leave it to the lawyer. He'll put in the notices. In fact it strikes me Rejean could help. His parents live in Montreal. We could put one in the *Montreal Star*. And that clears your responsibility. What are you thinking? You've gone far away again.'

66

'I was thinking. What do I know about Canada? It's a world away. I don't know anything about it except it's vast, vast enough to lose yourself in. The first time I saw the word was when I was just learning to read. I was going through Rab's stamp album from the beginning and came to Australia.'

'That's right. He kept only British Empire stamps.'

'I couldn't spell that out, too hard, so I turned the page and came to Canada. Now that was easy to spell. I asked Rab where Canada was and he told me it was a large, cold country and it spread all the way across to the top of the world. But he didn't tell me Stefan was there, and I would have understood even then.' She sighed, and he felt she was in danger of recasting all her memories in the light of this new information. 'Alexis, if it had been you in those circumstances, and from what you say there was very little difference between you at that time, could you have left your family behind?'

He juggled with her proposition and found it could not be answered with a yes or no. 'I could have left as he did and for the reasons that he did, but I would have had to come back to my own.'

'How could we mean so little? Is paternity such a casual affair that men spawn like fish in a pool?'

Only her serious expression kept him from laughing. 'Not entirely. But it's a more variable instinct than motherhood. Genealogy appeals to men. Children don't.'

He saw her mood change to one of self-pity. Why did my father not care for me? What was missing that I should be so neglected and forgotten? And he wished he could console her, sitting so forlornly on the settee opposite exactly where Rhona and Stefan had sat, laughing and flirting. Here she was, their progeny, desolate because they had not cared about her enough to care for each other. Any other woman of his acquaintance he could have comforted with an arm or the warmth of his side, wife, child, mother, mistress. But not Esme. She was utterly removed from him, inaccessible.

'But I am certain that not a day of his life has passed when he hasn't thought about you.'

'In ancient Rome, you know, they didn't count paternity as much. There was a ceremony carried out after the birth of a child, rather like our christening I suppose, where the mother placed the child on the ground in front of the household altar, and the father or any man who wished to assume responsibility for the infant picked it up and adopted it as his, gave it his name. Every child was assumed to be illegitimate.'

'Sensible precaution. It's a wise man that knows his own child.'

'It's a fortunate child that knows its own father.'

He longed then to hold out his hand to her, to cross the distance between their sofas and tuck her under his arm as a chick tucks under a wing. Human to human they might huddle, but he felt that would bridge a significant divide. They must not touch. Was it Mairi's purse-lipped denial that any human warmth could be innocent, or an acknowledgment entirely personal that he was putting himself in the way of temptation. No, he repudiated that. In loco parentis, that was all.

'I'm tired but not at all sleepy. What time is it? Late, it must be.'

'We needn't go to bed tonight. I'll make another drink and we can talk. No hurry. How is it you never know the time? Don't you have a wristwatch?'

'No, no I don't. I can guess near enough.'

They sat up all night, sharing that experience that comes from talking into the small hours. They tired and revived, drank a pot of coffee, turned up the fire as dark invaded the corners of the room. They saw images blur, recede, magnify in the strange sequences of optic fatigue, and at times their own voices boomed or fell silently whispering. And at four he found that she had dozed off, curled along the arm of the settee, and left her to wake at her leisure.

7

From where he sat in the office attached to the work sheds, Alexis had an unimpeded view, indeed almost a panoramic view on three sides. The office was the most southerly outhouse of the square that formed the buildings of the former farmhouse, byres and storerooms. Bit by bit he had been able to afford its conversion by planning, building and financing it himself, and his own office had been the last, and therefore the best development. It benefited from earlier mistakes, but independently of aesthetic judgments related to window frames, harmonious building materials and the like, it had the finest position on the quadrangle with windows all round. The northerly windows looked onto the main Perth – Lochearn road and took inspiration from the line of hills. The easterly aspect, though to be accurate the position was south-easterly, was on the boundary stream between his property and his neighbour's, a boundary they saw no need to reinforce with further impediment to an evening's stroll or conversation in the form of fence or hedge. From these windows the boathouse was some five hundred yards distant, but while the structure was in itself a form of temptation to go out and sail or row on the loch and forget the problems of the drawing board for an hour or two, the building actually hid the loch from sight and so minimised its disadvantage. The finest view of the loch was from the south-western window and in this portion of the room Alexis had made more of a study than a work area, with armchair, bookcase, reading light. Although it was his boast that he spent very little time indoors except in his office, a good proportion of the mellow hours of sunlight were passed at this end of the room, in meditation rather than in action.

But for a few days after his return there was such a backlog of work that he was more often than not at the architect's chest which housed his materials. It faced the sober admonishing hills and so for twenty minutes before Graeme Sutherland arrived at the rear entrance Alexis had time to prepare his reaction. Curiosity had vanquished his old friend then, and brought him swinging kilted down the hillside from the Curriedon estate, cutting his way through the dying bracken that coated his hose with golden dust. Now, that curiosity was the very reason Alexis had broken with the tradition of the past years, and avoided finding his way up to the gamekeeper's cottage where, settling in front of a peaty fire, he could give an account of the days he had passed in the capital. He had boycotted him, and had not even faced the reasons for his avoidance. He could not render the unease he felt about Esme in terms of fireside conversation, or, sitting back in an armchair, begin, I spent three days almost exclusively in her company, took her to the National Gallery, had lunch, picked apples. I think I am a little infatuated with the girl. Though like most private thoughts the idea did not present itself to him in words. It was merely a complex and pleasant sensation which he was still evaluating, enjoying to the point that he did not wish to categorise it for others.

'You've been away a good long time, man.'

'Too long, much too long, Graeme. All this to catch up on and more coming by the post every day. Sit down, please.'

'You're a lucky man that's so needed. You were with your niece, I hear. I came past the other morning when I had business in Lochearn and asked Mairi what you were up to.'

'Mairi's niece, yes. Some legal problems to sort out.'

'Oh, indeed. And you'd be much better suited than Mairi to dealing with those. Now this would be Rhona's lassie.'

'That's right. You shall meet her when she comes north.'

'You'll not be hurrying back, then?'

'No, my business is all finished,' but realising the truth of this assertion cost him a larger share of regret than he would have admitted out loud. He worked on for a while, head bowed. Graeme was used to these silent bouts and picked up a book from the shelf at his elbow. Alexis' table top was methodically organised and gave no impression of feverish industry; his regard for order some considered pedantic, for the rows and rows of felt-tipped pens with which he coloured most of his functional sketches were in strict ranks of shade, housed in a cantilevered box that made fine distinctions possible. He drew on graph paper, every block corresponding to a stitch in the finished garment. From a distance the patterns looked like musical notes dancing up and down the page, a weird and polychromic score. Each square was translated into a key at the bottom of the sheet and the machine operator followed this card on her knitting machine. For a long time he had been experimenting with different techniques of dyeing and blending of yarns, since he felt he had gone as far as he could in pure design. The shape of a garment was limited by its function; it was its texture, colour, quality that gave it the right to be considered as an art.

The raw wool, blended with cotton, silk or linen, was worked into a dozen different yarns, each batch of which was dyed into a score of colours. The dye ran differently in each batch, for the materials took up the colour at varying rates, one thread often an intertwining of blue and mauve, pink and russet. Their colours were as subtle and subdued as the landscape that was their inspiration. Bracken, peat and heather were duplicated in the dyes of the wool, the rough and hoary texture of the land that had passed into the fibre of the cloth. When these parti-coloured yarns were knitted into the designs, the effect was brilliant and three-dimensional. A flat surface became as glittering as a starling's wing, suggesting infinite variations. Very little was entirely what it seemed; a motif was repeated not in regular blocks, but diminishing by minute proportions to the top of the shoulder, so that the body tapered in perspective; a tartan overlay, far from being an arrangement of squares and lozenges, broke, merged in places, was reversed in its neighbour colour, re-formed boldly on a cuff or collar, like a theme which had gone underground for most of the symphony and re-emerged triumphant in the closing chords. Each was unique; each was priceless.

'Well, would you wear this with your kilt, Graeme?' And he pushed the paper out for comment.

'I think not. More for the ladies, that one.'

'The American gentlemen like these on the golf course.'

'Ay, well, that's as may be. My father kept to the Harris tweed jacket with his kilt, and I'm content to do the same.'

'Was he the gamekeeper at Curriedon before you?'

'No, he was on the Melville estate before it was sold in lots. And his father was a keeper too. He was a ghillie on the Balmoral estate when Queen Victoria was in her last years.'

'Does it go in families, then?'

'Oh yes, like poaching, there's no schools for it. You must learn it from somebody who has the skill.'

Alexis reflected on what had taken place in his absence, slotting back into old routines but with a sense of effort that made him feel something more than three days had elapsed. 'You've a quiet winter ahead of you now that the family's gone back.'

'There's plenty to do all the same. The hill fires we had in the summer cut down the ground cover and the grouse won't be breeding in the same numbers. I'll have to re-stock.' Graeme guarded the reputation of his estate for shooting the largest brace of grouse in the region.

'Aileen's fiancé would like to do some shooting next year. He shoots game in Canada and would like to keep his eye in.'

'Yes indeed. I forgot there was to be a wedding next summer.

You'll have your hands full.'

'Not me. There's to be caterers and wedding consultants and a trousseau ordered by the dozen from Jenners. I won't be needed.'

'A grand affair. We'll look forward to that.'

'I'm glad it's worked out so easily for her, but all the same . . . she's young, maybe too young to know her own mind.'

'You like the young man well enough?'

'Yes, no doubt about that.'

'Then stop havering. If you've done, take a turn down to the village with me.'

It was barely midday and the early exit from the office gave their walk the air of an escapade. The landscape was restrained, with autumn well advanced and the boughs of the trees that flanked the road and overhung from the odd wayside garden more in evidence than their leaves. But the copper glow of the beech, the golden powder of dying heath plants, the fitful sun added a piquancy to the day that belied the season. In one's heart it might be summer still.

They strode down the crown of the road, fearless of traffic. The butcher's van drew level and waited respectfully for them to pass, and the baker, coming to the end of his morning round, waved as he overtook them. His was a brown van with lurid facsimiles of his wares painted on the side panels. As they drew closer into the village they encountered more pedestrians laden with shopping or like themselves out to see and be seen. Those they met smiled, nodded, made some salutation on the fineness of the day, a courtesy Alexis took for granted in his normal routine but which struck him afresh on his periodic returns from the capital. They had manners, these people. They had time. But still he smiled to see that they universally acknowledged the gamekeeper first, and himself second. He might have lived in the strath half his life and be known outside – oh, all the way to Perth – but Sutherland was born and bred there. He was one of them, while Alexis' children and his children's children would always be descended from that foreign fellow at Inchcombe.

They took themselves automatically to the hotel where James Robertson poured them a hefty dram and ordered a plate of sandwiches, but no ordinary bar room sandwiches these. Soft baps filled with salmon from the local streams or thin shreds of pinky brown venison Sutherland had himself provided from the last shoot at Curriedon Lodge. Hung to perfection, it was served by the landlord as a rare enticement to diners who knew quality meat, and to no one else.

'I've not seen you since your do on the fifth. It was a grand night. You spent a bob or two that day. Here's to you. You must have a return visit, ay, come and eat the last of the venison if you will. I have a haunch left. By the end of the week, mind. It'll keep no longer. You and Mairi.'

'I'll get Mairi to phone down.'

The landlord nodded and attended to his other customers while Alexis and Graeme settled into the corner of the ingle-neuk, warmed in and out, while the view over the loch and the southerly hills was nourishment for the spirit.

'I have a very unpleasant task ahead,' said Graeme with a sigh.

'Why? What?' Alexis started almost guiltily. Their conversation was like the day, fitful, as it is between those who know each other so well that only drama to one or the other creates the impulse for dialogue. They were mostly happy to observe others and be silent, though Alexis knew if he pressed the saturnine Scot for an opinion he could be sure of a sound and balanced one, and was content to keep that in reserve.

'Ach, this morning I was up and about early. Can't seem to keep to my bed these days. It was no more than five and I was in the kitchen boiling my tea when I saw, or thought I saw, a body go past the window. Now nobody has any doings outside my cottage at five, so I nipped out as quick as you like, thinking it was a burglar afoot or a poacher, but I was too late. It was a young lad, eighteen, nineteen maybe, and he'd got down into the bracken by the stream and was away like a hare when he heard me. But he'd no bag of tools with him so he wasn't up to that mischief. Then at eight Mrs Dunlop, the cook, came up from her house and said she'd seen him too, and if I wanted her opinion, it was the lassie Fiona's boy.'

'Fiona? She's the maid?'

'She's the kitchen maid in the house. A daft-like lassie but works well enough. She's been there all the season and sleeps in the house. The family retained her over the winter to help old Max and his wife to keep an eye on things. It's too much for them now patrolling the grounds and locking up. Anyway, it seems she's the one that needs an eye kept on her. Mrs Dunlop had it out with her and she said, Yes, the boy had spent the night with her in the big house. Max might be blind as well as deaf for all he'd know, though he sleeps two doors away.'

'It's no concern of yours, surely?' But there Alexis was wrong and Graeme frowned at such ignorance of community law.

'I am in charge while the family is away and I cannot connive at this. We don't want babes in arms, do we?'

'No, I forgot.'

'Ay, you forget too much.'

'So what can you do? You're not thinking of sacking her?'

'Oh no. The girl will get no other work round here. I phoned the mother to come and meet me here at two when the bus calls past. We'll go up to the house and give Fiona a talking to. There's no harm in her but she's feckless. The mother's a widow and maybe the girl's not getting the firm hand she needs.'

'Rather you than me.'

'Well – you've no idea who the young man might be?'

'No, I was soundly in my bed at five.' But as he spoke, Alexis realised Graeme would not ask a question to which he did not already know the answer. After a moment's consideration of how his friend's mind would work, he asked, 'You think it's Ian?'

'More than that. I know it's him. They've been hanging around together all summer. He's a nice enough laddie but I came to you hoping you'd speak to him since you've influence over him, rather than his own father. He never did rub along with his father, which is maybe why he's taken to you. Would you have a word with him?'

'What about?' Alexis was on the point of saying it was a matter of indifference to him whether Ian sired a hundred good weavers in the valley, but he stopped himself short. He had no wish to antagonise his old friend by assaulting his somewhat pedantic moral code. And besides, an insidious memory crept in. Did men spawn so readily like fish in a pool? 'What do you want me to say?'

'Oh, don't be too hard on him. It's only nature, after all. What they do at his house, or hers, or in the bracken is their business. But not at Curriedon Lodge.'

But Alexis did not relish the prospect facing him after his solitary return journey, and strode out with an angry brow.

'A man,' he heard himself saying as he tried out his speech of

74

reproval, 'a man does not cavort, consort . . . copulate.' The right word refused to come to him. 'Cohabit?' But that was the trouble. A man did, if he were a man at all. Was he meant to reverse instinct?

At the turn of the road he found himself on a wide ledge of shingle overhung with silver birch, one of the few spots along the loch where the road actually ran down to the foreshore. This place Aileen had especially favoured as a child, making the longish walk from their own shore to play, and had called it for no apparent reason 'the animals' combination place'. Had she seen stags rutting here? Surely it was too open a piece of ground for deer to venture down from the hills. Or humans? That had been his own first introduction to sex. As a young boy he often went beach-combing and once, along the Atlantic edges of the Bordeaux country, wandered into a cave and found a couple engaged in the act of joy. Well, it was joy, or ought to be in sight and sound of the Atlantic breakers as they swept, sighed, pounded on the beach. Only at the time he had felt sorry for them, unknown man and woman, clumsily half dressed on cold slabs of rock, rocking gently to the crash of the foaming waves. They were illicit lovers, surely. All real lovers were hiding, cowering in sheltered places. Hardly man and wife out for an afternoon's fossil hunting. Now that was an indecent suggestion! He laughed out loud, then sobered, recollecting that anyone coming past at that moment would have thought he had encountered a madman, bellowing into emptiness.

He walked into the sheds where a dozen looms clattered in a ragged harmony, some heavy, some light, the weavers shuffling their feet on the pedals with the virtuosity of an organist, hands flying every bit as rapidly over the threads as they lifted the bobbins up and around the warp. Ian sat with his back to the door and Alexis had to lean over him to catch his attention and direct him to the office. Ian followed exultantly, the face that was often withdrawn and moody lit by anticipation. Perhaps he had an errand to perform, some prank the two of them would set out on, driving the van. That was better than a holiday when they went together to fish, to the wool sales, Mr Alexis talking to him as though he were an equal – him, an equal – buying him drinks, asking his opinion, sharing bread with him.

'You slept last night at Curriedon Lodge.' There was no

question in the statement and so it needed no refutal. 'Mr Sutherland and Mrs Dunlop saw you, and Mr Sutherland and the girl's mother, Fiona, isn't it, are up at the Lodge now giving her a sound scolding. As I am expected to do with you.'

'Yes, Mr Alexis.' He hung his head and braced himself for words of wrath.

Alexis ruminated and a smile stole out. 'How did you expect to get away with it at the Lodge?' and his voice creased with curiosity.

'I fell asleep. It's too cold for the hills and so we went inside and fell asleep. I only awoke when it was getting light. I knew Mr Sutherland had seen me but thought he wouldn't know me.'

'That was an ambitious prospect with Mr Sutherland. He knows the faces of sheep. How would he mistake a human being?'

A long silence fell while Alexis' eye lighted on a parcel of magazines and some letters delivered by the midday post and he fancied, quite without foundation, that one of them might be from Esme.

'Have I lost my job?' the youth interrupted at last with sheer dejection in his tone, for it was more than his livelihood. Each day was the best entertainment he had had in his life. He never tired of the patterns that grew under his hands, of learning the skill of the other weavers who had spent fifty years at the loom and knew some of its secrets.

'Don't be daft. Of course you haven't lost your job, or she hers. Tell me, is it Fiona you are keen on or having a girl?' he asked in amazement that this scrap of flesh in front of him was capable of paternity.

'A bit of both.'

'I mean, how keen are you on the girl?' Yes, Aileen had arranged things tidily. There was none of this mess of emotion with her. 'Because if you are keen, it's only reasonable to stand by her. I think she's probably having a fairly unpleasant time right now, and it might be best if you went and helped her out of it. If you want. It's not my concern, but you put Mr Sutherland in a difficult position. You were in fact trespassing.' He struggled to put it in terms the boy would understand, for he was blowed if he could work any moral blame into his diatribe.

Ian nodded. 'I'll take my bike.'

'And, Ian,' he cleared his throat, 'you are taking sensible precautions?' He was about to add, You don't want to be a father before you're a man, but decided it was less shaming to say, 'You don't want to be a father before you're ready.'

'I will, Mr Alexis. Thank you.'

And a few minutes later the boy's head could be seen bobbing up and down to the rhythm of his pedalling as he cycled past the hedge and along the winding road.

What follies were committed in a moment's weakness. The word would be all round the village in a few days, if he knew Mrs Dunlop's gossiping tongue, and the girl would be cast as a hussy for the rest of her unmarried life, and beyond. Not one of the good souls of the village would loosen his hold on the memory of Fiona's indiscretion. Gentle, tender, idle kissing led to the pit of sin.

No, there was no letter from Esme and in an instant he thought he would pen her a line. The postman could pick it up with the bundle and it would go straight to the post office as anonymously as an order, or a bill in a brown manila envelope.

'Dear Esme,' he began on a sheet of virgin paper embossed grandly with his own insignia.

'Dear Esme.' He stayed his hand for, as though by dictation, Graeme's voice came into his head.

Don't be a fool to yourself, man. What is there in it for you? Ach, I know you've always been a man for the ladies, a well turned ankle, a bonny smile. But look at the bother you got yourself into over her mother. You can tell me as long as you like that it was innocent enough, but did it look innocent? You won't marry again. You've stuck it out all these years because that's your mettle. It only made trouble for you at home. And if you didn't leave your wife over that one, you won't leave her over this one. Like mother, like daughter. And what point is there otherwise? If it's a thrash in the bracken or a roll in a bothy bed you're after, there's plenty of queans would take you on those terms. But if it's true you want to help the girl, if you're certain you want to help her for other reasons, then do her a real service. Leave her alone. You're too old to go running after wee lassies with half baked notions. That's kidding everyone. Of course, she'll be flattered that you pay her court. Of course she'll turn to you in need. But in time she'll need a young man more, and you've no business to stand in the way of that.

He pushed the notepaper away. There was nothing he could not have, nothing he could not buy, but perhaps this particular friendship came too dear.

8

It was true that from earliest schooldays Rab had boasted to anyone who was prepared to listen about Aileen's prowess. She worked hard. She was a happy combination of the best attributes of her parents: flair and doggedness.

Hers was a tidy mind. She did not miss a single lecture, or fail to check a reference, however hurriedly it had been cast out as an aside. A list of her prizes and bursaries made daunting reading, for it showed up not only intellect which could be put down to a form of birthright that was either granted or denied to the unsuspecting individual, but also a system of daily application that the lowliest might attain. Her contemporaries thought her a brilliant student and they borrowed her notes and passed them from hand to hand like distilled wisdom. They were accurate, concise, a perfect paraphrase that was often rather better than the original because it was succinct. Her genius was her method.

Aileen was not in the habit of looking back, however, even in self-congratulation. What was won yesterday was too easily lost tomorrow, so she never lifted her head from the present. The same workload that overwhelmed Esme, a prospect of weeks, months of toil for an intangible goal, Aileen accepted would not diminish in real terms. It was as infinite as knowledge itself. The more she mastered one area, the more vistas opened up on either side, of associated disciplines which she did not trouble herself with overmuch. The mainstream was what she sought to breach. Time later for peripheral discoveries. Day by day she toiled at her desk, as neatly ordered as her father's, gradually transferring tasks to be done to the side of tasks completed until eventually the books were returned to the shelves, her own or the Reading Room's, and the process re-started. Why was she so fortunate? She did not question too much. She trusted her teachers and strove in the direction they indicated. She always had one objective – I know where I'm going and I know who's going with me – and wasted no energy on superfluous considerations of how or why. Confident, controlled, she knew no indecision.

By comparison, Esme was hopelessly circuitous, adept only at the kind of thinking which was non-productive. She constantly overshot deadlines, not because she was idle but because she had become diverted in the course of the prescribed reading onto something more interesting than the narrow parameters of a given title, and rambled aimlessly over the shelves following her own likes. The days of her assignments ticked by and still not a word was committed to paper. Her notes were illegible even to herself, scrawls and curls and doodles all over the page, a grotesque cartoon of the labyrinthine process of thought and association that passed for study. Every day she thought she had made a mistake in following a line of argument, and like Penelope undid in the hours of darkness what she had achieved in the light.

Aileen had her own problems, but not the common ones. Nothing presented her with insurmountable difficulties, but at the same time nothing was irresistibly attractive and if now and then a shadow of unease clouded her efforts, it certainly was not why she should study – the question that bedevilled Esme – for education was liberty, far less how, but to what she should apply herself. Between the counter-attractions of philosophy, literature, history, politics and the social arts, she had chosen French as being the most useful, which was a kind of worldliness. But there she might have been wrong for the neat, analytical turns of her mind were more suited to the niceties of philosophy than to the trammels of literature.

In spite of the steady pace of her work, weekend visits to Lochearn, wedding details and the time spent with Rejean, she found space for her cousin in the winter and spring. The family respected Esme's wishes to stay on in the big house and did not badger her with tiresome practicalities. They began, as no urgent buyers presented themselves, to take her point that there might be some virtue in having the house occupied as an insurance against frozen pipes and a leaking roof, and grew more indulgent. But Mairi took away all the furniture she felt was valuable and Esme confined her life still further to the lower floor, shutting up the rooms above whose echoing solitariness struck with the cold chill of neglect.

When Aileen visited the house it was often driving down in the Mini late after a session at the library, and they closed the evening together at least twice a week. So it was that Esme, less fearsome about unlatching the front door than when her cousin first called, greeted her.

'Aileen, don't talk to me. I absolutely forbid you to talk to me. I must finish this wretched essay by midnight. It's sending me to sleep with tedium. What do we have? We have Restoration Comedy.' She wafted the pages in the air. 'The bawdy aftermath of Shakespeare. The rump of literature.'

The front room was strewn with papers and reference books which implied that Esme had achieved something in the way of self-instruction. But she read the critics only to refute them. I will not plagiarise, was the cornerstone of her study. Consequently every essay was an agony of creation where she attempted to say something that the academics had not already said, little realising that originality, if attainable, was certainly not what was required.

'Shall we tidy up a little to begin with? You may feel better if the papers aren't so messy.' Esme slumped carelessly in the nearest chair and Aileen took matters in hand. She turned up the fire, made fresh tea and with a gesture here, a straightening of the rug there, she succeeded in throwing over the room an entirely new aspect. Esme found she too was being pummelled by the other's busy manner, like a floppy cushion made to sit up and pay attention. It was impossible to resist the whirlwind of her activity. Through many evenings Esme had sat in contemplation of the cobweb round the central light fitment, a relic of Rab's art deco period. She was never utterly certain whether it was manufactured by a spider, ravelling his existence gently through hers, or whether it was the product of mere dirt, its traceries, if that were so, incongruously lovely against the brass. But either way it did not long survive Aileen's duster. Flick and it was gone.

'How simple things are for you!'

'Simple? Why?'

'You don't need to think in order to act. Perhaps that's why I'm not very good at either. They cancel each other out with me.'

'Oh, nonsense, Esme. Come. Let's be practical. What can I do to help?' She scanned the sheets on the floor, and in a few minutes made sense of her scrawlings. 'Where are you up to?'

'I'm at the last stages of transcribing it. But looking at my own writing makes me feel ill.'

'Oh, don't exaggerate, Esme. I'll dictate and you write it out in your best copperplate.'

'I'd be embarrassed. It's such drivel.'

'Get along with you or we'll be here all night.' And, patiently, she read to the scribe so that the work proceeded in double time, for whenever Esme's spirits flagged or the paragraphs seemed too banal for utterance, Aileen prodded, cajoled, threatened until at last the final word was written.

'Do you know what the Fine Art lecturer did to my last essay?' Esme declaimed, lying full length in front of the fire. Aileen wondered, Had he put a line through a page, refused to mark it because it was illegible? Such stories, though probably apocryphal, abounded.

'No, what?'

'He added commas to a sentence. What a piece of impertinence. You would think he could follow a sentence of more than twenty words without having it broken up for his digestion, like pulp food. That's what I'm expected to produce, a baby mush.'

Aileen laughed and looked over her shoulder at the offending additions. 'I think that's much more insulting,' and she put her finger on the comment at the end, 'Quite good for a beginner.'

'I know. What a cheek. And look at the mark, beta plus query plus. What kind of a Christian mark is that?'

'It's a pretty good one.'

'Is it?' She heaved a sigh that curled into the air like her question mark. 'I had a row with my English tutor today.'

'A row?' Aileen could not believe in such an eventuality.

'Oh, a nice academic row. The words were at least two syllables long.'

'What about?'

'Oh, something stupid. Sources in Shakespeare. We'd spent weeks going through Holinshed and I said I thought it was a complete waste of time. It didn't get you further into the text and it failed to take account of the other sources he might have used. My tutor' – this was a man known by reputation to Aileen as having the longest sleeves in the department, or possibly the shortest arms but the overhang was intriguing – 'said, "What sources?" So I replied, "Maybe *the* source, reality, life, what he did with himself at nights, the weather, the landscape." I couldn't get him to admit Shakespeare might have had a moment's inspiration. He doesn't know what original means. All he could fall back on was, "I think you've missed the point, Miss Rosowicz." I'll say I have. They're such bibliophiles, Aileen, that they can't see ideas may arise from other sources than books. What a load of rubbish the whole thing is.'

'Only a few more months,' she consoled, perceiving this to be a general condemnation of existence rather than of the essay alone.

'I defy you to be cheerful.'

'I'm sorry, I won't be uncheerful.'

'Then let me have a share. What have you got to be so blithe about? I expect you have worked like a storm all evening?'

'Yes, I did put in a good evening's work. Translated a passage from Gide. It's odd, you know, but I can compose a reasonable translation of traditional French. The idiom seems to come out quite naturally, but I can't get it right with modern French. It's either stilted or slangy and familiar. But the Gide came out without too much re-working.'

'What was it from?'

'The *Symphonie Pastorale,* where the pastor is falling for Gertrude as he teaches her to read, but doesn't realise it. It was fun working on the double meanings.'

'That's not much to be cheerful about. What else?'

'Rejean will be back again soon and has a whole fortnight free. We're going ski-ing. You will come to Lochearn for the Easter holiday, won't you? You can't stay by yourself. We felt dreadful leaving you out at Christmas.'

Esme shook her head. 'There's too much to catch up on.'

'How else will you learn that we're not all bears? Alexis invited you. I mean specifically invited you. I had this letter today.' She produced it from her bag, the wide writing curling over the page. Esme recognised the hand by now from the many cards and letters Aileen received from her father, embellished with drawings and diagrams, or odd pinmen adding a commentary in the margin. He phoned only in extremis. Why was there never one for her? If he wanted her to come, why didn't he ask her directly? For her there was never a thought, never a word. So many promises, so little follow through. People came and went, leaving her depleted.

'Let me see. "We expect the usual gathering and trust Esme will make one of us." You see, a proper invitation.'

She shook her head again, but smiled. It was something. 'You are too good to me, Aileen, too generous. One day you may regret it.'

'Goodness, why should you say that?'

'You are so unstinting. I have nothing to give you in return.'

'But I don't want anything.'

'I'm not used to being beholden, and when you are so thoughtful I either have to comply or be grateful, and I don't excel in either of those virtues. It puts a constraint on me. Now I have offended you.' The face of her cousin had become solemn.

'No, I'm not offended. I just feel so much solitude isn't good for you. But I won't ask you about Lochearn again. Instead, no, I won't leave you in peace, come to the Union with us on Saturday. Rejean should be back, but even if he's not it doesn't matter.'

'I've only been to the Union once and I loathed it.'

'Oh, Esme! What else are you going to do on a Saturday evening? I won't let you mope by yourself. It's not natural.'

'You do realise that you can make me do almost anything by telling me I'm abnormal if I don't? I don't know what normal is. I do what's natural for me. Isn't that enough?'

'No, it isn't. How are you going to meet anyone if you stay in all the time?'

'Anyone? I don't want to meet anyone.'

'How are you going to find a husband or a boyfriend, then?'

'I don't want to find a boyfriend and certainly not a husband. I can't think of anything worse than spending time with the boys in my lectures. They either talk about sport or bore you to death with how many references they appended to their latest essay, by way of footnote. They're not real.'

'Well, I don't know where the real people are for you. The ones I meet are real enough.'

'There you go making me feel a freak. Anyway, I've got nothing to wear to that sort of thing.'

'That's silly. You can borrow anything of mine.'

And they looked at each other and laughed at the impasse. 'Oh, all right, if I must.'

9

Rejean, making an early morning visit to the Botanic Gardens in Inverleith, was surprised to find Esme tending towards the hot-houses with her books.

'I didn't know you came here.'

'Yes, sometimes.'

'You like trees?'

'Of course I like trees. What is there to dislike about trees? But I come in cold weather to sit in the tropical houses. It's cheaper than heating my own room. Are you looking for something special? These are all ornamental trees, aren't they? I mean horticultural varieties. They won't grow commercially.'

'I haven't always got commercial interests at heart. I do occasionally think a tree looks good rather than wondering what its yield will be.'

They were winding slowly up the serpentine paths on the north side of the gardens. It was a bitter morning for the time of year, with a fine haar lying over the Forth which gave a creeping rawness to the climate, more insidious than low temperatures for it was a damp that seeped through layers of clothing and ate into the bones themselves.

'I'm on my way to the exhibition centre.'

But he was distracted from that aim by the sight of a columnar evergreen that in the middle of the frost-whitened shrubbery struck out with glints of yellow in its foliage and he dragged them towards it. 'What a marvellous creation, don't you think?' With respect that bordered on wonder he touched the fronds, handled the grey green berries.

'It's only a tree as far as I'm concerned.'

'Ah, then, you haven't looked at it properly. It's so perfectly adapted to its purpose. See, it's a conical shape so that it sheds the snow, and the boughs are light and airy to allow the wind to pass through in cold climates where your stout British trees would snap. And these needles, look, they have the minimum surface area to prevent loss of moisture while those that die form a thick carpet underneath that retains ground moisture but prevents other seedlings from taking root and depriving this tree of its substance. Now could you have created a better tree on a drawing board?'

She smiled at his eagerness and the wind-ruffled hair which undid his too regular manner. 'I am impressed.' Though she agreed to what he told her, she was more interested in the change that contact with the outdoors wrought in him. He was always unobjectionable, good company or so she had heard others call him, but in the open air he took on a freshness that was more appealing than the neutrality that the first commendation implied. Whereas the biting wind reduced her to a variable state of red and blue, a patchwork of misery, it called out in him haleness, a hearty ruddiness of complexion so that he exuded good health. He prided himself on being fit, a peak she had never aspired to, but for once she could appreciate the insularity physical well being provided against the daily onslaughts of cold, hunger or fatigue. She admired her cousin's choice more than she had done. He was the antidote to the grey dust of scholarship settling on them, a reminder of fresh air and open spaces, and minds uncluttered by minutiae.

'The whole of Canada is dotted with huge forests of conifer, mile after mile as far as the eye can see. You couldn't believe how majestic they look in a mass. One tree in a park, well, one is just a specimen.'

They gained the top of the knoll and paused to look back at the planting. 'You know,' she said, 'you are out of place here. I can feel how homesick you are in spite of everything.'

He faltered and his good-humoured smile died away.

'Oh, I am sorry. That was impertinent.'

'No, it's not impertinent. It's true, quite true, though I'm not too proud of being the victim of a rather ignoble sensation.'

'Is it ignoble – to miss home?'

'To suffer for it is.'

'I don't see it that way. It seems quite laudable to me to be attached to your homeland. What is it that you miss?'

'Space, more space, just miles of open space. I'm suffering from claustrophobia most of the time. Look at those gardens opposite.' She looked and saw the correct frontages of Inverleith, in the classical mould with basement steps and either no garden or a poky plot of grass. 'I can't stand that kind of garden, all those little spaces with railings separating them from other gardens as though the people were afraid that dogs and children might walk over their grass. What else is grass for but to walk on?'

'So you have open-plan gardens at home. But that can't make such a difference. There are other things.'

'If I'm honest, the people are enclosed here too. Yes, I know that's an unacceptable generalisation, but people are insular in Europe. It's a different way of doing things. I don't say it's wrong, but I miss the openness of my own way of life. I miss hearing French spoken. I still translate pounds into dollars and always will. The smells, the sounds, everything that is alien reminds me I'm not at home. I can't explain it to you without sounding feeble. It is simply being there that I miss. I don't know how to put it.'

'I would never have thought you were a candidate for nostalgia.'

'I'm not. I don't talk about it, and I don't let it get the better of me. I go ski-ing and walk on the hills at Lochearn when I can. That keeps it under control.'

'Good. You mustn't be unhappy while you're here.'

'Are you cold now? We've been out a long time and this fog doesn't seem to have lifted. We'll go to the hothouses if you like. They should be open.'

The park was empty and involuntarily their descent, which began sedately enough, gradually through the steepness of the slope and the lack of an inhibiting onlooker turned into a run and then into a race, where like children they took greater pleasure in impeding each other's progress than in making headway themselves. Rejean won by a foot or two, as he was prepared to cheat and jostle more outrageously. They collapsed in laughter at the front entrance to the tropical house and Rejean, exhilarated by the chase and the crisp air as well as the unburdening of a secret he had been able to confide to no one else, put his arm round her and kissed her, lingering for a second with his cheek against hers. 'Thank you for listening so patiently.'

The steamy warmth inside was like a sauna bath, so soporific that they were content to sit and doze under the dripping palms.

'Aileen tells me you had to see your lawyer last week.'

'Yes, he took me to lunch actually, at The George. That's

awfully posh, in case you didn't know it. I was most flattered.'

'Everything's straight now?'

'As straight as it will be. Legally we have acted correctly, but there will always be a doubt.'

'About what?'

'About whether my father is alive or not.'

'Forgive me saying so, but does it matter?'

'For those who don't know who their parents are, yes, it does matter. Now, you have told me you suffer from homesickness, that it's a feeling you can't rationalise or control, just an indefinable longing for something, somewhere that you've known since birth. It's the reverse with me. I'm insatiably curious about something I haven't known. I don't even know what my father's features were like. He's obliterated, and not knowing puts half of me in the dark. Half of me is hidden and I want to find it.'

'Would knowing him help you? Aren't the answers in yourself? The families I know seem to be half strangers to each other anyway, keeping secrets, divided by conflicts or different loyalties. There are no happy families. It seems to me you're lucky in having one side of your family line obscure. You'll experience only half the anxieties that afflict the rest of mankind.'

She listened with sorrow to this. There was rather more to Rejean Simard than she had first given him credit for. 'That is the cynicism of the whole man. I wish I could be cynical. Imagine if I told you that you would never see home again, never. That you were going to live in exile for the rest of your life. How would you feel? That's how I feel about being excluded from my patrimony.'

He pondered and could not disillusion her. Fathers were only men, and were liable to the sins of lying, cheating, drunkenness or debauchery as much as the remainder of the race. Was she in search of the unattainable ideal? He thought it better to know nothing than to know disappointment.

'Shall we move on? I want to see the work they're doing here on soil erosion, if you can bear it for a while.' The maps and diagrams meant little to Esme but he explained how trees were useful in preventing soil from being denuded through wind or water erosion which in some parts of the globe turned fertile land into desert.

'So you don't just cut trees down?'

'That's hardly a profitable enterprise. You do have to plant them again. You must go round some of the Forestry Commission plantations when you go to Lochearn. That taught me a good deal.'

'Is that what you're working on over here? Conservation?'

'Re-cycling and re-stocking maybe, rather than conservation. My father wanted me to take a degree in Economics at Laval, but I became interested in the other side of the business, land use and erosion, tree planting and ecology, or the part the tree plays in the ecological pattern. It wasn't exactly what he wanted, but two years spent here won't be wasted. I'm writing a report on lumbering techniques in Sweden at the moment. That's a bit dry.'

'You ought to try second ordinary English Literature. I'll swap any time.'

'Come on, I must drop you back home and get down to some work.'

But she would go no further than half way with him and insisted on walking the rest of the way.

'Are you sure? You'll notice the cold.'

'No, the sun's beginning to drizzle through. I'm fine, really.'

He didn't go inside directly after they parted, but watched her in the mirror as she receded, striding away from him into the distance. She shouldn't be on her own. The other fellows must be fools, and he turned the nose of the car towards the pend, not without a pang of regret that he was not entirely his own master any more.

Esme's mind was busy. She tried to focus on what they had said, but time and time again the action of the kiss intervened to gain some recognition from her. How did she place it? How could she judge it when she had no knowledge of these things? In a world where engaged couples cohabited, was such a casual kiss a trivial matter? Was it possible to be friends by means of lips and finger-tips? Perhaps it meant nothing more – to him. To her it was significant. When she walked abroad she invited attention. Only in the twoness of life was there some kind of sexual immunity, for a woman alone was a prey and she saw that her solitary mode of existence was not as simple as she had imagined. That was why Rhona had slunk against walls to avoid the workman's whistle which covered her with shame, rammed her profusion of red hair under a hat, always hid. Rhona was a victim, but Esme would not be cast in a passive role so easily. Perhaps it was time to do away with her diffidence, the source of virginity that says I am inviolable because I have no desire. For the appalling thing was that in Rejean Simard's embrace she had thought it might be no unpleasant thing to be his lover, clean limbed, blue-eyed, yes, hardy handsome. Among her darting sensations she had felt the lure of curiosity. What would it be like to be in such a man's bed? Oh no, acknowledging such a mean lust smote her with reproach and she turned to the only maxim that had been driven home to her for staying power – Thou shalt not.

When Esme had completed her lectures the following day she left George Square and walked up Middle Meadow Walk, her footsteps tending to the great public library on George IVth Bridge. She made a detour to the Royal Mile in search of a cake shop that might sell her the remnants of the day's stock cheaply for her meal, a crushed bridie, a pastry that would not be fresh in the morning, and lingered to eat them on the steps of St Giles. The Royal Mile was a remarkable slope, encompassing the events of ten centuries of history, from the heights of the ancient castle down to the more recent and somewhat barren Palace of Holyroodhouse. There was hardly a close or an alleyway in the Mile that had not housed a nobleman, or a murderer, raised a philosopher or a poet, witnessing together the rise and downfall of the house of Stuart. Covenanters and Jacobites alike had slunk against the stair walls on dark nights, meeting plot with counter-plot, matching attack with bloody revenge.

As the evening thickened, from her high window in the reference room she watched the vast concourse of people who swarmed up and down the broad street, students going to and from late lectures, early visitors come to taste the pleasures of the out of season capital, shoppers and shop-keepers, professional men like Mr Scott locking up their offices for the night, an unending passage of men and women going about their business. What limitless entertainment the streets afforded. How she would like to follow half a dozen of these anonymous folk, boarding their buses, unlocking their cars and see them through the nightways of the city into their homes. What would they tell her about themselves if she could sit by their hearth for an hour? About her own life she felt no curiosity, no momentum for change, but what a fund of intrigue was in other people's. She rubbed clean a lattice and saw a fine drizzle had started, dazzling the lights of the traffic and amplifying the sound of pneumatic tyres on tarmac. The headlights arced over the stones of the buildings opposite, and threw into definition the sills and lintels, supported by a curlicue and ogive, the heavy mannerisms of the pseudo-classical.

Now I came here for a purpose, she recalled, but what was it? Casting an eye round the shelves of the reference library she was again intimidated by what she did not know, could not acquire. Books on a shelf were as closed, as forbidding as people in cars. One had to take them out before one could begin to make progress. But which? Oh, yes. She was going to look up something about Poland. She knew nothing whatever about the country, or the language apart from the one word Alexis had used and jolted back her memory. Dushka. Dushka Esme. Once when Stefan and she had watched for the homing pigeons, Rab was called away on legal business, and when the first of the fluttering grey birds had touched down on the summerhouse she had run to tell him to trigger the stop-watch. She had fallen over and Stefan, hearing her cry out, had picked her up with the words, 'Dushka, dushka Esme', and the clock was forgotten for ten irrecoverable minutes while he bathed her cut knee. She had the scar still.

She read that at different times Poland had covered different areas, and from 1795 it disappeared altogether from the map of Europe as an independent state until it was resurrected in 1918 after the First World War. Twenty-one years later, its traditional enemies, Russia and Germany again tore Poland apart. It emerged in 1945 with its land devastated once more, and new boundaries.

The Poles, she learned, were an ancient branch of the Slavic people, dating back to the sixth century, who had made their home around the basin of the huge River Vistula and its tributaries, a plateau that lacked natural boundaries and merged imperceptibly into the dominating countries on either side. They were a peasant race, ruled by a warrior class of nobles, and surviving on meagre smallholdings. But gradually a culture emerged that looked to the West rather than the East, founded on the Church of Rome, the Latin alphabet and Renaissance-inspired teaching. In the previous two centuries these traditions and beliefs had been forced underground, but had not died, and in literature, music, science, Poland had given significant men and women to the world. It was a history, she learned, of suppression and enslavement of the population that had culminated in the annexation of Poland by Hitler in 1939, mass evacuation of workers, the exile of its ruling class throughout the crumbling capitals of Europe, had led to the Warsaw ghetto, the mystery of Katyn forest and the near extermination of an entire people.

Unaware of time now, or of the hush that had fallen in the emptying street below, Esme took herself to the biographies of Marie Curie, Chopin, Copernicus and Paderewski. Was this her birthright as much as Charles Edward Stuart and Sir Walter Scott, the philosopher Hume and Adam Smith? Did one learn of the past solely through association and direct teaching, or could something pass unconsciously into the blood along with one's genetic make-up? Marie Curie's biographer had written, 'Polish women are often very beautiful, brilliantly clever with great and enduring charm. Marie Curie had these qualities also, but her face wore the shadowed look of those who are born into an oppressed race.' Was it possible that there should be some national characteristic created by oppression, a look, a cast of the eye, a type of feature and, if so, did it afflict her personally? She knew she was apart, distinctive from her foster race, but whether this resulted from predominantly physical or mental properties she could not tell. In the past she had been gratified to be an only child. It conferred the status of being unique, but now she wished for siblings with whom she might compare her own hybrid state, in the search for what they had commonly inherited.

The librarian rang a bell at ten o'clock and Esme realised she had been there for more than five hours, and that she was famished. Outside, the night was wet and moonlessly dark, enveloping her quietly. No bus came, so impatiently she set out to walk the two miles to home. Merely to move was a relief. Sometimes, for weeks at a stretch, she felt her whole being was at a standstill, that she had made no advance in knowledge and that the stream of people who milled around and past her were bent on a course she could not see and did not understand. Being a student, serving an apprenticeship, struck her as a void. Yes, that was it. At her core there was a vacuum, a lack of urgency, something that was happy to fritter and dither and observe. Was it laziness, stupidity or self-indulgence that this evening when she should have been reading a critique on

Alexander Pope she had been following her fancy? Shame on you, she thought. Aileen would have filled half a notebook in this time, and she broke into a run as though to recoup some of the elusive commodity she had wasted.

10

By the first of May the sooty gardens of the suburbs had begun to stir with the promise of life. The hardy snowdrop had long been replaced by the spears of crocus which in their turn had given way to the rock plants that took kindly to the terraced layers of the town plot, aubretia, alyssum, snow-in-summer breaking out in riotous colour against the sun-warmed sandstone. Esme kept the window open all day to catch the aura of the new year, for she was too primaeval to believe it began with two-headed Janus at Hogmanay, and as the warm air blew the curtain into a sail and fluttered the pages of a book over and over she felt her attention wander, and hurried outside. The unpruned roses forged ahead with stems like trees and a store of fat buds already well developed; the apple blossom drifted gently down like snow, a mild pink snow that shrivelled in a day or two to a brown flake and she smiled to recall how under these boughs they had packed the cartons. The last apple had been eaten long ago, but along the branches another crop was revealed in the incipient fruit, no bigger than a pea sheltering behind a corona of pistils. She would not be there to eat them.

A drifting feather caught her attention and she looked up to see a handful of wheeling seagulls. They had been driven in by a storm out at sea, though it was hard to believe that on this mildest of days there might be a gale blowing a few miles away, on the North Sea. She watched their circular spirals intently as if they were an omen, sinister from the left or a harbinger of good tidings from the right. So Rab would stand, scanning the sky waiting for the pigeons to settle home. He had set off for the Waverley with baskets of the pigeons pecking nervously through the slats, winking bright eyes and cooing deeply in their throats. They might be transported to the south coast, to France or to Ireland. Occasionally, if they were set off nearby on the Calton Hills or at North Berwick, she would be taken along to watch them being released, spinning upwards and away in a cloud of feathers. But more enduring in her memory was this wait for them to return. The summerhouse was their favourite setting down point, and many long hours Rab spent with his binoculars trained over the garden and its neighbours, his hand poised to trigger the elaborate timing device that would ratify his entry. Sometimes, infuriatingly, the birds would circle before they landed and then he became inarticulate with rage, wanting to burst out but knowing full well that any demonstration would delay their landing.

She waited too, certain that she must not stir. She waited for a message, a signal, the merest reminder of her existence and that she was not deceived in the man.

In the garden at Inchcombe, Rejean lent a hand, for Alexis was intent on making the first cut of the long grass that flourished in the orchard. A mild winter in the strath had failed to check its growth which lay matted in thick tufts. The scythe was the answer and through the afternoon the rhythmic swish of its blade could be heard.

'Isn't this rather slow?' objected the visitor after an hour's work. It was clear that Alexis was the more talented reaper. He had the knack of lifting the fallen sheaf and depositing it in a pile at the end of each row of trees. Rejean swashbuckled with his blade and scattered grass everywhere. He couldn't clear the base of the trees, but left ragged sprouts behind.

'It's the time-honoured way. But we'll take a rest if you like. It's hot work.'

Aileen, who had the foresight to consider their thirst, brought out ginger beer and found them sprawled under the blossom-laden trees. She carried her revision with her in the form of a book of French idioms for Rejean to clarify several points, so while they talked in their secondary tongue Alexis took a wander about his territory, glass in hand.

He could feel justifiably pleased with the advent of the new season as he surveyed the roses, thought the hedge was suffering in a dry spell, remembered he had meant to tie the top growth of the clematis. A pleasant plot, he thought, scanning its range from the boundary of loch to road. It was informal but cogent and he had cultivated it singlehanded from the wilderness that stretched elsewhere along the shoreline. It was roughly broken into patches that retained the look of the landscape, a lightly wooded area, a screen of the native silver birch in front of the loch, one large oak which stood to the south-west of the house, providing shelter from wind and shade from heat. The formal garden was small and Mairi grew what flowers she wanted in that. For the rest, he had pruned rather than altered the elements of the foreshore. It all had its function prescribed apart from one area which he allowed to invade the order of the rest because of the possibilities it stimulated in his imagination. Like many tidy men he enjoyed the prospect of one extravagance he could not justify, a single self-indulgence he could not control. So the unkempt orchard of the old croft, which in husbandry could have provided more valuable food than its motley crop of tasteless apples, was his favourite retreat, in spite of its perennial couch grass and daisies and an old arbour which had reverted to an unpruned thatch of dog-roses. The orchard was alternately in prospect an efficient cottage garden, or a Tudor maze of yew bordering the thyme lawn he had wanted to experiment with for years past, a formal pleasance with a parterre of herbs, or maybe a miniature landscape of conifer and heather on scree, a microcosm of the natural setting of mountain and loch around him.

But the pleasure he derived from the old orchard was infinite because it was unspecified. He enjoyed the plans more than the execution, thumbing through seed catalogues and brochures which supplied the information for half a dozen designs laid to rest in a drawer, but he continued to relish it because he did nothing about it in the end and the permutations remained accessible. They were useless apples really, small and acid, fit for cider and nothing else. They weren't even worth peeling. In his mind's eye he saw Esme skinning an apple in one long curling curve. But he pushed the remembrance away.

He returned dismally to his work in a corner where he would be unobserved by Rejean and Aileen, whose voices rose and fell inconsequentially. He had been in a visible gloom of late for the interminable discussions on the wedding touched but did not involve him, and he was left to reflect that fathers were superfluous except when it came to footing the bill. Weddings were dreadful affairs, he felt, a mere ritual which in all other cases apart from his own daughter's he had stubbornly refused to attend. The business of eating to excess at every social function, Christmas, weddings, parties, infuriated him and he became more abstemious than usual in revolt. He had long considered that the sole purpose in gathering with one's fellow humans was the interchange of talk and that the accompanying actions of eating and drinking impaired this directly and through their after-effects. The stupor of food and alcohol was not the best adjunct to repartee or even good sense.

Morever, something in the form of the wedding service itself caused him dismay, its inflexibility perhaps, its chant-like responses, its lack of spontaneity, so that the words and ritual of the performance became a symbol of the union they inaugurated, dull, meaningless, endlessly repeated. Nor could he admire the insistence on contracting their marriage in the eyes of God by persons who had not sought his wisdom in the preceding twenty-five years of their life. It made a complicity of sham. And expense! Half of the country was to make a profit out of Aileen marrying the young man of her fancy, from lace, frills, flowers, lobster as well as salmon, air tickets to and from Canada, trestles, raw-cuffed waitresses from the surrounding villages. It was an indulgence of profligacy from which the ascetic in him recoiled. While he expressed his taste for craftsmanship, he begrudged paying for service. Couldn't a man stand up open to the sky with the woman of his choice and say 'I will, I do' without observing the stultifying form and ceremony of the times?

Then, pausing over his scythe, he heard the strains of a record Aileen had put on in her room and the words looped their way under the boughs.

Parlez-moi d'amour.
Redites-moi des choses tendres.
Votre beau discours,
Mon coeur n'est pas las de l'entendre.
Pourvu que toujours
Vous répétiez ces mots suprêmes –
Je vous aime!

The pure lyrical line of this mollified him. How succinct the

French were. Only Scots of the tongues known to him came near to it for the deftness of the language along the intonation of a song. He cursed himself for having become a cantankerous old fellow who had lived into the age of cynicism. Then bending down again he saw that Rejean had silently joined him, and felled the grass on the far side.

Rejean wasn't certain what he thought about the interior of the house. It proclaimed its origins rather too clearly for his taste, something that had worked for its living, farm, sheds, byre and outhouses. The rooms lacked elegant conception, either too small in their initial state, or over-large where two had been knocked together for expediency. Their furnishing was in a style he did not recognise as being grand, or modern, or expensive. Whitewashed walls, a sanded floor, a conscious rendering of the spirit of the peasantry which prevailed at the time of the building of the house. Indeed, there were antiques everywhere but their value and design were quite lost on the young mind and the attitudes of the new world. He did not appreciate that a Charles Rennie Mackintosh chair had been placed exactly at that point on the landing because its vertical shape countered the long low window, that a slatted bamboo shade was rolled as a blind and a lacquered table set beside the other pieces because they formed a neat visual group, beyond which there were many sub-strata, which it needed long experience to excavate. The Japanese mood, the vertical and horizontal balanced as neatly as the yin and yang of Taoism, the columnar chair, the circular table, but all achieved with materials essentially natural. The house was full of such puns and jokes and innuendo. But if Rejean was to give an opinion on it, all he could say was that it was interesting, which meant basically that he did not understand it.

But perhaps he was most baffled by the sudden changes in mood from room to room. They had arrived at a compromise whereby Mairi held sway in the dining room which was resplendent with silver, silver chafing dishes, silver trays, silver jugs of every denomination within the scope of pouring liquid, a Queen Anne silver teaset on its sideboard which, decked with this finery, looked more like an altar in some remote high Andean church than a simple serving table. Mairi could put on a polished show for her dinner guests. Over everything there hung an indefinable smell, of cleaning fluid and Mansion polish and a richness he had begun to think of as English in origin for he had not encountered it elsewhere north of the border, of thick gravies and Patum Peperium, the gentleman's relish, and Hellmann's mayonnaise. For Mairi gave dinners that were more lavish than any of her neighbours', except perhaps at Curriedon, for in the region 'come in and have a bite' was the norm of hospitality. She was proud of her glittering set pieces, hothouse grapes, imported cheese, flagons of wine carefully decanted in the old still room, north facing and a perfect wine cellar. But for all that hospitality was its function, her room did not exude warmth.

He was more able to relax in the parlour, as Alexis insisted on calling it, for what was its purpose but to talk in. This was his domain. There was nothing in the room that had not been mended or belonged at one time to someone else. It was the retreat of the conservator. One scarcely noticed the furnishings, merely hugely comfortable, used rather than preserved. Sitting with a glass in hand while the early evening fire emitted a thin blue smoke, he could admire whole-heartedly the pattern of light from both east and west which the windows threw across the room. Books filled the recesses of the fireplace and elsewhere Alexis' paintings gave the room its relief. Landscapes, they hung like secondary windows on blank walls, views of the glens and the mountain streams, spaced deliberately to give the place new perspectives by night when the curtains were closed and the natural outlook barred.

Alexis leaned against his mantelpiece and threw wood chippings on the fire. 'So you are quite set on this course?'

'Resolutely, yes. I know you think it's below par, but there's nothing else I want to do and it will be so useful. It's not just secretarial skills. It will use the French as well, and we do a class in Economics, and on the principles of Company Law. Ultimately I'm going to help Rejean in the business, and it will be invaluable for that.'

He grimaced at this estimable aim. He would much rather that she do something independent of her spouse, but then it was out of his hands. Mairi approved, naturally, of the acquiring of a practical skill, of the girl following in her own footsteps, and so his last hope of an ally was Rejean. 'You don't mind if your wife spends another year steeped in her books?'

'Not at all. I hope to be going home next spring . . .'

'And it will all fit in so well. If you are sure about us having the flat for another year.'

'Of course. You don't need to ask,' Alexis expostulated and turned to toast the other side of his legs.

'It's not going to be very convenient when either of us wants to come to town,' but this was taken as Mairi's traditional penny-worth of objection and ignored.

Alexis stood gloomily preoccupied in the idea that Aileen might make her home on the other side of the Atlantic. What a long desolation that would be.

'And then,' she rushed the fence, 'I've asked Esme to be my bridesmaid, and she's agreed.' This had been a long-standing problem. Aileen had innumerable friends but none of them especially favoured above the others. Her younger cousins, the children of her uncles, were likewise plentiful and that alone cancelled them out. She could not pick out one cherubic attendant and abandon all the rest. Esme was a godsend. There was only one of her and she was right. Rejean agreed readily, but his was not the greatest hurdle.

All this Mairi saw but the coolness that had blown in Esme's direction ever since the funeral was not likely to be tempered now. She was responsible for somehow inveigling (Mairi had a whole vocabulary of words associated with duress) Alexis to stay at the old house, most unsuitably; she had resisted Mairi's quite proper appropriation of her assets; she had entailed Aileen's affections, and worst of all she had not communicated as much as a scrape of the pen since November. That it might be incumbent upon her to do so and inquire after her niece's welfare did not occur to Mairi. So this was a facer. How to get out of it, or accept with no loss of credit? She clucked her tongue to stall. 'Well, if you've asked, it can't be withdrawn. I always did mean for her to have some time here, and if you're sure that's what you want, I'll abide by it. I expect we'll have to buy her dress for her. And of course if she comes here, as I suppose she will have to, and Rejean's parents are staying as well . . .'

'Oh no, my parents wouldn't dream of troubling you. I had a letter from my father a few days ago, and on his instructions I have booked us into Gleneagles. That will be much less trouble all round.'

Alexis was silent listening to them. He had given a whoop of joy when he heard of Aileen's divine intercession but composed himself to ask with studied nonchalance, 'How is Esme, by the way?'

'Up and down. The good days are pretty rare. I don't know what she does with herself all day. Every time I go round there she is drawing up a new programme of revision, but when I look at it I realise it's the same amount of work in less time.'

'What is she going to do next year?'

'No idea. Drifts, procrastinates, hopes something will turn up. She goes into a visible decline if I try and talk realities to her. She hates studying, so there's not much point in going on with that.'

'What does she do with herself, then?' pursued her father.

'I don't know. She never goes out. I forced her to come collecting with me in Rag Week. Didn't we look a sight, Rejean? We went up and down Princes Street all day as Siamese twins. Black trousers each and that enormous sweater you passed over to Rejean. We both got into it quite comfortably. We laughed so much, I'm sure it did Esme good. Though I was as stiff as a board for days afterwards. It was proof anyway that Esme's face is her fortune. All the men gave to Esme's collecting box and all the women to mine. Moral there. But then the evening was bad.'

'Why bad?' asked Mairi, who had returned with a pot of coffee.

'It was all my fault, I must confess. I said she should come with us to the Union and it just didn't work out.'

'Ah, do you still go to the Union?' asked Mairi and her face burst into a second of animation. 'Rhona and I used to go there.' She looked across at her husband but met no returning invitation to speak, in fact she met a hostile you-dare-say-a-word look, and dropped her eyes again. For that was where they had met, a casual wartime meeting at a dance hall. She was aware that the others waited politely for her to go on, but she was shy of recollection and they did not prompt. It was unfortunate that she was the least clever of her immediate circle; all her siblings had been through the University, as well as her child and her spouse, though his was an abbreviated qualification under post-war rules. And, knowingly or not, they dismissed her and her experience because she was merely practical, as though this were not as valuable a skill as bookishness. Her opinion was not consulted. They were foolish in this. Had they been kinder, she could have told them of the Palais and the Plaza dancing palaces. And that was what they were, arenas of sound, glittering cathedrals of glass and light, of jazz and jitterbugging and the big band sound – all first hand – and spoken wistfully of how she and Rhona saved their clothes coupons conjointly so that they could buy a blouse or a pair of shoes more quickly and appear in fashion. They had established an excellent trading system, two of this to one of that, four coupons and a sweater equals one wool skirt, though Rhona suffered in the exchange by being less than fastidious, and a point was deducted by her senior for every stain and smudge. She would have spoken of the eternal hunt for nylon stockings, virtually unobtainable and so the most prized gift which the brothers or the fiancés could bring back from a trip to America or London, and of dawn raids on the occasional shop which did manage to lay hands on a tiny stock. So precious were these nylons that businesses were founded just to repair them, and women sat up late mending ladders with spider-like thread and a small crochet hook, a shilling a time. More often than not, however, the search was futile and they had to resort to painting their legs with brown dye even in winter.

But they did not ask. The grief of her stillborn marriage lay over her like a shroud and made so much of the past inaccessible, too painful in retrospect. A happy woman would have leaned across the table and, seizing her husband by the power of memory, for what is shared is the strongest bond of all, said 'Do you remember how we used to . . .' and the vapour of joy would have ascended like the aura from candles and good wine, enveloping them all, from which the young couple beside them would have learned immeasurably. But they did not ask, and she and they were impoverished by it. By a bitter irony, only Esme of her acquaintance might have pursued the point and asked and asked and asked until the defences fell. But she turned away and performed one of the myriad domestic tasks for which she received no thanks or credit, and poured the coffee.

'Why didn't it work out?'

'Oh, we'd left her with a friend of ours and thought she was getting on fairly well with him, but someone else had cut in and made himself objectionable.'

'How objectionable?' he persevered, reconstructing in his mind's eye the rather gaunt debating chamber of the men's student union, which on Saturdays was given over, inappropriately, to dances. He doubted if they had improved since his day. The bar shut at ten and there was a general stampede of semi-drunken males onto the dance floor for half an hour, for a quick reconnoitre on the likeliest prospect to take home, in the hope that gratitude would be overwhelming. As far as he could remember the bar was a male province in a positively mediaeval segregation of the sexes.

Aileen prevaricated. 'The way a man can who knows what he is doing with a girl who doesn't.'

Alexis' face creased with pain, but she imagined it was anger.

'No, I realise I was to blame. I did make her go because I thought, She can't spend all her time in that gloomy house by herself. Then, upset, she came to find us in the Couples' Hall and was virtually thrown out by the doorman who thought she was a troublemaker. Till Rejean intervened.'

'How exactly was he objectionable?'

'I don't know that,' she answered patiently. 'But not indecently, I imagine. It was a public place.'

'What I can't see,' objected Rejean, 'is why you girls go there at all. It's so barbaric.'

'There isn't anywhere else. That's where everyone goes and if you want to see your friends, you go there too. What do you do in Canada? Fill in dance cards? And there is always the option of saying, No. Esme is such a little goose really. One does become exasperated in the end when she behaves like a protected species.'

Alexis admired his accomplishment, but with a sad inflection. He had made her secure all right. She could turn on her heel, give someone a mouthful if she really wanted to. She would never need to. Her whole bearing worked against exploitation. She knew where she stood in relation to the universe. But, shockingly, he had made her so secure she could not fathom insecurity in others. She cared, she took an interest. but was she truly sympathetic?

And then, to confound him, she went on, 'The trouble with Esme is she attracts the wrong sort of men, the undeserving.' This gave both her male interlocutors something of a pang. 'She is so overtly attractive, well, sexual, isn't she, that men look and admire without ever wondering what's inside her head. And as she doesn't know her own worth she'll always fall a prey to them.' That was better, he thought, that was nearer the truth, even though it did contain a barb.

'What do you mean, she doesn't know her own worth?' interrupted Mairi. 'I'm sorry, but I'm becoming so tired talking about Esme all the time. Six months ago we hardly heard her name. Now she's on everyone's tongue. And what I can't understand is why you all seem to think she's so extraordinary. I don't see it, but then I'm not a man and I may be immune to what you call her overt attractiveness. I want to know what she's done, and that doesn't sound so amazing to me. She'll have difficulty scraping together her degree from what you say. She doesn't work hard. And I ask myself, Why are we all sitting here taking an interest in someone who has never, as far as I know, done anything for us? Has she put herself out for you, Aileen? I'd like to know.'

'That's hardly fair,' the girl reasoned. 'She hasn't got anything to give, in your sense. I mean what could she possibly give me, or do for me? Look at us sitting here in this room, think about the meal we've just eaten. Well, Esme's sitting by one bulb eating bread and cheese for supper. I can promise that. And she's a person, she isn't a balance sheet of plus and minus and it's all got to come out at the end of the month with nothing owing. I'm not trying to patronise her, but she is worthy and I look on it as a pleasure to do anything for her. You can't imagine how hard it is to persuade her to accept. And all this giving or taking isn't the point. I'm fond of her. I won't let her down.'

Bravo, thought Alexis. I like you better every day, young woman.

'But you see,' objected Mairi with that slow satisfied smile of one who always knows best, 'you are raising your voice and making an issue over her. That is the thing about the Esmes of the world. They make trouble. You don't see it, but I have lived longer and I know. It isn't a matter of what she can afford, of course not. But she could think a little. A postcard doesn't cost much. Cooperation costs nothing.'

Rejean spoke up at last. 'She is someone whose qualities may seem frail or even negative, but I do believe she has never had a vicious thought in her life. I count it as a privilege to know her.'

But Mairi shrugged at this eulogy, the terms of which she was hardly equipped to assess, and Alexis thought despondently, Sometime, somehow, he will pay dearly for that commendation.

The inside of the church was cool and white. Behind the altar were heavy blue curtains and a simple cross. The fittings of the church, pews, balustrade, the gallery behind and its supports were of good weathered pine, but so old that they approximated more to the colour of oak and were polished by antique use to a sheen that pine seldom acquires. Mairi came weekly to this pew, and always alone. So the betrothed couple beside her made a stir of novelty and the nods and smiles were stronger than usual in anticipation of the great celebration that would attend their nuptials. Mairi's neighbours moved a little from their accustomed places to accommodate the newcomers, and only the most uncharitable thought it was a while since Aileen had seen fit to show her face inside the kirk door. Maybe she was a heathen like her father.

Aileen was oblivious to their censure. She saw the church interior not as a house of God, heavy with sublime meanings, but as a kind of public meeting place in which she was obliged by custom to hold her wedding. It had an entirely functional aspect, and she reviewed its assets, good capacity, excellent vision, wide aisles, fine organ, as critically as its defects which seemed to consist mainly of poor acoustics. Would banks of flowers take away the echo? She imagined two tall stands on either side of the altar and perhaps smaller posies on the pillars or the ends of the pews to give a more intimate air. What colour? she mused. Something warm in tone. Mairi had said to spend as much as she liked on flowers. Their supplier was a business friend and would give discount.

Rejean was less sanguine. The rarefied atmosphere of the chancel made him breathless, as though there were not enough oxygen in its corners, but he shook his head in an attempt to clear it of the stuffy air. He must have drunk too much wine at dinner the night before. But the feeling of anxiety persisted and he wondered if he was in awe of the place or if he felt himself to be under scrutiny. Indeed the examining of his conscience, which might be considered a necessary adjunct to his attendance in this place of contemplation, had proceeded intensively since the moment a few weeks before when, full of carefree abandonment, he had stooped to kiss the unsuspecting Esme.

Light in itself, a throwaway gesture, it had no profound moral significance. What worried and nagged at him and had run like a sub-current through the intervening weeks and his whole am- bivalent presence here, was that the kiss had revealed to him something he had only very lately begun to suspect. He did not want to marry Aileen at all.

The perfidy of that idea frightened him and he glanced at her to see if she registered the reaction away from her, but her eyes mutely followed the line of the psalm and her lips obeyed the paraphrase. Whatever did he have to complain of? She was the very model of his dreams, bright, fresh, a rare creature.

Was it then the married state he wished to avoid? Not in all honesty, for he knew himself well enough to realise he was tired of endless pursuit and was ready to move on to another phase of his being. He wanted a fellow traveller. But did he want some other form of alliance than this? They had lived together for almost a year and maybe that fluidity was an impediment to the definition of marriage.

He did not know. He was in a perfect muddle with himself. And then, miserably, he began to cough, irritatingly to the congre- gation who were in the middle of a prayer, that dry tickling cough which exacerbates itself. He felt as out of place as a dog in a concert hall. Eyes looked at him in sympathy and stole away again for shame. He was a sight now, bloated with coughing and puffy-eyed as he tried to restrain it. Mairi, ever resourceful, slipped him a pan drop and gradually it soothed the spasm. Aileen took his hand and smiled reassurance.

No, the unspoken link between these ideas that did not quite formulate into a cohesive argument was Esme. Place that chimera beside the certainty of a settled future with Aileen, and the choice was declared. He knew what to expect with Aileen. There were no surprises there, but with Esme there could be no such predict- ability.

And then the surroundings impinged on him again and he felt these were unholy thoughts. Here was the entire congregation (he did not appreciate how much larger a slice of the community had come to weigh him up) listening to his banns: Rejean Albert

Simard, bachelor, of the parish of St Jean des Prés in Montreal, Canada, and the whole cumbersome apparatus was set in motion. How could he think better of it? What talk there would be for Aileen, and for no good purpose; for something as fickle as a whimsy kiss not even, he remembered with regret, reciprocated.

After lunch, which was a cold collation, the men took their coffee to the office. The newspapers were spread over the desk and work tables, with books weighing the pages down or acting as column markers. Reading the Sunday news was a serious business. 'Do, feel at liberty,' Alexis indicated a chair, a supplement, but Rejean read a line or two, lost the place and began again disjointedly.

'I have something I would like to talk to you about, sir,' he said. 'Though perhaps I shouldn't.' He gestured hopelessly, and Alexis peering at him from the leader of the *Sunday Times* saw a worrying resemblance between his future son-in-law and the other young man who had stood idly and lovelorn in his office in the late days of the autumn. He put down the paper and paid attention, though the hard and concentrated gaze with which he signalled his full attention might have been less than conducive to a simple narrative.

'If my father were here, I suppose I would talk to him about it. But, as it is, I feel you are the only person I can consult. Though in truth . . .' he tailed off and looked for a long time into the garden, flicking the edge of his armchair abstractedly with his fingers, 'I don't entirely know how to say this, and you have every right to be livid with me, but I feel I can't go ahead with the wedding.'

Alexis folded the paper away. 'You haven't said anything to Aileen, otherwise you wouldn't have gone to hear the banns read.'

'That's right.' Rejean clung to some positive interpretation of his dilemma. 'It was while I was sitting there this morning that I felt – dwarfed by the prospect.'

'So it is a momentary feeling.'

'No, not entirely. We've been engaged what, nearly twelve months. For six of those I've felt doubtful but only today I felt it impossible to go on.'

Alexis heaved a sigh. 'Why?'

'I think, to be honest, it's no coincidence that in those six months I've known Esme.'

'So you and Esme are drawn together?'

Rejean sensed the sharpness of the question. Yes, it was asking much to forgive disaffection from his own daughter, but impossible to overlook what looked like a flirtation with her cousin. 'No, let me hasten to assure you. Esme would be dismayed to hear me talking like this. She and Aileen are devoted to each other. I had thought that was impossible until I met them. I have never heard a hard word between them and one of the reasons I'm so ashamed of my indecision is that Esme never has, or would, encourage anything sneaky.'

Mollified, Alexis probed, 'Then why, if not for the sake of another relationship, are you intent on ruining this one?'

'If I were going to make an honest marriage with Aileen, Esme shouldn't be in my thoughts at all.'

Alexis assembled these ideas before he answered. 'Do you really think that? That the moment you marry your attraction to – and for, let's consider that – all other women will magically cease? How very convenient if it were so. It's about as logical as saying because I own one painting, I may never look at another one. I see not the slightest error in seeking and enjoying the company of other women, apart from your wife.' But dammit, he was the last person to consult. Wasn't his about the most dismal record in marital contentment? How could he give honest advice based on an extension of his own experience as a man without at the same time betraying his daughter's interests? For ambiguous as Rejean's feelings might be, or even Esme's, Aileen was without equivocation. He knew how a jilting would affect her standing in this community. It would be whispered against her for years hence. No man in Christendom had a longer memory than a Scot when it came to scandal. On the other hand, did he not profoundly believe that he himself would be better off without the institution of matrimony, that a relationship founded on the tug-of-war between jealousy and indifference was dead before it began and he was deceiving the young man, son-in-law or none, to tell him to go ahead on such a false premise? That his difficulties would be resolved on the wedding day was a lie. Shouldn't he spare him his own anguish?

So he rationalised this way and that, effectively silenced by quite contradictory motives. 'I can't tell you to do anything.'

'At least you're not hostile.'

'Did you imagine I would be?'

'I deserve your wrath.'

Besides, Esme. There was Esme after all. The finest trees in the forest must have space and light, and he wanted to see a clearing round her for full growth. Was he truthful enough to admit it was a clearing for himself? Maybe not. He could not wholly equate his interest with the young man's, beyond seeing that she made a disruption, broke the calm pattern of existence for both of them.

'Tell me, have you taken against marriage itself or against Aileen?' Rejean looked scarcely able to decide so he began again. 'Are you postponing or cancelling?'

'Oh, postponing, until I can sort myself out.'

'But it's gone too far for that. To be stood up so soon before your wedding isn't something you recover from. Before the banns were read, perhaps, but not now. The old breach of promise law still carries some stigma here. If you break, you break for good.'

'Oh no, that's too harsh. I admire Aileen too much.' Alexis could have wished for a warmer commendation of his only child. 'Aileen is the perfect wife . . .'

'But Esme is the perfect mistress,' the older man added grimly.

Rejean looked surprised at finding his thoughts so neatly echoed.

'Console yourself that Esme's not made for monogamy. There's no man could hold her to that, so don't burn yourself out thinking you could. She's no captive.'

'Never?'

'Never.'

Rejean accepted his authority and, seeing him anxious to pursue the next paragraph of the *Times* leader, lifted his paper again to end the conversation. How very strangely the British spend their Sundays. At home, he would be at the lake on a weekend like this, swimming or water ski-ing, deepening his tan and renewing acquaintance with his lakeside neighbours over a barbecue, stretching himself in the grand outdoors of the banana belt. And a waft of nostalgia caught him and transported him where he longed to be, among his own folk and under the gilded sky of home.

'I think I'll go for a walk, if you'll excuse me.'

Left alone, Alexis feared he had done his child a disservice. Wasn't it the sense of not being paramount with each other that eroded confidence in a relationship, a gnawing jealousy that at last undermined the whole personality, at least of women? Could Aileen be cast in her mother's role of dissatisfied wife? He would move heaven and earth to prevent that. Well, she would never know of these premarital doubts unless Rejean himself admitted them, and then surely in the context of happiness rather than recrimination. Alexis for once doubted his own judgment, and would have liked a second opinion, but of the people concerned only Esme was capable of talking it over without heat or hurt, and she too might have a declared interest to throw her off balance. Best say nothing.

In the middle of the afternoon, remembering that Graeme was to join them for tea and fearful of missing the best of the day, Alexis struck out along the shore to intercept his friend, who would almost certainly walk the distance between Curriedon and Inchcombe.

Graeme saw him from afar and cut down from his vantage point on the hills and across the road to join him.

'I'm glad you've come,' he started as they sauntered by the water's edge. What did he want to say? He glanced back at the house again. Rejean was indoors and he and Aileen were occupied in a noisy squabble over the crossword. Laughter and teasing floated towards him. Was all well? Was the hesitancy in his mind only? Why open up doubts to the infection of calumny and rumour? And if he told the story whole, he might implicate himself and could not tolerate having Graeme think he had acted with bias. 'What's the thing you would most wish for your children, Graeme?'

'Nothing material. Not to make the same mistakes I have, I suppose.'

'How do you prevent that if the mistakes are in their nature?'

Graeme considered. 'You cannot. The sins of the fathers are visited on the children . . . Genetics undo us all.'

Alexis heaved. He was in no mood for the Presbyterian catechism today, and casting round him for some wonted relief in his plot, his personal landscape, saw only what was unfinished through idleness or despoiled by wind, rain, predators. Imperfection accused him. He should have worked harder, but he felt his life and his energy drain away in disappointment and failure.

Work, work, work, everything shouted at him and there was no surge of determination to cope.

This was mirrored on a face the gamekeeper knew too well to mistake. 'You're jaded, man, tired of the daily toil. What you need is a holiday.'

'Yes, you're right. I need a change.'

'When did you last have a break?'

'In the autumn. Remember, I stayed away for four days.'

'If you did it then, you can do it now. Before the wedding takes a hold of you and your energies. Away to the capital and have a good rest to yourself.'

This opened such entrancing possibilities that Alexis visibly brightened and he sat down on one of the circular benches at the base of the oak, more in contemplation of the inner prospect than the outer. What excuse was there to take him back to the city?

'Alexis,' Aileen called out, 'what do you make of this one?'

'Come out, I can't hear from in there.'

She came rustling the paper across the grass. 'Is it "Labor vincit omnia", or "Amor". We can't decide.'

'It's both. Virgil contradicts himself. He says both.'

'That's no earthly use. It's got to be "work" or "love".'

'Ask Mairi. She's the expert on crosswords.'

'Odious things. They never make sense.'

'Ay well,' contemplated Graeme as she swung away to the house, as limber and carefree as a young doe. 'No trouble there. She's a credit to you.'

11

He dressed with meticulous care. A three-piece suit of bird's eye tweed conveyed precisely the air of the squire in the city which he wished to assume. A white linen shirt of antique and voluminous cut, which had belonged to his father, set it off while from the tray of cufflinks he chose some made in oxydised silver. He wanted to appear casual, though this in itself was a mannerism, and deliberately selected what was used so that the exterior impression reflected his face and his person, worn but careful. Graeme Sutherland would have been reassured; this was the form of escapism he envisaged when he recommended the trip. It was time Alexis took to his old haunts, renewed acquaintance with the other side of his life which he had allowed to fall into abeyance over the winter. There was no need to work himself to a standstill when the routines of the city awaited him; a theatre trip, a jaunt round the galleries, a lunch with friends. He would have been less assured if he had known the real motive behind the visit, for Alexis seeking his own pretext had made the key for the wardrobe and opened it up.

When he brushed his hair into some semblance of order, for it generally went its own way, he caught sight of himself and looked away from the self-conscious gaze of his eyes. He was a dandy, though it was a brave man would tell him so to the bone of his nose and he was making a show of this swagger to cover the self-doubt he felt at his undertaking. He was being disingenuous. He knew he was going through an old ritual, as though his feelings were not sharply different from those that accompanied every other drive to the capital. He was going to see Esme. He was concealing the nature of his ploy. He had an errand and a legitimate one, but wasn't he approaching it in a way most calculated to gratify his wishes? He could send the contents on or deliver them by proxy, but instead he chose to go in person. He had not analysed his own conscience further than this but driving down through the passes of the gateway to the Highlands, and as the city itself drew into sight, the parallels between this and other journeys were too pressing to avoid notice. He did wonder if he was setting Esme up as a substitute for her mother, the perfect undemanding companion. Civilised, beautiful, responsive. No, he could not make the same mistake again. What, in all honesty, did he want from Esme? Was he being frank in averring he was in loco parentis? How certain was he that she would welcome an advance on that state of fatherly benevolence? His mind slewed away from answering these questions for he had arrived.

Esme had come back from her weekend shopping and was unlocking the door. The sun made the house look shabby, highlighting the peeling paint and the dusty windows which she cleaned at the rate of two a week, but the exercise was rather like the painting of the Forth bridge, for as soon as she had finished it was time to begin again and they were never entirely clean but in successive stages of dirtiness. The Rover pulling silently into the drive caught her off guard because it was so unpremeditated, although the second she saw him she ceased to be surprised; it was exactly what he would do, turn up at her door unannounced. Still, she was discountenanced as he lifted her trifling purchases from the doorstep. He followed her without a word through the maze of passages and doors to the scullery on the ground floor and deposited her messages.

'You are early this morning. Have you come from Lochearn or were you staying at Canonmills? I didn't know Aileen was expecting you.'

'She wasn't. I came straight here and in fact they don't know I'm in town. I gave out I was going to a meeting in Glasgow.'

'Why ever would you do that?' She paused in filling the kettle.

'Let's go upstairs and I'll tell you.'

He went ahead to the room by the main door but even when she joined him, carrying her sparsely laden tray, he took his time beginning. This room, now that it contained all her activities bar sleeping, was a strange mêlée of objects and functions, a radio perched on the table where she worked in the full light of the windows, books mixing with plates for she ate where she worked, her knitting scattered by the fire so that he could follow the course of her day like a trail. She saw him look round but pride prevented her from apologising for the disarray. She lived to suit herself.

'Do you remember how you asked me about the wardrobe that was delivered to Lochearn?'

'I thought you had forgotten.'

'No, I didn't forget entirely. It was pushed to one side and then, when Aileen talked of you last time she came home, I remembered that I hadn't fulfilled my undertaking.'

'You needn't have come all this way for a few sheets.' She was grateful all the same. She was tired of making do. 'Did it take you long?'

'An hour or two. The things are in the car.' He stood up from his place by the fire and went to the window. He was tempted at this late stage to suppress the real nature of his errand. What if he opened a Pandora's box of evil, without as much as hope to rectify the balance. 'But I didn't come for those. That would have done any time, but this was rather more urgent and I wanted to give it to you myself.' From the inner pocket of his jacket he pulled a fairly large brown envelope which he handed to her. 'I found it in the middle of the linen. It was quite undisturbed, exactly as Rhona left it.'

It smelt of the garden lavender Rhona had sewn into bags to keep their household linen fresh. It was addressed simply to Mrs Rhona Rosowicz. Nothing ominous in that, surely. It was a moderately heavy package and Esme tipped the contents onto the work table. Some thirty photographs spilled out and she wonderingly picked them up in turn and after a glance passed them to Alexis who had seated himself at her side, or dropped them in favour of others in the bundle. They were snapshots of her, principally, during the early years of her childhood.

Some she recognised as having seen before for Rab had taken them all. They were of the garden in its heyday, of Calton Hill with the pigeons, of the beach at Gullane, and copies had been made in his dark room for whoever was included or wanted one. They catalogued exactly that period Alexis had described to her, had brought out of obscurity, between her birth and the age of three or four. Every one contained her: frowning, smiling, busy at play with the activities of the child, bathing a doll, holding a top and whip on the garage forecourt, balancing on the swing. They were all monochrome, a few so old that they were printed on sepia and the absence of colour made them appear bleached, ancient relics of a former existence so remote it bordered on the meaningless. Some were new to her. Esme stared long at these views of herself in poses she did not recognise. The Muslims were right; making a replica of the human form gave the owner power over whoever was represented. Someone, a cousin, a friend, whoever had returned them, had kept this ownership over her for years and not shared it. She was unsettled that they should be returned to her at this juncture when she was unlikely to obtain a satisfactory explanation of how or why.

Again she picked up these new discoveries. The man with Rhona must be Stefan. The face compelled her attention as forcibly as Ferdinand's did Miranda. If it was the first male face she had set eyes on, it could not have drawn her more. And yet, why should it be so surprising? They were her own features recast.

It was the same disposition of eyes, nose, mouth, a little distorted by looking into the sun, except that over his was thrown a shadow not wholly attributable to a difference in age (for there was none) or in sex. He was more gaunt, more hollow by nature. The image evoked no memory. She simply did not know him and would almost have preferred to have maintained ignorance about his exterior resemblance if the man himself were to remain obscure.

'It is Stefan?'

'Yes, of course. Who else?'

'I can't understand why Rhona kept these hidden for years. Why didn't she want me to see them?'

Alexis was turning the envelope over and over in his hands. 'I don't think she did keep them for very long. They were sent to her, judging by the postmark, only a few weeks before she died. The packet was already open, so I didn't feel I was overstepping my authority in looking inside. There was nothing further in it, no note, no covering letter.'

'Well, thank you. It is interesting of course, especially to see a likeness of Stefan, and I hope it hasn't taken up too much of your attention.'

'I think,' he said rolling the words deliberately, 'perhaps it has taken up all my attention since I found it. I wouldn't be here otherwise.' He had the knowledge to deceive her, or at least forestall the guess she would eventually make. 'The writing is your father's.'

She lifted the envelope and pored over it as though the individual letters might reveal something other than their formal copperplate calligraphy. 'You're sure?'

'Quite. I knew the handwriting the moment I picked it up.'

She was caught, pulled by a thousand thoughts, and paramount was the sensation of incredulity. Alexis, relieved at last to have unburdened himself of this private knowledge, sat back and admired her composure. It was more than his when he had first found the packet. Would the past always be coming back to hinder their progress, a bond and a distancer so that they might not stand in direct relationship with each other but were always having to realign according to the pattern of their forebears, departed, alien but so powerfully present? She was distraught. The set of the head, the movement of the eyes observed so assiduously told him that,

113

although the temporary loss of self-control would go unnoticed to all but the expert eye.

'Why didn't she tell me! Why would she lock them away and say nothing? She must have hidden the key and I thought it was only mislaid in all the confusion. Don't you think? She hid it?'

'It seems probable.'

'But why?'

'Perhaps she knew she was ill and couldn't thrust this on you as well.'

'But it's the doubt that is intolerable. Whatever I don't know is so much more disturbing than the realities. I can always learn to cope with them. If I had known more details about the delayed wedding, or Stefan going to Canada, or about this, I would have been prepared. I had an interest in the matter.'

'You've some justification for being angry, Esme, but don't judge your mother too harshly. For her it was an episode she wanted to blot out. Talking about it, regenerating the old strife was pointless.' He leaned forward and methodically dropped the photographs back into their hiding place.

'It means he is alive, doesn't it, or that he was alive last year in spite of our having no replies to the notices. So all those months we've lost. What a waste.'

His heart sank as he pursued her line of intent. He hesitated to disillusion her, but objected, 'Does it mean he's alive, Esme? Why would he send it after all this time if it were to stir old memories, retie old bonds? He could have done that at any time. To me there is something more significant about the timing. It has a valedictory air.'

'Why? Why do you think that?'

'I think this was despatched by an executor. It's a natural enough package to leave with a lawyer, "In the event of my death".'

She scarcely heard him. The facts were unimportant if they disguised hope. 'The stamp is Canadian, and the postmark, look, can you read it? Saguenay?'

He bent over her hands. 'Yes, I made that out.'

'Do you know where that is in Canada?'

'In Quebec. It's the name of a river that flows into the St Lawrence. Do you want to look at the atlas?'

'In a bit.' She sat back in her chair and leaned her head against the wall. 'So that's what you really think? That he's dead. But I can't square that with Rhona's silence. If she had reason to believe that, say if there were a note she destroyed, why didn't she say straight out when it arrived.'

He pondered how much more he should divulge to her. 'Rhona blotted him out for reasons of her own. She didn't wish to enlarge on his existence for you because of some feeling of guilt, yes I think I can say she felt some guilt about the causes of his disaffection, but she didn't want to malign him. There's something I didn't see fit to explain to you before because it made no difference to things as they affected you and I saw no need to hurt you wilfully, but within a short time of settling in Canada Stefan met another woman and was living with her, till the point where the correspondence ceased. I presume he continued to live with her. Perhaps she had sent this envelope found among his effects. But that, fundamentally, is why he never sent for you and Rhona.'

'And any children?'

'Possibly. I don't know.'

The sadness caused by her father's neglect and indifference was slightly mitigated by this turn of events. To abandon them for no reason was attributable only to disinclination. Another bond, another child perhaps was cause enough. She saw Stefan trapped between conflicting ties of there and here, neither being home to him, or wife and mistress, distant child well cared for by a large and doting family, and this one, more immediate, more fragile, and forgave him the choice he made in his insoluble dilemma.

'Tell me what to do. Should I go and look for him and my half brothers?'

Still the prospect did not endear Esme towards the remote Stefan whose single message was an anonymous and somehow final envoy, as though he returned even his memories with bad grace. If Esme had been moved to envy, if she could have harnessed such devotion to herself by deed of transfer from her cousin, she might have envied Aileen her father. How easy her life was, all decisions negotiated. It did not strike her that a life without stress could make her into an emotional pauper.

'Don't ask me. I have no rights in the matter.'

Yes, she was madcap enough to do it, to go streaking off on so futile a voyage as retracing a twenty-year-old pilgrimage, following leads, knocking on doors, asking questions of strangers in a strange land. He quailed at the thought of her vulnerability. How could he spare her such exposure? How much more would it need to prevent her embarking on the chase? For he was convinced of Stefan's demise, although if he examined the idea objectively there was no concrete evidence for that supposition stronger than his own wish to have him gone. And why? So that Esme's absence did not force the four walls of his existence to take on an utter vacancy. What had Stefan done for her that she should show him allegiance? Even if he did exist, a being warmly breathing somewhere on the face of the earth, hidden from sight in the vast North American continent, what would he want with this girl knocking on his door to claim remembrance? Oh no. He knew them both, and it would not do. They shared the same name, they shared the same face, but beyond such communalities of blood they were aliens. They had nothing in common, not even language, just as it had been for Rhona.

Nevertheless, the inevitable appeal of belonging struck him on her behalf and he felt how difficult it would be for her to turn her back on the sentimental aspects of the search. He had been sorely tempted, anticipating her impulses, to destroy the envelope, unknown, unseen by anyone. Yes, he would have done that. He would perjure himself in the interests of right. Right? Oh, right indeed. What claim had he to pervert the course of her decision? She was autonomous and he had no business to meddle with her choices. Her confusion arose from the fact that nobody had been honest with her, but out of pity more than cruelty had allowed her to cocoon herself in dreams of an ideal faceless father. Things had so conspired to enhance that image, the tall, the grey, the deep-eyed doting father, and how little it corresponded with reality.

Still he drew back from the power of his influence over her. It would be pleasant to keep a cooing dove in his dovecote, wandering no further than the perimeter of the garden hedge, but he wanted Esme free and independent, not with clipped wings. To adore her wildness and to admit she would not be ringed by him, that was the paradox he juggled with.

'Oh, I can't think of this.' She pushed the books around on her desk. 'There is so much else to do. My degree exams begin in a couple of weeks.'

'I know. I wondered if I ought to defer it, but didn't want to appear to prejudge the issue.'

'Yes, I realise. I am glad you came at once.' She was immobilised, stultified by the information.

'Come now. Let's be entertained. Are you too busy or can I take you to lunch?'

'I meant to look in at the Gallery for some revision.'

'That sounds painless revision. We'll settle for that and go on to dinner. Better still.'

She looked at the books, lying open and half read, spines creased and words imperfectly recalled. Here was a critique of Shakespeare, oh so heavily embellished with footnotes they positively weighed it down. And in the middle of the page, a two line quotation from *Macbeth*, pathetically alone in that mass of commentary, a fragile raft in a huge and unwelcoming sea. That decided her. Living took precedence over literature. She was going with him.

He took her to Houston House Hotel, a fine example of a Scots tower house, vertical as a fort but also warm and expansive. They sat in the garden, in a secluded corner where the trapped sun drew out the smell of carnations and pinks, and made the drink before dinner a heady combination of day and evening. And he allowed the problems which were besetting him to overflow.

'I'm tired of the business. That's what it comes down to. It's booming, so I must be the only man in the world who's not pleased with success. I've been swamped by an order from America which I must have been a fool to take on, all things considered.'

'What sort of order?'

'Several gross of knitwear, which sounds wonderful, but they don't come off the production line so easily. They are individual, and though I've worked my way through the designs, the making of them is up to others and when you are under that pressure quality goes. Like William Morris, I know the counting house is the enemy of the workshop. I can make work for some and money for all, but it's not a craft that way. I'm no more than a high-class manufacturer.'

Esme was flattered but also dismayed that he launched on a topic so removed from her knowledge. She did not want to look a fool in front of him. She hesitated in one of the thinking silences he relished in her company. 'That's the price of success, surely? I mean you don't want to stop at being a cottage industry. You're not interested in making a garment for the hill shepherd or the local bowls champion. Homespun is not your style. You set out to make something for sophisticated tastes, and you can't be surprised when only the cosmopolitan can afford the finished product.'

'No, I can't complain about success. But it does prevent the creative impulse from being sustained. You repeat what you have already done because it sells. I don't complain about making a profit, but that profit detracts inevitably from aesthetics. God or Mammon, serving both is hard. But my immediate problem is that I have had to employ six temporary workers to fill this order, and then I will have to sack them at the end of the summer.'

'That's fair enough.'

'No, it isn't. I don't fire good workers.'

'Isn't some work better than none from their point of view? I expect the training or the experience they get with you will be a passport elsewhere. No?'

'In a sense you're right. I was able to take on three of my apprentices from last year who would have lain fallow over the summer. But this is just the start. I have reached the point where it is all or nothing. If I go on with it, the business will have to be more mechanised. And I don't want to go mechanical.'

She tried to jolly him. 'I noticed Jenners were featuring your cloth and knitwear last week, and I was immensely proud each time I walked past the windows, and so should you be.'

'Imagine if I overtook whisky as the largest national export.'

'Don't you weave any more? I thought weaving was your forte.'

'It was, but you can't do a great deal that's innovative with cloth. There's more design potential with knitwear, though that remains basically body-shaped. The design comes in the making up with cloth, I've always felt. The actual process of weaving I find a chore nowadays. I seldom do more than three or four inches. I haven't finished a bolt in years.'

'Why not?'

'It's too predictable. The pattern is set from the beginning, in the first few lines, and at a certain point no matter how large your motif is, there comes a repeat in the pattern and you have to go through the same sequence all over again. I lose interest at that.'

'What would keep you interested? Jacquard weaving?'

'Weaving in circles perhaps. If one could invent a loom that was circular so there was no need to cut the cloth, which is wasteful and expensive. A fusion of the two skills, a kind of knitting machine without stitches.'

'That's impossible,' objected Esme.

'That's why it's intriguing. The possible is too easily achieved to sustain the imagination.'

She laughed at him. 'I believe you lie awake at night composing these conundrums.'

While they were talking, totally absorbed, two figures appeared at the main window of the dining room on the first floor, about fifty yards from where the outdoor couple sat. They were a young woman and her husband, somewhere between the ages of the two they regarded with such piercing interest.

'It is Alexis, isn't it? At the far end of the lawn.'

'Who is his lady friend? The reason we've not seen him for the last six months I suppose.'

'Are you coming to say hello?'

He looked again. Normally, a greeting would be automatic but there was just that kind of closeness in the heads, a tension in Alexis' frame that stayed interruption. 'No, not today. I think we'd be *de trop*.'

It was an Italian supper at Houston House. The hotel served a set meal and each day's menu was different over a period of about a month, French provincial, Russian, Indian in an alternation that encouraged the newcomer to sample, the initiated to experiment.

She was fun to be with. She noticed everything and he openly toyed with her interest in the variable shapes of glasses, why King's pattern was so called, the symbols of silversmithing. As in the Gallery, she was naïve in her experience but sound in her judgment. He didn't set out for self-aggrandisement, being the know-all male bored him to tears, but let her have her say and pushed out the barque of her inquiry into the ocean of what there is to know.

'The best bit of *Osso Buco* is meant to be the marrow, see.'

'How inaccessible. Why doesn't it boil out in the sauce?'

'It doesn't. I believe in polite company you take a teaspoon to eat it.'

She tried. 'OK. Not great.'

He smiled. He imagined, in a reverie, taking her to supper nightly in this room, working their way through the catalogue of dishes, *poivré, Diane, fricassée, bonne femme,* and his thoughts descended in this way down a long spiral to nowhere. He jolted himself out of it. What was he planning? A Volpone type seduction –

> and could we get the phoenix
> Though nature lost her kind, she were our dish

endless variety to revive the tired satyr?

Over coffee, he said, 'Are you embarrassed to be seen with me?'

'Goodness, why should I be embarrassed?'

'I am rather old to be escorting you.'

'I have never found my own generation very rewarding. I don't feel at ease with them.'

'Why is that?'

'They are too competitive, too material. I know I am an anachronism but I don't care for my contemporaries.'

'Apart from Aileen and Rejean?'

She nodded. 'Yes, they are the exception.' He had made the first reference to their being a pair, a man and a woman, conforming to social mores, or not conforming, as he seemed to imply. Did she care to be seen with an older man? Did she know? Did it matter what she or anyone thought if it were a simple and predictable meeting of relations, compatible but distant? There was a consciousness that it was not so behind the question, the unacknowledged complicity of their being here and together. And it was the unseen she responded to.

Leaving the hotel at sunset, slow and exquisitely delicate like northern lights over the city, they drove in silence for some time. 'Where shall we go, Esme, a casino, a night club?'

'Are there such things in Edinburgh?'

'Yes indeed. Or do you want to dance the night away? You tell me. I'll drive you there.'

She considered. 'I would like to go to the sea. I haven't been for such a long time. But it will be dark by the time we arrive.'

'Have you swum at midnight?'

'No.'

'It's warm at night. The water has had time to come over the sand and absorb its heat. The foreshore is quite inviting. We could go to Gullane. You are invisible in the dunes.'

It enticed, a night mirage. 'No,' she rejected the prospect, 'let's go home.'

'Of course, why did I ask? Esme wants to go home.' He headed the car north and left it in a side street rather than conspicuously in the drive. They had only just unlocked the house, however, and switched on the light in the front room when a ring at the door made them start.

'Who can be calling for you?'

'Aileen.' She blanched. 'She often calls in the evening.'

'I don't particularly want to be seen here.'

'No.' The bell sounded again. It was useless to try and ignore it when the light shone out. 'She doesn't stay long. Hide in here.' She opened the largest of the many cupboards in the hall, full of meters and bed ends and old blankets. He walked in obligingly as she closed the door on him, and as an afterthought she locked it.

When she pulled back the main door, however, she discovered it was not Aileen after all, but a couple who had visited Mr Scott to make an appointment to view the house. Unable to reach her in the afternoon, they had come back before driving home to Hawick, on the off chance that she had returned and gratefully saw her light shine out into the street.

Esme's heart sank. She could hardly turn them away and judging by their tenacity they intended to make an interminable inspection. She couldn't let Alexis out before their eyes, so passing the door to the cupboard she slipped the key into her pocket in case they showed any inquisitiveness in that direction. They were thorough. They looked at every room from every angle, tested each sash window and even ran the water in the taps. They made a minute inventory of plumbing, wiring, heating, north-south orientation, while Esme grew more and more frantic thinking of

Alexis stifling in the cubby hole below. What a fool idea to lock the door! If she had left it open, he could at least have moved from room to room behind them, or gone out to the car. There wasn't as much as a light in it, she remembered. An hour passed and the prospective buyers showed no inclination to leave but absorbed her in detailed questions of how long, how old, how much to which she could give no more than bare and disjointed replies.

As soon as she had shut the main door on them again, she flew back to the cupboard. No Alexis! Just piles of old furniture. She couldn't hear breathing. Surely she had killed him by leaving him to suffocate in an airless box. She dropped on her hands and knees and crawled over the floor, patting the ground for a trace of reassuring warmth. 'Alexis, Alexis.' He was dead. She groped in the dark and could see nothing. Then a hand tightened over hers and an eye opened on her out of the gloom. 'Oh, you've been lying doggo. How you frightened me.' In her relief that he had not after all snuffed it in her box room, she squatted beside him on a heap of rough grey army blankets and nestled him in her arms.

'You scared me deliberately!'

'No, not really. I became very bored after a while and decided to make myself a mattress of blankets and then I fell asleep, most pleasantly. How long have you been away?'

She grasped his hand and pressed it against her cheek, her lips, her forehead to convince herself that he was quick.

'Oh yes, I am alive all right.'

'The thing is, I think they will actually buy it. Their surveyor is coming next week, and they want it for the Festival. They are going to turn it into a boarding house.'

'Shh. Don't think about that. Things will fall into place.' Her arm lay negligently along his shoulder and without moving he found he could kiss his way from her ear to her mouth. 'What would you have done if I had died?'

'Given you the kiss of life.'

'That's good, but not worth dying for.'

'No?' She persuaded him otherwise. Her embraces were unabashed, even accomplished as her mouth insisted against his, shaped, receded, reformed. Lying back in the unlikeliest bower of his experience, he allowed himself to be seduced. She found the space between his clothing and kept up over the whole width of his frame a caressing that ravished him, as her hands passed and re-passed in a steady constant rhythm to which her kisses were a melodic harmony, with something of the cradle, a compassionate rocking. What fool was it said lovemaking was an expression of the male drive. He had not progressed beyond the kindergarten of sexual understanding. It was to a woman that sensuousness belonged, by which burrowing into the imagination she took hold of the very nerve ends of a man's being.

'Sleep with me.'

'This is forbidden.'

'I don't forbid it.'

He had not imagined he would ever sleep in that room, or in that bed. They undressed by the open window and met chilled under the covers. When they had warmed a little, he moved her to sit across him and was astonished anew at the curvature of the female body. Painters made much of breast and leg, but he admired most the shoulders and back. Full breasts and slender legs were commonplace; magnificent shoulders were a rarity. The interplay of width and slenderness, the exact depth of the clavicle so that it suggested rigidity and structure without being bony, and the superb tapering of the back into the waist; these gave supreme pleasure. He admired as a tailor or an artist admires hoping to recreate the vision, but knowing reproduction will elude him. The lines of light and shade as he passed his hand along them were too delicate for the draughtsman. No Venus or Maja came close to reality.

Such lovemaking was exquisite. By degrees she was etched into his memory, stroke by stroke as his hand came and went, retreated, stopped and began again. He was like a blind man in a familiar place for whom touch is the sole confirmation. Esme felt her body, in which she took negligible interest, change and reform under his flattery of its dimensions, as though she were molten and could liquefy or solidify at his will, the raw substance for a cast he had moulded. So her breasts could swell, her waist narrow, her loins – she hardly knew how else to denote those vague internal reaches – contract in waves, as an ingot melts progressively. When he took her breast to his lips, the sensations within her became too intense, till reaching a climax she took her pleasure alone.

She lay for a while on his chest before she spoke. 'I am so sorry.'

'Why are you sorry?'

'Because you are not satisfied.'

'Oh, my dear, I am satisfied.' He smoothed the hair by her ear and kissed her lobe. 'Are you tired? Do you want to sleep?' His lips burned.

'For a little while. It has been such a strange day. Wake me when you want.'

He watched while she fell asleep, and after a while got up and put on an old coat he found behind a door to go outside. Having slept himself, he had no idea what time it was. The sun had gone down, but a speck of brilliant light was focused in the west which, as he watched, was further and further compressed under the weight of the night clouds till it disappeared. He walked in front of the summerhouse which brought back the long twilight of Esme's childhood, and his own spent in itinerant exile, the dusk of the war years with the ominous growing night, the stillness of the natural world he had observed immemorially on those crescent evenings long ago. It was twenty years since he had kept these vigils, noticed the musk of roses at the end of a May evening, heard stalks rustle and birds prepare for sleep.

The moon broke out, as opaquely white as the curl of her ear against a pillow. She could become his whole cosmology; she made him radiant to the sun and immune to the cold. The vicissitudes of age, labour, disappointment she could diminish by youth, hope and inspiration. She was a resurrection and a new life. Perhaps, after all, the care of one human being for another, of which he had begun to despair not only for himself but for all men, could be a talisman against loneliness.

He reflected that he had acted on impulse, however, and that he would be wise to heed the advice he had meted out to Ian, and take sensible precautions. They did not want babes in arms after all. Nor did he want to burden her with these considerations; there were more urgent things to say. He flattered himself that he had outgrown the carnal importunity of young men, the rough and ready and needy. His needs were more diffuse. To withhold was the token of his intensity. The boiling world of lust held no attraction for him compared with the slow enjoyment of sensuality. The contemplation of an object, mere appraisal of whether he should or should not pursue it, became a substitute that was better than possession. And so by stages he had rationalised the baser instincts of passion and purified them to a lingering residue that he found more exciting because it was more subversive; longing, the commission of adultery in the heart. He would let the romance of the imagination take its flight.

In the morning Esme awoke, uncomfortably aware that the presence of Alexis in bed had troubled her all night. He slept on. Towards the inert male form, brown, yes, attractive certainly, she felt an antipathy so strong that she found it hard to lie still. How curiously spare in face and chest where she was plump, heavy at the shoulder and wrist where she was narrow, altogether unrecognisable as a human counterpart to her own self. Then he awoke and out of his eyes shone the divine intelligence, humour, patience that in any dark night would make her seek shelter with him. His hand moved and touched her face.

'Is it a good day?'

'The best.'

He shaved. Her cheek fitted into his and the coolness of the lean male face was good. Days were not worth having together without nights. They skipped a page, missed a beat, so that meeting again they had to bridge an interregnum of mood or place or occupation. The important thing was to keep their hands in touch and she saw that, like any other relationship, marriage was a mosaic of daily acts.

12

Aileen had moved back to Lochearn after her finals and vacated the flat at Canonmills. Rejean subsequently cleared out his belongings from the office at Goldenacre and transferred them to the flat as a first step towards taking up permanent residence. It had been scoured out and smelt strongly of antiseptic and old dust combined, the twin aromas of spring cleaning. He took a certain pleasure in re-arranging his possessions in drawers left open to air. There were three rooms in the flat, a bedroom centrally, flanked by a lounge at one side and a kitchen on the other with a large recess where they ate. At one time the recesses in these old apartments had been curtained and held a double bed. In one exactly like this, he had been told, a family of five children had been raised. With his preconceptions of living space he found this very hard to credit. When two of them were in it all day it felt crowded, so that at times he was as awkward as a giant in a doll's house. The wash basin was so small he could not put his hands into it without splashing water on the surround and floor. But he admitted it was a great improvement on the room at the back of the office where he had slotted in as neatly as a file. Still, he felt as all the spouses had done who moved into the top flat at the big house, that he had released the last hold on his own self-determination and was drawn irrevocably within the family group.

From the bottom of his suitcase he took out some papers he had brought from the office to consider and amend, and put them by the easy chair to look at when he had finished with his installation.

On the dressing table he placed the boxes from Hamilton and Inches where they had chosen their wedding rings. They had been specially made up to their requirements, being a composite of standard designs. Looking at them again, he was not sure if he still liked them. They were ornate and showy in white gold to match the metal of the engagement ring; that looked well with diamonds, but he thought he might have preferred a plain band after all. There was something about the tight circumference of the ring itself that struck him for the first time as constricting, like wearing a metal tourniquet on one's finger. Curious idea and faintly barbarous, not being substantially different from a bull having a ring through his nose by which he could be more easily tethered. He slipped his on and loathed it more and more. He thought of the enormous sum it had cost; and why, to satisfy vanity and convention. They had even been engraved inside with their Christian names and the date. Well, what a piece of nonsense and, worse, it was a form of hubris, positively endangering the happiness of a successful outcome. What difference did all this paraphernalia make to the core of the relationship? None. All that mattered was human certainty, and on that he was far from definite.

That was enough. He was committed. He would not disappoint.

However, his chest hurt with the anxiety of these thoughts. Irritably he tossed the rings to the back of the table and went down below to the dairy under the block of flats to see what he might eat for dinner.

Afterwards he wrote to his father:

'Everything is ready, virtually, and I will meet your flight to Prestwick as arranged. Bookings are all made but I do feel your stop-over is going to be hectic. Seven cities in twelve days is a concept they laugh at in the UK. You must learn to slow to walking pace.

'Aileen went north yesterday and I am moving into the flat. The only development over here is an odd one. Esme (the fetching cousin) found a packet of photographs sent to her mother just before she died, by the man we placed notices for in the *Star*. Address? Only Saguenay. Is that not exceptional? So he seems to have been there quite recently.

'I wonder if Aileen and I could fit in a trip home before her term starts. I certainly would like to be home in the fall. Give it some consideration.'

He put down the letter and thought back to the day he had called in at the big house with a message from Aileen, and Esme had asked him, 'Tell me, Rejean, where is the Saguenay in Canada?'

'About a hundred and fifty miles north of Quebec City. It's a region in Quebec province.'

'A long way from where you live?'

'Not by my standards, but by yours, yes, a very long way.'

'And tell me something about it. Is it like Montreal?'

'No, it's about as unlike as you can get. In fact I know the area better than most Canadians because my father has a small sub-office in a place called Port Alfred. It's a centre for timber. But why do you want to know about a place like the Saguenay? Most people haven't even heard of it.'

She considered. She had meant to say nothing, but mulling over the facts by herself had reinforced the need to know more if she was to square her interests here with her interests there. She explained about the photographs and how the postmark supplied a lead that had been missing in spite of their advertisements.

'Of course the *Montreal Star* is an English paper, and not generally read in the Saguenay. We should have thought he might be in a French speaking area. There will be few people of Polish extraction there. You're thinking of going, naturally.'

'You say that so simply.'

'What is there to keep you here?'

She avoided his look. How would he react if she told him? 'Tell me more. You've been up there?'

'Yes, I spent a summer there during my college days. It's a beautiful place in summer, fearsome in winter.' Shuffling her books and the objects on the table around he outlined on the cloth a river represented by pencils, flowing from west to east. 'Saguenay into the St Lawrence. Main town Chicoutimi, which is Indian for "as far as it is deep".' He placed a rubber half way along the southern shore. 'A big town, on hills with a lot of older colonial type buildings. You know, no skyscrapers. Then there are smaller towns, Port Alfred and Bagotville to the east.' A drawing pin and a paper clip. 'One is mainly a railway terminal for freight and the other has a Canadian Air Force base. I've a good friend who was serving there the last time I heard. And Arvida to the west. That's the only English town in what is a fiercely nationalist, maybe even separatist region. They feel the way the Scots do about the English. Arvida has an enormous aluminum smelting plant, aluminium to you. It's the largest in the world, I believe.'

'And north. What's up here?' She waved above the pencil line.

'Not much. Wild areas, small farms, forests no one has ever crossed.'

'It sounds formidable.' She was daunted.

'That's north. The areas by the river are quite hospitable.'

'How about the countryside and the people?'

'It's a very mellow landscape, rounded and good farming. Like the very far north of Scotland. The people are small, dark, usually French stock from the early settlers.'

'How early?'

'Eighteen thirties. One of the first to set foot was a Simard and they and the Tremblays are rife in the area.'

'And what would a Polish émigré do?'

He shrugged. 'Anything. He spoke French, you said.'

'So I believe.'

'I don't know. But he wouldn't be hard to find.'

'I wonder if you would keep this to yourself for a while. I want to make up my own mind.'

'We could all fly over together in the fall. I would so like to show you my home.'

Recounting this picture of his homeland brought back its nostalgic appeal for him, open spaces, clear skies day after day, biting cold that challenged and braced you – what a country!

He turned to the notes at the side of his chair. They were rough chapter headings and jottings for a book that had slowly taken shape during the course of his research over the year. He did not know exactly what he wanted to write. Certain chapters formed crisply but the connection between them did not and so he could come to no conclusion about the purpose of the book. Tree conservation of course was what it was about. So much had happened in forestry in the previous twenty years that needed to be summarised. Aerial and infra-red photography had shown things barely guessed before about the importance of the tree in the pattern of world ecology; technology had proved the dramatic effect on soil if roots were removed and showed the influence of rain forests on the world's climate. All these needed to be re-stated and backed up with current research. But still not enough was being done internationally to correct or stabilise the maintenance of forests. Countries worked piecemeal within national boundaries and what one country achieved was undone by its neighbours. He wanted to write a definitive text and in vainglorious moments imagined being subsidised by the Agricultural and Fisheries Agency of the United Nations, and a synopsis of his work being circulated to interested scientific and political bodies, worldwide. But he did not divulge such an ambition to anyone else. Aileen, to whom he had mentioned the idea of the book, had dismissed it as not being essentially marketable. So he felt a little ashamed of the manuscript and kept it locked in an office drawer to be taken out and worked on in secret, as are all ambitions.

What fascinated him most was the interdependence of seed stock and actual growing conditions in the full-size tree. So little had been done to analyse the mutations brought about in seed development by the influence of climate and soil. It took too long. How interesting it would be to have a controlled experiment of seeds from the same tree planted in entirely different conditions to see how their growth rate and eventual height, flowering and seed production compared. Further still to see how the subsequent generations of each tree diverged from these 'norms' of growth pattern. The variability of factors influencing growth was so great, however, that they precluded a reasoned conclusion and the debate was likely to be as endless as nature versus nurture, heredity against environment in the human species.

He crossed the room and found what was to him his most valued belonging, a fossil of probably neolithic origin in which the lace frond of a fern leaf was imprinted. It was not very different from the ferns that covered the slopes above Inchcombe, except that this had come from the region of Latvia. Its whorls, its spores were as detailed as the fingerprint of his own hand, minute traceries of the utmost delicacy engraved in stone. He had not found it himself and was a little reluctant to admit to anyone who saw it that he had bought it prosaically from an archaeologist he had met on one of his trips to Scandinavia. This man had become interested in forestry through the process of dendrochronology and the fossilised bark and seeds he had found. One evening he had produced drawings which were an artist's impression of pre-historic European forests based on existing fossils. Rejean imagined Europe supporting huge virgin forests of sequoia, the dinosaurs of plant life. How long would such a tree take to mature? How long before it denuded its own soil and died? How long to decompose?

He rubbed his fingertips over the grooves of the fossil, fearful, in spite of the pleasure he derived from it, that in time he would wear them away with touching, and wondered again at the power by which one element is changed into another, the soft into the hard, the durable into gases. He could never burn coal or peat without feeling in some respect that he committed a sacrilege against a divine order of which this metamorphosis was the most tangible expression.

Maurice Simard sat later than usual at his desk in the covered concourse of downtown Montreal. The office was empty on a Saturday and the precinct in which it was sited rang to the footsteps of idle shoppers. Husbands sat, hunched in boredom, on the benches of the open square while around them dogs and children played until the wives appeared with full trolleys or cartons to be loaded into the cars parked in the underground bay. Above them the Hotel Montreal towered, a-bustle with preparations, activated between those lunching late and dining early. A few swimmers took to the rooftop pool and ordered warming glasses afterwards.

Maurice Simard was glad he had had the foresight to buy shares in the hotel when the precinct was built, glad that the subterranean shops brought such profit to the hotel and him, insulated underground from heat and cold alike. That was business acumen. He was an empire builder, of the new rather than the old world type. The failure of dominion by the ancients and the Europeans was in imagining that natives could be harnessed by slavery to provide labour which would make them wealthy, without perceiving that the subjugated eventually rebelled. The invasions of Hun and Goth, the rebellions of Carthage, Egypt, Israel against Rome, the growing independence of the exploited continents of India and Africa from the British bore testimony to the weakness of the imperialist. Such empires crumbled. A twentieth-century Canadian knew people could be harnessed by the profit motive and nothing else. There must be a small share of incentive for every man in an organisation and then he would work harder to increase that share.

As a young man, starting with a derelict lumber yard left to him by an uncle, he could have prospered greatly by extortion. When the city of Montreal was spreading its boundaries by half a mile a year, he could have charged exorbitant prices for timber and made a quick fortune. Instead he maintained a modest profit margin and made himself respected for honesty. He visited the Scandinavian countries where design was more advanced than at home, and bought the blueprint for modular, self-built houses. With a little adaptation to Canadian requirements, these kit homes sold in thousands and he supplied the timber and the window frames ready prepared. By the ingenious system of franchise, he found himself in possession of a monopoly. He paid fair wages; was liberal with bonus payment and discount to employees; he donated a sizeable portion of excess profit to charity, for it was tax deductible and it was publicity. He began to be known as a powerful man, one whom the Mayor of Montreal made sure he invited to the annual civic dinner. He was even thought of as a philanthropist, and that was more important than being a millionaire.

The prospect pleased him. He rolled down the blind and thought about what pleased him less. Rejean was not a worker. That did not surprise him, for he had not educated or trained the boy to be a worker. Only necessity made men work as hard as he himself had done, and necessity was an ugliness that had been carefully excised from Rejean's life by his money and his wife's breeding. Still, he had not foreseeen that the boy might turn effete. He had anticipated at least common sense in his own progeny. He sent him to Laval to acquire a degree in Economics and he had come back with a head full of ideas about land conservation, the preservation of universal ecology, whatever that was, and spoke at length about the tree and climate. He had sent him to Europe to learn a little of the business, and a modicum of those commodities in which he himself had never dealt: culture, background, education. And after three months he had come back with a new fiancée and ideas more wild and fantastic than ever. The latest craze for writing a book, Aileen had told him of it quite by chance, positively alarmed him with its eccentricity. What practical purpose did it serve? The way to change people's attitudes was to get out there and show them. Talking didn't do it, and writing never convinced anybody of anything. Yes, he was profoundly disappointed. He had fathered a dreamer.

So he kept him at a distance without intentionally being cruel. He imagined he was doing his son a favour for he thought of him as a European, a throwback dredged from their past ancestry. Paradoxically, he hoped his son might become sated with dreams and turn into a realist; this way he had cured him of the vices of drinking and smoking through a bloated surfeit. Surely one grew tired of concerts and ancient monuments.

His ulterior motive for keeping Rejean in Europe was a personal vanity, however, for he ambitiously conceived that the Simard empire might extend beyond his native continent from the Mackenzie to the St Lawrence, to gain a foothold in the old world, in a gesture that symbolised both independence and defiance. The colonial power colonised. In the same way, established firms boasted, 'By Appointment to Her Majesty' as proof of excellence which some attributed to an entirely natural snobbery. At a lowlier level, research students had their own jargon of achievement. BTA

– been to America – was on a par with a PhD, or was at least a pre-requirement for its award in some research subjects. It hardly seemed to matter that the foothold was one and a half rooms in a small thoroughfare like Goldenacre in the suburban environs of a middle-size city, or that it produced no measurable business. The claim sufficed; it was 'my office in the UK'. It looked well on the letter heading.

Rejean's latest note lay on his desk, and that perhaps was what had given rise to the bout of unease. It troubled him how frequently the fetching cousin was mentioned in the last few months, although to begin with he too had been intrigued by the searches. More than his name, they now possessed the single fact that Stefan Rosowicz had put a package into the post office at a Saguenay depot within the last year. Sending packages of photographs over the world without a covering letter, that is couching the intimate in such negligent terms, seemed a peculiar way to run one's life and Maurice thought, What is he getting himself into this time? What kind of people are these? He checked his watch and confirmed that he might catch an old friend who was ex-Mayor of Chicoutimi at home. He lifted the receiver and dialled.

Putting the stone back, Rejean glanced out of the window and saw that it was quite late. The shops were closed; a hazy sunset lit the windows of the houses opposite, then as he waited the colour that had temporarily transformed the sandstone into sheets of burnished copper faded and the grey crept back in again. All muted and sunless and enclosed. He detested the greyness of the Edinburgh streets. Alexis and Esme told him they were beautiful, pointed out this and that architectural curl and folderol. He was blind to them. The monochrome, the very powder of antiquity that in the fossil was alive and real to his mind, when translated to the buildings of the city was faintly dirty and drab. The fossil was pure and unalloyed. The houses were tainted by human occupation, which brought with it soot, grease, leaking rone pipes and bad drains.

He put on a record of Tchaikovsky's 'Pathétique', and lying on the settee allowed himself to be swept along in reminiscence. He imagined the ageing composer working in New York in 1891, tired, genuinely sick from ill-defined causes and pining to return from the self-imposed exile. He was a success, they mobbed his concerts, but still he longed for . . . what? Rejean listened acutely to the second movement for some solace that would heal his own nostalgia. He listened for people, voices, the shape of home but beyond the dreadful yearning found nothing concrete except the sighing of wind through the ancestral trees of the homeland. It was the contours of the land he missed, climate and soil interwoven, and no amount of reasoning could help him take comfort in the similarities. Yes, the same sky, the same sea enveloped all. True, the landscape was like that of Canada, but it was not it. Though the elements did not alter, three thousand miles' removal made a difference. There were discrepancies of scale; there was nothing in the world like the sweep of a Canadian hillside in the fall when the high tints of the deciduous trees, and especially the field maple, flamed out against the sober evergreen. His eye longed for that dappling, and could not find rest in the lamplit street, the cramped room, or the empty armchairs. He felt the exclusion that nostalgia brings, the divorce from what sustains, and to his own surprise the anxious chords of the movement produced tears of total sympathy and identification that fell sideways from his eyes onto the cushions. But it hurt him to cry, not physically for the tears rolled away quite independently of his volition and he did not make a sound or utter a sob, but in his thoughts he knew he would not be whole again.

13

They corresponded.

I am sitting alone at nightfall. The lamps are lit. Beside me the window is open and through it I can see the loch. It is quite still. A perfect evening and I ought to be content with it, going off to find wood or for a ramble like a good boy scout, but I am not content because I think persistently of you and what is here seems less than what is not. All day you've been hovering in the background like this, interrupting conversations and distracting me from what I'm doing but at the moment you've settled in the chair opposite where the breeze lifts your hair, and I can give you full attention.

In a little while you will be under my roof. I keep changing the pictures round and I know it's to be sure they please you. This is a mild state of insanity, so pity me and hope it will not last too long. The prospect of your coming is almost enough to chasten me from self-indulgent thoughts. How dangerously we choose to live. Your being here may have a devastating effect, blow the top off things for good. But I don't care any more. Control is slipping. My own life is in abeyance, takes second place, and I am tired of waiting for all the tomorrows to unfold and divulge you, for nothing seems real unless you share it.

I know. I'm haunted too. What is this man at my elbow, never stays but never goes away? When I have a spare moment in the middle of packing up the last of my things, working for the finals, I turn round and tell you about this or that. I hold these interminable dialogues with you wherever we go, though I admit they're beginning to wear thin. I'm flagging in imagination through having to make up your part as well as my own, a duet for two voices but I'm both of them. That's a strain on the vocal chords and I'm no ventriloquist. It's a very second-rate, second-hand Alexis who speaks for you in my head. So coming between Delacroix and *Hamlet*, your letter is a welcome diversion. It revives me. It starts off a chain reaction of quite new conversations about new things. I wish you could hear them. You might be amused at what you are saying.

You mention Delacroix. Why? Why just him? As I read your letter in the office, I see there's a catalogue of the exhibition sitting on my desk. No other. Just that one. It has fallen open at his 'Murder of Polonius'. I didn't put it there. It happened. What power do you have to recognise the inevitable – or do you instigate the inevitable by observing it? A fearful prescience, this. Beware. Those who are always right are never believed. That is the penalty they pay. Sybil and Cassandra would tell you that.

But seriously, it does make me wonder who you are that you're so in key with what's going on around and in me. It must be more than the harmony people are said to achieve when they live together for a long time, prompting the same refrain in their minds at the same moment. The moments we have spent together are so few I can practically count them. Whatever it is, I give you full credit for it. It hasn't happened to me before. Similarity, yes. Identification, no. You teach me who I am. I feel as though I'd been strumming out a rhythm in the background and suddenly you come in fitting the melody round it and I realise I've only been playing an accompaniment and disguising from myself the fact that it's poor, thin stuff with no depth in it at all. I am not made for solo performances. I am a symphony man, and didn't know it.

Who are you anyway, coming along like this and reversing all my hard-won suppositions about myself? I was very smug and sewn up. Now I feel turned inside out.

How do you know without being told? One part of me thinks that you are an expert in camouflage: you can blend and fuse with your surroundings. But I don't like the idea very much. It makes you too neutral. Certainly you don't seem to thrive on the assertiveness of a good many women I've known, which tends towards a shrill recital of likes and dislikes that they imagine comprises character. But I worry about this. I worry about everything. Such sympathy can be a dangerous aptitude. Who else will you sympathise with? If you are endowed with these unusual levels of tolerance, that would mean that the cause of any agreement and mutuality between us operated equally for everyone you know. And I would like to believe I am more singular. Vanity? Yes, I do have to fight vanity in myself.

It isn't either that you just think the same as I do. That *would* be a limitation. I do like your challenge, but deep down the empathy is more enduring. The sense I have of the same image being in your brain, but seen from the other side. The mirrored view that completes mine and shows me the whole. I don't know the overall picture until I see it in your mind.

Is it possible, that kind of mental bonding, that synchronisation if you like? It's so obscure in concept and so new to me, I can hardly believe it, never mind fathom its origins. To define it seems to be committing a grossness. But tonight, sitting here alone with hardly enough light to write by because I can't bear to get up and put the lamps on when you're so close, so here, and moving might drive you away, I want to say it. I want to say what can't be said. Between men and women there is such a limited vocabulary of reaction, isn't there, just a handful of tired phrases which we press into service again and again, like our bodies, defying isolation and at the same time pretending the everyday is unique. One must avoid self-deception. And then it does strike me that humans are fools to try and categorise their feelings in the first place. Sometimes one ought to resist the impulse to embalm sentiments in words, for badly done it may hasten the process of disintegration. The words I have to use are overlaid with accepted meanings, an accretion of abuse by other people and myself that dims their freshness. I can't invent anything new – new words are even less meaningful than old ones – but I would like to think there is something original I can offer you in language and in thought. Part-sibling, part-wife, part-child but none specifically, if a little of all of them. But I see to my surprise that I employ the language of kinship. I feel kinned, maybe for the first time in my life truly kinned. I feel your hurt and rejoice in your happiness. I want to share every unconscious impulse you have, but I feel I don't need to touch you or even to talk to you to do it. The bond is subcutaneous.

But I fail. I don't know who you are or what you are to me. I am content for the layers of your personality to be revealed to me, though I may never come up with the final phrase. You inspire me with multiplicity. I haven't said what I meant and when I turn round to see how you take this extraordinary declaration – I know it is rapturous, you have let out that demon romance in me and I was trying so hard to control it – I find you are gone. You got up and walked away and I am left inveighing against the space that separates us because if you were here in person I would convince you.

I have had the strangest experience today. It is like a bad dream you will have to interpret for me.

I walked back from Adam House (the last of the Fine Art exams, tolerable) and was lured into Princes Street Gardens by the sun and the flowers on the clock and the cheerful gaudiness of people outdoors in a summer swelter. There were children playing all round me and I sat down on one of the park benches beside a woman who had two school-age daughters. The sun was warm and I was inclined to be indolent and didn't pay much attention, but I

137

could see that for some reason the woman was intrigued by me. She stared, almost disconcertingly.

Eventually, the girls went down to the ice-cream kiosk, the taller leading her sister by the hand, and the woman suddenly said, 'My name is Sandy Pollock. You don't know who I am but I saw you with a friend of mine at Houston House Hotel a couple of weeks ago, one Saturday evening you may recall.'

Now I opened my eyes at this and looked more closely. No, I certainly didn't recognise her but it gave me a shock that I had been seen, been identified. I gave her marks for observation but would much rather have been anonymous. 'Yes, we were having dinner there.'

'My husband and I were at a wedding reception which had gone on later than expected and we saw you from the windows, sitting in the garden, quite tucked out of the way. We very nearly came to say hello. It's such a long time since Alexis called on us. He used to call regularly when he came to Edinburgh.'

'Yes, you should have come to speak to him.'

She cast over me a curious sidelong glance, that one where women who are not naturally forthright appraise each other's likely reaction and modify their speech accordingly. I must admit, I liked the look of her and, yes, I did want to speak to someone who knew you. The very mention of your name guaranteed her my attention. 'Can you guess why we didn't?'

No, I couldn't and it showed.

'We would so obviously have been interrupting a tête-à-tête.' How that innocent word could take on profligate overtones I don't know, but it did. When the Scots want to be salacious they slip into French. I was overwhelmed with embarrassment, a kind of retro-active guilt because at Houston House I was aware of absolutely no colouring in our behaviour which might have suggested the in-decency she attached to a single drink in the garden. But was it there? 'And then if you were the reason he had kept away, he wouldn't want to come face to face with us.'

I was dumbfounded and could find nothing whatever to say. I never felt so young in all my life, tongue-twisted and awkward.

'I've known Alexis a long, long time. Duncan worked with him at one point. Well, we take him as he comes and don't ask too many questions. He never did let the right hand know what the left hand was doing. You are involved with him?' she probed, but gently.

'Yes, I am involved with him.'

'It's absolutely none of my business and you've been most restrained not telling me so already. But if in ten years' time one of my girls brought home a man like Alexis, I would move heaven and earth to stop it.'

My dismay by this time was patent, yet she so genuinely meant well that I was fascinated by why. If she had passed me slips of paper at a seance or breathed over a gypsy ball, it would have been more in keeping than this very calm recital against the brass band booming out Strauss down in the gardens and the steady clicking of the floral clock. She had me spellbound and it wasn't even the Ides of March.

My eyes asked why. I could say nothing.

'My dear, it's a recipe for misery. Whatever can your mother be thinking of?'

'I am over the age of consent.' Was this not feeble?

'But there is an unbridgeable gulf, not just of years but of the life he's led. Edinburgh's man about town. And married women are much more his ticket.'

I haven't been properly calm ever since. What is she that she should so prophesy against us, our Sybil or Cassandra indeed. Or just a jilted lover. Is one of those girls playing by the bandstand yours? Her imputation is that of the worldly-wise; what do I know, I am a child, I am being used.

Oh Alexis, reassure me. I wait here day after day for your letters, there is simply nothing else, wait to see you and there's a great rebellion in me at having to be so reliant on you. I am not a dependant by nature. And if I think that you are after all half-hearted then I must quit now while I am still intact.

Yes, I am more sorry than I can say for not having prevented that, sorry for many reasons. I saw the Pollocks and read perfectly well that I was in disgrace for dining out a girl of Aileen's age. (You may recall I asked at dinner if you were embarrassed to be seen with me. Their cold shoulder had made me so self-conscious.) They are very *upright* bohemians. Nevertheless, I should have been wise and gone to see them on that Sunday, made all well, given a discreet explanation, but time with you was more of a priority.

Secondly, I'm sorry because of the character my past actions have given me. I would like to disown them – they misrepresent what I would like to be, with you and for you – and I appreciate that you don't confront me with the shortfall between reality and the ideal. I am not blameless, Esme, though both Sandy Pollock's children are Duncan's as it happens. I am probably amoral in that I have taken laissez-faire, if that isn't too much of a French euphemism, to its fullest limits. But have I disappointed you? That is much more important.

What dismayed you? Let's be honest. I am old enough to be your father. I have been married for more years than you have been alive. I have loved more women than I can effortlessly remember, but never made love without affection. And I did not once promise anything I could not fulfil.

Will you still have me on the premise of the naked truth? I am not a very statesmanlike lover, no bouquets, no gifts, no speeches. In fact it strikes me I have not bought you a single present, and may never because you are in the grain of my life. I feel I do not need to woo you. But if you are willing, I bring you all there is of that most characteristic commodity, myself. Wherever you go, I will go with you and for as long as you wish. If you want me to buy a house in Edinburgh, I will join you. Elsewhere, yes, say the word. Life here would be too complex. I cannot entirely see me flaunting you in the glens, but I could live in Perth and conduct my business. That is an undertaking.

The one thing I do ask is that we wait till the wedding is over. I suppose it's a commonplace that I have maintained the semblance of normality for Aileen's sake, but there is no sense in breaking it for the gain of a few weeks.

You have humbled me. I didn't ask for so much. Proofs, demonstrations, shows of strength appal me, turning this fragile poise of affection, need, longing into a ghastly account sheet, credit and debit. What do I stand to gain? I will not enter into any form of barter with you but what you offer, yourself and so open-handedly I am dazzled with. I am in the whirlwind of change. Yes and soon.

These leaden days! When was July so tedious? I have never wished my life away like this. Hurry I say to noon, come quickly to nightfall. I work like a demon to make time pass, cannot sleep, cannot rest till you come. People say, you're up early, you're working late. Early and late I have lost track of in this welter of impatience. A week. Eternity.

Oh Esme at thy window be
It is the wished, the trysted hour.
Those smiles and glances let me see
That make the rich man's treasure poor.

14

The day passed in a ferment of anxiety for Aileen. The Simards were coming over for dinner from Gleneagles, plus the minister Galbraith and his wife, an ill-assorted combination Mairi had foisted on her as something within the bounds of duty, and finally Esme and Rejean were driving north together. Each of these held its own pressure but she had looked forward to Rejean's help in coping with the medley of guests who did not know her or each other well enough to make for a smooth evening.

She ironed her dress, detested it when she tried it on again for the mirror, chose another and ironed it. The house was fretful with preparation, Mairi punctilious with the girl Fiona who had given up her day off from the Lodge to help. She was saving hard towards her engagement to Ian. But she cut the vegetables badly and laid the table left to right so that everything she touched had to be re-worked. Alexis was no better. He hid in the office begging a mass of letters as his excuse. He disliked the second dress and she began again.

All day she expected her cousin and fiancé to arrive. It was perhaps unreasonable to look for them before noon, but the hourly chime increased her frenzy. Mairi, consulted, took on a long face. 'They may have stopped somewhere. For lunch. Very thoughtless.'

'They weren't going to Gleneagles first?'

'There's no knowing what they may have done.'

'I think not. I don't think that was the arrangement.'

But as time wore on, it became feasible that they had stopped for tea as well as lunch. Or, she kept the idea at bay as long as possible although it began to invade every moment like a stain that grew and spread, had they had an accident? She retraced the road. The Highland line, Callander, bonny Strathyre. The road wound tortuously with many a blind corner. Pretty enough for eyes to wander from the way ahead. Where were they? Should she call the police station or the hospital? No, that was to make fear concrete. She went out and picked cider apples from the floor of the orchard in order to busy her hands but the lengthening shadows reminded her of how she waited alone and their coolness under the boughs reinforced the chill around her heart.

At long last the skirl of wheels on the road announced their arrival, but it was almost seven and the Simards were due in half an hour. Aileen's face was white as she ran to the five-bar gate.

'You're so late. Whatever kept you? Were you delayed starting out? I honestly thought something must have happened.' She leaned against the mudguard of the car and rode impromptu for the hundred yards until they were inside the courtyard.

Turning off the engine, Rejean stepped out of the car and finally spoke to her. 'Don't fuss, Aileen. We stopped at Linlithgow for the afternoon but we're here now. What more do you want?' And he went indoors without further greeting or embrace.

She looked after him, baffled, and turned to Esme who stood by with a valise in her hand. 'That's not all you've brought, is it?'

'It's all I have. The bridesmaid dress is here, isn't it?'

'I suppose I can lend you something. Come, you had better get ready. The others are dressing. It was bad of you, really, Esme, to keep him so long on the road. I know that you haven't seen Linlithgow, but another time would have done.'

'I'm sorry but I have to put you right on that. I had the greatest difficulty getting him here at all. If it weren't for bringing me, I doubt if he would have come.'

They paused on the landing. 'You don't mean it? Well, why ever . . .' and moved forward into Esme's assigned room.

Esme was kind. 'I get the feeling he is reluctant, no that's too strong, anxious about seeing his father.'

'But he worships his father.'

'He could feel both.'

'What did he say?'

But Esme valued his confidence too highly to break it. 'Nothing substantial.'

The older girl wrung her hands and carried out tiny, unconscious acts, turning back the sheets, adjusting a curtain. She was on edge with nerves. However wrought she was, it did not impair her thinking, and she came to the same conclusion as Esme had done but dared not proclaim. 'We're all feeling the stress of this wedding. I shall be so glad when Saturday is over.'

'Won't we all? But look forward to it, Aileen. You are going to enjoy the day?'

'Perhaps. If the sun shines. Look, you carry on. Everything is here. The bathroom is on the left. Only you and I use that one. Don't be long and I'll see you downstairs.' She ran away along the corridor and going below to pour sherry and make sure the room was perfect, flowers crisp, cushions plump for their guests, she thought she heard footsteps on the landing over her head as someone went into Esme's room and shut the door, but dismissed it as imagination.

It was Alexis and they stood together a long time while he caressed her hair, kissed her eyelids and her cheeks.

'You didn't come to greet me.'

'I daren't. I have been in a torment all day and so has Aileen. You were very late.'

She leaned away, though her arms were still round him, and looked into his face. The quizzical line that shot her eyebrow told him much. Rejean was breaking under the strain of his double life.

'He spoke to you, did he?' he asked.

'Yes, I thought you might know something. He is in despair, the despair of wanting to be decent as much as anything.'

'What did he say?'

'He was desperate to go home and couldn't face another year of exile.' Ah, that was all. Enough but less than the chasm that might have split them. 'Aileen thought we had had a crash and I don't know how we avoided it. He was in such a state,' she went on. 'There were tears. Can you imagine that? I've never seen a man cry before and I was alarmed, for both of us. He was driving like a maniac and he simply couldn't see. I think he's ill. He thinks he's ill.'

'Mentally?'

'Goodness knows.'

'What did you tell him?'

'That he'd be going home for good shortly. That he must speak to Aileen about it if she's to understand. I was in such a state of compression myself about the next few days that I could hardly concentrate on his problems for paying attention to my own.'

He let her go and then, feeling the withdrawal of her warmth, put an arm round her shoulder again. 'This is all wrong. Your relationship with me is against your impulse. You should be a free agent and I am cramping you, cramping these people near me. It may always be like this, Esme, deceit and guilt. Can you face such unremitting subterfuge?'

'No, I can't. But after Saturday it will be better. How odd it is you care about hurting your daughter and not about your wife.'

'There's much to tell on that score. Wait a while.'

'And us?'

'Be patient.' He heard a sound as a car nosed its way along the drive. 'There they are. I must go.'

'Must you?' She encircled him more closely, anxious to prolong the moment. 'Will it be impossible here?'

'I think it will.'

A voice cut through their isolation. Mairi reaching the landing called, 'Everyone downstairs. They're here.'

'This house does not feel good. It's restive,' she whispered.

'It is tonight. If we can get through the next few days without calamity, I'll be surprised. Don't be long.' He broke away.

She washed and changed while the talking swelled below; someone had a raucous laugh, the door bell rang again, voices eddied at the foot of the stairs. Alone, her courage misgave. How superficial and unimportant she was to this occasion, an intruder in the calm flow of things, present only because of the insistent kindness of Aileen in wishing to involve her. How had she repaid the kindness! What a huge disturbance she was about to make. In his home context Alexis was another man, father, husband, employer, pillar of

144

respectability which she was about to destroy in one move and stigmatise him as an adulterer and deserter. She was going to transform him into the man she resented in her father. It seemed too cruel to impose her own fate on Aileen. How could she look her cousin in the eye again?

The lure of the empty rooms upstairs was greater than the social ones below. She wandered unimpeded round the upper floor taking in the views of the courtyards, the sheds opposite, the archway over which Alexis' bedroom projected. Was she prying? Only indirectly. She wasn't concerned about their belongings or the tidiness of their rooms or whatever else might concern the owners at such an inspection behind their backs. She wondered how people slept in this house; obviously not together. Celibacy must be maintained under this roof. Four single rooms for four single people and Rejean sublet to a hotel with his parents. Well, well.

Downstairs Mairi fumed. Esme was, of course, the last guest to appear, and she an inmate. What atrocities was Fiona perpetrating on the carefully balanced meal while they waited? How inconsiderate of her niece. Twice in one day to keep them hanging on. Whatever had she and Rejean been up to, to be so tardy on the road? Where was she now? What a loiterer. Poking about in corners and making them all look fools downstairs as they waited on the most insignificant member of the party. Even Alexis glanced at his watch. It was sheer self-importance to focus attention on herself this way. It was to have been Aileen's special evening and somehow the intrusive cousin, the cuckoo, was going to spoil it all.

At last she stood in the doorway and the heads turned, the conversation died. They were all curious, Claire Simard kindly, her husband dispassionately so; Graeme who had been asked to equalise numbers – how awkward Esme had no escort – was quietly watchful. Even the Galbraiths had heard of her strange circumstances and looked with interest. What did they see in the girl who paused in the doorway, hesitant as to what was expected of her? They saw nothing. They were uniformly disappointed that she was herself and not closer to whatever fantasy they had projected onto her.

'Ah, Esme,' cried her aunt. 'How naughty of you to keep us in suspense. And you were so late arriving, I haven't had a chance to welcome you yet.' She placed a strong hand on each shoulder and grasping her niece kissed her on both cheeks. It was a predatory kiss. It was so uncalled for, so icy that it made the girl shiver in apprehension. She knew how lambs felt when they were seized by an eagle unawares. She detested gratuitous touching, as an animal reared alone will not submit to being handled, and she reneged on the round of handshakes which might have been suggested by the ring of men who had stood up politely at her entry.

The talk rose again and she submerged gratefully under it. Claire who sat nearby was sweetness itself and engaged her in the kind of talk known as small which is not to imply that it is purposeless, until gradually Esme recovered her composure, becoming less afraid that her secrets betrayed themselves. Only Alexis might notice the palpitations the scene brought out in her, a room full of strangers in itself an ordeal, though he forbade himself to look at her. The room swam less in front of her eyes. She saw it more for what it was, his own place in which she too could feel at ease. She was particularly intrigued that every chair in it was different, not a single matching pair with all periods included; club, basket, Orkney, easy chair, chaise longue and she herself had landed on a prie-dieu. Of course his was the eclectic style of the impulsive, but she thought it might well be a game he played, to see how men and women sat themselves.

Mairi rose shortly, annoyed that Fiona had forgotten her instructions to announce dinner and had to fetch her personally, which seemed to everyone else a circuitous way of doing things. She was so flustered by this and the antagonism aroused by her niece that she forgot her seating plan and people placed themselves as they liked. Esme, whom she had consigned to obscurity at the kitchen end of the table where Fiona would pass repeatedly and where she might be cajoled into making herself useful, won pride of place. She sat between the two garden side windows with the lamp of the sideboard behind her which lent her an aureole of light once it was switched on at sunset. She was flanked by Maurice and Alexis, who had gone ahead to shut a French door against the evening air and ensure his nearness to her chosen place.

'Rab's desk?' she inquired, pausing to caress the flutes of the roll-top, under which a copy of *The Master Builder* lay, spine bent, and a pile of poetry books as well as the day's copy of the *Scotsman* folded open.

Fiona clattered around with soup bowls looking distinctly inexpert and uncomfortable. She was forced to wear a cap from which by degrees the blue black hair escaped as wayward as seaweed that someone had tried to net. Esme smiled, but Fiona thought she mocked and did not smile back.

'Do you think she hates us?' she asked Alexis.

'Who?'

'The girl who is waiting at table.'

'Why should she hate us? We are giving her a job.'

'She's serving us food she probably hasn't eaten, except in kitchen scraps, salmon, asparagus, and yet it's the food of this part of the country.'

'I wouldn't worry about it too much. Fiona doesn't know fresh from tinned salmon. She's just a village girl.'

'Don't be so dismissive. She would know the difference if someone showed her.'

'There you're wrong. She would think it silly and pretentious. Gentry talk.'

'And are we gentry to her? How grim. I would hate to wait on someone's table and know my place.'

'Aren't you hungry?' whispered Aileen as Rejean pushed away his soup, left the salmon almost untasted.

'It's choking me.'

She could see now that she had time to look at him properly that he was thinner. Had he lost weight or was it the dark suit? 'Tell me,' she said to divert her mind from the possibilities laid open to her, 'what did you think of Linlithgow?'

Alexis heard the question spoken on the far side and repeated it to Esme. 'A romantic ruin?'

'Romantic? No, I did not think it was romantic. It was much too desolate for that.'

'Wasn't it the birthplace of Mary Queen of Scots?' he recalled.

'As well as the place where she was seduced by Bothwell,' added Aileen. She and Rejean sat directly opposite her father and Esme near the middle of the oval table and theirs formed a nucleus of dialogue which divided itself from that at the ends. The plan had gone wrong.

'These are hardly glamorous episodes, you'll agree,' said Esme. 'Her father was lying ill as she was born, wounded at Solway Moss. And he was so disappointed at siring a daughter he gave up altogether and died.'

' "It cam' wi' a lass, and it will gang wi' a lass," ' supplied Aileen.

'Not an auspicious omen. And Bothwell's seduction did help the prophecy along. Poor Mary.'

'Why poor?' asked the cousin across the table.

'Because she had no skill with men. She had the talents of her cousin Elizabeth, scholar, musician, she inspired devotion in those who served her. Why else would Babington and the others have risked their lives? But she was such a fool with it.'

Alexis smiled. 'You don't admire her, then?'

'You have to admire anyone who is so magnificently wrong all the time, but I respect Elizabeth more for being magnificently right.'

He teased. 'The Virgin Queen. A heroine of yours?'

'Oh yes.' She took up the challenge. 'Elizabeth never lost her wits over her lovers. Mary was much too soft, too yielding. She gave up power to the men who married her but Elizabeth knew marrying meant losing control.'

'Stern words on the eve of a wedding,' said Rejean. 'So women must not surrender power to men?'

'Not if they're sixteenth-century queens.'

'I'm glad of the conditional. You still haven't told me why it was desolate.'

Esme glanced over at Rejean to sound his opinion too, but saw his mother had captured his attention. 'It seemed a symbol of Mary's failure and of Scotland's, simply by being a ruin. It was set on fire by an English army, even if it was accidental, and left to burn for a fortnight while the people looted what was removable. It should have been whole, full of its original furniture and hangings instead of being open to the sky. And then it felt so impregnable, less a palace than a prison with dungeons and walls ten foot thick.'

'Imagine that,' interrupted Rejean again, 'living out of the light. You could shout for a lifetime and nobody hear you.'

'It was the tenor of the times,' was Alexis' consolation.

His attention was drawn away from her by the minister's wife who asked about the business, his unfavourite topic for social events. Esme, left to surface into the wider pool heard Claire Simard admire a French ormolu clock which sat on a side table.

'It *is* valuable,' admitted her hostess with the simulacrum of reluctance. 'We bought it from a friend of ours, a very old friend in Edinburgh. She runs a fine antique shop in George Street. Do make a point of going while you are there, and mention our name. She'd be so pleased to look after you. It came from the sale of King Farouk's palace, and apparently when the bidding was in progress Mrs James leaned over and kissed the clock. The auctioneer called out, "Now that Mrs James has kissed it, it's worth twice as much." Of course, she had to buy it after that.'

The table laughed along its length, though Alexis commented under his breath to her that he thought it hideously ugly and suspected Mrs James appended the story to every clock she sold. The tale sent a shiver down Esme's spine. In the world of ormolu clocks, kissed or unkissed, she had little purchasing power.

'Now in Canada that would fetch a king's ransom. It is impossible . . .' but Claire Simard was drowned out by laughter at her unintentional double meaning.

Maurice took the first opportunity that presented itself and turned to his right. 'So you are undecided about the trip to Canada after all?'

Esme re-directed her gaze. He was a heavy man, most unlike his son in manner. He was little given to talking and there was a lowering, even a truculent quality in his face, thickly browed, dominantly featured. Esme was at once in awe of him and the silent power he wielded, as most people only learned to be.

'I think myself into and out of it.' And of course in his hearing this sounded like a weakness even to her. 'It's strange that you are here after a ten hour flight and I ought to know it's not an irrecoverable step, but I hesitate all the same.'

'Why, you're not frightened of flying, are you? Fly back with us if you're nervous.' He did not try to charm her in making this suggestion, for he had no charm to spare. He tended to make one gesture towards people, a take it or leave it offer. No haggling.

'When do you go?'

'In a week's time.'

'That's too soon.'

'As you wish. Think it over. It will need you to work on it if you are to find anything out. I did all I could . . .'

'Yes, I'm grateful.'

'You don't need to be grateful with me, we're almost relations, just honest. I didn't achieve a whole lot as it is. I called an old friend when I heard from Rejean recently, about the package you had in the mail. He's a past Mayor of Chicoutimi but, though he knows where to look for information, we don't unfortunately have anything like your register of births, marriages and deaths or a census which would record all the persons living in an area. These are with independent parish priests, and the records are not collated in the same way. But there are a number of Poles in the region and descendants of Polish refugees. They're to be found in the telephone directory.'

'A Rosowicz?'

'There are several examples of Rosowicz but no S. I copied these out.' He passed her a slip of paper on which five names and addresses were written, but he was right. None contained an S even as a middle initial. Esme looked at the addresses with numbers of over a thousand. Did this imply the enormity of scale Rejean had hinted at? There were streets with names she found puzzling and unfamiliar, and yet one might conceal a step-mother, a half-brother.

She put it in her pocket. 'I find it hard to envisage.'

'Nothing easier than going to look. Think about it.'

Esme felt stranded. She was at this dinner table, but not of it. The two men beside her pulled her towards a common past, her father, her origins, but in diametrically opposite futures, neither of which was certain. The constraints on her truthfulness as well as her liberty were a torment to her. She wanted to say to Maurice, I may well go in time but with Alexis as my companion. But a second impulse pulled her. Did she want him along on such a journey? She was used to doing exactly as she wanted without reference to others and the compromise involved in pausing to consider Alexis made her feel clipped and pinioned. This dependence was a curb not a liberator.

The women talked of shortbread.

'I call it shortcake of course.'

'I think you'll find that's a little different,' corrected the minister's wife who regarded herself as the local authority on the national sweetmeat. 'Now, our shortbread . . .'

'My recipe includes rice flour,' intercepted Mairi.

'Oh, but that's so gritty.' And she felt it between her teeth.

'And I insist on using unsalted butter whatever the books say.'

Heaven save her from domesticity. Wasn't talking about food obscene? Like making love, cooking was a thing one did, not talked about in public. And Alexis' raised eyebrow imitated hers.

Rejean was in improved spirits. He pursued the minister into a dialectic about banns and why they were required for three weeks, which was answered only indirectly.

'In Scotland, the age of consent was sixteen years of age while it was twenty-one in England and many runaway heiresses went north to marry their man. You've heard of the smithy at Gretna Green?'

'No.'

'Well then, the blacksmith's cottage at Gretna Green was just over the border into the land of licence and the local churchman performed many a ceremony at the forge between eloping lovers while father came hotfoot behind in his carriage.'

'Like the father of fair Ellen in "Lochinvar",' added Esme and at once wished she had kept silent, since an explanation would have to follow for the benefit of the questioner and she knew if the duty fell to her it would not be an easy recital.

At Rejean's query she moved her hand towards the host, and he took up the tale on her behalf. 'As I recall, Young Lochinvar rides out of the west like yourself but there, I trust, the analogy ends. His beloved fair Ellen of Netherby Hall has been forced to marry her cousin, a foppish fellow who dangles his bonnet and plume while Lochinvar interrupts the wedding feast and claims a measure with his former sweetheart. And of course, seeing the handsome pair, the bridesmaids conclude,

'Twere better by far,
To have match'd our fair cousin with young Lochinvar.

They elope on his noble steed and are consequently pursued up and down the brakes by irate father and kinsmen. Read it yourself in Scott. He does it rather better.'

'I don't see why Lochinvar should be such a hero,' objected Aileen. 'Ellen and her cousin were already married. He was an interloper.'

'In ceremony,' retorted the punctilious minister. 'It had not been consummated.'

'You're not on the side of Lochinvar?' asked Mairi. 'Surely it was abduction, not elopement.'

'Oh, indubitably I am on his side. The lack of consummation does make a difference. Even the Church of Rome would have granted an annulment.'

'But to get back to Gretna,' pursued Rejean. 'These marriages were legal south of the border?'

'Quite so. A mere quirk caused by the juxtaposition of countries united in language, government, freedom of movement but not law or religion. Once performed, however, the ceremony was perfectly acceptable. But in church we do feel that the banns prevent such haste in requiring proof of residency.'

'Do you think,' asked Esme, 'that fair Ellen ever regretted living outside her marriage? She had no status beyond being a gallant's concubine.'

Alexis found the question more amusing than she. 'Status was a small price to pay, surely, for wandering into the sunset of romance?'

'But I wonder if she got awfully tired of sitting on the back of that charger.'

There was a moment's pause before he led the laughter. She had a way of speaking so simply that it was disarming and the lilt she gave to these unplanned utterances took her hearers by surprise.

'Write a postscript, Esme. The unballading of Walter Scott.'

Graeme was troubled and remained silent throughout most of the meal. He hadn't been mistaken in the source of his friend's malaise. They were discreet, oh yes, but the signs were there for him to interpret. Track and stalk, he knew them. It was as he had feared. He had been ready to dismiss her as a flibbertigibbet, but looked again and failed to find the lass newly out of her teens whom he could put down as worthy of no particular respect, beyond what is accorded to a pretty face and a lively spirit. He looked beyond his prejudice and saw a woman of substantial quality. It was her gravity that held him, the way she slipped the sheet of paper into her pocket without arousing comment. Contrary to what Mairi believed, she was self-effacing by instinct. She had not laughed all evening but had bent her ear in the right places. He could not fault her, try as he might. And Alexis was interested beyond the ordinary measure. As the couple sat opposite him and talked together or across each other, he felt himself in the pull of two magnetic fields that were complementary in strength. Anode and cathode, they could go on satisfying, sustaining, recharging each other for ever.

Such a startling consideration bemused him. His own marriage had been a workaday affair, and though he missed his wife grievously it was in the sense of a yoked drayhorse who found he had to cut his furrow alone. The daily burden was doubled, that was all. There was no mystique for him in womankind. Having that extra dimension forced on him was painful more than diverting, for it threw into consternation his habits of thinking. Life became complex.

Honour? Duty? Self-sacrifice? He glanced to the wife, assuredly wronged and wronged again. What was there useful one could say about other people's marriages? He had as much respect for Mairi as for her husband, if rather less fondness. He admired her wholeheartedly. Of Mairi's good work within the strath he probably knew more than anyone else, even the minister who instigated much of it. She undertook hospital visiting, had made his own wife's last weeks lighter with thoughtful errands, made rounds to the elderly who were housebound, daily, tiresome, thankless tasks – well, maybe her marriage had fitted her for those. Her works of charity were innumerable and there was hardly a woman's committee in Lochearn that did not admit her as its mainstay. She was the best fund-raiser in the district. She was the cornerstone of Alexis' business and had plied her energies and her skill to his purpose. Why could he not acknowledge that and rest content? Here were two people with such a store of good, but unable to see it in each other. Why? What was missing? Was it the power of sexual attraction, or the sweetness of sexual content that filled the cells of marriage like a honeycomb till it was brimming, and withered them without. Or was it the unarrestable diminution of will power in the face of setbacks, signal of the fact that there is no experience which does not disappoint?

15

He was so perturbed that in the lull between dinner and coffee, while cigars were lit on the verandah and the liqueurs passed from hand to hand, he took the unusual step of pressing Maurice Simard to walk outdoors. 'I must show you something of the loch. Terrible to leave Lochearn and not even get your feet wet. And a perfect evening for it. We'll be back for coffee, Mairi, never fear.'

Rejean watched them wistfully as they disappeared round the side of the oak tree. He hovered a moment and said to Mairi in the tones of formal politeness that best endeared him to her, 'Would you mind, ma'am, if I took a stroll? I feel in need of some fresh air.'

'Fresh air! Why, you've been in the open air all day, haven't you, at the palace and in the sports car? What a greedy boy you are! Off you go then, and take Aileen too. She's looking rather peaky.'

Uninvited but included nonetheless, Aileen put her arm through his and sauntered towards the wood of birch and elder.

'Now, Esme,' said Alexis, 'you haven't seen the loch either. Shall we follow suit? We'll be back before the others,' he assured the hostess who began to feel the evening slip irreparably away from her.

She sat musing as their backs turned. In spite of all her hard work! What was going wrong? What could she do to put it right? Her estimate of a successful dinner party was not a very elevated one, being like Cleopatra's conditioned by the cost of the banquet. Certain quantities of certain foods consumed meant she was on line for a memorable evening. She flattered herself that she was a notable hostess; in another age, Hume, Scott and John Stuart Mill would have sat at her table and after-dinner conversation have fostered the spirit of an epoch. She could not guess how far short of reality this was, having no understanding of the subtle alchemy of people. Many famous contemporaries had passed through her door, but she did not recognise them for what they were and, even if she had, would have been amazed to learn that they remembered neither a word she said nor one iota of the food she had given them.

She turned to their depleted party. What must the minister think at all these departures? But the minister did not think anything amiss, being ideally happy in the company of women for most of his flock were of the feminine gender. He found it an ideal opportunity to hold forth on why the Church of Scotland does not adhere to the doctrine of the Trinity.

Graeme turned sharply, almost with annoyance in case he had been overheard, when other footsteps were heard on the shore, and discovered behind him the topic of his dialogue. The two men froze.

'You see my meaning?'

'I cannot believe you,' said Maurice Simard.

'Look again. She is the light of his eye.'

'Why do you want me to do this for you?'

'For him, for her, not for me. Well, if there is something in it for me, I believe every man has his place. Alexis's place is here. Inchcombe is his work as well as his home.'

'How do you know it has come to this? And, if it has, isn't it up to him?'

Graeme pressed. 'We may need to tie Ulysses to the mast till he is out of danger.'

Alexis called out, 'Aileen and Rejean have taken the other path through the wood.'

'Good. We'll meet them on the way back,' and the two men by consent moved on ahead towards the small bay Aileen had termed 'the animals' combination place' so many years before.

It was a fine view, and Esme turned it over and over in her head so that she would not forget it. The sun had dipped behind the western hills that separated Lochearn from Loch Voil and Balquhidder. They cut off the direct rays, which gave to the landscape the quality of refracted light that was so distinctive, light seen through water that softened and blurred. Under her feet were flat stones, ideal for skimming, and she launched one or two over the surface of the loch so that they dipped and span in satisfying whirls. Where the wood had crept too far towards the shore bare roots of trees were exposed and had turned rotten in places. There was a wide shingle at this point and every hundred yards or so there was a slip of water from a field drain or a mountain spring, making its delta of effluent, courses which as a child Aileen loved to dam.

What a place it must have been to grow up in.

He leaned against the stump of a felled spruce, one foot raised as he bent over in contemplation of her. 'What do you think?'

'Of what?'

'Of the place.'

'Oh, I have seen it all before.'

'When?' he frowned, puzzled.

'In your paintings. I recognise it all.'

'Ah well, at least I am realistic if nothing more.'

'Tell me,' they walked on, forgetful of time and assignations, 'why don't you paint people? There aren't any people in your work.'

'That's my weakness. I'm a good colourist and a hopeless draughtsman. Apart from not being able to draw people, I find them too contemporary. They push everything else out. You look at them and think, Why is that man running, doesn't he have a funny hat, I wonder what he does for a living? They are too immediate.'

'But they give a scale.'

'That I do admit. They give a scale.'

Meanwhile Rejean and Aileen, equally oblivious, had reached the bay with its ring of birches. By now it was almost dark for they had walked a longish way, predominantly in silence. Rejean sat down to rest and Aileen looked back tremulously, thinking they had exceeded the limits of courtesy.

'Don't worry. They like to think we are alone.'

She gauged his state. He seemed puffed and was certainly drawn and white. Best to let him rest. She perched near him on a boulder which had been eroded into a convenient seat. Gradually, he got his wind back – how had he become so unfit? – and started to look about him with interest at the bay and its shingle.

Shuffling the stones at his feet, he came across a strange rock. Grey and smooth on one side, it was on the underside split clean across, so that it lay along his palm as neatly humped as a curled hedgehog. Now what could have split it? Not a storm in all likelihood, for the valley was sheltered. Nor the action of a tide. An avalanche perhaps, and he scanned the hills above; a weak promontory, a sudden landslide could have done it. Maybe frost had found the weak spot in the strata and cleft it in two.

'Do you think if we searched long enough we might find the other half?'

'It could have been cast up anywhere along the shore.'

'Not necessarily. It could have sheered in half in this bay.'

'I certainly don't want to get down and comb this beach for a broken stone that looks like every other pebble.'

But he persevered for a while, raking the water margin with the toepiece of his shoe. 'Do stop, Rejean. It's a waste of time. That noise is dreadful. Sit down, will you.'

'It would have been interesting to put the two halves together. Don't you find it extraordinary that there are two exactly matching halves along this shore?'

'No, I do not. You see these all the time. There must be a geological fault.'

'I'll hang on to it all the same. It will make a useful paperweight.'

She groaned inwardly. Another one to his collection of stones. Soon there would be no room for them at Canonmills, ousted by rows of dusty grey rocks. To divert him she said, 'I haven't told you yet. But my results arrived this morning. I wanted you to hear before anyone else. I got a first.'

'A first what?'

'A first-class degree, of course.'

'Oh, yes, how stupid. I was hardly listening. That is marvellous. But you've worked for it. Will it make next year easier?'

'No, not a bit.'

'And are Alexis and Mairi pleased?'

She stared at him. 'I said I hadn't told them. I went to endless trouble to intercept the postman before he got to the office.'

He knew he was being churlish and stopped himself. 'Oh, I am sorry. I am being very dull. Come, let me apologise.' They kissed and he left his hand at the base of her neck. That was the loveliest part of her. She had indifferent shoulders and limbs, but her neck, swept continually by the long pale hair, was magnificent. She had such carriage about her head, a quickness in her movement that made her seem bright, alive, determined to go and do. He adored that. The hair fell straight and thick, cut just at that point where it might become inconvenient, and intriguingly coloured. Often in the early days of their courtship he had tried to define the colour, honey, ash, gold, no, none was near enough. It was in fact precisely

157

the colour of sugar when it is heated and starts to colour, the second before it burns and goes bitterly dark. As her kitchen menial, his mother had taught him to watch for that trace of caramel as she prepared for the deluge of entertaining in autumn feasts, thanksgiving, harvest festivals.

'Make love to me.'

'Here? In this spot? We cannot.'

But he pulled her down against the cold rocks before she had time to stand. 'Rejean, be sensible. We are overdue.'

'Are we to be separated all this time?'

'It was unavoidable.' As he touched her again, she had confirmation of what she had suspected at dinner. He was thin. His body, more familiar to her than any bar her own, took on a strangeness and this, allied to his odd, obsessive behaviour this evening, filled her with revulsion. There was in it all an aura of sickness, mental or physical, which was so contrary to the Rejean she had engaged herself to that she felt she was dealing with someone unknown. He was becoming unwholesome.

'It's dark now. No one will come,' he urged.

'But only sluts lie outdoors.'

He released her and lay on his back watching the formative stars. 'How very nice you are. But I remember when you were not so fastidious. Be careful that you don't incubate your mother's malady. Frigid women are easy to dismiss from the round of one's pleasures.'

She rose indignantly, prepared to hear no more. What did he know about her mother! Surely Alexis did not speak of that? 'You are not yourself,' she said haughtily.

He rolled over on his side to look at her, lunar pale. 'Of course I wouldn't expect you to make love out here. But I would have been interested to see if you were willing.'

'Don't lay traps for me like that.'

But before he could reply her face, which had contracted for a second, collected itself. 'We're over here,' she called. 'Graeme and your father. We're not so late after all.' And with relief she ran across to join them. Could he move her? Had he elicited fury in that single spasm of the eyebrow. Ultimately, what did the girl feel? How different would Esme have been? the thought nagged.

Would she have lain with her betrothed under the stars and admitted no shame?

Alexis kept a wary look out for signs of the return, loath to end the interview with her prematurely, though the voices on the verandah rose and fell like warning signals. They strolled side by side at the edge of the lapping water. They did not touch and though they had embraced at her arrival, they had not kissed. He had thought the moment ill-considered and yet, for all his restraint, he was in the grip of an erotic delirium which had ravaged him since May. He hoped her presence would reduce the nightmare-like frenzy of these imaginings: mere furniture, a rocking chair, a stool, a waist-high table that he leaned against to draw suggested forms of intercourse that drove him to the verge of insanity. He was obsessed with his own physical movements. Sitting, standing, squatting developed a new intrigue as he watched his frame perform these common acts, which were transposed from words to deeds and by extension into metaphor. They were symbols of the lust that tormented him. The tiniest action such as the strokes he employed to paint took on a sexual colouring, the square masculine, the round feminine, until his whole life became patterned like a Klimt canvas. Ixion on his wheel, Tantalus forever thirsty and unslaked knew no greater agony of mind and body than he did.

This she divined. Next time there would be no half measures.

Under the hubbub of the foregathering to take coffee, Mairi asked her daughter, 'When you met, what were they talking about?'

Aileen guessed it rightly it was Alexis she inquired after. 'Ibsen, I think.' Had she known it, either of the other dialogues on the shore that evening would have been much more instructive to her way of thinking, but she was pacified.

'Is that all?'

She could not be expected to know that Hilde Wangel had come to haunt her household.

16

Celebrations were halted the following morning. It was the second Thursday of the month and Mairi was preoccupied. She had the accounts to attend to and having confirmed the engagements of the day (Aileen had a final fitting, business as usual for Alexis, dinner at Gleneagles and Esme could do as she liked) she took herself off to the work room.

Languidly, as though it had not been her intention all along, Esme followed Alexis out to the sheds. No one knew why they were called sheds for the weavers and knitters were housed in a byre quite as solidly constructed as the house. Inside the door, she was daunted by the noise. Twelve looms as varied as their occupants clattered as pedals fell, heddle rose and the shuttle flew side to side. No sign of Alexis, however. The adjoining room she peered into was worse, with the mechanical grating of the knitting machines, while every eye looked frank interest at her dress, her hair, her features. Aileen's cousin. They liked Aileen fine, but this one, if Fiona was to be believed, was like a May storm, all smiles and showers so you didn't know where you were with her.

'You'll be wanting Mr Alexis,' interrupted a voice behind her as Ian, bolder than the rest, directed her. 'He's upstairs.' And he nodded to a wooden staircase leading to the loft which she climbed, emerging into an Aladdin's cave of colour. This was where Alexis stored his wool.

'Ah, you've come. Good. You can help sort these out.'

'What are you doing?'

'Tidying.' Behind her, cones of wool were stacked on open shelves, protected from dust by thin curtains of butter muslin. Every hue, every fibre, every combination of the two blazed out at her. At his feet were baskets of partly used cones. 'Find the colour code and match it up with those on the shelves. But, if there isn't one, put the cone on the back shelves here.'

'What do you do with these?'

'I make up samples or special orders. Or I amuse myself by

weaving short lengths like these.' He showed her one or two hangings into which he had incorporated the rough wool of the hedgerows or short strips of bark or twig. 'They go to bazaars and suchlike charity. That's my tithe.' Up here too were the vats where he did his dyeing and more shelves with the natural dyestuffs he liked, indigo she found them labelled, kermes, poplar and osier twigs, the roots of the walnut tree. 'Rejean has got hold of some interesting new bark dyes for me. The most difficult thing,' he confided, 'is obtaining a good blood red.'

'Not cochineal?'

'That's rather pink, I find. I've been using the roots and petals of several red flowers, but with dilution they all turn pink.' He showed her an array of test tubes containing, as he said, rather pale colours, cyclamen, rose, petunia, no blood red.

'So what do you do?'

'I have to use chemical dyes. But they glare. Acceptable on mixed fibres where you get dual tones anyway. I'm going to make up a batch on Sunday if you'd like to help.'

'Is this the vat?' She looked inside a capacious steel drum he had installed in the ante-room with inlet and outflow pipes and a boiler for heating the contents. 'Looks like Hannah's washing machine. What a splendid way to go to work.'

'Delightful work, hard for the body, easy for the mind. Are you tempted?'

'To what?'

'To join me?'

'Oh, I . . .' She laughed but the idea assaulted her with its attractiveness. 'I'm not qualified to do anything useful.'

'You can read and write, can't you? Weigh quantities and mix ingredients?'

'The Sorcerer's Apprentice? No, I don't think so.'

'You could do worse.'

'I probably shall.' They worked till the wool was sorted and stacked and Esme returned to the kitchen to make coffee. By the time he joined her, she was deep in a book. She picked up any book that was to hand and sat absorbed by the Aga with her feet resting against the wall by the flue pipe of the stove. 'Can you possibly be comfortable like that? Your feet are higher than your head. No, don't move. I'll pour my own.'

'There is something I meant to ask you.' She thought back to the details and put her book down while she concentrated. 'Last night, do bear with me, I dreamed something I think may have been an invention. And yet I feel it was so real. It may have been a memory.'

'Yes?' He settled himself beside her.

'It was dark and I was small, very small, perhaps only three or four. I was in a strange bed, maybe sleeping away from home for the first time. But this was a public dormitory or a ward in a hospital, I don't know. All round the bed were children who were bigger than me and they stared at me curiously. It was a frightening room with a crucifix in the wall and long shadows that fell into alcoves. I was so scared I hardly dared lift my head from the pillows. In fact I tried to keep my eyes shut.' She was so serious in this recital he had to smile under cover of his coffee. 'The worst thing was they were talking in a foreign language and they were so suspicious of me because I wasn't one of them. I thought I had died in my sleep and this was how it would be afterwards, being locked out. I felt so repressed and alien. And there was nothing I could do. If I told them to go away, they wouldn't understand and if I shouted for help, well, who could I shout to? I was one and they were so many and I knew they were going to torture me, even by silence, for I was helpless and alone. So I burrowed further under the covers and pretended they weren't there. I thought like tormentors they would abandon an inert bait.'

His smile died as the recollection unfolded. What a fearful power of recall that could reconstruct a living nightmare so many years later. Would the past ever go away? 'Yes, that happened. I didn't know about the children. I expect they were simply interested in a newcomer. But I know exactly where you were and when. That was a residential nursery for young children and a good many of them were foreigners, Polish and French. It was at Ravelston.'

'But what was I doing there?'

'Let me see. Stefan was still in the Navy, as I was. Rhona was working and there was no one to look after you. She had to go on earning. I seem to think Rab and Hannah were on holiday. The nursery was a stop gap. You were there about a month in all. There's nothing else you can remember?'

She shook her head and cast about for some other shadow thrown by the dream. 'Perhaps standing waiting with Rhona and a stranger at a bus stop.'

'The stranger was me. I used to come on Saturdays, for I was based at Rosyth, and I would take you out or meet Rhona. She was very low then.'

'I see. Well, thank you for that, belatedly.'

'No thanks are due. It was my privilege.'

In the work room, Mairi stuck to her tally. The accounts had become increasingly complicated as the business grew, and in exasperated moments she wished for a full-time book-keeper in addition to the accountant, whose input seemed to be limited to making their returns to the Inland Revenue and overseeing her entries, tasks which hardly merited his fee. She did the work and he was paid for it. The lists of figures dazed her. Once a hundred pounds was an event. Now most were four figure items and they dealt with manifold outlets and suppliers. The bills were endless and she often emptied a cheque book at a sitting. And then there was the invoicing and filing, and careful cross-reference. It had begun to eat into more and more time. A whole day a month was not enough. But for all that, she was reluctant to give up her influence and control. This way she could account for every penny, could oversee how and where money was being spent. No tax inspector could have faulted Mairi's ledgers. She was correct to the last column. When occasionally an official from the Highlands and Islands Development Board came to review their annual grant for training new weavers or the apprentices from Perth, he handed back the books with the commendation, It's a pleasure to see accounts as well kept as these. Mairi wanted no higher praise. Efficiency and economy were her watchwords, and when they went hand in hand, as in an ideal world she was certain they did, her satisfaction was boundless.

The business was her work; it was her achievement. Alexis, indeed, had had the inspiration. He saw it could and should be done before the hand loom tradition died out altogether and he had the expertise to mend the abandoned looms they found in work-shops and salerooms, to persuade others to resume their half-forgotten craft, and train a new generation in its continuance.

But once he germinated the idea, he lost interest. He spent more time drawing and paddling in dye than in the work sheds, and had not woven a length of cloth singlehanded for years. The weavers, young and old, admitted that his skill and knowledge far outdistanced theirs, but knowing with Alexis was enough. There was no need to capitalise on that skill. To her had fallen the task of making an income from his talent, of shaping, encouraging, finding buyers, markets, arranging visits while he dissipated his energies in all the inconsequential jobs he had burdened himself with needlessly. If he had driven himself in one direction, instead of footling along, how wealthy they might have been. Maurice Simard was a real businessman. He had his own light aircraft, his yacht with which he plied the great lakes. They had a sailing boat. New machines, faster techniques could quadruple their output, but he wouldn't hear of it, insisting it was a hand craft first and last and that the exigencies of fashion were hard enough to bear without making them an aim. He wanted to drop the ghastly commercial lines and concentrate on something durable. She replied that mechanisation would free him from drudgery so that he could concentrate on design, perfecting techniques, anything he chose. How often did they lose time waiting for old looms to be mended, or replacement parts to be crafted by a joiner, when new machines would at least work and have spare parts in production. But he was obdurate, or silent, and there the debate ended.

So, watching Esme and him together, her anxiety was two-fold. He should not be so exclusively in her company, Mairi was certain, but uneasily so without concrete reasons. Further, she mistrusted the privacy they entered together of books and paintings which in twenty years had brought them no profit and less happiness. That was a distraction, art, culture, the vague longings for artistic expression. He ought to invest his time in something more solid, not speechify to giddy girls. But she compressed her lips and dared say nothing. He could kill with a look.

Going to prepare lunch she found Esme ensconced by the Aga feet on the wall, and her disapproval filled the room as she assembled her utensils.

'Can I help?'

'Why, thank you. You'll find another apron behind the cupboard door. The vegetables are in the water. I think you'll find the small knife is best.' She watched Esme's efforts with suspicion and, Not thorough, was her conclusion. There was a real art in vegetable preparation, wasn't there? 'Perhaps if you cut the carrots from the broad end first you would get on faster. No, diagonally, that's better.'

But the sun rounded the corner of the building, enticing the girl away. It was a blustery day, the wind whipping up edges of cloud into a froth and taunting her with reminders of better places to be and better things to do. She bent her will. Never let it be said that a plate of carrots had defeated her.

'You've got nothing in particular lined up for next year?' started Mairi, seeing that her niece was at a disadvantage.

Indeed, Esme was almost caught off balance and looked round alarmed. But no, there was no knowledge in that face. 'I have a lot of things in mind, but I don't know if I shall see any of them through.'

'Have you had your money from Mr Scott?'

'No, I haven't.' But, really, was that a question one asked!

'It'll come any day now, but it won't last for ever. I mean you can't live on that. What you should do is put it on deposit till you decide. Are you going to buy a flat in town? A small maisonette should do you and your share will stretch to that. Nothing too pretentious of course. You shouldn't be too ambitious, though it will seem a come-down after living in that big house.'

Esme was stubbornly silent.

'You didn't apply to Moray House?'

'No.'

'A pity. Teaching is such a good profession for a woman. Or the Civil Service. Now, your mother had a first-rate post in the library service, went straight in after her degree and was heading for higher things. She was picked out for training as an archivist. Quite remarkable and endless prospects. It was Stefan's fault she lost that. He was all set for Canada and she resigned. Then, when it didn't work out, she had to start at the bottom again and times were different. There were a lot of senior and experienced men returning from the war and of course the men had to have priority. She lost her chance. A great pity.'

'She never enjoyed her work.'

'Enjoy? That's not the point. What would she have done

without it? She didn't have a husband to support her, remember. She would have had to rely on charity and handouts.' She looked over Esme's shoulder at her work. 'Yes, that's all right. You could lay the table now. I'm going over to the dairy.'

So for five minutes while she was released from the constricting nosiness of her aunt, work, money, plans, what impertinence, Esme laid the table in a whirlwind of activity. The room span as she opened cupboards, shook the cloth, skimmed the dishes onto the surface, flashed cutlery and all at top speed. Alexis, coming back for lunch, was in time to catch sight of her at the moment when she fell into repose with her book again, tucked in her corner by the Aga, picking it up without hesitation at the correct line and re-entering whatever world she had temporarily abandoned.

Mairi inspected the cloth. 'I think we had better have a clean one. I can't imagine who put that away dirty.' Then, halfway through the reiterated chore, she looked out and said, 'Perhaps we should eat outside for once. It is a lovely day,' thereby forcing the girl to do what she could least tolerate, repeat a task.

Her quickness annoyed Mairi who liked to delay over the method of execution. That was all important to her. Esme was more masculine in finding results the only significant criterion. It did not matter to Esme if a plate were out of line, or a fork unpolished, as long as the essentials were there; eating was a prelude to conversation, work a necessity to be got through before the real business of the day started, though what that was she could not convincingly say.

But the talk of work had its effect on her and, dread it as she did, she turned her mind around to face it. She looked on employment as a monotony that would dull her living, and it was one of the insidious attractions of living with Alexis, that he removed any need to structure a career.

As long as she could recall she had wanted time to pass and take her further into maturity, so that she could make her own decisions instead of obeying a time span imposed on her by outside forces. Her education had been a series of deadlines to meet, of restrictions on her freedom so that she was constantly saying to herself, If only it were summer, Christmas, next year. She had merely done what was expected of her, following the aspirations of others towards an unknown and generally undesirable goal. Teaching?

The Civil Service! That was the toll of doom. It was not that she was lazy. When imperative, that is immediately before any of her deadlines elapsed, she could work for twelve hours at a stretch, scrub the house from top to bottom before she left it, write a thousand words an hour. But all her efforts must be exceptional. She could move a mountain – once. The thought of tomorrow being the same as today, bringing the same chores and the same faces, stifled her and compelled her to renege on the routines of normal life.

But her aunt's advice contained a useful pointer. Here she was for the first time free to make a decision and she was in danger of encumbering it again with clauses. She must choose wisely or find herself in a path directed by others. Living with Alexis was not terminal. She must have her own orbit. Whatever happened, she would not be a kept woman. But what contribution could she make? What could she do that would not conflict with his lifestyle? There it was again. She encountered even in herself the malleable stuff that women are made of which prevents them from being any more than their men want them to be.

'What are you thinking?' he asked quietly when, between courses, Mairi and Aileen bustled like trains in a siding.

'Ineffable thoughts.'

17

Aileen and Esme had worked out a system of interchange in their clothes which inevitably favoured Esme. She owned no more than half a dozen dubiously maintained garments, a correct brown suit (Aileen insisted it was a costume), a blue peasant dress so heavily embroidered that nobody but Esme would have worn it in daylight, a skirt or two and a few blouses supplemented by her re-cycled knitwear. Aileen possessed dozens of different outfits stored in a box room, a profusion which inspired her to largesse. Mairi could not grasp this one-sided borrowing. If she saw her daughter in any of Esme's clothes, and who would want to aspire to such threadbare respectability, she would say, 'Oh, you have a new sweater.' If the situation were reversed and the changeling appeared in Aileen's guise, her comment was, 'That's your cousin's, isn't it?' and her eye poked into every seam to guard against the abuse of a tear or a missing button. For only half of Polonius' injunction went home to Mairi.

Alexis followed these matinal apparitions closely and enjoined them to behold the lilies of the field.

Esme's method of dressing in particular he could not fathom. She might borrow an item from Aileen, but it underwent a metamorphosis in her hands. Everything she owned did multiple service so that the same yardage of raw silk was alternately a float of scarf, a bandanna wound fantastically like a crest when she had been swimming and walked up from the loch, a belt or a sash to define a length of robe, or in the evening a shawl, spread out and fluttering behind her, lambent and diaphanous as the filament of flying things. She dressed like a peasant, for whom there is no fashion but utility, no beauty beyond practicality, but the functional aspect evolved itself as decoration. Fluidity as all-important. Nothing was constant, fixed or defined.

She had the knack of serendipity; took up a handful of thrums cast off by the loom and knotted them into tassels with which she embellished a bodice; found the knee breeches he had worn as a boy still intact in a press and putting them on with brogues, hose and waistcoat became a hoyden, skimming the heather as neatly as any tyke or tousle-headed ragamuffin out of school.

Mairi looked askance as she asked permission for these. 'Wherever was she rummaging?'

'No matter. Let her have them.'

'I hardly think it's suitable.'

'Why not. I'll not get into them again.'

'Men's clothing! Well, I see I must look to my closets.'

The truth was he could not take his eyes off her. Her inventiveness intrigued him, and work alone barred him from being exclusively in her company.

To Mairi, possessions were power, but to Alexis the use to which these objects were applied transcended their face value. Mairi was offended if a teapot, a chair, a silver teaspoon she considered valuable were pressed into service because abuse might damage it, might undermine its market price. Alexis thought the chair became most fully what it was by being used; function was sacred. The most beloved article, whatever was truly favourite, was the thing man had shaped to his purpose, which evolved as a portion of each task so that it shared his labour and was elevated at last to the rank of companion. To have something he did not use, that existed from superfluity and show was vulgar and merely possessive.

So when one of the girls came into a room and asked, 'Is it all right if I borrow this pen? I can't find mine,' Mairi's response, irrespective of who asked, would be to hesitate. If the pen were broken it would cost money to replace it, and that was labour; it would cause inconvenience; blame attached to the neglect of the original pen. And, besides, things had their place and their owner, and she was abrogating some of her proper authority by diminishing her store of its symbols. Or, if she did lend, she felt she was gaining control over the borrower through the object. What are you intending to do with it, where are you going with it, isn't it the best pen you ever used? There was no absolute giving in her vocabulary. It was always to be returned with interest, if of nothing more than indebtedness.

Alexis could as little deny them affection as withhold the trivial object they requested. To ask and to give were bonds of devotion. The contents of his house and the reward of his labour were to serve their purposes. There was no yours and mine in his establishment and all the mansions of his dwelling place were open to them. 'Take it, take it,' was his response whereas Mairi, having acceded would admonish, 'And remember to put it back afterwards.'

In unobserved moments, Esme would seek him out and silently bunch against a wall to watch him work. He had shown her a great deal, how to cut a mount, how to shape a mitre for a frame, distress wood and thin varnish and she was never-endingly intrigued by his diverse occupations. She cast her eyes about the walls of his office, for they were hung with strange and inconsequential clutter he had at one time admired, or things he wished to draw, a sampler with mottoes in cross-stitch he had found in a barn, walking sticks new and old in every native wood, quotations that had struck him deeply, copied out.

'Getting and spending, we lay waste our powers.'

'How long has she been posing for you?' asked Mairi when she came into the office to collect the invoice and found a sketch pad on top of the desk. It was an innocent enough drawing made while she read in sunlight with her eyes shaded by a hand.

He refused to make an incriminating reply. 'Good, isn't it? A good likeness.'

'Oh, I don't know. I think you've prettied her up a little.'

'No, you're wrong. You must take another look. I couldn't do her justice.'

Discreet as they were, it was impossible to hide altogether. A shrewd observer would have noticed the change in his pattern, an excuse to linger over the locking up at night, a protracted visit to the dairy cold store, or how even in their communal evenings in the muted parlour a chair would be minutely adjusted to give a side-long view of a window-seat where Esme perched over her copy of Palgrave's *Golden Treasury*. And that sober volume went between them like a philtre. By a wordless arrangement, each left the book face down at a page the other was to read and take to heart, through deduction or by the hint of the slightest pencil line drawn parallel in the margin.

Live with me and be my love,
And we will all the pleasures prove.

Had she come all the way for this,
To part at last without a kiss?

Beside the haystack in the floods.

All optimism and joy were on her side; fear and dejection on his. Once she burst out laughing at the day's quotation

Shall I part my hair behind? Do I dare to eat a peach?
I shall wear white flannel trousers, and walk upon the beach.
I have heard the mermaids singing, each to each,

I do not think that they will sing to me.

until the waves of her laughter rebounded off the walls in a scale of ascending notes, shook against the ceiling, made the fire dance so that Mairi and Aileen raised their eyes in astonishment. Whoever laughed at the *Golden Treasury*? The affair progressed vicariously, leaving traces too subtle for detection though at times there was an alteration in the air no greater than the exploratory thread of the spider that may cross the path of morning walkers.

They did not touch, but standing side by side they emitted the unmistakable frisson of man and woman, so that admiring the profuse growth of a herbaceous border, poppy, love-in-a-mist, forget-me-not, standing on either side of a doorway to say good-night with a hand on the latch, settling back against the inviting cushions of the sofa became each a voluptuous experience through which they tarried with a self-denial of real gratification that was almost ascetic.

18

Rejean came alone on the last day before his wedding. The weather was set for a warm spell. It was the midsummer heat that can descend on the central Highlands and embalm them in a vapour for days on end, a heat haze in the morning, an incubating cloud overnight. He found Esme by herself in the orchard, resting her back against a tree, for in the suffocating humidity this was the coolest place.

'Where is everyone?'

'Alexis had to make a trip to Perth. Mairi and Aileen are doing the rounds of Lochearn, visiting people who gave you presents but aren't invited tomorrow. What are Claire and Maurice doing?'

He was amused that two days' acquaintance gave Esme familiarity with his parents' Christian names. He would be formal with his mother-in-law till the day he died. 'He's playing a round of golf.'

'I didn't know he played golf.'

'He doesn't. Not well. But it's impressive to say he played Gleneagles King's Course, and photography to prove it. My mother went to the Caithness glass factory.'

'But they're coming over for the dance this evening?'

'What could keep them away?' He had settled comfortably with his back against the same tree. 'Why are these people not invited tomorrow if they have given a present?'

'I think it's the other way round. Aileen's rather like nobility round here. People give because of who she is and don't expect an invitation because they're not grand enough.'

'What do you mean "like nobility"? Like royalty?'

'Hardly. But she's well known. A lot of the village call her "Miss Aileen" just as they call him "Mr Alexis". Haven't you noticed?'

'Odd. That seems very old-fashioned to me.'

'And to me.'

'Actually, it was a present that brought me here this morning. Or rather two. Did you know it was customary for the groom to give the bridesmaid a gift?'

'No, I expected nothing.'

'Properly speaking, I should have kept this till tomorrow. But I knew I wouldn't see you alone. It's not a very conventional gift, I'm afraid. I think a silver bracelet is more the norm.' He handed her an envelope without inscription or card. It was flimsy, unsealed, and as she opened the flap in trepidation she thought, I have grown nervous of envelopes.

'I fear the Canadians even when they are bringing gifts.' It contained a ticket about the size of a cheque, which with greatest worldliness she would have recognised as an airline ticket. But the words Air Canada, Prestwick, Montreal and even the date swam before her and made no impression. What was the thing? She turned it over and glanced down endless regulations about baggage allowance, check-in times and insurance liability, none of which had the least relevance to her. It was not what she would have looked for from Rejean and then it flashed into her mind how it had come about. 'This was Maurice's idea.'

He faltered a second. 'Yes, how quickly you found me out.'

'And he wanted you to pass it on to me as your gift, not his?'

'Yes, substantially.'

'But he paid for it?'

'True again.'

'Well, thank you but it is much too expensive, not perhaps in his terms but in mine. It's dated next week. That's rather precipitate. He wants to rush me.'

'It's valid for a year.'

'Still, I would feel next Friday started the clock ticking. It would be like a time bomb under me. The ticket', she looked more closely, 'is only one way.'

'You may like it, Esme. You may want to stay. It's a marvellous country, air, space, freedom. It's a young man's country with so much opportunity.' He flung his arms out and for a moment grew expansive. 'I can't understand why you are so reluctant to go.'

'Perhaps I am not ambitious. At any rate, thank you.'

'The best thanks would be for you to use it. If nothing else, it's exciting to see. Go for a month. Settle your mind. You've got nothing to lose.'

She followed the path of his enthusiasm, but did not go down it with him. 'What a pity the ticket was not intended for you.'

Well, that was true enough. Late the previous evening, after their dinner guests had taken their leave, Maurice took him into the smoking room and giving him the envelope, said, 'I hope you can use this wisely.'

The ticket had given him a surge of the heart it failed to arouse in Esme. He thought, My father understands how I feel. In spite of his disinterest, these gestures he fobs me off with, he has realised how unwilling I am and agrees I should go home rather than prolong a stale relationship. This is my release. Go home! He could drop the charade and with his father's blessing. There would be time for swimming and a fishing trip and weekends by the lake. He flashed him a look of the uttermost gratitude, which unhappily missed its mark.

Maurice lit a cigar, talked of golf, said Esme was the sort of person who needed to have things decided for her, charming, attractive and vacillating. At every syllable Rejean saw his reverie crumble. He was not wanted. He was not so much as thought about. For a second he touched the low point of despair, of the absolute annihilation of self. The man had more concern for this two day stranger than for his own son. To whom could he turn now? No one. But this final rejection had the inverse effect of steeling his will. No one but himself. At a stroke, he threw away the expectation of personal happiness. He shed the last husk of adolescence which looks on self as central, and espoused instead a goal, a principle. His mind turned back to the hidden chapters waiting in a drawer at Canonmills. When he got back he was going to take them to a publisher. He would find a sponsor, somehow, if not his father or his would-be wife. No one could cheat him of that accomplishment. 'Labor vincit omnia' superseded 'Amor'.

'What do you want me to do with it?' he asked Maurice.

'It can be your idea. Don't mention me.' Rejean rose. 'Are you going? Sit down till I finish this cigar.'

'No. We shouldn't overdo things. And the smell offends me, though you may not have noticed. I'll leave you to enjoy it. Good night.'

The hotel was quiet. The bars were closed. In the dining room the three-piece band was packing up, and down the corridors guests passed and said good night. The lights were on in the billiard room and he thought of joining the earnest male voices for a game. But instead he found the key of the swimming pool, having been judiciously polite to the attendant during his stay, and a midnight swim alone in the dark pool was much more to his taste. He plied it length by length, for he swam powerfully, indeed had worked as a life guard in a college vacation on the Great Lakes. He slept well and awoke refreshed and determined.

'What was the second present?' she coaxed.

He smiled. 'Quite absurd. I found this stone the other evening on the beach. It intrigued me because of the way it split in two, and I hoped . . .' He passed over the grey shape and was rewarded that she cradled it.

'How beautiful. Does it contain a fossil?'

'No, it isn't old enough. And even if it did, we would destroy the fossil by looking for it. A fossil is only a space where something once was.'

'Thank you. I shall keep this by me always.'

'I hoped you might stumble on the other half. I expect you will be here more often than I.' She cupped the tumulus-shaped stone in her hands and wondered if that were true, and why he said it. 'Are they coming back for lunch? Well then, why don't we take a picnic to the shore? Will you swim?'

Esme thought of her hair laboriously washed for the evening's entertainment but she would have to do it again later. She did not have the heart to disappoint him.

'You find towels and things. I'll find the food.'

The heat dissipated them. They swam and ate and lay in a fringe of shelter from the beating sun cast by the silver birches, half asleep. Around them was a low drone as farmers reaped an early crop and the threshing machinery buzzed and whirred in the fields above. Boys went by on a lumbering haycart and called to each other, but the heavy air capped their shouting so that nothing more invasive than a muffled voice reached them. Fishermen cast wide. Their weights dropped into the glaze of the loch almost soundlessly, and as silently the fish bit and were landed. In late afternoon the sun began to cloud a little; a fine haze set round the hillside at two hundred feet like a thread spun into a cocoon.

'Does anything change?' he murmured drowsily, face down.

'Round here? I doubt it. I wonder what your parents think of it. It's all so slow. You'll see this evening. It will be dancing in the old style.'

He moved his head up into the pressure of the air. 'The old style? Not minuets?'

'No, not that far back. Scottish country dancing.'

Invigorated by the prospect, he stood up and assumed the pose of a Highland dancer, while she watched his capers from below.

'No, not that way. That's exhibition dancing. Imagine doing that for three hours. You'd be dead from exhaustion. No, what we do,' she accepted his hand up, 'is dance in sets. Look.' She placed him opposite her and indicated a row of three more imaginary couples. 'Now, you must bow to my curtsey and when the Master of Ceremonies says "cross" you do it like this and then the step you use, don't look at me, look at your feet for a minute, is toe and heel, like a step and a shuffle. Do you follow?'

'And bagpipes?'

'Definitely not. They're an outdoor sound. We'll have an accordion and a few fiddles. Violins to you.'

'Violins? You dance to violins? Marvellous.' And he laughed incredulously.

'Come on. Dance or you'll disgrace yourself. It's very accurate, Scottish country dancing. If you get in a mess, the whole set goes out of order. Now this is how you do a wheel, and a chain.'

She hummed a plaintive air to keep time, and Rejean did not attempt to tell her that even in remote Canadian schools the principles of this dance, so akin to square dancing, were taught for he was enjoying the stern chiding of her instruction and the cool clasp of her palm as they moved up and down the set, represented only by the serried trees. He was neat footed and could turn on a pin, so they moved happily in unison. 'You'll do,' she concluded after a breathless Petronella.

'Will I?' but he did not release her crossed hands until he had out-challenged her evasive eyes.

And Mairi, coming to investigate and announce their return, found them standing hand in hand at the water's edge.

Alexis was late back. Esme left a note on his desk with the ticket. 'Maurice's idea – via Rejean. I feel I am being jostled. What say you?'

The village was a scattered collection of buildings, originally farmhouses and an inn. In the nineteenth century, however, the country was opened up as English landlords bought vast tracts of land, like the Powell-Jones family, and turned them into shooting estates. Fishing, game, fine wool from the hillside flocks made the native community prosper, if rather less than the landed gentry, and a church was built at one end of the straggling village with a good stone manse nearby. It conformed to the archetypal pattern, with a porch and three gable windows on the attic storey. Belatedly a hall was added a quarter of a mile away on a small rise of ground at one end of the churchyard where the rock was too flinty for grave-digging. The spot threatened to be sepulchral, with gloomy overgrown cypresses and a pair of yew trees, but by a happy accident it fronted on the yard of the inn, now the hotel, and in the evening enjoyed the double benefit of proximity to the licensed bar and the reflection of the warm lights inside, magnified by the water winking two hundred yards away.

Punctual as they were, the hall was already tuneful. The accordionist, Graeme Sutherland's nephew who served with a Highland regiment but was fortunately home on leave, entertained the assembly with the fine Scottish airs of his repertory. The dance was not restricted to the village but was a valley affair, and in the summer months when the numbers were swollen by friends and visitors it was a capacity crowd. Everyone came. Everyone who could walk could dance. There was the minister and his wife, to oversee correctness, Mrs Dunlop pushing her man along ahead of her, Fiona and Ian, the neighbours who had attended Alexis' bonfire celebration the previous November, and even Curriedon had sent down a party of house guests. Now that the season was open, the house was full of Englishmen intending to shoot but avoid being bagged themselves by Miss Jane, a debutante daughter. Mr and Mrs P-J were benignly in attendance till they saw things were proceeding normally and they could retire to a quiet night at their own fireside. The Master of Ceremonies was James Robertson who left the hotel to his steward and took on himself with due pomposity the duties of the occasion. And, finally, their own party who had sat round the table on the evening of Esme's arrival.

The village hall performed many functions since it was the only public building in the strath. It doubled as scout hall on Fridays, cinema every second Saturday with Graeme Sutherland's other nephew as projectionist, hall for the flower show, accommodation for the Women's Institute when once a month they sold their produce, honey, pickle in jars, seasonal jams and preserves from local fruit, and occasionally even a theatre; but it was acknowledged that when the high green curtains were drawn and the fiddlers tuned their strings for the dance, the hall came into its own.

They played liltingly, not the great songs of the country which are all of loss and leaving and the heartbreak of exile, but the second strand of airs that were fitting accompaniment to the jig, the reel, the Strathspey. The music curled round the walls and by enchantment set the feet of the assembly itching. It caught them up, grandfathers, children, couples who had chosen each other and couples who were still in process of choosing, whose shy footings gave rise to delighted conjecture on the part of their elders. The dainty reels taught in dancing classes could not survive the first scurry on the floor. Arms were linked, feet flew faster than the notes, the men stamped and dashed with their partners as insistently as rutting stags, winding them up the set to first couple, and no dancer worth his sporran made a wrong step or lost his girl in the affray. Highland youths knew what girls were for and were unabashed in approaching them. They'd come to dance, hadn't they, and unlike the callow young men of the city had no notion of hanging round a bar or talking to each other when there was good blood-heating dancing to be had. Aileen and Esme were much in demand, Aileen because she was known and liked and it was good fun to rag her on her wedding eve; Esme because she appealed to the large, sandy coloured Highlanders, neat and dark and darting like a southern swallow.

The energetic dance brought out her colour and the pleasure of release into movement that was disciplined but oh so free added to her features a kind of fire that was generally kept latent. She flew. She was like a skimming stone touching the surface so rarely, so lightly that it was difficult to believe in her substantiality. For three hours she hardly stopped or rested. But in one pause, for the benefit of the instrumentalists, a stranger who was evidently not of the region came and asked her to take the floor with him.

Mrs Dunlop put round the rumour that he was a guest from the Lodge.

'Are you from the valley?' he asked.

'Oh no.'

'Where are you from?' he pursued.

'Well now, guess.'

He danced with some regularity and it was in truth a relief to take the steps precisely and slow to walking pace. He was an upper-class Englishman with a curt accent but a rounded manner, so that she warmed to him and his futile questioning about her place of residence, to which her laughs and her shaking head produced no clue.

'I'm in transit,' she avowed, 'and that's the truth.'

As she spoke, the music ended and distractedly he continued to hold her hand while the Master of Ceremonies announced a Dashing White Sergeant. For this dance each man required two partners so Rejean, seeing what the others were about, whirled Aileen over the floor and caught Esme by the right hand while Aileen, his previous partner, he held by the left. Esme stood irresolute but Rejean was the more insistent of her claimants, so that the Englishman resigned her with a nod and the three formed themselves in a line to begin the hurried informality of the tripartite dance.

Whoops and cries went up for this was a great favourite in the valley; it gave a man the opportunity to flirt with anyone, within the bounds of decorum, to taste the joys of dancing simultaneously with two girls and deciding the finer points of their skill. Why, it made you dizzy with excitement. If Rejean twirled Aileen with punctilious grace, it was to Esme that he returned with devilment and zest; Aileen he touched, Esme he grasped. When they moved up the line of dancers weaving their way among lesser beauties, it was the dark head that bobbed the more brightly for him.

Alexis made himself agreeable, although Esme's note had upset his equilibrium. Thinking back over the events of the last few days, he perceived the ticket was no more Maurice's notion than Rejean's and put his finger on the very spot. In this black mood he would not dance; if he could not take her exclusively, he would have no one. He preferred to go from one group to another talking. The minister bent his ear about the hymns chosen for the wedding – all news to Alexis – and how the organist and the choir were coping admirably with the Bach to try and do them justice on the morrow. Ian came self-consciously with Fiona. Mr Powell-Jones confessed it was to be a poor year for the grouse. It was always a poor year for something, according to him. And so by slow degrees he perambulated the entire hall, glancing from time to time at the stags' heads which surveyed the scene with glaucous eye and the sombre panelling which gave the place the air of a sedate Edinburgh tea room.

Try as he might to be amusing or amused, his attention wandered back to the dancing and sought her out from among the rest.

Aileen came and insisted that he partner her.

'Oh, not me, I'm feeling antediluvian this evening.'

'Rubbish. You're the best dancer of the lot when you step out. This is such an easy one.'

'I know the steps well enough,' he said grudgingly.

'Don't hum.'

'I like humming. I like this melody.'

'And I absolutely forbid you to whistle if they play "The Road to the Isles".'

'But I requested that especially.' He feigned dismay.

'It wouldn't surprise me.'

They parted company when the gentlemen and ladies made separate wheels and when they came back together again he asked, 'Are you happy? You look happy.'

'Yes, of course I'm happy. Why shouldn't I be?'

'How very sensible you are. I admire your cool, my lady, really I do.' They peeled off as top couple for a minute before joining hands again at the bottom. 'You cope so well.' She smiled at this rare compliment and moved away to ask Maurice to join the next dance.

As Alexis took a respite from this strenuous haul up the floor, Graeme Sutherland walked up. 'You're not fit, man. You're out of puff.'

'Who is fit for this kind of dancing?' And he scowled.

'The youngsters take to it easily enough.' He nodded to the floor where, as glidingly as a swan, the unruffled Aileen set to her partner. 'Your niece has a new admirer.'

'Yes, so I see.'

'They make a bonny pair. But Miss Jane won't be pleased. He was her front runner for the season.'

'Who is he?'

'His family is in fruit importing but they took a step up last year when his sister married a minor royal.'

'Or down.'

'Come now, don't unleash all that pent-up socialism at a friendly gathering. You wouldn't stand in the young woman's way, would you?'

Alexis, impelled by this remark, took his old friend by the elbow and guided him towards the open door. 'There is something I cannot say in here. The air will be cooler outside.' Graeme went in awe of this gravity and allowed himself to be led down the path towards the church gate, under the dark boughs of the cypresses. 'I am right in thinking it was you who planted the idea of the ticket?' Alexis, rare for him, was furious. He found stress could only be worked off, not vented in words, and avoided the heat of argument when he could. He would much rather have challenged Graeme to a boxing match or a longstaff competition, Robin to Little John, than waste breath in futile anger.

Graeme, stalked where he thought he had done the stalking, was confounded. 'Yes, I spoke of it first.'

'Wasn't that meddlesome of you? Don't ever, I warn you, interfere with me and my doings again. Confine yourself to your natives. I am out of your sphere.'

But this denial was a confirmation in Graeme's reading. 'I did it for the best,' he said helplessly.

'That's the excuse of all do-gooders. It won't serve. Your best is not my best and I must enjoin you, whatever motives prompt you, not to be my keeper. That is between me and my conscience.'

For a minute the older man was intimidated and felt inclined to leave the matter there, before they fell out seriously and the unforgivable was said. But the course of their long friendship stood between them as a reproach against cowardice. Honesty must out. 'I beg you not to do this thing.'

'Why? What difference does it make to you?'

'You are anchored here. If you cut yourself loose, you may drift for ever. A man has his place and it doesn't do to go transplanting late in life.'

'I am not late in life. I am forty-three years of age. And I am entitled, as all men are, to a fragment of happiness. You have known it and you know I have not. Why would you deny me my portion?'

'But not with her.'

'Why not?'

'Think of the girl. You will ruin her.'

He expostulated. Words followed an explosion of sound. 'I suppose this has to be the perfect setting for such a Presbyterian utterance.'

'Don't dismiss what I say. I don't mean morally. I mean you will spoil her, indulge her. How can she be your peer? And what else can there be in life for her after you? She is too close to you. Why must you set your heart on these women who are forbidden to you? Your wife's sister and then her child. Why, it borders on the unnatural.'

Alexis bit his lip and bowed his head. 'You push me too far. I can tell you it is not I who am unnatural, although when you live as I have done you lose sight of what is right or wrong. I have forgotten what normal people do. Once you enter that downward spiral, there's no way of pulling out of it. But I have some justice on my side. I won't ask for your understanding. I've kept my silence all this time and won't break it now. You've never heard me say one word against my wife or my marriage, but don't imagine that what you see is all there is. I have some cause to feel aggrieved. I don't want to think about that. It's gone. It's over.'

Talking, Alexis had walked up and down the grass verge between the graves, pent with rage and the physical containment enforced on him. In such a mood, and against a lesser adversary he could have fought to the point of bloodshed. Only character, disgust that he might sink to bestiality, kept him from breaking out. But to be chastised, curbed by another was intolerable. He would not submit to anyone's correction bar his own. He came back down the path to face the gamekeeper and leaned forward on an ancient tombstone. His foot came to rest on the boundary rail of the grave, on which his shoe made an imprint in consecrated soil. Graeme saw him go over the edge, unheeding in his rage. He looked and did not know the man. He felt a total repugnance against the invader, the foreigner, the violator of what he held holy. He could not summon the words to express such alienation.

'Remove your foot, man. You unhallow the dead.'

The iconoclast obeyed. 'Tomorrow I am divorcing her. No, not literally. How easy if I could do it like an Arab and say three times, I hereby renounce you, and have done. But there will be interminable wrangling and no consent. She doesn't want me, but she wants a husband. But tomorrow the knot that ties Aileen loosens me. I'm going.'

'Have you decided then?'

'Irrevocably. There's no stopping me now.'

The sceptic was intrigued. 'Why her, after all this time?'

Alexis considered. 'She is the one woman in a million without spite.'

Graeme sucked his cheeks in. 'Give her time.'

'If you had lived out of the light for twenty years, you wouldn't deny his freedom to a fellow inmate. Good night.' And turning round on the path, he added, 'Goodbye.'

Graeme walked up and down under the sighing yews for some time. The weight of this unhappiness pulled him down and he could not face the hall and the dancing again. He was dismissed and knew they would not take hands again in friendship this side of a miracle. But still he could not begrudge his admiration. Cause, yes, he had no doubt there was cause, but was relieved that it went unspoken. That was the great dormant strength of the man, the ability to be his own counsel.

Inside the hall again, Alexis was free to watch her uninterrupted. The Master of Ceremonies knew his programme. Towards the end of the evening, he announced dances that were both slower for tired feet, and more deliberate, even intricate. The eight sets on the floor were well spaced for the first time, as old or under-aged took quiet leave to their beds. These were the dedicated performers, young and lithe, who took some pride in the execution of their steps.

This format had long fascinated him. It was only folk dancing but it had a complexity in its progression that was as involved as the sophisticated waltz, mazurka, minuet. The figure of eight was tight, self-contained, a shape of absolute symmetry and performed well it was a delicate harmony, each move total in itself but related to the whole while the variables of the four couples, it had often struck him, provided the minimum number for self-perpetuation. It was a counterpoise of men and women, lines and wheels, the solitary step as against the action of the group. He could watch all evening the gradations by which the lower half of the set moved up and overtook the positions of first and second couple. An eight was the numerical symbol for infinity, laid on its side, and, like it, capable of being endlessly reproduced without a break.

It was true, Esme was back with her English milord. She went flitting across the room in those intricate weaving patterns, pulling her less able but obedient partner along, exasperated with him and amused at the same time. Yes, she showed every evidence of liking him. They set, crossed hands, set to their corners, made a circle of four, crossed again, danced outside the set and up again. Nobody could deny they were the most striking couple in the hall, exuberantly, youthfully, enviably handsome. They moved well together, dark and dark, loch and sky reflecting each other, a matched pair, so that his heart ached with crude envy at the tangible union of their bodies.

Why should he stand in the young woman's way? In his quiet moments he had evaluated the problems of a life with Esme realistically. He could not look forward to leaving Lochearn. His workers were indigenous and if he himself was a nomad, as he had averred to Esme, he still respected stability for its own sake. His upheaval would shake others. Conversely, how could he introduce her to the strath on a permanent basis, as his mistress, his common law wife? The goodly people in this hall knew how to shun and they would ostracise them both if she crossed his threshold as other than his kinswoman. And even if she were willing to accept so circumscribed a life, what agonies would he have to undergo every time a young man came a-knocking on his door? He was deeply wrought that the ideal, so nearly in his grasp, should be attenuated by secrecy, fear, deceit and all the other ugliness that ran most counter to his personality. He was not greedy, he was not possessive, but the dread of dereliction almost eroded the joy of seeing her smile across the hall at him. Could he live with himself in this degraded state?

These were the ignoble passions. He pushed them away with all the force of one who has learned to master his instincts since adult life began. In these thoughts, self was uppermost. He admonished himself that self did not matter. Practicalities would resolve themselves. He was rich enough, he was even powerful enough to arrange anything. What mattered was that he did not, by the exercise of his personality and his superior years, over-influence Esme. Yes, she would be flattered if he courted her, yes she would turn to him in need, but these were not the absolutes of free will. They were the results of a dependency brought about by her exceptional circumstances, so that he accused himself of taking unfair advantage in tying her down to him. His were the jesses by which the hawk soaring became entrammelled in the branches of a tree and died. He folded his arms and stared into a bleak future with her, bleaker still without her. Let her go, he commanded himself. He consigned her in his wishes to a hallowed end but he must terminate his authority over her now. Let her go with his blessing. He turned round and made for the door.

Meantime the Englishman had made his advance. To most young men, women are rather like commodities, valuable according to their rarity. Almost no one could instinctively see the merit in a lump of uncut crystallised carbon, or yellow ore that was in its unrefined state. Having been assured that there is a limited supply of diamonds or gold, however, who could resist the temptation to corner a share of the market and lay up his individual store of what is most prized by his fellows? A pretty face, ready wit alerted him to the fact that she was above the commonplace and gave hint of more durable qualities. If the Englishman, and he was to remain nameless to Esme, cast his mind back, there was not a single girl of his acquaintance who would have dropped his hand to take another's. When a man meets this hard core for the first time he must either say, I find diamonds worthless and gold lacklustre, or make his bid.

'I wonder if I might see you home? You are living locally. Or, wherever it is, I can drive you.'

' "Through all the wide Border his steed was the best." ' Then she grew silent, seeing he was serious and intense. No, he hadn't been refused before. 'I am so sorry, but I am already spoken for.'

'But you are not with anyone.' He had made his own inquiries during the course of the evening and watched her party. There was the young couple who had interrupted them earlier, others had told him they were to be married the following day, and his parents as well as the girl's parents. Who was she with? Or had someone in the assembly beaten him to the question? Glancing round, he thought not.

'I am so sorry. I can't.'

He frowned and wanted to object, but his breeding held. He did not question further, except with a look, and assumed the lady declined for the primary reason, that she did not care for him. Sadly, Esme realised that if a few months earlier he had materialised at a Union sortie, or in one of her classes, he would have done very well indeed.

She caught Alexis by the arm just as he reached the cool draught of the outer porch. 'Where are you going to? You haven't danced with me yet, and if you won't ask me I must be forward enough to ask you.'

'Where has your Adonis gone?'

'Gone, that's all. Will you dance?' She held out her hand in offer and he led her back to the floor where the final dance was being announced. The non-dancers straggled back to watch the last fling, so that the participants moved under the gaze of many an eye.

'This is too energetic. I like close dancing.'

Their eyes travelled over each other's face, asking, answering. Of all her partners that evening, this was the one she waited for. How could she tell him that?

This was a progressive dance allowing late arrivals entry at any point, and the reels with their compact formations were abandoned for the evening. The eights merged into a homogeneous whole, women to the inside, men outside, separate but linked in two enormous concentric wheels that revolved filling the room. Each couple performed a design of hands and feet, crossing, turning, back to back, before they spun, broke and moved on to the next partner to conclude the movement. But as the wheel rotated by which Esme would be carried forward and away from Alexis, she took a look behind and in an unprecedented blunder, stepped backwards and searched for his hand to begin the recurring phase.

The result of her action was catastrophic on the exacting progress of the group. The dancers cannoned on both sides, with an effect like a row of dominoes a child pushes to collide with each other in a gradual and cumulative collapse. The confusion reigned for a few seconds, and only she and Alexis moved sure-footed through the remainder of that sequence. In a minute the others reassembled and passed off her clumsiness as a joke.

Not so Mairi. She stood bolt upright, her eyes ablaze and in such aspect she was a fearsome object. So far Esme had confined her tricks to the private scene, but to bring her shameless seeking for attention into public view was beyond impertinence.

Five times when it was their turn to divide and move on, Alexis and Esme ignored the rules of the dance. They stepped outside the circles and re-entered together as a pair, or more simply formed an arch through which the others passed. The dancers took it humorously. It was a little saucy in this context to make so definite a preference clear, but at the late hour and because of Alexis' standing it was overlooked. But the Master of Ceremonies was put out at this tampering with the due order of things as they were laid down, and called the evening summarily to a halt.

Approaching midnight, the air was still warm. The hills enclosed the heat of the day and the fine shawl of cloud that had drifted over in the late afternoon insulated them from night vapours. But it was pitch black. In accordance with custom the hall lights were doused before the stroke of twelve, and the revellers left to grope their way home. The party attached to Inchcombe split up, the Simards heading off separately while Alexis said to Mairi and Aileen who were already seated in the car, 'We will walk back. It's a perfect evening,' and turned on his heel to obliterate objections.

Many dancers threaded back along the highway and after

quarter of an hour the cars ceased to weave amongst them. The walkers thinned, peeling off from the main road to garden paths or the hillside tracks that led to home. Left alone, utterly alone on the last stretches of the broad road, they linked arms and, by entwining, clapsed their hands together.

'You're a bonny dancer.'

'You are not so bad when you warm to it.'

'I fear, Esme, that you drew attention to us.'

'Does it matter now?'

'No, it's beyond mattering. Come, this road's too hard on feet that are sore from dancing. Let's take the shore.' They cut through a wood of birches laced with a network of thin streams over which he handed her for safety. After a few minutes the ground broke free from stones and they found themselves on sand. He paused, remembering the place, and almost without caring whether they were seen or not kissed her for the first time since her arrival. Esme's kisses were addictive. One simply did not finish, but each ran into another the way a pianist practises an opening phrase with different emphasis, staccato, pianissimo, moderato and a repeated trill as, drawing away from his mouth to cool her lips on his cheek, his jaw, the socket of his eye, she would return again andante.

Why her? Why not her! But once in a lifetime, in ten thousand lives was a man fortunate enough to meet his equal, physical and mental. Every man kept in the corner of his yearning the image of a woman who was not passive, acquiescent merely in loveplay; a woman who occasionally sought and, undoing one by one the knots of convention, ravished him. Here she was, quiet, modest and yet, unleashed, a sensualist. Whatever she was or was not was paramount. She filled the space of today.

Heady they fell softly to the sand. 'This is crazy. Anyone could come along here. It's open ground.' He forced himself to consider their position but only between embraces that gave the lie to caution.

'Shall we use the boathouse?'

They stood again and under cover of the overhanging boughs reached the dark sanctuary of the shed. The slip of water in which the boat gently rocked gave back a little light, while one window southward showed house lamps at a distance. She undressed and lay down beside him in the boat among the tarpaulins that had warmed him on the night of the bonfire. Adrift, they were soon out of all consciousness, drugged by the benign air, the dancing, the release of tension after so many days and weeks of waiting. The water lapped round them in their coracle and a fusion took place in his mind between this moment and eternity as he set about rediscovering the body he had but partially known.

They did not hear the door open and for a few seconds were invisible as well as silent themselves. Then a movement betrayed them and a girl's voice said, 'There's somebody here.'

Esme sat up, then, clutching some discarded clothing, stood. Alexis put his arm up to restrain her but too late. The girl giggled and her companion turned round and saw, in the reflected arc of a car headbeam passing on the road, his master in the midst of adultery.

Ian and Fiona had followed the same track to this spot, but lagged a ten minute interval behind.

Ian was staggered and for some seconds stood immobilised. He had seen the female form in parts, but this whole nudity rising out of the boat made him gawp. Such a marble statue he had seen once, of a woman standing on a shell, but that was cold and white. This made you want to turn your hands to the blaze.

He pushed Fiona out of the door. 'I'm sorry, Mr Alexis, I'm very sorry.'

And he too retreated to the edge of the wood where Fiona waited for him. 'Not a stitch on. Did you see?'

'Yes, I saw.'

Fiona chortled, then a more wicked thought still entered her head. 'Isn't she his niece? I had a notion that was incest. Is that not incest, Ian, like brother and sister? Remember the McDonald girl had that funny misshapen baby and everyone said it was her brother's.'

'Hush. She's his wife's niece, not his. It's only if they're blood relations.'

'At least he had his clothes on. Imagine if he'd been down to his buffs as well,' she simpered.

'Be quiet you silly besom. And not a word of this to anyone, mind.'

Esme dressing heard the tittering note which was loud enough to bring a battery of lights into play from the upper windows of the house. After a few minutes she and Alexis left the boathouse as shamefaced and averted as Adam and Eve expelled from Eden by the all-seeing eye of retribution.

19

It was a day of glassy perfection. When Esme went early to the office to pick up the mail for the house, her degree pass forwarded, a letter from Mr Scott with a cheque, the stones under her feet were already warm. The door stood open and he sat with his back to the sun poring over papers. She slipped her arms around him and leaned her head against his. He dropped the work and putting his hand up behind him touched her warm head and her sunstruck hair.

'Good morning. Are you cross with me?'

'Should I be?'

'I keep bringing trouble to your door.'

He swivelled round to look at her. 'Hard to believe, isn't it, when you have a morning as peaceful as this, that the volcano is going to erupt in a day or two? This can't go on. We must find time to talk later and arrange things, though I don't know when. Perhaps tomorrow when they have all gone. This is to be a twelve-hour marathon. A thousand people will be coming to shake my hand today, so don't be disappointed if I'm never with you.'

He kissed her for her result and laughed at Mr Scott's cheque which was an enormous sum to her, and a meagre portion to him. 'At least I shall not be marrying a pauper.'

'Don't say that,' she corrected sharply.

'I'm sorry. I didn't mean to jibe at the amount.'

'Don't say "marry". We may never marry.'

'So be it. I undertake this venture on your terms,' and he smoothed away the creases of anxiety. 'Go and dress now. I'll be along when the clattering has died down.'

Left alone, he sorted through the telegrams which had been arriving all week and put them into piles: those to be read out at the reception, those to be merely mentioned. One caught his eye because it came from the post office of Chicoutimi, Quebec, and read 'Congratulations on your timely capitulation. Mabon Caulderwood.' He grimaced at the cross in the corner. Aileen had vetoed that one.

If he had set out to paint a canvas of the day, he would have gone to the bright end of his palette, little employed, pearl, coral and turquoise, though these were his favourite colours and his favourite gems, so rich and rare in their milkiness, their dull opaque softness, that they were to be reserved exclusively for high days, not to be abraded by exposure to the dailiness of life. It was a day of melting beauty, clear skies overhead of an extraordinary translucent aquamarine, the shade created by a water colour artist when he runs a wash down his page so thinly it allows the creaminess of the paper to shine through, an ethereal tint. A little cloud puffed up on the horizon but never endangered the sun which rose and rose, and hung at the meridian like a silver pendant which as the day advanced was debased by the increased depth of its colour, from pewter to brass and in the early evening turned to a flat copper disc.

Aileen was ivory, pale as a lily in a scoop of satin. The sight of her made him tenderly preoccupied, for she was a lovely creature, fragile boned, strong willed, and a greater paradox in that she was his flesh and still a mystery to him. Silent, unshakeable, she managed to look in the midst of turmoil as though the sack of Rome could not assail her constancy. She moved effortlessly through the day, gracious, gliding, reminding him of the essential goodness of life which might in another age, another place, truly be a land flowing with milk and honey. He could rest content that in this, at least, he had done his duty.

Esme wore a dress of coral, a bold pink he told her was the one colour in the spectrum a man could not wear. The thing was of some silk she called tussore and its long skirts crackled like flame when she went past. It would be easy to denote Aileen's cool passivity on paper; it only needed a little deckling, a crinkle of the parchment to imply all was not entirely flat in her refinement. But how on earth could the static medium denote her cousin's restless movement, since for the duration of a second she was conspicuous in every group she highlighted, and was gone. How could he begin to paint the incandescent, the sense that every fire must give of contagion and roaring out of control, or the subdued and utterly necessary comforting warmth? Wasn't it a cardinal rule of art that a painting could not contain an image of the sun, except on the point of setting, because its chromatic intensity would blanch out lesser colours? He might do it by a corona of warm tones to make a framework for the central portrait, an allegory of sensuousness to contrast with the pellucid chastity of things bridal – he did not know how it could be done. But all day she flickered and distracted like a sun spot before the eye.

These colours were picked up in the florist's art. Every greenhouse and every nursery for fifty miles around had been plundered for blooms that accorded with the scheme. Bud roses, dawn gladioli, a cream convolvulus binding the looseness of the rest, carnations the colour of ripened peaches.

Turquoise was Mairi's choice and it became her. Transformed by a smile, she was a handsome woman with straight shoulders and erect carriage. She bore her part nobly and he admitted that in the anonymous social milieu, he milord, she milady, they were in synchronisation, or was it like Jack Sprat and his wife or the couple in the weather house, they agreed in function although they were diametrically opposed in spirit.

Against these high tones, he must set the sober colouring of the men, the dark grey stonework of the church, the sombre trees of the valley, something subfusc to denote the serious undertow of the celebration. In this the words were implicit. To the young people the vows were a song sung because it trilled easily off the tongue, some of the best known poetry in the language lurking in the staid canon of the Book of Common Prayer. 'Forsaking all other, keep thee only unto her.' 'To have and to hold from this day forward, for better for worse, for richer for poorer, in sickness and in health, to love and to cherish till death us do part, according to God's holy ordinance, and thereto I plight thee my troth.'

These promises were too eternal. Hearing them irked him because he thought the undertaking a sham, fealty and bondage disguised as high romance. And yet here at his elbow was Esme holding out a hymn sheet, all things bright and beautiful, by her person a living contradiction of his black thoughts. How could he be such a cynic?

The music they played that day overwhelmed him and gave him

a measure of how limited his chosen art was. These were the liquid emotions, more immediate and more vibrant than anything he could paint. Delighting the eye was nothing compared with stirring the heart. Here were Bach, Vivaldi, Palestrina chosen by Rejean, pure as song birds heard in the morning air. He wished he were not musically illiterate; that his education, so admirable in other fields, had given him the ability to untwist the hidden strands of harmony, see more, feel more, but also provide him with a critical vocabulary behind which he could build a defence. As it was, he was pulp in the hands of the orchestrators, and the first note of the organ confused his heart and his head so much that sense departed and he was swept by wave after wave of rending emotion. The choral solemnity of these works rose and drowned him as time and time again the melodic line of the instrument parted from the aching descant of human voices. When they sang, after the signing of the register, the plangent notes of 'The lark in the clear air ascending' he feared that he would sob outright and be humiliated. Why had he selected that with its spiralling hopes, of all things, to walk down the aisle to?

But conventions were also secularly served. The photographic session took almost an hour. Every individual participant of the scene was shot with every other individual, until Alexis began to suspect that the photographer was attempting an arithmetic calculation on the laws of probability; then groups of numbers, three, four, five, six people and finally the entire assembly. How many times was he going to be asked to smile? At last the official car arrived and Aileen, standing on tiptoe on the steps, threw her bouquet into the air. It arced in several parabolas before it was caught, quite unintentionally, by Esme who was not looking and did not know of the legend. Its artifice displeased her, but she broke off one of the apricot coloured carnations and gave it to Alexis to replace his tired buttonhole. Then round the car there was a shout and a scramble, while they all stopped from their talking to look for a second. The urchins of the village sprawled and felt along the ground because Rejean had thrown the traditional bounty of the pour-out, a bagful of silver coins which fell in a shower and bowled down the road in all directions.

A piper heralded the cortège as it took its stately drive down the half mile to Inchcombe, his plaid lifting behind him as he piped.

Droves of guests swept through the gatehouse as insistently as the waves beating on the shore. For they had taken a chance on the weather and all two hundred guests were seated at trestle tables laid out as though for a mediaeval banquet in the courtyard. The finest linen tablecloths, scrolled with amaranthus, the heaviest silver, posies of cream and coral in memory of those in church garlanded the tables which were spread down their length with ashets whose contents made decoration superfluous.

Whole lobster, crab and salmon were garnished in glittering simulacra of the living fish; innumerable fowl presented their snowy whiteness to the carver, filled with an array of stuffings from the humble meal through to refined chestnut; pressed meats abounded, liver and duck pâtés, terrines, the homely haslet, all quivering in their gelatinous juices. It was a tableau by Veronese or Titian, a still life pushed into a corner of a great history painting to indicate the sumptuousness of Venetian life. Men and women working out their drama still fingered a cluster of grapes from a cornucopia.

The sun cast its shadow round the walls of the courtyard as round a dial, suffused his guests with light then little by little withdrew again. This huge assembly had not happened before and would not again, so there was a special excitement generated for him in seeing his familiar surroundings decked out for the unique festivity, but behind that the sadness of valediction. His speech, which he had intended to be gay, insouciant, turned melancholy instead and he mourned the loss of his child more than he had meant.

It was left to Rejean to entertain the table with a fine politic speech that played on the sympathies of the listeners and ended: 'There is a continuing bond between the nations of France and Scotland, fused in your history, evident in the legacy of your language. My welcome here is an example of the hospitality that is extended everywhere and, if a French Canadian may be regarded as French by proxy, to your neighbours across the water in particular. Aileen and I are gratified if we have advanced the aims of the Auld Alliance to some small degree. For your kindness, your gifts, your warmth, I thank you as a stranger who is in no hurry to leave. If this is what it is to be a Scot, I shall work to be worthy of being called a native at last.'

Amid the applause for this, the sentiments of which surprised no one but Esme who recognised a saving lie, Maurice and Alexis shook hands; their children were happy, their wives approved, they liked each other and so they set the seal on their lineage.

The piper took his chanter and struck up. There was a high squeal as the sound of the pipes severed the air, and then settled into the heavy drone while the throng dispersed to listen, to drink, to dance, to talk or walk along the shore as it took their inclination.

Mairi sitting at the top table had her reward. It was the apogee of a life lived vicariously. As the two-seater left the portal gateway and purred into the distance and out of sight, she knew her efforts were crowned. Aileen was safely accounted for, and she herself had been the instrument of success in this day. Esme might laugh under a tree and half a dozen faces turn to hers in attestation of her power; half a dozen menfolk queue up to dance with her as they were doing now, poor fools, but Aileen had won the day. Passing along the road, a late traveller who discovered the time between afternoon and dusk might hear the heart aching lilt of the pipes and the voices lifted in the songs of parting and exile which pervade the Celtic mind, and wonder who and why. Well, it was Aileen they fêted, even if Esme remained more hauntingly in the consciousness.

Oh ye'll tak' the high road and I'll tak' the low road,
And I'll be in Scotland afore ye;
But I and my true love will never meet again
On the bonny, bonny banks of Loch Lomond.

Will ye no' come back again?
Better lo'ed ye canna be . . .

The words died across the evening bay and the refrain came beating back on the flow of the wave.

From the lone sheiling of the misty island
Mountains divide us, and the waste of seas –
Yet still the blood is strong, the heart is Highland,
And we in dreams behold the Hebrides.

20

Graeme stopped on the road to pick Mairi up and take her to the kirk for Sunday morning service. It had been a huge success, there was no doubt of that, and Graeme patted her arm in congratulation. 'You did us proud, lass.' They would be the talk of the strath for a twelvemonth after staging such an event. It was the apotheosis of weddings and Mairi sat back warm in self-congratulation that this morning the buzz about her household would oust all else.

Alexis was intent on his dyeing. The skeins were prepared in the loft, waxy hanks of wool in its natural state, and he attended to this urgently. Esme, seeing the promised heat of the day, decided to wash a few things by hand and put them to dry on a line she found in the corner of the yard. When she joined him he was already up to his oxters in the dye vat, dipping a sample length. He heated the brew, timed its simmering and added further colour and fixative until he was finally satisfied with the intensity of the shade. He had not achieved quite a true red, but rested there.

'Rinse these, will you?'

'How?'

'There's a hose outside. Hang the wool on the line and spray it.'

She looked down at her clothes, a wash dress bleached by age and use, and without objection kirtled it into her underwear in the manner of young girls who execute handstands, or play with handballs against a wall. Bare-legged, she ran up and down stairs with his dripping hanks of wool wound into a bucket, hung them on the line and doused them until the water ran clear. The work continued for an hour, by which time they were both hot and bedraggled, and as curiously soaked in dye as Hardy's reddleman.

Well satisfied with his labours, he switched off the heat of the drum and they rested for a while, dangling their legs from the parapet of the loft into the cooler air of the yard. They watched the skeins dripping gently onto the cobblestones below.

'A hundred pounds of wool and a good batch of colour. Are you worn out?'

'Not at all. Do you wind by hand?'

'I can do, but I have a device for winding it evenly.'

'I shall help you then.'

'I think perhaps,' he weighed the choices, 'you shouldn't be here that long.'

'What do you want me to do?'

'Tomorrow I have to go to Edinburgh to see a wool merchant who supplies me. It's a good opportunity to take you back without arousing comment. You can use the flat at Canonmills until Rejean and Aileen come back from honeymoon. What's that? Nearly a fortnight. I will come back down at the weekend and we can decide what to do from there. Where would you like to live, Esme?' and he hugged her shoulders.

'I would like to live here.'

'Yes, I know. So would I.'

'I can't decide. I can't visualise things until they happen. I don't know how you're going to carry on working here but not living in the house. I feel you haven't really thought about it. You don't want to leave at all.'

'I'll talk to Mairi when you've gone. A separation isn't going to take her by surprise, and for all I know she may be eager to leave.'

'You don't want me to be here when you broach it?'

'Oh no. Can you imagine? She would take you apart. I don't want you to have to face up to that yet.' He hastened to protect his Aegina from the revenges of jealous Hera.

'I will have to sometime.'

'But later. When we have had some time together.'

Mairi did not hear out the service. She did not last as long as the sermon, but passed a note to Graeme saying she was not herself and would go home alone. He was not to wait for her. She struck out along the shore road.

The sun had reached its zenith. The valley stifled in an unaccustomed heat to which neither animate nor inanimate was adapted. The short trees gave almost no shade, being either sparsely leafed or conifer along that stretch of the route. She marched determinedly along the crown of the road, her feet seared by the molten tarmacadam which here and there formed rivulets of bitumen running like lava to meet the verges. Her elegant costume was as constricting as plate armour, every seam binding into her, the waistband a girdle of fire. She removed her jacket, undid the neck of her blouse, rolled up her sleeves. The sun beat down remorselessly. She halted, wondering if she should take the shore-line, but her shoes were hopelessly inadequate and she would not be reduced to stocking soles or bare feet to cope with the pebbles. She stuck to her path although the fieriness of the noonday very nearly crippled her and her face burned red, for shame or heat she could not say.

Coming into the courtyard, she found the culprits. Her eyes moved up and down Esme like a blow torch withering paint. The dress tucked into the knickers suggested much more of the latter than the former. Their bare legs and arms, the disarray of their attitude, dye seeping slowly into their clothes, the runnels of sweat at temple and neck contrasted too forcibly with the covered decorum of the band of worshippers. Their smiles died at this long scathing look, so strong were the texts in her disapproving stare. They stood condemned by their appearances.

'We do not hang our laundry out on Sundays.'

'Is that all?' Esme jumped down obligingly to remove it, but could not restrain herself from adding, 'I thought cleanliness was next to godliness.'

Alexis laughed, not loudly but audibly enough, and the breeze that fluttered the corner of a petticoat was the only thing that stirred. 'How,' he continued lazily, 'how does it differ from my dyeing wool? That's been washed and rinsed and laid out to dry too.' Mairi now saw clearly into the corners of the yard where before she had been sun-blinded, and amidst the draining puddles recognised the spindles of yarn. 'Are we not to work on Sundays? How is that different from the breakfast you cooked, or would you turn us all into Wee Frees. Keep your Sabbath precepts intact or they may turn into hypocrisy.'

Mairi turned on her heel while Esme, bemused, followed her afraid that after all the inadvertent washing was a major offence.

Her aunt lowered herself into a chair at the kitchen table, her eye taking in a faintly grey patch on the wall by the Aga, as she mopped her brow with a handkerchief. 'Are you sure you are quite well?' asked Esme, concerned that the indomitable Mairi should be so overcome.

The woman turned to the door as Alexis' footstep was heard entering and her face blistered as she said, 'Did you enjoy my husband?'

The clock ticked, a floorboard creaked.

'The church was full,' she went on, 'and everybody seemed to know. The girl Fiona had prattled to Mrs Dunlop, and you can be sure she wasn't slow to pass it on. The whole village came to stare at me and whisper. I was humiliated, can you imagine? I couldn't sit there a minute longer with every neck craned to look at me and see how I was taking it. My husband and my niece and on my very doorstep. That was the best morsel they've had in years.' She ran her eye over Esme again, disbelieving. 'I am ashamed for you. I am ashamed for our common parentage. What would Hannah have said to you today? And such timing. All I've worked for thrown away because of you. How am I to show my face again? It is true?' She turned suddenly before Esme had time to prepare a lie.

'Yes, it's true.'

Looking up to catch the words, Mairi saw through the door of the kitchen to the dining room and her array of silver. Her eye travelled back as it does from the distant to the nearer prospect, encountering like mountain ranges the furniture she polished weekly, chairs newly covered under her direction, a quarry tiled floor she'd scrubbed three days before, while Esme sat with her feet up in the sun. Around her the hired crockery for the wedding day piled in hundreds, washed and dried by her own hands late into the night and again from six that morning.

'Do you really think you are going to sit in my place here? That I'm going to move over obligingly and let you in?'

'No. We'll go away.'

'Go away, will you? He's been going away all his life, my child, with one woman or another.'

To Esme's questioning glance, Alexis shook his head and her anxiety subsided marginally.

'So you will go away and live in three rooms at Canonmills, content to be his whore.' There was something unusually obscene about this word when it hung on the lips of a woman like Mairi, so otherwise respectable, like drunkenness or tobacco smoke, an additional grossness because it sat strangely with her elegance and her demeanour at other times. 'Well, why not? Your mother was his Edinburgh whore before you.' She felt the thrill of wounding when Esme winced at this defamation. 'Didn't you know that? Well, he has been remiss in his narrative, missing out whole chapters here and there.'

Esme ignored the slander to herself, absorbed as she was by the one against her mother. 'That's not right?' She looked to Alexis for confirmation, though without a word from him clouds parted in her mind and revealed a connective whole rather than the fragments she had pretended to herself made sense.

'Oh, yes, it is,' interrupted her aunt. 'My sister's gone and I shouldn't speak ill of her, but she was the ruination of my marriage. She was always Rachel to my Leah.' Her voice took on the bitterness of the woman who is habitually overlooked and unwanted. Coming in as a stranger, Esme would have pitied that note.

He came and stood between them, and seemed to wish Esme out of it. 'I won't deny that. We were good friends.'

'Oh yes, such friends. Through thick and thin they were friends.' She addressed nothing to him but vented her wrath on more impressionable material. Her hysteria rose and Alexis, forewarned by the new factor of publicity when this was generally his private counsel, put his hand under Esme's to propel her towards the door, but she removed hers. Whatever was going to be said would not be said behind her back. 'The proxy husband.'

'I don't believe you.'

'Ask any of my brothers. They remember. He was seeing her until just before she died.'

'That is quite true,' said Alexis, walking round the room negligently, 'but the slant you put on it is your surmise.'

'No, it's not surmise.' She turned to Esme, impaled by these darting accusations. 'What has he told you about the reasons for Stefan leaving your mother? That they were too poor to manage? That he was proud and didn't want to live off his wife's income and with her family? That's only half the story. He left when he saw what was going on between his wife and his so-called friend.'

'But that has nothing to do with my case,' said Esme, seeing that they would make no progress on the rights and wrongs of the past, but she stumbled over the words.

'Oh, yes, it has. It has everything to do with you.' She saw the faces in church again, the sly looks and snickering smiles she tried to ignore haughtily but which became too much for her, accumulated in their hundreds. She foresaw herself as the abandoned wife and knew what a come-down it would be. Her entry into that society was assured because of him. 'I've played this game before, you see, and you haven't. I'm not going to be cast off now. For more than twenty years I've kept my marriage going and I will not give it up without a struggle. I will do anything to keep you out. I breathed a sigh of relief when Rhona died last year, but I never thought you would come along like a reincarnation of your mother and start it all up again. I suppose your kind of wickedness doesn't stop. There will always be girls who can't say no.'

Esme was abashed, but equally confused by these wholesale condemnations. 'Perhaps ugliness is in the eye of the beholder.'

Mairi moved quickly before Alexis could prevent it, and seized her niece's hand against the edge of the table where she imprisoned it with a strength the girl fought against for a moment but could not match, so she left it pinned on the corner which cut into her. 'My conscience is quite clear. Make no mistake about that. I don't go to bed with other women's husbands.'

Esme thought of many answers, but without voicing them she knew their weakness. She was guilty on fact, and on theory she was juvenile. Her aunt had the edge. 'But he is not,' she corrected gently after a moment, 'not your husband any more than you are his wife.'

'What am I, then? Tell me what you know about it. I am so anxious to hear what experience has taught you on the subject of being a wife. You imagine it's some sort of romantic swoon, reading poetry together. I've seen you sneaking off. But it's nothing like that. It's years of work, real work not book work, day after day of work, planning and building, getting dust in your eyes and dirt in your fingernails. And doing it alone without a smile or a thank you. You look at me and think – she's just a wife. That's easy. But how do you know? There might be other things I wanted to do apart from lift and lay after other people. When you destroy my marriage you take away my accomplishment but, worse than that, you take away the things I might have done. Ask yourself if you could do it. I don't think so. You haven't got it in you. You're like Rhona, all pretty show and no staying power. She couldn't hang onto her husband but I kept mine. You're nothing, either of you. Learn to be a woman before you come telling me where I've gone wrong as a wife. You can draw the men after you but that doesn't make you special. Every little tart does that. In my book, you're very ordinary.'

During this eclogue, which Alexis had heard more or less, adapted according to circumstance, at periodic intervals over half his lifetime and was therefore deaf to, he had wandered to the window, distraught in one part that Esme should be so baptised, but in another bored by the whole hysterical proceeding. She did herself more harm by these outbursts than by anything else. He heard the poverty of her mind announced in every word, her shoddy thinking, her second-rate attitudes, and was appalled once again at himself for enduring the commonplace so long. He had made up his mind. Why could they, the gamekeeper, the wife, the people of the region, not accept that, without forcing him to go through an explanation? He knew exactly where he was in relation to his own escapism; why must he re-enact the processes for them?

Esme, the uninitiate, could not be so disinterested. Was she a little tart? She remembered men in cars crawling by the kerb she walked home along at night, and being told to move off her patch by a prostitute at the West End while she waited innocuously. She remembered the words the interrupting stranger spoke on the dance floor of the Union, and reddened. To be so frequently mistaken for a whore, she must have whoring in her face; why couldn't the facts proclaim themselves instead of some fleshly allure she did not want, did not foster, couldn't recognise herself? She pulled her hand away from the crushing pressure of her aunt's, as if she was trying to pull away her battered emotions and regain self-possession. But as she wrenched it, Mairi grasped the hand to prevent her release and seized on the thumb, which became dislocated from its socket.

There was a second of almost unendurable pain that made the blood flow from her head till she thought she would faint and fall, then a contrary flush as the body assembled its defences. She lifted her left hand with the right and looked at the joint, which was already swollen and distended. This is not my pain, she told herself, but a measure of the pain I have caused her. I must bear it.

'You've broken my hand,' she said, fearing the worst.

'So what? You break easily.' Mairi was in fact filled with horror but when she was already puffed with venom the feeling served to increase her conviction of being woefully abused.

Alexis heard the wrench. He thought a plate fell or a pane of glass cracked in the concentrated heat of the midday sun. He turned round and saw Esme flinch and then stand straight with the simple dignity that capsized his own responses. How could he not have stopped it? He should have seen it coming.

He put his arm round her and examined the joint. 'You must go and have it set,' he said so quietly the sound barely carried on the air. 'How could you do a thing like that?'

The sight of him nursing her in his arms was unbearable to Mairi, for the gesture measured the distance between them, the care he had never lavished on her, its rightful recipient, and worse, the loving-kindness that was still in him, untapped. Hers had drained away; his was a flooded reservoir. For him to have a store of compassion was a double cheat on her and she felt infinitely more abused that he could feel tenderly for one girl than if he had seduced a whole bevy of women, cynically. She faced the fact that she had lost him. She would go to her grave unloved, and probably unloving. Love was the price she would not pay, and could not therefore exact.

'Don't touch her.'

They did not move apart.

'Don't touch her,' she repeated and lifted from the hod beside her the poker with which they riddled the Aga. It was three foot long and weighed two pounds in tempered steel. Using it like a rapier, she cut between them as they stood, severing their proximity from the shoulder to the waist. The poker left a smear of soot down their damp arms. 'Touch her again and I'll break her arm,' she threatened.

'Don't be so ridiculously melodramatic.'

'You think I wouldn't do it?'

Esme looked incredulously at her aunt. The ugliness of mind had its effect. In spite of her urbane dress, the accoutrements of civilisation, her face was masked in hatred. She had become the witch, the step-mother, the hag of all ingrained fear.

'No, I believe you,' said Alexis.

She lowered the poker and with it her rage seemed to fade.

Alexis turned his back on her and said in a low voice, 'We must take you to a casualty hospital.' He racked his brain for which was nearer, or which had an emergency unit that would attend to her on a Sunday. 'Sit down,' he said as she seemed to sink with the weight of what she must face up to, being prodded, examined, going through the doors of the infirmary as a maimed and ir-reparable being. 'Are you all right? I'll have to wash first. I'm not fit to be seen like this.' He left them alone for a moment.

The two women sat in silence at first and when Mairi did speak again, it was in an altered tone, of utter reason. 'I'm afraid you can't go with him, you know. It's not right. It's not decent. I'm surprised it hasn't occurred to you already. He was your mother's lover, though that doesn't seem to shock you. Isn't it strange how alike you are, you and he, much more than Aileen? You enjoy the same things, feel the same. Haven't you told yourselves that in the past? It's not a happy accident. It's natural. He's your father. It's so simple. Your love affair is incest.'

Alexis was in time to hear this, and at last she had succeeded in making an impression on him. 'You liar,' he said in a voice that made Esme congeal with fright. 'You would murder with a lie.'

'Disprove it,' she challenged. 'Rhona told me so herself.'

He took the road to Callander, afraid that the nearer cottage hospital did not deal with emergencies and that they might have to back-track or drive on much further. They sat dejected in the surgery and a remarkable object of pity in that setting. The red dye which he had marginally removed with his clothing, and she not at all, lent them the macabre aspect of being horribly blood-spattered and everyone who saw them recoiled as from victims who were badly mutilated and likely to be suffering the multiple injuries of a car crash. Esme's pathetic thumb hardly warranted the medical attention lavished on it.

'How did you dislocate it?' was the inevitable question which had not struck either of them, and they had no alibi.

'I think it was a domestic brawl,' conceded Esme. The duty doctor raised an eyebrow to Alexis and asked no more.

They waited for the X-ray plate to be developed, in a bay serviced by the local Women's Institute, and took tea.

'Tell me it isn't true.'

'Which bit of it first?'

'About you and my mother.'

'You must have guessed by now that I was attached to Rhona.'

'But how attached?'

'I don't know how to measure these things for you. In cubic metres?'

'Don't be facetious.'

'Ask yourself this. Need it have been more than between you and me. In Mairi's eyes and no doubt in the sight of half this country, we are sinful. But what we have done doesn't amount to transgression as far as I define it. If you condemn the affection I had for Rhona, you condemn yourself.'

'I feel that's not a straight answer.'

'Does it really matter?'

'Don't tie me in knots. Tell me you're not my father.'

'I'm not. That's easily said.'

'You are being so hard on me. Why don't you look at me? You were stunned when she accused you of being my father. Is it possible?'

'No, it is not possible. Don't you see she found the one thing to say that could separate us? And she's succeeded,' he added with some bitterness. 'If you let that absurd suggestion work on you, you'll succumb to her warped thinking. I was,' he thought back with effort to the time and place, 'I was on board one of His Majesty's destroyers in the South Atlantic, if I remember rightly, at the time you were conceived. I can look up my service record if you want.' And he glanced down at Esme's withdrawn face, which recorded a doubt enforced by the mystery and secretiveness now ineradicably printed for her on the word 'father'. He congratulated himself ironically on how far he had come; he could read her thoughts. 'Oh, this is ridiculous. I can offer you no better proof than the evidence of your own eyes. The face of Stefan Rosowicz, isn't that a mirror image of your own? You saw that yourself when I brought you those photographs. Among a thousand men, he would have to be your father, it's an indelible stamp, a fingerprint.

He was your father, he married your mother, and he left for the reasons I told you.'

'But why would Mairi invent such calumny?'

And he saw that after all the bitterness and anger would not pass away merely from his own volition. He would have to say it out loud. 'Because thinking the whole world is corrupt gives her such opportunity to be sanctimonious. She believes in natural sin. I questioned her about it once. She swallows the Old Testament whole, the fruit of the forbidden tree, creation in the seven days, an absolute fundamentalist. And then,' he sighed, 'it was convenient to develop the lies about Rhona and myself because it was the perfect excuse for her own shortcomings. After Aileen was born, we had no sexual contact, of any kind or degree.'

'Is that possible?'

'Oh yes, it's possible if you are determined or disinclined enough. It happens to a few women, I now know. Motherhood overtakes them and they reject their mate. It was my misfortune that Mairi was one of these, and hers that I was not biologically equipped to deal with it. We should have sought help, I know, but to cover that disinclination which was quite genuine, she loathed sex, she invented adulteries for me and occasionally I obliged. My weakness compounded hers and for a score of years we outdid each other in animosity. Rhona was the opposite. She became Madonna-like, voluptuous but irreproachable. Can you blame me for feeling hard done by, or for trying to make it up to Rhona? She suffered much more by the slander than I did. People are so determined to think the worst, you know. I don't suppose even the family gave us the benefit of the doubt. They always did think I was a blackguard. We were a man and a woman and we liked each other's company. It wasn't possible for us to keep out of each other's bed, they thought. And after all this time, the story is still malicious. It still causes grief to you.'

'Why,' Esme embarked on the question that had prompted her from the beginning, but did not dare to ask itself before, 'why did you marry her?'

'Good question.' He heaved, disliking all self-exposition. 'Think of the girls I'd known till then. Boys' boarding school. My mother was downright decadent and we lived the queerest life, always on the move. We changed house every eighteen months on average and we were never there anyway. She was a perennial malcontent. I'd met society girls, all glistening and oozing charm and about as substantial as a mouthful of candy floss. Then when war broke out and I joined the Navy I encountered the others, the prehensile camp followers. At least they were honestly dishonest. They did give full measure. When I met Mairi, I was impressed by how hard she worked, I think. Only a clerical accountant, but she was given all the important work and it was perfectly done. She was neat, she was new, she was scrubbed. But what finally did for me was the family. An only child is intrigued by families. I couldn't believe that house. It was like a helter-skelter, people up and down, noise, radios, boys laughing, mending their bikes in the bedroom, dynamos, crystal sets, meccano on the floor. It was a revelation to me, like being in the middle of a cub pack and not being killed. I staggered out each day amazed I'd survived. That was what I wanted. But that wasn't what I got.'

The nurse returned with Esme's documents and the hand was soon re-set and bandaged.

'Come back in a week's time and we'll change the dressing and see if it's healing properly.' She was brisk and cheery, so that Esme listened to her as if she were talking in a foreign language.

'I am visiting,' she said, 'and will be gone by then.'

'Then you can go to any hospital.'

'In Edinburgh?'

'Yes, the Royal Infirmary if you like.'

When they got back to the car, Esme asked, 'Do you think I am weak?'

'No, of course not.'

'Perhaps I am compared with her. She has such reserves of hatred and venom to make her strong.' She shuddered at the memory of the wrenching tissue, the cold steel drawn down the length of her arm, the second when she had expected a glancing blow to the crown of her head and blood to spout like a fountain, soaking her neck and shoulders. That was it. She had tasted fear. Never in solitude, in deprivation, in the stress points of her brief years had she been afraid. Situations she could cope with; people might defeat her. And she knew in her heart that she would not be whole again. 'She may have found the vulnerable spot in my nature. I don't think I have got her grit.'

'Where are we going now?' He started the engine and idled while she made up her mind.

She looked down at her stained dress and patchy legs. 'I'll have to have a bath and change somewhere before I can go out.'

'We'll need to go back to Inchcombe for that.'

'I can't go in.' She recoiled.

'No, no of course not. I'll get your things together.'

'And I can't stay there tonight. Are you still going to Edinburgh in the morning? Then I'll come with you. Can't I spend one night in a hotel?'

'That's what I was thinking. But you'll be known at Lochearn or St Fillans, and that will start off a whole chain reaction of rumour and questions.' He frowned that the world had to be inhabited by other people. 'And Crieff will be absolutely full. It's the height of their season, and a gala week of some sort in Comrie.'

'What about Gleneagles? Sunday night won't be too popular.'

'But the Simards are there.'

'No, they were checking out this morning. They were driving down to spend a few days at the Edinburgh Festival.'

'Well, if you're sure of that, it seems the best place. No one will know you there.'

'I want to feel safe. I don't feel safe now.'

'I know. I know how you feel. I will take care of that.'

He left the Rover parked at some distance and slipped into the house to pack her belongings without seeing Mairi. He took the dry clothes off the line and put them in the small case he found in the bottom of her wardrobe together with the items he saw about the room. A book at the bedside, a mole-shaped lump of grey stone propping it open, the packet of photographs stashed in a drawer with half a dozen envelopes and pieces of paper he did not examine, and her very few clothes. Heavens, was this all the girl owned? He recalled Aileen's going away trousseau, boxes and boxes of clothes, hats, shoes wrapped in tissue to cover every eventuality. He should have taken more care of Esme, been more concerned, asked more questions. He would not make the same mistake again. He picked up a cloth and towel and some astringent cleaner so that she could remove the worst marks before she entered the hotel, and after a change of dress in a lay-by she emerged rather less besmirched.

He booked her in and they took tea in the lounge overlooking the south-facing gardens and the lake which masked the golf course, but it was a pensive, constrained meal. They could not talk there and scarcely felt inclined to be alone. 'Do you want me to stay? I'll stay till nightfall, or overnight if you prefer.'

'No. I will wait for you coming back in the morning. I'm going to have a bath and go to sleep.'

'Ask for whatever you want. If you prefer, dinner in your room.'

'Yes, I will.' She walked out to the car with him but it was hard to say goodbye in a car park, and they parted at last without a kiss because the touch of her lips was never so lightly given as in a public endearment.

He wound down the window. 'I will be early. Be ready.'

She smiled, but as he drove away the sense of dereliction caught up with her and she was weighed down by exhaustion and a nagging pain now that the first protective shock injury had worn off.

The Simards, who had not gone as planned that morning but extended their stay to accommodate a fellow guest from the hotel, on a trip to Inverness and down the three lochs of the great canal in pursuit of the fabled monster, crossed her in the foyer.

Esme had no art in pretending. Besides, there was the bandage that required some explanation. They drew her into the empty lounge and heard everything. Esme, weary and quite woebegone, did not mind that Claire Simard's arm went round her and drew the girl's head to her shoulder.

'My dear, this is no good for you. This is simply not fair.' She consulted her husband with her eyes and he nodded. 'Let us take care of everything. You don't need to worry any more. We will see to it all.'

Mairi capitulated. She sat in the kitchen for half an hour after she heard the car drive away and read by the sound, evaporating into the distance, what their likely movements were. She was bemused at first, shaken by her own vulgar lack of dignity. In all, she prided herself in doing nothing that was unbecoming. But the parasite had drained her, and lived on; and in the core of that idea she perceived it was impossible for her to sustain her fight with him. If she did, if she stayed here embattled, they would not both come out of it alive. To salvage something, regain her self-respect, she must move on. Like a commander who knows his troops outnumbered, she planned a strategic withdrawal rather than endure a rout.

A practical woman, she found practical solutions. She made a mental inventory of the fabric of the house. By opening each door in turn she could take stock. She knew the contents of every drawer without looking, and separated them into projective piles of his and hers. The partitioning she arrived at was fair; any divorce court would have applauded her impartiality, though the judicial scale by which she weighed was obscure. It certainly was not Esme's in similar circumstances, where every item independent of its final destination had a story, an association, a place in her heart. It became the furniture of her mind. Some belongings Mairi denoted by family rites, like the antique dinner service patterned with grotesque phoenixes passed down from his mother; others he had bought and worked on, his dues; but a problem arose over pieces like the roll-top desk which had been her father's but was recognised as Alexis' when it was sanctified by use. Which was more important? Which claim was more pressing, inheritance or usage? Should things belong, as Brecht averred, to those who were best for them? Was there, as Forster maintained, such a thing as a spiritual heir for property which had a quite different material owner? She didn't phrase it like this to herself, but standing puzzled with her hand on the roll top acknowledged the conundrum. Really, she didn't like it and it wasn't valuable, so his dowry was swollen many times by default.

She heard him come back but didn't intervene in his packing of the case and then much later, after she had started to pack a suitcase of her own, heard him return again and worked out where the girl was and what they intended to do. She heard him working on till nightfall, taking in the wool, winding some of it mechanically, going at last to bed. And, hearing that, rose herself in the small hours to occupy her fevered hands with something.

She wondered then at the advisability of leaving the field clear. Each view, each room was attenuated by the sickening prospect of their sharing it together. Every chair proclaimed her anticipated presence. Even her grey footmark remained beside the Aga, the ghost of her slouching attitudes. Impelled by temper, Mairi snatched a cloth and washed it vigorously away, rubbing fiercely in circles. And was satisfied as she looked closely that she had absterged the stain altogether. But as the water dried out, it became clear that she had removed a thin coat of emulsion from the wall and a larger, deeper patch of grey was ingrained into the spot.

She could then have caught up the poker and smashed every one of the belongings she had deemed his. The attraction of a scorched earth policy beckoned to her: leave nothing behind which they could use, let them start out with nothing as she had. And then, realising that this was a limited revenge against someone like Alexis who could afford to replace the old things without penance, and better them, she stumbled on a neater ploy. Like a guerrilla army, she could have a protracted victory if she took time to poison all the wells. A few words, a hint or two dropped Iago-like to spread and fester. Let them lie comfortably three a-bed with incest in the sheets.

Part two
21

For five days Alexis' activity verged on the demonic.

He returned to Gleneagles early on the Monday morning intending to pay Esme's bill and drive her to Edinburgh. She could still stay at Canonmills as they had planned, although her sojourn would have a different bias. But the receptionist told him there was no bill to be settled. Miss Rosowicz had not stayed overnight in the hotel but had checked out the previous evening along with Mr and Mrs Simard. She had a copy of their account duly receipted in her hands and passed it to him. He read it blind. It meant nothing, words and figures all nonsense.

'Have they left a forwarding address?'

The girl flicked through a separate register. 'Their home address in Canada I believe is . . .'

'I know that. Did they go by train?'

The girl was taken aback. He stood suavely suited, a gentleman, and then brusquely turned on her with a rasp and she felt the brunt of something sterner. 'Mr Simard hired a car for the whole week. I think he kept that on. But I'm afraid I don't know which agent he used.' She frowned for he unnerved her, worrying in case she had omitted something.

Alexis drove to Edinburgh before midday and from the flat telephoned all the likely hotels, The George, The Caledonian, The North British but meeting with negative responses cast a wider and wider net until by late afternoon he had made fifty calls. No one had a Simard or a Rosowicz registered. The Festival had opened and the hotels were full. Swedes, Germans, Americans brought a complement of strange names the receptionists struggled with. Each call took him five minutes of explanation. He abandoned this technique and took to driving the streets looking for them in person, calling at any guest house or private establishment en route. At ten o'clock in the evening, Princes Street was thronged with people walking three abreast on the pavements. There was a breathless sunset over the city making the visitors linger. Theatre and concert goers ambled back through the gardens, until there was a mass of perhaps a thousand people on the walkways. Imprisoned in traffic lanes, Alexis could only fume. She was here. Somewhere she was near him if he could stop and find her. What could he do, climb to the top of the Scott monument and like a muezzin cry his message over the city? Where is Esme? Find Esme for me!

On his return, frustrated and impatient, he started to phone the golfing hotels on the outskirts of the city as far as North Berwick, The Open Arms, Greywalls, Marine, but with no more success. The endeavour was futile and he spent his first sleepless night.

In the morning he called at the old house. A woman came to the door through plasterer's buckets and step ladders. Yes, there was a forwarding address. She ferreted in a box and brought out a slip of paper which bore, in Esme's handwriting, his own name and address, written a week before in good faith.

Mr Scott regarded his request and his demanding, almost hostile presence suspiciously. 'I have had no contact with Miss Rosowicz for some time. I have not personally seen her since the sale of the house was finalised. I sent her a cheque covering her portion, let me see, a week ago exactly. That was the end of my business.'

'Yes, I was there when she opened that.' His heart sank to think how and when. He remembered the joke she had not taken to and he was loath to say more but saw he would proceed no further with the professional man unless he was specific, and went on, 'But there has been a family quarrel since then and I am anxious to trace her whereabouts. She left in a hurry and without goodbyes.'

'How little things change.' He said this so sardonically that Alexis looked up for explanation. 'You recall it was much the same mission that brought you here together last November, to look for her father.' Alexis nodded sadly at his own mismanagement. She had trusted in him then, and had learned to trust less since. 'Ah dear. In that case, should she contact me, I will advise her of your concern. But I think that most unlikely.' This negation produced such a downcast look that Mr Scott grew less steely. 'There is just one possibility.' He lifted the telephone and dialled from memory. 'Our bankers may have had the cheque drawn against our account. You don't happen to know the name and address of Miss Rosowicz' bank? Pity.' But after a few minutes he returned the mouthpiece to the receiver. 'No. Early days, of course, if you say she received my forwarded letter on Saturday. She may take a day or two to pay it into her account, especially if, as you infer, she is in an emotional state. Should that occur, however, I will let you know at your home address or, yes, this is your Edinburgh number. I will instruct the bank to telephone me the moment the cheque is presented. But you must realise it is valid internationally. It could be cashed anywhere, from here to Hong Kong.'

He drove back to Lochearn, distraught as much at being helpless to retrace her as by her disappearance. No word came from the lawyer by Saturday when at daybreak he set out for Prestwick to try and intercept her flight to Montreal if she intended to take it, or interrogate the Simards if she did not. The airport was unusually busy and finding out the most basic information involved waiting in a series of queues or among crowds of jostling people, laden with documents or luggage. At last he found the international departure area but no official was prepared to divulge which passengers had already checked in. He found the Air Canada desk where a girl informed him that there was neither a Simard nor a Rosowicz on the passenger list for that day's flight. They had cancelled their tickets and booked instead on the outward journey to Montreal the previous day.

When he got back to Inchcombe, there was a telegram waiting for him in the office. 'Arrived safely Montreal. Will write, Esme.' The staccato words perforated him. How inadequate. How banal. Could she not know that all he asked was that he should not be forgotten, that going out of a door for the last time she might have turned and wished him farewell?

He was dismayed by the ominous repetition of her father's journey. No voyage was undertaken with a premonition of gloom and disaster. Merely to step out was to announce a belief in arrival, but the little they had heard of Stefan after landing was circumstantial; the unknown remained indelibly. He had not returned and he had not prospered on the other side to the extent that he wished his progress to be made general knowledge. He prayed Esme might do better but sighed that ultimately they might both be touched with a fatalism that was unable to admit its own failure, covering itself instead with the dignity of silence and withdrawal.

The days wore away with the slow repetitive insistence of a

nightmare. It was impossible for him to believe, on waking, that the terrors of the night occupied a few minutes of sleeping experience. Those grinding horrors which aged him, punctured holes in his self-esteem through which fear seeped, catastrophe, untold and untellable indignities performed on him and by him, until his whole well-being was infected – could these be the work of seconds? Was it really only ten, twenty, thirty days since she had left? He became an insomniac, raging wordlessly night after night against the prison of his body, the cruelty of his torturing mind which prodded him awake through endless grey dawns and would not let him rest. Conversations were reconstructed whole by his feverish memory, for there is no rationale at two in the morning, and phrases wounded him all over again so that by sun-up he was a mass of disconnected nerves, dragging himself into action with the single formulated thought: How can I manage to get through today?

He'd been standing on a fault line, in the middle of an earthquake zone and not noticed till the disaster happened. The land masses of his life had come adrift. Aileen had gone. His break with Graeme left him more isolated than he had foreseen. At the time, when he quarrelled angrily in the churchyard, he had been looking forward positively to something new, and a friend was dispensable. Now he was sunk back into the old constraints but without a companion to share them in the easy, desultory manner of undemanding friendship. He would have given a whole month's sleep to walk up the hillside and knock at Graeme's front door, knowing there would be a fire, a chair, a glass for Auld Lang Syne. But that was gone too. He had dismissed it arbitrarily, sealed off his own welcome with a lack of anticipation that merited his exclusion. With Ian there was necessarily a hiatus. The boy was respectful, never alluded to the incident, in fact he even stuck up for him. Alexis heard he punched a youth in a brawl for passing some insulting remark, and got a broken tooth for his loyalty. He had sent the perfidious Fiona packing, and Alexis wanted to say this justice was too strict, but could not find the words. There was a difference. The camaraderie was gone. And the rift with Mairi was unbreachable.

Without Esme, he did not want to go on. He could not face tomorrow without her, or at least the hope she illuminated the future with. He had worn thin the optimism of youth that is confident it will turn out for the best. The age of cynicism ensured he was not too utopian in outlook. In the twentieth century no one sane believed in eternity, certainly not an eternity of joy, whether sublime Christian or orgiastic Muslim. But for her to come within his grasp and be withdrawn again was too spiteful a malice, especially when he felt he was responsible for the loss himself. He could have guarded against it, the slip 'twixt lip and cup and walking abroad in the late and early hours, reviewing the sad futility of his garden, he cursed his lack of absolute tenacity, his holding power.

One dream he had persistently. He stood on an ice floe in the Arctic. He felt secure until he noticed that the ice was cracking up underneath him, and almost instinctively he jumped onto the larger of the two pieces at his feet and breathed a sigh of relief. But in turn this island broke, started to melt and turn watery so he leapt from patch to patch looking for some sort of foothold. All the time the black water welled up to meet him, eroding by minute degrees the land he stood on – except that it was not land, it was melting snow and what he feared and what saved him were the same element, one in their chill immensity. This black water he drowned in nightly. It was the blackness of memory, too insistently recalled, of a madness he felt was beginning to impinge on his tired brain, even of the wish to die. Against such hopelessness, only his will to survive could prevail.

At length she wrote.

My dear Alexis,

Yes I know how long it is that you've been without news of me, and I am feeling guilty about it but I have needed all this time to think, adjust and recover. I am sorry that I didn't say goodbye. I should have done, I know, should have at least told you where I was and what I was going to do, but I knew perfectly well you would make it impossible for me to leave. I know you are feeling bereft, as I am. I didn't know such pain was possible, that you could have withdrawal symptoms from a person. But I have had the advantage of doing something new, of walking away in fact while you stay on and cope with difficulties that are maybe immeasurable.

Doing this has clarified some issues and I am grateful for that. I can see you more precisely at a distance. I am still – what can I write that is intelligible – enthralled. I know you are a great man, great in capacity at any rate. I am not sure about application. Yes, everything I say to you on the subject of talent sounds like effrontery because you have achieved and I have not. But that is precisely my point. Close up, you threaten to overpower me. You are so large that you stand between me and the sun, and I will not live like Brand on the shadow side of the mountain. Maybe all women feel that about all men, but I am not at this moment resigned to be secondary. If I accuse you of anything it is of not being absolutely honest with me, not treating me as your equal although I know that is your instinctive nature, to be egalitarian. You eked out information piecemeal, as it suited you, and that won't do. I won't have you editing my version for me. I may need to grow a little before we stand shoulder to shoulder. Above all, I do not want to be my mother's ghost and I must exorcise her spirit before we can proceed.

As for the practical, well, my hand mends. Slowly. What if it does sit a little crooked? I have been so busy I have hardly looked at it. I am driving. Yes, I am driving. Maurice pushed me through a test, the one specially designed for incompetents and I have spent some of my substance on riotous living, namely a car. This is an object of some joy to me. I do wish you could see it, my first possession, a moveable house which I sweep, polish, furnish with bric-à-brac and quite definitely dote on. So the snail is not without its shelter in the storm.

I also have work. Maurice insisted on making phone calls on my behalf, though I do detest the sense of pulling strings for I suspect in time they may have a retroactive power, and I will be pulled by them. It transpires the head of an English-speaking school in the Saguenay requires a remedial teacher for a term. And that is me, an uncertificated novice who has never done a day's work in her life. Does any class deserve to have me foisted on it?

So I have transport and I have work. I am equipped for the 20th century. This is good for me, Alexis. Do not fret. I am finding out about things like driving licences and health insurance and income tax forms. I am becoming worldly-wise. It is mundane, I agree. But these are the gizzard stones of life.

Montreal I like. It's on the move, going somewhere. I'm not sure where that is, but I like the bustle and the way Maurice and Claire fill the time. Every day is large and I can see why Aileen found the way of life captivating when she was here last summer. Maurice is taking me up to Chicoutimi at the weekend and he'll see to some business at the Port Alfred office while I find somewhere to stay. He won't leave till I am settled.

There is quite a debate going on about whether Rejean will come over in the autumn for the AGM of shareholders. Maurice's company went public two years ago and Rejean has prepared a paper he wants to present in person. Maurice mutters about it being a waste of money, and time. What can Rejean possibly have to say to interest the company etc etc. I wonder why he doesn't care for his son more? Doesn't that strike you as odd, that you don't like your child simply because you do not understand him?

Nevertheless, he is good to me, a man who should have had daughters just as you should have had sons. Maurice could have eaten of the fruit of the Lotos without ill effect, trustworthy but not dull. A little more teasing, a little less uxorious respect would have softened his crustiness. As it is, he plays the tyrant and generally gets away with it. English is his mother tongue – why do we say that, but fatherland? – and French is Claire's though they are both Québècois and they are getting me into training for the Saguenay which is French-speaking, exclusively. The bilingual conversation keeps me agile. My French is astonishingly bad, text-book inflexible. They say they have to speak 17th century immigrant stuff to make me understand. Do you know the dialect is called Jeval from the way a French Canadian pronounced 'cheval'! I am accepted at once if I say I am a Scot. Half of Canada has a Scottish grandmother. Anglais is mistrusted, Ecossais is blood brother. But Montreal is cosmopolitan enough to be non-divisive, and I may meet more resistance in the Saguenay which is fiercely separatist, so they say.

I hope Rejean comes across. I know he wants to, very badly, and I want to see him, well with one reservation. The Simards have kept my confidence so far, but with Rejean here in person will they or I say something? I will try to be discreet. I don't want to indict you or prevent this lull from being a useful reappraisal. After all, you are free to re-think, as I am. I presume Aileen knows nothing and will continue in this assumption.

I have made firm friends with Claire. She is so very organised, charming, sophisticated, has this house cool and beautiful in blond tones, Swedish lines, natural. You would approve of her chastened eye. I believe she thinks she has taken me in hand. That is, she has introduced me to her tailoress, given me at least half of the bolts of cloth she brought back from the woollen mills and I emerge sleek, overhauled, professional. But is it me? I am a tearaway at heart and like it to show. There is quite a lot of pleasure to be had from this sort of unreflecting relationship, and I am not demeaning it by that word. I would like to be unreflecting, natural, not contorted the way I can be. But Claire is an object exercise on how to extract the most from your resources. Not a beauty, not a savante, she is still astute enough to avoid looking gauche in either category. And I do envy that succinctness of effort.

So I am well and fear you are not. I think of you, oh inexorably. You once said of Stefan that there was not a day in his life when he did not think of me. I feel that might be true now. It is certainly true for me. With you I am whole, apart I am merely functionary.

No, it didn't do. It didn't come close. The girl tried. She probably was sad and lonely and afraid, but these were pallid emotions compared with his consuming passion. The letter did not restore her and in failing to do that, it could not restore him either. Its palliatives did not mend his broken aspirations. She intended to spend her term away from him, looking for Stefan against his advice and against the current of their relationship. He felt the mental removal more forcibly than the physical one. That she could leave him exposed the huge rift in their differing evaluation of the commitment to each other. To him it was absolute and imperative. To her it was optional, could be put down and taken up again at will.

He wondered if he was being unfair to her. Maybe she was more sagacious than he realised in saying she needed to grow a little before they matched as equals. She was not his equal, not because of lack of quality but because the quality was untried. She did not know who she was as well as he knew it, and what distanced them were the aeons of experience which enabled him to recognise perfection out of the context of the flawed, and prevented her from doing so. In that lay the imperfection which debarred heaven from being too often materialised on earth. What time would maturing take, and what suffering? He could not measure it but feared that like any child, in growing up, she might grow away.

He could have lain along the ground and bellowed out his hurt and anger like a wounded stag.

22

The graph paper in front of him was half blocked in, but for nearly an hour past he had sat passively at the desk. To be fair, he was passive as far as motion went, his pen inert, his body static as though frozen in the chair, but mentally he was active.

No matter how he tried, he could not make his hand move. The page he worked on sporadically represented nothing new; there was no novelty in his occupation, no sense of challenge, for its potential was exhausted. What was a sleeve but a sleeve, essentially man-shaped? How could he vary the patterns he had already developed in his youth, in his fertile phases, except by stable repetition, pretending to himself that a minor adjustment of colour or stitch could alter the basic theme of his labour, to elevate the useful into the beautiful? But in the hunt for innovation he was endangering both qualities. The craftsmen of Harris and Lewis, the spinsters and knitters in the sun of Fair Isle and Shetland had discovered all that was significant a century ago. Esme, hand-winding wool over the backs of chairs, had more contact with the craft than he did. With deadlines to meet, orders to fill in their hundreds, he had lost the freshness of design which resided exclusively in uniqueness. There was no such thing as batch inspiration. He had lost his touch.

He ran a pencil over the grain of the paper. The fact was the whole game was an affectation and the high principles he had started out with, to revive the fading art, foundered on the commercialism of success. The best that could be said of him was that he employed twenty workers; their days were meaningful, though his as overseer were not. He could not take the refuge in self-esteem that consoled most men, 'What I do is important because I do it.' He viewed himself too dispassionately for that, and suspected he was no more than an entrepreneur or, worse, a capitalist. He had poured himself into too many tasks, designing, painting, weaving, doing none to perfection, and ultimately would be judged like Rab or the earnest amateurs who made up the field of also rans, a smatterer. He had filled his life with smallness and there was no room left in it for an original.

As he swung into this restless and unchannelled state, Mairi was in a counterbalance of optimism. She heard from Aileen on her return that Esme was in Montreal, but of the exact cause and nature of her departure they both remained ignorant, and Mairi did not enlighten her daughter further. She put her own bias on it. She imagined that Alexis had thought better of his desertion, that her outbreak had had its effect. Or had Esme turned him down when she saw the problems ahead? No, she thought not. Only one woman had turned Alexis down and that was herself. He had decided to stay of his own free will and, giving thanks for this, she did her best to make the return to the daily conduct of their lives as painless as possible. She did not refer to Esme. She did not upbraid but allowed him to dictate by his silence, by his absence, by the long night hours she knew he spent pacing, the way they were to behave and accepted it as normal.

She whitewashed the kitchen walls herself, giving two coats to the spot by the Aga, and was satisfied when she had obliterated all trace of her niece. She tidied the room which had been Esme's, and left it bare, deliberately removing the coverlet so that it looked as spartan and inhospitable as a cell. She did not know that in the small hours he went to that room and lay on the bed to watch the orbit of the stars through its uncurtained window. It emanated its own comfort, the comfort of a strung hammock to exhausted limbs, of a bivouac under a crevasse to a mountaineer. He had grown too lax, too idle with the years and, lying in the dark, he thought it was time again to expose the lean sinews of endeavour. He made up his mind under the guiding auspices of the pole star that before his life became overlaid with the minute accretions of conformity, adherence to the relentless social code based on eating, rising, working to a pattern imposed by habit rather than will, he would try to discover in himself some alternative. Take no thought for the morrow, wasn't that the principle he admired most and still it was the antithesis of his routine. The carefree pose he struck disguised a rigid structuring in his lifestyle. But how could he break it when the impetus for change had gone? He felt like an athlete who has lost a marathon by a hair's breadth but knows his training programme, his efforts towards fitness are to be redoubled if he is going to maintain the will to win. What, where could he begin?

Mairi too realised that some restructuring was necessary. She had made her own plans and said one morning at breakfast before the day gave cause for division between them, 'I was thinking of taking on a housekeeper.'

He put down the *Scotsman*. 'Is that essential?'

'It will give me more time for the business. The accounts are too complicated for me to go on dealing with them part-time. I must reorganise.' This made her defensive because she knew the financial intricacies were an aspect he almost disregarded, like her own importance, but she was determined to side-step a quarrel, as he was. He swithered. If he wanted less of the routine, wasn't it sensible to give her more, even if he did resent her financial management?

'Who did you have in mind, or will you advertise?'

'I thought,' she hesitated, amazed at his capitulation, 'that Ian's mother would be ideal. She is a good cook.' Good in Mairi's terminology meant plain and unimaginative.

'Does she need the work?'

'John Galashan is shiftless. He's been dismissed from his work on the Melville estates.'

'Why?'

'Drunk, I think. Something not finished. The new owners are in a hurry to complete maintenance before the winter sets in and John's a layabout.'

He was annoyed that his source of local information had dried up and felt his isolation more keenly. 'So they're on hard times? Well, you'd better speak to her. But I'm not used to having people under my feet. She doesn't clack all hours, I trust.'

'Oh no, she's very discreet,' she replied, taking the other meaning from the one he intended, and was surprised at the hardness of the look he threw her. He imagined this was an oblique reference to Fiona's tattle and it gave rise to the instant suspicion that she could ring him with spies and informants. Confused at his hostility when a moment before he had been compliant, she objected at last, 'It's simply too much work.'

'Yes.' That was true. She had never had help in the house except for special occasions and it wasn't an easy one to run, for it was an office, a factory, a showpiece for every casual visitor who cared to look up his name and address in a trade index. He conceded in all, and foresaw that the biddable woman might be a relief from the monotony of his wife's company indoors.

'What are you doing today?' she asked, emboldened by his apparent lenience of mood.

'I'm going over to the Foresty Commission to see the Green Man. I feel like a walk while I'm there. I haven't had any exercise for weeks. So don't expect me back. I'll be late.'

'Do you want sandwiches if you're on the hills?'

'No, I don't –' and then he softened his flat denial by adding after a peculiar pause, 'don't think I do.'

His expedition to see the Green Man, so denominated by Aileen partly because he drove round his territory in a green Land Rover, was an impulse rather than a plan. His house was about five miles from Inchcombe and Alexis decided he would walk all the way there, and set out in good heart. He anticipated his welcome, all the better for being infrequently called upon. They would walk up on some job or other, maybe sit in the Land Rover and drive up to the higher corries where the Forestry Commission lands ended and those of the Powell-Jones family began.

He headed through the lower glades of the Commission, up the gully of a burn and over a wide moss-grown bridge until he found the arterial road, wide enough for a vehicle to cut its way between the trees. The forest was scrubby and mangled at first with the upheaval of recent planting, he noticed, and further on there was some established young growth, waist high. Then presently the road seemed to dip and he found himself in a cavern of green, where huge pines and some deciduous patterned the sky. The growth on either side was impenetrable beyond a few yards and the forest floor was so dense with decades of pine needles that the most tentative step from the cleared path made him sink and slither as though touching on the crust of an avalanche that at a tremor would slide downwards through the brake of trees.

To be out was better than to be in. He strode along in good fettle with himself and the day. It is not so bad, he said to himself, when one has somewhere to go, though he did not push himself further into an exact definition of what was not so bad or where he was going.

There was no vehicle outside the house which stood on an isolated shelf a thousand feet above the level of the loch, and he began to have misgivings. He knocked at the door and then put his head round it, for doors were kept on the latch in these parts on the assumption that if you thought there was anything worth stealing you were a poor devil who needed it more than the owner, and then he called out. Hello there. But no one answered and his own voice in the emptiness of the spot resonated strangely, as if the forest were a sounding board multiplying the solitude. He stepped inside, feeling slighted that there was no one there to greet him when he should chance to call once in a half year. He glanced round the worn and shabby room, which would have sparkled out with life and gaiety if the man or his wife had been in residence, but finding no one he left and descended the hillside to the loch precipitately instead of taking the long route round by the path.

He was as disappointed as a child and his spirits that were buoyant on the upwards march plummeted as steeply as the downward one. Now, this fluctuation of mood was patently unreasonable, and he tried to chivvy himself into a more balanced frame of mind. He could not go on soaring and diving like this. He must level out. The trouble was he was dying of loneliness. In the middle of what seemed abundant and rewarding, he was on his own, again. He was dying of the internal monologue of existence which met with no returning shout of warmth or welcome from another being. No friend, no wife, no child, no lover, no one. In this, he realised there was an inversion in their lives, his and Esme's, whereby she had passed onto him her state of being friendless and alone, while she moved into his once peopled existence. While he was glad he had transmitted some of his vigour, glad she was independent and her own woman first of all, he blamed her bitterly too for not sticking it out with him. So he bounced backwards and forwards between varying states of rejoicing and reproach which left him no peace. If this was love, he didn't think much of it. Perhaps he should have stuck to simple adultery after all. Ah. He was in his dotage. He was even lying to himself.

And the things he had poured his talents into turned round and fled him too. He could not derive one germ of satisfaction from anything, his garden, his house, or his labour. He despised and hated every one of his achievements because he saw they were temporal not final and went on demanding more and more effort from him to maintain what he had already accomplished. Revolving this in the chamber of his mind, he realised he had imagined there was a static phase, a kind of perfection which was attainable by objects and people. That vase would stand immemorially in that spot. But it was not so. The patterns were constantly shifting; the selling turned into buying; leaves grew and dropped, were swept, decayed and fed the tree again; snow fell and melted; he read and forgot and read again – and in all the busyness, the activity of mind and body in acquisition of one kind or another, the prefixed destination was a mirage he and other men laboured towards as an ideal, a conquerable fact. But fixed states had at their core the flux of change, the impulse of creation and ambition. There was no actual arrival. He would always be travelling.

He had come in his ramblings to the edge of the water again, and stood looking east and west along the length of the valley, bound in by its mountain ranges and hills at hand. Those which rose behind him were warmly patched with heather, while here and there on the hillside were dotted the prosperous stone built dwellings of the farmers. Opposite, however, the view was over a bleaker range, sun-denied, with vegetation that was scrubby and land difficult to till. Occasionally the road opened out on a clearing and then he had a sight of meagre farms and homesteads. They punctuated the vast hillsides, still glacial with the blueness of things recently thawed, it seemed to him, in spurts of colour, a red cloth on a washing line, a child running in a yard, a yellow boat drawn up on the shore, but these were insignificant dots on a landscape that was insuperable. In waterlogged pastures, land reclaimed by natural force, fields abandoned to weeds and boulders there was something too awesome for majesty.

It turned cold as the afternoon sun fell behind the hill. He dug his hands into his waterproof pocket and discovered a package he had overlooked on his walk up the hill. Drawing it out, he saw it was a brown paper bag filled with sandwiches which she had made and wrapped for him in spite of his injunction. He puckered in distaste. He prised them open. Lavish fillings, cut with care. They made his gorge rise. Titbits of flesh embedded in fat. He was famished but he would not eat at her behest.

He tore them into fragments and fed them to the birds. A farmer taking a tractor to high ground heard the commotion and looked down. A man alone on a promontory was encircled by gull, crow, thrush, rising and wheeling like a pillar of smoke. What was he feeding them on to make them so rabid? He seemed to have the power of a St Francis or an Orpheus, and then he went on to think less charitably that he was encouraging peckers to come and molest his fields and wished he had his gun with him to shoot the marauders.

Into all these elements Alexis read the frailty of mankind. The huge mountains crushed. The water drowned. His scale and his power were minuscule in comparison with theirs. He was daunted over and over again by the challenge they presented him with. He was nothing more than a slip stream to this minor water course, a trickle that merged underground below a tussock of grass and was lost in subterranean futility. Why, if he walked into the loch, and he imagined the pull of its water against his clothes, filling his pockets, weighing him down, he could be out of sight in three minutes, toe to head. The water would seep into his ears, nose, mouth and through the sieve of his orifices would filter into his stomach, an algae brackish taste he foresaw, and then into his lungs. His body would fight, he thought, make a display of choking and rejection of the hostile element (how long did it take to drown if you committed yourself to it?). But after maybe five more minutes, his bloated, water-weighted frame would sink without trace. The loch would obliterate him and those fragile cells in himself he had fed, fostered, worshipped sometimes, brain and body for so long. One speck he was, one mote in eternity.

He saw his corpse, once it had risen to the surface again after a day or two from the gases of decomposition, carried to the shore and wondered where the wreckage of his carcase might beach up. He watched the ripples on the surface and decided it would be on the eastern stretch of Earn. On that point would his cairn be raised.

He put his foot to the water's edge and embraced the likelihood of death, letting the waters of oblivion rise above his head.

Although he knew perfectly well that he would not affront whatever luckless passer-by might have to pull the fat slug out, the Green Man maybe doing a statutory inspection in the woods up that end. He would not disgrace his own memory by such cowardice. The heroes of myth and epic made their quietus by falling on a sword, pushing a pillar, cutting their adversary down in combat. But civilisation had advanced to the point where he could not look on the death of himself or an enemy as a convincing victory. It was not even an aesthetic solution. How many modern heroes died in the last act? He had always felt consummately cross with Dido for throwing herself on the pyre the moment the white sail of the departing Aeneas was seen on the horizon, that wet boy Romeo dying for love. Real heroes, that is the unsung, began again. Starting at nothing; back to square one, a new apprentice fresh, anxious as himself every September, a new bolt of cloth, a new idea, a new day. What else was there to do? Life was the victory. If he must fall in time, it would be face to the battle.

Turning away, his eyes caught sight of the hill range and a waterfall spilling over one of the rocky ledges of the face. That, as he remembered, was one of Bruce's caves, one of the many. Every pot hole in Scotland had been occupied by Bruce or by Rob Roy and turned into a tourist trail. But it jerked his mind back to the tale of Bruce's spider which six times attempted to bridge a span with its web before it succeeded on the seventh, and the routed general took the moral to heart and thought, If the instinctive creature can prevail over circumstance, why not the rational one. Now that was his history hero, the man who endured. Let him strive in imitation.

But he foresaw a long, hard winter of it.

He installed a loom in the end bedroom and to counteract the ravages of sleeplessness, to give invention to his hands, would weave late and early. It took him many days to cut the warp threads with a yardstick, for he was determined that this length would be perfect. Setting up the threads absorbed several more, each knot in place as though it were a demonstration piece. Looking lengthwise across the taut threads, the joins could be seen to form a furrow, straight as a ridge on a plain. He had no concept of what he wanted to achieve, raploch or barathea, but took half-used spools at random from his shelves and attempted in his selection to deny that very act. It was to be freehand. He was reminded of the gesture by which a gardener naturalises bulbs, by throwing them on the ground willy-nilly and planting them where they fall. It was artless just as much as it was artificial but the haphazard appealed to him at that moment.

When he started the weft, the same principle applied. It was a tonal exercise rather than true weaving, perhaps an extension of the little pieces with bark and hedgerow wool he made up for his own amusement. He looked for yarn that was thick and thin, and padded this in place as a bird theeks its nest. The thudding shuttle as it swept to and fro allowed him to be an automaton, bent on covering a certain distance, an inch or two of space, before night fell or the sun rose and called him to other work. But often daylight revealed that errors had crept in; the idea was flawed, uncertain and imprecise though it was, and he undid in the hours of day what he had achieved by night.

She watched the decay of order with growing alarm. He was always prone to heavy bouts of labour, driving, punishing himself beyond what normal men could endure. The need for sleep and food and variation was expunged at these times, and in the past he had often paid off a loan in this way, purchased a loom or a knitting machine, created the cash for Aileen's schooling or her private lessons or her travel abroad. Latterly, since affluence had overtaken them, these spells had become more remedial than economic in purpose. He liked to work himself to the bone, despised luxury and his own softening hands, and would flay himself with corrective toil. The self-flagellation over, he would collapse exhausted but feeling purged.

This phase was different. It was not so temporary. It went on for weeks, showed no sign of ending. He did not go to bed. She was sure of that. In the mornings when she came downstairs, she could chart his progress during the previous night. He ate sparsely, if at all, but a knife out of place or a mug would reconstruct for her his movements, even his diet. His books would be disturbed, some opened, read and marked. She came across a copy of Burns, folded with a letter as marker and the Canadian stamp told its authorship. She would not stoop to reading it, but felt it was humiliating beyond endurance to have them communicate behind her back. It was not entirely over, then. She might come back over the water to wreak havoc again.

The book could have told her that. His own characteristic line of pencil highlighted

Ae fond kiss, and then we sever!
Ae farewell, alas, for ever!
Had we never lov'd sae blindly,
Never met – or never parted,
We had ne'er been broken hearted.

She was alternately furious and despairing. If Esme had been within range, she would have boxed her ears. To think that Alexis was spending his evenings in this chair, reading this rubbish, yes, deliberately reconstructing the image of Esme. She was disgusted that such sentimentality could afflict a man who in all reason was beyond the age of romance. She would rather Esme were here, under her eyes, than an absent insidious spirit whose influence she could not measure or curtail.

And then she noticed above and to her left a smudge on the wall exactly as Esme had left it when she was reading. The sight shocked her. For a second she felt as if it were the blood of a murder victim seeping back to accuse the perpetrator, as Rizzio's was meant to do in the great hall of Holyroodhouse or the head of Lorenzo forever flowering in its pot of basil. It seemed a spontaneous manifestation, almost the act of a poltergeist. Then scepticism overcame her and she looked more closely. It was worse than she had thought. Nightly he was sitting in this chair, unconsciously perhaps in imitation of her action, feet above his head against the wall, lost in a book. She could wash it away again, paint it over, but time and again it would reappear to mock and haunt her. She wept. She raged, and knew the utter defeat that no one would come and no one would see and no one would care.

He walked in and looked round the knitting shed without closing the door. It ought to have been dull and routine but he was tense with excitement. A clean slate. A new September. Each year it was the same. There were maybe a dozen aspirants at their places, eyeing him under his reputation. Were they terrified of him, terrified of revealing their fragle talent for his inspection?

'Throw the windows open. It's too warm for work.'

This was the usual bunch, opinionated, proud of a book of samples or a single idea they pinned their faith on, and day after day he would have to wean them away from egotism. He didn't speak much. His words were emitted too thoughtfully for exuberance. He did not instruct them at all. He let them work and make their own mistakes and correct each other. They shied away from holding their designs up to the group, but what else were they aiming at? This was the first blast of scorn that would blow against them all their lives. It whipped off the superfluous.

He wondered going around the room what they saw in him, a bison of a man, the bull of a dying tribe. An old master, fudging on with outworn standards. All he ever tried to tell them was that the future springs from the past, that no art can afford to ignore its own origins, that they would invent nothing in the course of their working lives. They were shocked at this year after year, when he said, All my best is shaping old things new. They thought they were original, unique, maybe even geniuses. And year after year he levelled their good opinion of themselves. One glance at a half-finished article revealed to him its flaws. Here and here, he said, You've made a mistake in the pattern. Rip it down and begin again. Nothing less than perfection will do. And they hated him and fought against him and were always convinced by the rightness of what he told them to do, because they did it.

Once in a while, maybe once in five years, he came across a brilliant, innovative mind. Then what a game it was. Pitch and toss, the ball returned with interest. You dare; I will do it; you'll see it'll go wrong. The boys and once a girl grew up and looked him in the eye. They never forgot him or he them, and when they turned up with their successes to show him he felt that the bread he had cast upon the waters had come back to him after many days.

23

The trees of Europe grow in Canada, but differently. Spruce, pine, birch, some oak are there, but of all the trees which characterise the Canadian champaign it is probably the emblematic maple which lends its distinctive features to the autumn. The lobed leaf turns to variegated shades of amber, gold or scarlet at the first frost when the traveller waits for it to fall. Instead, it adheres to the tree for a further month or more, so that the season which in Europe is a quite brief interlude, measured at times in days rather than weeks, in North America establishes something of a permanence. It actually deepens. The hillsides can flare in colour, sweeps of deciduous alternating with the sombre foil of evergreen, hill beyond hill beyond hill.

This was Rejean's country, then. She measured his description against the real and felt the difference was his homesickness. At each turn of the road Esme thought there must be an end, a disappointment, at least an anticlimax compared with what she had already seen on the road from Montreal. At first the water of the St Lawrence shone through the interstices of the forest on her right, or a lake signalled waiting, unspoiled promise. Each new view brought fresh delight or variation until, when they turned into the Laurentides Park north of Quebec City, she felt that the scenery through which they moved might indeed be never-ending since it had no visible perimeters, and her admiration for it became tinged with awe when she reflected that it was possible to drive from Quebec to Chicoutimi, that is, from Edinburgh to Inverness, without passing a house, a garage, or any evidence of human habitation on the main highway through the province. What happens, she wondered as Maurice steered her car relentlessly north, what happens if you have a breakdown?

But she admonished herself for her timidity, remembering the early Scots who moved across the continent before her, the victims of the Highland Clearances, the political refugees fleeing retribution for their support of the fated Stuarts, the misguided emigrants in the Darien scheme and others who, having survived the sea passage, were faced with the struggle to maintain an existence in primitive conditions, planting crops, building shelter in the middle of the friendless unknown, and had outwitted enemies, the cold, endemic disease to lend their name to rivers, mountains and the townships they founded. These were her people. She must not dishonour them.

It was only the scale, she told herself, that was overwhelming. The trees, the lakes, the sky were all similarly composed to those at home except that they were immense and the eye which was used to the scope of the domestic landscape broken by a wisp of smoke, a sheep-cote, a pile of logs under a dry-stane dyke, became tired in its search for the familiarly inhabited. The road itself was the single piece of evidence that they were not entering virgin territory. Otherwise, the densely packed forest on either side gave no clue as to their location, or their direction, and no welcome.

Maurice noticed her silence and, to divert her, told her how a friend, running out of petrol in January on this very stretch, had left his car at the roadside but when he returned later with a breakdown truck could find no trace of it buried under drifting snow. It was not recovered until the spring thaw three months later in April.

19th September
Dear Aileen,

Thank you for your card. 'Welcome to your new home' cheered a heavy day. Actually my flat – sorry apartment – does feel tolerably like home. I found it through a register of houses to let which is kept at the local post office, curious but convenient notion. It's the basement of a big house on a corner site in Arvida. The couple who rent it to me, Monsieur and Madame Chantal, are quite charming and helpful, two school age daughters, *not* my pupils. These girls are superbly bilingual. I would suffer from verbal schizophrenia in the circumstances but they pop in and out of the two languages without pause. I have learned always to try my French on the unsuspecting Québècois and once I have established my goodwill, they come forward with impeccable English, which they keep well hidden if you don't. I have a lounge, kitchen, bathroom and two bedrooms with central heating for ninety-five dollars a month, whatever that is worth in equivalent terms, and I consider myself very well off. Basement implies a gloomy sub-terranean den, but there are full-sized windows in every room bar one which has high lights, if no outlook, and the outer door leads up a flight of steps to the garden. I am very comfortable and contained.

The house is within walking distance of the school; not such good news there. I imagined I was being employed to be the remedial teacher in a basic skill – reading, writing – to a few select individuals. Not so. I am the remedial teacher to the whole failed tenth grade, a dozen recalcitrant sixteen year olds (I'm not that much older myself, for goodness sake) who informed me on my first day that they were going to get jobs the day they left, earning every bit as much as me, so I needn't push books, hard work and all that learning stuff at *them*.

The headmaster is an ingenious con man, never admits there's a problem and attacks others whenever his system is found to be imperfect. The difficulty is geographical, I've discovered. The whole area is French to the bone – the slogan PRESERVONS NOTRE AME ET NOTRE LANGUE FRANCAISE painted on the side wall of a school near here is a pointer to the way the people feel – and the English are a tiny minority because they only come up here when the company sends them. The company is either the aluminium plant at Arvida, or the hydro-electricity station at Shipshaw, or the Air Force. The RCAF has a base at Bagotville. They all seem to look on two years as exile and three as eternal damnation. Why, I don't know, but everyone mutters darkly about the winter. Well, how can you teach children who are always on the move and always have been? Can you remember much rolling stock at school? In my form, two girls came and three left. That was over a period of seven years. I simply didn't realise what stability was. I wonder if Edinburgh is the last city state in the world. It's solidified, hasn't it? Nobody moves house. It's big enough and varied enough to educate and employ its young people, a self-perpetuating fountain.

Anyway, a side-effect is the non-availability of staff. I see the redoubtable Don Elphick is up against it there, and that makes him descend to low cunning in employing half-wits like me. Nobody will come, and if they're good they don't stay long. One ingénue has left already. Mostly wives or qualified sons and daughters of servicemen or middle managers. They're all putting in time. They know the children of ambitious parents are boarded out in Montreal, or Winnipeg, or Vancouver, sent to one of the outward-bound schools.

I am supposed to teach, wait for it, English, Geography and History (an agglomerate known as Social Science) to three classes and otherwise babysit the remedial tenth. It's taking me all my time to know what they're *saying* and they fall about laughing at my pronunciation, itch instead of haitch in spelling is an infallible precursor to gorilla scratching. Oh dear. The absurd thing is we are meant to teach by rote, every Canadian child in every school in the tenth grade is doing the same page of the manual on the same day. Ugh! Imagine how spontaneous I feel about that. I told Mr E on the first day that that was unworkable with educational drop-outs, and he tacitly agreed. So I have carte blanche to do what I want with them as long as

a) they make no noise

b) they do not deface the desks.

He has a mania for desk tops. They appear in every report on staff or buildings that he has ever written e.g. The desks remain in an appalling condition but this will not be remedied until they are replaced by plastic covered work tops. So much for educational theory. Personally, I enjoy the graffiti. 'Hot legs Esme.'

I actually wish I knew something about teaching. I see now how admirably we were taught, but also how very teachable we were. Did we ever argue except dialectically? Did we ever complain about our marks or the books we had to read? (And in case you're smiling, second ordinary English Literature was different.) I don't get through a day without a storm of protest. There are work-sheets, answers to which are devious beyond my ken, for they rely on a method known as multiple choice which might be renamed multiple confusion as the alternatives seem to be chosen for their almost indistinguishable inaptness. Isn't one of the assets of English the fact that it has no synonyms? I have avoided these since I got into my first fandangle with them.

I talk to them instead. They have no notion of how to conduct a meaningful dialogue, don't listen to each other or think their ideas are important at all. I ask them about themselves. I try to make

233

lessons out of their answers. They teach *me* the geography of Canada. We read plays in funny accents and occasionally, miraculously, laugh together.

I have gone vegetarian, temporarily I suspect, and mostly because it's a cheaper way to eat than meat. The fruit and vegetables are superb, and I am drunk on apple juice. Stay me with flagons. Comfort me with apples. There are fresh pineapples from Hawaii, all sorts of mangoes and lychees and yams and pawpaw fruit. I am having a feast, but the best was a box of Red Delicious from British Columbia I bought in the supermarket. It brought back incredibly happy memories of the old house. I spend ten minutes polishing each one before I can bear to eat it. Each has a perfect five point star at the base, so bright and waxy it looks artificial.

As for the rest, I have made hardly any advance in the Rosowicz affair. I took the car and went to see the Air Force Chaplain who lives in a married quarter on the base about fifteen miles from here. Bob Findlay, Scots great-grandfather, six foot four, rangy and disjointed, very likeable. He was most sympathetic considering all the warning he had was a telephone call. Actually, sitting on his chesterfield, I couldn't help thinking it all sounded damned silly and much less urgent than it was a thousand miles away. But I will press on. He has given me the name of a priest to contact and I still have the five names Maurice gave me to be going on with.

When will we see you? Can't you come over with Rejean next month? I would so enjoy hearing how things are with you, and how they are at home.

Esme hesitated for a long time before appending the words 'at home', playing with the various levels of meaning and interpretation Aileen could place on them, but then decided if she really did know nothing there was no harm in what was the most natural phrase.

Reading this letter one Saturday morning reinforced a mood of gloom in Aileen that was outside the normal range of her personality. She was gloomy a good deal these days. Rejean was away on a field trip, again, though that was almost a relief even if she did suspect he took the outlet more often than he had to, prolonged his stay abroad with days visiting the homes of friends he made, days shooting at country lodges in Sweden, days lost somewhere unknown to her. If she counted back, in the six weeks since they were married they had spent a total of one week together. In truth, the flat was too small for both of them full time, the cupboards overflowing with sports equipment and shoes of every denomination she could imagine, trainers, spikes, mountain boots, golf shoes, ski boots. Where did they all come from? A man made a mess and didn't tidy it up afterwards. He ate too much, was altogether too labour intensive and she persuaded herself she didn't have time to see to it.

This led her to the major cause of her gloom, the fact that for the first time she had come up against something she could not do. Shorthand had for Aileen this unique property. It produced tears that neither Virgil nor Racine, John Stuart Mill nor Kant had summoned. Against them she was ready to pit her will, notion for notion, line for line, until they fell and displayed their meaning to her. Breached, they were generous and gave back knowledge, and sometimes wisdom. They sat memorably in the brain so that in a quiet moment, alone or in company, one could be entertained by thinking

Infandum, regina, iubes renovare dolorem

or by pondering, if one really must, the categorical imperative and put it down to experience. Shorthand had no such recompense. Wrestle with it as she might, it was not memorable, it did not fall and display anything, it was not entertaining alone or in company. It was the hieroglyphic of despair.

Sometimes poring over her table amidst the singular debris which those who live without witnesses accumulate, unremoved salt and pepper mills, a mug washed out before each use, a permanently laid mat, she would smile thinking that however onerous the task of chastening these symbols was to her it would have been beyond the patience of Esme. Her shadow, evoked by the letter, lurked in the room. Aileen could see her tearing her hair out at the uselessness of what was proposed – oh, her heart went out to Mr Elphick – storming, raging and subsiding at last into twenty minutes' furious learning, while she jotted and prepared to make a brilliant stand against the title or the tutor or the system.

What would Esme make of international shipping regulations, customs transfer and bills of lading? Rip-roaring stuff. If only her cousin could be persuaded to make a stand *for* something.

Well, they were supposed to be such clever girls, and what were they doing with it? Frittering it into mechanical tasks, taking down notes from other people's mouths, writing verbatim transcripts of drivel and, in Esme's case, correcting endless reams of mis-spelt, mis-constructed prose. Could it be prose in the tenth grade? No, it was drivel too. Should their education have fitted them for work, or was their working life an irrelevancy in the middle of their on-going education? Certainly it was not possible to live by Virgil or Kant, stimulating companions though they might be. A vocation was called for, but they had settled for the humble middle-women vocations of secretary and teacher through which the twentieth century transmitted the bulk of non-creative learning. Scribe and tutor, then. The work was necessary, it was traditional, it was respectable. But was it all that they could do? Weren't there some more automatic, passive minds than theirs that would be content with such an intermediary role; for it was hard to believe that their degrees had made their execution of these tasks at all better, whether that was faster or more accurate. Wasn't this circuitous daydream proof that she was loath to return to the notebook full of transcription or translation? She was slower at shorthand than many a quick-wristed sixteen year old, her mind straying off into systems of logic or mathematics or coding to help her explain the symbols to herself. Or she saw analogies with Arabic lettering, consonants first, vowels a dotted afterthought. The narrow mind was blind to these digressions. Could these be the ciphers which made life meaningful? And she wasn't even, and did not pretend to be, original, creative, daring. If she felt these frustrations against the dailiness of life, what did Esme feel champing at the bit, impatient with what was not busy, quick, inventive?

No, hold. There had been alternatives. Alexis had always insisted on her acknowledging the possibility of creative work, undertaken by the practical artisan. A skill, a trade could have been theirs every bit as much as a profession. Or they could have studied law or medicine, but there was no avoiding their disinclination for either discipline as well as a few problems with

Physics. They chose from a limited sphere of personal objectives because, and it was not easy to make the confession to herself, because of their nature. They lacked the drive to choose differently. They were unprepared to make the effort to launch themselves into some wider, more demanding seam because always and inevitably they held something in reserve for their careers as women. No amount of work or education could quite remove the image of Young Lochinvar. Here she was already married, and Esme probably not far away in spite of swearing she would stay fancy free. Systems of logic were powerless against the systems of the body. Biology took over; it enforced the bonds of marriage; it created children and against these forces the demands of scribe and tutor were negligible, instantly forgettable.

She saw at once what she had not admitted to herself before, that it was quite wrong of her to have pursued her goals towards qualifying in opposition to her life with Rejean. She had scarcely asked his opinion, though she knew he wanted to return to Canada and did not enjoy staying on to accommodate her. But it was too late now to change her course. She would have to put it right at the end of the year. She modified the pangs of conscience at neglecting him and her marriage by turning back to Esme's final suggestion. Why should she not go to Montreal with him! Hurriedly consulting her diary, she realised that she could join him for the week of her mid-term which, with weekends included, could be extended to a holiday of ten days in all.

Esme's composure was for show. Underneath, she was as confused and self-contradictory as her cousin – and every bit as lonely. The flat at Canonmills was not less populous than the apartment in Arvida, and the letter which went between the two addresses bridged similar moods, even if it did not express them. Perhaps it would have been better for both recipient and sender if it had, instead of letting their confidentiality lapse, but Esme's honesty wavered at the prospect of more exposure and she could not bring to the surface the cause of pain and withdrawal which, spoken, might have found her a sympathetic ally. Habit was strong. She kept it to herself, nursing her own grief till she was sound enough to face the world in a less vulnerable state. Pride and accustomed solitude kept her silent.

And silent she was. The rooms through which she threaded her evenings were empty after Maurice left. They gave her adequate space for reflection, and she was not short on self-reproach. She had leapt into a void, then stopped to look. The hasty act of removal, which had seemed tiny and temporary, became immense in retrospect as she underwent a continental drift where landforms that had been locked together floated apart. A breathing space? Recuperation, well and good. But she had not simply taken a fortnight off in Bath or Tunbridge Wells or Malvern or any other inland watering place to convalesce. She had flown. And overseas. The intervening medium of time was enlarged by the concern of her protectors, though she couldn't blame the Simards for acting on an impulse which was, at the outset, hers. The decision to run away, or in other terms not to decide, was culpable. She knew it. She faced it. She did not exonerate herself from the accusation that in a crisis, her courage misgave.

She tried out half a dozen excuses for the rebound, but none fitted. True, she was young, unsure, afraid of launching herself into an adulterous union without a fund of normality in her experience, or was daunted by the new territories of scandal and opposition; each served a turn but was not final even in conjunction with another. No, the missing factor was that at the sticking point, she stuck. She did not have the faith in one other human being which would have guided her into the future, and could not waive her own doubts on the evidence of the invisible or the unproveable. It was easy to gauge the strength of Alexis' attraction. It was not so easy to assess the strength of his feelings, when he kept their power under such rigorous suppression. Here the disparity in age was manifest. A younger man would have swept her along regardless. He, in allowing her space and choice, gave her the opportunity for his own exclusion.

Not, of course, that he was excluded from her thoughts. The lamp at nightfall burned out in a dark that was resonant with vacancy. He expanded the room even in absence and the dialogues she held with him were more intense than ever. No idle chat. By the day and by the hour, the conversation swelled with things done, said, shared experience, and the half-made moments of their encounter were fulfilled.

Mindful of him, she was inclined within the very first week to make a double vault. Jump backwards. It was no worse than jumping forwards, except that she was tired of movement and the friction burn caused by molecular collision with the air. Hold still, she said. Make a go of something for a change. The second crossing would not cancel out the first unless she had something to show for it. So she came to a halt, not knowing that the wounded bird in flight is rarely caught but grounded, becomes an easy prey. Her scars might heal but she was vulnerable nonetheless.

24

Second time around, Montreal was less appealing. It had been dusty and hot in August but city streets in North America take on a limpid sultriness in those conditions, the parks of La Fontaine and Mont-Royal like oases, while broad, tree-planted boulevards in the suburbs took off the glare of day-round, week-round sun. Water had seemed a central feature of downtown Montreal, the river winding sluggishly, cool fountains breaking on the stones, while sun and glass created their own illusion of glamour, the city full of winking mirrors, cars idling at lights, windowed skyscrapers taller than anything she had seen.

But the turn in the weather exposed that, underneath the patina of summer, much of the housing was shabby and less well maintained than her native city had brought her to expect was an urban norm. There were fine civic buildings, imposing churches and in the new districts there were rolling estates in various styles, Spanish Colonial, pillared White House replicas or Rancher homesteads, mid-west fashion. They had frontages like film sets: trees in tubs, trained Virginia creeper and landscaped gardens of evergreen. But the new went cheek by jowl with the old and for someone raised in a homogenous approach, where layouts could be different but compatibly so, this was disconcerting. The concrete new style she loathed. It aged conspicuously in five or ten years and was most farcical when poured into wood lined moulds to simulate timber. It was already pitted and weather-stained.

Evidently a different standard prevailed here. She had been

greatly struck by coming across a settlement in one of her forays into the Laurentides. She had driven at random along a road, and stopped out of interest when she came to a break in the even pattern of the forest. In a clearing there was an enclave of farm buildings which had been abandoned. There was a pervading sense of decay about them which she hadn't expected in the tidy Saguenay. The buildings were already far deteriorated, the wood eaten into and eroded with fungus and mildew. Frost had expanded and split the fibres, loosening nails and corroding them with rust which had run down and further stained the wood. Paint, creosote or tar wash had long been absent. The farm had reached the stage of being irretrievable and after another winter would revert wholly to the invasive forest, dead wood rotting back into green again.

Who could afford to build short term like this, in urban or rural settings? Who could afford, or bear, to abandon a home to the wilderness? What social factor was at work that made built-in obsolescence a norm? Were they so rich, were they so mobile or was the weather a predatory element? She recalled the solid tenements of home and thought they were not so shabby after all; they stood against wind and time. Only fire could gut them. Newness mattered here, brightness that was replaceable as soon as it faded. The suburbs did not have sidewalks or kerbstones or street lights, and the whole unfinishedness was tiresome after a while, like wearing a coat with a button missing. It was a small omission in the overall scale of things, but it detracted from the vital function.

The house too disturbed her in the change of the year. It was one of Maurice's own modular buildings – he was not too proud to live in what had made him affluent – a bungalow built in a rectangle with an open square in the middle which was planted with shrubs and some flowering trees, magnolia, almond, a tulip tree, around which the rooms flowed in an undefined sequence. One could sit or eat in several places according to mood, in or outdoors, by sliding back a partition of wood or glass or curtain, in Japanese style, and step into a greatly enlarged area. Now in good weather this was delightful and had appealed to her new emancipation. One could float through space without impediment.

In the grey days, in rain, she looked for a door to shut behind her, and finding none glanced over her shoulder every few minutes to guard some privacy. There was a roof but it was an invisible roof, sloping inwards so that the constant gush of rainwater into the drains of the courtyard was depressing. Outer walls comprised entirely of glass could not shut out a view of the sodden garden, while the ever present drab of the courtyard shrubbery was like living with a sarcophagus in the same room. When she walked, she walked on parquet wooden blocks, and the self-conscious sound of her own footsteps drove her frantic, a timpani of notes she never got used to but which infallibly made her turn round to see who was following.

And then there was the real cause of her edginess – for there was not one discernible factor different between the new and charming place of summer and the dull and dispirited one of autumn apart from the weather and she actually preferred the temperate season – no, the real cause of her malaise was that she missed what she had left. She missed the place but not so much as she missed the man. A few weeks in August constituted a holiday. By October she realised she was half way through the stint to which she was contracted, that she could not decently return till she had spent Christmas with the Simards, and that she was in the same situation she had perennially been in, of wanting time to hurry her ahead without the bother of living through the intervening space. Reality, today, the insistent present, was her problem and she was discovering it did not go away.

Claire refused to be daunted by either weather or mood, however, although observing none of the young people was in the best of tempers. There was one thing she liked better than a party and that was a party of house guests. With residents, every day was a festival and she was dedicated to giving the girls the break she was sure they deserved. She marvelled at their independence, or said she did for she was a feminist of a very pale colour, and much preferred to charge her clothes to someone else's account. Each day was planned for them: a drive to friends who were taking a late weekend at the lake, shopping for fripperies, looking for things to match other things bought on a previous outing, a trip to a new museum on Canadian heritage, and Esme must see Ottawa. Can we fit in Niagara? was a daily hare run to exhaust debate. Maurice complained at the pace and said he had a business to manage, but spent most days with them all the same.

Rejean's visit was not social, however. If Maurice was pleased to drive around Ontario with his bevy behind, Rejean was not. He closeted himself for hours in the office or at home and worked out his strategy. The AGM was on Friday and he and Aileen were scheduled to fly back on Sunday, the day Esme left. He had to work quickly to make sure of his ground. He passed Esme late at night with a sheaf of papers in his hand and noticed her for the first time that day.

'You're working too hard. I never see you,' she complained. He turned back from the door to the study and held it wide for her to go through. The desk was strewn with sheets, and glancing at them she saw they were filled with figures and calculations. 'What is it that you are doing?'

'Backing up the paper I'm presenting tomorrow. I want to put certain measures through.'

'What certain measures? Tell me.'

'Well, we're living on borrowed time at the moment. I want to establish a development fund, say five per cent of gross annual turnover which could be tax deductible, to go towards acquisition and replanting. For now, we buy timber on site but that can't go on for ever. The ecologists are being heard and if timber becomes scarce – well, it is a shrinking world commodity so I don't know why I say "if" – we must grow our own. I've done the research to show it can be done profitably for the fine woods. Slow financial return but assured. And a development fund would pay for new machinery. We're an old firm. Our frame-cutting equipment is out of date. It's all hand operated. They're doing new studies in Japan and the States with a kind of thinking robot, a computer machine that can calculate and store information about sizes and measurements. We want to look into that, be first in the field.'

'Why does it matter so much to you? It doesn't sound like your area at all.'

'The business is my future too. And no business runs except on sound economics.'

'Will Maurice comply with these changes?'

'There was no hope before we went public. He's one of the old brigade. What was good enough twenty years ago still goes. But he'll have to agree if the shareholders vote it in. So I must be convincing. He won't be pleased at having things turned around and there'll be a tussle. He's one of the exploiters, you know.' He smiled that Esme was surprised at this application. 'No, I mean he's generous as a person, if you don't argue, but he's not much idea of paying back the soil or the long term. He tends to think, Me, now, and blow the future.'

'So tomorrow may be unpleasant?'

'I hope not. But either way, it's a day of reckoning for me.' The tone in which this was said did not move her to ask why. He had withdrawn from them and was absorbed in himself and his own ideas. He was changing. One part of her believed this was not possible, that people only developed. But with him she saw a grain thicken, an attitude of mind become set. He wasn't as open or trusting as he had been a year before. She fancied he had hardened a little. Or was she wrong? When he shielded his eyes it was only against too much glare. In soft light he would take his hand away again and the look shine out as clear and honest as ever.

But she was anxious when they were late back for dinner which was routinely at seven. The candles had begun to gutter and the vichyssoise threatened to curdle. And then they heard the car sweep down the drive and voices grow loudly towards them, but not in animosity.

Rejean came through the door first and a glance told Esme he had won the day. Maurice followed, shaking the incessant rain of that autumn off his Burberry and there was an aversion in his movements, or an elaborate stiffness not natural in him, as when he turned round to the third man who made up the party and who had waited till the others were well inside before making himself obvious.

'Can we dine one more?' Maurice consulted his wife. 'Guess who we ran into as we were leaving the office? Five minutes later and he would have missed us.' The newcomer, arriving just at that point when they were first alone and things were liable to be said, had spared them a confrontation. Behind Maurice in the doorway stood their chance encounter, obviously no stranger to Claire who embraced him French fashion and fussed and petted him as a well known visitor. He was a man of about Rejean's age, conspicuously dressed in the uniform Esme recognised from her sorties to Chicoutimi as that of the Royal Canadian Air Force. 'Could you believe it? He only came down today and we bumped into each other in the street. So we decided to come back for dinner. You don't mind? We should have called first.'

Claire waived protocol.

Their guest came forward to shake hands with Esme and Aileen and Rejean introduced him as an old friend from college and ski-ing circles, Mabon Caulderwood.

Esme was alerted. 'Oh, yes, of course, the telegram.'

'That's right. I'd forgotten,' said Aileen, taking the proffered hand and holding it while she recollected the wording which was sufficiently pert to be barred at the reception. 'You haven't capitulated yet?'

The stranger smiled unperturbed. He had probably never said anything he had lived to regret, but turned what might have looked like an offence to the bride into swift flattery. 'If I had met you before Rejean did, I might have done.' He made a nod over the hand he held, not quite as formal as a bow but it was a gesture with enough antiquated gallantry to take away from the speciousness of the remark, and so to make his forgiveness complete.

'Do come and sit down now,' Claire insisted. 'Everything will spoil if we leave it. I do apologise for rushing you but we eat at seven normally. An unfashionable hour, I know.' Claire led him away by the arm.

'Not at all. The apologies are all mine for imposing on you. You don't need to worry. Nothing is ever less than perfect in this house.'

Rejean waited behind a moment while his father and Aileen went to the dining table. To Esme's raised eyebrows he answered, 'Yes, I got my motion through, but narrowly. We are not pleased. He had inserted the item in the agenda and hadn't as much as read what I was going to say, though I left a copy with him. So he was caught off guard.' They turned and followed. 'Still, there will be worse to come.'

They were interrupted by laughter, that particular laughter that accompanies social banter. The stranger had changed the ambience of their evening, and in the circumstances probably for the better. They were determined to be humorous for him. 'What did you say he was doing here?' asked Esme.

'He's a trusted messenger.'

'What's that? Or is he Mercury in modern dress?'

'Oh, much more prosaic. He's allowed to carry documents which are too secret to go through the mail. A private postman for the RCAF. But of course he can't say anything, so don't ask.'

Esme looked into the bay ahead where they waited to be seated, and saw him lean earnestly over towards his hostess. 'I wouldn't trust him very far.'

Rejean was surprised and not just at what he thought was the almost indelicate haste behind the judgment. This was his friend. Wasn't that credential enough? Why should Esme take against him? Then he gave her a little more credit for her opinion and said, 'If I were a woman, I might think so too.'

'Don't worry, I'll be polite.' But she was glad all the same that the newcomer was seated between the two other women. This did mean that she was presented with him full on and could not easily look away or deflect phrases that came in her direction from time to time, especially when Aileen and Claire disappeared into the kitchen and she was left, not altogether unwillingly, with the men. Sport and careers were better than straining vegetables, and Claire's culinary fantasies wore her out.

As soon as they came back, laden with a tray or a serving dish, the guest rose to his feet and relieved them of it, held the door open, performed intricate moves with chairs or table mats to accommodate whatever food appeared. He did all this neatly, in fact invisibly to everyone but Esme. He was obviously an expert diner-out. He talked on through it all.

'Yes, I'm going ski-ing at New Year. I've been doing a lot of competitive ski-ing and I want to get faster. Do you get much in? The snow's kind of wet in the UK from what I hear. Slow.'

Rejean admitted it was slow in the UK and so acknowledged indirectly that if it came to a race between the two of them, he would be the loser. In the time that had elapsed since they were rivals, he had slipped and the other had gained.

'No, sir, I've no family left. A sister married to an embassy official. She's in Brazil at the moment.'

Or, paying attention to the ladies, say, 'This is looking superb, Claire. How can you cook Cordon Bleu and stay so svelte?'

How did he know that the one compliment Claire found over-whelming was contained in the word svelte? Had he been lucky?

Had he stored the fact from long ago and brought it out of a register of what women liked to hear? Esme tightened her lips and set out to resist the charm of his fine manners, which was not hard. Aileen began to flirt with him strenuously. Her long cope of fair hair swung in his direction time after time, made a kind of secret chamber in which they sat apart talking inconsequently, in tones which occasionally filtered out and were even by their tremor suggestive. This was new to Esme, who thought sexual teasing was anathema. One did or one didn't, but should not pretend one might. She had not imagined sex was a social asset to be paraded at a dinner table, and with a stranger. Why was Aileen doing it? she asked herself. Perhaps she was feeling her husband's week-long neglect and was prompting him towards some greater show of interest. If this were so, she was falling far short of her goal. Rejean hardly observed them. Then Esme remembered her cousin had been cooped with a class of women, taking down shorthand for two months. That was enough to make anyone react to the first attractive man like a schoolgirl out of convent. Attractive? Esme looked over at the conspirator and wondered if she read in his eye just such an objectivity as in her own, or did he think he was irresistible? Again, in contemplating these strange modes of behaviour, Esme came up against her ignorance of what was or was not done. Instinct was evidently not enough.

At the other end of the table talk drifted towards business, and to avert this Esme asked, 'Tell me, why do you build in wood when it perishes so easily? You're always pulling houses down and putting them back up again. Why not build once and for all?' And she told them about the farm in the backwoods.

'They must have over-cultivated there,' said Rejean. 'A farm in the middle of woods isn't a good idea, is it? No nourishment left in the soil and not much sun.'

'There's nothing wrong with a wooden house,' Maurice told her.

Inquiry along this line was maybe unwise with a man who made his fortune selling timber to replace old timber and to whom decay might therefore appear an advantage, but such niceties of tact tended to be lost on Esme when she wanted to know. 'Nothing wrong except that it doesn't last. There are no archaeological remains of a civilisation that built in wood.'

Rejean waited for a scalding reply. His father was quite capable of arguing that the Pyramids were made of wood if it suited him, but to his surprise the older man creased in a smile. 'So? Who builds to be an archaeological remain? I don't think the Romans had that idea up front when they built the Colosseum. And what do you want us to build in? Stone? We haven't any. Bricks are expensive to manufacture and they crack in extremes of cold. The best building material is always what is to hand and if there isn't one, chances are people shouldn't live there in the first place. Trees are our natural resource. So timber-frame houses are cheap and quick. A man can build his own, thankfully. That's what made my business flourish. You need a mason for a stone house, and he comes dear. Your buildings are fine for your country where they're all packed up tight and you don't want to see or hear your neighbours. But here we've room to spread ourselves. Add on a new den or a nursery at the back. We don't want to be calcified, thank you. We want to live now, not in two thousand years' time.'

Esme smiled, liking this roguish tone in him and his licence with her meant she could reciprocate. 'Well, I don't care for the makeshift. What roots can you put down when you're always on the move? Tear this house down, it's ten years old, or leave it to rot and move on.'

'People make their own permanence. It's like different species of tree, some deep, some shallow rooting. We don't go in much for old things but we can put our house on the back of a lorry if we want, and drive it a hundred miles down the road to another site. What could be more convenient? You don't even need to pack up to move house. Great.'

Terminating this conversation in what he thought was a perfect victory put him in good form. He opened another bottle of wine and went out to his pantry to look for a case of vintage Cognac he had laid down some time before.

In his absence, they drifted away from the table, the others to talk of holidays and travel, Esme to the long windows which gave a view of Montreal waterfront by night, lights winking on ships destined for a thousand ports, berthing in its giant tideless dock. St Helen's Island was adrift in the middle of the current like an ocean-going liner, heading out of the St Lawrence to home. Street lights spattered the city, clustered or thinning where there was a park, a garden, a factory. She found the central heating of these homes oppressive and slipped open the latch which released her into the garden and blissful solitude. All this activity and hardly a sound. Fine for Maurice to talk of neighbours. There wasn't a house within a hundred yards of his.

It was later before Rejean got round to suggesting that Mabon return the following evening, an idea that gave Esme a transitory pang. Their last evening together and him to share it! And then the guest declined. He had a prior engagement. You would have, thought Esme, while he continued, 'And if you are going away Sunday this must be the last time. I'll have to be up early myself to catch a plane back to Bagotville.' He gestured apologetically.

'Bagotville! You're not still there? I'd guessed you were at the end of that tour. Esme here is living in Arvida.'

The two looked at each other with altered recognition but before Esme could divert the proposition, Aileen said, 'If you go back on Sunday, why don't you drive with Esme? It's such a long way on your own.'

Esme was stumped. She had made so much of her fears about the long return journey, especially if the rain drummed down all the way, that she couldn't dodge his company. She would have appreciated sharing the driving, but not with a semi-stranger five hours of whose company would wear her smile out. He was too flash by half. So she couldn't make a better response than be taciturn.

He flicked a glance over the state of affairs and demurred, 'No, it's too much of an imposition. You probably have other plans.'

But the absolute rudeness of her stony silence weakened her. He was their friend and she was beholden to them. She felt the pull of a string and gave way, 'Not at all. I'd rather navigate than drive if that would suit you.'

So it was decided for her. She would pick him up at his hotel which was en route and they parted without further exchange, though he delivered lengthy and elaborate thanks or congratulations all round, whichever was appropriate, while she went away out of earshot.

When the door was closed on him, Aileen said, 'Oh Esme, how lucky that was. Imagine going back with that divine man.'

'Was he divine? It's a shame I'm not one of the converted.'

Maurice, locking up for the night, said, 'Don't be misled. He has more muscle than he showed us on this occasion.'

At breakfast the following morning, Rejean dropped his bombshell as they sat round the kitchen table.

'I've cancelled my return flight to Prestwick.' This was delivered in a matter of fact tone and he proceeded to finish his coffee, so the others were nonplussed. Only Esme sitting beside him could gauge the pulse of anxiety that throbbed under the statement.

'Why?' asked Maurice, thinking of a technical delay, an urgent meeting or some tangible cause to account for unaccountable behaviour.

'Because I've finished my work in the UK. I can do more here and now that I've taken these plans in hand, I want to see them through. They're my ideas and I can't delegate them to some manager. All right?'

Maurice and Aileen looked over at each other with astonishment, like a doubles partnership in tennis which knows a ball has been hit clean down the middle of the court and left both of them standing. Rejean had counted on this. They each assumed he had negotiated it beforehand with the other, and showed more delicacy in their respect for each other's feelings than they would have done with his. That momentary glance galled him. It proved what he had suspected, how little he mattered to either of them. They did not turn once to him but to each other, thinking, If it's been agreed with him, or her, then I can't oppose it. He was the outsider.

'You will lose the refund on your flight,' observed his wife.

'No doubt.'

'It's a three month ticket,' said Maurice quickly. 'You are going back within three months?'

'That depends on how involved I become here.'

'You expect Aileen to go back and live by herself all that time?'

'Aileen is by herself most of the time as it is. And there is another option. She can stay here. I would appreciate that.'

Esme wished they would not talk about his wife in the third person, or that yards of table did not stretch between them. She was the one person there who wanted to lean over and put a hand on his arm, the only one perhaps who had an inkling of why he was doing this, of the ravages of homesickness, not for them any more, but the place, the land, the treescape. Restored, he was not going to leave it again. But she didn't dare say a word on his behalf in case it was used in evidence against her.

'I can't do that,' objected Aileen. 'I've got my course to think of.'

'How much does that matter?' He leaned over nonchalantly to pour himself another cup of coffee. What he wanted an answer to was, Did it matter more than him?

'I am not used to cutting on things I've started.'

'No, I don't suppose you are anything less than single-minded. But it would have come to this anyway at the end of the year. It's always been understood we'd make our home here.'

Aileen folded her napkin into immaculate quarters and laid it on the table before her. 'Has it? I don't remember ever discussing it. I said I intended to help you in the business, but until today there was a business on both sides of the Atlantic. I never said I would live here all the time.'

'Then we are both mistaken.'

She rose from the table, deftly and coolly and went to her room. They watched, afraid more of acquiescent silence than the marital storm that might have broken. Claire did not disagree with her husband. She said yes to everything and then did exactly what she wanted later on, pretending she had forgotten. Esme recognised the frigidity of her cousin's tone and it filled her all over again with foreboding and the helpless despair of the child who cannot make grown-up people agree. Maurice caught her eye and by the power of his look conveyed to her that she should go to her cousin. 'Shall I?' she muttered dubiously, rising, and he nodded.

A dozen steps from the table, she looked over her shoulder and found him at her elbow, and they walked down the back corridor together for some way. The sun had come out at last and filled the inner court. It seemed a stupid morning to argue and fall out.

'Make him go back,' he said and, when she looked inquiringly to see if this really was his priority, added, 'or make her stay.'

'Make is outside my competence.' Why me? she thought. Why not him, why not Rejean's mother, why don't they all speak to Aileen directly? Why do it through an interpreter? 'But I'll try.' Did he ask her as a test of her involvement? She had fleeting glimpses of a suspicion in him that she was more the husband's than the cousin's friend; when Rejean insisted on flying over this time; when they spent two hours talking in the study late at night and he had little more than two minutes' dialogue with Aileen; when the wife paraded for a stranger to arouse jealousy; the way he always said, Have you heard from Rejean? – not from Aileen; all these and many more instances came to mind. They puzzled and hurt her by their obviousness. Was she to choose between them in friendship, or was she not to befriend the man at all and so drive him out from the compatibility with wife, father, companion? No, she would not do that. She felt the way an accused witch must have done put to the mediaeval water test – if they remained apart she failed and she was guilty of not trying because she wanted him here, if he went back it was because she had too much influence over him and so she succeeded and was guilty – sink or swim, she was a witch. 'I will try, but I am powerless to do anything but listen.'

He did an unusual thing for Maurice. He patted her shoulder. 'The marriage first. Careers must come second.' And he went back to the table.

He had waited patiently for a man who did not normally cogitate. He decided first and then made circumstances conspire to ensure his decision was the right one. He had to hand it to Rejean for upstaging him like this, so he resumed his place half angry and half admiring. 'And what exactly do you plan to do while you are here?'

Now this was not as wily a question as Maurice hoped. He thought his empire was as impregnable as Frontenac or Castle Rock, so that the young man would find no foothold in it. But Rejean had been doing his homework in quiet hours in the office. The business was under-capitalised, he told his father. They were holding on to far too large a proportion of the shares. They were too diffuse with sub-offices here and there. He proposed to be overseer of the regional offices. Maurice would still have absolute sway in the Montreal complex. Investment, trading, manufacture would still come under his aegis, but Rejean proposed an itinerant schedule for himself, which would suit his habits well and also keep him out of too close contact with his father. He could prove diagrammatically that there was a flaw in the management structure of the business, too many delegated responsibilities with

251

managers here and there and not enough integration. He could administer the provincial offices and pull the thing together.

Maurice was dumbfounded, but hid it well. 'Ah, so. That's what you think is wrong.'

'Not wrong. Just improveable.'

His common sense told him there was truth in these observations, so much truth that he hesitated to probe further in case his son had figures memorised to back him up. He did not care to lose face in front of his wife. Damn that year in Economics at Laval. He could not gainsay him so he tried a different front. 'And what about the office in Edinburgh?'

'I've always said it was good real estate and bad business.' Reading into the books, he was convinced that it had always been a money loser. He had been farmed out to pasture. Well, never again. 'Put it up for sale. Give it to Mr Scott to put on the market.'

'Have you been talking to the accountant?'

'No, I haven't, but if he's been saying the same thing I stand corroborated.'

Maurice was irritated that he had let himself in for that one. He would have to give in with a bad grace or submit to further humiliation. He looked down the table at his son who appeared composed, in charge of all his faculties, and wondered how calculated his timing had been. He had been determined to come back at this time but had not expected Aileen to accompany him. Had he intended to leave her all along? He glanced over his head, through the inner yard and out at the other side, hoping Esme was doing better than himself. What was he to make of it? This was not characteristic behaviour for Rejean. Who had put some backbone into him? *Was* she the undeclared partner in his plans?

'And you actually think you're going to come back here to live as in your bachelor days?'

'Maurice,' his wife interjected. 'Assez. Ça suffit.'

Claire was deeply unhappy. Listening to them wrangle, she realised they had always wrangled and could not understand why her affection could not bond them. They had jostled for position since Rejean could run, because in a very little time he could outpace his father who turned, by necessity, into coach and onlooker. His prowess at all games and sports should have been a mutual interest; did it matter who was better if they enjoyed playing them together? Slamming his tackle back into a boat, when with all conditions equal Rejean even caught more fish, his father obviously thought so, and reverted to the sports his son had no interest in. Though calling them the sedentary ones did not ease relations. Maurice had a way of picking up a book Rejean was reading as though it were a pernicious form of self-indulgence, a kind of mental onanism of which he could not approve and really did not want to know the details, but at the same time infer he was paying for all this education, so Rejean had better come up with a respectable degree. The change from economics to ecology was too much to bear. He could condone the useful; the theoretical was profligacy. He washed his hands of him.

Seeing both sides in turn, Claire was immobilised. She could not decide who was right and who was wrong. That would be like deciding which was better, her right or her left hand. She happened to need both, for one was hardly functional without the other and to choose between them was to throw out her own balance. So she sat mute, and weak according to some, until she heard that note of cruelty enter and then appealed in the language of their courtship and to them of emotion, and he desisted at once.

Aileen moved about the bedroom crisply, opening drawers and selecting items in order of creasing. The crushable would not go in till the last minute, the next morning. 'I seem to have twice what I came with. I suppose I could use one of Rejean's cases since he won't be needing them.' She paused in her perambulations. 'Did he send you?'

Esme sat in the light uncurling. 'No. Maurice did.'

'And I've to stay, have I, and do what they want?'

'I came to see if you were all right.'

'Of course I am.'

Esme tried to focus the dilemma in terms Aileen would respond to. An emotional outburst would not win her. 'Remember there's no choice for Rejean and there is for you.'

'Why is there no choice for him?'

'Because he's so unhappy living in Edinburgh.'

'It was his decision.'

'But sometimes we cannot endure what we decide.'

'I'm sorry, but I don't see that. You stick by what you decide whatever. You can't throw things over on a whim and walk out.'

Esme felt this remark was sharpened for her too. 'I don't think the work he has put into this plan is a whim.'

'No? Well I may find it strange he never consulted me,' and then she knew she was condemned out of her own mouth for she had done the same. She sat down at last, and weighed the imponderables. 'No, I know he feels frustrated and idle. It wears him out more than working hard and I'm almost relieved he's going to do what he wants instead of being squeezed into what other people want. But that goes for me too, you know.'

'But you detest shorthand and everything about this course.'

Aileen smiled in spite of herself to recall those hair-tearing evenings over essays at the big house. That might be cause enough to abandon it in Esme's view, but not in hers. 'You would despise a man for giving up because he didn't enjoy his studies, but not a woman. You finish what you start. It's that simple. I agree it's the most annihilatingly boring and maddening thing I've ever done, but I will master it in the end. It can't defeat me.' She read scepticism in Esme's face. 'I can't duck out on a challenge. You know that much about me. I can't explain it to them.' She threw a look towards the kitchen. 'The Simards think I'm a wife. Full stop. They're probably thinking it's high time I produced a grandchild and heir to the empire. But I'm not in such a hurry. That's their ambition, not mine. And we never did think of ourselves as somebody else's property, did we, spoken for since birth. I'll make my own decisions.' Esme heard the teaching of Alexis in this. Would he approve of their application?

'And there's something else. That's not the whole of it.' They looked across at each other and between their eyes passed the spectre of Alexis pacing the boards at Inchcombe. She turned to her compatriot, her fellow friend. 'What do you think, incidentally?'

'I can't say,' replied Esme, challenged. 'I honestly can't give an opinion.'

'Funny. That's exactly what he'd say.' Perhaps Esme was the wrong person to consult. She had gone native herself. If Aileen looked on the old and new worlds as a scale, her staying would put all the weight on this side, and that was an imbalance that offended her sense of justice. They owed something to the old country, she and Esme. 'I couldn't leave him without saying goodbye.'

Ah, the barb! Had anything been said about the terms of her defection? Esme grew agitated wondering if now was the moment to speak. What if she said, You stay here and I'll fly back on your ticket? The precipitate action thrilled her. Alexis would come to meet the plane at Prestwick on Sunday, expecting Aileen and Rejean, and she was flooded with a recollection so close up of his arms, leaning into that husk and being folded out of sight. But to think that in Aileen's presence was almost an indecency, she felt. What words were there to say to his daughter, her cousin and her friend, to indicate what she intended? She could not steel herself to deliver a second blow today. Would it make any difference to Aileen's decision and, if not, was there any point in broaching it and adding to the fraught parting between the married couples a further layer of doubt and agony about the unmarried one? Let her not forget, she had to serve out her own term. And Aileen was going back to finish out the year. A year – alone – what courage!

'We mustn't act in haste,' Aileen concluded. 'There is no sense in doing now what can't be undone by a later decision. If he is resolved to stay, fine, I can't actually stop him but I have my obligations too. I finish early in June and we can review things then. But go back I must.'

For all her sangfroid, Aileen was shaken. She knew things were not going well between them, but this division needed explanation when she got back and what explanation was there? She heard herself making light of it, We agreed it would be best. Maurice has so much on his plate . . . but neither Alexis nor Mairi would be taken in. Who could know more about alienation than they did? This struggle over position and territory, the pecking order of squabbling sparrows, was the most obvious clash. But to her parents all the other clashes would be manifest, right down to the most basic of human failures, the inability to compromise between me and you. I will not lose myself in you was the sum of marital hostility, and even so forewarned by experience and example she would not lose herself in him or he in her.

On Sunday morning Mabon Caulderwood was fresher than on their first meeting, and fresher than Esme. There was little sleep to be had on taut nerves and, though she gave him a shallow explanation of events, he grasped at once what it meant and was silent on the subject.

He was out of uniform, which he carried in a bag over his arm and placed with care along the rear seat. He took over the driving seat without a word. He knew the car by instinct, but even this facility she grudged him saying to herself, He's a pilot, isn't he? What's a car in comparison with an aeroplane? His hand flew to the controls with an assurance that far outstripped hers. His training meant he had only to glance at the fascia to understand it. He drove at almost twice her normal speed and with such confidence on the road that she did feel utterly safe and could relax a little more in his presence.

She prepared herself for tedium, and instead found she was entertained. She was not fascinated by what he had to tell her about the places they passed through, for it smacked too much of the guide book or the Geography lesson, but she was entertained all the same and adjusted her opinion of him. He knew his stuff.

In the position of passenger, she was forced into addressing the profile, a more arresting view than the features which met her straight on. He was even darker than she was, as near to being black haired as Caucasians can be, and had a face which belonged to statuary. Not of the classical type, but a modern piece cast in bronze or a terracotta bust. There was strong colour and substantial vigour in the face, as though a sculptor had taken a chisel to stone and left odd projectiles and roughness, or a potter stuck on patches of clay which he left unsmoothed. The cheek bones protruded and yet she couldn't say he was lean faced, and the ridge of the eyebrow, jaw and nose were similarly prominent. It was a stronger face in daylight than she remembered, not at all effete or self-conscious.

But it was intriguing to her sideways glance because of a quirk of physiology. His mouth closed was wholly normal, but when he opened it to speak the upper lip moving away from the lower revealed two exceptionally long canine teeth. In repose he was – attractive, she gave out the word to herself as though it were a slur; in speech he was wolverine. She waited for the second of transition, mesmerised, and after half an hour in his close company felt it was the menace of the second that gave character to the first.

Without those teeth he would have been conventionally good looking. With them he had the potential for ugliness, the brutal disregard for aesthetics, and that was much more watchable.

'Rejean tells me you're looking for a relative in the Saguenay.'

'Yes. It's almost as unusual a reason as my father's for going there.'

'What was that?'

'To lose his.'

Esme deprecated the likelihood of self-analysis with him, as she had done with Rejean. She erroneously thought them the same type at the outset, simple, outdoor men who were not liable to develop, reliable characters who would not disappoint even if they failed marginally to excite. No, he was not introspective, but he had common sense enough to see that was her appraisal of him. It irritated him to be summed up and despatched as dull, especially by the first unusual woman to come into the Saguenay in his time. To make any impression he must move onto his own ground and not follow her into abstraction where he knew with infallible reflex that he would be trounced, and he was not used to being put down by women.

'What progress so far?'

The question came like the report from a gun. Was this how he was accustomed to addressing the men under his command? Esme felt its reverberation all round the car and it had its effect. She came out of theory and into fact. 'I telephoned the five people called Rosowicz in the region but they were no wiser than I, and said they had no relative by the name of Stefan who wasn't listed in the telephone directory. Everyone seems to have a telephone here. It's as good as an electoral register, though I took the precaution of consulting that too.'

'Why go on?'

'I think he may well have changed his name. He didn't want to be traced by my mother, I suspect, and I have a feeling he may have remarried, or committed bigamy if you like plain speaking, or simply be living with another woman and want to be anonymous for that reason.' She explained about the packet of photographs and how it proved he or a family member or an executor had been in the Saguenay something like a year before. The trail was not entirely cold.

He assimilated the facts with speed, and with some ingenuity followed the puzzle through its maze of blocks and bars and saw an outlet. 'What was his profession?' he asked, since that was invariably for him the starting point.

'His family were tailors. I think he was.'

'Chicoutimi has a large textile industry. Do you have a photograph of him?'

'Not recent. I think I would know him if I saw him.'

And, like her, he began to adjust his opinion. He had thought her practical and go-ahead. But she was also a dreamer and the logical question of why bother, if he was only a tailor after all, not a doctor or a judge, would meet with hedging answers and half truths, so he did not put it.

'I went to see your Chaplain a while ago, Bob Findlay.'

'Oh, did you? That was enterprising. You went to the Base? What did you think of it?'

'Well, I couldn't get into the security areas, could I, but the married quarters looked like a bad dream. I bet everyone knows when you sneeze there.'

'And some.' An isolated laugh shook the car which bounced along the highway to the bypass round Quebec City. 'How long do you plan on staying?'

'I have signed a contract for a term. The headmaster would like me to stay for a year, but I won't commit myself.'

'Oh, you ought to stay over the winter. That's the best time here. We have a Carnival week in February with winter sports competitions between the sections. Fiercely contested too. And they build ice palaces on the compound. Have you seen an ice palace? Then you shouldn't miss that. First you make an igloo-type building with blocks of snow and then you hose it down. Overnight it freezes and the water turns to glass.'

'It's that cold?'

'Oh, cold! People make so much of that. It's nothing. The roads are kept clear with snow ploughs. You lose a few days' flying, that's all.'

Before they turned into the long dreariness of the Laurentides Park, he suggested they ate something at a wayside restaurant he knew. After the stop, she found herself almost drowsy, and involuntarily closed her eyes, in part against the soul-destroying monotony of the park.

'Do you want to sleep?' he asked at once. 'I can move my things and you lie down in the back. You look worn out.'

She shook her head. She didn't trust herself to be wholly unconscious in his presence.

'Well then, put my coat around you. It's heavier than yours. You doze off if you want. The road is easy.' He stopped the car by the ditch that formed the road verge and unpacked his greatcoat, an impressive garment of wool broadcloth made into flapping skirts and double lapels. There was a moment's embarrassment as he went to put the coat round her and, seeing her shrink by a fraction from contact with him, drew away again. She adjusted it herself, ashamed at her recoil.

In fact she fell fast asleep in spite of her resolution, and woke better tempered. Looking out she saw they had reached the roundabout south of Chicoutimi where the road divides right to Bagotville and left to Arvida. 'I'll get out now and hitch a lift to the Base. No, there's no call for you to go out of your way. A friend will be sure to come along any time. The servicemen are always passing. If I could have my coat back.'

She shivered as she stood up without it to change to the driver's seat and at the open door he made the funny bow she had seen before.

'I'm grateful for the lift and your company. Thank you.'

She watched him from the insular warmth of the car, striding out with his kit slung over his back.

Within two minutes, a car slewed to a halt beside him and without a backward glance or a wave he disappeared inside.

25

Half an hour after Esme had dropped him off at the Chicoutimi roundabout, Mabon Caulderwood crossed the road from the sentry box at the Bagotville Base and headed towards the densely wooded area west of the married quarters which lay opposite the gates. It was a walk of only a mile or so, but he undertook it reluctantly, side-stepping the deep ruts made in the ground by trampling and the wheels of a jeep going to and fro over the terrain.

Ahead of him, he could see two other officers walking tentatively between the trees, scanning the churned-up earth as warily as he did himself. They were maybe a quarter of a mile distant and had not observed him, so he hung back, in no hurry to catch them up but equally determined to accomplish what he had set out to do. He waited, hoping they would take a detour and leave the site for him to inspect alone.

The first of these men was Bob Findlay, accurately described by Esme as six foot four, rangy and disjointed and very likeable. Few people came to know the Chaplain better than that. The other was Charles Cartier who was the second in command at the Base. Mabon guessed that like himself he had come back that afternoon from Montreal where he kept a house and where his two sons were being educated at boarding school. Apart from being among the most distinctive personnel stationed at Bagotville at that time, these men had nothing in common, so Mabon knew it was from duty rather than inclination that they strode out in each other's company.

Charles Cartier was distinctive because he was the most successful officer of his generation. His pedigree had been impeccable for promotion. He scaled the ascending echelons of seniority in such record time that Mabon and his rank of junior officers were left, if they were forced to admit it, dizzy with envy. Some of this success was due to his own ability, sure; the personality no one found offensive and the meticulous exercise of each new role assigned to him. Mabon respected that. But he had too the luck of birth. He was descended on his mother's side from a family of Ottawa-based politicians (an uncle had been Minister of Defence in an undistinguished administration). He had been educated at the foremost private school in Canada and subsequently at McGill University where he took a degree in Physics, developed after joining the service as a pilot, into an expertise in Nuclear Physics. On top of all this, however, it was his bilinguality that set him apart. Few English-born Canadians mastered their sibling tongue as completely as most French born. Mabon for example had no French. So to have a foot in both camps, to be thoroughly French without going all the way to separatism, was an asset when it came to negotiating in the delicate border areas of national defence. He was highly prized in the internal diplomacy of the defence department, where he was privy to the highest policy-making committees on nuclear tactics, somewhat over the head of the Commanding Officer who was a militarist first and last. It was acknowledged he was biding his time at Bagotville, putting in eighteen months in an operational post before being detailed to a major area.

He walked out now because the CO had informed him by telephone that there had been an accident at the Base. Two airmen, one of them a trainee pilot, had tried to bring their Voodoo down at night. The circumstances of the crash were not generally known as yet but they had overshot the runway, according to the control tower, turned to try for another touchdown but by this time had lost altitude and dropped speed dramatically. When this happened in the Voodoo, the plane was notorious for flipping up its nose, and the pilot, although he was experienced with the craft and the position, lost control and ploughed into the wood, killing both crew members outright.

The Chaplain had been backwards and forwards several times and led them to the spot. All round the point of impact, in heavy growth of pine and spruce, the debris of the crash was scattered. The fuselage was broken in two and every extraneous part of the plane – nose, flaps, wings, tailplane and wheels lowered for the abortive landing – had been whipped off and pulverised by the force of the collision. They were reduced to splinters and fragments no bigger than cigarette cartons strewn on the ground while the internal apparatus of the machine hung in strips from the branches of the trees. These too suffered damage, some trees being denuded below the crown, while smaller specimens were felled or stripped of foliage on the side that faced the aircraft.

To these men, imbued with absolute belief in the power of the mechanical birds, it was a holocaust of destruction. It undermined faith. Cartier, who had seen fewer operational actions than the Chaplain, could hardly disguise his nausea. He would not tread further into the debris.

'The medics have been in. They were over as soon as it happened

261

and then at first light to clean up.'

Mabon did not advance towards them but stayed downwind. The acuteness of his hearing, like an Indian scout's, meant the words were received by his ear with syllabic precision. He lost nothing.

Charles Cartier had to ask. 'Was there no hope?'

The Chaplain looked at him sceptically. 'What chance was there when the plane broke up like this? There wasn't enough left to do an autopsy.' The other walked on and Bob addressed his back. 'Has the flight recorder given any clues?'

Cartier turned and acknowledged one of the sentries who guarded the wreckage but was awkward about saluting. He wished he had had time to change into uniform and appear correctly. 'The CO was listening when I came away. He's been on the telephone to Ottawa ever since it happened. It's bad publicity for the Base especially when we have such a fine safety record.' He caught sight of the Chaplain's inimical expression. 'No, don't get me wrong. This is bad all round. Wilkes was a married man, wasn't he? And how old was the Flying Officer? Twenty-one? Imagine being a CO and calling the next of kin. It's not even war. It wasn't an exercise or bad weather, just a routine training flight. Are the funerals going to be here?'

All three men thought how difficult such funerals were, however frequent, but the Chaplain shook his head.

'That's as well. This is going to need very discreet handling.'

The Chaplain was sure these were the right things to say but still wished the other wouldn't say them. 'It won't do morale any good.'

'Oh, I don't know about that. The men often rally after a crisis like this.'

Bob crossed his arms and put his head down. He couldn't stick the way Cartier played at toy soldiers. He sat at his desk and juggled nuclear fall-out statistics, the range of inter-ballistic missiles and, in the meantime, overlooked the fact that men died. He'd been out in the middle of the night himself to help cut down empty flying harness from the branches and could have choked with futility about the young men wasted, although he'd seen it all a dozen times before. He'd learned to cope with everything except officialese.

Mabon shared this annoyance with the administrative mind of

the man who sat inside a shelter and told the others how to do it, documenting only. He could no longer conceal his presence, or his curiosity, and moved forward to announce himself.

The others were startled to hear someone else approaching through the undergrowth and turned round to see Flight Lieutenant Caulderwood walk into the arena. He stopped to talk to the sentry before he came towards them and involuntarily their stance changed as they prepared to greet him. That change, which would have been obvious to any outsider, was prompted partly by professional distinctions. He was junior in age and rank to either of them. The older men were never wholly familiar with each other, but they used their Christian names from time to time and knew that because of their exceptional status they were automatically off the record and could relax. The Chaplain of course had everyone's confidence, but not Mabon's. He sought no confessor. They adjusted their attitudes to him as a colleague, but also as an individual, though why they could not say. They knew him to be exceptionally competitive, which meant he was the best pilot at Bagotville, they knew his popularity with his own and junior ranks outstripped theirs, they knew he had a remarkable success with women although he was never caught in an indiscretion and played away from Base which was all that could be asked of any officer; these were the prestigious assets. So why did they cold shoulder him? They did not know either, unless it was jealousy.

'I just arrived back, sir. Trenton.' Mabon addressed the name to Cartier, knowing this would communicate that he had been on service duties, not pleasurable ones.

The senior officer was not pleased to find the junior treading so closely on his heels. 'John Wilkes wasn't in your squadron, was he?' This was almost a challenge to Caulderwood's right to come there in the first place, for it was reducing him to the level of a sightseer.

'We went through training school together and we served in the same squadron at Moose Jaw. I was his best man.' The Chaplain was more informed and would not have asked to see his pass. They were longstanding friends, Wilkes and Caulderwood, and he had come to the spot because he could not believe in the fatality, not to gape. They went over the same facts, diluted for repetition in the Mess. The other officers must be craving news and they might as well let Caulderwood disperse it. But Mabon was a flier and knew more about the Voodoo than they or any flight recorder could tell him.

He studied the lie of the land, the direction of the flight path in relation to the runway and said, 'Of course, John could have saved himself if he had used the ejection seat.'

'There wasn't time,' objected Cartier.

'Oh, there was time. I reckon he ran out of fuel because he was a good enough pilot to climb if he got the boost. But there's been no fire which you would expect with this impact, and I think that shows he was empty. He must have known it was touch and go when he failed to land first time and he could have ejected then. But,' he turned round like the aircraft to face north-north-west, 'that would have left the Voodoo an undirected missile, heading towards the married quarters. He stayed with it.'

Neither of the others had worked out this factor and yet it was so reasonable they did not try to contradict him. 'If I could ask you to keep that to yourself until we have confirmation.'

'Of course, sir.'

Cartier excused himself and hurried back through the woods, ready to repeat this aspect to the CO as his own deduction, and concurrently thinking through the list of those he would have to contact in the next twenty-four hours.

Bob Findlay too headed towards the road, but Mabon turned and went with him, although the Chaplain strode out as rapidly as he could in the hope of outdistancing his unchosen companion.

'I drove up with someone who knows you, Esme Rosowicz,' said Mabon. Meeting with no response, he confirmed. 'I think she said she came to see you. Or don't you remember?'

The other stopped. His brows did not lift. 'I remember.'

'I met her at the house of a Montreal friend.'

'Simard fils,' supplied the Chaplain, on whom no detail of Saguenay life was wasted. He was displeased. The habit of secrecy extended to his private life and he neither divulged his acquaintances nor name-dropped for effect. There was something excessively disagreeable to him about the thought of these two people together, of the way in which the pilot introduced her name almost as a boast. He didn't want to know the way the world was going, and shook his junior off at the junction of the roads to the Base and the quarters without another word.

Mabon's reception was very different in the Mess where he lived in, together with about fifty other bachelors. Perhaps half of these were in the bar when he arrived, walking past with his baggage on his way to his room. His name ran like a refrain down the passage as men hailed him, and in a moment his own navigator, Tom Westwater, found him and they walked back together.

'Have you heard?'

'Yes, I've just been over there.'

'Did they let you in? We were all told to stay clear.'

'I hadn't heard that order. I only got back half an hour ago. Demoine picked me up at Chicoutimi roundabout and he told me. Anyway, I knew the MP and he didn't challenge me. Cartier and the padre were there.'

'Oh, what do they know? Have they found the flight recorder?'

And to the largish group which had by now collected, like atoms round a nucleus, Mabon repeated the information he had gleaned from his superior officers, together with his first-hand impressions of the site, the broken craft, the strewn litter of the crash, knowing he was more than a reporter. Like him, they would not believe it till they had seen it for themselves. He omitted the supposition he had made about the nature of the pilot's sacrifice. Men drifted over to where he sat and asked a question or two in supplement and drifted away again to distribute whatever answer he had given verbatim.

The death of their colleague had an effect on the air crew that was a composite of the attitudes of Cartier and Findlay. They knew all about human wastage. They knew their skills were more specialised than the average doctor's; the best of them were as rare as brain surgeons. Years of costly training, years of experience, years of dedication went into the making of a fighter pilot. He was the century's most expensive man. They knew their own value and felt in the circumstances loss of life was pointless, though this expressed itself no more forcibly than the repeated phrase, It's a bad deal. It's a bad break. It was a statistical fact that by the age of forty, even in peacetime conditions when chances of survival were good, half of a pilot's age group would have been killed. Their families collected as many insurance policies as pensions. At the same time danger was their most intimate companion. They liked it and doing daily battle with the elements, the machine and their own fallibility was one of the reasons they had chosen their rarefied way of life. So they were not sunk in gloom, as the Chaplain had predicted. The adrenalin of imminent death pumped through them and they were not fearful. They did rally, if only to outwit the laws of selection, and survive themselves against the calculated, actuarial odds.

Mabon listened and thought of the man who had told a wicked story well, and who would be missed. 'Has anyone from his squadron been over to see Mary Wilkes?' he asked. No one knew. The question was repeated all round the room.

'The CO went over last night,' someone said.

'But from the squadron?' He stood up.

'No, I don't think so,' Tom answered. They looked round. The Squadron Leader of 425 was away for the weekend and probably didn't know about the crash.

'Then, I think I'll go over there. It's Chicoutimi north, isn't it?' he asked Tom. 'Yes, I remember where it is now. Over the bridge, second left, up the hill.'

Tom nodded. 'Why don't you wait till after supper? It's nearly time.'

'No. Get the blonde stewardess to make me up a few sandwiches, and put them in my room. Tell her it's for me.'

He left the Mess and found the black sedan which he kept parked to the rear of the complex. As he drove out of the gates, he knew that behind him in the other corner of the bar some wit would make the audible quip, It's kind of early for his condolences, isn't it? and another reply, D'you reckon he'll send the CO or Cartier a memo to say he's been? And they would laugh.

He regretted that in the middle of the admiration for him as an officer and a pilot, for his function, there was this malice in some quarters against him as a man. He couldn't say any more than Cartier or Findlay or the two air crew who had made these predictable sallies behind his back why it was. He was careful not to give cause by dropping slanderous comments that were invariably circulated back to the subject. Esme Rosowicz had been right in that reading of their claustrophobic intimacy. A hundred officers and their families knew everything that could be repeated about each other, and a good deal that couldn't.

Still, he could not understand it. He was, within his code, strictly honourable. He gave every man his due and twice if he was senior. He did not boast. His question about Esme to the padre was made in a spirit of friendly inquiry, but of course was misinterpreted. He did not drink. He did not smash up furniture or cars or aeroplanes. He did not sleep with fellow officers' wives. So why did they gripe about him? Just because he did none of these things, but carried about with him that aura of insularity from their bad opinion, which they longed to perforate. He was simply better than them on all counts. To most, he was a hero to emulate, and to a few a rival and a measure of their own limitation, whose stature they must reduce if they could thereby increase their own. Devotion or hatred. He never provoked indifference.

And Bob Findlay, why was he unusual?

He looked odd. He was too big and spare and uniform sat absurdly on him, tailored elegance on a scarecrow. Going back alone to his quarter, three houses up from the CO, he loped over the gardens as ungainly as a giraffe. When he stopped to speak to a couple of teenage boys who were zigzagging down the road on bicycles, he could not bend in half but dropped his neck forward to address them from a height. He questioned them closely about their wonderful machines, the flags and badges they sported on the handlebars and frame, and all parted company well satisfied. He did not speak to his flock about God unsolicited, his, theirs or anyone else's. This was regarded as a point of supreme tact. The boys knew they would not be press-ganged into youth clubs, or scouts, Sunday service or what have you but could remain happy heathens and he would still go on talking to them about their fishing tackle or their tennis racquets or whatever was seasonal.

Bob Findlay was not in close enough communion with the Almighty to press his acquaintance on anybody else. God would have to make his own introductions. And though the Chaplain was not diffident about the existence of his father in heaven, he did not conclusively know by what name to call him. He had undergone a change of religious conviction when he was young, a fact he did not publicise because religious converts are almost as heinous as political turncoats. He had been born in the plains of Alberta, adjacent to the American frontier and in a town where there was a fair-sized population of Mormons, but no Mormon school. He had gone to the state institution and then a high school in Lethbridge which was the nearest large town, and in both of these he had taken in his share of Bible reading, so that the two doctrines of Christ and Joseph Smith co-existed in him. His great grandfather had been one of the early band of pioneers who settled in Utah and saw the miraculous flock of seagulls save the crop from the ravages of the cricket. He was able to trace with linear clarity through the records kept in Salt Lake City that his forebears had come from Cupar in Fife, Scotland. When he was required to go, as all young Mormons were at eighteen, as a missionary to the unconverted European, he was able to spend his year in Fife, based in the dreary, washed-out town of Kirkcaldy.

But his mission failed. Some of the canny Scots admitted him and his brother in Christ, a few argued on the doorstep, many more shut the door promptly in his face. But the informed handful he came across in his time there revealed two facts which it was hard to argue away. The Bible was better poetry than Joseph Smith's garbled testimony which began to read more and more like the plagiarised *Hamlet*, rendered into a Germanic version with Rosencrantz and Guildenstern as the heroes. And bad poetry was sufficient reason for his apostasy. He was certain his creator spoke in divine tongues.

The second was that his faith contained at its centre an inequality in its treatment of women and black peoples. They could not come to the inner sanctuary of the temple, and he was bemused by the tortuous logic employed to validate this fact. It was through the agency of their husband, or the moral quality of father, brother or male supporter that a woman was vouchsafed access to heaven. Did that imply that she had no direct rights to a share in the hereafter? If so, this did not strike him as egalitarian or consistent with true Christianity, and the Church of Scotland minister who first trounced him on that score turned missionary instead. In his maturity, he realised that the major religions were sexist and racist, if not explicitly in their doctrine implicitly in their practice. Could he envisage a black Pope, a woman Archbishop of Canterbury or Chief Rabbi? The Western world had a few centuries of evolution to go through before that was feasible.

Moreover, his wanderings turned him into a wanderer. The shifting career of a navigator pleased him. It was an excuse not to settle down as a tenant farmer and marry the girl next door. That would have shown up too clearly his disaffection from the Latter Day Saints. He admired the way of life they inculcated, and came to the conclusion that the best of religion was the society it engendered. Strong religious communities did not abuse or exploit their young, allow of wholesale adultery and divorce, or abandon their old to infirmity or neglect. But he couldn't stay inside for the comforts and ignore the creed. He would have to take his tithe elsewhere. He left the sect and merged in the free flow of Christian philosophy, a humanitarian more than anything.

Habits died hard of course. Though he served coffee and tea and liquor in his house, he could not drink them himself and invented a quite fictitious liver complaint to explain the abstinence. For all that he felt at home nowhere in particular and could not be pinpointed on an issue, theological or military, he was well respected by the air crew. It wasn't an easy job in peacetime. Operational bases like Bagotville were the best because there was some cohesion and purpose about them. He was needed to marry and baptise in abundance when the remaining churches were in the diocese of Rome. He had become attached to its bleakness, fond of its people. He had asked for a second tour of duty, and in that too he was unusual.

26

He telephoned and she accepted.

Afterwards she was puzzled by the shattered resolution, and went to buy a dress.

Chicoutimi, for all its remoteness, regarded itself as a very modish city, importing the latest vogue as far north as it was likely to be worn in the hemisphere. As she went from shop to shop down the main street and up the hill again, she was baffled by the choice and did not know where to begin.

Two things had happened since she dropped him off at the

roundabout on Sunday. The first was one break when she was sitting by herself in the staff room. She always sat by herself, because she found the endless recital of wrongdoings and petty misdemeanours more wearing than the acts themselves. The classroom was a sanctuary in comparison. At lunchtime she could escape home, eat quietly, wash, lie down if she wanted. It took all her strength to keep to a routine, and the drawback of teaching was it couldn't be carried out in spurts like study, and reflect her output of energy. She could easily have worked eight hours a day, at her discretion, putting in a couple of hours before midnight and the rest before noon with the best of the day to herself. Working from nine to four ran counter to her nervous system, and then she had to find another burst of enthusiasm for the hundred books she ought to decipher. It whittled away the *joie de vivre*. She needed time alone to revive.

So one coffee break early in the week she sat semi-conscious in a corner when her attention was arrested by a familiar name. Any other name but Mabon she might have overlooked, but it caught her ear down all the lanes of conversation and she fastened onto it, having no compunction about the innocent pastime of eaves-dropping.

'They say he puts in a hundred hours some weeks.'

'No, not flying. But I suppose he has to log it up. Montreal every other weekend. Some schedule.' It was a man who spoke to a woman. 'He's working towards his promotion to Squadron Leader of course.'

'He's young for a Squadron Leader, isn't he?'

'Oh, the way he's going, he'll be the youngest CO in the force. He's a demon for work.'

Then the bell rang and cut them off, but during the free lesson she had afterwards Esme had time to piece out the fragments of their dialogue. There had been admiration in her colleague's voice, and she echoed it. A hundred hours, Esme calculated by her new timescale, a hundred hours constituted at least two weeks of her daily existence, including the work at home. That is, for every week she lived, he lived two. Did he not sleep? Did he not rest or play? And yet he gave time to certain priorities. She realised, now that her mind was less occupied by antipathy, that a return flight from Montreal to Bagotville airport would have been faster than the alternative she offered. He had come with her as a deliberate policy, in contradiction of that speed that was essential to him. Why? She certainly had given no clues about favouring him. To know her, to help her? And then, having arrived, he had gone off on foot to circumvent her detour. Only chance had brought him another lift. She modified her impression of the courteous reprobate, too dashing by half. Maurice was right, there was some grit in his character that wasn't to be overlooked so easily.

And there was another thing. She had formulated the opinion early on, maybe even when he walked into the Simards' hallway and stood immaculately accoutred, cap-à-pie, that he would pay attention to her, make a pass at her the moment they were alone. Perhaps that was why she hadn't rushed to welcome him as a passenger, assuming he might get – fresh – and that was her explanation of the shrinking from his gesture of solicitude. He looked like a man who was used to being accorded greater liberties than hers. And then, when he behaved rather better than she had expected, rather better than herself, she was piqued and thought she was presumptuous. The man couldn't win. She was at a loose end, wasn't she? There was no social life here for an English girl apart from at the Base. He was a way into that. Wouldn't he have passed as an escort for six weeks? He might put her on the right path to finding out something conclusive in that time. He had the contacts, he knew the organisation, to establish whether Stefan existed and, if he did, where.

She looked at the racks of dresses and did not know what she wanted. She had had so little occasion to choose. Normally she bought at random, whatever took her fancy. That was why she bought so little. Not much did. Today, she was purchasing with an event in mind and felt she should conform to some standard. But what was the standard? Not hers. She abandoned all her preconceptions, and submitted to the dazzling choice. Colours she would not have worn in Edinburgh or Lochearn against their sober, chaste background enticed her here. Pale, pastel, impractical things sought out her eye. Gathers, ruffles, braids seduced and rippling folds, when normally she chose plain. She tried to marshal these conflicting attractions by an exercise of logic. The dress she selected must be serviceable, unobtrusive if she wished to wear it often – and she caught herself thinking he might ask her out again –

but sophisticated, even soignée. As she paraded in front of the mirrors of a downtown store, she saw herself with other eyes, and knew it was Mabon's approval she was seeking, rather than her own, and chose accordingly.

Rejean had telephoned one evening. 'You got back safely? Yes, I thought he would make it in record time. I had a call from Aileen. The flight was good. No hitches. Well, there's not much I can say, is there? I'm busy if nothing else. I'm sorting out a schedule for myself, making a report on the various sub-offices. Have you heard from Mabon, by the way? He called to thank Claire for dinner and I spoke to him. He wanted to know your number. Apparently you're too new to be in the book and they can't trace your name in the records. You'd better check yourself and see Bell telephone get it right. Anyway, you don't mind that I gave it to him? I felt I could hardly refuse to give it but thought I'd warn you first. No, I don't know what for. Would I recommend it? Why not? What else are you doing nights? I was thinking of coming up myself in the next few weeks but that can wait. Good luck. I'll be in touch.'

So when Mabon did call and asked her to a party at the Officers' Mess, his reception had been prepared and she found she put down the receiver smilingly. It was not good humour that made her smile, but his insolent self-assurance that she could not possibly say no.

When she laid the dress out on the bed, she had misgivings. Alexis had shown her a yard of handloom tweed and said its merit was partly its quality; the dyes, the threads had substance and because of that it had longevity. A lifetime could not wear it out. The wretched dress accused her with its flimsiness. It was tricky, badly finished on the inside, and she suspected that it would degenerate into shabbiness before long.

He came to pick her up. Civility prevailed over common sense which suggested she drive herself, instead of the double trip he would have to make. He made the right remarks, helped her on with her coat as though she were armless, guided her unerringly to the car door. She submitted so far, although it was a social code that made her out to be a simpleton.

The drive to the Base was the first time she had been out in the evening since she arrived. Sitting beside him in his car was an unnerving, motionless experience. The Simards had taken her to a drive-in movie in Montreal, waiting for nightfall for the show to begin, by which time she was too tired to notice or care what she watched. But the spectacle was the same. The countryside unrolled as though it were on the move and not the car or them. It was in a strip, like a film which could be seen with one eye or the other. Focus was the pair in synchronisation. There was a breathless air of suspense, waiting for the lights to dim, the scenario to loom on the screen.

The dark sky suppressed the contours of the terrain, a heavily glaciated landscape with low trees, soft undifferentiated fields without hedgerow or fence. The country rolled without drama, although the northern coast of the Saguenay was marked by a line of hills as definitely as the Forth, and there were mountain peaks beyond. Space was limitless. There were minutes of silence between houses. Each homestead sprawled, and it did not matter. The encroaching forest could always be made to recede a mile or two to allow for the negligent horizontal development.

The perimeter of the Base was well defined with wire and fenceposts, and the gates through which they drove by courtesy of the official pass in Mabon's windscreen were flanked by two armed guards. Inside, the station was a warren of assorted buildings, mostly prefabricated shelters reminiscent of wartime constructions, cylindrical corrugated shapes against the lowering sky and hangars that faced the aerodrome where, even on so still an evening, winds congregated in the yellow wind-sock and pointed to a prevailing north-westerly. Bleak it was and unbeautiful, but standing on the edge of the unknown Esme experienced the thrill of activity, of dawn operations and encounters in cloudy skies, of men and machinery outside her range.

But when he took her arm across the compound she had to say, 'Please would you not do that?'

'Do what?'

'Hold my elbow.'

'Why?'

'Because . . .' Because I can't bear to be touched casually? 'Because I can manage quite well by myself.'

He dropped his hand and moved away.

Once inside, he introduced her to the CO and his wife but

almost immediately they were divided. Mabon was re-routed by friends while Esme recognised the Chaplain as they crossed.

'How are you?'

'Better for being away a week.'

'Yes, I met Mabon the day you drove back.'

Their eyes lifted and they read each other's thoughts. She smiled at the smallness of their world in spite of its acreage. 'That wasn't prying. I meant I knew you'd been in Montreal.'

She turned her back on Mabon and the room and its throng. The music at the end was too loud for conversation and so they drew to one side.

'Actually I've been meaning to phone you but couldn't get hold of your number. I should have taken a note of it. You haven't had any luck?'

'No. All blanks.'

'Well, I was out visiting a family recently who have Polish connections. They tell me – this is an odd topic for a party. Do you mind?'

'The odder the better. Go on.'

'They tell me there's an old man who lives in Mistassini and he knows everything about the Poles in the area. He's not your father,' he hastened to assure her, 'he's been there since the First World War I gather, and he's too old. He's almost a hermit but he keeps in touch with expatriates and goes to a Polish reunion in Montreal once a year. That kind of thing.'

'How far is it?'

'About two hours' drive. He's called "Le Polonais" and "Polski" by the English. These people didn't know his real name. They're not Polish themselves. But he's a celebrity. You won't have any difficulty finding him.'

Her eye drifted across the room as he talked, asking her who she had seen, how she was settling in the area.

The Mess was a typical club room, to be found inside every golf club or cricket pavilion, a male enclave with few concessions to the feminine. The floor was spartan, the tables and chairs functional, the curtains chosen because they would not need too many trips to the dry cleaner's. The bar was busy, curving between two doors so that the comings and goings at either end multiplied its business. She had heard somewhere that the air crew drank heavily, for some technical reason to do with depressurisation, and it was true the bar was the most lively and warm spot in the place. The noise it generated drowned out the musical trio at the other end. But, for all that pints flowed and glasses filled and emptied all evening, there was no loss of demeanour. Of course the presence of the CO was an inhibition. They were not fully off duty in his presence and every man feared that a social indiscretion would be remembered against him in his career.

'Tell me who they are,' she said to Bob.

'All of them?'

'Only some. Who's the man who is talking to Mabon?'

'That's Charles Cartier. He's our once and future king. And his wife Yvonne.'

'Ah yes, a Guinevere. Is this Camelot, then?'

'Could be.' He smiled at the reference hauled back from long ago. 'Arthur and Lancelot would do quite well. They're great rivals, though they don't acknowledge it themselves. Cartier's our desk man – this is all treasonable, by the way – and Mabon's the operations man.'

'Thinkers and doers?'

'If you like. They've got their followers who keep things lively.'

'But they seem very amicable.'

'Oh yes,' he dragged out. 'Everybody's good buddies.' After some moments, he said, 'I'm sorry, I never got the coordination right for dancing. Would you like me to take you over to Mabon?'

'No, he can come and find me if he wants. I like spying out the land. Unless I'm keeping you?' And he gave a very definite shake of the head. 'Tell me who the man is . . .' though she watched Mabon all the same out of the corner of her eye. He didn't miss her. He was encapsulated in his own good opinion, self-sufficient to the end. He stood in the centre of a group of men, his navigator, Bob said, other fliers, some wives, and it was noticeable that they became animated when he spoke, passive when he didn't. A smile from him was signal for a laugh from them.

Someone called Bob's attention and he excused himself.

Mabon caught her eye and seemed to hover for a moment in indecision before he left the party of his friends to rejoin her, though their looks followed him across the room. I wonder, she thought, if I would be acceptable here whatever I did or said, because I am with him. Though she felt no special joy at being with the man of the moment, his presence was a reassurance. Solecisms were unthinkable with him. He made whatever he did or endorsed the norm. Even her dress, picked with his eye, was right. It was in the manner of a score of other dresses and gave her the camouflage of anonymity. Would anyone notice there was a different person inside it from the dummy on display? Would she be content with this for long?

'Don't you want to meet my friends?'

'Not especially.' Strange; from her this sounded intimate.

The CO left the Mess, removing the last remnants of restraint. The music was played a little louder, the spirits gushed, dancing became more frenzied. He took her hand.

He steered her to the centre of the floor. The chairs round the outside were cleared to make a ring for dancing. She hadn't considered what his style might be, so it was all guesswork what she would have to improvise. He jived modernly. What else? It was a dance she had only watched, but grasped the idea at once, and he was pleased how well she followed. His version was his own. He danced it like Flamenco, in which the national dance imitates the national sport. He used her the way a matador uses a cape, sweeping with long decoys in front and behind to torment the bull with a vivid, flickering movement like a sunspot in the eye. They did not make contact by eye or body, but the space of air between them vibrated and shimmered as though they gave off thermal currents. It was an exhilarating paso doble as she turned, twirled, retreated under his arm while he remained almost static and impassive at her flounces, the most solemn of toreros.

Other dancers gave way a little and watched their exhibition. They were good. And the band, seeing the pair in demonstration, repeated the number without stopping.

Behind them, a contest was drawn up. Two men, Tom Westwater and a rival from Cartier's camp, had called each other out. Along the bar half a dozen glasses were ranged at their elbows on either side. The attention of the dancers was diverted from Mabon and Esme when a barracking roar went up as the two officers started on their first pint. The object was to drink quickly and drink steadily without lowering the glass. By the end of the third pint, Tom was half a glass behind and the other side, scenting victory, chanted like a chorus of baying hounds. The end of the pint brought a roar that stopped the beat of the room, then the music reasserted itself. Tom downed the next two more quickly and they entered upon the last, to the accompaniment of a steady rhythmical hand-clapping, at the same moment. His opponent was slipping behind, gulp by gulp, but before the finish he spluttered and coughed and having to put his glass down admitted defeat. There was no mercy for the loser, a runner who did not even cross the tape, and the laughter and the accolades all went Tom's way, flushed and bloated but victorious.

Mabon smiled wryly. He was genuinely amused or indulgent. Esme was not. Her eye alone went to the beaten man. Why did they set themselves up to be knocked down? Would he come back again tomorrow or next week for this pointless contest? Her smile withered. She looked round for an older face sitting in a corner, half hidden in the shade of a lamp. He would scowl in disapproval at the vapidity of their concerns. She could hear him say, High living and plain thinking. How she would like to sit down at that moment by his side and talk it all over with him. How she would like to hear him say, under his breath, Come, my bonny burde, let's do a Schottische and show them how to move. She would glide away with him and never look back.

'I'm sorry, I'm much too hot in here. I'll go outside for a breath of fresh air if you don't object.'

He conceded, but advised that she take her coat. She did not halt outside but took insistent footsteps away from the Mess. She turned and twisted among the shed-like offices of the various sections, denoted by a code of letters. And still he dogged her.

'You don't need to come with me,' she objected, turning round.

'Yes, I do.'

'Why? I am all right on my own.'

He looked at the strange hostility of her expression and felt he could not say he was her escort and stayed with her whatever happened. 'This is out of bounds to civilian personnel.'

'Ah, I should have known there would be an official reason.'

He went up and tried to speak to her face to face. 'Why are you bitter?'

'I don't want to be here. I don't want to be here at all.' She looked out over the blank horizon and saw nothing but desolation and solitary, uninhabited wastes. And then to soften the imputation these words made against him, that she had come to the Base against her will, she added, 'I ran away from someone. But he followed all the same and will not go away.'

The hand that should have rested on her shoulder as a gesture of concern did not alight but fluttered into space.

It was cold by night and she shivered slightly at the unaccustomed temperature. 'Could I look at one of the hangars? Do you have the authority?'

'Well, maybe mine. It's out of the way.' He led her diagonally across a square of glittering dark tarmac to the hangar which was used by his squadron and unlocked the side entrance which led into an office he shared with several others.

She had imagined he would have more lavish accommodation. This was no bigger than a cupboard, and was badly arranged with a long narrow entrance flanked by shoulder high files and, at the end, three desks arranged in a group. His, she guessed, was the tidy one. She took in a dusty glazed partition, a pin-marked notice board on which orders and a diary of events for the month fluttered, and above shelves filled with flying manuals and maps for aerial reconnaissance.

'How very austere.'

From a drawer of his filing cabinet he produced a bottle of rye. 'All we have, I'm afraid, or would you rather have some coffee?'

'Coffee.' She sat and waited while he arranged things compactly around her. 'How much time do you spend here? It's fitted out like home.'

'All my working day when we're not in the air.'

'But you sleep in the Mess?'

He weighed this question for a long time, trying to guess at what answer she might expect, and her reasons for asking it. 'Most of the bachelors do. It's cheaper and easier than an apartment, and when you're on standby you must be near the Base.' He produced palatable coffee.

'It strikes me as oddly monastic, as though you'd taken your vows to the service.'

Again he could not decide whether this was a taunt or not, being a literalist. He sat down at one of the other desks and measured her remotely, sitting in a strange abstraction an arm's length away.

'Yes, in fact we do take an oath of allegiance, to the Armed Forces and to the Queen when we join the service. And I am dedicated to my work, if that is what you mean. I couldn't do it otherwise. But I wouldn't go as far as saying it was a monastic life. We live elsewhere.'

'Such icons.' She looked at a row of pin-ups on the wall opposite, to prove her point.

'Not mine. I don't go in for images.'

'You believe in what you do?'

'Yes, of course. It is important work. Militaristically, it is very important.' And he frowned, by which she divined that for once she had ruffled his composure.

'May I look at a plane, or is that out of bounds to a woman too?'

He got up and opened the door for her to follow. They went into the main arena of the hangar which housed several machines, vastly different even to her untutored eye from the placid vehicle which had driven her across the Atlantic. The purpose of this machine was war. It was designed for killing. That was borne out by the drooping nose and the tapered wings which ensured speed and manoeuvrability to roll and tumble out of firing range in the sky, under cover of which it could deliver its lethal charge.

Close to, it dominated the human. At a distance, flying overhead in the sky, it was on a controllable scale. But when she stood beside it she was daunted by its bulk, more than three times her height and longer than a railway carriage. In answer to her questions, he told her it could weigh up to fifty thousand pounds and it was inconceivable to the lay mind that an engine could lift and sustain the inert metal casing for – how many miles had he said? – almost three thousand with extra fuel tanks. He walked round it with her, explaining the terms supersonic and twin jet and how the after-burners provided a boost of power which left the vapour trails she might have seen over the Saguenay skies. He told her about the parachute that aided tricky landing when the wrong winds blew.

'And weapons?'

'Yes, it has weapons. Two nuclear and three guided missiles.' He simplified but was satisfied that she asked more, and satisfied that he could give her the names of Douglas Genie and Hughes Falcon, explain the difference between those carried internally and externally and the methods of firing. 'Of course, I've never discharged missiles like those and probably never will.'

She looked upwards and noticed above the wing tips a painting of a bird enclosed in a circle.

'L'hirondelle,' he said, answering her look. 'We're L'hirondelle squadron.'

'Are they all named after birds?'

'No, some are known by numbers but this is the only French-Canadian squadron and it is reckoned to be unlike the others.' He stood back admiringly, as though the heavy machine were more than metal. For him it was the sum of the efforts of the men who cared for it, their pride, their skill, the man-hours which were devoted to maintaining it in flawless condition.

He locked up again when she had seen all she wanted. The wind had picked up while they were indoors, and whined slightly against the few objects that offered resistance in its path across the runway, a clump of thinning spruce, a wooden shack.

'We're night flying tomorrow,' he told her, consulting the lie of the stars. 'I hope this weather holds.'

On the way back to Arvida, she told him about the Chaplain's suggestion and he volunteered to drive her to Mistassini when they had a mutual free weekend. He refused to come into the apartment for he liked to disappoint her expectations of him, and bade her a cordial good night.

Driving on the solitary return journey, he underwent such a mixture of reactions about the outcome of the evening that he had to consider what they were. There was no doubt the best moments were when he was in control, when he was driving, when they danced, when he was able to explain some portion of what he did in the Voodoo. Not that she was a negligible element at these times. She enabled him to review what he was and take an added pleasure in it.

He was less happy about the instants when she asserted herself. When she had drawn his eye over the room, there was that second when he hesitated to join her, when he felt that most of the women he had known would have come across the floor to him and shared the limelight he enjoyed. She attracted him, oh yes, there was that naging impulse to the relationship. It was a long time since he had met a woman so close to his ideals of physical beauty, well covered but mobile in face and body. But even that she seemed to under-employ. She did not behave like a beautiful woman, display herself according to the dictates of corporeal excellence. She should have fluttered, flirted a little, behaved in a way that gave rise to laughter and teasing. That was the way a lovely woman passed an evening in the company of men, wasn't it?

He had waited in the hangar for a specific encouragement towards a conventional embrace, but instead she made it clear she did not want to be touched or made a fuss of, carrying with her the memory of the other man who would not go away. And he set his jaw for combat.

Then puzzlement warmed into annoyance when he thought of them spending an evening in the hangar. Quirks of behaviour seemed right in her presence, and utterly absurd out of it. It was not normal, it was not cautious. What did he know finally about her or her background? The office was deep in confidential reports and documents, not classified, but restricted all the same. He felt he had abused the trust placed in him by taking her there. He grew sober thinking what might have happened if, say, Charles Cartier had come across them, or even one of the sentries. How to explain that! For all he or anyone else knew, she might be an infiltrator, a journalist, an agitator from the anti-nuclear camp. He must be careful with her. She got under his defences the way other women had not. Monastic indeed!

Pleasant or vexing, he realised he was moving out of the sphere of his normal operations.

Esme was no more satisfied. She felt she failed to make any impression on him. She was baffled most of all by what they did not talk about. She had heard of the crash in the adjacent woods, in Arvida, and it had been covered in the local press and radio. But he did not mention what seemed to her a perfectly natural subject. Fearing a close friend had been killed, she desisted and left it at tact. But she would have thought it easy to refer to Aileen and Rejean. That must look odd to him, and having spoken to Rejean himself he knew the score. It was as though he chose from the narrowest possible range of topics, nothing controversial, nothing difficult and above all, nothing of which he was ignorant.

When she watched him across the room, she felt the principal cause of his fascination, and fascination it was for the men as well as the women around him, lay in the fact that he was negligent about the effect he created. The manners, the smile, the slow, wry drawl of his speech were habits he assumed or doffed at will. The relaxation of his style indicated a supreme egotism. She realised she had been quite wrong in coupling the two men as the same type: Rejean's was the politeness of concern; Mabon's was the politeness of indifference.

27

My dear Esme,

Five days in the Hebrides, painting and paddling. It is too cold for literal paddling, but the weather has the bonus of keeping away obnoxious tourists. (Notice that all tourists are obnoxious except me.)

The weather is bracing. That means in layman's terms it rains most days, but I don't mind. I have a wondrous waterproof I bought from Cairds in Perth which has so many flaps, double pockets, studs, secret corners and ingenious devices that one day it will complete its transmogrification and walk out wearing me.

I have taken a cottage at the end of an inlet, one of half a dozen fishermen's cottages stoutly constructed in boulders with a lee-ward door and hasps as big as my hand. Unhappily, the inside has been tricked out with modern pine and looks twee and countrified. I would have liked to see the old range. There was one at the old house long ago. Don't know if you remember it. A monster of sliding doors with an oven and rails on the side for drying clothes. It was a boiler and a cooker and an open fire all in one. It was the bane of Hannah's life, stoking that furnace and black-leading it with an array of sooty brushes and a polish called Zebrite. Isn't that a fearsome connotation!

There must have been a loom here once, installed in the alcove of the living room where the good wife would put in her spare hours making the tweed. It is a natty dinette area today. You may be surprised to learn I have woven a whole bolt, singlehanded. It's like no other cloth you have ever seen and it breaks most of the rules of good weaving. It is loose and open and rather lumpy but I am as proud of it as a cuckoo would be if it ever built a nest. I have had it lying around the office to test reactions, and everyone who comes in comments on it and, better still, touches it, infallibly. Even the postie and he's a surly customer. Now isn't that a good sign. If people want to touch, they want to own. So when I go back I am going to hawk it round the manufacturers and see what they think. It will be hard to cut because of the thickness of the fibres. The ends will need to be taped, the whole garment blocked and maybe interfaced, and it will have to be made up in large soft shapes, but all the same I have a feeling that this may be the winner.

This holiday has been my reward. It has been all hard work since you left and I remind myself that Jack becomes a dull boy. I often wonder how work suits you. I could never work in a group. Even my loom has to be well away from other people. The frustration of working with colleagues, whatever its attractions, is that some of the success depends on integration within the group. And as far as my experience goes, such equalities are rare. You may be luckier. Always with teaching I come up against the lack of measure, but it's my bribe to conscience and I go on with it hoping conscience will not cheat on the bargain. My apprentices bend slowly to instruction, like seasoning wood, and end up true.

Out here, stuck in the crevice of a rock, I am alone with what I like doing. No one interferes, no one argues, no one even knows. What comes out, line, shape, colour, is under my direction and I can blame no one else for my product.

And what am I doing? Trying to be a better draughtsman. Drawing is the basis of art, they tell me, and so if I want to be better I must begin again at the beginning. Every day I go out with a clean sketch pad and every evening when I come back and settle in front of my peat fire, I discover each page is covered. I am as surprised as anyone. I recognise the objects I have drawn, I remember them, but I am amazed at such fecundity, such release. My worries about this flow are connected; that I will not get everything down fast enough before the stream dries up (it cannot go on in such spate for ever) and that something strong, important, irreplaceable will elude me. So I am working, working feverishly, all the time.

I have three canvases on the go at the moment. I am gradually putting together the pieces for a landscape, greatly foreshortened, of the whole of Loch Earn. I saw it one night when I was on Ben

Vorlich, soaked to the skin and all that drenching rain was pouring down the hillside and into the loch, then – in the diagrammatic form you see in geography books – down the watershed and into the sea. So I shall put the sea in. An impossibility but never mind. I suspect that if you flew a very few hundred feet above the loch you could catch a glimpse of the North Sea. The colour is almost monochromatic, which I hope suggests the kind of continuity I am after, but that is difficult, calling for great restraint in mixing.

The others are domestic snatches, things I use and see every day. One of the loom threaded. Have you seen the oil by Van Gogh of a man weaving? He is dressed in blue, and you see him from the back, no face. He puts me in mind of Stefan. And I am doing a little sampler of the cobbles of the courtyard which is turning out very well. I am painting this as superimposed images, which look like photographic slides with heavy frames, or sections the way you see an Edinburgh garden through the railings, with an altered image through each slot. Colour is depth. Every brush load suggests meal and honey, tissue – look at all the various tones in your skin – stone and mould. It is too tempting. I have to ration myself, content that in voluntary abstinence there is almost an ecstasy.

I wrote all that yesterday. I came in full of it and of myself and thought, I must talk to someone, and of course it was you. Today I am not so full of it. I am rather empty because the person I conjured up in my head talking to you, at least on paper, is at one remove.

Aileen says you have met another man who she thinks will be important to you. I have pumped her all I can without being totally conspicuous about it, but that's not much and so I reserve judgment till you tell me yourself how things lie.

But I want you to know that of all the advantages I have wished for you, freedom of choice was paramount. You said in your letter I wasn't honest with you and that implies I didn't tell you the truth. But I don't begin to know where the truth is. There are tiny and broken fragments of it here and there and I did give you these piecemeal, not as I selected them, but as I came across them by chance. I give you my truth; the absolute truth you will have to reconstruct for yourself.

Be free in your choice, Esme. Listen to the dictates of your — what? I don't know how to name it but it was once called conscience or soul or heart, though these are defunct terms. No one listens to their heart any more. They listen to their sex organs. Be advised by the recalcitrant, seeking, unshakeable person that is *you*. Please discount any loyalties you think you have to me. Tell yourself I am an old man and I will have many dry months from now on. There is no need to carry Anchises on your back from the ruins of Troy. There is a new world, new life, new civilisation waiting for you and who's to say they aren't better than the old? Don't forget how many ways there are to be alive. I am the past. I send you with all godspeed to the future.

28

Paulette Chantal came downstairs with this letter which had inadvertently been put into her mailbox. She was a dainty woman of the type the valley had evolved after a hundred years of close breeding, so dark and bright-eyed one would have wagered the Indian had passed into the immigrant. But she was a French-woman with all the assets of the Parisienne, a fine cook, with a strong nurture of home, and a figure that had been honed down to qualify as petite. She was ideally happy in her marriage and constructed make-believe fantasies about the life of her tenant who remained maddeningly unattached. Esme kept her informed about the search for her father as a decoy from discussion about the search for a mate.

She spoke the oddest English, not in her adult life having read a page of the language. So she spoke fluently, but in a patois which was an amalgam picked up from radio broadcasts, the occasional American film and a literal translation of the form and syntax of French.

'So you go to Mistassini with your friend?'

Esme turned the letter over and over and wished the woman would go away and let her read it. 'No, he's either been flying or away in Montreal the last two or three weekends.'

'You have to go before the snow comes,' she reminded the uninitiate.

January? 'Oh, I think I'll be gone altogether before the snow comes.'

'Sure.'

'Perhaps I ought to go on my own. It's not so far.'

'But it's better that you go with a man. It's a funny place.'

'No one's going to set about me on the road from here to Mistassini?'

Madame was horrified. 'Eh, no. The Saguenay people they are . . . serious. There is no crime. The Church is too strong. Since it was first settled, there has never been a murder in the valley, not one, and we have a big population. You can go anywhere in safety of your life. A woman alone too is,' she gestured meaningfully, 'is quite safe. But better if you have a man to go with. He can ask questions.'

Esme was taken with this frequently repeated eulogy on the virtues of the Saguenay and put her letter down, seeing there would be no immediate release. She gestured to the landlady to sit down and did so herself. 'You're so proud of Quebec, aren't you? Wouldn't you like to be separate from the rest of Canada and be truly independent?'

'Maybe, sometimes. We don't like to be a minority, only one French province and all the others English. But Canada is not one country. It is ten different countries with one government.' Esme liked the way, mid-flow, she would pronounce a word in French, 'gouvernement'. 'You have a problem like this in Scotland, I read in a journal. Once you marry another country, how do you break away? Separatist. That's a popular word but we know we are not rich. We stay with our partner, yes, because we cannot afford a divorce. General de Gaulle when he comes to visit he makes a grand speech from the balcony to all the silly boys and girls, the students you know, "Québec libre!" It's not Vichy France, it's not nineteen forty-five, it's not the German army of occupation. We must be sensible and go on living tomorrow not throw it all away on a grand gesture.'

'But you still don't like the English Canadians?'

Madame dimpled her cheeks in deprecation. 'I like some, sure.

They are some very nice people. But I don't make too many friends. They don't mix too well with the French. They always say, Come on, you speak to us in English. English, English, always English. Why can't they learn French? And even the young Québécois talk in this terrible franglais. Qu'est-ce que c'est qu'une canne de beans? Soon we will have no language. A word here, a word there. All the time you hear people say "correct".' She said it as Esme had first heard it pronounced kirek and thought it was a cricket chirruping. 'There is no "kirek" in French. It's a horrible sound.'

'Préservons notre âme et notre langue française.'

'Bien entendu. But there's a problem. We are not français. We are French Canadians. We are, I think you say, hybrids. We are Europeans in North America and North Americans in Europe. In France they think we are peasants. So we are nobody. It's lonely, you know.'

Esme glanced inevitably towards the letter, the address of which was facing towards Madame. 'Such a fine, strong handwriting,' she enthused.

She could have said it was from her bank manager, or Mr Scott but of all the feasible explanations the one she landed on was, 'My godfather.'

Mabon and Esme set aside a Saturday to drive to Mistassini. There were not many Saturdays left before the end of her term and she was conscious of another deadline catching up with her. Teaching made that difference; time flew. The work days were five giant strides, the weekend an objective which she reached only to find it was a hurdle propelling her forward into the following week. Mr Elphick had approached her almost deferentially and asked, 'I am arranging the timetable for next term and wondered what your plans were?'

'I haven't decided what I'm doing. I think maybe instead of keeping you waiting I should say I'll be leaving at the end of term and let you look for someone else.'

'Ah,' he hedged, 'but that's not fair to you if you change your mind. I would like you to stay, of course. I can't replace someone like you easily.' Esme knew enough to see that this was a sop. His pleasure would be withdrawn at the first new inscription on the desks. 'We'll give it a little longer. Tell me a week before the end of term if you want to renew your contract.'

She could not make final arrangements till she had been to see the old man. If he had something definite to say, what point was there in going home in the New Year without having made contact? Stefan might be on her doorstep.

She wavered and agreed.

Mabon picked her up in the black sedan, punctual to the minute they had arranged. They had met a few times in the interval, once for lunch, another time when he had called in passing through Arvida but he had had Tom Westwater with him and did not stay long. They had met by accident in Chicoutimi when Esme was looking for Christmas presents for the Simards, having agreed that whatever the outcome she would spend the holiday with them.

At these times there had been hesitations, silent adjustments when like cautious strangers in new territory they took their bearings and lifted a finger to the wind. Not the least of these hesitations was the fact that he had never indicated the slightest desire to touch her, and although she was relieved not to have to make any decision in that direction there was the hint of indignation that he could find her so resistible. She knew he was not passionless. He bore himself with the tension of the physically aware. The casual holding of hands, the cheerful bussing when they met was not within his range. There were no throwaway gestures with Mabon. She tried to assess what she wanted from him and decided, shamefully, it was an advance she could repel. She had come down to the terrible feminine cheat of coquetry.

They swept out of the upper end of the valley of the river Saguenay into full view of the basin of waters known as Lac St Jean. It was a fine stretch of lake which accommodated ski-ing, fishing and boating in the summer months. Even so late in the year the lake was piercingly blue, like the clear sky it reflected, and almost as immense. The villages and small townships were prettier than the workmanlike encampments of the valley, each one clustered round its mother church with the recurring architectural motifs of wooden boarding, wide verandahs and the steep roofs of the French colonial style.

Mistassini, at the north-west tip of the lake, was a small market town, of a few thousand inhabitants and just at the verge of civilisation beyond which life could not be supported, which meant that it was in all likelihood fixed in time. Here a Trappist monastery had been founded, an outlandish setting, or was the crown of encircling peaks, already deeply encrusted with snow, a reminder of the ultimate silence in which the philosophy found itself at home?

He parked. 'Where now?'

'I'll ask someone, shall I?' She waited till a likely shopper drifted down the main street towards them and went out with her prepared question. 'Pardon. Pourriez-vous m'aider? Je cherche un homme qui est connu par le nom "Le Polonais".'

Mabon watched her through the windscreen, as ever a little amused by her antics, her enchanting inability to do what was normal. What a diversion she had been and only a huge workload had prevented him from being further diverted. Out there she was an object that drew eyes, a woman no man in his senses bypassed, gesticulating, smiling, frowning as she followed directions. In here she would be cool, withdrawn, appraising, the damnable thinking faculty getting in the way of him and her. However did you go about seducing a woman who said with her eyes, Seduce me but I will despise you for being so obvious? It was the double edge in her that caught him on the raw every time.

He opened the door, leaning across. 'Yes, I saw. He's up the main highway half a mile or so, and on the left.'

'Can you lip read?'

'Not in French.'

The directions led to an older house on the far side of the township, with an open run of tufty grass and steps to a verandah on which in summer days a wicker chair would rock. It was taken inside under cover now against the coming weather, and the outer door which was fitted with a fine mesh to deter the invading insects of a heatwave was spuriously redundant.

She was overcome with misgivings and could not leave her seat. He opened his door and shut it again when she made no move.

'You can't come all this way and fail at the last.'

'But what if I don't want to find out what he has to tell me?'

'You accepted that a long time ago. You wouldn't have started if you didn't mean to finish.'

It was all very well for him. He'd never reflected in his life.

She rang the door bell and waited. Rang again and thought really it was stupid to have come all this way without a prior phone call. Mabon had every right to look as though his restraint might crack. Eventually they heard the scrape of a door opening far away down a passage, and after two or three minutes an old man did hesitatingly pull the overlapping doors ajar.

He was evidently old, maybe eighty, but age had manifested itself in a wholesale bleaching of his face in which there was not a crease or a line. The hair was a white shock and eyebrows, lashes and beard were similarly drained of colour. But it was a well disposed face, so Esme launched into the preamble of which she was so nervous that she had taken the precaution of writing it down and memorising it.

'Bonjour, Monsieur. Je m'appelle Esme Rosowicz. On m'a dit que . . .' But that patronym was sufficient passport to his home, his hospitality. A girl with a Polish name, a girl who spoke French, a girl who was English. He must resolve the enigma. He drew them down the passage talking half in French, half in English, neither clear, and once he had seated them in his living room went away again to make them a concoction he called 'le thé anglais'. He did not consult their taste as regards cream or sugar, far less lemon, but served it as he thought it ought to be taken and ladled it in cups like broth. It tasted of dust and soot but they endured it rather than give offence.

She had managed to convey her errand between his comings and goings but it was half an hour before he sat down and gave her his full attention. Every single item in the room where they sat was red, chairs, curtains, carpet, a table covering which was a square of antique chenille. None of these specifically matched, and with the onslaughts of sun and age were faded into every shade between rose, madder and burgundy. The extraordinary contrast between the pale-haired man and his vivid setting made her think he was a replica of Father Christmas in a seasonal grotto and herself a child asking for the unattainable.

'We are not so many Poles in the Saguenay, though the Polish people speak good French but not me, I regret. I came here by accident, many years ago. In nineteen hundred and six my family left Poland to go to America. My father was a churchman who had abandoned his vows and married. There was no future for such a man and we left Poland to go to England first, yes I was there, in

Liverpool where we found a ship to take us to San Francisco, through the canal. But as we were ready to go, only a day or two and our passage paid, we heard of a great earthquake that had flattened the city, and that fires were raging through what was left. But the shipping company said they would change our booking and we came to Montreal instead. My father and mother and brothers and I. Not greater than the chance that brings you here, or your father twenty years ago. Do you have brothers at home?'

'No, there is no one.'

'There is always someone. Il y a quelqu'un là bas qui vous attend.'

'Peut-être.'

He nodded to Mabon who sat in a gloomy corner. 'C'est votre bon homme?'

'Non, un ami qui m'aide.'

'Alors, this father matters to you because you have no one else. But do you think you matter to him?'

'No, except for the gesture of the photographs.'

'Yes, it would be interesting to know why. Mais, je vous avis, do not seek to disturb too much. If this man does not want to be found, he will not be. If it happens, it is right, and if it does not, that is right too. There is nothing more interesting than what really happens.'

'But you don't know him?' she urged. How easy if this were he. She could accommodate this snowy being in her iconography. Why could we not have the parents we wanted?

'There was a man who came after the war, the second war. I did not meet him but I heard of him and I remembered him because he did not come to see me and I am Le Polonais. Although he was a Pole, he wanted to forget that he was Polish. Men do not give away their nationality unless there is a reason. I thought maybe he was a deserter who had changed his name and was afraid. But I would not have blamed him. He came without a wife and without a child, but very soon he married, yes he did marry a Frenchwoman born in the region. He had children if I remember, two or maybe one. I think he is your man.'

'But where?'

He shook his head regretfully. 'I do not know. But he was a tailor. That was sure.'

'And of course he wasn't a Rosowicz.'

'No, the name he used was Roberval, Stefan Roberval.'

In the shadow, Mabon stirred and when he spoke his voice had a sharpness to cut through uncertainty.

'Do you know where he worked?'

'No.'

The old man was tired now and flagging. He rarely spoke so long, but his farewells were kind. He took Esme's hand in his and made her promise to tell him of the outcome. December days did not often bring so choice a visitor.

They walked back to the car, parked some way from the house which had no drive. The low afternoon sun went down behind them over the lake and night fell precipitately without an inter-mediate twilight. It was cold at once, the temperature falling sharply and she shivered. Alexis or Rejean would have put a compassionate arm through hers, offered a jacket or a scarf, taken a quicker step to the car. He commented her coat was too thin for someone who wasn't acclimatised. She was either hot indoors or cold out.

'Are you out of patience with all this? I am. I feel I have come back to the start. Roberval now.'

'There were not so many men called Rosowicz. There will be fewer Robervals.'

'Do you think?'

But the subject for him had no interest when it could not be acted upon. He had finished with it and turned to the course of that evening and their share in it instead.

'Shall we go back by a different route, explore a little? I don't come this way often.'

'Whatever you want. I'm in no hurry.'

He turned the car away from the road that had brought them in and nosed his way down a turning.

Stars rose and above them all was the pole star, luminously clear.

He did not know where he was going, but that did not matter. He was a brilliant navigator. He did not have to depend on the automatic instruments of flying which had to some extent under-mined the human skill. If he had been stranded at night in a forest, without compass, he could sense his direction like an Indian by finding the mossy side of tree bark, or by day wait twelve hours for the sun-seeking leaves to turn and show him south. He would

convolutions of his thinking were simply linear compared with the miracles of his anatomy.

He took her home. She was sleepy. 'I shouldn't drink wine, you know.' And she curled on the settee while he made the coffee. He came back after a long interval with two cups and put one down beside her.

'I couldn't find the instant kind.'

'Oh, I don't use it. I should have said.'

'I managed.'

He kissed her and found that without benefit of words they were in rather better agreement. Not that she was suddenly compliant. Oh, never that easy. She played games, hid and withdrew her mouth, said no to the male kiss and insisted on the female one, made with the barest degree of pressure but how feelingly. She was the most articulate of lovers, never sloppy or meaningless or tiresomely repetitive and he was stunned that thinking could express itself so corporeally.

What started as a frolic, both feeling vaguely, It's expected, became earnest. They could not kiss and part. Esme, chilled more than once by the cool draught of his self-possession, was cheered that she could elicit emotion from him at least in this. She could extort his volition, while admitting hers went soaring with it.

She despised herself. What had happened to one man, one woman? She had sworn her own fealty to Alexis, and yet at the first opportunity here she was shaping herself round another. It was a time-worn form of oblivion, forgetting one man in the arms of another and simply enjoying it, simply being curious did not excuse her promiscuity. She was, she regretted to admit, not entirely nice.

She hadn't paid attention to its details before, but the dress was buttoned down the back and there were small apertures between the fastenings. Without noticeable indecency, he could insert his fingers between these and caress the naked centre of her spine. He found that there was a ripple of hairs in her back longer than is usual, feathering to a taper at the point where the waist is narrowest. This intrigued him and he circled it for some time, well aware that it produced almost unbearable sensation in her, until when he lifted the v-shaped formation, she shuddered and held

297

herself against him for a moment.

Then moved a fraction and away from him again. 'The coffee's cold,' she laughed it off. 'Shall I heat it?' And, rising, she walked away.

The nature of that involuntary spasm kept him guessing. He wondered if it was an orgasm, but on second thoughts, no, it was the precursive signal of the experienced woman. But in these circumstances it was to him an unparalleled occurrence. What was she, after all?

She came back with two fresh cups and was more composed.

But he was tired of protracted courtship and leaned forward to the chair where she sat away from him. 'Can I sleep here tonight?'

She turned away from the absolute question. 'No,' she answered quietly.

'Will you come to bed with me?' he rephrased it, thinking she objected to the different interpretation.

'No,' she answered again.

'Why not? It's not as though it's the first time.'

'That's a facile assumption, don't you think?' She was hiding behind words again, and to assert his own authority he reached for her hand as the most accessible part. She pulled away as she had done when he went to arrange the coat. 'Don't. It's not fair to touch me. You know I am susceptible.'

He had to agree that if it were a contest, he might be using unfair means to swing her round, but was surprised all the same at the switch in her tactics.

'I know. I know I am being unreasonable. I never meant for one second to mislead you but I am not, categorically not, available. I have no idea what we are doing. We don't even like each other.'

He became more and more puzzled by her reactions. 'I would never have asked you out if I didn't like you.'

She eyed him over her cup. How could she tell him that the greater part was missing. If she could have delved into semantics with him, she might have established that what he meant by the word 'like' was closer to admire or feel attraction for, in her terms, but he would have every right to grow exasperated with the quibble. 'Let's not quarrel. I have had a most pleasant day, the best day I've had since I came to Canada.' He did smile at the concession. 'And I know I owe it to you. Can we leave it at that this evening? If you want to go on, call me, and if you don't I'll understand, perfectly.'

He stood to go. It was after midnight and these non-sequiturs of hers could go on for ever. Imitating his move, she found herself face to face with him again. 'What I admire about you is that you don't lie.' As a substitute for the embrace which was presumably barred, he placed his fist against her cheek and nudged it slightly. In someone else it might have been a playful gesture.

And of course she had to spoil it by saying, 'You just haven't found me out yet.'

She woke in the night to the sound of screaming.

It was a screaming so terrible and protracted that it wounded her and blotted out her other senses. It rose and fell over a register of half a dozen notes that mocked harmonics. It would have been the score to Rodin's 'Gates of Hell' if they had moved into life, or death, the vocal anguish emitted by the head of Despair. What could it be? It was a scream that curdled blood, the scream of unchristened children, murdered victims, women taken in adultery stoned at the gates, all those who were condemned to purgatory and everlasting damnation because their souls had not been cleansed. A wail, a human wail. It denoted a distress so unbearable that she wanted to shutter her ears against it, and clapped her hands over her head. But still the sound pierced her refusal to hear it. It was no good. She couldn't ignore it. She would have to get up and alleviate the condition, whatever it was, that was causing such torment. Somebody upstairs must be ill, but why didn't they see to it? Was it outside? She quailed at the thought of going out in the dark to attend to people wounded in a crash and yet the sound, that subhuman shrieking, must be silenced.

And then it went. All was quiet, the loudest sound her own heartbeat. It was a nightmare after all.

In the morning she wondered. Things were not right. It was dark but her body told her she had slept long after the interruption. She went into the living room and switched on the light. But she couldn't see out. A thick fog seemed to envelop everything, muffling sight and sound. The clock told her it was eleven, but surely it lied. She was utterly disoriented. Was it night or day, which day was it and where was she? Was she dreaming or was she really back at the big house or Inchcombe, safe indoors with Alexis in the next room? The solitude of her position, with only her own senses, and those dimmed, for reassurance, was born in on her, lost, sunk in a subterranean night.

A repeated tapping roused her from the settee where she had lowered herself. She traced the source of the tapping to the internal door of her apartment and, opening it, found nothing more alarming than Monsieur Chantal dressed for the outdoors with boots, hat, parka and carrying a shovel.

'Eh, you are OK? You are too pale.'

'I was frightened by the dark.'

'We have the first storm of the winter. It's not so bad. But the wind. You hear the wind in the night?'

She nodded. That was the source of the keening. Wind, trapped at the corner of the house, could imitate the human voice. That was all, but still the memory of that death cry made her shudder.

'I have to dig you out. The wind makes the snow to drift on this side. Please.' He excused himself as he went past her. He went to the outer door but saw with his practised eye that the drifting had completely filled the well of the stair to the basement and he would have no leverage from below. 'No, it's too much. I go upstairs to try. You will hear me going along the windows, OK?'

After she had dressed and the stair was cleared, she went outside to review the results of the storm. The things of the neighbourhood she had hardly had time to get used to, roads, houses, green verges, were as unfamiliar as when she first arrived. Everything had been transformed overnight. The view that had sparkled in yesterday's sunshine was turned to monotonous white. The snow bleached the landscape to a dead tissue. Close up, handfuls of the stuff revealed its crystalline hexagons. The sharpness of the cold made huge flakes and preserved them intact. It was not cold as she understood cold. It was not raw or bitter, but dry enough to make the bones crack, and as Mabon had predicted the sun blazed in a brilliant sky. The Chantals' daughters came out and threw scoopfuls of the snow at each other, a novelty they tired of quickly. No child could roll this stuff into a snowball or fashion a snowman for hours towards sunset. It was too crisp to cling, like granules of polystyrene.

'You don't stand about in the wind,' advised their father,

clearing the last of her windows. 'It will burn your legs.'

'Burn my legs?' she asked stupidly.

'Sure. The heat burns and the cold burns, both the same. You must have your legs covered on a day like today when there is wind. You be careful.' He shook his head. 'These winters, you know, j'en suis fatigué. I am from Quebec and three months is OK but five,' and he shook his head dolefully again, leaning on his spade. 'My wife, she likes it. She goes ski-ing. You can fall in a mountain of snow and not come out wet. You want to learn to ski if you live here. But for the rest of us, this is exile.'

Exile! That was exile then, even for a man a hundred and fifty miles from his birthplace. It was being in one spot and craving for another, being cold and wanting to be warmed by temperate winds, seeing white with your eyes when your mind longed for colour. Generation after generation coming to colonise in hope, in good faith, yearned for home and still in dreams beheld the Hebrides.

He telephoned at the end of the week.

'Hello. I didn't really expect to hear from you again.'

But he knew better than to go down that road. 'There's a foreign film being shown at the Mess on Sunday. *Last Year In Marienbad*. Have you heard of it? They show it after dinner to which guests are invited and I wondered if you'd care to come.'

And yes she had, and yes she would but there was something else to say first. 'I've signed my contract for the rest of the year.'

'So you did, after all. Why didn't you tell me?'

'I am telling you.'

He had to smile at her obtuseness. 'Why didn't you tell me before? What changed your mind?'

That was the question she had shied away from herself, because it wasn't a matter of thinking it out to a logical conclusion. She had weighed half a dozen conflicting emotions. She hadn't done what she came to do, find Stefan. But she was beginning to see that the closer she came to finding him, past or present, the less willing she was to make contact, actually to discover in case she found an emptiness where something should have been. She shilly-shallied and put things off, knowing all the while that if she was to have any credibility she would have to decide to push on, or invent an excuse that would mask her unwillingness. Then there was Rejean, who phoned her every two or three days and promised to come, but never did. He leaned on her insidiously for support and a little encouragement, though he was doing well in his sphere, but liked to hear her say so. She was on this side, on his side, and that mattered to him.

Equally, on the other side of the water, things had not simplified. He had not made the break on his own. And Aileen was there. If Aileen had not been a third party complicating the issue, she might have been more inclined to go and face all the unpleasant consequences of choosing so unlikely a partner. The inclination was there, nightly conjured. She could face Mairi, the uncles, the Pollocks and the Sutherlands but Aileen's arguments she could not counter. But by the summer they could cross, change places and each be in their rightful homes without her cousin being on hand to witness and condemn. That was rank cowardice, she knew. There was the school. The most unruly of her boys had said, You're not leaving, are you, miss? We'll never get a better teacher. And that was the most seductive compliment of all. It flattered, but it created obligations. She worried about them, the sinners, the tares, the lost sheep, and fell into the utmost vanity of thinking herself indispensable. And finally Mabon, the unfinished business, the question mark of who was uppermost. It really ought to be a championship bout and go fifteen rounds.

'I changed my mind because it seemed right.'

'That's good. I'm glad to hear it. Glad you're staying.' That was the most personal thing he had said to her and she found herself flushing with pleasure down the telephone.

Later, she was annoyed with herself. She had allowed the directness of her first intention, to stay a measured time and do what she must within that time, to be hatched over with the fine etching of indecision and delay. She had overrun her boundaries again.

29

'I want you to go back,' said Alexis at the end of Aileen's term.

He took another break. Most things nowadays were a diversion from the main purpose.

But Edinburgh in December was as dispiriting as the Hebrides the month before, and as lonely. The shops along Princes Street where he took gloomy saunters were full of the gimcrackery of Christmas, a combination of the useless and the ugly and all decked out with painted baubles and scenes of festive mirth, which were gratuitously embellished with synthetic snow. Stilted robins, plastic-berried holly, cheap ribbon gleamed at him redly. It was a pastiche of bad taste, visual as well as gastronomic. What could he do? Go into retreat for the duration? For years he had planned a major rebellion against institutionalised Xmas, but had not landed on the formula which would excuse him his share of the ritual gorging. Never did Wiliam Morris's phrase about the capitalist as a 'purse-proud digesting machine' strike so true. He saw the turkeys trussed up in the butcher's window, their necks knotted in a loop. His system groaned at what it must accept. Could he be ill this year? Could he invent a fictitious ailment, some passing melancholia, a three-day contagion which would debar him from being jolly? He prayed annually for lightning to strike and save him. But it did not. Perhaps the elements too recognised a heretic, or a high day worshipper.

'Go back? Where? Oh, Montreal. Why do you want me to do that?'

'Because I think you should be together at Christmas.'

She swivelled round from her notebooks and gave him an enlightened look. 'When did you start turning into Pèrc Noël?'

'Do as I say, and ignore my appalling example. I mean you don't want to grow up like me, do you? What could be worse? It's not right this being apart.'

'No, I don't suppose it is. But he can come and find me if he wants to. He knows where I live.'

She turned back again and a silence fell between them which was involuntary on both sides but they did not know how to interrupt it. So she went on writing words on the pad, and he watched the traffic on the road and thought; another evening. He stretched out for the *Evening News*, hoping there would be a film, or maybe a concert at the Usher Hall. But nothing sounded interesting, although he had not been to the Cameo or heard Alexander Gibson conduct the Scottish National Orchestra for a long time. Distance did not lend enchantment. And yet if she had been there. He turned a corner in his memory and glimpsed her unawares. For long periods he forgot about her, or released his hold on her persona although the vacuum she left remained an empty space. A man can learn to use one hand but never forgets he used to have two. A small thing would trigger off the ache. Turning the pages of the evening paper, his eye lighted on an advertisement for the exhibition at the Royal Scottish Academy, for which he had had three paintings accepted. He could not even be bothered going to look at them and flung the paper away.

'I can't believe you are so dispassionate. You must feel it.'

She gave him space again mid-sentence.

'You must want to be with him.'

She sighed and looked into her feelings but they were so far away below layers of other and more pressing considerations such as a Christmas shopping list, and what they would have for dinner, and company law as it related to contracts. 'Once entered into, a contract between two parties, that is the signatories to the agreement, is binding in so far as . . .' What could she say?

'Is there anything wrong – physically?'

She looked surprised.

'I don't suppose your mother will ever get round to asking you about it. So I must.'

'No,' she said slyly, drawing out the word till it sounded like a query, 'but I'm tempted to answer "yes" just for the fun of hearing what you'd say. What would you say?'

'Be patient and be kind.'

'Pooh. I've got better advice for myself than that. No, I wish it were so simple. I would know how to put that right. People don't have those problems nowadays, you know. They can talk about their sexual performance.'

Well, well. Performance? What were they – circus artists?

Obviously, this assurance was a good thing and there was no correlation whatever between such desirable freedom and the mounting divorce rate. The problem must lie elsewhere. He thought that perhaps men and women really were different in prehistory when he was young. The tragedy in life was not to die too young but to live too long, to outlive all your generation till there was nobody left to talk to. Speaking to her, he felt his language had suddenly become obsolete.

'Then, if it's not that simple, what is it?'

'Oh, I don't know,' she said testily at last. 'Does it really matter if it can't be helped?'

'Of course it matters. You achieve nothing while you're unhappy.'

'But you did.' She meant this as acknowledgement of his determination, and couldn't see it inflicted a degree of pain.

'Do you imagine I wouldn't have traded it all in for personal happiness?'

'All your success? Would you? I don't believe you would, you know. And anyway, some people couldn't be happy no matter how they tried, or who they tried with,' she consoled him, but it was a shabby consolation. 'It's all perfectly friendly, so I don't see why you're concerned. We'll get together sometime.'

He did not dare to tell her Rhona had thought the same. What about the meantime? They lost the habit of sharing. They lost the time together. They forgot how to make allowances. Could she be content to let things fall out the way they would? Or was he guilty of projecting onto her the distress he felt at his own abandonment? Was he speaking all through not to her, but to Esme, desperate to elicit some felt response because this self-containment cut him out too coldly? He must put his faith in reconciliation, not for Aileen, but himself. It was cruel to imagine Esme might be talking about him, thinking about him in these distant terms. He felt the gulf immeasurably.

'I still think,' he harked back to his original contention, 'that you shouldn't leave Rejean alone at Christmas.'

'Oh, he won't be on his own. Maurice and Claire are there.'

'What bachelor fare is that?'

'And Esme's going down apparently, with the pilot. Quite a ménage, you see.'

'Ah. So. That's not so bad then, is it? Esme and the pilot.' He prised open the self-inflicted wound and seemed surprised it hurt.

'Hm. Looking serious, isn't it? I wonder if she'll marry him.'

He was dumb.

'It's a bit off, isn't it?'

'What?'

'Everyone deserting and going over to the other side.'

He got up and put his hand heavily on her shoulder as he passed, making for the door.

'If you're going out, get something for dinner.'

30

'You're late,' said Maurice when they arrived.

'We went a hundred miles an hour as it was.'

'He drives too fast. Were you canoodling all the way?'

'Not simultaneously, no.'

She found him in the study. It was her favourite room in the Simard house. Books floor to ceiling made it warm and enclosed. She had admired it on her first visit, running her hands over the shelves. 'And I didn't buy them by the yard, missie,' he had forestalled on that occasion.

'Oh, it's simple to buy them. Have you read any of them?'

'Nope. But Claire has. And Rejean, of course.'

'Do you know you have a first edition of Byron's *Don Juan* here?'

'Who's Byron?'

'Don't pretend to be such a Philistine.'

'Good investment.'

The room was advantageously placed. It had the best drawing fire in the house, the clearest view of the drive and whoever was passing to the main entrance. It led off the living area where Claire and Rejean finished decorating the tree, a ten foot fir which reached up into the exposed pitch of the roof. He was near enough to give instructions and gratuitous comment on how they were doing it, without of course being obliged to hold a single bauble. Claire had her own preconceptions about a tree. Silver and gold were all she permitted in her decorations, a restraint he admired but thought rather sombre.

Mabon came and went in front of the window, carrying cases, and then they heard him shut the main door and follow Claire towards the kitchen end of the house.

'Are you going to make an honest man of him, Esme?'

'Why, is he dishonest?'

'Don't mess with me. Will you marry him? Claire would like it.'

'But I might not.'

She got up from her chair and went to stand by the fireplace where the logs crumbled and broke into ash. It was a peculiar fireplace by her standards, more like a picture frame let into the wall at floor level, and in front of the blaze were two mesh curtains like chain mail to guard against spurting.

'I'm pleased too. When I first met you , that unfortunate evening in Lochearn – Come back and sit down, I can't address your shoulder – that first evening I wondered if you were a mischief-maker. No, I did. I suspected you, I don't know quite of what, of scheming. Before I came over I fancied you might be making it with Rejean. No, you don't need to tell me I was wrong. I'm apologising now for doing you evil in my thoughts. Claire and I are fonder of you than I would have imagined. Fonder than of Aileen, I'm afraid.'

'Maurice, don't make those comparisons, please. Care for me, and I am glad of it, but not at Aileen's expense. Otherwise I feel I've robbed her.'

'She's robbed herself. Why isn't she here with us now? What's up between her and Rejean? I tell you, I wish you had made it a little harder with Rejean. He can't even choose the right woman.'

She looked at him aghast. Were there not complications enough without adding Rejean to them? 'That's a dreadful thing to say, Maurice, a dreadful responsibility to put on me. You make me feel so disloyal to Aileen, and my life has changed out of all recognition because she came and knocked on my door one night from kindness. She has her own sense of duty.'

'Was that the sense of duty that kept your parents on different sides of the Atlantic, Esme? I don't like it. I didn't mean to say this much. Maybe I have got it out of proportion seeing Rejean living back here when he's a married man. Yes, she's a different breed from us. But husbands and wives ought to be together. That's basic, isn't it? You would think after all that nature would speak. She's a cold fish, I reckon. There may be extenuating circumstances, but if she wanted, really wanted, nothing would keep her away from her man.'

Esme could find no contradiction. The logic of someone else's point of view was always more powerful than her own, because it was expressed while hers was only felt on the way to expression. It took her a long time to weigh the balance. Besides, there was a slur in those words if she was sensitive to it. If she really wanted, why wasn't she with her man too?

He patted the hand on his shoulder. 'You and Mabon, well, that puts you out of reach. And I'm pleased you're staying on in Arvida.'

On Christmas Eve the Simards, like their friends and neighbours, celebrated the Nativity at Midnight Mass. All five of them went in Maurice's car to the church of Notre-Dame.

It was already crowded when they arrived and there were no seats left. Men and women of all ages took up the pews by the sacristy and overflowed into the wooden chairs behind. These were the rickety oak chairs with a shelf behind the back stay where a prayer book or a breviary might be lodged, the same the world over. They found Claire a single free seat but Esme and the men stood among a hundred others at the rear of the chapel and listened to the organ playing while the choir assembled behind the reredos. Then they filtered into the stalls and began their recital. Agnus Dei, Kyrie eleison, Tantum ergo sacramentum. The priest and his servers performed the rituals of the mass, remotely by the altar from which Esme was distracted by the hum and business of the place. It was somewhat less solemn than in the presbytery. People came and went through the curtained door behind her. Small children, awake at midnight, crawled and scrambled for attention. Old men mumbled to their neighbours and over all this there was a discreet scampering of movement from the service, wine and wafers served, the bobbing of communicants, the priest touring the aisles and chancel while the acolyte swung the incense cup, singing those beautiful and moving incantations. A woman came forward and touched the hem of the priest's surplice, and the procession passed by, a blend of familial and mystical.

'Do you do this?' she asked Mabon as the congregation broke ranks and packed towards the door.

'Used to. Used to serve mass at five on Sunday mornings. I am one of the fallen.'

'I expect you will go back to it.'

But he looked sceptical. Of them all, the only one affected by the mass was Esme. Lack of religious training made her more susceptible to the experience and for a long time afterwards she pondered the meaning of it and wondered at the symbols of the interior. The table on which votary candles were placed, in successive stages of melting until there were curtains of wax hanging from the edges; was it ever cleared of wax and, if so, at what intervals? What was burned as incense? What was in the sacred wafers? But most of all, she guessed at the state of faith that made the woman touch the lace hem of the surplice, in imitation of the gesture of Mary of Magdala. An act of penance or simple belief? She did not know.

They returned towards one in the morning and kept open house for anyone who wanted to drop in, till dawn. The house went like a fairground. Lights blazed throughout. She recalled some stern injunction to save electricity when she was young. She repeated this to Maurice who blew it away. Let them burn. He would be a long time in the dark.

Their visitors were old friends of Mabon's and, feeling at a disadvantage when they had so much to say directly to each other, she would slip out quietly to serve drinks and food and relieve the hosts of some obligation. There were so many, she would hardly be missed.

He came and found her once in the pantry. He slipped his arms round hers and pinned her behind the door, and when she complied, retorted, 'Don't you know only sluts kiss in doorways?'

'You should know. Besides, I am a slut with you.'

He kissed her again. 'That's the only way to get you to agree to anything. Will you come to my room tonight?'

'No.'

'Shall I come to yours?'

'No. Don't you get tired of asking the same question and getting the same answer?'

'Your words tell me no. Your body tells me differently.

Sometime your body will win.'

'Or lose. But for the moment, I am keeping my sluttishness under control.'

For all that, meeting his mouth with a smile was good, indefinably good, like the tension of the muscles after exercise, warmth in the sun, the joy of simply being in one's skin. She relished her sexual emancipation, knowing enough about herself to realise it was a self-engendered pleasure and needed no specific objective. It was convenient to have him as an aide. Often, in conversation, she had discovered that her interlocutor said nothing interesting but his very anonymity might be the stimulus she needed to voice her thoughts aloud. With Mabon she could express her sexuality, but she did not interact with his. It was a monologue with interruptions.

'Go back and be charming to their visitors. You impress them. No, I mean it. The room grows colder when you leave. Take these things will you? I wonder what's in them. They look unspeakably contorted.' She picked up savoury biscuits wound into strange and, one would have thought, inedible shapes. 'Do they even eat bark and twigs in this part of the world?'

She was still pottering about when a man came out to find more ice. 'Oh, hello. Have I seen you? Oh yes, you're Mabon's fiancée.'

'No, we're not engaged.'

'Sorry.' He was rather tipsy and gave her a wink. 'Just living together, eh?'

'No.'

'Boy, is he slipping.'

At Lochearn it was a more reticent gathering. Neighbours stayed away. It was felt the weaver had been less hospitable than of yore; there had been no bonfire party for the first time during his residence. There were one or two dinner debts that had gone unpaid for a longer period than was normal, than was polite, and it was noticed that Graeme Sutherland did not call any more except when the master was not at home. Tongues might have wagged had the mistress been anyone bar Mairi, but her propriety held good. There were still nods of acknowledgement when she went to church for morning service, and her presence there weekly gave the lie to silly Fiona's story which only half of them had heard and less than half credited. The niece, or whatever, had been summarily dismissed, but all the same it was a good yarn. It gave the lady her come-uppance and everybody likes to see the mighty fall. It fairly took the edge off any crowing about My daughter in Edinburgh or My daughter in Montreal and made the metropolitan quite commonplace after all.

So folk side-stepped them and Aileen, feeling a chill of reproof in the air, was bemused and asked why established practice had been broken, why there was no party. All she received was the excuse, too age-old for credence, of work. There had been too much work to organise it. True, even on Christmas morning he found something to occupy him and she had to go out to the sheds to fetch him back for the present-opening ceremony.

Rare visitor that she was to the work rooms, she noticed something had changed. 'Isn't it unusual for all the looms to be on the same cloth? Oh, is this the tweed you were telling me about? I'd forgotten.' She looked into it more closely. 'Well, I wouldn't buy it. It looks lumpy, like congealed porridge.'

'You are looking at gold, my lass, solid gold. You won't be anybody in a year's time if you haven't got a coat of that.'

'It's that successful?'

He brushed the pile with the flat of his hand. 'Preposterously so. I can't quite fathom it because I agree with you, there's something horribly – ecological about it, as though I were re-cycling waste product and hadn't got rid of all the old bits. But it's going to be the cloth of the decade. I've had more orders for this than for any other fabric I've ever produced, in toto, and I've only been doing it for four months. It'll be one of those definitive fabrics that appear in textbooks and people in a hundred years' time will think we were mad putting that on our backs.'

'It's outrageously romantic.'

'Is it? I didn't think about that. Why do you say so?'

'Those cloudy colours are excessively wistful, and the softness of it. Has it got some mohair in? It's wholly feminine.'

'You may be right. That's a fault. The next batch I'll make up in indigo and juniper.'

'Come back now. It's present-opening time.' He grimaced. 'Try. You haven't had any breakfast, have you?' She linked her arm through his and led him away.

311

The presents were piled in an elaborate triangle at three points on the dining-room table, in the way a zealous grocer displays his produce to be more eye-catching. Mairi made a fetish of wrapping paper and stick-on bows and cards that compulsorily matched the paper. Her warmest commendation of any box she undid was 'beautifully gift-wrapped' or 'expensive paper' or 'I haven't seen that design before' until he could have bellowed at the irrelevance of it. Her pile was grotesquely swollen by donations from several unlikely sources, chocolates which he considered the most feeble and ungiveable of gifts, from old ladies she visited, people she gave lifts to or saw regularly round the village and who had no one else on whom to lavish the affectionate vacuities of Yuletide. Likewise presents addressed to them jointly found their way into her hoard, carefully garnered and encouraged by reciprocal largesse over a three month period. It was a satisfying visual proof, at least once a year, of how much more she mattered than he did.

Her present to him was a letter opener, a flat silver blade, thin enough to slice skin if it had been whetted, and a handle like a poniard fashioned in silver gilt and chased in the manner of the craftsmen of Toledo. He did not think it appropriate or amusing.

No word. No card. No gift of the Magi. He turned aside with the dulling grief of it. Loss? It was more than loss, for to lose something implies you have mislaid it and may find it again. He was wrenched. The girl grown into him, from him, had pulled away and the wound made by the severance bled daily. It would not heal. It was not a death over which time must close, but a recurring lesion, an endemic infection of the spirit which would return in bouts when he was most whole, most sound, and sicken him. There was no avoiding it. It was in his bloodstream.

The Simards gave Esme a record player. She played Rejean's music non-stop when she was there. He had a pantheistic collection of records, some in Montreal, some at Canonmills and duplicates in both places of those pieces he could not be without for long. His present to her was half a dozen of these works she played over and over again – It's self-interest because you're wearing my versions out! – and one record by the Indian singer Buffy Sainte-Marie whose songs were heard in every corner of the house when

312

Rejean was home. She sang the traditional ballads, like 'Sir Patrick Spens',

Long, long may the ladies sit
With the gold combs in their hair
A-waiting for their own dear loves
For them they'll see no more.

And then there were her own songs, intoned to the accompaniment of the mouth-bow which was a cross between pipe and a single string lyre, the strange pulsing of which put Rejean and Esme into a state of trance no one else could share.

'Oh Rejean, do turn that dirge off. It's Christmas.'

'This is Esme's.'

'The same applies. Not today, not this moment, please.'

They turned down the volume in the study to oblige.

The disadvantage of this from their point of view was that it gave space to talk, which up till then they had avoided, there being no subject which was not fraught. He did not want to discuss Mabon any more than she wanted to discuss Aileen with him. They wheeled silently over neutral ground. He thought she looked well, that is he found her more attractive than before. She had done something with her hair he could not quite figure, but it suited her. She smiled and laughed more than she had done on her own soil. More than all this, however, when she sat on the floor and laid her cheek along an arm rest, there was no need to say anything. Her silences were sympathetic.

He had put off going to Port Alfred, had gone to Ontario and British Columbia instead, made notes, carried out some research, visited an old friend in Washington which was his favoured state. He drove down the coast road from Seattle, along the cliff tops which descended into horseshoe bays and sandy coves that made lagoons of the trapped water behind, where horsemen rode through surf, but came back always to the unasked questions. From time to time he took a deep inrush of breath, prepared himself to speak and then found the record must be changed, the fire adjusted to someone would pass the door and inhibit his speech.

'You're cheating,' said Claire, coming to find them. 'Switch it off and be sociable. Where's Mabon? How can you be such a terrible host. You know Maurice has gone to fetch your grandmother. See to the wine now, Rejean.'

Esme's gift to Mabon had cost her some thought. She supposed she must give something and at last decided on the white silk scarf with fringes which was worn by the other pilots but which, she had asked Tom Westwater indirectly, he did not own. But the decision turned out to be the easiest part of it. They were not sold commercially. She had to telephone the supply store on the Base which dealt with officers' uniforms and then order one, for they were out of stock. Then, because she had no entry permit to the camp, it had to be sent to her and arrived, as it befell, the day they left for Montreal.

Still, she was rewarded by his genuine pleasure, not so much at the thing (he had already worn one out and neglected to replace it) as at the trouble he appreciated she had gone to. His reply was less auspicious, a four inch square box placed on the table at the end of dinner. Dismantled, it proved to be a chocolate orange which was a novelty in that these were English and imported.

'Have you seen these before?' he asked. No one else had.

'Yes, I've seen them,' she faltered. She should not have put in so much effort, for it showed up the paltriness of his. She was acutely embarrassed at the gaucheness of not anticipating theirs would be a dollar forty-nine exchange.

'Won't you unwrap it?' he pushed.

Could she say she disliked chocolate now and add insult to ineptitude? 'Would anyone else like some?' Perhaps mercifully, no one would and she could quietly forget it without having to simulate pleasure.

'I rather think I could find a corner,' said Maurice, sensing the hiatus.

'Should you?' warned Claire.

'On top of what I've just eaten, it can make no difference whatsoever.'

Obligingly, Esme unfolded the box and took out the ball wrapped in orange coloured foil and carefully undid it. As it fell apart into segments, it revealed that one had been removed and replaced by a cardboard wedge so that from the outside it was still a perfect sphere. Under the cardboard was a curl of tissue paper in

314

which he had folded a ring, a thing perfectly devised for hiding in the angle of the section.

They applauded as she held it out. 'Now that is something.'

'How ingenious. How did you wrap it up so carefully again? That is the most entertaining thing I've seen for a long time.'

She tried the ring on. Of course it fitted. How should he overlook the obvious? He could gauge the circumference of her finger by looking at it. It was of gold, an antique ring with a pale amethyst in a raised setting which was decorated with four hearts, one on each side. It outshone all else given and received that day as well as everything she owned, but she did not find it either amusing or appropriate; her thank yous were muffled by the obligation to say them, and the weight of what the Simards must read into such a present given in such a way.

They dined at Gleneagles. It seemed less of a failure so, among the other lost revellers. He looked round at the men sitting at table and wondered how many of them bore his stigmata. Were they too driven from home by its unbearable pressures, or by their own hollowness which did not manifest to them the futility of doing things like this, in style, spending a working man's wage on an evening's food and wine, showing off in front of those who were being shown off, being seen to be seen?

All the same, he refused to be absolutely boorish now that he was bibbed and tuckered.

'When I was a boy, I never once ate Christmas dinner.'

'Never?' Aileen could not believe such an omission.

'Not in the conventional sense, no. I never sat down to a dinner at home. My mother wouldn't stay in Scotland over the winter. She wouldn't stay over the summer either but the winters she deplored. She used to take her furs and set off for Europe. She liked crisp weather, snow, frost, anything but damp. I did think she was a reincarnation of the Snow Queen when I read Hans Anderson. We trudged round the Mediterranean for three or four weeks every year. I'm sure she sent me to boarding school so that I could have interminable holidays to traipse round the continent with her. My father couldn't leave. If he didn't sell rings at Christmas he was never going to sell them. So I was a kind of chaperone to my mother, and a pretext! Can't you see how pale he is? He must get away from this wretched fog.

'So there we were, Anya and I, stranded in some hotel on the Côte d'Azur that had virtually shut down for the winter and would serve you gruel and brisket on Christmas day if there were two in the dining room. Anya could have gone and rolled her sleeves up, and cooked a dinner for them, but it wasn't her style to have her hands smelling of onions and chicken stock. Latterly we took a villa, anything that came to hand, Greece, the Adriatic, it didn't matter where. But she wasn't going to sit at home with her son on Christmas day, that was much too dull. She would sound out the local gentry or anyone interesting, bohemian would do but she preferred rich, and she sent them a card when she arrived. She had taken the soubriquet Baroness which was quite unwarranted, well no, her father was a Baron though he utterly disowned her when she married trade, but it did look good on her visiting card. It didn't matter to her that visiting cards had gone out of fashion twenty years before when the telephone arrived. Out of a dozen sent in any district she descended on, maybe half paid off. Some lady or gentleman came to call. She did well with the ladies. She did rather better with the gentlemen. She spoke all the European languages, so conversation was no problem, and she invariably charmed her way into a household for the festive period. She was a natural sponger, instinctive, had no qualms about it. Maybe she belonged to a period of broader hospitality when the Baron had house guests a batch at a time, tutors for his children and walkers for his dogs. She did have her standards. She wouldn't take outright. She always stumped up somehow. She used to carry little presents with her ready wrapped to make her welcome complete. The trouble was, she couldn't remember what was in them and would spend hours deciphering them by feel. She had an embroidered carpet bag of things she considered private, that is out of bounds to me. "What was this? The silver thimble. That will do for Madame, but Monsieur will have to have the snuff box. Alexis, have you hidden the snuff box? I thought you took rather a fancy to it for fish hooks."

'So we gained entry into a dozen different Christmases. Other people's celebrations are so much more interesting than your own, and the men and women who were prepared to put up with her, not to say me, were unusual people to begin with. Displaced persons like herself, displaced in time, living out their anachronisms of a way of life long gone, or refugees from one sort of persecution or another. They were the old Europeans who could sit down and talk, truly talk to each other about last year in Marienbad, the latest champagne festival at Montreux, the restoration of the Sistine Chapel. These were shared experiences. There was a communality of interest. They took care to keep themselves informed. And on top of that she was a vagrant, quite rootless beyond feeling she was a citizen of the world. She once told me she had slept with every nationality of European except her own.' He waved his hand in apology in case this was indelicate over dinner.

'I didn't always get to sit at table. I think some of her hosts thought I was an elaborate page boy in my knickerbockers, and despatched me to the kitchen. I don't think Anya was too clear on my filial status when it behoved otherwise. She could ignore the specifics of a situation very well. "The boy" she would call me vaguely. But I had rather better fun below stairs than she imagined. Occasionally it came off and we were feasted royally. There was a party once, I was older then, fifteen or sixteen, in an Austrian Schloss. Everyone nearby talked about the place because the princeling had paid off his gambling debts by hiring it out as the set of a war film, though I was personally convinced it was Count Dracula's castle. He sent his Rolls-Royce to pick us up on Christmas day, which I was impressed by at the time. I think he was rather taken with the Baroness, but I was under strict instructions never to leave her alone with any of her admirers. That could be awkward, being a six foot putto stuck behind a screen, constrained between his go and her stay. She was very wicked and used to tell me of her exploits, she had no one else to boast of these conquests to, but the facts were carefully excised. I could guess pretty well what pages had been turned too quickly for me to see. But for her day she was a very liberated lady.'

'You never told me any of this before.'

He adjusted the remaining implements of his place setting and then looked sideways at his daughter. 'Of course not. I've only this second made it up.'

He was silent driving home, spent an hour playing the 'Enigma' variations before he went to bed. He pushed the curtains wide in his room when he did retire so that he might have a view while he fell asleep and could be awakened naturally at dawn, provided that sleep came at all.

He was at the point of dropping off when the door of his room silently opened and admitted Mairi.

Such an unprecedented intrusion called for alarm. Was there bad news from the other side of the Atlantic, he wondered, or was Aileen suddenly taken ill? He waited for doom, but she walked in softly slippered and to his continuing surprise closed the curtains again to shut off the light from the half moon.

He sat up to address her. She was robed in a nightdress and peignoir of satin weighted with Brussels lace. Was this how she was attired in her own room, in her own bed? His house was a mystery of revelation. He had thought her strictly flannelette. She sat on the edge of his bed and it came over him that she was a somnambulist he must not disturb. How then could he direct her back to her own chamber without rousing her? And yet the hand that leaned forward and touched his bare chest seemed conscious enough, its pressure deliberate. He removed it, kindly, but it returned again and he was impelled to speak.

'It would be better if you went back to your room.'

To his utter dismay, she began to remove the film of the dressing gown till he stopped her with a hand. She was, when all was said and done, a handsome woman. She had not broadened or thickened over the years and if it were left to externals he might have welcomed these advances. A waft of pity came over him for the waste they had incurred. She could have succeeded with someone else.

'I think,' he whispered, 'I think that you should go to bed.'

'Why not here?'

He pulled the shoulders of the robe together. Her nakedness was the greatest obscenity to him, more than his mother's with whose nude lounging from the bath or poolside he was intimate.

'We are too damaged. Let us leave it at that.'

'It is what you wanted, or was it others and not me?'

'Shh. Let us leave each other self-respect.'

'Is it still her?'

He turned and refused to answer but she repeated it louder and

318

or two as harmless as a grain of salt in a brine solution lying in a laboratory dish. Each day the rime grew thicker and stronger, while the inky blue waters were compressed into a smaller area, until the day came when she stood on the southern shore and in either direction, the river was white. It was submerged under an ice-cap. The theory of polar waste growing towards the temperate regions and affecting their climate did not strike her as remote or absurd any longer. This was the primaeval force. This made land into wilderness, sea into land, forests into coal, made food scarce, animals extinct. Man bowed to it. When the polar ice-cap relented, man flourished. But his migration north was bounded by a definition of hardship, the absolute barrier where it caused pain to breathe, exhaustion to walk.

Already, by the end of January, she was unspeakably tired of things white. The monochrome hurt the eyes. An etiolated landscape had no perspectives. Where were the blue hills of Fife when she looked north? Where were the sounds of bustle, a ship's hooter, the distant roll of the sea, the dimension of largeness in other people's lives? Everything was silent. Silent, deadened, frozen in. Or when the snow-laden winds did come, once or twice a week, there was such a howling, an other-wordly scraich of souls in torment, all the damned foregathered on the shores of Styx and forbidden to cross, that silence was preferable.

There had been a lull. Most weekends she stayed indoors while Mabon stuck close to Base, or so he said, expecting to be called out on the quick sorties which were all that could be gained in the way of flying time in such unpredictable conditions. But Carnival week had come round and she had promised him at Christmas that she would go and watch the ski-ing competition in which he was entered as the representative of his squadron. It was scheduled to take place on the slopes of the golf club at Grande-Baie. The weather had been clear for some days, with bitterly cold night temperatures which seldom rose above freezing in the day, but the skies were brilliant and there was neither wind nor snow. Though Esme had no particular relish for the expedition, the weather for once provided no excuse.

She set out to meet him at Grande-Baie as planned. Clouds had started to pile up at dawn and the experienced eye took warning.

Storm shutters were fitted, cars parked in more sheltered areas downwind, what was loose-tied, what was animate brought indoors.

Esme's eye was not experienced. No one had told her about real cold. No one could have done. How can you convey any sensation to someone who has not known it for himself, the blueness of blue, the flavour of an apple or what is warm inside a kiss? Mabon might say, Your coat is inadequate, or Maurice, Make sure your car battery is kept warm, but without the value of first-hand knowledge, these timely admonitions missed their mark. Esme went unprepared into the Saguenay winter. It was almost as negligent as a high-altitude pilot forgetting his oxygen equipment, or an astronaut disregarding his exercises for weightlessness. She had no shield of anticipation with which to protect herself. The natives were short and compact. Esme was too long and her body was wasteful of heat. They knew the tricks of dressing and moving which they had acquired from infancy – several thin layers tied at the waist, close cuffs, nothing over the mouth because the breath would condense and eventually freeze into a chapping and uncomfortable muzzle. They knew how to turn against the wind, how to stay indoors on certain days and perform a multitude of errands on others, not to touch exposed metal with a bare hand because the flesh would stick and tear before it came loose. Frostbite. Yes, these were new possibilities. The art of survival was hard learned.

She had thought that the human body was infinitely adapted to the planet it inhabited. It was not. The frail housing was not proof against the shocks of cold, heat or drought. It would freeze or scorch or dehydrate every bit as readily as a botanical specimen transplanted into a foreign clime. The body was a stranger in its own environment. These extremes could be minimised by some degree of preparation, but nothing could counter the most invasive element, fear: fear of the unknown and the unpremeditated which brought her up against the terminal nature of her own resources.

Her fears as she took the eastbound road out of Arvida that day were nameless and formless, laughable to the long-standing resident who was not likely to think he was going to perish at every turn of the road. The sky was still blue and she told herself she could easily drive out to the Baie des Ha-Ha and back before nightfall, when admittedly poor visibility would make the judgment of distances more difficult. The Saguenay roads, like most in Canada, were built high to shed snow, with deep ditches on either side, and were usually without the benefit of cat's eyes, so that at night the road merged into the ditch and more than one driver pitched up, relatively unharmed, in a wall of snow. Even in the towns she found the lack of pavement disconcerting since it provided an edge to miss or aim at. Driving on the right-hand side of the road, when she was accustomed to walking on the left and looking for oncoming traffic in that direction, was strange and confusing. Her brain had to invert.

She nosed her way along the empty road, bounded in white, but thinly. There were no drifts. The winds had cleared the surface of snow. It showed through black in patches all the way to Grande-Baie and she laughed at her own timidity.

One of the hills of the golf course was bustling with activity. She parked nearby and got out to walk that way. The slopes were cleared for the competition, which was well advanced to judge by the compaction of the snow surface. On the edge of the run maybe a hundred spectators had gathered and their clothes showed up in vivid spots of colour, the primary paint-box red, blue and yellow against the backdrop of snow. They were, she noticed, all suitably clad in boots and ski-wear. Tom Westwater came over when he saw her, leaving the group of his fellow supporters.

'Gee, you look blue.'

'I know. I've got on everything I possess and I'm still frozen.'

'You'll be OK next winter. You'll acclimatise.'

Esme did not tell him that she bitterly regretted letting herself in for this one, and was not going to stay for another.

He explained what was happening. It was a slalom competition against the clock. As they watched, skiers floated down between the markers. Mabon and Charles Cartier were the leaders of their sections and would represent them in the final having made the fastest time in the preliminary heats. She smiled at Tom's enthusiasm. The gauntlet had been thrown down; honour was at stake. They were like knights in a tourney taking up a challenge on behalf of some obscure code of chivalry, inter-squadron envy, ground versus air, she didn't know what.

She didn't need to be told which was Mabon. Dressed in black, he was conspicuously poised at the starting point. He was coiled in a ball and, when the flag dropped, he shot out of the starting gate as though he had been released with a spring into the air and began his long swooping descent. Esme did not think he was the best of the skiers she had watched in ten minutes at the slope. There were others with more grace, more style perhaps, but he had determination seamed into every line of his body. His agility and flexion at the turns of the flag markers was pronounced. He took them without hesitation, weaving in and out while his rivals seemed to hesitate a fraction of a second and go round the outside of each. When the last spray from his heels went up at the finishing tape, a spontaneous cheer went out over the snow, whatever the clock said. He was a trier and his allies tried with him all the way.

He plodded over to her and removed the goggles. 'I didn't think you'd come.'

'Why not?'

'Didn't you hear the storm warning on the radio first thing?' She shivered ignorance. 'You must learn to put the radio on when you wake up. In fact I called you to say stay put, but you had already gone.'

'That was . . .' But any commendation of his thoughtfulness he would refute as merely being sensible. 'Have you won?'

'I don't know yet. I don't care as long as I beat Cartier. I improved on my time.' He glanced over to where the judge held up marks to indicate his speed while he thought over to himself how in the middle section he could have improved. The snow was fast now, iced over with the drop in temperature. By greater effort, lower dipping, he could have picked up a second or two and he was annoyed with himself. 'He comes last because he was faster on the first run. Can't you stop your teeth chattering?'

'When will the storm come?' she managed to hold her jaw steady enough to say recognisably.

'Later this afternoon. We're all right for now. Relax. Do you want to go back to my car and I'll be down in a few minutes.' She had discovered that his questions were always imperatives, politely phrased, so she conceded and, taking his keys, went down to the parked car which was warm inside because he had placed it butting a wall where it was in full light.

Charles Cartier's flag went down. He was an accomplished skier but he was altogether heavier than Mabon who, like the knowing pilot he was, had calculated that the force of gravity would not be fully counteracted by the effects of wind resistance on that large frame. And youth gave him the edge, as well as weeks of practice. The older man could not manoeuvre so deftly round the markers, and ended a second or two slower, to the delight of all the junior officers who were rooting for the reprobate. She smiled too, relieved that he had won the joust.

He received their congratulations as his due, easy, unperturbed when he spoke to them. He was well pleased when he joined her, bringing his kit from the boot to change out of the ski-ing suit in the back of the car. 'What do we do now?' He consulted his watch first and then the sky, hazing over to the north but not dramatically so. 'I reckon we've another two hours. Let's go into Chicoutimi and buy you a coat. I am sick of seeing you look frozen.'

This did not strike her as such a bad idea. If she was to outlast this winter, she must put another layer between herself and the elements. 'In both cars?'

He examined the logistics of the journey. He made a reckoning of distance versus weather versus time and knew she relied implicitly on his decision. 'We'll take the sedan, and come back for your car later. It's so much slower. We'll be there and back in an hour in this.' So saying, he spun it round and headed along the coast road from Grande-Baie to Chicoutimi.

On the shore was the office and lumber plant, boasting in twelve inch characters *Maurice Simard et Fils*, abandoned too to frozen inactivity. A tall derrick stood out into the river, which stripped the raw barks from the timber which was floated downstream from the dense forests up country. A pile of prepared logs, maybe ten or fifteen hundred pieces, mast long, lay on the formed ice waiting for the thaw and the journey in a boom down the St Lawrence to the manufacturing towns of Ontario. They looked at this distance and in their spilled carelessness like straw, or a handful of matchwood. How immense were the resources of the country when trees could be plundered so voraciously. At the end of the chute a single trunk hung frozen in the air, suspended against gravity as though it were attached to the end of the conveyor belt by magnetic force. In a few days, perhaps, the air would warm sufficiently to break its hold, melt the adhesion of ice, and it would crash down fifty feet to join the cataract below.

Further on, she noticed huts on the ice like sentry boxes and asked what they were.

'Men use them for fishing.'

'But it's frozen. How can they fish in that water?'

'They cut a hole like Eskimoes and the fish come up for air. It's easy fishing.'

'But how can the fish be alive when the river is iced over?'

'God, Esme, you are so ignorant. Their gills filter oxygen. What *is* surprising is that the fishermen take out fires, braziers with charcoal to keep themselves warm while they are waiting, and the fire doesn't melt the ice.'

She pondered this inconceivable paradox to herself. Fire did not melt ice. Trees hung in air. How?

They went at once to the shop where she had bought her dress and flatteringly the assistant remembered her, L'écossaise naturellement, and because the shop was quieter than usual on a Saturday they received more than their share of attention. The owner joined them at one point in the fitting room, inflating the quality of the merchandise with tales of how she brought the latest fashions directly from Montreal, and how they did not have their duplicate in the Saguenay. Each item she sold was unique, she assured.

Mabon sat patiently by while the assistant brought garment after garment to them, and as choice became ever more elusive for Esme (when had she decided anything except by default?) he was drawn deeper and deeper into comment and stood to adjust and assist.

'That's too bulky for the car. That's too bright and showy,' he would say at once and send things back without a second look.

She was self-conscious. She was not free to relax in these various shapes superimposed by the tailor's cut, and moreover trying coats on and taking them off brought her into physical contact with him. She found that if she remained about two feet away from him she could see him in focus. Outside his magnetic field, her actions were unimpaired. But the moment they moved closer, her will, her judgment, her very brain seemed to dwindle into a helpless reliance on him. As he smoothed a shoulder, straightened a lapel, she could not see his hands as practical functionaries. They flattered, stimulated, were outrageously personal. At times, fluttering like restless pigeons round her form, she could wish that they might settle where they liked, if only to be still.

The owner played her master stroke. 'La jeune demoiselle vient d'Ecosse. Nous avons ici un manteau tout à fait exceptionel qui vient aussi d'Ecosse.'

She brought the coat in with her, over her arm. The sight of it was adequate proof for Esme. The label at the neck with Alexis' signature was unnecessary corroboration. It had passed through his hands. Everything about the coat declared that fact, the subtlety of the dyes, the quality of the yarn, the weave of thick and thin pieces.

'You must understand this cloth is hand woven and that makes it quite special. No two are the same. Ah see, it could have been made for you. Perfect.'

'What colour would you call it? Blue?' he asked.

She stared into it fathomlessly. It was every colour in a starling's wing, a midnight blue, but a blue that travelled well along the light. It did not die in the air like azure or the thin colour of woad, unstable and streaky. This was strong and intense. She saw him mixing, weighing, crushing this and that, dipping the hanks, a form of occupation and excellence so remote from anything she knew now that it was next to impossible to believe it had come from his looms a small month before. She looked at it with as little familiarity as if it were chain mail hanging in a museum exhibit. 'Made in Scotland, you see,' confirmed the assistant holding out the label.

'This is the best. This will do.' He had decided for her. She stood inertly like a child and let him button up the garment. 'Turn.'

She turned, dumbly.

'Do you like it?' Time was running on. He wanted to get back before the storm closed in.

She had no idea if she liked it. She hadn't as much as looked at it, had no notion of detail or fit or cut. She only knew it was indigo and juniper, that it had a thread of mohair and one of flax that did not entirely take up the colour. 'It's rather dear, I think.'

'Then let me buy it for you.'

The assistant discreetly removed herself from the scene of financial altercation, especially when she could assume it was a form of barter.

'Oh no, I didn't expect you to do that.'

'I don't imagine you did. I will pay for it now and we can argue about it later.'

She wore it at once and the old coat was packed into a carton, though he was all for throwing it away. They emerged into a deserted street. People had retreated indoors for the wind was picking up fragments of snow and turning them unpleasantly into a flying shrapnel of ice. Mabon and Esme dodged and herringboned their way uphill to the car park, taking momentary respite in the arcade of shop fronts. When they reached the black sedan, they found the locks were frozen over, but he carried a spray of some kind on him which warmed and released them. On the windward side of the vehicle, snow and ice caked together in rivulets. The wheels when they started were solid and did not roll so much as bump them along.

'I made a mistake,' he admitted. 'We should have brought both cars and made sure you got back. I haven't seen the weather change this quickly for a long time.'

She was instantly terrified. 'What will happen?'

'We do one of two things. Take you to Arvida, hope I get back to the Base and abandon your car altogether at Grande-Baie, or do it in reverse. It's so maddening being stuck here in the middle, with your car as far as it could be from home.'

'How long is this wind likely to keep up?'

'Maybe days.'

'We can't leave the car all that time without a block warmer.' She remembered Maurice's tale of the car lost in the drifts till the spring thaw. 'We'll have to go to Grande-Baie.'

But the drive was much worse than either of them had anticipated. He had made his second mistake in underestimating the deterioration of the weather. One moment the sky was clear, the next they were in a white tunnel. Mabon tried to disguise from her the extremity of the road conditions, knowing how timorous she was against the massive whiteness of the landscape. The one factor to their advantage was daylight, though that hardly counted for much when there was zero visibility. They did not pass or meet another car on the return journey to Port Alfred, or rather they did not see one because the driven snow fell on them so suddenly that they might have been in a convoy of traffic, obliterated by the opaque windscreen. He still had to drive as though there might be other fools on the road besides themselves.

The wipers failed to clear the heavy falls. They clogged, froze, lay idly groaning under the impossible task of lifting the accumulated weight. Time and time again Esme had to wind down her window, which at once admitted a maelstrom of wind and stinging hail, lean out over the windscreen and shovel the snow away by hand, or scrape the ice off the wiper blades. They said nothing. The high whine of the wind, the drone of the labouring engine, made speech a chore, and there was between them the unspoken coordination which comes of adversity, of needing each other to prevail. He was determined they should reach Grande-Baie at least. A walk of two or three miles, if they had to abandon the car, was a risk he was not hasty to undertake. He glanced over at her. The coat would rebuff the storm, but she was not adequately shod for long walking. Goddam her for a liability. The inconvenience of two frozen cars and both away from Base was another major deterrent, even if the walk to shelter was accomplished safely. He coaxed the engine yard by yard along the shoreline, oblivious of anything but the whirling white that enveloped them. Fishing boxes, log boom, railway depot, all were wiped out. All he could attend to was the imperative need to keep moving east, to keep the motor running without a stall. Once when she leaned out to clear the windscreen of its packed load the blizzard whipped the white silk scarf from round his neck and it was irretrievably gone.

The hill into Bagotville town gave relief. They were within sight of houses, and the leeward dip of the bay shaded the colony from the worst of the blast. They found Esme's car smothered, but functional.

'What do we do now? I can't drive to Arvida by myself in this.'

'We're in a fix and whatever we do will probably be wrong. You can't go back on your own, that's for sure. I think we're best to go back to the Base, and wait there till the worst is over. You can stay for dinner in the Mess, and when the snow stops or the wind dies down we'll get you back somehow.'

'Will we get that far?'

'The back road is more sheltered than this coast road and I can attach a tow line if you break down. We'll make it.'

Esme was too afraid to ask what would happen if the storm did not abate. The immediate was too pressing. The dread of their drive together was nothing compared with being on her own in the white dark. She concentrated on the fact that she would be indoors again, under a roof, in half an hour and could wipe out the sights and sounds of that day. The last leg of their cross-country staging was difficult in that they had to traverse the wind which poured down from the north, but that very factor kept the windscreens clear, and they were able to maintain motion till the gates of the Base grew into sight.

The station was in chaos. The condition of white-out was sufficiently rare to be a talking point. Today it had become dangerous because it had blanketed over so suddenly that the normal procedures could not be carried out. A routine airline flight was expected down in twenty minutes but the snow ploughs were failing to keep the runway clear. The storm had descended before the pilot could be alerted at Montreal, nor would there be time to refuel or turn round to make a half turn to Quebec. The plane must land and on a sheet of frozen ice. No one there could forget the accident three months before and fatalities loomed again. That pilot had known the Base; this one was a comparative stranger. In these conditions houses, fields, runway and forest became indistinguishable.

Mabon settled Esme into the Mess and went to his room to find his heavy overshoes. Then he connected both cars to the tether of the block warmer, and went out to help if a dangerous landing was inevitable.

The room was empty apart from two or three wives who had come across to collect the mail from the post office boxes, and they twittered excitedly about the storm before feeling their way back the few hundred yards to their homes. They reckoned it was as well there was no social event planned at the Mess, this being a major furlough weekend, because nobody would have been able to drive out, and they would have had to sleep inside the Base. This gave rise to many conjectured pairings, the burden of which troubled Esme not at all.

How could such men be married to such women! Two dozen were out there now, Mabon among them, doing whatever was needed to ensure the safety of an aircraft and its passengers. There would be ambulances on standby, men reading radar screens for pinpoint accuracy, others on the tailboard of a fire engine. Some man ran, head bent into the wind, to place flares at the perimeter edge of the runway in the hope that they would illuminate it and give the pilot a sighting, to make that marginal difference between safety and catastrophe. How did he know the plane would not fall from the sky and crush him? How did the men in the flight control tower know the incoming craft would not drop a foot or two and collide with them? On such a day radar was only as effective as the men who read the signals and passed on the messages. She could not do what they were doing, endanger her life to protect another, never. And the pilot, even if he did have ground-controlled assistance, how could he see flying blind? She could not see to drive at a fraction of his speed, and with the confirmation of a road under her, not in shifting skies. These were skills so far outwith her knowledge that she looked on these men as demi-gods. She marvelled at the prototype of the modern hero, the twentieth century explorer, pilot and navigator, the sailor of the skies. No other profession conjoined glamour and responsibility in equal part. He was what every man at some point in his career admired and wished to be, and at that moment Esme worshipped him too.

Gradually, she was left alone. The wives shunned her as an oddity, an outsider. Through the muffled silence of the storm she waited, tense, for some reading as to what was taking place outdoors. She heard rather than saw the plane come down. Its engines throbbed overhead for a few seconds before the sound was swallowed up, and she prayed with all her strength that no one might be injured, that is she kept her attention unwaveringly on that spot and trusted to the professionalism and dedication of the men, rather than rely on a deity whose actions to date had been ambiguous. The men who helped to guide the craft down said she slewed over the runway as if it were a skating rink and came to rest with her nose in a mound of discarded snow.

The passengers were only a dozen in number, and were glad of the refuge offered at the Mess. A few at a time, officers and civilians, filtered back across the snowbound tarmac and brought good spirits to the room. The lights went on, the bar was opened. Dinner was proposed as a panacea to all temporary ills. The evening was under way but Mabon was still missing. Some officers from the quarters brought their wives over to join the resident bachelors for the meal, anxious to be where the events were, to be in the focus of today.

That was the least of Esme's intentions. She wanted to be as far away from that scene of howling desolation as she could imagine. The others seemed able to turn their backs to the staring window, the empty lifeless view it framed. They lifted their glasses as inconsequently as ever and she could almost envy their blinkered vision. The desire to return home was strong in her, to sit in her own chair, sleep in her own bed. The white abyss which separated her from them made their attractions the more reassuring.

Bob Findlay came over and spoke to her. 'What are you doing so far from Arvida?'

'We were caught in the storm, driving back from Chicoutimi.'

'I'm surprised. Mabon should have known better.'

At that moment, Mabon joined them unsmilingly. 'It looks bad. I've been over to the Met office and they say the storm isn't expected to pass over till two in the morning. The gale is force nine and strengthening with heavy precipitation. In other words, we're in for a bad night.'

'There's isn't a great deal we can do then, is there? We'll have dinner first.' And she turned to include Bob at their table but he had already left his seat.

The night carried all the ingredients for a spontaneous party that no one there would forget. It was the high spot of the year, a head-shaking event that remained a by-word for a long time after. They were adrift, removed from the constraints of normality. The blizzard of wind and snow heightened their pleasure in the warmth and conviviality of each other's company. Officers who passed surly from some old slight clapped each other on the back as they heard and told of their own heroism. Strangers were present who must be entertained, made welcome so that they carried away a legendary account of Air Force hospitality. The bar did not close all night and those whose senses were not completely dimmed gave out the vaguest hints of the bacchanalian scene. Charles Cartier, the senior officer there, set the tone by flirting openly with every one of the fifteen or so women present. Yvonne was in Ottawa with her mother, and servicemen did not tell tales, never knowing when they might require the mumness of mutual secrecy. If Charles Cartier could persuade any woman to cross the storm-swept arena to his vacant bed that night, good luck to him.

The lights went out at nine thirty. The electricity lines had been cut at Shipshaw and though the station had its own emergency generator the Mess was not reconnected for lighting. Installations and monitoring systems were the priority. No one minded. Adults could play at being children and grope in the dark. Candles came out. Someone fairly enterprising came across with batteries for the music machine. And in the corner a game of poker lit by a heavy car torch vied for supremacy and noisiness over the dancing.

Charles Cartier commanded her in a quick-step, though his performance of this was rather slower than the beat of the music. 'We're having a party for some friends when my wife comes back. Would you and Mabon like to come? We would be delighted if you could both make it.'

She tried to move out of the vice of his grip actually to look at him while accepting this invitation, but had to be content with a cliff-face view of his shoulder. How she hated dancing plastered up against a man, no room to move your feet but at his direction. She remembered the precise aesthetics of a reel where the tip of the fingers was the point of contact and feet went to and fro with the delicacy of a lacemaker's bobbins. Oh, the decorum of the past.

She switched to Mabon at the end of that record and he was impressed by the invitation she had obtained for them both. He imagined he would be one of the most junior officers there. He was penetrating the inner circle. What power Esme had to effect these entries he could not imagine. He could identify that she had some strength of individuality, but while this did very well in private life he had not thought it would be of any use in his professional one. Now he felt she could open doors for him that would remain closed much longer otherwise, until the due process of time and rank and seniority was fulfilled. Esme was a step in the right direction for more reasons than one, personally desirable, but also a means of access, a social asset.

She leaned on him willingly in answer to the irresistible pressure of the dancer's hand in the small of her back. She ought to be going but, oh, not just yet.

Charles Cartier came forward suddenly and switched off the music. He waited till dead silence fell before he spoke, taking his stand easily as the man in charge. 'The control room has called through to say the storm has set in for the night and a general statement is being broadcast by our own and the French radio station, warning personnel not to go outside unnecessarily. The temperature has dropped to thirty below, with a wind factor, and it is feared that either frostbite or permanent tissue damage could result from quite brief exposure. We don't want that happening. I believe that, unprecedentedly in the valley, divine service and Mass will not be said in church tomorrow morning to encourage the community to stay at home. So please be alert and do not venture outside unless you are equipped with survival suits.

'Now our immediate problem is that all fifty of us must stay here for the night. As far as I know from checking duty rosters, some fifteen officers are absent on weekend leave, and these rooms will be made available for our civilian guests. There are spare supplies of bedding in the ward room at the back of the Mess and I am afraid station personnel must make the best of a night on a mattress on the floor. It should be a friendly night.'

A mêlée ensued of jamboree proportions. Mattresses were heaved down the corridor from the ward room. Men and women collapsed laughing or drunken. Shouts were raised. A brawl broke out between two officers over one secretary. The civilians had the time of their lives. They cavorted joyfully together. Two business-men from Montreal wondered independently how they could switch their wives. If they had only spoken to each other, they might have brought it off.

Mabon and Esme stepped out of the confusion into his room, and shut the door.

'So this is the cell?'

A hand torch revealed it was as impersonal as her own room. A flying manual propped up a series of aerial reconnaissance maps. A clipboard with a sheaf of virgin paper lay on the bed. The armchair was tucked away in an inaccessible position, between the bed and the radiator, seldom required. It was that unique combination of the spartan and the ugly with which rented accommodation is equipped. Its utilitarian function notwithstanding, Esme con-ceded it was tidy. The man hated a clutter of unnecessary accre-tions. He did not live here but, if not, where did he live?

'You will be more comfortable here,' he said. 'I'll sleep in the Mess lounge with the others.'

'You're going?'

There was no space to stand two feet apart. He moved towards her. He had been patient, after all. He had driven her here and there, guided her through the snow to safety, warmth, the comfort of shelter. He had bought the coat which remained an unsettled bargain between them. She owed him a little kindness in return. And, besides, in this white wilderness, he was all she knew. Whatever he was or was not, he filled the space of today. Leading

334

his hands around her back, she abandoned herself to eventuality.

He did try. But there is a limit to what a man can accomplish in a bed meant for one person. The Royal Canadian Air Force did not intentionally encourage its officers to double up. He was tired. It had been a gut wrenching day. Even men of his stamina grow tired after a morning ski-ing, an arduous drive in blizzard conditions, standing by for an emergency landing and all followed by a hectic party with far too much liquor flowing. It blunted the edge of feeling. And then the object, undressed in the double helix of the torch light, exciting enough a prospect to make anyone lose absolute control.

Perhaps he had not been wise to undertake it at all, but he did try to raise some flicker of the bodily enjoyment that he had confirmed lurked in her somewhere. He tried too hard. Esme felt herself to be a ski-run down which he was practising various jumps, knee-bends, reflexes and all against the clock. In some moods these sexual gymnastics might have been diverting, a textbook exercise in instruction, if nothing else. Stimulus, erogenous, clitoris, immissio penis were clinical terms that touched her, moved her as little as the technicalities of stem-christy, bogen, snow-plough or telemark turns. She was immune to such forms of seduction. The exclusively physical was about as erotic as a weekend spent with a map and compass orienteering in rough country. The mind had such recesses in which it hid. It viewed all dispassionately and would not be wooed. She could not concentrate on these passes because of the howling of the wind, the rattle of the glass in its frame, the flickering light he insisted on keeping switched on. It was to be expected that at the moment when he might come close to knowing her, impressing her, if ever, he took his pleasure alone. She neither knew nor cared, but he consoled himself with the confident opinion that there would be other times when it would be better.

The assembly wore a different look in the morning. Charles Cartier arose from two bottles of whisky unimpaired and manned the radio for further news. He decided to make a foray as far as the CO's house and strapped on his flying suit as Knights Templar fitted helm, targe and breastplate. By the time he returned with the orders of the day, those of the company who were awake had breakfasted, avoiding each other's eye. Bob Findlay collided with Esme coming from the room where, door ajar, Mabon lay abed.

The Chaplain averted his face. His friends called Mabon the most talked about junior officer; his enemies the most slept about. He had expected better of her somehow.

The sky mocked yesterday's blizzard. The wind still whined high in the wires, but power had been restored along them. There were deep chasms of snow as evidence of the storm, stretching in places from rooftop to rooftop like tents, but it was fine, crisp snow the wind would blow away in an hour or two. The eerie stillness of Sunday morning on the Base, with flying suspended, activity at a standstill, made it hard to credit that last night they had behaved with such frenzy, as if the dawn would not break again, or the rage of the storm abate. They had acted faithlessly, as though the ark would not come to rest on Ararat.

She stepped outside to find her car. It was tied up like a patient horse to a corral, absolutely clear of snow because of a freak of wind direction. The engine started first time. She went back indoors to tell Mabon she would risk the drive to Arvida, whether there was a daylight curfew or not. He was asleep with the admirable capacity he had of committing himself wholly to whatever was in hand, even an inert function. Sprawled, informal, he did not seem any more familiar to her than the evening before and, as she knelt at his bedside to wake him, she was still excluded from intimacy with his body. She could not take liberties with him beyond nudging him awake.

Opening his eyes, he wondered who she was and why she was in his room, till the night re-formed in his memory.

'You're dressed.'

'And breakfasted. The company is all up and about. I'm going back. I've work to do before tomorrow and the sky is quite clear. Fallen snow is preferable to falling and the ploughs have been along this morning.'

He did not offer to accompany her and when she had gone turned over and fell asleep again.

When he did rouse himself later in the day to go for a shower, he was surprised and a little displeased to find that she had written out a cheque covering the price of the coat, and left it on his dressing table.

Rejean sat at his desk and looked down on the precinct. It was not a comfortable scene. The winter had been less severe in Montreal than in the Saguenay, but it was dragging on interminably. By early March spring ought to have been imminent, but this year the earth was as hard and unreceptive to growth as he could recall. Had his two seasons away depressurised him, made him less hardy for the vigorous energising winter he had so relished in the old days before he went away?

The previous week he had gone ski-ing with a party of friends and persuaded Claire to come with him. It was as well he had taken her. He was out of breath by the time he had strapped on his boots, and the pain in his chest continued all the time he was sitting on the chair lift beside her, so much so that he felt nauseated and could not acknowledge the waves of old acquaintances, far less feel any urge to compete, or outdo their expertise. He wished himself anywhere but there. He dismounted and turned to find the best angle for his descent. There were two routes. A broad, rather easy piste that undulated over hillocks, and a narrower defile that was very much faster and was avoided by all but the experts. Out of vanity, he chose the latter. He pushed himself off unsteadily and almost unwillingly for he felt giddy, as though he were having an attack of vertigo. His legs were heavy and would not perform on the turns. His knee-caps felt rusty, and creaking joints suggested he might be unfit, out of training for such strenuous exercise. But he forced himself on. There was no way but down.

Claire overtook him on the next bend and shouted gaily as she swept past. His mortification was tripled. He braced himself for the steep downward rush. Normally he found the intake of cold air into his lungs exhilarating; today it was too literally breathtaking. He swore he could feel the sharp air seep like a poisonous gas into his trachea, through his bronchial passages and into his lungs, stifling and suffocating him like mustard gas in trench warfare. But this wasn't poison. It was pure unadulterated open air. It cracked him. The two halves of his chest seemed to split asunder and his heart, desperately racing like an over-strained engine, trying to keep the two parts in synchronisation, felt swollen to bursting. Every orifice was on fire, ears, nose, eyes, mouth. He could not see, he could not breathe. It was a miracle he did not collide with another skier or fall himself and break a bone. He was hurtling down totally out of control, a driver in a runaway car, relying on past performance to keep himself out of danger. He landed up at the foot of the slope among a brake of trees. He was still attached to his skis but he was bent double coughing, trying to expel the bitter air. Claire, seeing her son in some distress, came over to where he stood alone. He turned and was violently sick, staining the snow with an indelible patch.

She was riven by that stain. She found a handkerchief for him to wipe his mouth, and made someone fetch him a drink from the refreshment kiosk. He could not speak for some minutes and she was in a full flood of horror as he retched and gasped alternately He clung onto her shoulder and coughed repeatedly, racked with spasms that bent him in half.

She managed to unbuckle his skis and support him and them back to the car. He could not drive and relied on her to get them home safely. Though the seizure calmed a little during the half-hour journey, he was white-faced and badly shaken by the instantaneous collapse of his bodily system.

The doctor was not a great enlightener. He proposed variously that Rejean was unfit, had an upper respiratory infection, was suffering from congestion of the bronchial tract and recommended lots of glucose drinks. He regarded this as a much less dramatic manifestation of illness than many that came his way and privately thought the young man was over-reacting. No spots. No temperature.

One question he asked set Rejean's mind racing, however, when he was left alone and had time to consider. Have you had any previous history of asthma or respiratory problems? To which the instant answer was no, never. As he lay and cast his thoughts back over the previous year, he recollected the time in church when he had felt the constriction of the chest followed by the bout of coughing. Then there flitted back tiny episodes, pressure, aching, attacks of sneezing and fatigue when he was exerted. Also there had been his dramatic weight loss. No. He could not say this was a sudden and unprecedented attack. Without specifying what he was doing to anyone else, he made an appointment with a specialist who arranged to see him almost immediately.

His thorough tests and questioning revealed a diagnosis that imputed so much against Rejean's own view of his manliness that he refused to believe the outcome for some days. He went about in a morose condition, taking the pink and white layered tablets he had been prescribed and privately thinking they were a placebo.

Maybe he had been overworking. The desk was piled high with financial reports he was obliged to read but did not understand readily. He had committed long hard hours to slogging over them. Page after page of figures, debit, credit, balance sheet, margin of profit expressed as a percentage of gross annual turnover . . . it made his eyes swim, his head ache as he tried to work out the message the digits effectively concealed from him. How well were they doing? Had they indeed peaked five years before? Were they in a downward spiral from which only massive investment could save them? Was the input to be achieved by increased cash flow, the introduction of the new ideas he had been formulating, or old-fashioned hard work, longer hours, smaller salaries for himself and his father, fewer luxuries? He had given a direct instruction to Mr Scott about the sale of the property in Edinburgh and had in his hands a letter agreeing terms of sale. It was final. He wondered if he would ever stand on Scottish soil again and he felt the loss of something he had not noticed at the time, and regretted he had not made more of the experience.

This started off a long chain of association which ended up inevitably with Esme. They hadn't seen her all term. How was she? She answered his telephone calls but that wasn't the same thing at all. He checked his watch. What would be going up at midday on a Saturday? He telephoned the airport but the Air Canada desk reported that their only flight to Bagotville that day had already taxied out. Did he want a booking for Monday? The Sunday flight was cancelled. No. He hung up. There was nothing for it but to drive. He called Claire and asked her to make up a bag for him. He told Maurice quality control was slipping at Port Alfred. He would be back early in the week. He packed up his reports and filed them away, emptied the desk of papers and turned over the blotting pad.

Esme sat on the floor of her basement living room, pinning tissue paper to cloth. The Chantals were away for the weekend visiting his brother in Quebec and had taken the girls with them. She listened occasionally, and did not know what she was listening for.

She was more accustomed to the silence of the place than at the beginning, but it was comparatively recently that she had pin-pointed the exact cause of the creeping stillness that unsettled her. There were no song birds. There was no dawn chorus. In winter in Britain birds could be heard and seen even on the coldest day. In the last three months she had not heard the pure notes of bird call, except for Madame's canary upstairs singing its heart out in a filigree cage. She had broken a coconut in half and attached it to the parapet of her staircase but no bird came to swing and peck. Monsieur looked on the contraption as a symbol of witchcraft and removed it tactfully, pretending the wind had rubbed the twine that held it thin.

One afternoon, in fact, during a storm she had seen her first bird and hoped it was a sign of spring. Noah did not look more anxiously over the flooded waters for the returning dove than Esme glimpsing the bird that blew past her window. It was an anonymous species. Thrush, crow, blackbird, she did not know. It could have been anything. It was a dark mass of feathers hurtling across the flat space in front of the window, unrecognisable because of its wind-doubled size. It had torn and ruffled wings. It was perhaps a migrant bird blown off course, its transitory passage delayed too long so that it was caught a prisoner in a hostile environment. Again and again the bird attempted to rise, moving downwind to assist its take-off, but again and again it was beaten down by the tourbillion and reshaped on the ground, a squalid heap of feathers and bone. Snow clung to its wing tips. Its force was spent. Esme could do nothing. She could not keep a wild bird alive in her apartment, could not set a broken wing. It would die of terror at her ministrations, she of its fluttering. She let it blow heedlessly out of sight and hoped that the struggle would soon be over, that the power of the wind would snuff it mercifully out.

As soon as the thaw came and the atrophy of her will power was over . . . as soon as the thaw came she would leave the snowbound hemisphere and follow the sun.

She snipped, head down at the cloth. When she glanced up for a second with a mouthful of pins, she was in time to see a man stumble down her steps, not much better assembled than the hapless bird. She ran to let him in and found, under the enveloping parka, that it was Rejean.

'What are you doing here?'

'Trying to kill myself.'

She helped him out of his things and let him collapse in a heap on her settee. He was an alarming sight, heaving and puffing like a steam engine which can't take a hill. Her questions were a hindrance and she bottled them up. Quietly she folded away the scattered remnants on the floor and let him pull himself together. She thought for a moment he had fallen asleep, a rudeness that at one time would have been unthinkable for him.

'Are you expecting Mabon?' he asked, opening his eyes and staring up.

'No. If you drove up, then you probably passed him on the road. He's driving to Montreal today and then going on to a training course in Trenton for a fortnight.'

He swung his legs round and sat rubbing his eyes and cheeks. 'Isn't it inconsiderate to barge in on you like this? I wanted to surprise you, and I certainly succeeded.' He drew his breath more steadily, so that she became less anxious for him.

'Have you been unwell?'

He ignored the question and got up to poke about in her kitchen and find something to eat for he was famished after his long uninterrupted drive. 'Have you been baking bread?' Six loaves lay on a cooling tray, swollen and yeasty and burnished with glaze. 'Are you laying in for a siege? How are you going to eat all this?'

'Oh, I knew you were coming,' she said.

'Who taught you to bake bread?'

'The person who taught me to read.'

He cut off a crust and approved. 'Butter?'

'Come and sit down properly if you're going to woof.' She laid the table while he sorted through her minimal record collection.

'Haven't you bought anything since Christmas?'

'No, I'm saving.'

'What for?'

'To buy my passage out of here.'

He came and looked at her expression to see if she meant it seriously and apparently she did.

'Where are you going?'

She shrugged. 'Play Buffy.'

'Aren't you tired of it yet?'

'Why should I get tired of something I like?'

'Very commendable.'

He sat and ate the simple meal. More colour came back into his face but he had lost the patina of good health and robustness, the

341

sense that he could take all-comers he had exuded in Edinburgh. In his own terrain, he too had a smaller scale. That evening he was almost raw and transparent. She noticed a vein ticking under his left eye, and that the line he shaved to was sharply differentiated from the texture of the rest of his face. The eyes still held their good humour, but behind them was a new look, puzzlement, anxiety. It endeared him immeasurably to her. As the too-handsomeness fell away, it revealed more of the internal man. He was always the most likeable and honest of men, but that combination of virtue didn't do much to interest her. Suffering of one kind or another had sharpened him, given him a rough edge that was rather better than the bland or the smooth.

He was maybe the only person she could share a room with in companionable silence. There was no ebb and flow of tension. If he felt like it, he could turn aside and read her newspaper, she pick up a piece of sewing, either of them shift the record over when it halted, without a word being exchanged. And for all that there were vast areas they did not wish to lay bare, there was no real restriction. It was not the consuming vitality of an evening spent with Alexis where this placidity was unthinkable. Passing Alexis on the stairs, she felt transfused by whatever was in his mind at the time, and drained of what was in hers, empty and full in alternation, a pulse of response going between them every second. Rejean was more peaceable as a companion. It was possible to be herself with him, and that was a blessing. She did not need to contort herself to suit his whims. He had none. His was the tenor of equanimity.

'I should have asked you to dinner. I meant to, but I'm not very sociable at the moment. Do you mind?'

She shook her head. 'No, I don't feel up to the public glare either.'

'Will you come out for a while? Not in the car. I never want to sit in that car again. I'd like to stretch my legs. What has Arvida got to offer?'

'There's an English cinema. I haven't been to a proper cinema for years. Could you bear it?'

'It wasn't what I had in mind but we can walk there and back. Hasn't it started? What's on anyway?'

'I've no idea. Let's go and see.' She went to fetch her coat which he helped her on with and let his hands fall down the material of the sleeves.

'Nice.'

'Should be. It cost plenty.'

'That is not an urbane thing to say, Esme.'

'I never did pretend to be urbane.'

They headed out towards the main square of Arvida, a low, flat township built on a plateau which was chosen as the site of the aluminium plant for that very reason. The streets were wide and spaciously verged in green borders down which trees had been planted, still snowed over. One day they would be quite genteel boulevards. At the moment, the architecture of the functional was too prominent.

Rejean was enchanted with her movie house. It reminded them both of the Cameo at Tollcross where they had sat separately through a hundred French films, which gave rise to a long catalogue of, Did you see . . . and what about . . . I preferred the early silent version. They bought their tickets which shot out of a metal dispenser, added sticks of liquorice to their store of comforts, huddling in the velveteen back stalls like teenagers looking for chummy seats, a helpful variation on the Victorian courting couch which allowed for osculation and no other form of bodily contact. The décor took Esme back to even earlier cinema visits, to the Alhambra or the Playhouse or the Savoy on wet Saturday afternoons when she would be accompanied by the youngest uncle. The whole expedition including bus fare would cost half a crown, and then she realised that any translation for Rejean's benefit was false. She was talking the currency of the past again. What ghastly films had they sat through, horror and science fiction when her uncle's choice prevailed, less often the lushy gushy spectaculars when it was hers.

This evening it was a Boulting brothers comedy from the Ealing studios, a black and white relic that was quite lost on the audience because all the jokes were English and parochial. Only one other person in the darkened auditorium laughed apart from Esme. She wished she could find out who the expatriate was, a man, perhaps a serviceman on exchange. But when the lights went up at the end there was no one who corresponded to her image of an Englishman abroad, What was she expecting, a top hat and riding breeches? What could a fellow stranger see in her, either? She was half-naturalised.

'That was simply awful, Esme.'

'I know, wasn't it? But you'll always remember how dreadful it was.'

'I never met an Englishman who talked like that.'

'Haven't you noticed, we only export the atypical.'

He walked her down towards the frozen inlet and they meandered along the silent streets by skirting the water and came by a slow periphery to the dam at Shipshaw, whitely looming in the night. She came across something she hadn't seen before, a slip stream to the side of the dam which trickled over rocks. In summer it would make a small waterfall, maybe ten feet high, into the arterial Saguenay. In winter it had frozen into a huge stalactite, like the table of votary candles at Notre-Dame, hundreds and thousands of hours of congealed drips, a glacier before her eyes. Yes, she could accept glaciers in Greenland, shuddering firths of ice, but on her doorstep it was ominous. How could rapidly flowing water freeze? It could, inch by inch, molecule by molecule. If she stood long enough without herself turning into a pillar of ice, she might see the grains thicken inwards from the edge of the bank, crystals shaping, not as symmetrically as the hexagonal snowflakes, but gradually like Japanese paper flowers unfolding in water. This was not pretty. The progressive calcification was complete. The current was solid. How was such inversion possible! It was a sculpture of liquidity. A thousand gargoyles protruded from the ice-face, bearing hideous lumps and distortions, goitres, dropsy, boils and livid purpling bruises. It was an illustration by Blake for Dante's Inferno. But this hell was ice-bound.

He put his arm through hers and walked on. 'The thaw will start soon. You picked a bad winter. It isn't normally so long.'

'Why is it always the hottest summer or the coldest winter when I go anywhere? I expect I'm in for the wettest spring on record. Not a flower in sight.'

'Misery.'

He took her back to the house which was warm and welcoming and still untidy from their hasty exit, as though they had not really left it and met themselves coming back. He did not want to anticipate the moment when he would have to go out into the sharp night again and sat irresolute while she made good the room. They lit a lamp and made coffee. Talk was easy, endless. It was not hard to sit under the same arc of light together and roll time away towards midnight. When a room empties of sound, the slightest movement makes a great disturbance, and they sat perhaps longer than they should, and said more than they ought, inevitable when there are only two beings moving in the universe. He put his head in her lap for comfort and Esme stroked his head in an aimless caress. Here it was Mabon had first embraced her, but how much more at ease she was tonight than with the other. From where he lay outstretched, his view was of her upturned chin, which with a drowsy eye he could pursue to the mobile neck and shoulders. She was deep-gorged, voluptuous as a pouter-pigeon, reminding him of down-filled pillows and sleep.

'Esme?' the trill went out and broke into the shadows of the room.

'Yes, you can stay the night if you want to.'

'Can I sleep in your bed?'

'Well, I . . .' Her doubts formed on her brow.

'I mean sleep. I'm in such pathetic physical condition I doubt if I could manage anything risqué. I just want to be beside another human being.'

She bent over him and tousled his hair. 'You're always too neat and regular. I expect you wake up with your hair brushed. But you smell of pine needles. Yes, if you want. We can sleep with the sword of Damocles between us.'

That was easily said. When she appeared in her shift, scrubbed like an infant, he thought the sword of Damocles might fail. He spoke to her over her shoulder while he lay, he felt with absolute rectitude, on his back, both hands pinioned beneath his head. 'Do you remember the manuscript I told you about at Christmas, Esme?'

'Yes, have you been working on it?'

'I'm taking it to a publisher next week when I get back. They seem interested in it. I've been checking all the references. Dull stuff.'

'It hasn't got a thousand footnotes, has it?'

'They're in the text.'

There was a long silence.

'Have you still got that stone I found at Lochearn?'

But there was no reply.

He woke at four in the morning with the worst attack he had had so far. Esme was awake the instant he coughed and switched on the light at her bedside. She sat through five minutes of racking spasms. He made inhuman gestures, reminding her of a drowning man, a whale spouting, so terrible and out of keeping in this gentle being that she was riveted by not being able to help him. He was dying. She was certain he was going to die. Scraps of half-learned first aid came to mind. His throat was unimpeded. He wasn't actually being strangled even if it sounded as though he were. How could she get air into him and stop that desperate gasping? She turned him round to begin the slow rhythmic exercises of artificial respiration. She lifted, counted, held, lowered in sequence for several minutes, too anxious to pause and check if he had actually stopped breathing or not. Her hands grew hot from the friction against his skin as she shaped out the triangle of his lungs. In the next break she listened. He was quiet. The rasping had petered out and he simply heaved up and down but he was alive.

Face downwards on the sheet, he said, 'Thank you but I prefer the kiss of life.'

'I thought if I did that you might pass away altogether.'

'I just might. Pummel my back, will you? Where you were rubbing.' She made her hands into fists and banged down the spinal column in response to his instructions, higher, lower, harder, and gave up only when her hands could take the pounding no more. When she looked at the palms, she could see that they were bruised, tiny points of blood showing under the skin. 'That is out of this world. Better than making love.'

'It sounded good.' She pushed his head round a little so that she could see into it. 'Rejean, what is the matter with you? Do you know?'

He rolled onto his back and looked up at her as she sat squatting like an urchin on her knees. 'Yes, I know. That was an asthmatic attack I just had. Apparently I can look forward to a lifetime of those and be grateful I come out of them. Some people don't, or not as quickly as I do.'

'But I thought people were born with asthma.'

'Most are. It's quite rare for an adult to develop it. Come under the bedclothes. You'll get cold.' She put her arm around his neck and put his cheek on the width of her shoulder, stroking and smoothing it abstractedly. 'It's allergy-based. You go along quite happily living with egg white, cat hair, dust or whatever, then one day, bang, your body reacts and you're allergic to it. Feathers and house dust for me, not easy to avoid. In fact it's not the dust at all but microscopic mites which live off the dust. They are breathed in and irritate the lining of the lungs.'

'But Rejean, that's too sinister, to fall victim to something you can't even see.'

'It's ironical, I'll give you that.'

'Why does the body react suddenly?'

'Stress. The specialist assures me it can happen to anyone. A specific illness shows up where the body's defence mechanism is weakest.'

'But you must get better. You've always been so fit.'

'That's what I can't take. I'd rather break a leg than live in a padded cell like Proust, breathing rarefied air. In my case, I'm worse than a cripple. I don't know if I can ever swim or ski or run again. I don't know if I can do a job of work. God knows what Maurice will say. He's never had a day off sick in thirty years. Can you imagine how proud he'll be of an asthmatic son?'

'Did the specialist think it was inevitable, for you?'

'In the sense that it is my specific weakness, yes, it was likely to come out. But the stress-related factors, no, I induced those myself. If you like, environment was mutable, heredity was inevitable.'

'And what were the stress factors?'

Now if circumstances were conducive to being honest they were then, with his head on her breast, lapped in her arms, physically contained by her goodness. And it was something to Rejean's credit that he did not take advantage of them. He bit the inside of his lip and said nothing.

'Rejean, what were they?'

'If I tell you, you'll have to hear everything.'

This said in a strained undertone of unwillingness forewarned her for the pan drop in church, the confession to Alexis who had neither sided nor blamed, the drive through Linlithgow when at each turn of the road he had ordered himself to stop and tell her, deterred by her lack of knowledge of what he was about, by the way she looked straight down the road ahead. The sham wedding, the sham marriage. The disaffected months when he knew he must come home, redoubled by the fact that she was there and that long or short term, Mabon or not, he must speak to her.

'Why did you tell Alexis? Did you think he was capable of being impartial?'

'But he was. Considering I was preparing to jettison his daughter, he was remarkably disinterested.'

'I would like to think so.' She put her head in her hands and it was several minutes before she formulated a reply. 'You have just made me responsible for two things, your illness and the break-down of your marriage. I can't accept that. I didn't know and I protest my innocence. Even if I had done, I'm sorry Rejean, but like Alexis I would have said you had to hold to your engagement. I never wanted to rob Aileen of anything.'

'I wasn't blaming. I was giving you an explanation. I should have let it out and I'm suffering from my own dishonesty. I've tried not to believe in the psychosomatic element in this illness, but at heart I know it's probably the strongest of all. More than the allergy, more than the cold that brought the first bad attack on, it's what's in my mind I can't fight.'

'And all Aileen did wrong was knock at my door. It's so unfair.'

She looked round abashed at their relative positions and drew away. An internal consciousness made her reticent. She could hold him without desire but if there was a hint of sexuality she must decline.

Moving unsettled her. She leaned over to the bedside table where the lamp burned, and with one hand pulled open the drawer and unwrapped a sweet in a tube and put it in her mouth. It was expertly done and she lay back pale on the pillows again. It was the first time he had seen her eat sugar.

'Barley sugar,' she explained. 'It helps to keep the morning sickness at bay. It is morning now, isn't it, or is it still the middle of the night?'

He revolved this slowly in his mind. Sitting hunched up, she was not much more than a child, barely pubescent out of her clothes, wiped clean of everything female. 'How long?'

'A month. It was the night of the storm I told you about. The

Base was snowed in and I slept in Mabon's room.'

'Once?'

'Just once. I'm fated.'

The proposition that had been formulating in his head, that had in the main brought him all this way to speak to her directly at last, crumbled. 'Have you had confirmation?'

'You mean have I seen a doctor? No, I don't need to. I know.'

'And what does Mabon say?'

'Oh, he doesn't know. In fact I haven't seen him since, though he has phoned several times. I've tried to keep out of his way, said I was busy.'

'Don't you think he should know soon?'

'Why?'

'He has some responsibility.'

'No he doesn't. Sex is a reflex action with men like Mabon. He simply tries with every woman who comes his way. He doesn't follow through to consequences. That was up to me, so I'm perfectly prepared to . . . take the rap.'

He looked astonished at the fragile form behind such resolution. 'And you won't consider any alternatives?'

'An abortion? No. I'm the sort of person for whom those alternatives don't exist. This child was conceived against the laws of nature. Oh, I'd done my calculations. I wasn't completely naïve about it, but genetics were stronger. This child has a will already. It's a survivor and I am going to see it does survive. The only bitterness I feel is that I was caught, when to be quite frank people like you and Aileen and half the world, it seems, were cohabiting on a rather more regular basis. If your life is fraught with its ironies, so is mine.'

'Much good it did us. Would you marry Mabon if he asked?'

'No, I would not. And I don't even want him to come and ask. He would look on it as doing me a favour. My life would be hell for ever after.'

'Esme.' He caught her elbows and made her turn to look at him, for the plan recently abandoned reshaped itself in a different guise, like the best plans adaptable to the minute. 'There's a job in British Columbia. On Vancouver Island they're building a new lumber mill, a whole township going up in the north. I could get the management of that site if I wanted. I have all the qualifications. I've actually done the work, and the climate would suit me better on the west. I would go, if you came with me.'

'As man and wife?'

'Yes, to begin with it would be pretence. But absolutely what you want. No one is to know this child isn't mine. I would make it mine.'

She examined the proposal and admired its appositeness. It fitted. Yes, it all fell into place. Alexis said to the newly pregnant Rhona, I care for you more than my wife in whom I am disappointed. I will leave her for you and take the other man's child as mine.

Thou wilt not with Predestination round
Enmesh me, and impute my Fall to Sin?

She was not going to be limited by the past. She would make her own choices, free and unencumbered, but now circumscribed already was that freedom.

'You are charging me with an intolerable burden.'

'I want to help you bear yours.'

She looked clear into the eyes and found out their frankness. 'I need a friend more than a husband, Rejean. There is not that between us that makes a marriage and never will be. I think I am a figment of your imagination, someone on whom you can project your needs, your romance if you like, when the everyday becomes too boring. It's just because we agree so well, but don't be deluded by that. Compatibility isn't everything.' Or was she reconstructing the present to make the past fit? If Alexis did not stand a giant, casting a giant shadow, could she have settled for the man before her and said, He is a good-enough-husband? Could she compromise the chance of a great love for the security of a safe one? Whose love did move the sun and the stars in their places? It was all delusion. But if her mother had said no to her second suitor, that freed Alexis for Esme and she must say no to this one too. Echo, Echo like the captive nymph with no voice of her own. 'At some point we will be accused, you know. And I want to be able to say *I did not* with absolute conviction. I did not commit adultery.'

'You could pretend to be tempted.'

'Be my friend, Rejean. The whole world wants men and women

to fail at that. Sex is easy compared with friendship.'

'Can't you have both?'

'No. Sexual relationships are terminal. They either lead to marriage or the end of friendship, which is the same thing.'

When he fell asleep again, curled into her back, she could not be sure that the prohibition would work. She was afraid that the avenging angel of the Lord must come and make a cross on her door for her misdeeds, done unawares but momentous all the same.

33

She looked up the international telephone code for the British Isles and wrote it down. Then she followed it by the area code for Lochearn and finally added the number of Inchcombe. Seventeen digits. Perhaps it would take her seventeen seconds to dial them. There would be a pause while it connected down the obscure registers of trans-Atlantic wiring, a click and then it would start to ring at the other end. It would recall him from whatever task he was busy with. Midday. She added on the extra hours to arrive at Greenwich Mean Time. It wasn't British summer time yet. He wouldn't have gone into the house. He would be at the other end of the office. A bird's eye view of the room showed him crossing it, hand on the receiver: Yes? Alexis speaking.

She shook with the audacity of making the call. Seventeen digits. Were they the ciphers that made life meaningful? She was tempted to try them out for the simple pleasure of hearing his voice, and hang up again without breathing or daring to speak. And then she thought, How adolescent. Why didn't she grow up, but her heart pounded at the prospect and was hardly stilled by the internal chiding she gave herself.

Exactly what did she expect him to do? Repeat Rejean's offer, a quick recapitulation on the past, his and hers?

How could she deliver the news without tears at the shame of her own culpability in letting him down, at her fickleness, and what was the point of crying three thousand miles down a telephone?

She wanted him, his arms, his reassurance, his reality and she didn't deserve them. She knew those minimal pauses when he flicked over an idea in his brain like a playing card on a vingt-et-un table. Buy a card. Twist. Bust. This would be a hand he threw in. The additions were so simple as to be visual. Esme he wanted. Esme and child was quite another sum. It was unreasonable to think he would encumber himself with a child and the child's child. How long were the continuation dots supposed to go on? Were they some sort of arithmetic progression towards infinity?

He would not warm to her. He would shelter behind that calculation and she would be left to assume a rejection. All things considered, Esme . . . If he advised Rejean that it was too late to recant, what other advice was he to proffer her? She knelt in front of the telephone, one of the lares and penates of the modern household, and dared not call on the oracle for fear it gave back an evil prophecy.

If only, she had said all her days in these despairing moments, if only I had a father to turn to, someone who would give me impartial advice, but that wish was proving to be the ultimate in self-deception. Why had she come to look for her father? He was a stranger in a strange land. It wasn't to confirm to herself that Alexis was not her father. She knew that in her marrow. Whatever fused them it was not consanguinity. Mairi's hateful hypothesis was a spur to the journey which she had contemplated since she first knew of Stefan's defection to the North American continent. She had come because she vaguely fancied he might add another dimension, that they would have hand-held conversations on a verandah and he would paint pictures that enlarged her view, or that he would step out of obscurity and be all the support she wanted, father, mother, Rab, Hannah rolled into one. But how could she expect him to be strong who had always been weak?

Parallel to the fact of his nearness, and she had an almost definite sighting, was Mabon's, a counter-force which seemed to prove that she had been correct in her first guess: men did spawn like fish in a pool. What contact had Mabon made with her beyond the superficial and derisory? Fatherhood was a lottery. In spite of which, the social fabric of name and property was based on proveable genealogy. Proveable indeed! That was the cause of man's obsession with the chastity of his womenfolk, not to mix his seed and another's indiscriminately. Gradually she perceived that the physical father counted for nothing, the social father everything. And there she was the child of Rab and her uncles, who had been guides as well as companions, and of Alexis, and of another being who was starting to reveal himself to her little by little, for out of all of these his was the strongest tie, the abstract figure of the fatherland.

But at bottom she had no right to expect men to solve her dilemmas. She was as fond of Rejean as a woman could be of a man without a trace of passion, but he had no business to unburden himself on her. She was not implicit in his failures; and Alexis was not implicit in hers any more than Stefan or Mabon was. It was an impertinence to assume any of these men would come and disentangle her from her own meshes. There were no Lochinvars. It would be easier if there were, because without the shield of a husband or a father she was defenceless against the public virtue of respectability. She had no status. Without a father she had been a dubious commodity. Without a husband she was inadmissible. A woman who had an established relationship, however dismal or meaningless or destructive, was acceptable to society. A woman alone was not. She understood that without a man she would have to make her own decisions, earn her own living, guide two lives without a stay, as her mother had. How could she escape the snare of heredity? Abused children became child abusers. The offspring of single parents became single parents themselves. How should she do any better? She was autonomous at last. She needed no one.

She was afraid of such independence which amounted to wilfulness in herself. It seemed unnatural. Self-reliance was the prerogative of men, or so she had been taught. They were linear, logical, directed because they had uncluttered minds. Women were deferential, hesitant, lateral. But Esme could see these characteristics were hopelessly transposed in her. A life spent without male example or influence had forced her to produce compensatory tendencies in herself. In her teens she had not once been alone with a man; between Rab going and Alexis entering no man had walked into a private room where she sat. She had had to develop the inclination to decide for herself because no one would advise her, and whose advice would she take anyway? She did not decide well. She did not do anything well, but made all her mistakes firsthand.

If she tried to think about herself objectively, and how it was that she was different from the other women she met, she could see that they were more feminine than she was and more content. She remembered how George Sand wore men's clothing and used the French adjective in its masculine form about herself, and yet was the lover of men like Chopin. Something of that accrued to her. She felt not wholly woman and thought it the greatest affliction to be born with a mind and body that contradicted each other. There was a rift between the two down which her personality fell. The body attracted the male, but it was in a false guise. Under the skin she was something other than they expected.

There were many ways of expressing the paradox. The great Elizabeth claimed she had a man's mind in a woman's body, but that did not solve the discomfiture of being a hermaphrodite in a heterosexual world. The id was female, the ego male, to use the jargon of the psychoanalyst. The x factor in her proposed, the y in her mentality criticised. The creator was extravagant and impulsive, the effector drew back and evaluated the end product first. She must direct, but she did not know in what direction. Was it any surprise that she achieved so little? In fits and starts between motive and effect she jerked along, not simply wayward but devastatingly critical of her own non-productiveness.

How could she expect anyone to live with her? She was impossible.

Maurice was distracted by the hand that lay half open on the top sheet in the hospital.

The chamber where they sat was hushed with the religiose composure of the sick room. The sheets were tucked in with mitred corners, the pillows lay closed end towards the door, the coverlet fell within an inch of the ground; and the patient, he lay as flat and folded as linen in a press.

They went up Monday at midday on the first flight after Esme's call. Rejean had been well on Sunday and then in the afternoon went into an asthmatic attack from which he threatened not to emerge. She said that the sight of him staggering round her room,

354

bent double over a table, coughing, wheezing, blowing to expel the air that was suffocating him was too much for her. She had feared a dozen deaths for him, heart failure, blood pressure, that he would fall into a coma from oxygen starvation to the brain. She did not know what to do any more and telephoned her doctor who committed him on sight to the Hôtel Dieu St Vallier in Chicoutimi. He could not be allowed to drive back to Montreal in his present condition and she could not nurse him adequately in the flat.

She followed the ambulance down the rutted roads and waited while he was admitted and taken to one of the men's medical wards. It was a massive teaching hospital and said to be one of the best in Canada. Silent nuns wheeled past her, busy, bowed, wordlessly efficient. Maurice was appalled at the appearance of his son, a collapsed athlete, yellow, feverish, straining for breath. His first impulse was that immediate relief must be available. An oxygen flask would purify his lungs. Some life-support machine was surely to hand. But the specialist who waited to speak to them explained that he had ordered an injection of cortisone to relax the spasms and give his body time to rest and muster its defences. The system must filter its own air. What was life worth if one was dependent on machinery? He had already contacted the first consultant in Montreal and they were agreed on this procedure.

'Of course,' he finished, 'he was unwise to undertake the drive to Chicoutimi. Rest and medication are what was ordered but he chose to ignore that.'

Esme, calling in from work, was too far gone herself to care that this seemed her fault. What was the point of saying again she had not known and the way people round her conducted their lives was none of her doing? The barley sugar hadn't worked that morning. She was dragging herself through the days in a semi-conscious state, trusting to the better nature of her classes not to create uproar when she was incapable of disciplining them.

Maurice watched the hand and the distended veins that flowed into it. It took him back to the childhood illnesses when the boy's mother sat like this holding his hand, putting a damp cloth on his forehead, giving medicine gingerly from a spoon and the infant life, imperilled by nothing worse than chicken pox or measles, seemed infinitely precious. In those days they had been able to behave naturally together, played rough and tumble, tickled and laughed in unison. Was it the advent of maleness that separated them? He thought it strange no circumstance on earth would make him take that hand in his. The embrace they had let fall long ago and handshakes followed soon after. This was his issue, his son and heir, but he would not dream of touching him.

An Irish nun came in with a drink. She smiled, recognising Esme from the day before. She spoke in the soft cooing tones that would reassure under death sentence. 'You needn't look so worried. We have a wonderful doctor in ENT. He will do every-thing that can be done. So never fear. Trust in God. Sure your young man will be all right.'

Maurice looked at her. 'She made the assumption and the lie was simpler,' she explained as the nurse went out and closed the door.

Trust in God. Well, he was not quite so hopeful on divine intervention, and thought the surgeon looked a better bet.

He fretted at the restriction of the room, and the sickness that is anathema to the healthy. They waited pointlessly. They had come pointlessly for there was nothing they could do. He remembered the list of engagements he had had to cancel. How could they possibly be fitted into next week's diary? Perhaps he would fly down again tomorrow or the day after. Go over to Grande-Baie first and have a look at things himself. The manager really was not reliable. He saw the building with the nameboard *Maurice Simard et Fils* looming to meet him. Et Fils! How proud he had been when the insignia was added at Rejean's coming of age. It put the business into perpetuity, gave a successor to the empire and made it as far as he could ensure immortal, through a son in whom he was nevertheless not pleased.

Why not? A deep antipathy in the blood. He did not like him, did not know him. He was a stranger to his own flesh. Terrible: he recognised it was a terrible admission. It was the worst form of aberration in a father not to care for his own son. It cut across the fundamental tenets of parenthood and of life if it were to continue. But what diabolical work was it on the part of the Almighty to seed birches from oaks, doves from falcons? Didn't a man have the right to recognise his own stock?

And all his daughters stillborn.

He and Esme left Claire at the bedside and drove back to Arvida in the dark.

'The first thing I must do,' he said, 'is phone Aileen. You haven't done it already?'

'No, I didn't want to call.'

'I thought we should wait till we had seen him. It's hardly a glowing picture I can paint, but it's less alarming to do it this way than to wire. Do you mind?'

'No, go ahead.'

'Do you want to speak to her?' He put his hand on the receiver.

'No, I've nothing to say.'

She agonised to see him heedlessly go through the motions she had drawn back from, look up the international dialling code, then that for Edinburgh and add finally the number of the flat at Canonmills. 'Don't forget to let me pay you.' What if Alexis were there by chance, listening to one half of the dialogue and knowing she must be at the other end of the room? She went into the bedroom so as not to hear him talk but even from there she could detect the ease with which a cable spanned three thousand miles, and quailed at the thought of the connection.

After some minutes he followed her unthinkingly, preoccupied with what he could not say to his son's wife. Their alienation made him feel the more unnatural by his. He sat down in an armchair while Esme brushed her hair. She bent her head over and brushed from the nape to the crown. When she leaned back, sparks crackled from the current she had activated.

'I'll call again tomorrow, if I may. She'll have had time to think out what this means. Aileen is very polite. She doesn't ask why he comes to see you. Should I be polite as well?'

She put the brush down and sat on the edge of the bed.

'He came to tell me he was ill.'

'But not us. Not his wife. It's news to me he's seen a specialist.'

'He didn't like what he heard.'

'But how are we supposed to understand if he keeps everything to himself? I can't read his mind. Now don't give me that look, Esme.'

'Just support him.'

'Support him! What else have I been doing for the last thirty years, near enough? I know human children are dependent for a long time but this is becoming absurd. Where does dependence stop? When he draws state pension? He's a man, isn't he? When I was his age . . .'

'You know I don't mean financially.'

'What then? Physically? It does look as though I'll be carrying him for the rest of my days.'

'He's sedated now. He'll get better.'

'I would like to share your optimism. He looked as ill to me as anybody can be.'

'He said you'd reject him because he was sick.' But at least he had noticed.

'I have no time for someone who is weak.'

'He is not weak, Maurice. He has different forms of strength from you, that's all.'

'This illness . . .'

'You can hardly blame him for being ill. Remember the pressure is on him. It's easy to be a first generation success. What do you do for an encore?'

'It is not easy to be a first generation success,' he corrected.

'No. I'm sorry. It's easier.'

He paused and thought there might be something in what she said. Perhaps he did not give enough credit because, looking down from his achievement, that of others following seemed foreshortened.

'Am I really a bad father, Esme? I have tried to be fair and let him do what he wanted, but it rebounds on me time after time. He turns round at the end and says, It wasn't what I wanted after all. He's not my – type. I don't get him.'

'I'm not the person to answer that, am I? To me, any father is better than no father.'

He was silenced on that score.

They were easier with one another. They felt they had cleared the air without giving or taking offence, and this inspired him to ask the insistent question. 'Just tell me simply, so I don't put my foot in it later, what is it between you two? He was staying here.' His clothes lay around. Why dispute it?

She had not thought the accusation would come so soon, but was glad she could look him in the eye and say, 'One married man is enough in anybody's address book.'

He nodded. She had to give him some leeway for the patience, the discretion he had shown over her precipitate flight from the enchanter, and allowed him a follow-up. 'Is he still in yours, Aileen's father?'

'Oh, I never forget my friends.'

Maurice and Claire took a room at the Manoir du Saguenay until Rejean's progress could be monitored. They visited him every day in the afternoon, while Esme went to Chicoutimi in the evening. His improvement was dramatic. The cortisone reacted as the surgeon had intended. He had no side-effects apart from loss of appetite, and by the end of the week, Maurice having already left by air, he was able to go with Claire in the car back to Montreal.

The last evening, when she went to see him, he was dressed and they sat at the window of his room overlooking the bay that formed the deep-water harbour of Chicoutimi, still thickly frozen over. He passed her a letter he had received that morning.

Dear Rejean,

Aileen called as soon as she heard from Maurice and I am putting this down at once in the hope that it catches you in Chicoutimi. I have been looking at the map to locate you. What splendid names, Mistassini, Chibougamau, Cap Eternité, Ile Maligne – wouldn't they tempt the most stay-at-home to spread their wings? Or is it like the renamed Cape of Good Hope, an inverse prognosis of what one may reasonably expect? In that case I take Ile Maligne as a synonym for Paradise.

The illness I am heartily sorry about but have rung up a chemical researcher I know, and he assures me it is controllable these days. (That is astoundingly facile of me standing on the bank shouting 'swim' while you are being swept out to sea, but you know what I mean.) The Hôtel Dieu sounds a pretty remedial sort of place – is it a joke? – but it augurs well.

There are other things that worry me more than your illness. Maybe this is the wrong time to set them down, maybe not. If you feel this is clumsy and ill-advised, forgive me for meddling.

I was anxious when Aileen came back without you in November and I wish the separation, which she said was to be for a very short time and was mutually agreed, had not drawn out as far as March – as I see it is by the calendar. I know how these divisions harden and would ask that you do not become too entrenched. I have said exactly the same to her so I'm not being partisan. Men are often too proud to make the emotional appeal and wait in a form of haughtiness for women to give in. They can wait a long time for that. Women have a much tougher emotional base, they can actually make it on their own and an attack of the vapours doesn't do a man's case any good at all.

I don't know what's behind it. I haven't asked, or rather I haven't asked to the point of obtaining a satisfactory answer. I rule out the obvious things and am left with the shifts and balances of character. Here I feel – involved. You spoke to me that Sunday almost a year ago, and I gave you advice you acted on, not solely at my behest I hope. But I do wonder if, as things have turned out, I should have been more candid. As I recall, I said there were two options, to proceed or to recant absolutely. No half measures. I'm quite an expert on half measures myself so I try to warn other people off them.

What I wanted to say is that I am convinced it is a matter of trying hard. Any decision is workable if you put enough into it. The most unlikely couples seem to rub along together and that must reaffirm the importance of effort versus choice. In marriage, the whole is very much greater than the sum of the parts, though you are entitled to put your tongue in your cheek to hear me say it. Besides, people, like language, are constantly changing. You have to pray sometimes that you aren't saying or doing the opposite of what you mean or that some fearful inference hasn't crept in of which you were unaware. I am having to relinquish half the words in the dictionary because they carry such innuendo. To talk to each other is the most important thing. I once knew a girl who said she was buying a marriage bed big enough to take the huff in. Huffs are very dangerous things.

I am sorry. I digress, which is the main pleasure in writing a letter.

Aileen intends to fly over to Montreal at Easter. I think her term ends in three or four weeks. She is concerned, she does care. Underneath that infuriatingly calm exterior she is having a mammoth struggle with her priorities. Emancipation makes it hard to be male, but it makes it ten times harder to be female.

I have decided to franchise two or three products for manufacture under licence: a new tweed which has taken off with the energy of an intergalactic missile, making me rich but not idle, and a couple of the perennial sweaters which have arrived at the nauseating stagnation of becoming classics. I am tired of seeing them on the machines and want to try something new. I am not wild to go mechanical myself but I enjoy the prospect of royalties from an idea someone else can incubate. I am looking for a piece of land to buy and could do with your advice. I can't decide if I want working land or leisure land, a farming estate or a shooting estate or an island off the western shore where I can fade into a personified sunset. There is a vile new idea at large about time-sharing where you sell fifty unsuspecting people a week's respite from their lives in a spa or a shooting lodge or a ski resort and keep two weeks for yourself. Did you ever hear of such a promiscuous form of cohabitation? Though I predict I would want to be greedy and have it all to myself. Would you like to come in with me on a grouse moor, somewhere with fishing rights and a loch big enough for water ski-ing? We could do it properly. Sell your book and we could go halvers. That, by the way, is a Scotticism I am very partial to.

I am glad you are near Esme. It is a long time since I had news of her. Drop me a line when you can. I have never been in hospital and imagine it is execrable.

She was consumed with jealousy over this letter. It brought back the evenings when Aileen came down to visit her with his embroidered cards and letters bearing pin men and none for her. If only it had been written to her, what a change it would make in her outlook. Had he had an inkling that she might read it? That assumption would be based on complete confidence between herself and Rejean. Had he divined so much? Was that the cause for being candid with him, belatedly? But still he did not speak as though to say, You tell him about us, lady, if you will, and if you do it is because it is not important any longer. But she held her tongue. They had moved on several paces since last May but it was not a tellable progression.

'You said something about your book when I was half asleep. You've finished?'

'There will be some re-writing, which I can't face up to.'

'If Aileen is coming over, she will help. She did it once for me. She's the perfect amanuensis.'

361

'Is Mabon back?'

'No, I haven't heard.'

'Will you call him?'

'I doubt it.'

She made her plans independently. On review, her prospects were not so fearsome. The money from the sale of her grandparents' house was intact, bar the purchase price of the car, and was banked in Edinburgh. Her account in the Bank of Canada in Arvida showed that she had spent very little of her salary beyond her basic needs, and so she had saved approximately half of it. She reckoned she could still appear respectably in public till July and the termination of her contract. Thereafter the problems arose. Where was she going to go? She had consulted a gynaecologist, who confirmed the pregnancy as positive with an expected date of delivery in November. What was she to do from July till November? And what later? The questions mounted, multiplied. Did she want to live in Montreal, or Edinburgh, or anywhere? She did not want to go where she was known. She did not want to go where she was unknown. She would have liked to cut herself adrift on a raft, away from all habitation and all faces, and sail out of sight of the world, obscure and private to the last.

34

Mabon telephoned the Friday evening he came back from Trenton. She had had a card from him with a photograph of a Voodoo jet on the front, for which he apologised, but he mis-spelt her name, for which he did not. He had called in at the Simards' by chance and so had recent news of Rejean. But she found she could not ask or listen properly because the voice with its patient, lazy drawl, which bore no resemblance to his nature, unnerved her.

'Charles Cartier is having his party tomorrow and reminds me you promised to come. Can I pick you up before eight?'

She wavered.

'You did accept for both of us.'

'Then, yes, I'll come since I said I would. Don't you think I should drive myself?'

'No, I want to come for you. I haven't seen you for six weeks.'

Oh hell, she thought, putting the phone down, what does that mean? She had anticipated the problem of telling him, but overlooked the inconsistencies in not telling him.

He kissed her frankly when they met and she thought, I cannot hold out. I cannot do it. On what grounds can I say no having already said yes. I could lie but I will not perjure myself to him.

On the way to Chicoutimi, to obviate the personal questions, she asked, 'What were you doing in Trenton, if it isn't classified?'

'No. I was on a training course for new jets we are buying to replace the Voodoos.' Esme had to smile at this fondness for the official, or was it the matrimonial, "we". 'From America. But it's highly controversial. Buying these will make the Voodoos scrap overnight. Some of the top brass think we should buy updated stock, even though they're heavy and slow and don't manoeuvre too well. It's a powerful lobby and I may never get to fly one of the Yank jets.'

'How many pilots were there? Not everyone, surely?'

'No. About a dozen.'

'From all over Canada?'

'Yes.'

'Wasn't that a privilege to be chosen?'

He was never certain whether she probed out of interest, or to mock at his replies, to turn them round and show him their hollow innards. 'Yes. I will have to help train other air crew under my command if we go ahead.'

She watched the rough face and wondered how it would age and weather; what patterns it carried to her child that even though she knew him were unguessable.

'What makes you a good pilot?'

He shrugged and diverted the question away from himself. 'Some people have a kind of instinct. The feel of the machine. You can't fly on instruments all the time. It's when the machine breaks down that the pilot comes into his own. I suppose speed of reaction between reading the panel and changing controls to suit wind and weather. You've got to be calm when there's an emergency.' He hadn't given it much thought before and found it hard to visualise what he did exactly. He just did it. 'What else?'

'Leadership?'

He appreciated the prompt. 'Yes, you have got to be able to get along with the air crew and the ground crew, trust your navigator and he trust you so that when you're in a tight corner you're not both asking if the other one has made a mistake. Stamina. An hour and a half in the air with the full high-altitude equipment is damned tiring.'

'Who's better than you?'

'At Bagotville? Nobody. But we're talking about peacetime conditions. In war, there's a combat hardiness that they say matters. I don't know if I have that till I'm in it. We're more than twenty years since the last war arena. I'm likely to be over the hill by the time another war comes along.'

'When is over the hill?'

'Thirty-five. Forty.'

She smiled. 'You can get in a few flying hours before that calamity occurs.'

He looked over, wondering what point her banter had this time. Must they always be out of harmony? 'We're here.'

Yvonne Cartier, who came forward to answer their ring, was a beautifully kept woman. She had the same physique as the other wives: waistlines rigorously restrained by meagre pecking, long flicking fingernails that suggested to Esme the battery of machines performing their chores for them, mixers, vacuums, fridges, washing machines. The important thing was not to come into contact with the substances, flour, dirt, water and fibres being deleterious to the gloss of their polish. On their heads they wore elegantly poised combs and headpieces. Esme felt a dowdy hen in comparison. There must be chalk on her shoe, there always was; her nails broke constantly on the scraping blackboard; there was probably a loose button somewhere disguised among the folds; her hair was merely shiny.

'Yvonne,' he said, stooping to the statutory embrace, 'that is a gorgeous dress you've nearly got on.'

She left him to his act, certain he would enjoy flirting with his rival's wife without her eavesdropping. Six weeks' celibacy? She thought not.

She struck out on her own. The Cartiers had spent a tour of duty in Belgium and came back with a houseful of Flanders furniture, massive pieces carved in oak. On bookcase, sideboard, tables, were alabaster ornaments, a Botticelli Venus and a copy of the Discobolus. Amber brocade curtains fell ruched from floor to ceiling. It was not her taste but that was immaterial. It was different from the anticipated and harked back to something she remembered.

They had opened up their basement as well as the living room. The senior officers and those in Cartier's section and their wives went up and down the stairs, trying to lose each other on the way. Esme, looking round at faces she recognised but was not propelled into talking to, found Bob Findlay hiding like herself. They sat at the bottom of the steps to the upper storey where no one would pass and disturb them. He smiled to see the non-conformist.

'Any news?'

'The old story. Yes and no.' She told him of the trip to Mistassini and the new name which had been suggested.

'And?'

'There was only one listed in the directory but I could get no reply. This was in December before I went away for Christmas. When I got back I rang through to Inquiries and apparently the telephone was disconnected in November and the number has since been removed from the directory.'

'But you have an address?'

She prevaricated. Someone put a glass of liquid in her hand, and looking up she saw it was Charles Cartier who had sought her out. She nodded thanks and turned away to the Chaplain again.

'Champagne cocktails. Be careful of those,' he warned so low the host could not hear. Cartier brought with him a trail of officers who enjoyed a little reflected glory, and their noise drowned out this aside. 'You have an address you can visit?'

'Kenogami.'

'That's five miles from where you are.'

'The weather's been so bad.'

'You're chickening out.'

'Yes, I am. And other things.'

His eyes bored through her motives but he had been a professional a long time and did not ask till he was invited. 'Give me a ring if you need help with it.'

'I may do that.'

'You are a sadist,' one of the officers said to his host. 'I can't drink these with the tests on Monday. One and I'm on my knees. Two I'm anybody's.'

'In the shape you're in, half a dozen won't make the slightest difference to the outcome. It's a big "grounded" for you.'

'Roberts has got five pounds to lose tomorrow. He can't get his flying suit done up, or if he can, he daren't sit down in it. It's an open and shut case.'

Bob explained. The air crew had to pass an annual medical check, not strenuous, but they had to have satisfactory blood pressure and performance on several tests. They went in fear of losing their fitness certificate, and therefore their flying pay, if they were grounded.

'Does anyone ever fail?' Esme asked her host who leaned on the banister.

'We bribe the doctor. He wouldn't be too popular at CHQ if he started laying off all the air crew.'

'Central Head Quarters,' whispered Bob. 'He always talks in jargon.'

'They live like virgins for a month,' said Cartier. 'No meat, no alcohol, and no sex. It does them good once a year.'

'Early for Lent, isn't it?' she said.

'I still reckon you called this party deliberately to hang us up.'

'That's the way to dry some people out, I believe.'

The other was not so far gone that he did not sense the rebuff from the senior man, and wisely departed.

When she turned back from watching the nature of this dismissal and how it was meekly accepted, she heard Cartier say, 'No, I don't regard the incidence of alcoholism in the service as greater than in civilian life. On the whole, I feel social drinking is necessary. Our men work hard and they are entitled to relaxation like anyone else. Occasionally, I admit, an individual does have a greater than usual problem with drink, but the service is very tolerant, indeed quite helpful until he gets over it.'

'Yes, but what are you judging by?' said Esme. 'Drink here is cheap, it's available and it seems to be condoned as socially acceptable, to go by what you say. Are you sure it's the same in civilian life?' She did not care one way or the other but was determined to fragment his monologue.

Cartier summed up her value as a witness, remembering that she had first-hand knowledge of the night of the storm, when admittedly things had got a little out of hand, and she might have a tale to tell if he provoked her. As a woman, and a woman who was not even a wife, she was quite worthless in his milieu. She was, however, an outsider and he felt he must defend his stance. The fact that she worked and charged her clothes to her own account gave her marginally more significance. A pay packet did give her some right to her own opinion.

But like a good diplomat he avoided the central issue and gave a polite reply. 'It's fashionable to decry life at the Base, but if you examine the facilities available it would be hard to better them, certainly in comparison with the home town most men are returning to. The cities, I grant you –' He made a large exception with his hand. 'We provide clubs of all types, there's a bank, a post office, a Base newspaper, library, its own telephone exchange in addition to the very considerable sports and recreation facilities, and these make it truly self-contained. A beauty parlour for the ladies,' he conceded to Esme, who was reeling in disbelief. 'Take the cinema, for example. Unless you have a particular interest in the continental, foreign-language film, I think the Base here and the Arvida theatre provide you with a very adequate selection of North American films, if you enjoy North American films, that is.'

This was felt to be a comprehensive reply.

'I must say, sir, I feel the morale of the Base is higher than at any time while I have been here. The spirits of the men are very good. It's the dependants who find it hardest to adjust. There aren't the same amenities in the surrounding areas, and rightly or wrongly wives do feel cut off.'

'Why do they keep calling each other "sir"?' Esme asked Bob. 'Aren't they off duty?'

'An officer is never off duty. Unquote. Especially when he can earn points.'

Mabon stopped dancing with his hostess and came to look for his partner. It took him some time to find her behind a row of backs, but he was pleased to see she was keeping the right sort of company. The glass was still full to the brim.

'I hear they are introducing a new aircraft, sir, the S62 from the States.'

This was a presumption on the part of the officer, as the matter was still subjudice in Ottawa. Mabon and Cartier exchanged glances as the only men present who knew anything official. The others listened with bated breath for the inner council view. This was hot news. This was repeatable. 'I can say no more at this time, but I do hope the decision will be thoroughly investigated before the force takes delivery. It's going to cost us many millions of dollars in re-training and adjustments of, for example, hangar accommodation and servicing equipment from the extant fleet.'

'Then why,' queried Esme, maddened by their respectful silence for the great man in their midst, 'if it's superfluous?'

'That is classified information,' Cartier corrected gently.

'Oh, you mean it has a nuclear warhead. That's not classified information. Every boy in the tenth grade knows Bagotville is a nuclear base using American weapons which are directed over the North Pole at the USSR.'

At that moment Mabon would have appreciated the facility of vertical take-off, or an ejector seat to catapult him out of the room. Here was Esme, a guest, a stranger, a woman, actually spreading sensitive information. First of all women did not argue, or hold the floor, and secondly it would be recorded against him personally. He foresaw a squeamish interview with the CO about his security rating, and perhaps a review of his hard-won status as trusted messenger.

Bob Findlay was enjoying himself hugely. His neutral position allowed him to stand on the sidelines of the struggle between the powers of light and darkness, dedicated and sceptical, male and female.

'Every boy in the tenth grade might be wrong. It is not good form to discuss the situation socially.' As her escort, Mabon was the one person fitted to deliver this mild rebuke. Unsettled as he was, he had his reward since his superior officer thought he was handling the matter judiciously, and nodded.

'For heaven's sake, why not socially?'

'One never knows, absolutely, who is listening.'

'You mean because of security? But this is not a time of war or national crisis. I can't be content, I'm sorry, to feel others are making decisions that may lead to war without having my say. Yes, I know you're all thinking, what right have I? I'm only a foreigner and a non-combatant at that. I'm not likely to have to lay my life on the line. But doesn't it touch us all? War can hardly be looked on as a national pastime in the twentieth century. I mean,' she turned to Cartier, 'you are in the business of legalised warfare.'

He smiled thinly. This was not a breed of woman he knew too well. Yes, they had their shrill activists on Parliament Hill, writing under-punctuated sentences in the Ottawa press, but here, domestically, the shrillness was tempered by charm as well as male control. 'Yes, in essence. We are all committed to the concept of military defence and intervention on behalf of peace-keeping forces, if required. But in the West, I think I can truly say, we will never be the aggressors.'

'Don't you think nuclear stock-piles are their own aggression? If it's communism you are fighting, I can only say that communism is an idea and has to be ousted by a better idea.'

'I am no more afraid of ideas than you.' This was taken by them all as a handsome compliment, 'But I am afraid of the Soviets when they use armed aggression to enforce adherence to their principles. And you can't deny that they do, from the evidence of their actions in the post-war period, in any continent in the world.'

Mabon felt the argument was becoming too polarised, the burden of debate falling too heavily on the older man. 'What do you suggest, Esme?' she heard him say. 'The Soviet threat isn't going to go away of its own accord. What solutions are posed in Britain?'

The question was clever, and she knew it. Easy to tell them what they were doing wrong; another matter to say how it should be put right. 'Nothing new. Détente, SALT talks, cultural relations for what they're worth. Diplomacy. Nothing new.'

Charles Cartier had a moment or two to marshal his thoughts and gave out his edict. 'The weakness of democracy is that it eliminates coercion from a man's vocabulary, and it isn't till a man is forced against his will to vote, read, speak, write, in a way he does not want to, that he is prepared to stand and fight for his freedom not to be coerced. To me, communism is not an evil of the first magnitude. This is off the record,' he added jocularly, and they obliged with a laugh. 'It is a superb ideal that is attainable only in reality through the corruption of those ideals.'

He had spoken. He was not displeased with himself, nor with Esme for giving him the pretext to show off the middle of the road attitudes which had made him a successful negotiator.

'How serious we've become! I'm sorry, Mabon, I'm pulling rank on you. You'll have to wait your turn.' He lifted Esme sedately by the hand from her nook in the stairwell and took her onto the square of parquet he had cleared for dancing.

It was all right then. She had not made a social gaffe. He felt as relieved as when he had pulled an aircraft out of a steep nose dive, and went outside to clear his head.

Bob thought she was spectacular when she shot her man down in flames. He liked it. He liked the modern way of women, the new women which the old world was breeding. What a partnership they would make if they could desist from exterminating one another.

Yvonne guided her to the powder room later in the evening. Did she need powder?

'My dear, I do like your dress. I nearly bought one like that last season. So useful.'

'It has been. It's the only one I've got but I don't suppose I get as much use out of these clothes as you.' She sat down at a mirror in a spacious bedroom and brushed her hair, the only repair she would make in public.

Other wives and women came upstairs behind them and delayed what Yvonne had come to say. In the bedroom as downstairs, a different standard was predominant. Everything was expensive, not old, not rare, not mended by any means. It had its price tag, although she could see that in the hands of people such as these the nouveau was not necessarily loud or ostentatious.

'You know,' one of the newly arrived wives said to the confidante, 'when Jerry got his report in February, the senior officer, and you know what an old bear he is normally, had written in it, "A most capable officer, enhanced by the social expertise of his gracious wife." ' The recipient of the compliment preened herself for gasps of admiration and envy. Had Esme been around longer she would not have wondered if the phrase were repeated intentionally in Yvonne's hearing, as wife to the heir apparent. She would have known the wives had a ranking of seniority as strict as their husbands'.

'It's often wise,' said the hostess, *sotto voce*, 'to let the men do the arguing. They understand these things so much better than we do.'

She's right of course, thought Esme. I can't resist jumping up on every platform that comes along, bawling my head off. I don't even care all that passionately on any issue. I can't bear to sit through a one-sided argument and let them pontificate without some opposition. She asked herself where the lie was in education that taught both sides of a debate mattered to a fair conclusion. Obviously life and education did not concur in this regard.

'It is frightening,' she looked at Esme with total candour, 'what is remembered against a man during his career.' And then she smiled, fussed a little more over her and took her downstairs again, having delivered the homily she had been enjoined to do.

Oh no, reflected the novice, I am being told to toe the party line. It's get on or get out all over again. I've to think and act the same as my man. I must get out of this. The implicit loss of her identity hit her with a blow.

He fell into the easy assumption of continuance.

In the dark, he stretched out in the one chair of her living room, a black vinyl monstrosity that both rocked and swivelled. She stayed out of range in the kitchen, delaying the moment when she would have to make a start on denial, and listened to the rocking chair creak a little on its base. He did not speak. She came through eventually. He knew she would invariably come to see what he was doing if he was silent long enough.

She sat where he indicated, on his knee.

'You are fluttering.'

'Yes, I am nervous.' She had made up her mind, but her body was coming to another conclusion altogether. She could not fuse the two in opposition to the intolerable excitement created by his presence, his sexual immediacy. And she was physically shy for the first time in her life in case she betrayed change in every pore.

He went on kissing her in the way he had of kissing on the transverse so that she was pinned by those teeth, a sensation not displeasing.

'You can relax. I'm off duty till Monday. I can stay the night.' He undid the back of the dress and, in doing so, brushed against the sensory pads of her vertebrae.

'Aren't you subject to Lenten fasts?'

'I didn't touch the champagne. That's my contribution. If I don't pass, who will?' He removed the shoulder pieces and discarded the garment on the floor.

'Mabon.'

His reply was to kiss the profile of the breast he had exposed.

'Please.'

'Please yes or please no?'

'Please let me go.'

'It will be different, I promise.'

This was schizophrenia, the two masks of Greek drama overlapping, tragi-comic. Be happy, said the corporeal woman. Be chaste, said the thinking one. Compromise, said the realist. Take him as your lover and reject him as your husband.

'You use the room on the left, don't you?'

He was as good as his word. She discovered at last the fusion of intimacy, the simultaneous exchange, and did not think that really she had been cheated. Not by him. Maybe by the writers, Hardy, Lawrence and the other men who told her what to expect, down to the technique-ridden modernists, the exponents of images of fire and water and earthquake which fell far short of the real. The word excited the brain, the picture the eye, a chord the ear, but they achieved nothing more than a simulation of what they reproduced. Art was a substitute, which gave back a false note when there was no experience at the core. Experience was the true note and art a reminder of it. In enacting the real, Mabon was a million times more eloquent than they were in description. Living took precedence over literature. Alexis had told her she would have to reconstruct the absolute truth for herself and he was right in that as in everything. She could not take it as read. She would have to go back to the beginning and do it all again.

Mabon was more practical than she. In a thousand meals, and after all some men eat three times a day, why does one remain as memorable? She was that to him; balance, variation, the timbre of the unexpected all struck him as the culmination of whatever it is one seeks. He liked it. He liked her company. He thought the two were inseparable. He thought he knew everything there was to know about women but he didn't realise that she could hold an image of him in her body and the image of another man in her mind. He was the instrument. The other was the impulse. They mistook each other. The cause of their division was that while she had the words, she did not have the large experience which gave a point of comparison. She did not know what it was worth, physical happiness, thought it was easy, rather common, accessible to everyone. He was wiser. He knew what it was worth, but his limitation was language and he could not tell her.

He watched her pleasure with a touch of envy.

'I never wished I was a woman before.'

'I wish I were a lady.'

'Don't ladies do this?'

'No. Ladies do not.'

'I don't know many ladies.'

He got up. The light went on in the bathroom, then the kitchen and after a few minutes he re-appeared with a tray and switched on the bedside lamp. He managed her all the time, she thought, circumvented, manoeuvred, deserted her even according to a plan. He was a puzzle to her. She recognised the calculated moves of a seduction, set steps in a dance, a sequence he went through without an original concept. She saw the coldness and anonymity of his way of life, the exclusive maleness which made her wonder if he was more than an automaton. Then, just as she was poised to say goodbye, enough, he would demonstrate, well more than prowess, but he waited till the extreme edge of her rebuttal before he did it. He was so maddeningly contained, unmoved. Even this tray was laid as an expert laid a tray, in perfect neatness with a cloth underneath. He knew the contents of her cupboards better than she did and could put his hand on everything to order.

He was strangely accoutred in her bath robe. He handed her a cup and went to sit in the armchair at the far side, watching her without necessarily looking in her direction. In all that he did there was a weight, a pause that unhinged her response. He would let a sentence drop and she was left straining for its reverberations, in the way a single drumbeat makes the jungle tense.

'Having established that, I think it's time we talked.'

She heard the customary note of command and knew she had been subordinated to the ranks.

'How long were you planning to wait before you told me?'

Ah. So she had given herself away. It was a futile aim to try and deceive him. How could she keep it from a man who read the path of the wind by the salt on his lips?

'What have you done about it?'

'It's certain.'

'And is it mine?'

'That's a very flattering inference.'

'If you won't tell me, I must ask.'

'Yes, it's yours.'

'That was careless of you.'

'Or you.'

'I assumed, wrongly, that you were experienced. Or are you? You didn't conceive deliberately?'

She was panicking. To whatever fault she answered, whether she was insatiable, ignorant, rapacious or lying, she seemed to incur blame. 'You must draw your own conclusions.' There was a lump lodged between her breasts that expanded and contracted at a great rate, nearly choking her and stilling all rational debate. She realised she was about to do that most untypical thing, and cry. Maternity was making her into two people, in one of whom she did not recognise herself. She must not cry in front of him. In tears she proclaimed herself weak and emotion was so uncalled for. She looked down into the cup and cursed the slow ooze. Her humiliation was total.

'Easter is a month away. That gives me time to arrange things.' He looked at his watch, incongruously Esme thought until she remembered the pilot's issue watch carried a record of the date. What was he going to arrange for her? Pillory in the stocks, the ducking stool, branding with irons? This woman is an adulteress and a witch. 'Do you intend to hand in your resignation?'

'No.' But perhaps, when they discovered, they would insist. She recalled a tale from long ago of a woman sacked for 'moral culpability'.

'It will have to be the Protestant Chapel at the Base. Do you want to see Bob Findlay or should I?'

What for? The rites of exorcism. What auto-da-fé must she enact? She shook her head wonderingly.

'It will have to be one of us.' His voice grew more authoritarian. 'Say something.'

The folly with tears was, they were meant to call out sympathy and instead they often enraged, for their ugliness as much as their mute misery. Was she hoping he would see and desist from his inquisition? The one fallen tear that cut into her face like an ice floe, but which she would not condescend to wipe away, was on the far side from him in the shadow of her face. It dried out slowly, puckering her skin.

'I don't know what you mean.'

'He must have some warning if he is to marry us.'

She looked up. 'But I'm sorry. You misunderstood. I won't marry you.'

'But you must.'

'Why must I?'

'It's not going to look good if I'm living with a woman who is the mother of my child without marrying her.'

'Ah I see. That's easy. I'm not going to live with you either.'

He pursued her line of reasoning to its logical end. 'What are you going to do, then? Disappear over the horizon like a Montagnais Indian with a papoose strapped to your back?' She squirmed agreement. 'You are pathetic, you know. I wouldn't say you were the prime frontierswoman, would you? A keg of powder and a sack of flour? I can't see it myself. You haven't got it in you. You go white when you haven't passed a house in ten minutes. Be realistic, for once. You can't make it on your own, anywhere. Whatever you think about yourself, you are not the sort of woman who goes through life without a man.' He had come involuntarily to the idea of marriage but, having made the liberal gesture, was exasperated when she drew back. Men prevaricated about committing themselves, not women; and certainly not women who were pregnant. He realised what a laughing stock this would make of him. Caught at last, they would say, caught at last. All those faces in the Mess jeered at him for his lack of efficiency in what he was supposed to be so almighty good at.

'I don't want to live with you, or marry you. I still do not think I like you when it comes down to it.'

This really was the final insult. He thought himself a considerable catch, and was in truth if one weighed looks, ability, prospects, popularity, social flair as the ultimate code of value. He was stung. 'Isn't it rather late to decide that? And are you the only one who matters? What if I claim my rights over this child?'

She floundered. It was one of Aileen's arguments. This is the current of normality, submit to it. If he said he had rights in the matter – did he actually have legal rights of access if she refused wedlock – how could she deny him? Morally speaking, his willingness to undertake them did bestow them. She had passed into the phase of supernumerary, with no rights of her own.

He saw this was the strongest line of persuasion and pressed forward. 'Remember why you came here in the first instance. You travelled three thousand miles on the slender chance that you might find your father. Why was it so important? You must have missed something, not having a father, not having two parents. This child has the right to know its father, don't you think? Or are you determined to perpetuate the mistakes of others indefinitely? You can cut and run on your own account but can you honestly speak for my child?'

That was an irrefutable argument, unless she perjured herself. Mabon's will at this and every moment was stronger than hers and she deferred to it. She wilted. To soften the impact of his absolute superiority, he came to the bed again and kissed her, tasting the tear runnel in her cheek with a double victory. She clung to him the way a brain-washed victim will cling to his tormentor in a moment of relenting kindness.

35

Contrition set in with the thaw.

It happened over a weekend. The long icicles melted away into puddles. The snow thinned in patches and showed up the wan-thriven grass which had all but died in the four dreary months since it saw the sun. A sound of dripping was constant where before the wind was the accompaniment of solitary reading. Drains and gutters filled, then overflowed. The roads widened again and were black and purring beneath the tyres. At length the Saguenay showed through, in dark blue bruises underneath the ice. The swell of the thaw brought down torrents of water from the round glaciated hills, and swirled away the edges of the stiffened pools. Green became a new reality. Over four days the deadened branches broke wood, put out buds and curled into new leaf. There was no protracted twilight of change, February snowdrops leading into the crescendo of crocus, anemone, daffodil through a shifting orchestration of warm winds and chilly dawns. A new backdrop had been unfurled, one she could not have pre-supposed from the evidence of two weeks before, or of the rich autumnal landscape at her arrival. The view was either green, or white, or red. There was no interaction.

Adventure beckoned her. She could walk to the verges of the scene unhindered, dip down lanes, find ancient tracks which pioneer horses and the guiding farmer had plodded into shape along the lie of the land. This was the King's Domain, held in fealty for a warlord three thousand miles away in Europe. The Seigneurs to whom it was leased had cut the fields into strips which radiated from the river. It was the principle of settlement which had shaped the whole of Quebec along its waterways, though by the second half of the twentieth century the feudal system was intact in no more than half a dozen places, mechanisation in the form of roads, railways and large scale farming having cross-banded the plain. The strip, up to an arpent in area and ten times as long as it was wide, ensured fair distribution of the rich alluvial soil as well as the poor stretches of the inner shield, and gave access to the transportation of the river, the connective St Lawrence which opened out into the Atlantic and the homelands of France.

The land was rich, its perma-frost notwithstanding. Every-where the vegetation burst forth luxuriantly, so prolific even in new growth she had to brush it aside to pass. The plants were recognisable, but different. Grass was grass, one would have thought, but this stuff was short, thick and tough, full of fibre rather than the long silky stems that fringed the hedgerows at home. It grew closer to the earth in rounded, moulded clumps that followed its contours and dared not rise too high into the blasting winds, so much wiser was vegetable than human evolution.

Ahead of her lay three unpleasant tasks; she must write to Alexis, she must approach Bob Findlay for his consent and to fix a date, and interconnected with these was the pressing visit to Stefan Roberval, which she couldn't defer any longer. It was not prin-cipled to let her wedding pass ten miles away without communicating it to him and extending, if he were her father indeed, an invitation to attend.

She went to Kenogami.

As she expected, the address she located in the telephone book turned out to be a ramshackle barrack of a house which was reached by an unpaved road of mud in winter, dust in summer and perennially rutted. It had been overtaken by smarter houses which turned their back on it. It was well on its way to the state of delapidation of the abandoned farm enclave in the woods, planks splintering and peeling, from the shingle of the roof to the first step of the porch. Not affluent, anyway. Not active. A pot of paint didn't cost so very much and soap and water were virtually free. She prepared herself for decrepitude.

She knocked. She had a choice of parts prepared as an alibi in case the man appeared before her and she found herself unable to go on. In her bag was the envelope with the photographs but she found neither of these a source of fortification.

It was a boy who answered, not much younger than herself and not much taller.

'Bonjou. C'est ici la maison de Stefan Roberval?'

'Mais oui.'

'Puis-je vous parler un instant?'

He looked at her suspiciously, her smart clothes, her bulging bag, her foreign air. She did not look like a debt collector.

He was a sallow-faced youth. To judge by the nervous hesitancy of his movements, he was anxious not to offend but was easily downcast. 'Entrez, je vous en prie.' He held the storm door ajar with his foot, in which pose he was so gawkily spreadeagled she practically laughed as she went past. There were two rooms in the place, the door giving direct access to a living room which comprised kitchen, dining and living area.

'Would it be possible to speak to Monsieur Roberval?' She could cope with this after all, though she was embarrassed by her blatant opulence in a context where not one item rose above the level of the essential. He was worse off than she had been at that age. Her, opulent! Who would have thought it? She sat on the edge of the settee, covered with a blanket of Indian colours and pattern. He looked so surprised at her question, she added, 'He does live here?'

'My father?'

'And he's away?'

'He's dead.'

How oafish of her not to perceive the cause of dereliction in the house. It was a place without a man, and she should know. She felt impatient at having to talk through the intermediary language which wouldn't express her meaning accurately. Alexis had been right then. The package was a valediction. She could have saved herself a journey and a bit besides. 'I am very sorry. I wouldn't have troubled you if I had known.' Her alternative came into operation. 'I am working for an agency looking for Polish nationals who have lost contact with the country since the war. Your father was Polish?'

'Yes.'

'Do you know where he came from, which town? You don't mind my asking? There may be benefits for expatriates.'

'He never talked about Poland or his life there. He wanted to forget everything before he came to Canada.'

'Is there anything, I wonder, that would connect him with Poland, a passport or an entry visa to Canada?'

'No. He was robbed soon after he arrived. Thieves broke into the house where he was living in Montreal and took his things. I think he had war service medals. They even took his bicycle and he couldn't get to work. But he lost all his papers.'

'What was his work?'

'He was a tailor.' The boy began to warm to her questioning, lost his lethargic dreamy air and looked more vital than when she came to the door.

'You don't have a photograph, I suppose?'

He obliged and rummaged in a drawer of an old-fashioned dresser, smothered in layers of paint. He came forward with a snapshot taken in high summer, but the high tones were so bright they effectively masked his features. 'I wonder if you would say this was the same man?' She drew out of her bag one of the better pictures of Stefan, wearing a short cotton jacket with a small collar and rolled up sleeves, his face already at twenty-three or -four deeply crinkled in its smile, but from leanness not age or disease.

'This could be. But it's so old it's hard to tell. A brother?'

The boy spoke beautifully in French. He painted the words in the air, using the conditional when correct instead of lazily lumping his sentences into the present tense. He spoke with the pure accent of classic French, not in the local patois, and there was the equipoise between mind and tongue which is so often found in good French speakers, following the dicta of the Académie Française to resist the deterioration into slang and slovenliness. Here it was almost a humorous anachronism. On the table behind him, she had seen when he turned round for the photograph, was a scatter of books, face down or places held open by an apple or a ruler and there was a notepad down which he chased line after line in the fluent copperplate still being taught in the established schools. He was a student in the agony of an essay.

'Are you at school?'

'Yes, I go to the seminary in Chicoutimi. I take my final exams in the summer.' He smiled wanly.

'Will you enter the priesthood?'

'No, not the priesthood but I had hoped to go to Quebec University in Montreal. I have a place for next year, to study modern languages.'

'And can't you?'

'It will be too expensive. My father was ill for a long time and he couldn't work, for maybe the last two years of his life. My mother has had to pay off those debts and the hospital bill at L'Hôtel Dieu.'

She realised even dying wasn't free. 'He died recently?'

'No, eighteen months ago.'

Esme thought backwards. 'When?'

'A year and a half,' he repeated, thinking she had not followed the numerals in French.

'Which month?'

'November,' he obliged.

'And the date?'

'November the fifth.'

'You are quite sure?'

'Yes, how could I make a mistake? All our neighbours were having a party with fireworks and we had to go and get a taxi to the hospital. C'était trop amer.' The way he said 'amer' had a mordancy she could not overlook.

'At night, then?'

'Yes, he died before midnight.'

At least going out of that door for the last time they had gone compatibly. She reconstructed the distant days in the hospital, with the sounds and the sights of the Forth in the background, the gulls, the sea traffic wending its way to the expansive communal ocean. Was it so different for him? The two of them had kept their vigil at the same hour.

The lad was not stupid. He responded to the close questioning, and her interest fed his about these long ago events. He started to wonder himself, to throw her under cover of his lashes the long glances she gave him.

'Your mother is not here?'

'No, she's in Montreal. I will move there as soon as I have finished at the seminary.'

'You're selling this house?'

'No one will buy this place.' He smiled or almost smiled. 'It's falling down. I can put my fist through the wall in several places. When we go, the neighbours will take the land and add it to their own, perhaps make a swimming pool. I am living here alone. My mother has re-married.'

'That's good.'

'Is it?'

'Won't your step-father help finance you through the degree?'

He shook his head, and there was no arguing with the mordancy of that expression.

'So what will you do?'

'Go to work, I expect. A shop, or a factory.'

'You've no brothers or sisters?'

'No, I am alone.'

They eyed each other. Esme very nearly spoke up, but if it were true that they were siblings, how did it advance their knowledge of each other to claim kinship? They did not have one memory in common, or share the bond of language. If they were strangers rather than brother and sister, their alienation could not have been more final. Environment mattered more. The nuances of flesh which tantalised across a room, across a continent wouldn't come down to specifics. Whether he was her clone or not was not proveable. And if she pronounced her legitimacy, she denied his.

'You said there might be benefits.'

'A fund, I believe. But we have no proof that he was Polish, I'm afraid.'

She understood the barrenness of the house. The mother had moved on and left him to fend for himself in a shell, cleared out her best furniture and belongings and he could follow as he willed. The neglect showed. He was at the point of development when the body is fully grown in size but hasn't filled – the warp set, the weft to come – which makes the adolescent male vulnerable along one grain, fibrous but not bonded. She looked on him as a sapling, full of vigour and potential, which needs light and air to grow to splendid maturity. But here? In a shop? In a factory!

She rose to go, feeling a terminal exhaustion at the things she could not change. 'Where is he buried?'

'The pauper's end of the churchyard.'

'In Kenogami?'

'Yes.' He took her cue and went to open the door.

She hovered on the steps, half turned, and in departing asked, 'What is your name?'

'Alexis,' but with a precise intelligence he did not add the patronym.

'I am Esme Rosowicz. You may hear from me again,' she stammered out so hesitantly he did not for a second believe her.

J'étais bouleversée. J'étais bouleversée, went over and over in her head.

She drove over to the Base to call on Bob Findlay. She found him in his garden, wearing an old parka and overshoes to try and prompt his tender specimens into life. He had a stand of roses pruned in the autumn, when he had wrapped them in sackcloth against the cold season, but they had died back further and he was cutting away this briar with clips of his secateurs. 'You don't mind if I finish this? I'll be five minutes. You're not cold?'

'No, I'm not cold now.' She told him of the meeting she had had and he pushed his collar back as he straightened up, to see her better. She looked composed, but she always did.

'Yes or no?'

'That's where the trail goes cold anyway.'

'How did it feel?'

'That's a very subjective approach you're encouraging me to follow. Or is the Anglican Church dealing in the mysteries of spiritualism nowadays? You didn't learn that in the Presbyterian kirk. It felt sad, pointless really.' The ground was like a sponge, wet and seeping under her shoes. She moved to a path. Not one thing on her horizon amounted to the spectacular. Trees, houses, camp, were all flat and grey. Space, yes, there was endless unpunctuated space all right. Space without people, without point, without connective tissue in her life. The spine of the chapel tapered a fragile mast into the sky and that was it. The air was raw cold, wet cold for once. 'This is a bleak place, Bob.'

'Don't let it get you down. Go and see your friends in Montreal tomorrow.'

'Montreal tomorrow? That's a jaunt I need a week to recover from. I'm used to thinking that thirty miles is an undertaking.'

'How is the one who's ill, Simard fils?'

'He seems better, but he's unhappy. I can't face seeing him at the moment.' She stamped her feet to regain circulation in the damp soles. She stayed deliberately at an angle when she asked, 'Are you booked up for weddings in the next month? Easter's the commonest time to get married, I understand.'

He folded his secateurs in his pocket. He revolved half a dozen answers in his head and couldn't find the power of utterance for one of them. He put his hand under her elbow and led her indoors. His housekeeper made Esme a pot of tea and left them to it in the study.

'Don't scold me, Bob. I've had enough of that already.'

'He's not pleased?'

'Not this way, no. He's very conventional. Underneath that devil-may-care he likes to do things properly.'

He read her objectivity, which was a departure from the starry-eyed who sought his blessing thirty Saturdays a year. 'He's very highly thought of, Esme.'

'By you?'

'By the service.'

'Actually, I don't know why he's marrying me. He's in wedlock to the RCAF. It will be a bigamous union.'

'Yes, the Force is hard on young officers. They never know what they're competing for or against. Some of them are rank mad.

When the promotions are announced in the New Year they're scaling themselves up or down, against their training year. And if they haven't got the extra stripe they don't know why, so they go on working their hearts out to earn it. For the men of his calibre the career is a sickness really, a compulsion. Women have to wait around for the –'

'Scraps?'

'No, I mean the rewards which will come later, and I don't mean financial.'

'You're not trying to sell me heaven? I don't think I can wait that long.'

But he was too fragile on that point himself for humour. 'You can be sure he's going places, Esme. He's a very single-minded person.'

She weighed this commendation and found that it lacked. 'You don't like him, do you? No, I'm sorry, that's not fair.'

'He's not easy to know, and I've been around with him a long time. I was in BC at his first posting after officer training. He had that mark of distinction even before he was twenty. I know where I'm going and I know who's going with me. Nothing would stand in his way. I remember when he left that squadron, there was the usual presentation from the officers and the CO. But, as well, the ground staff, the men had a separate ceremony. They'd clubbed together and bought him something. I can't remember what, was it a tray? But they'd had it engraved and did it all by the book. Now that didn't happen for other officers. I can't explain it. He bullied the men, gave them real stick when things weren't the way they should be. He never let anyone off. But in the end they thought he was a great guy.'

'So do I as long as he isn't mine.'

He wished he could see more warmth in her for the prospect. Where did his duty lie? To encourage her towards a union which he thought was headed for difficulties above the normal expectation, or cast one more fatherless infant adrift in a basket of rushes?

Esme was ashamed at having let such a remark slip. She stood by a very simple code of conduct: put up with it or change it but don't complain. She had scolded Rejean mentally for unburdening himself on her and here she was doing the same.

She suddenly turned on him with a whoop and said, 'Do you bob? We don't bob in Scotland so I'll need some instruction. Isn't that typical? The Scots won't get on their knees even to their Maker.'

She'll be fine, he thought.

She drove to Arvida along the back road and realised Mabon should be there before her. He had moved in, virtually from the first evening. Madame had dimpled with pleasure to see the black sedan parked outside all night and she was ecstatic that there was to be an Easter wedding. Quelle joie.

He brought with him so little in the way of moveables it was almost touching. He owned as little as she had brought in her case, but these were all his wordly goods after ten years' work. When his parents died, hadn't there been a house and contents? He shrugged. That was a long time ago was all the answer he would give. What difference had he made? Some. She saw him as seldom as before. Since the thaw, flying schedules had resumed and he was committed to his workload of a hundred hours a week.

But she couldn't find him in the living room, reading a manual while he waited for her, or catch sight of his car sweeping round the block without the dredging thrill of expectation. He moved her. She did not know why. If it lay in the set of his mouth, the flutter of his hands, some mental abstraction in him that at the end of every encounter left her puzzled and curious, wishing to ask more, probe to the core of his elusive, sideways personality, but knowing quite well he would not answer her searches about himself and his motives. He wasn't interested. Why should she be? But his silences continued to entrance her where speech would have dulled.

It was the honeymoon of their union, the month of honey aptly named. It was perhaps a modern paradox that it anteceded the wedding proper, but the function was constant, the indulgence of the body together with the suspension of the mind. Her first impression had been wrong. He was a skilled and caring lover. She was intrigued enough with the loquacity of that dialogue to overlook the poverty of the other. Five times on the night of the party he had brought her to fulfilment, with or without him, five times between midnight and noon. She did not know whether to be amazed or ashamed. She had no idea what her body was capable of and he did; that was cause enough for fascination.

Starting her letter to Alexis that evening, she underwent some change of heart. She remembered her critique of decent behaviour. Promiscuity perhaps, but never without affection. And judged by that yardstick she had failed him, and herself. She was not fond of the man who spread his charts on her table and plotted a course from take-off to rendezvous, logging with meticulous exactitude the length and path of the flight and the consumption of fuel. The night at the Base was a breach of faith with Alexis. She had no business being there if integrity mattered. He would not have done it in her place, she was sure of that. But it was less important as an act of disloyalty because she could suffer like a martyr behind her frigid response and blame him, blame fate, blame the colossal prince of the world.

The second night was a much worse perfidy against herself. She had made a decision to become an isolate and was diverted from it by carnality, physical greed, all the besetting vices of which Mairi had accused her. She was ordinary after all.

She came by a long route back to incidents in the past which she had glossed over at the time but in an accumulation were beginning to look like an indictment. Why had she locked Alexis into that cupboard? Common sense told her he could have several chances in the maze of rooms to escape detection, to escape altogether if she left the door open. Hadn't she, if she was truthful, wanted to keep him there to play with the licentiate urge which had been the undertow of her existence since the day she met him? Not conclusive, perhaps.

Then there was the moment in the boathouse when they were discovered. She stood up. She made a gesture even more conspicuous than extracting Alexis from the routine dance. Did she want them to be exposed? Was she a sensation-monger underneath? Hadn't she enjoyed the gawp of that boy – he wouldn't look upon the like again. Was it the same relish for voyeurism which had made her undress at Mabon's bedside? He was about to leave without demur. The action had been a conscious one. No force, abuse, coercion mitigated it. She was the one who made trouble. She was the agent provocateur. She judged her own case and held herself in contempt.

In some effort at self-defence, she cast her mind back and recalled that at least with Rejean she had been in a compromising position and had not been compromised. But, if she was frank, he had asked, not acted. Had he put his hand under the shift to feel how the pigeon pouted, she might have been swayed. Let's face it, she always was swayed. She was powerless against the groundswell of her own nature. Was there any man she could say no to, any knack or novelty she would not come out of her horny shell for, the carapace of modesty drawn back to reveal the soft and succulent? She was a wanton.

36

Alexis, up and about before daybreak, worked in the office, burrowing into the hollow chamber of the early morning. The silence outside seemed impenetrable; then little by little broke under the imminent day. A car went from the direction of Lochearnhead towards St Fillans, the tyres unzipping on the surface. A spray of rain must have fallen. The dusk thinned, turps mixed in an oil base, and let the texture of the day show through.

In the birch wood on his right the first note was heard, some aggressive cock sparrow twittering over his territory. Mine, it said, keep out. Others, not to be ousted, voiced their opposition and the group, a chamber orchestra, started in on the musical debate. Four notes, pause. Repeat. Four notes again but spoken from a handful of instruments, not quite in rhythm yet. Stronger voices were heard staking their claim, finch, wren, until the harangue swelled into a rondel for several voices, the same theme overlapping to prevent discordant jars, insistently rephrased so that where one part finished another began. Where could it end? The deeper notes were heard. A bassoon dove that had gone wild added a motet, a thrush in cor anglais performed a solo and suddenly there burst out the clarion blackbird, soaring over all the minions of that demesne. That heralded a new phase. The orchestra was at full complement. First violin and woodwind strummed out their interplay, cadence on cadence filling the room, the wood, the valley and no one to hear it but himself. When the last note fell he knew he had missed the cuckoo as so often in the 'Pastoral', overlooked the summer sound. He would have to listen again tomorrow.

Why did they do it, bargaining for position, he who shouts loudest eats first, might in the animal kingdom being supposedly right? But sparrows took on thrushes. They stole from them when they weren't looking, flutter and away before the clumsy bird could turn round. Other forms of hierarchy than that pecking order prevailed. They were more vociferous in spring but it wasn't exclusively a mating call. A warning cry, a bush telegraph? Or just an interchange on the unreflecting happiness of being alive and in the sun? Nothing more. Why rationalise it?

He remembered there were men who went about recording birdsong and others who imitated it, sometimes making a living from their aptitude. He had heard one of them, a Larry Adler of the hand, who could mimic every bird suggested by the audience, and he marvelled at the forms of human ingenuity. Why would someone want to do that, go round lecturing to groups and societies, entertaining old ladies with this expertise? Odd. Then he recalled that, when he was a boy, there had been a fashion for hooting like an owl. Sitting on top of a bank that looked towards the moor, he and his friends would cup their hands over their mouths, blow into the aperture of their thumbs and fan the outer fingers to resemble the 'Whoo Whoo' of the night owl. How many hours had they invested in the perfecting of that quite useless skill? Inane, really, the things boys vied with each other in. He used to be able to whistle melodiously and, just thinking of it, pursed his lips and blew. He produced an apology of a note, a flat dead tone all air and no vibrancy. He smiled at its sheer horribleness. He tried again. There was a knack to it, funnelling the out breath, rolling the tongue, compressing the lips just so. And he did it. A globe of sound floated out into the room. It was the very shape of happiness. He was so pleased with it, he laughed out loud in exultation, and then grew self-conscious when the laugh ricocheted back.

But there were tunes, weren't there, to test his re-discovered genius, better than stray balloons of notes? He fluted a phrase or two by way of practice and lay back in his chair with his hands behind his head, his feet resting on an open drawer, abandoned to the pursuit of excellence. He fell spontaneously into a song that was suited in its highs and lows, its simple swooping dips to being whistled and only when he had reached the end of the melodic line realised it was

If I were a blackbird
I'd whistle and sing
And follow the ship
My true love sails in.

The postman arriving before the milk found him trilling his heart out fit to burst.

The birds did it better anyway.

He took the pile of letters over to the kitchen to open during breakfast and in amongst a toll of business mail, bills, orders, manila, white or buff, came across the envelope with the Canadian stamp addressed to him in a strange handwriting. He fancied it was Rejean's reply to his letter and was perked at the pleasures the morning was bringing. It might be a good day. Or a better day at least.

The housekeeper came over to the table with his regular breakfast. Her presence allowed Mairi to lady it a bit more. She would sit through the meal drawing up plans and lists for the day. Alexis knew he had been wrong to resist employing Ian's mother; he liked the homely woman. Her quiet body padded the house. He took some comfort in her antique ways. She wore her hair in a style he hadn't seen for years, a roll going from ear to ear at the back, pinned like a swathe. She was garbed in a series of cross-over aprons in a print material edged plainly, and alternated these day by day. He thought these had gone out in the 'twenties. He wondered if he could ask where she managed to buy such relics. Was there some corner draper shop in Comrie, the type that sported ladies' underwear like armoury, with a surplus stock of several hundred destined to keep her going for a lifetime? He resisted. The woman would have been mortified to be noticed. She tended to walk away backwards when she met him and left a room as soon as he entered it. He was 'the Maister' after all.

It was her custom to serve and clear breakfast. Mairi and he did not speak more than perfunctorily, so she could hardly be an eavesdropper. He had come to look forward to these attendances of hers. If he were very lucky he might earn a smile from her; on high days a word.

Two enclosures fell from the envelope, the first a letter of some thickness in Esme's hand. He put it up quickly before it drew attention to itself. Underneath was the thick card of the invitation which in a gesture of some magnanimity was addressed to both of them. This and the envelope were in the same calligraphy. The black embossing of the words did not need to be read. They were self-proclaiming, and their import drained him of sense and feeling. His last thought before he closed his mind over it was, Good taste at any rate, no silver, no lovers' knots or hideous bells. But he would not whistle or sing or smile or laugh or dance or shout again.

The woman filled his cup. He dared not lift it in case his hand shook and he dropped the thing.

She was gone, removed, forever absent and changed.

What forms of mourning, he wondered, were ratified for the living, for living loss? The conventional seemed inappropriate. He could wear black, band his sleeve, don sackcloth, rub ashes on his head or commission envelopes with a black edge. But these were phases, symbols. They held good for a week or a year or three years before they were put aside. He needed a continual observance, the death of joy, the wearing underneath normality of the shirt of Nessus to prod the bereaved into interminable pain.

And then, growing wider in his perspective, he could see that this form of daily grief afflicted more than himself. Esme's loss of her father was as incalculable to her as this to him. Hadn't Rhona winced at being so shunned by her siblings, her remote spouse? There was the mourning by children of a parent in divorce, a man of his abducted child, the unbridgeable estrangement between members of the same family or even in the same household. Mairi, sitting apart, wore that mantle too. He needn't imagine it had been fashioned for him exclusively. He was just the latest to fall under its shadow. He could have sent up a ululation of despair, except that these women taught him something of dignity and forbearance. He must not indulge himself with the vanity of thinking he was at all exceptional. There had always been someone there before him.

Mairi picked it up and read through the direction line by line, aloud. She succeeded tolerably well in disguising her relish that the outcome had been as predicted. Her eyebrow raised a fraction. Her lips closed more firmly as she finished her perusal. She had a terrifying cast of hardness in her face. 'That was quick. Is this the playboy pilot, or someone new?'

'Yes, the pilot.'

'I wonder if Aileen's received one. I must make a note to give her a ring this evening.' She screwed round to consult her diary of events. 'Three weeks. Shotgun, I suppose. Really, she has a remarkable facility for not learning by her mother's mistakes. Will you go?' She played a double role. She hoped to wound him of course by slander, by casual diffidence. But she was also ambitious that the third party behind her would hear and repeat round the village . . . and the mistress said, having a bairn, nothing in the other. In this she underestimated the quality of the servant.

'If I –'

'Aileen has booked her seat already to see Rejean. Come to think of it, it would be a good time to go together, Aileen and I if you can't spare the time. I always wanted to see Canada, take that scenic train through the Rockies. Beautiful card.' She flexed its deckled edge and ran her thumb nail over the print. 'The Protestant Chapel, Bagotville, Manoir du Saguenay. It certainly sounds quite a do. I wonder who's giving her away. She hasn't asked you, has she? I mean you would be quite a good person to do it.'

He did not trust himself to reply in front of the woman whose sensibilities he respected. He rose from the table and took his coffee to the office, shutting the door behind him and locking it. He wanted no intruders. He was alarmed by his inability to focus on the pages in front of him. Be rational, he chided himself. Read what she has to say. He unfolded the sheets of the letter, flimsies that instantly fell about the floor. Then, when he reassembled them, he found she had forgotten to number the pages, and he had to place them according to the folds of the paper. No appellation and no signature made the jigsaw more frustrating.

'I am having his baby and he wants to marry me, so I must seem to want it too. I am outnumbered in this. He and his are stronger than me.'

The morning he saw born was fully grown. It was heart-breakingly bright and cheerful. Clouds puffed on the hills and collapsed out of sight on the other side, rollicking merrily along like children on a bobsleigh. The land was most beautiful, poised, regenerated, full of hope for the new season. But she was gone, removed, forever absent and changed. The landscape was nothing but a mirage, the birds chattered and made a tinny sound that grated on his ears when he felt sae weary, fu' o' care. Thou'll break my heart, thou warbling bird. He went and shut the window before he sat down to her letter.

'I can't make excuses because I haven't been able to absolve myself from culpability and maybe never will expiate that particular flaw. I won't harrow you with the circumstances but, believe me, it was the next-to-immaculate conception.'

Reading this, he fell into self-blame and cursed his own fastidiousness. If he had consummated their relationship, he might incidentally have taught her something about self-protection. Had anyone said as much to her as he had to Ian? Had Rhona carried out any part of mothering? He doubted it. They were not that wise and wily breed, a far cry from his daughter. Who could Esme have asked but himself? But he never had helped or probed, preferring her cocooned.

And then he was seized by an obscure and paralysing jealousy. If there had to be a child in the inevitable sequence of things, why not his? If that were her lot, how much better his than another man's. His child and Esme's. The possibility had entered his head the night they slept together in the old house, as a fear, and he had not pressed out of scrupulousness. So many scruples turned around to mock a man. Time had given him a second chance and time had found him out a fool twice over.

He turned back to the letter and tried to excise the me from his feelings, as he went about in his search for the thee.

She talked of absolution, expiation, culpability. The tone of her confession suggested she had received nothing but opprobrium; she was ranked among the profligate even by herself. This was so far from the truth he was almost out of temper with her, could shake her to a more whole and wholesome view of things. But what did the girl judge by? He knew there was no original sin. He believed the babe, the Christ-child, was innocent and that life began in a state of goodness however it was conceived, from which the world and its societies corrupted it. Esme had no adult vice because she had no knowledge. She had lived in her tower for twenty years almost a freak of nature, which had protected her by isolation till she became a single island strain of a species unadulterated by other forms of contact, *avis rara in terris*.

He thought of the true venery of which she knew nothing, the perversions of degraded lust, the nightspots of San Francisco, the brothels of Soho, the red lights of Amsterdam. As a young officer in His Majesty's fleet, caught up with the boys, hadn't he been repelled that his fellow man, the noble and infinite piece of work, could applaud and participate in these couplings which amounted to the vile and debasing use of each other by men and women?

The fitchew nor the soiled horse goes to't
With a more riotous appetite.

Why, there were a million sins more chargeable than hers. How could she feel that the life-giving moment and the beauty – he repeated to himself that it was beauty – mystery, grace that surrounded it was a sin? To make and cherish life was the absolute benediction. Had anyone put an arm round her shoulder and said, Blessed art thou among women?

And that was his failure too. What had he shown her but the dark side of human love, secrecy, shame? He was hardly in pristine condition, the last man to sermonise about the sacred shrine image. He remembered Sandy Pollock's intervention as a reminder of his gross unsuitability. He remembered the boatshed. That was a singular piece of idiocy which mortified him all over again at the visible disgrace. So much for self-restraint. That calamity had precipitated this. He couldn't conceal from himself the connection between her fear, her flight, her vulnerability.

He turned over the envelope again, his finger as sensitive to the grooves made by the other hand in heavy oblique strokes as to the dots of Braille. Who was he that she mentioned him not once by name? Mairi's phrase stuck. A playboy. Surely Esme could choose more wisely. He feared for her, by extension from his own service days. Not just the man he abhorred, but the ethos of his way of life. Did he have any idea what her mind was capable of, or was he a base Indian who could throw a pearl away richer than all his tribe, from overwhelming ignorance of what he had in his grasp?

For her to be unhappy was a worse agony to him than his own.

But self would not be stilled entirely. He was grateful for the invitation, but could he face going to see it enacted? He read on.

'I include Mairi. Her omission would be more complicated to explain. Her presence is the price I am willing to pay for yours. Will you come? It is the only thing in the day I will look forward to.

'Enough. I am committed. I will not disappoint.

'Maurice has agreed to give me away, what there is left to give, and Rejean will be best man.'

Of course he had to go, if only to know. Or did a secret hope curl undetected in his planning, that like an older and less agile Lochinvar he might divert the proceedings, escape with her in a waiting vehicle and run, run, run for the horizon?

In minute detail she reconstructed for him the visit to Kenogami. He put the letter down at last, bemused that Stefan should choose to pass his name on to his son. Why? Was it the coin of conscience, the payment of some unweighable debt? Certainly it wasn't done for spite and he acknowledged over the years a friendliness of intention that gave the lie to Mairi's slur.

By the same post, Mr Scott received a communication from Esme Rosowicz which he duly filed among her other, growing documents.

'I seem to be behind with all my correspondence and am suddenly aware that I have never thanked you for finalising the estate of my mother, and for the subsequent payment of the residue. You may or may not know that I left Scotland in August, ostensibly to look for Stefan more thoroughly than I could by proxy. More probably I was looking for a change, which I have undoubtedly found. I have been working in a high school this year and am to be married next month.

'I think I have come to the end of the road as far as Stefan goes. A man who tallies with the facts we have died in hospital here before I actually knew he was still alive, so I don't feel too great a sense of loss or guilt at not looking harder, sooner. However, I have met his son, my half-brother in all likelihood though he does not know it. The position is this as I see it.

'Stefan was alive *after* my mother, briefly but after. As she died intestate, a portion of her estate should pass under Scots law to him. Even if they were estranged, they were not divorced. A half, a

394

third, I don't know what proportion is involved, but that money would have gone in turn to his son and heir. I know the law on this is suspect, distance, custom and consent being prejudicial to any claim the boy might have, but I feel the justice of his claim is strong. The spirit not the letter. He is likeable, clever, despondent because he sees no way ahead. The mother I bypass. I didn't meet her. She has remarried and wouldn't appreciate my coming along to say she had lived out of wedlock all these years or that her subsequent marriage must be re-registered. It does call for some tact.

'This is what I want to do. I wish you to put in hand, for I have no idea how it is to be done, an educational trust for the boy:

Alexis Roberval,
No 1007 rue Gingras,
Kenogami, Chicoutimi,
Quebec.

'I am enclosing a business card from a firm of Montreal solicitors who may have to administer the trust from this side. I wish to put aside half of my inheritance to help him graduate. He has a place at. Quebec University for next year to read languages but no money, and of course there is no state award here. I don't want my name to be used. He must believe it is from a fund for Polish expatriates or something such, for which he happens to qualify. The money must be used exclusively for fees and books, for which he should produce receipts or bills of some kind. No living expenses. He'll have to go and sweep a supermarket floor for those. If the money is not taken up, it will revert to me, but I hold my offer open for a year.

'Is this feasible? You know my bankers. The money is still in that account. If you need power of attorney or written permission, of course I will reply by return.

'Finally, my future husband doesn't know of this scheme and might very sensibly object. I would like it to be enacted as soon as possible and would appreciate if all communication about it were addressed in my maiden name.'

An inspired plan, he thought. He wondered if she knew that Rhona had benefited by just such a scheme as she had hit upon, a

Polish ex-servicemen's fund set up after the war which enabled her to complete her degree which otherwise, by the exigencies of her marriage, she might have had to abandon.

Esme's last note was to Maurice. She thanked him for his acceptance to officiate at her wedding and included, with some apology in case it seemed ungrateful, a cheque to cover the amount of her single air ticket from Prestwick to Montreal.

Having paid off these outstanding debts to the past, Esme turned round to give attention to the man of the present. She felt it was underhanded not to tell him about the Roberval household, though the trust she would divulge to no one. He sat at the far end of the table, poring over his maps, an aerial blow-up of Labrador dominated by the concentric circles of the contour lines, while compass points and bearings were scheduled on a timetable at his side. He was calculating furiously and did not appreciate her interruption with this long, rambling and to him quite inconsequential tale.

'Yes, I thought it must be him when the old man said the name at Mistassini.' He lifted his head and looked straight into the light. The pupils did not contract by more than a fraction, leaving the iris a thin rim as in the hollow-eyed statues of Auguste Rodin.

'You mean you knew him?'

'Knew him? Yes, met him. He was one of the tailors at the Base when I first arrived. He made a uniform for me. I knew he'd died.'

'But why didn't you tell me?'

He put his pen down and tried to remember that far back. 'I didn't see what difference it made. It was before Christmas, wasn't it? I thought you would leave at once if I told you.'

She was too flabbergasted to object at this decision, or to feel, as some women might, pleased with the unspoken compliment. 'What was he like?'

'I honestly don't remember.'

She let him go back to his plans.

The next time she sorted through his wardrobe she found a Mess uniform she had not seen him in and, checking to see if it should be dry cleaned, came across the label on the inside pocket which announced in woven letters:

She ran her finger over the cross stitches that held it in place. That was the nearest she would get to him.

37

Mairi and Alexis set out in good time from Lochearn. The plan was complex: it reflected the trapezial shape of the journey. Drive to Edinburgh, pick up Aileen, drive to Prestwick. Fly overnight to Montreal arriving, because they flew with the international clock, in the early hours but with time enough to snatch some rest before they drove, all six in two cars, with the Simards to Bagotville. The service was a tardy afternoon affair. They realised it was a punishing programme, but trans-Atlantic tickets were selling out and they were lucky to secure the last two on Aileen's flight.

Alexis had said nothing but submitted himself dumbly to the plans made round him. Mairi read this as acquiescence, but seldom wisely quiet said the unforgivable whenever she could. At most times he could walk away, but closeted in the car with her there was no escape. She had kitted herself out completely for a long stay. Having made the crossing, she was determined to make the most of it and do the tour of North America she had talked about for years. A cousin in Alberta, a school friend in Seattle would pace her across the continent. The phone had buzzed with these interactions for so long that he knew her schedule by heart. He had already discovered that travel was the most vapid form of entertainment and would fly home by return, leaving her to wander back in her own time.

It was a bright morning, of luminous intensity. He tried to cut himself off from what impinged on his enjoyment of the day: his errand, her company in the confines of the Rover, the pressure of air travel. Since his last drive to Edinburgh, the Forth Road Bridge had opened and he did hesitate for a while about which route to take, the high road, the low road, the known or the new. He plumped for the Strathyre road as being a slightly safer choice when time was short. He could not gauge exactly how long the toll would take or where the roads merged on the other side.

'I wonder if she's showing yet. I suppose we must be glad we didn't have these problems with Aileen. She's a good girl.'

He looked at the hills, furred with growth, each leaf burst achingly into the void of the air. There was no more tender colour than this first show of tips along the hedgerows, a shade on hawthorn and beech that was almost transparent. Pigment could not imitate it. In light all the colours of the spectrum made white, but mixed together in pigment they made black, and so paint was always cloudy and opaque. Translucent watercolour, which might have come close, did not have the solidity to give that promissory note of future growth.

'Don't you think,' she interrupted the reverie, 'it's odd that Rejean hasn't come back for six months? Six months almost exactly. I would have thought, in the normal course of events, that he might make the effort at Christmas.'

'I think he was probably ill even then,' he excused.

But she was like the sly cat not willing to release her prey, not hasty to come to the point of killing it because it was such fun pouncing again and again. 'He practically lived here when he and Aileen were first engaged. He kept his clothes in the far room even when he was back at Goldenacre.'

They passed through Callander and the road untwisted, a riband sometimes silver, sometimes grey according to how the sun shot it with light. It flowed along the crest of the land like a lava stream always by the easiest route, a drop of mercury coursing from hilltop to sea.

'He came very seldom after, let me see, after Rhona's funeral.'

'Wasn't Aileen doing her finals by then? She hardly came either.' He was irked at being forced to justify his young friend who only incidentally was his son-in-law.

She corrected the flaw in the logic of this. 'But there had been times earlier when he came on his own for the fishing and shooting. Don't you remember?'

The highway was traversed by access roads, tracks leading to farms, offshoots in both directions. For all that I have travelled down here a hundred times in both directions, he thought, I have never branched off and explored those diversions. I must go down them one day.

'When did Aileen say the baby was due?'

He consciously held the wheel tighter. He had avoided being drawn into dialogue along this line though she tried over and over again to cajole him into some response. 'November.' She knew perfectly well what Aileen had said, but she insisted on counting back the statutory nine months and arrived accurately enough at February. The woman somehow managed to make every hair on his body stand on end; her speech which affected refinement and ignored the hearty origins of Scots, the numerical accuracy of everything she did, the way she sat cross-legged draping her hands in space. It made him wince with foreknowledge. He realised with sickening apprehension that he might somewhere in the next week be expected to share a room with her. Maybe a bed. He had overlooked that. He tried to shift his mind out of this gear but the scenery was small antidote to her overburdening presence.

'November. That's what she says, at any rate.'

He glanced across at her, almost intrigued that she could make the simplest remark into a gloat, every statement a lie. She systematically took the lowest interpretation of human behaviour and was incapable of seeing she herself was debased by that. 'What reason is there to fabricate a story? The truth appears vivid enough in most instances.'

At last she had his attention. She had him riveted. 'Perhaps she had something to lie about. Do we have any proof it is this man's? It could just as easily be Rejean's, given that she's that sort of person. Maybe she doesn't know herself. I've seen her and Rejean together. Why else would he stay there when Aileen is here? And it was so strange he was in her house when he took ill.'

The words made a pattern he did not immediately absorb. He was checking whether the road behind him were clear, in the wing and then in the inside mirror. He saw an image of reality down the receding road he had just travelled along but it was a distorted view, a fading emprint. His mind knew that what the reverse image showed him was not accurate, a backwards glance, an inversion, a negative from a photographic plate. If the present and the past were set up as two reflecting surfaces at the correct angle, the future became a mirror image endlessly repeated until it faded into infinity. And always his own eyes looking at himself growing smaller and smaller and smaller.

Why did she say it? She didn't mean it, didn't believe it any more than the other fabrications. It was intended as the extortion fee for his good behaviour. One step out of line, my manikin, and I will say it in the right ears. He believed her. He gazed at her for a long moment and thought, Whatever comes I cannot immure myself with such sickness and remain healthy. She was a plague, a leper he must shun or seal into a lazar house before she infected everyone.

Below Callander there is a blind corner, well known to locals. In fact a convex mirror has been cemented into the bank opposite to allow drivers issuing from the slip road a better view of oncoming traffic. It was perhaps unfortunate that on this day, at this moment, the drivers of both vehicles were less than knowledgeable, less than attentive. A car drew out of the siding without due care and attention; Alexis sped on in a second of road blindness, occupied with the inner view.

They did not collide. They missed each other by a hair's breadth. As the smaller vehicle cut across its bows, the Rover swerved and careered off at an angle. The first driver accelerated out of danger and turned the corner safely. Alexis felt the adhesion of the tyres to the road surface was wrong and the impelling curvature of the machine took over, making whatever efforts he could produce at holding the wheel steady or correcting the angle of impact spurious. He hit the bank, spun over once and the car turned into a cartridge fired at high velocity shooting down an air space, a beetle capsized and helpless on its back. Sparks flew from the friction of metal on the gritty surface of the roadway and after some five interminable seconds the missile came to rest on the bank of the opposite side of the road, so that it faced the oncoming traffic, and tipping against the verge righted itself with every incongruous appearance of normality.

Alexis knew he had survived, but he remembered throwing out a hand to save Mairi from going through the windscreen and that it was shattered. The wheel had effectively kept him in place during the corkscrew turn but his chest had been jolted against it and there was damage there. His brain was in a spin and for some seconds he had no notion of what to do. The road was deserted.

The other car had driven off and left him to it.

A van overtook him going north. The driver realised that Alexis' car was facing the wrong direction as it straddled the road. He reversed till he was a few yards from the scratched but otherwise intact vehicle. A man in overalls stopped and got slowly out to see what was up. Providence could not have worn a more unlikely face than the Scot, truculent in speech, utterly obliging in deed, who leaned on the open window by which Alexis slumped, trying to staunch the flow of his own blood, and asked, 'Are you all right, pal?'

Am I all right, pal? No, how can I be all right? I am hurt when I could be whole. I am alive when I could be dead. I am a man in his middle years who knows he has a vista of disappointments to look down, and the first of these is that I will not even reach my destination.

'I am going to go into shock in a few minutes. I've broken several bones. Don't worry if I'm sick. There's a blanket in the back and a coat, if you would cover me. And then call an ambulance. And the police.'

'How about your wife? Anything I can do for her?'

He looked over to the averted head. 'No, she won't mind how long you take.'

They weren't easy to trace, just far enough from home to be outside their known circumference. He seemed to have no documents on him, and the policemen had to go through the hand luggage to find the tickets and papers which had been packed. Tracing the car took time. Tracing the next of kin took more.

Aileen phoned every quarter of an hour to Inchcombe, playing in reverse the torments of the long wait for Rejean and Esme when they drove north. Eventually she called the police station at Lochearn just as the inspector from the Edinburgh constabulary and an accompanying woman sergeant came to the door.

She telephoned Montreal immediately and told Rejean he must fly back to help her, but he refused until he had performed his role at Esme's wedding. No, it might not be important to her but it was important to him. He would leave at once after it. It sounded anyway as though there was nothing he could do, and the argument that she needed moral back-up sounded strange from her lips. She would have to manage by herself.

She phoned again in the morning with the latest bulletin and so delayed their start. Rejean realised they were likely to be late and called Esme to explain they had been held up and would go straight to the Chapel. Would she mind going in the official car by herself?

He did not have the heart to spoil her wedding day by saying that none of her immediate family would be present after all, or why.

The fixed points of ceremony were unalterable. The Protestant wedding service, vows, hymns, blessing, the signing of register, was a standard practice. Coming so close to the only other wedding she had attended, Esme felt she knew the rigmarole too well. It sounded second hand, a blurred repeat.

More importantly, the similarities revealed to her how shoddily different this day was in essence. She couldn't avoid comparison between Aileen's celebration and her own, the fuss, the cost, the breathless adulation of a whole community turning out for their prominent family. These contrasted too forcibly with her own abandonment and neglect, of herself and by herself primarily.

She was sick again after a sleepless night. Mabon removed himself to sleep at the Base. She thought it was a hypocrisy, but the evening coincided with his stag night at the Mess and that would have been wild enough for her to be relieved he did not come back. Just as well they weren't on view till three, by which time the trusty Tom would see to it that the pilot was immaculate. She tried to picture Mabon out of control and could not.

They fell out over the dress. He bought a crinoline thing from Chicoutimi. He knew her dimensions, fashioned her taste, paid the bill outright. He insisted she try it on for him in the living room, dismissing as nonsense the idea that this was bad luck. She could always leave something off, couldn't she, the headpiece or whatever? She slipped obediently among the ice-cool folds of cloth and stood to be adjusted, pulled, fitted until he was at last satisfied with the result. She was not. Whoever elected white the colour of brides suffered from a wicked sense of humour. It embalmed too much. It mummified the wearer. To her it was a potent reminder of the vanishing snow, the soft, the suffocating stuff. Its purity was not apt. She felt stiff in it, peaks of meringue, an iced cake tier on tier. She would not, she insisted, wear it.

'Don't you like the material?'

'C'est du beau tissu.' She mimicked what the shop assistant would have said to clinch the sale.

'It's peau de soie.'

And that, neatly, was the cause of her unease, the feeling that the elaborate confection of the dress would become part of his erotic range and she saw herself in it some tired sad strumpet labouring to please him long after the day of public wearing.

However, she was learning when and how to make a fuss. Later she would face him. She returned it by herself and exchanged it for what Aileen, oh Aileen, how she missed the friend, would have called a serviceable costume. Putting it on now, she thought it matched her perfectly, the ivory wool as scoured as the face it framed. Wasn't she wise to choose a lustreless cloth, eschewing the gloss of satin, silk or brocade? This was the stuff of nuns' habits, the rough weave of hospital gowns, the fibre of the humdrum. It suited the emotional drudgery of their lives.

She remembered she had no flowers. Mabon had seen to buttonholes but shouldn't she have some nosegay, some tribute to the spring? She went out into the garden and searched along the paths for something she could pin to her lapel but it was an arid season and the best she could discover was a battered aconite which, cased in green ivy and a sheath of silver foil from the kitchen, did well enough for her. It was a touch druidical.

Painted, rouged, buffed into a simulacrum of normality, she looked better. What drained her every time her mind returned to it was the meeting between Alexis and Mabon. How could she not introduce them? What could they talk about? She kept seeing them at the end of a perspective, baffled, wholly baffled by each other as she was by her involvement with them both. Of course, she was wrong to prejudge their meeting. They would have found the common strain.

She tried seriously to compose herself. Her nerves were getting the better of her. Stage fright, she told herself, that's all I'm suffering from. She tried to abstract herself from what was about to be. The performance was what mattered. She must give them good value.

In fact she gave a tour de force. Mabon and all the other doubters who waited for her to fluff a line, miss a cue, were agreeably surprised. A Garbo hat of plaited straw, black-edged, hid her from too much inquiry. He was convincing in the part. Like a great actor, he delivered the words as though he had invented them a minute before and believed fundamentally in something they encapsulated. And it was done, not to be undone. The performance was live and enacted once and for all. No encore. The scene as she projected it became real and instantly faded like a shot from a zoom lens, distancing every minute under the impact of new footage, the here and now future.

'Where are they?' she asked Rejean in the vestry when they went to sign their names.

'Delayed. I'll tell you about it at the reception.' He held both her hands and kissed her unexceptionally before she was overtaken by other congratulations.

'How was the stag night?' he asked Mabon.

'Rough.' They went into the shadow boxing routines of men, how much, how late, how often, trying to knock each other down with words.

Others clamoured round her and she enjoyed the instantaneous glamour of the starlet. Tomorrow it would be someone else, thank goodness.

At the Manoir du Saguenay it was difficult to see Rejean alone. They or rather he had decided on a buffet meal, anticipating, with more concern than she gave him credit for, that a protracted session at table would tire her. So people constantly claimed her attention, the Chantals, the Cartiers, Bob Findlay, colleagues from Arvida. Mabon had asked the CO and his wife as a duty, and was astonished when they had accepted. One up to Flight Lieutenant Caulderwood. But where were her own folk?

She left them all and went to search for Rejean. She tracked him down eventually by a long window, forking a plateful of food with no interest.

'I'm staying till the speeches, Esme, and then I have to get back to Montreal,' he apologised.

'But you still haven't said why they didn't come with you. Did they change their minds? I was sure Aileen would come up with you from Montreal anyway, even if Alexis and Mairi thought better of it.'

He had intended to falsify but he saw she was hurt. She thought they were in Montreal and had simply found something better to do with the day. He put his plate down on a brocaded chair and led her outside the window to the terrace where the sun warmed the corners under an incipient wisteria. She leaned against a balustrade and he walked up and down the verandah wondering how one said these things.

'They had a car crash between Lochearn and Edinburgh. It would be early yesterday morning our time.' His pallor said more than his words. She put herself in his hands.

'Tell me.'

'I feel it's so unfair, today especially.'

'Just tell me.'

'Mairi was killed outright. Alexis has a broken hand and maybe serious internal injuries. They don't know yet.'

'Aileen?'

'She was waiting for them to pick her up.'

'And you are flying out tonight?'

'Yes, I booked my seat as soon as I heard.'

'Let me come with you.'

He looked surprised and then thought, Well, they were her closest relatives, the only ones prepared to come today. 'I can't say yes to that. You're going away on your honeymoon, aren't you?'

'Yes, he's allocating me two days in Quebec. That doesn't matter. He'll hardly notice.'

'You don't mean that. You're wrought.'

'Why didn't you tell me when you phoned this morning?'

'I thought it unfair to you.'

'Unfair. Yes, it is unfair.' He took her clenching hands to keep them still. 'I am married now and I cannot be unmarried.'

He read this as a symptom of regret that there were no witnesses to the fact on her side. 'You don't want to come. It'll be dismal. Who wants to go all that way for a funeral?'

'Is it any stranger than coming all this way for a wedding? I would make that journey for that funeral. Mairi. Imagine that. Killed with one blow. She seemed so very unkillable. How bad is Alexis, do you think?'

'I really don't know. Last night Aileen had none but the baldest news because she hadn't seen him and this morning we were rushing to get off.'

She looked around her at the formal gardens of the hotel, an oasis in the muted landscape that from now on she must call home. How could she have been so foolish as to sign away her birthright, release her freedom, change even her name? Who was she now? Why did it have to be that his release was bought at the price of her bondage? If she had not acted so precipitately but had kept faith with her own instinct, she could have been going home to him this day; with him; from him.

He stood in the frame of the window. 'Do come and be civil, Esme. The CO and his wife have another engagement and are waiting to say goodbye.'

She excused herself to Rejean.

Alexis grasped the hand that came to his and felt that it was strong. Opening his eyes from one of the cyclic reveries that made up most of his day, and night, he saw it was Graeme Sutherland. He knew how weak he was by the overwhelming surge of gratitude he felt at this restoration. It was almost worth the wound to have such healing. He brought the air indoors and the burrs of a thistle head clung to his sleeve where he had brushed past.

He forced his mind out of the penumbra of what had happened. He knew only death would have brought him back unsolicited, without the apology that was due from his side first.

'I didn't kill her.'

'I never thought for one minute you did.'

'It was a broken neck, wasn't it?'

'Yes. A quick exit. All you can ask.'

The survivor leaned forward and encountered the padding round his midriff. 'What the hell have they got me in, a corset?'

'Of sorts. Two broken ribs. Be grateful it's nothing worse.'

He looked at his hand, bandaged into a fist. 'Has Aileen been?'

'Yes, Rejean is due in this afternoon so she's gone to pick him up at Prestwick.'

'It seems to have happened the wrong way round.' He lay on his back again, suddenly exhausted. 'Yes, Rejean. I missed it in the end. How did it go?'

'What do you want me to say?'

'That life's worth living after all. I want you to say some miracle happened when she heard about the accident and that she didn't go through with it. That she's as free as I am.'

'No, she is not.' He spoke this with such affirmation it almost cancelled out the negatives. 'She is safely wed.'

'Safely! How could you say that to me? You mean safely out of my reach.' He rolled his head over and met the gamekeeper's eye. 'You still think you were right?'

Graeme had had a lonely season too. He missed companionship but he missed peace of mind more. He had come determined to heal the breach and would not be deflected by anything but absolute refusal. They had shaken hands on meeting and that was a pact.

'Ach, let's not bicker now.'

Alexis consented to that injunction. 'Tell me, what's been happening in the strath? I've missed your broadsheets.'

He listened to the sing-song voice reel out the great minutiae of the parish, who'd come, who'd gone and who kept to their places. It did him more good than a transfusion.

They walked through the gardens above the Heights of Abraham. The Château Frontenac gleamed in the distance, its copper roof green with verdigris. Below them were the straits where a Scot changed the history of the nation. He knew his French, having fought for the Stuart Pretenders, exiled in France. On the side now of the Hanoverian George, he challenged the watchman and spoke well enough to deceive him. He persuaded him to put up his rifle and the heights fell.

Behind, the narrow cobbleways hid courtyards hung with geraniums in white-painted baskets, corner cafés with a dozen scrolled chairs optimistically set on the pavement and painters transported half a world away from Montmartre. An artist begged to draw her and Mabon encouraged it, but she refused. Horse-drawn fiacres passed. She expected to see Emma Bovary, Odette de Crécy settle into the upholstery hidden behind a veil en route to an assignation. He said they should hire one of these carriages and make a tour of the city but she refused. So they walked silently through the gardens above the Heights of Abraham, turning heads but not each other's.

Esme started again, hesitantly. She tried to unburden herself of what she felt to be the curse of predestination. To Mabon's ears words like shadow and sequence sounded strange. One point he fastened on however: the idea that his appearance at the Simards' was parallel to Stefan's, that their meeting had been a chance one but preordained in time, and that inevitably he was playing out her father's role.

He thought he mitigated this impression by saying, 'Do you think I came by accident? No, I'd seen you in Chicoutimi maybe a day or two after you arrived in September. I thought when you were with Maurice that you were Rejean's wife and I was in too much of a hurry to stop the car and talk, or ask where Rejean was. Then a friend at the Arvida school said there was a new teacher straight out from the UK and described you. The next time I was in Montreal I followed it up. I knew you'd gone to the Simards' for the week and that I'd meet you there. I only went because of you.'

Instead of shedding the sense of being caught in the snare of her ancestry, Esme felt more entrammelled, bound by an invisible force she refused to name or even acknowledge directly in case, by invoking the mysterious power of Jahveh, hubris, genie, the three self-cancelling wishes of folklore, destiny, the will of Allah or voodoo, she might fall victim to the returning prophecies of her own theology, however obscure or diverse it might be in origin. She was afraid to breathe in the corners of a shadowy crypt in case she brushed against the statue of a superstitious god.

It was a good turnout.

Mairi had capped the attendance at Aileen's wedding. For a time the traffic was halted along the main road through the village and two policemen were sent out on patrol to clear the bottleneck. The church was full, with even the gallery crowded. The Reverend Galbraith was impaled between envy that his ministry could not draw such a packed house on Sundays, and a reflected glow that a believer had her just rewards. It proved the existence of a deity.

Alexis, of course, was more objective. They came from duty, these mourners, or in search of sensation, for the crash coming on a dull day received media coverage, but mostly because he was a known commodity, a brand name and readily identifiable. They came to stare and carry away reports.

The yew-bound churchyard was awash with wreaths, fanciful, gaudily intricate. He remembered sadly the insignificant tributes to Rhona, specks on the enormity of indifference. These in reality were a testament to his success, an unlooked-for accolade. Flowers, strange. The Jews banned them as emblems of celebration and he might himself have preferred laurel, juniper or cypress or the monochrome flowers with a touch of sobriety. Some restraining discipline was needed.

He was not entirely well. He was strapped heavily and resented the constriction more than the pain. His left hand hurt; thank heaven or whatever powers that be, his left. He obdurately refused to wear it in a sling and propped it instead inside his jacket lapel. Aileen told him he lacked only a tricorn to become a Buonoparte. He was equally obdurate about a reading. Everyone objected. It was not the custom. Custom be blowed. He was here because there was no secular place appointed for such ritual, and as she had been a confirmed Christian he was obliged to pay his last respects in church.

They sang some dirge. 'Nearer my God to thee.' Couldn't Rejean have come up with something better? Galbraith spoke of her goodly works and went as far as quoting the virtuous woman whose price was above rubies, which made him shudder as much at the obvious as at the too literally true.

Aileen was seized with nerves as he got up to make his reading. The church fell into an uncanny hush, curious to see how he disposed himself. Twice in one year inside the kirk, she could hear them think. She wished she knew what he was going to say or read. They watched him as they might have watched Samson mount the steps between the pillars. He could do anything, rain Ahab curses, use the pulpit as the rostra to deliver a philippic, spout a lewd passage from the *Metamorphoses* and none of them the wiser.

But today he was the douce and canny man.

He read a lament by W.W. Gibson. It had taken him a day and a half to trace it among his books, for it was the last line that stuck with him as it tended to be with Esme's letters, and he had neither author nor title to go on. He hunted systematically in his anthologies, reading into the night and thinking, If she were here, she would find it at once. I am sure she would. She might even know it. At that, the book he was holding fell open at the place revealing what he had searched for so long.

We who are left, how shall we look again
Happily on the sun or feel the rain
Without remembering how they who went
Ungrudgingly and spent
Their lives for us, loved, too, the sun and the rain?

A bird among the rain-wet lilac sings –
But we, how shall we turn to little things
And listen to the birds and winds and streams
Made holy by their dreams,
Nor feel the heart-break in the heart of things?

A part of Aileen thought, He got out of that one well, and a part
was genuinely moved by the voice resonating through these
unlikely halls. Its quality was not lost in amplification. It was not
swallowed up by the occasion. It did not become pompous. Its
origins remained untraceable, like his own, sometimes English in
enunciation but Scots in its emphasis, its hearty vowels, its way of
saying the elusive meaningfully and the meaningless with humour.
Well, his accent was like a chameleon and took on the colouring of
his surroundings. She'd heard him talk the roughest vernacular
with hill farmers and then outpoint them all in colloquy with
Powell-Jones. She loved him. What more was there to say? She
loved her father. No man could come close. Her heart stilled with
apprehension when she thought how near she'd been to losing
him. It fired her with pride that such a man should be her progenitor.

He was satisfied. That was the best he could do. He was sure that
his wife was consigned to earth a fulfilled woman. She had had her
strongest if not her last wish, for he had never left her and their
marriage, as far as the world at large could judge, had been a
success. She would not live with the stigma of being the deserted
wife. She triumphed in death, but not for the same reasons
generally attributable to her religion. It was timely. He would not
have spent one more day under the same roof as her. No one knew
of the cause of their alienation apart from Esme, and he believed
fervently that the blight had worked itself out at last, that the
ground was cleared of sorrel, the rose of canker.

She found the headstone, as she had assumed, in a quiet and tidy
corner, deeply shaded.

410

The inscription read simply

Stefan Roberval

Beloved husband of Marie-Anne

father of Alexis

Sunt Lacrimae Rerum

The boy must have added the Latin tag.

She stooped to lay her spray of roses. The corner was as lonely as an arctic cairn, wind-blown and bleak. What a place to be laid to earth, cold and shadowy as his existence.

A gardener rounded the corner, hoe in hand, but seeing her at her oblations he respectfully went to a remoter spot and weeded with the gentle circular motion of the unhurried expert.

38

Rejean and Aileen were alone at Inchcombe for a day before Alexis was discharged from hospital in time for the funeral. It was difficult to avoid each other, though they were kept busy answering the telephone and opening the scores of letters and cards that came by every post. For a week the mail came by parcel load in a van, too heavy for the sack of the man who delivered by bicycle. Replying would take most of her holiday, Aileen judged.

So they fell into the occupations of mourning which disguised for a while whether they missed the subject or not. They missed Alexis. He was the connective thread in the functions of the place. Without him the workers stared blankly at the end of a piece and wondered what to do next. Mrs Galashan tidied up tidiness in his absence. People came and went without being answered. Everyone waited for his instructions. The house reverberated emptily without him. How could he have filled it all?

At sunset they stood at the open window and wondered individually how they should sleep. In the old days he had gone to bed in the adjoining room and when the house grew quiet stepped lightly to her door. Alexis knew early, catching sight of him going

411

back at six one morning, bleary and mother naked. They had no inhibition then about give and take. Was it exciting only when it was unlicensed? She, hand on a chair back, had the same thoughts. Still, memory could be a barrier as well as a bond and she found it hard to ignore the interregnum, the vacant space in their relationship. He had changed and so had she because of it.

'Are you really better now?' Once she would not have asked but established her own assurances.

He would not discuss it. A broken leg he would have refractured and reset a hundred times rather than admit to this weakness, which was worse than a mental breakdown to him. He was painfully ashamed of the disability because he thought it was an unmanly complaint. It often estranged him from those who found his manner tense, because he would not explain himself and say the easy thing. 'Intal works. But I may become resistant to it in time.' He sat on the chair and leaned over the sill. The loch, a miniature in silver, mirrored the encasing sky. Beautiful, beautiful place. Why couldn't he like it better than he did?

She put her hand tentatively on his head and felt the familiar strange texture of it. Not thirty, he was going grey with a line of coarseness at the temples and, sampling it between her fingers, she found it tough and wiry in the context of the soft capillary darkness. He rested his head on her hip and girded her with his left arm.

'This house is too quiet.'

'I know.'

They heard the cries of children playing on the far shore, too remote to seem significant. But the sound carried and was magnified by the water and the wind direction, a sound like a ripple from a single stone widening until it beat against the sand and was absorbed. What were they playing? Tig, Blind Man's Buff, chasing each other in the twilight, or following one another down the helter-skelter of a municipal playground.

'That used to be me,' she said. 'You probably think I spent my childhood looking like Shirley Temple. But I was a tomboy, or tried to be, always outside when I was young. I grew up here. I mean really grew up. Not many people live in one house all their lives. I know every stone, every path, every leaf. Alexis made it. But it made me. Adults know places from the outside, already finished, but children grow inside and see them differently. I could walk blindfold from here to St Fillans along the shore or the road, and I could describe what it looked like every ten yards as we went, what rocks jut out, what trees grow in that spot. I know it off by heart, the way Graeme knows the moors. It's like a poem I say over and over to myself, a mantra.'

She went on stroking the hair at her side. 'When I was small I was very timorous, physically afraid. I used to set myself progressive tasks to try and get over it. Make myself walk home through the woods at night when I was terrified and the trees were leering at me the way they did at Snow White in the film. And there's a crag towards the Melville estate that's like a knob of rock. It was my Tarpeian rock. It goes sheer over your head. The lads went up like mountain goats but I struggled to get my foothold on it at all and I looked such an idiot having to scramble round it on the grass verge while they all waited for me at the top. I was afraid of heights, though I didn't know it. I used to go up there on my own and practise and practise and practise till I could scale it as quickly as them. I wasn't going to hold anyone up.

'We had a gang. We called it a gang, anyway, though we didn't rough-house people. Almost a dozen of us, mostly boys. I don't think anyone here knew I hung about with the village children, though I went to school in the village till I was eleven. They were a scruffy lot, and some of them were so poor I can still think of one or two who never wore proper shoes, only rubber gym shoes.'

'What did your gang do?' he asked.

'Played games, made up teams for rounders, the boys made guiders. Do you know what a guider is?' She smiled at the recollection. 'It's a kind of primitive car. I don't know what you'd call it, a go-cart, a bogey made from the chassis of an old pram with an inset of wood over the metal spars for you to sit on. The front wheels are pivoted so that you can steer with a rope, preferably a bit of your mother's washing line. I wonder if boys still make them? Gie's a hurl on your guider, they used to say. The boy with the best guider was leader without dispute. It gave you a lot of bargaining power. Girls didn't make guiders. I was infinitely annoyed I couldn't be leader. I didn't think I was very well suited for it, but I would have liked the chance. Some bossy girls came near the top of the order. When they got themselves organised they could shout down the opposition and have their own way at least part of the time. But I was a mouse who followed on.

'We used to go carol singing and guising, trick or treat to you, and Easter egg rolling and it was good because they were always there if you wanted them. I wonder if children play in the streets any more? I don't see them, but maybe I'm out at different times. Between tea and bed, that was the time, till it was dark in the summer evenings. All those wonderful games: What's the Time Mr Wolf, Statues, Hospital Tig. I would hate to think they're lost. I can't even remember the rules or what the point of half of them was.

'But the best times were when I was on my own. I don't recall having many toys. A few dolls I used to prop up in front of cases and pretend they were school desks. I liked the real things, boxes, baking tins, a proper trowel Alexis let me have. I spent hours by the slip stream trying to dig it into a new channel. Put a boulder in the way and watch the stream fork. But no matter how I tried it went back to its original course. It knew its own energy and I was wasting mine.'

He thought this over for a long time while she paused, fretfully rubbing the stones of the sill while the sun sank, the noises receded from over the water and the children vanished indoors. 'I won't ask you to give this up again.'

She sighed. 'Perhaps I've always tried things that are too hard for me. I imagine I can do everything, and at once, but I can't. I can do a very little well. One thing at a time. People have always thought me so clever that I believed I was. But I'm only theoretically clever, nothing more. I don't know what to apply it to. I could go on accumulating degrees for the rest of my life, but whatever for? To prove I could be leader if only I were a man?'

He pulled her down and she knelt beside his chair. It was good to be together, face against his shoulder evoking a half-forgotten desire. No, not desire. Stupid words. A known place with a known person. It was the reverse side, ease, comfort, tenderness. It never was desire. 'Tell me what it is you want to do,' he said.

'I don't know what I want to do. I am perfectly capable of thinking myself to a a standstill. I want to be with you, I want to be independent. I want to live here, but I do like there. I can't focus on a single decision and say categorically that's what I'll do. I am turning into what I most fear and despise, believe me I do, the instrumental female. I have a terrifying apprehension that I'll achieve nothing on my own, except being the medium for achievement in others. I want to be upsides with the men and I can't. I am debarred from my view of heaven which is being what a man is. I haven't got a new thought in my head. I can crib well, that's all. You,' she said, 'you are more innovative than I am and that makes me very bitter because I didn't even recognise it. I pooh-poohed your ambitions because they were outside my scope. What can I say, except that I was envious and I was wrong? But how can I accommodate my own limitations?'

In the face of such an outburst which he would not have foreseen from her, for the cool blonde restraint was implicit in her attitudes, he could find nothing to say. It wasn't any easier to be male? She could reduce her sense of limitation by helping him to overcome his? Enjoy it in me, you may beget the other sex? To be so patronising was impertinent. What on earth could he say that wasn't dismissive of her heart-soreness? There was no consolation for the missing gene. They looked at each other over the huge divide and prompted by Alexis he said the only thing he could.

'I can't make it without you.'

In the morning they set to work in tandem.

The original scattered jottings he had carted across the world several times in the bottom of a suitcase had formulated themselves into more than chapter headings and stray ideas. He saw ahead the shape of several books, untravelled continents that would keep him occupied in exploration for a quarter of a century. The Montreal publisher had been helpful in highlighting this. Festina lente. One book at a time. So he took a single segment of what he wanted to say and hoped that eventually the other segments would be written to form a corporate whole.

He dictated the final changes in this manuscript to Aileen, sitting on either side of her father's desk which the two of them, working over like a see-saw, did not fill. They talked, they argued. That isn't clear. Find another word. You used that idea on page seventy-three. That's slang. What kind of North-Americanese is that? You've used it transitively and it's intransitive. She might have the soul of a grammarian but he had to defer to her grounding in both the languages of his heritage. Besides, her impudence had always made him laugh. She channelled the wayward current of his mind. When she typed the sheets, the thing that came out was maybe his at source, but it was her conception, her moulding that systematised it. He recalled Elgar's wife patiently drawing groups of five lines across paper because they could not afford to buy manuscript sheets for him to compose on; Hardy's despised Emma filling his day book with quotations at his behest. He was humbled by such sacrifice of labour. What inscription, what dedication on a fly-leaf could men make that in any part paid off their indebtedness? 'To my dear wife without whom . . .' How inadequate.

He let her go alone when they had finished the morning session, to pick Alexis up from the hospital. He paced along the foreshore by himself, passing the spot where he had found the broken stone he gave to Esme's keeping. As he remembered that, she came welling up again like the pools of water that collected in the footprints that he made, every one behind him along the beach. She brought back the other shore where she was a stranger as he was here. Poise and counterpoise, he had to recognise they would never but never be in alignment, in the same spot at the same time.

And that made him discontent, to be invariably second best with her, not to a specific man as he understood it, certainly not to Mabon, but second best to her ideal which she kept intact. Well, he said he renounced the ultimate in human goals. Did it exist, the love that moved the sun and the stars in their places, or was it all like his, a workaday affair? He needed them both, the light and the dark, the achieved and the yearning. He could not live on a diet of air, but he had the patience to wait a lifetime for the fulfilling passion or, never finding it, still believe in its possibility, as Esme did. It was in their dreams that they were most alike.

This compromise in his thinking led him to another. He had undergone a battery of tests in a hospital unit in Montreal, the results of which came in a written report on his damaged frame. It made gruesome reading. Wet rales, dry rales, he sounded like a house with nail sickness. He put it away, for knowing didn't fundamentally help. The physician admitted that the extremes of the Canadian winter were likely to place recurring stress on his body's defences. He must not spend another winter on the dry eastern seaboard of his native country. He was allergic to his own place. He could go to British Columbia, or California, or seek a temperate zone which provided the balance of wet and dry, hot and cold his make-up seemed to need.

He must exile himself, and that being so he felt he should seek exile where he was known. The best balance he could arrive at was to spend eight months of the year, the summer season, at home in Canada and the other four months of the winter solstice at home in Britain.

This role as eternal migrant recommended itself to him in many ways. It pleased him more nearly than any other solution. The work in Montreal was practical, go out and do, show, talk, visit. The active appealed to him and always would more than the sedentary life he was having to succumb to. But the last six months in his father's office had made their relative positions clear. His father was a doer, one who created his own luck, but who also was mortal and fallible and was something of a prevaricator in the face of change. He had no vision outside the conventional. Rejean had been able to place his own begetter in the scheme of things and found himself superior. He knew that he had the potential to be a thinker and that was an added dimension. Action and reflection, that was what the two continents represented to him, North America, Britain, the new world and the old. A summer in the field, a winter writing. He struck his balance.

He'd be unhappy. Wherever he was, he would want the other but with less urgency than before. He needed them both, needed even the grit under the skull which produced the pearl. Without that malaise he was a nonentity, a nice guy who never got going. What was home anyway, an illusion, a reconstruction of childhood phases of dependency like Aileen's, a mirage you walked towards and through and didn't touch. Home was his luggage, what he carried in his case, in his head, on his person. Home was his own kind of people, wherever they were scattered. Home was his writing, the place where he was born, was nourished and which one day would provide his epitaph. Home was himself.

When they came back, his sympathies were evoked for the pain visible in the suffering of the man he worshipped this side idolatry and on whom he modelled himself, know it or not. He could say with some conviction, 'I've been looking up the Property Guide in the *Scotsman*. There's a house in Inverleith I like the sound of, opposite the Botanic Gardens. I'd like to go and have a look at it. Could we all go next week when we're down at the lawyer's? The money from Goldenacre could be the deposit. It's still banked here.'

He dreaded the poky gardens, the railings that kept people bound in and out, the dead grey stones, but he accepted their circumscription as inevitable.

Part three
39

Esme had crossed the divide which separates the wed from the unwed and waited for the change to strike her. In some ways she was more liberated. The summer term soon span away and left her unoccupied, and then she was free – through another's labour – to indulge her own pursuits. As a wife, she was issued with her own pass to the Base and visited the library every week, the only one in the region where English books could be had. The books, bandaged in red, green and yellow sticky tape, were whole at heart even if Proust's recherches stopped at volume six. Authors she had tasted in passing, between one urgency and another, she devoured whole. Basking in the suntrap of the courtyard (Mabon said, I want you to get brown this summer; I prefer tanned skin) she took Somerset Maugham at a gulp, Thomas Hardy in long and steady draughts, D.H. Lawrence in hurried gluttony. How pleasant it was to be married after all in such men's company.

Externally there was a change, but limited. The great exodus, the significant removal to the bridgegroom's house, was missing. She and Aileen had imported their mates into their own established environment so, while she missed a certain flurry of homemaking, there was no new routine to be absorbed. Sometimes when she faced a night of solitude or expectancy she found herself towards evening wishing that someone would call; Bob Findlay, Rejean descend amusing and impulsive. But no one did. That was the divide, not in herself or by herself, but in the minds of others. Mabon had become a guardian, a Cerberus warding off the casual caller.

She took to driving somewhere every day, telling herself it was to buy provisions. The supermarkets depressed her on daily acquaintance. The phrasing taunted. Eviscerated turkey. Tenderised meat. Barbecue flavour. Sharp frozen strawberries and jam that was 'like home-made'. As far as she knew, it either was or it wasn't. There was no *like* about it. The smell of the kitchen at the old house wafted towards her on boiling days, the elusive pungency of pectin and sugar. Didn't these selling gimmicks debase language as well as the product? Everything seemed second rate. Under the pall of newness things were rotten. Where was the flavour of life, the clotted cream, the sweet stalk of a fresh tomato, the free-range eggs from Dirleton? With a fraction more care the apples could have been unbruised, and the cheese less flaccid.

Once it got too much for her. Pushing the trolley down interminable twists and alleyways, while it grew heavier and heavier, she became exhausted. The cart rolled away from her and her feet seemed to slip on wet flooring. She felt faint and retreated to the car, leaving the half-filled trolley in a corner. She couldn't make herself go back to it and went home empty handed. Mabon, waiting for a meal, was furious: For God's sake, woman, can't you even do the shopping? He went back with her and bought everything that made her squeamish, blood red meat, wet fish and sugared foods. He had a sweet tooth.

'You need to make sure of an impression at the Wives' Club. They have meetings once a month and do a lot of good work. Charity, visiting. Shall I ask Yvonne to introduce you?' He couldn't understand why she groaned aloud.

Notwithstanding, she was drawn into it.

She received an invitation to a garden party. This was in June and it was inscribed by the CO's wife. Formal dress. This meant the full regalia whereby legs, hands and head were covered when, according to the temperature and humidity reading, they should have been sensibly bare. She was at the height of discomfort even before she arrived. Apparently no suitable garden had suggested itself, and so a hundred scorching wives met indoors in the Mess. The afternoon was breathless, the windows tightly shut in the belief that the air conditioning worked better that way. She didn't think it worked at all, or was it the furnace inside her that made her warmer than anyone else?

She listened at first to the drifts of conversation around her, hoping to find something she could latch on to.

'The barbecue was good, but you know I can't eat a whole T-bone and the dog had half. Jerry's salads are wonderful but he does cut such man-size portions of potato.'

'And you should just have seen the CO's face when her top came off.'

420

'I was wearing my cerise gown and the only other chic woman at the ball said to her escort that she recognised mine at once as a designer model. And it was he who told me.'

'He had a girl in his room, and Lord, if he wasn't called out on scramble before dawn. She couldn't walk through the Mess at eight a.m. and ask for breakfast, so she had to sit there all day until it got dark. He takes a risk. You have to admire him for that.'

'She was livid. She paid a fortune to have the suite re-covered, had it done in Montreal at a continental upholsterers. The best. I mean. And when Mary went to see it, what did she say? "I adore your loose covers. Did they come from Simpsons-Sears catalogue?" '

She tried to concentrate on the proceedings. They wanted a rota for the charity shop, tickets for the summer ball weren't selling well because the date was inopportunely close to summer leave, the primary school at the Base was losing a teacher. They looked at Esme and she had to explain she taught something different from first grade math.

They seemed interested in what was going on, all of them, as she glanced from face to face. She recognised them as the women who patrolled the supermarkets, hunting in pairs, swooping on special offers with enthusiastic noises, filling cart after cart headed for the freezer and calling out to each other across the gangways vital information about the best buys.

She was baffled, more than if they had been talking to her in French. The range of their concerns – summer storage of their furs, censure of the women who didn't do their bit or alternately tried too hard to jostle their husband up the promotion ladder – convinced Esme she wasn't a woman at all.

She went to the Ladies' Room, always a sanctuary at the Union, doubly so when escaping her own sex. Why did she have to suffer from such exclusiveness? Couldn't she be more like her kind, roll her eyes in horror, filter gossip through clenched teeth? She couldn't go back into that stuffy hothouse atmosphere, but on the other hand she couldn't exactly walk out in full view of the wives.

The night of the storm had graphed out the ground plan of the building, and knowing that mid-afternoon on a Saturday she was unlikely to meet anyone she edged down the corridor of the bachelor's quarters. There was a fire exit door at the bottom which she lifted from the latch and slipped behind, into the crushing heat.

And three yards away Bob Findlay crossed in front of her, astonished to see her appear from a blank wall, open sesame.

'Oh Bob, why do you always see me doing what I shouldn't? I've just run away from the garden party. I'll never go to another.'

He stooped his neck and his jacket rode up six inches at the back. 'That bad? Come on, we'll go and have a proper garden party at home. I can at least offer you some English tea.'

'Can you really? And talk. Can you put me in a deck chair in the shade? How marvellous. You won't split on me?'

'Oh, the ladies will do that for me, never fear.'

He was right. Yvonne Cartier saw she hadn't returned and so sweetly asked if she hadn't been well. Mabon was less tolerant than Bob. He had more to lose.

'But what can I talk to them about?'

'You shouldn't have to ask me what you can talk to other women about. You should know. Talk about women's things, the home, children. They might be helpful to you. You haven't done much to get ready.'

'Actually, you think being women is all we need in common, as though there weren't different kinds of women apart of course from pretty ones and ugly ones. That's the important distinction. You could get on with them better than I can. I cannot find a single point to talk about.'

He gave this some consideration and rejected its validity because 'I could talk to any man I met for half an hour.'

'Oh, so could I. Make no mistake about that. It's women who confound me. I don't know why, so don't ask me. I don't understand what they're saying. They don't listen to each other for a start. I gave Yvonne ten minutes about her house re-fit in Montreal. New drapes, new cushions. I have been stitched into every pleat of those cushions. I know the cloth and the colour and the problems with the piping. But when I got a word in about Quebec, she cut me off. I mean she's presumably been to Quebec City. I wasn't trying to talk to her about funny old Europe, where, Gee, it's so quaint. I was trying quite hard to move inside her experience and find out what she thought on a subject of mutual interest, but I get the erase button. The message is, nothing I have to say matters. It would, of course, if you were senior to her husband. They're paralysing me with boredom. They're not even funny, except unintentionally.'

Esme told the truth but a lie would have been more circumspect. Yvonne Cartier was for Mabon the epitome of wifehood, the woman who did it all impeccably and was still very toothsome, the most attractive spouse on the camp apart from his own, of course, but four and a half months pregnant she was past her best. They had flirted for so long together at parties, he and Yvonne, that their relationship was almost a status symbol, a man and a woman who would if they could, the only one each would breach their regulations for. So she chose the wrong god to slander.

'What makes you so special, I would like to know, that you set yourself above them?'

'Nothing. I'm not special. I'm as ordinary as the dirt under your shoe. You're right to castigate me. But I am not gregarious. I am not the bird that flocks and I just want them to go away and leave me alone.'

'But you can't avoid it. You have your duty as my wife.'

'Do I?'

'I don't intend to live like a hermit. You must take your place in public with me and do the things the other wives do.'

'I didn't bargain for that. Can't I duck out?'

'No. Not without comment, and for me as much as you.'

His face as he produced this ultimatum was puzzled. Normally his features were aloof but secure in their rightness for the occasion. He gave very little away. The two extremes of his countenance were total relaxation and total concentration. He did not betray emotion in the whole gamut of his expressions, so this frown, this compression of the lips, was as close as he came to the tremulous state of uncertainty. And he deeply resented that she should ruffle his composure.

Bed and board she could cope with, but the public face was one she could not wear. They sat looking into the heart of the paradox. The things that attracted him to her, made him pursue her more avidly than any woman before, disturbed his judgment to the point of sleeping with her incautiously, and marrying her – the thing that did all this was her uniqueness in his experience.

But a wife was not unique. She was a woman who conformed to

wifeliness, doing the done, saying the unobjectionable. The person she had been would not do service now. She must change with the metamorphosis of growth. Inside every woman were these other people, his wife and his children, the parasites the man released to eat into her innards like a tapeworm, till she was consumed entirely and there was nothing left of self.

'You must try harder.'

'To be what? Different from what I am? Nearer what you would like if you could buy me in kit form? I am so sorry I don't have the right component parts. If only you could give me a brain transplant. I would be much less difficult.'

They lifted their eyes to each other and acknowledged haggardly the scarring of their union.

He walked away, mortified by her lack of understanding.

She, as she always did, escaped. She withdrew inside her head. She went elsewhere for companionship in quiet hours.

She saw Alexis more dimly now, uncertain of the difference his injury made, but more pervasively too. She could not open a book without turning to him to share it. The *Golden Treasury* became her Bible, though she used it secularly. She let it fall open the way the Romans did with Virgil's *Aeneid* or the superstitious mediaeval mind the Apocrypha, to take a reading from it. Not that she was looking for a prognosis for tomorrow: tomorrow was too far away for certainty, or for her to want to change the causal balance of its outcome. She took a reading for today, trying to find conviction that another like mind existed in the universe, as confirmation of her own. Not 'Puto ergo sum' but 'Putat ergo sum' was her creed; thought is possible and therefore I exist. What is he thinking now? she asked, spreading her hands over the pages.

She tried hard to see the landscape through which she took her daily drive impartially, that is, through his eyes. Was it beautiful? Was it frightening? Why did she not like it better? Did the roads lack something, and if so, what? Was their omission in her unfamiliarity with where they led? Was it her own limitation she was bounded by, which made her incapable of responding to the thing that was not known? But she could not make him give an answer to specifics. The disincarnate voice would not contradict her. She missed the reality that was beyond her call.

He was in her growing solitude a constant friend, ready with a laugh or a comment, the person she directed her life towards. He was the perfect counter-agent to her mood because she summoned and controlled him, though from time to time he was obdurately silent and she lost contact, as though perception were faint, trans-Atlantic signals weak.

True, at these times he had switched off the transmitter. Give her marriage a chance, he said to himself.

40

Graeme stood at nightfall in one of the high corries of the Curriedon estate, a shallow bowl of moorland with a copse on the western slopes which was frequented in season by a herd of stags before they broke up and followed the hind. It was a favoured spot of his too, a trap of afternoon heat because of the convex curvature of the land as well as being sheltered by the trees from breezes that might have cooled it in the evening. It was always still in this cup of land, always mild. It was a short mile from his own threshold and very often he walked that way as a stroll at the end of a day when he had been too much in his Land Rover and too little on his feet.

The epicentre of the depression gave a spectacular view down to Loch Earn. The greenery of the vegetation broke up the natural fall of the land which was precipitate at this point, and showed the zigzag of the gully in high relief. Daylight had virtually gone. The light he saw by was a reflected glow, as though the elements of the landscape could absorb light as well as warmth and continue to emit it for a while after sunlight had failed. It was the best time of the day as far as he was concerned. Day is done, gone the sun from the hills, from the sea, from the sky. It brought to mind vespers, the bells of evensong and a gratitude for simple tasks he had been able to complete.

A wisp of grey in the deepening blue of the evening was the first indication he had. Away to his right there was a bonfire, just a trace of smoke. By concentrating fixedly on that spot, in the way an eagle hoods his eyes not to miss a flicker of movement, he could pick out the flame that generated it. It was not an ordinary bonfire.

Not leaves. Not garden waste. Not ordinary wood. There was an acrid edge to it, a curl now and then of the dead black which no natural product emitted. And by veering downwind he could establish the direction. It was Alexis who made that bonfire on the foreshore at Inchcombe. A smaller fire than his great November conflagration. More secretive. He was annoyed that he would have to wait another day for explanation.

Aileen sat on the same evening with a piece of paper in front of her and juggled the figures. Every now and then she spoke to Rejean who was writing letters to Esme, to his publisher, to his mother and checked the numerical accuracy of a sum.

They had come back from their third visit to the house in Inverleith, two of which were made before they submitted their offer through Mr Scott. The second of these was ratified by the approval, albeit mixed, of Alexis who had driven down for the official reading and executry of Mairi's will. The garden at Inverleith was a tangle, the décor bizarre and nothing was helped by the tumbling raucous sunshine of late spring which showed up deficiencies of taste and maintenance cruelly. Still, it was convenient. It was the end of the row with windows to the south, the orientation prized in Edinburgh houses. Their offer had been accepted, which was what they wanted, but it led to the disagreeable suspicion that they had bid too high. No recanting now. The problem was finance.

Aileen had reason to be well pleased with her mother's bequest. She left all her assets to her daughter, which included her portion of the sale of the big house and a sizeable sum accumulated over the years which was her salary as book-keeper in her husband's business. This was a tax dodge operated by many families, nominal directors earning exorbitant consulting fees. Mairi tolerated no such evasion. She had paid herself on the nail. Aileen jotted down these totals, added the value of the office at Goldenacre, and found she was able to deduct the cost of Inverleith and leave enough for legal costs, removal expenses and some refurbishment. She was well pleased.

Then there was the furniture which Mairi considered hers to give, a list devised long ago as she projected their divorce. This inventory was so comprehensive she and Alexis had argued for

some time about the rightfulness of her abstracting it from Inchcombe. It would leave the house half empty, she protested. She
would leave him sitting on orange boxes. No, no. He did not mind
in the least. So that was a great bonus. They started out with the
cushion of material possessions which would guard them from
want, which enabled them to direct their energy to something
other than nest-building; it made for happiness. So she was happy,
furnishing the prospective rooms. She drew up plans according to
scale and fitted things here and there, just so. It was profoundly
satisfying that the proportion of rooms to fittings agreed. Her taste
was her mother's after all.

The strangest bequest was to Esme, in the last sentence or two.
'I would like to leave something to my sister's daughter, Esme
Rosowicz. I think the contents of my bedroom at Inchcombe
would be appropriate.' She interrupted Rejean yet again.

'Don't you think that was exceptionally thoughtful, to leave
something to Esme, when you consider that they didn't really hit it
off?' He looked up but added nothing. 'I suppose it was to pay back
what she took from the big house when Rhona died.' She tried to
recall the room in question and could remember little of value, a
narrow oak bed, a chest of indiscriminate origin, some clothes.
Strange choice. A token gesture. 'Not much there but kind all the
same.'

Alexis had caught sight of his face one morning in May when he
was shaving and decided he was mighty tired of it. Now women
had the edge in this. Make-up gave them a new face for a new
season. They could change their sexual ambience with a different
palette of colours, a different cut of gown. He wandered along this
topic, scraping away, and wondered if he could persuade one of his
apprentices to write a piece on the connotations of changing
fashion. The highlighting of one erotic zone after another to arouse
flagging interest was a perplexing device, far more complex than
the displays of peacock and bower bird where obtaining a mate was
the priority. In humans, did clothing simulate posture as well as
the basic anatomy it indicated? He went on listing questions in his
head, lines of argument, possible references. Would any woman
interviewed admit that her plunging back tempted touching, that
she invited in her dress its undoing?

But his own face remained, immutable, looking back at him the way Rembrandt's did, a mixture of cynical detachment from the outer and compassion for the inner man.

So he grew a beard – not, he discovered, an easy process. It grew in patches and for a while he had the appearance of a bird in half moult or a piebald fledgling. Weak areas of growth showed up along the cheek and sometimes the apparition in the morning made him burst out laughing at himself. His intimates averted their eye as from an affliction too great for words of comfort, best passed over in silence. Graeme told him outright he was a sight to behold. He had always been clean-shaven (this being parallel to clean living) and he had no patience with the bohemian.

But he persevered, intrigued by how it would turn out – neat van Dyck or bushy W.G. Grace. He began to consult textbooks on the art of the hirsute and was enchanted by the Assyrian knotted beard, the Germanic military moustache, the forked variety (was that pomaded?) or the long dundrearies beloved by Scots Victorian fathers. Some cultures forbad the wearing of facial hair by men and others compelled it. Alexander the Great prevented his soldiery from sporting beards because it made them too vulnerable to attack; didn't the Tudors regard the pulling of a beard as a major insult, while the Egyptians made stylised versions for kings and queens to wear on ceremonial occasions. So he read on, discovering in himself a fund of ignorance.

Mr Scott opened the safe to lock away overnight some documents more valuable than the usual trivia that lay stashed in piles round the shelves of the room. He paused before turning the handle and revolving the combination lock, and opened it up again. He put his hand on the original of Mairi's will, thumbed so often in the past six months he knew precisely where it sat amongst a bundle of others.

It was not, properly speaking, a last will and testament, but a holograph, undoubtedly in her own hand and sent to him with a covering letter. Her family had authenticated the writing so there was no reason to doubt its validity. He thought it on the whole a fair execution of her wishes, and her temperament, apart from the one word he returned to again and again.

He wondered if his clients realised how much lawyers know. He was cognisant of the most intimate details of one side of their lives, what they bought and sold and who they left it to. How one set of effects went through a transmutation and became another set, often through his agency. He could tell the parsimonious from the spendthrift, the wise from the impulsive by their account with him. He had learned to read character by how a man phrased his will. It was more lucid than a novel to him. He was a palmist in his way, shrewd, accurate along a very limited line of information. He did not think the Inverleith house a good buy for that stretch was damp but he forebore to say so. He knew likewise that there was more to Alexis' visit in August than had been divulged but he was content to wait until the pieces fell into place. He had never had the least satisfaction from asking his clients their motives; those told him nothing, because on the rare occasions when they knew the answer they falsified. He waited for the actions themselves to make motive clear, because they were irrefutable.

The last paragraph in the original ran, 'I would like to leave something to my sister's daughter, Esme Rosowicz. I think the contents of my bedroom at Inchcombe would be suitable. I leave it to my husband to provide in other material ways for his child.'

Now that, in any man's language, had one interpretation and one alone. For many, many hours he had fingered the idea. His mind was not as cluttered as might be supposed about its feasibility. He had a long memory for human detail, never confused issues or incidents, and some individuals who came his way were etched with graphic clarity into the retrieval cells of his brain. He remembered the girl Esme's reaction to news of her resurrected father, sitting in this office on a late autumn afternoon eighteen months ago. November the eleventh without consulting his diary. He remembered Alexis' reaction too. His guardedness had not been the guardedness of self-defence. As the executor, he alone was in a position to know of Esme's gift to her assumed brother. Really, how many relatives these people kept coming across in his office. Quite a litter of them. So untidy.

The word 'child' troubled him all the same. He did not care to be a go-between and on many evenings evocative of the one when they had come together to his door he reviewed their case. Were they father and daughter? If so, what was behind the curious pent-up rage the man had emitted during the August visit? What family quarrel did he refer to in the course of his explanation? How much did subservience to the letter of the will matter compared with a decent code of ethics which enabled him and them to face the future?

He put the original back. He had made and distributed photocopies for their use – Alexis, his daughter, her husband – because a photocopy does not reveal an alteration. He did not like the slander. It did not fit with things as he felt them to be and so in the single instance during the whole of his professional career he committed a felony, he tampered with the facts. It was a grave offence, to substitute the five letter word 'niece' for the five letter word 'child'. He salved his conscience by telling himself it made no material difference to the contents of the document, and he did not feel it was part of his function to perpetuate a malicious rumour which the tendency of his experience contradicted.

Mrs Galashan did as she was bidden to do on the Monday morning and washed down the walls of the empty bedroom. He had worked all the previous day to gut it, coming back late from Edinburgh on Saturday evening. She had not expected him for a day or two, thought he would sojourn with the young folk. But he would take these mad rushes at things and there was no staying him.

He said to her, Do you care for the curtains or the carpet? I haven't the heart to throw them away. These curtains came from Lord Gilmour's estate at Dunblane when it was broken up. My mother bought them and they've been with me all this time. Just think. Queen Victoria may have handled them when she stopped on her way to Balmoral. They must be a hundred years old and not a threadbare patch.

And when she agreed, standing in the courtyard where he had lugged them down, saying that she could do with them fine, he answered, I must have them cleaned for you and then I'll send them over.

How could such a man be bothered?

The floor was stoury. She set to work with her mop and metal pail, soaking the mop head in the water, squeezing it through the sieve of the bucket till it was moist but not dripping, and swilling it over the floorboards. She lifted off the worst of the glaur. Then she got down on her kneeling pad and started to scrub with bleach and wire wool as he had asked. I'm sorry, says he, this is heavy work I would normally do myself. But I overdid it yesterday and I'd better give my hand a rest. If you're not able, I'll ask Ian.

Goodness, and her own son know she was afraid to get down on her hunkers.

Besides, it was none of Ian's business how things lay upstairs. She did not agree that master and mistress should keep separate rooms but she said not a word. She'd been an orra woman, her mistress, not easy to take to. Now he had a way of asking you to do something that melted your heart. They said she was a good woman, but it was a goodness that set your teeth on edge. The way she corrected you. No, Mrs Galashan, that's wrong, making a triangle of your name, the middle bit three foot higher than the rest. Edinburgh style, that was. Running her finger along a mantelpiece to see if you'd dusted. What was the matter with the woman that she didn't want to cuddle up to a comely man like that. Still, she'd heard only the poor slept together. And she thought of sleeping with her own man, the shiftless John, not the other thing, just sleeping and how it was the best bit of the whole business, putting your arm round someone in the dead of night, in winter storms, when you were sick and tired.

Well, what was he to do now? Nobody at all in the place and young and lusty still she had no doubt. He had that twinkle in his eye as though he hadn't forgotten and never would forget. And yet a perfect gentleman not like that auld goat, and her mind went soaring up the hill to Curriedon where a good few years ago she had worked a brief fortnight, giving the hill too steep for her bicycle as an excuse for leaving. She'd not have her backside pinched even by gentry.

Bit by bit he put it back together. It was a good room; he had forgotten how good, with a double aspect like the dining room below it, her other province. The oak tree which grew so near was fully leafed and the southern set of windows looked into it, like a child's playhouse 'bosom'd high in tufted trees'. He flung the windows wide the evening he came back from the solicitor to let out the stale and fusty air of the chamber which had been effectively sealed since the day of the crash.

He had felt like a tomb robber in the Valley of the Kings at

431

Luxor when he had penetrated there. He had no knowledge of what she bought for herself or her boudoir, had refused to set foot inside the door, but here it all was, everything intact that would be required for a journey into the hereafter. Things beautiful in themselves, cashmere, silk he had not as much as noticed on her. Her wearing had despoiled them. A fifteen foot run of wardrobe packed with all she had worn in her adult life. Perfectly preserved, it was a museum of apparel, and the labels! Had some man, somewhere, thought she was elegant in Dior and Chanel? He hoped so, heaving them out of the open window in armfuls, watching them catch and float on the eddy of wind and fall like multi-coloured floral wreaths on the garden stones.

He was determined nothing should remain.

As Scott read down the paraphrase of her wishes, Alexis had begun to hold his breath in fear. She had been fair to him, left him the very small proportion of her interest in Inchcombe, provided he did not sell it in his working lifetime. So much of it had been mortgaged commercially in the beginning that it was in his name for the most part. But somehow even the exacting fairness of her partition grated on him. That he should stay at her injunction took away the pleasure he had in staying at his own.

Fair to Aileen.

But then the last footnote, the slur of the second best bed to my successor. He had wanted to leap out of his chair in astonishment. But the others took it naturally enough. The last sentence he hung on. Yes, she could do it. She could write it and in the deepest conviction of her rectitude perjure her way to heaven. The lie would live. So when it came out as it did, he almost shook with relief, and had to get away from them as soon as he could to think. The last sentence he revolved as many times as the professional man, weighing its balance, its truth. Esme was not his niece. Mairi would never have included that false note. The curve of the sentence was to something else. The whole bias of the piece, its generosity, its considered tone was to give ballast in support of the final word 'child' which no one alive could contradict and which must sever them for ever, even though she was in the grave.

At what point had it changed between the first and final draft? Had she thought better of malice, or had the grey and scholarly man done his own revision? Which of the two was less impossible, for neither was likely? He could hardly decide. Why should the independent arbiter act as his witness before God and the Day of Judgment?

With immense relief he saw the last shoe burn, the last bed-rail consumed in the heat of the blast. He had felt she could leave a message in a pocket, an old coat hanging on the back of a door that could hide a letter, a sentence on a piece of paper which would perpetuate the falsehood. He believed her power to be like that of the Borgias, ingenious in the administering of poison. A ring, a shoe, a letter, an apple, a piece of glass in the eye, all these could cause fatal wounds. Only once the room was bare, scrubbed with lye, whitewashed could he himself feel clean and cauterised.

Then he said to himself, Forget. Begin at the beginning and choose what you know to be useful or believe to be beautiful. That was truly an inspirational man, the Renaissance prototype, whom he worshipped this side idolatry and on whom he modelled himself, know it or not.

A few weeks later, in the idleness of summer, he went to a house sale on the far side of Perth. It was one of the nineteenth-century houses built by a territorial baron whose empire had foundered on the regulations of surtax, death duties and capital gains tax, an indefinite series of deductions until there was nothing left. It was a good sale of fine pieces, some of them Georgian, a couple of Restoration coffers though it was a style he couldn't live with. What he enjoyed was the buzz of the rooms, the crucial excitement of the auction when the bidding went fast and high and his wits ran to keep pace with the leaps in price.

It turned out he knew the auctioneer, who pointed out some of the better pieces in the catalogue. What took his eye was an eighteenth century lady's escritoire. It was English and delicate, three large drawers and one small one, a sloped bureau with several compartments in good condition underneath a glazed bookcase that ended in a dome. He had always had a penchant for furniture that moved, a table that became library steps, a chair where you lifted the arm rests and released a sliding mechanism that reclined. The immoveable into the flexible was the best expression of the skill of the cabinet-maker, as he thought. Cogs, ratchets, runners, the wheel fascinated him. The thing also pleased the aesthetic sense. Six foot tall in mahogany inlaid with satin or box wood at a guess. He fell for it.

But not quite. The reserve price was prohibitive and that by itself made him wary of committing himself too far. Thinking he could not afford it in the face of city dealers, he began to criticise it objectively. The inlay and marquetry were a feat of patience, scrolls of ribbon and never-fading amaranthus on the flap. On closer inspection he noticed discrepancies between the banding on the bookcase and the bureau. It was the same pattern on the two halves, but a narrower line above. This alerted him. He asked the porter to move it a foot or two from the wall so that he could inspect it fully. He tapped the sides, examined the fittings at the back and the jointing of the two halves. Turning his attention to the inside, he found the mechanism of the secret drawer behind one of the compartments was jammed. The thing had been subjected to rough joinery and he told the auctioneeer before the bidding opened that he believed it was not what it purported to be at all, but a marriage of similar though mis-matched pieces. Commercially its value was substantially reduced.

The auctioneer took his word for it but was bound to consult the expert in attendance. There was a lull in the proceedings. A later lot was brought up the list. The expert confirmed Alexis' view and in hurried consultation the reserve price was reduced.

When this was announced prior to auction, it produced a rapid deflation of interest amongst the ring. The item was suspect, a botch job. There is nothing more unsaleable than a pedigree piece that somehow mislaid its pedigree. It looked like a fraudulent deal and nobody would touch it. Alexis was almost unopposed in the bidding apart from a dotty schoolmistress who thought it was a nice colour.

So that was the first piece. He spent hours sitting on the bare floor with the window open so that his head was practically in the tree tops, admiring it. He waxed the runners, cleaned the wood, polished it to a lustrous patina. Did it matter to him that it was a misalliance? Not a bit of it. He liked it the way it was.

Mr Scott wrote to Esme to explain the terms of her late aunt's will and that the lady's husband had guaranteed to see all the contents of the room were safeguarded awaiting her instructions, or her return to claim them.

Secondly, the fund set aside for the education of Alexis Roberval had been taken up. He was in receipt of a notice from a seminary in Chicoutimi and the Registrar of the University of Quebec, in Montreal, confirming that the boy had been guaranteed his place to commence study in October of the current year. There was also a letter of thanks from the recipient which he had duplicated for her benefit. He considered the writer of such a letter – phrased punctiliously – was worthy of her assistance, and hoped he did not overstep the mark in saying so.

41

He carried out the before flight inspection meticulously. The engineers had already completed their routine check before they signed over the aircraft to him, and he noted the minor unservice-abilities they listed. He took nothing for granted. Tyres, oil spots on the ground, a dead fly on the wind shield that in flight could be mistaken for another plane. He saw to everything.

This done, he climbed into the cockpit and fastened on the helmet and ejection harness, removing the pins top and bottom. At once he felt at home. The outside looked best to him through the radial spars of the cockpit window which made their own grid pattern on the contours of the landscape. Dissected, the sky was comprehensible.

He waited patiently while the mobile generator was moved into position and its power applied to the Voodoo. He looked out at the monochrome of the runway and the flat glaciated landscape behind it, which was far from dreary to his eye. The lack of feature or variety from the ground was immaterial from the air, when all these things were foreshortened and underwent the change of perspective which made them interesting. The ground view was not the only one.

'Time?'

'Eight fifty-three and ten seconds.'

He double-checked his own watch and, with a speed of reflex and registering of details which the untrained mind could not follow or appreciate, he read the relevant dials of the aircraft's instrument panel. Temperature, fuel gauge, revs, wing flaps, tailboard; his eye alighted on each in turn and moved on. All was fit.

He asked the navigator to run through the schedule again and mentally affirmed each detail. The written word he had to memorise. The spoken word he could absorb at once.

He received clearance to taxi out and the chocks were removed by the ground crew. The plane taxied out onto the duty runway while he waited for permission for take-off, then he swung it into the flight path of the main runway. The machine vibrated in every plate and rivet with the burst of energy as he allowed the forward thrust of the engine to be converted into motion, slowly at first, though this slowness was comparative, and then with gathering speed until he reached the end of the runway and was minimally aloft.

The jets screamed their high-pitched wail as they broke free of the ground. They were airborne. The plane climbed steeply for several minutes while he worked intensively during this most vulnerable period of take-off, checking speed, direction, fuel injection, cross-winds, to keep in balance the variables of flight.

When they reached thirty thousand feet he could relax and look below him. The land north of the Saguenay was bleak: virgin forests broken by fragmentary lakes, a pattern of light and dark pieces which would be confusing to the layman but was graphic to him. He knew exactly where he was on the grid. He could place an aerial photograph of two square miles accurately in the entire map of Quebec Province and Newfoundland, no problem.

He veered north-east, changing course by three degrees. He flew over an air corridor between mountain ranges that made for easy flying in light planes because there was no buffeting from prevailing winds. The snag with this channel was that migrating flocks used its thermal currents in spring and autumn, so he avoided it then. The risk of bird strike was greatly increased during seasonal migrations when a bird could collide with the jet, even denting the fuselage. A very large bird could foul the engine up, though most were pulped. Once he had to bring a plane down with a faulty engine. It was annoying to think that a bird, composed of nothing more substantial than splinter bone and feather, could impede the mighty jet.

Today he was safe and climbing higher; he passed through the cloud barrier and entered the fourth real dimension, of the stratosphere or upper air. It was a naked, newly created world up here, the world at its primaeval birth. The air at high altitude was pure, clear and heady, an intoxicating mixture which had to be supplemented by oxygen to the lungs, heart and brain.

Light was of a different spectrum from that which fell to earth, grimed as that was through layers of dirt, pollutant, the dust cloud of human habitation. Maybe at the polar ice-caps or in the equatorial rain forests it reached the ground with this blinding clarity, without having first gone through the prism of soiling smoke. A pure blue aether shone endlessly. The cloud bank which formed the roof of the heavens from below was inverted to make the earthscape underneath him. But it was a shifting, undulating land in process of evolution. Earth and sea were fused, rolling by in a kind of soup of creation, the liquid and solid still not separated. There were hills, dips suggestive of valleys and craters but the mass was on the move, its seething topography too indistinct for his eye to catch and hold.

This was the miraculous state, to defy gravity and to rise above the drag of the earth to a pure eminence. It was release from the mundane, from the human. Up here he needed no one else; he could pilot this airship without navigator or ground crew, and at times wished he had been born in the pioneer days of aviation when there were greater risks, greater solitude, stronger contact with the air and the cloud formation in the open cockpit of a small buzzing single-seater, all alone. Still, it was a feat that this plane, fifty thousand pounds of pressed steel and fittings, got off the ground, that the insubstantial air could support the clattering mechanical bird in flight.

It was a phenomenon too that his body which was limited and earthbound in its capacities could be sustained out of its element. He had once come very close to the brain-crushing eight gs in a loop he had turned too tightly through another's mistake and knew the feel of death as blood pooled in the legs, and brain and body became dislocated from each other. The thinness of the air was kept at bay in a depressurised cabin; the air he breathed could be supplemented by artifice; his land-locked form was in truth deified by the machine he flew in. He was Icarus, or better. He did not fly too near the sun and fall from the sky. He was Mercury in a capsule. He soared.

It was in this rarefied atmosphere that he came as close as he knew to happiness, a suspension of conscious thought as he found the balance of his physical strength and his practical skill. For him, flying was like the elation of the skier who has laboriously traversed a hillside in mist. Then when he reaches the crest of the mountain, he finds sun and a clear surface. He sweeps down with perfect aerial ease; all his training, his native skill, his being coalesce into an instant of pure joy.

On that journey he was overtaken by an insight that illuminated life for years ahead. He was the succeeder. He was the survivor. Neither man nor beast nor god nor machine would stand as an impediment to his inevitable rise. Around him there rolled a great panorama of his own potential where he shouted, I will because I can, to the resounding spaces of the sky.

42

She wrote:

How can I begin to tell you how fractious we are with each other?

Last week we went to dinner with the CO and his wife. I looked on it as a polite return for their invitation to the wedding party, but apparently for someone as junior as Mabon to be asked to a domestic event (how they categorise these things I don't know) is bordering on the revolutionary. He was in a state of high tension all day and I knew without telling that he was mostly nervous about me, though he would not have been considered without me. I was ordered to buy a new dress and refused. Yvonne Cartier would just have to go on thinking how useful this one was for a bit longer.

But getting into it, I was not so sure. Five and a half months is pushing it.

There were a dozen of us altogether and the CO's wife, who is a very pleasant and absolutely anonymous person, had engaged a young girl, French, delightfully pretty, to help at table. She reminded me so much of Fiona it was uncanny, gawky, anxious to please but not quite so inept. I wondered who she was, a student at a conservatoire. She had the fingers of a pianist. We had a rapport, she and I. She did an extra deep curtsey every time she served me. The others alarmed her too much, and on that we were in agreement too. She was frankly the only person I was interested in and I wanted them all to disappear with their ponderous talk and leave us to communicate with more than eyes.

The men are overwhelmingly courteous. It makes me want to rebel. They have a strange way of serving food in dishes that are held for you. Now this is most awkward, turning ninety degrees to the man on your left, digging out vegetables with two spoons while your left elbow is wound into him or yourself. Then you have to go through the whole process for the person next down the line. Why they can't leave things on the table, I don't know. Mad. It is so finical. But I dare say nothing in the way of adverse comment. I am enjoined to silence by every look he gives me. I wonder sometimes if I am such a social liability.

Dessert was my undoing. I had been very peaceable till then. The girl was cumbered with much serving and as she leant over me with, dear oh dear, chocolate mousse and Baked Alaska, I said, 'Tu portes un véritable Mont Blanc. Ne glisses pas dedans.' The whole table stopped talking just in time to hear us both laugh. I knew they looked askance. Nothing must interrupt the flow of the inane. What a lovely accent, commented Yvonne, getting maximum mileage out of the incident. Hasn't she, Charles? I didn't know you spoke French. If only she did, she would know how bad I am at it but in the country of the blind . . .

Now it is a sad fact that the enceinte cannot eat much. Three mouthfuls and I am full. Besides, those two desserts would not tempt me if I were starving. The knife went through the layers of white meringue into the ice cold confection and brought out gasps of admiration.

A dozen eggs, no really! Fabulous.

I demurred, knowing I could not. No thank you, I said.

Just a little, she urged.

No really, and I got up watched by all eyes and went to the fruit bowl and found myself a superb green apple, hard and crunchy.

My dear, says she, you've no need to worry about your figure yet.

The yet spoke volumes, common acknowledgment that my pregnancy is more advanced than my marriage. I was mortified. I actually thought that was much more rude than my apparent misdemeanours (anon) but in this opinion I am obviously singular. I waited for someone to say something on my behalf, intervene or gloss over the moment, but it would not go away.

Let Berthe get you a knife. I don't think you've got one there. And a side plate.

On and on while the whole proceedings are held up and everyone is waiting for me to be seated and served. And the Alaska thaws.

As I suspected, he was not pleased with me. Why can't I be inconspicuous? he asks on the way home in the car. Why must I draw attention to myself? Why can't I be discreet and give no cause for comment? I don't need to talk to servants do I, and in French which is my way of showing everyone else up.

This is so farcical I can find nothing to say. And how can I explain why I liked Berthe? That she reminded me of someone else, that I feel guilty when we, the English Canadians, are living in luxury which the workers of Quebec cannot afford, artichokes and venison and such waste on every plate. How I said something maybe as a way of telling Fiona there were no hard feelings for clyping on me, as though one could apologise retrospectively. If I tried to say that to him, he would think me insane, and maybe I am too. There is nothing of the me in me he understands. With him I cannot begin to be myself, and feel constantly repressed into another form of existence. I become unnatural and tense, always waiting for criticism and the shortfall to be specified when it comes to debriefing time. This is what you should have done, after the event.

So we lay awake in mutual antipathy, wanting to hide from the people we make each other into.

The phone went at about five in the morning, a ghostly hour, when neither of us was rested but raw and out of sorts. I blundered about in the half light, feeling stunned from lack of sleep. He got to the phone first. I heard him speaking intently. Right. Message

440

received. Five-o-seven. He put the receiver down and then made three outgoing calls in rapid succession to numbers he had evidently memorised. Each time he gave his name and rank and serial number, and a time check. This whole process, which was alarmingly efficient and rehearsed, took maybe five minutes from start to finish, the longest pause in his activity being the wait for someone at the other end to reply.

I managed to raise myself and staggered into the kitchen to fill the kettle. He went back to the bedroom and got dressed in seconds, wearing the flying suit he usually carries with him. I sensed the urgency of whatever he was doing. No, he had no time to drink anything, no he didn't know when he would be back, no he couldn't explain then. And as he went out the dreadful fear overcame me that it was, as they say, for real.

'We're not at war?'

He turned round at the door and gave me a withering look. 'Don't be so bloody facetious.'

How do I win? On every front I am the loser.

The debate is continued when he comes back, earlier than usual when I am not quite recovered, not quite altogether. Of course I am obliged to have a meal ready within ten minutes of his return, which is unannounced and can take place – the high spot of my life – at any hour between four and midnight. I had got as far as the cookery book, which has the most fascinating photographs and anecdotes . . . however that is the sort of thing I must not say. He has not eaten since the previous evening. Is there anything in the house, or does he have to go to the supermarket first? Hostile activities have not been suspended. I go to pieces under this sort of barrage. My past was the worst possible preparation for my present life. I have never had to fight my corner and look a simpleton in the face of opposition.

I fire things into pots. I have the heat so high, the sides of the pan sizzle. How he survives all day without eating, I don't know. Has the stomach of a camel. A yell comes from the bathroom and when I go to see if he has drowned, fallen and broken his head in two, stood on a razor blade, I discover he has knocked my book which was resting at the tap end into the water. It is floating sadly wet, seeping red colour from the binding. I pick it out. It doesn't matter. I'll tell the librarian. I'll make it good.

Why can't I put things away when I have finished with them? Why can't I be neat? The apartment is littered with books left open all over the place. This is true. I pick something up when I am bored with housework, which is rather often, and keep about ten going concurrently. To Mabon, a closed book is so much neater than an open one. I will try, I am untidy, don't beat me massa.

I go back when I have got things cooking to try and mollify him. I can see he is exhausted. I do care that I am a source of disappointment to him, but I cannot comfort him physically. We do not touch other than sexually and that has ceased since I lost the absolute slimness of silhouette he demands. We do not kiss except as a prelude. Not for fun. Not for the gratuitous enjoyment of contact. Not for recollected passion. We simply copulate.

He explains at last what he was doing. He thinks I am glaringly stupid on things practical and can't really be bothered to tell me. So he drones it out, a dull lesson to a dull pupil. It was a war exercise he was called out on in the morning, rather like a fire drill when they are all timed to the Base. There is a pyramid of command and each man calls several more down the chain. He was later than usual to arrive at the Base because of the drive from Arvida and then he couldn't park the car because all the spaces were taken near the hangar, and so he had to put it in a restricted area with an Immune badge on it which promptly fell down when he closed the door. He got back from flying to discover it had been technically impounded, and his name would appear on a quite nominal charge sheet even though there were extenuating circumstances. I know he becomes coldly furious when what he does is less than perfect. Somehow it is my fault he is late, that we live in Arvida, that the sticker fell off.

I persevere with the war game. What is it about? They simulate interception of the enemy aircraft and missiles. That was what he was doing. What do the others do who are not air crew? Some have Immune badges and go on with essential work, others wait in the bunkers till the alert is over. And would this happen in a real emergency? Yes. What about the families? There's no room for dependants. 'Dependants', oh that word they all use. They can't say 'my wife and children', 'my family'. It's always dependants.

Aren't you?

No, I don't think I am.

I keep you.

Yes, you keep me.

I point out I think it's a bit hard on families to be within range of nuclear or even conventional attack and be offered no protection. But he says the entire defence network of North America would have to collapse for it to come to that.

Then he suddenly said, and its perception took me by surprise, You despise what I do, don't you? You think what I do is unimportant. This way of life, the armed forces, is the enemy of your way of life. And you think I'm illiterate because I don't read your books.

I protest this is an exaggeration.

But basically, that's what you feel. The service is the antithesis of culture as you know it.

And I had to agree they didn't have much in common, his life and mine, his people and mine.

He reminds me that there have been other civilisations before the European one, the cultures of Egypt, Greece and Rome. I almost thrill to hear the names conspicuously on his tongue. Yes, I learned some history along the way. And those empires, each and every one of them, crumbled because the military defence broke down. Didn't they? The civilisation of Rome came to an end when Alaric stormed the city. Now your culture is practically at its end. It should really have died out with the British Empire in 1918 but the thing that has kept it going is the support of its Commonwealth, NATO and the other English speaking countries who feel some loyalty. Alone, your little island would have sunk. Its strategic importance is minimal. Its contribution to the arms race is derisory. Britain is being supported by her powerful allies. It is incapable of defending itself, as Egypt and Athens and Rome were in the end.

I say I do not know enough about armaments to dispute that.

Take my word for it. But what I am trying to tell you is that without people like me, people like you can't survive. You British are all talk and no action, which is why you achieve so little.

In one sense this is so patently true that I have no reply. He says it with the limitless patience of someone speaking to an idiot or a child and so it does make an impression on me. I can understand how infuriating I am to him, smugly clever and not turning over a penny while he slogs all the working hours a man can. What it shows me is that when he gets into that aircraft he becomes superhuman. It transforms him. He doesn't work as hard as he does solely for personal ambition. He believes in the camaraderie with his men. He believes in the meaning of his labour. He has a certain dedication to his role as guardian of Western civilisation and whatever that implies for personal freedom, his, mine, our children's. I admire the theory wholeheartedly.

In another way, I am indignant at his limited scale. How dare he decry my nation and my island. Civis Romanus sum! I am a citizen of the world. My passport is international tender. Cartier is correct; you don't appreciate the meaning of patriotism till it is threatened, freedom till it is taken away. Love of my country is my last remaining bastion. I have abandoned my virtue; I have abandoned my name; I have resigned my independence. My birthright I would die to preserve. Unfashionable sentiment, but how can I apologise for being what I am? Not to him, anyway.

The form of military authority he describes probably is an integral part of freedom and he opens my eyes to the fact that the major cultures were reinforced by arms for defence and expansion. There is no great world power without power. But there are other forms of freedom and other sanctions. Can he forget that his law and his parliament, and half the world's to boot, are derived from my country's? Agreed, through militarism and colonisation, but they would not have survived if they had not been sound. If our shrinking waters leave behind on foreign shores the residue of democracy or of language, need one be ashamed of being British? Under-achievement? I am proud of it. There is also the thing one fights to protect as well as the fight itself, the raison d'être he overlooks.

However, such discussion is futile with him. I am at the third remove from his ideology: the wrong sex, the wrong nationality, the wrong type. If any one of these factors were different, we could have a dialogue. I feel I understand him better after this, but I don't sympathise with him any more. Defining the chasm doesn't help me bridge it. We look across the gulf of nationality, entrenched, unreasonable. There will be no truce on this or any other day.

And I don't really like to be reminded that I am on the point of extinction.

She wrote this not knowing to whom it was addressed, Rejean at some times, at others Alexis, but ultimately herself. By the time she finished she knew it was too grim to send, too personal. She folded it away among her papers, though it lay like an unspoken deceit against him in her mind.

43

Graeme arranged for Rejean and Alexis to join a shoot for eight guns that went out from Curriedon at the end of the month. The grouse had been moderately plentiful and Graeme was well satisfied with the number of brace he had dispatched to Perth butchers in the square osier baskets time-honoured for the purpose. The house consumed a good few birds each week, when there were up to ten guests being entertained at a time. Fiona and Mrs Dunlop and old Max and his wife were quite flummoxed with running after them, but Mrs Dunlop was a silly woman at the kindest, who fussed about putting jam scones in your midday lunch instead of a lump of meat and a flask. That was all anyone wanted on the hills.

They drove in three vehicles from Curriedon for almost half an hour over Powell-Jones' estate, covering rough tracks of moorland until they came to the north-easterly extremity. This was a plateau of ground that seemed barren, a rolling plain whose verges were indicated by deeper or paler shades of heather and other moorland plants rather than by differentiation of feature. It was like a calm sea which nevertheless has slight gradations of level and tone. One area had been given over to the cutting of peat blocks. Sods were stacked ready for transportation back to the house when the Land Rover was not full of people.

Here the grouse nested in the spring, in shallow and absurdly vulnerable dips, which necessitated the protection of the species by law until the glorious twelfth when the birds were grown and capable of flight. The beaters, students happy to earn a pittance out of doors, walked over the moor in the direction of the hides, shouting or ruffling the heather with sticks, and the alarmed grouse rose ahead of them, flapping noisily with their over-heavy body and cumbersome wings.

Rejean was a fine shot, easily as good as the more practised English guests at the Lodge. He was able to lift his shotgun and train his eye along the sight in movement, projecting with almost infallible accuracy the flight path of the bird and the counterflow of wind. Alexis had to bring his gun to rest before he focused, by which time the bird had long gone. Rejean, standing in the same turf-sided butt as his father-in-law, laughed over and over again at the unwieldy motion and the expletives which followed it. He lost more quarry through that than a wayward pot at target. Rab had been a crack shot, competing many times at Bisley, and Alexis knew he was hopelessly outclassed on both sides. The young man's bag grew steadily all day as the sun radiated from south-east to south to south-west, scorching them with a dry sirocco wind.

They broke at lunch time. The Englishmen, clad in their plus-four suits of camouflage tweed, took to Rejean and involved him in eager questions about game and conditions in the newcomer's homeland. They drew him off to one side and shared their lunch with him. What calibre gun did he use at home? Was there more rough or organised shooting? Were deer beaten out or stalked?

Alexis was relieved to abandon his post and deck down in the warm heather tufts beside Graeme who, knowing his place, did not fraternise with the gentry.

'I'm particularly useless at this.'

'Your left hand being injured has made you slower than you were,' agreed the gamekeeper. 'You're not shooting clean but lifting the gun. You've missed a hundred.'

'Thanks. Perhaps I'll go and help the beaters this afternoon.' He looked over to where the young men were in conclave about their sporting exploits. 'Don't you mind that all this is colonised by England?'

'Colonised. That's putting it a bit strong, is it not?'

'Maybe. But it grieves me that much.'

'You must accept the order of things more.'

'How can I when the order is so much in favour of one sector at the cost of another?'

'What am I to do? Set fire to the heather because it is not mine? You forget I am not a socialist.' He pronounced this in four syllables. 'I cannot afford such principles.'

A rasp of the saw-edged English tongue came towards them over the native heath and they both, being soft-spoken, felt some repugnance. The arrogance of that particular strain emptied many a bar when the season was high. Geordie, Brummie, Dalesman welcome but not the southern haw.

Alexis lay back on his elbow on the aromatic bed of heather, clover, erica of various shade. 'I think it's a disgrace all this belongs to one man, just a playground for fifty people one month a year. Then they trot back to the Home Counties and the land is abandoned for another twelvemonth.'

'Ach, what else would it be used for? It's only moorland.'

'It wasn't always moor. There were crofters on this land before P-J's great-grandfather bought it for a groat an acre. I was reading recently that you can do a lot to reclaim bog land nowadays, clear the grass and flatten it to allow water to drain. Then you feed the soil and grow good hill grass. Rejean can tell you. There are new strains being developed that are suitable for grazing at this high altitude. Then you can bring in flocks of sheep, make pellets for the winter and the land is back in gainful use.'

'Who can afford to do all that?' asked the sceptic.

'It's work, not money, that does the job. And there's another way that's even easier. Feed the soil, encourage new growth and when the first shoots appear you send cattle up the hillside. The cow dung fertilises and sweetens the ground and slowly, yes I admit it's slowly, the moss and lichen die out and the pasture grass flourishes.'

'Why,' laughed Graeme, 'you'll turn farmer yet. No. You're a visionary, I'll grant you, but you cannot change the old ways in a generation. If the estate went under the hammer, maybe something could be done with the moorland, but I'm not so sure even then. Look at the old Melville estates at Dunira. When the house burned down, nobody could take it over in the same way. Those wonderful gardens all overgrown, the lilies gone to riot in the fountains. Once those big estates change hands, they're gone forever.'

Knowing the full force of his friend's conservatism which amounted almost to fear of change, Alexis grew silent; but what hope was there when man raped the landscape? A summer of over-use, a winter of neglect. It would have to lie fallow for another generation through lack of insight.

'Doesn't P-J come up here himself any more? He used to be a keen shot. The man isn't seventy yet. He hasn't taken to his chair, surely?'

'Ach no. He's not the mettle of his father. He spends his afternoon stomping up and down the garden, making sure nobody gets a free keek over the wall at his flowers without paying the shilling entry fee.'

'No! Does he really?' A solitary grouse flew overhead, startled at the shout of laughter Alexis sent up at this picture of the misanthropist.

After lunch, Alexis left the shoot to the experts and headed over the moor away from the firing so that he would not disturb the flight of the grouse, or end up wingshot himself.

There was a stony path from the parked vehicles striking north, which he followed for some way until it dipped into a coomb, invisible on the tableland from any distance further than a few yards. It was like the crater of a small volcano, moist at the bottom and sheltering a few blaeberry bushes which he squatted beside and cropped. He ate the berries raw, relishing their acid bite which cleansed the palate they excited. He wished he had a container to make it worthwhile culling more, but he had left the game pouch with his half dozen grouse behind.

It was warm on the bank of the crater and he was inclined to doze out of the bothersome wind. Here he felt directly under the sky, recumbent on a plane with the weight of air evenly distributed like a coverlet. He shut his eyes and let himself go. He was not sure whether he dropped off or not; he thought it rather better to go all the way to the edge of sleep and come back again, but he was startled, awake or not, by a squeal somewhere on the bank above his head. He sat upright, then scrambled to the top of the ledge and looked about. The guns were distant and downwind. He did not think that was the source. He found the path again, intensely

448

curious, and on a loop maybe fifteen yards from where he had been lying he came upon the inert form of a wild brown rabbit, warmly dead.

He put his hand on it instinctively, and felt its life grow chill. Behind the ears at the nape of the neck was a circle of blood and he realised this was a common occurrence he had heard about, but never personally witnessed in all his years at Lochearn. He looked round but could see no sign of the weasel responsible for the killing. He had been told the predator hypnotised the rabbit which stood stock still, too frightened to pass its assailant, or to retreat. Why ever didn't the stupid animal make a run for it? It lost either way, but at least running it died creditably, not a palpitating mass of nerves.

Now, he thought, this is illogical. Why do I sympathise with the rabbit and hate the weasel? They are both despoilers in their way. But because the rabbit is softly furred and has a sensitive muzzle and the weasel is elongated and ugly, with legs too low and head too small, I prejudge them. Are my attitudes so easily to fall victim to aesthetics? Or must sentiment rouse in favour of the weaker creature?

Still, the weasel would not come back to gorge on this corpse. He picked up the rabbit by the ears and found that digging the grave he intended was not so easy in the stubborn terrain. His choice was between a boulder-strewn pathway, compacted by the passage of Land Rovers and parched by the sun, or a tough, rooty peat bog. Nor did he have an implement, neither knife nor file. And he stood cursing this act he had to stumble on, and trembling from head to toe incomprehensibly.

Mrs Galashan was in the kitchen when he and Rejean returned. 'Do you care for game?' he asked her. 'There are only half a dozen but you're welcome to them if you can be bothered with the hanging and plucking.'

'I like them fine. But will you not want them for yourself?'

'No, you take them by all means.' He turned to go and bathe and change and lose all contact with the killing day. 'I never want you to cook game for me again.'

Well, she wondered, stirring their broth, what has scunnered him now against blood and blood sports?

They lit the lamps at nightfall and filled the house with shadows.

The rooms had vacant spaces, where things had been adjusted to cover the blank walls. Not one of them remained as it had been. Alexis enjoyed the lunar landscape: muted walls, reflections, stark furniture seen in clear space. He enjoyed arranging things without reference to anyone else. It was the greatest luxury, even if it implied the greatest loneliness.

'There is something I would like to talk to you about, Rejean. Though you are perhaps not the ideal person to ask and normally I would say nothing. But it's constantly on my mind and I can't rest till I know.'

At one time, Rejean would have prepared himself to discuss a painting, a design, a purchase, however extraneous to his powers of judgment. Alexis liked to test unwary opinion. He found that was a more useful exercise than consulting experts whose responses were blunted by familiarity. The freshest ideas were the untutored ones. This evening, however, he was alerted by a different tone and knew he would be called upon to discuss a person. He put down the gun that he was cleaning.

'When you fly back to Montreal next week, I want to ask you very particularly if you would go and see Esme. And then write and let me know.' He crossed one foot on the other knee in front of what was a superfluous fire, but gathering the driftwood was a ritual that needed a function and he already had a year's supply stored Swiss fashion against an outhouse wall.

'Does she not write to you herself?'

'She has sent me two letters in the last year, one explaining why she left, the second why she was getting married. I have to deduce what her mental state is. And I can't be so stoical with myself any longer.'

Rejean listened intently. He did not often hear that lower register. There was a special timbre to the silence in the room when he had finished speaking, broken by spurts of flame from drying wood, the sudden hiss and explosion as heat met a deep pocket of moisture, as blue and green entered the red heart of the fire. He watched the ash turn grey and falling from the apex of the heat whiten and grow cold at the edge. Thirty years' growth died in thirty seconds.

'You are in love with her.'

Alexis did not move. His hand grasped the crossed left foot

which seemed uncomfortably poised but was fully at rest. 'Those are your terms, not mine. I would put it differently if other words existed, but those will have to do.'

Rejean could put his head back and let the various phases tumble into place. How foolish of him not to perceive the obvious before. The nature of their individual answers to him was the same, tense, expectant, loath to hurt and, underneath the silence, utterly conjoined. 'You didn't tell me, either of you.'

'There was so little to tell. I didn't know how she felt at the beginning. I was backpedalling, trying not to get us into an unholy mess. In fact I backpedalled so hard I fell off. Your parents know. In fact I'm surprised they didn't confide in you. They whisked Esme away before I could intervene, on that wretched ticket you gave her. I was ready to leave this house and live with her at that point, work things out somehow, but when Mairi discovered, there was a fracas. All in all, I mismanaged things very badly. I think I suffer from delayed reactions. I see the lights turn red but I still go through them.'

Gradually Rejean saw more and more of his own implicit involvement in the separation of these two people. The ticket, yes, that had been palmed on him and he wondered if his father were more perceptive than himself. But Mabon was his acquaintance, introduced by him and in his house. He had urged Esme towards the marriage, and then failed to appreciate the significance of her anguish on that day as she heard of the crash, realising more than he had done how Alexis' injury was concomitant with his freedom. So much for friendship. In everything he had succeeded in guiding her away from the one man he did not mind consigning her to, although the vision he had of their completeness together in this house, in this room, side by side over a book, a sketch pad, a child, inspired in him a terrifying envy.

'How do I make amends.'

'I am afraid for her. Irrationally afraid. Do something to help her. I don't know what to suggest. I don't even know what she wants any more.'

'She doesn't want him.'

'For heaven's sake, don't tell me that. I can't take it. I try to tell myself she may want the marriage, or the child, or the father. You know she found Stefan had died? These things are not separable. I could fly over tomorrow, all the way to Bagotville aerodrome, and say, Come home with me, Esme. But I don't know if she wants my interference. I feel she must come to her own settlement in her own time. But I fear that, like me, she may delay too long.'

Each formulated questions which they dared not ask because the reply might be intolerable. Do you think he will be good to her? What would Aileen say if she were here with us now? Could Esme abandon her husband and her child and live with you so totally in the wrong? Did you turn the wheel against your wife? What is the breaking point of stress in these unquantifiable factors? Who suffers most? He suffers most who suffers in the mind.

44

Esme prepared as best she could for the arrival of her child. She went regularly to see her physician, a Dr Cleophas whose English was as idiosyncratic as her French, so they spent many interesting hours not understanding each other, two deaf people whose attempts at speech seemed to confuse the issue. Still, he told her she looked wonderful at the end of every session and she assumed this was a medical diagnosis.

She resorted to textbooks for specifics. The pregnancy was normal; all these changes were in evidence, but after a while she closed the books again, horrified that the insidious processes were going on beyond her control. Why, her very tissue, her cells, were caught up in the climacteric of change. Let it happen how it would.

But as she walked down Chicoutimi High Street her feet involuntarily slowed in front of the baby shops. So many gadgets, accoutrements, bits of cloth and clothing were needed! Wouldn't it be easier to build a nest, lay an egg or two, or cub one's young under a bush, prairie fashion, compared with the complexities of being a human mother. Instinct had so deserted her species that a whole industry had grown up to tell parents how to rear their offspring. It provided the paraphernalia which would make the interlude as brief and effortless as possible.

Dimly, she recalled that in Britain she had seen little women steering huge prams, and in the house opposite a young child had been permanently installed in such a vehicle to review the passing world at leisure, rain or shine. She entered the world of babydom to ask for such a pram, but the shop assistant smiled. Canadian babies did not use prams. It was too cold to leave a baby outdoors except in the height of summer, and of course a wheeled carriage was quite useless in the winter. He suggested a small folding pram which would adapt to a child lying or sitting in it, and could be put away in the car trunk. She would also need a sledge with a hoop of wood behind to cup the child in place. She acceded, for instinct and custom together failed her.

She reverted to the half forgotten art of knitting. The action soothed, filling long lonely hours in which she seemed adrift among the purposeful occupations of mankind, waiting out her time. They progressed; she was static. But by applying her mind to the next row and the one after that, or the anticipation of a change of stitch, she could avoid the crawling slowness of her life.

She turned out a shawl of cobweb transparency. Didn't they say the test of fineness was whether it could be pulled through a wedding ring? She removed hers and slotted the thread-like netting through. But either the ring was too small or the fibre she had used too coarse; she could not pull it more than half way and retracted it.

If she ran out of yarn she became almost demented with the insistent turmoil of her thoughts, caught between the powerful cross-currents of variable impulse. She had a sledge in readiness, but did she want another winter here? She was having a child by this marriage, but did one compensate for the other? To justify what she had already done, was she compelled to go on doing it? Soon, the season would begin its cycle of departure again, while she would be left behind, maimed, winged, grounded. She watched the flocks gather in the morning sun with a wistful eye. Where would they go? Were they flying across the Atlantic? In these emissary droves was there one bird that would land on his roof, eat his grain, gain one second of his attention? A single carrier pigeon with a single message was enough to save the castaway.

Rejean came back invigorated by his Scottish summer. It would be a short mid-season spell in Montreal, for he too must fly away at the onset of winter. His mother, assessing him with the undemonstrative care of adult parenthood, saw he was on the mend. His book had been accepted for publication in the spring. He was reconciled with his wife. Aileen completed her diploma, passing out with the highest marks in languages and shorthand, a tribute to endeavour. She threw herself with equal verve into her post with the firm, her renewed marriage, her hectic social programme. She wanted to know everyone and do everything. She filled up her diary of engagements a fortnight ahead of the day and sometimes found it difficult to have an evening free during the week. Clubs, societies, discussion groups – she joined them all. A fraction of these sorties would be jointly undertaken by husband and wife, but the mother sighed and said nothing though at times she thought poignantly of Esme as someone who conformed more to her own view of wifeliness, the home bird.

Claire found it hard to understand the split life her son intended to lead, going seasonally to and fro across the ocean. Eight months to four on her side seemed not a bad proportion, but she saw it as a strange rootless existence and inveighed against the day Maurice had seen fit to open his office in the UK. There were foreseeable compensations. She was impatient to see the house in Inverleith. She anticipated New Year visits to savour Hogmanay and more protracted stays when or if they ever got round to furnishing a nursery. She noticed there was a discrepancy in their enthusiasm for the house. He had said it was old and stone built, and nothing more. She wondered what flaw it hid. And because of these improvements his health was better too. He had not had a major attack since leaving Chicoutimi, and it looked as though whatever had riven him could heal over. His life began to mesh – as far as a mother could see.

It was October before he found a weekend free to visit Esme. At first he fought against the instinct to go alone, impatient and curious together, but waited for the lumbering caravanserai of family life to transport him there at its convenience. However, either one or other of them was engaged and in the end he went by himself, knowing how Alexis waited for his news.

They sat in the corner of the Chantals' garden, on a bench where the last sun of the year gathered its rays.

'Late November?'

'So he says. I hope it is. I am petrified of it going on into December when there's snow on the ground. I have a mental picture of trying to get to Chicoutimi through snow drifts and giving birth in a ditch at the side of the road. Appropriate, perhaps, but not very reassuring. Mabon points out I am hardly the first woman to have had a child in the Saguenay.'

'You look well. I suppose we both look better than we did the last time we were here together.'

'Oh don't talk about that. It seems so long ago. I've missed you these six months. Missed phoning you.'

'You could phone Lochearn.'

She glanced along the bench at him but he kept a studied gaze ahead. 'That's a poor substitute for reality.'

'Better than nothing.'

'No, you're wrong there. Having nothing is preferable to substitutes.'

A robin came and perched on an ornamental tree, not the dainty robin but the gross russet North American variety. Very soon it would make its preparation for the crossing, and leave the underworld to Persephone and Pluto in the cold, unleafed, unfruitful solstice. The bird found a worm and flew away with it.

'Are you happier now?'

'Happier than when?'

'Than at the wedding. Than when I was here and was taken ill. You were so adamant about not marrying. I never understood why you changed your mind.'

'I didn't change my mind. I changed my body. He doesn't need to do very much to reduce me to a hedgerow prostitute.'

He looked intently to see if she meant this as a flippancy but apparently she did not, and he was wordless in the face of such despair.

'I know. Why did I fall for him? I ask myself that every minute of every day. How I came to be such a fool. I think the balance of my mind was disturbed. I was impressed by him, by the way other people follow him with their eyes. Have you seen that? It's true. He never enters or leaves a room unnoticed. I think it's called glamour. He's the charismatic male. What makes me feel guilty is that he could have succeeded with someone who was not me. He's somebody's ideal. He's very well equipped to deal with happiness and normality. But not with me.'

'Why?'

'I'm too diffuse. He can't bear it that I'm homesick, at bottom because he can't do anything about it, and he rejects me when I'm unhappy. So I hide from him, and hide what I feel.'

'I know that place and that there's nothing anyone can do.'

'He could listen. All I want is some assurance that in spite of my deviousness, which I am not comfortable with any more than he is, straight aims exist and matter. But he's a fair weather husband, I'm afraid.' She shook her head. 'You shouldn't make me say these things. They harden.'

'Can it improve?'

'Maybe with the baby. I'm not certain. He's so bitterly disappointed at what I've turned out to be, not a career wife, not fast or slick the way he thought I was simply because I was – bright.' She shrugged.

'Why do you stay?'

'I'm in the trap now. How do I get out? I'm married, no grounds for separation, expecting a baby in a few weeks. Where do I go?'

He took a breath as divers do and plunged. 'Alexis would have you back.'

She shivered and looked about for the cause in the flickering day. 'This sun isn't as warm as it looks. I suppose we're being over-optimistic sitting out at this time of the year.'

'He would, you know.'

She considered it head on. 'Did he say that or is it your inference?'

'Yes, he said it. His actual words to me before I left were, "I could fly over tomorrow and say, Come home with me, Esme, but I don't know if she wants my interference." '

She revolved this and found its many facets. 'Did he tell you spontaneously?'

'Yes. He was anxious to know how you were.'

'I was sure he would be ashamed of me. He didn't answer my letter apart from accepting the invitation. I wonder if I would have gone ahead with it if I had seen him before the wedding. I think I was waiting for him to stand at the church door and say, "Forget it, Esme. You don't need to marry the man to give your child a father." But that didn't happen, and doesn't out of imagination.

You pick up your own bill every time. Pay it in effort and tears.'

'You don't cry, do you? He doesn't make you cry?'

'Mabon? No, I don't care that much about him. And I'm clever. I can make myself cry.'

He took her hand in his. 'What's stopping you from going now?'

'This perhaps.' She put her free hand on her abdomen and felt the infant move. 'It's not Alexis' child. If I abduct it now or later, what trouble could Mabon make for all of us? He has a territorial stake in me. I don't want to lose my child by putting myself in the wrong, and I can't run away from circumstances again. How many times can you show yourself a coward without despising what you are? On the other hand, I can't see him agreeing to let me go. He would lose too much face.' She smiled ruefully. 'And I am so ugly pregnant. I find it hard to cast myself in the role of any man's paramour. I fight the adipose, but it is there.'

In the plummet of her self-esteem, this point seemed to him the lowest. 'Esme, don't you know?' he asked, amazed that her husband could not reassure her that beauty moved in other phases besides the sexual one. And indeed, reflected in his pupils, she did not seem too plain. 'There is nothing more tender.'

She covered the hand that held hers. 'Hurry up and be a father, Rejean. You're wasted.'

He watched the greedy robin return to his plundering attacks on the grass. 'Just one more thing that eludes me. It is proving not possible.' Her eye inquired but she let him pause and re-assemble under his confusion the things he had not meant to say. 'Six months. We decided as soon as I went back that we had waited long enough. Strange after three years avoiding conception to think there may have been nothing to avoid after all.'

'But that's not conclusive. Six months is not so long.'

'It's a long time when you're waiting. We'll see what happens over the winter, and then go to a clinic when we're back in Edinburgh. It's less public there.'

'Why have there got to be these hideous inequalities? You probably want this child more than either of us.'

'Never mind. I'll be godfather.'

'Is Aileen disappointed?'

'Not as much as I am. She carries on dauntless.'

'You are together anyway.'

He opened his mouth to say something, to clarify but changed direction and, in any case, Mabon came round the corner himself at that moment, having returned early to take them out to dinner, and found them hand in hand under the thinning boughs.

On Hallowe'en Esme and Mabon went out to a lakeside cabin east of Grande-Baie, near St Felix d'Otis, where one of the officers was holding a party. The fine weather held, warm days, close nights and they were able to sit outside, about twenty guests, keeping the insects and the dark at bay with flares Mabon had bought from supply. They burned like gigantic Roman Candles along the edge of the water. They gave out a warm, fulvous light beside which the encroaching dark took on a velvet purple. The subdued colourings of shale and pebble deepened, the spars of fir and pine went midnight blue round the perimeter of the lake and she had to marvel at the dark open spaces of the shield without a single point of definition as far as the eye could see except the dim interior of the cabin close to hand.

The wind blew from the west into their faces, so the men put up a sheet of plastic between stakes to act as a break. Two barbecues were installed in a sheltered spot, sending out the aroma of meat and spice and charcoal, over vivid glowing beds. She was introduced to an English girl, married to a Squadron Leader from the Royal Air Force on a year's exchange to Bagotville, but for the most part she was content to enjoy the balmy night and her own thoughts.

Until, when they had eaten and the beer flowed, a hundred cans at their feet, the jokes started.

The evening was lurid, highlights too intense and incongruous against the soft night. The stories were more lurid still, rupturing the steady flow of her internal monologue. At the first she felt a pang of distaste, but turning away to the horizon tried to blot it out. Innocent though she was, she had inferred as much from Union bar talk, and girls told these stories as well if anyone were prepared to listen. She remembered giggling corners she had walked past. The smut was too banal for repetition, imperfect either in fact or expression.

'And so he went into the drug store for the third time and the assistant said, Have you made up your mind what it's to be yet, mate?'

The punch lines rolled out one after the other as the men outdid themselves in vulgarity. She wondered why they loathed her sex so, loathed its physical propensities, the act of coupling they were intent on all their waking lives and most of their sleeping ones. Mabon once told her of a competition they had held, where the air crew wrote down every time they had a specifically sexual thought in the course of one sortie, no cheating. He won outright. Was this an expurgation, a catharsis, to hate and revile and cheapen the female who stole so much of his energy? Was it a form of vicarious excitement for the impoverished mind, a verbal pornography that was a tiny portion of the whole exploitation of sex? Or was she being, as usual, absurdly intense? The other women laughed. Mabon laughed, though give him his due he did not add to the fund except in a mild and genuinely humorous degree. She could not laugh.

At one outburst of mirth she thought no one could top, someone whose face was hidden in the dark launched out, 'Have you heard the one about the farmer and his wife who grew corn on the cob?'

Esme thought, I really can't stand much more of this. I can't tell them to stop. I can't tell them what I think without looking a prude. So she got up and walked along the back of the plastic screen and reached the steps of the cabin without arousing conspicuous attention, but at the top of the flight she was in time to hear the denouement which made her wince in pain.

She quivered from head to toe in indignation. What was the matter with her that she had to be so serious? Why couldn't she laugh it off like the other women and say, He's a marvellous raconteur. It wasn't her idea of a ranc.onteur or her idea of an evening's entertainment. Could it be her pregnancy that made her susceptible to what she felt was wholesale slander?

The cabin was in darkness and quaking she felt for a chair, and drew some relief from the black pipe stove which burned logs, sending out a glow in the room along with the pungent resin of woodsmoke. She lay back and put her stockinged feet automatically on the pine-grooved walls. Did Rejean and Alexis spend evenings in this way, dishing the dirt? She tried to imagine the words she had heard on their lips, and could not. Those men did not fit with the salacious. What would Alexis have done, finding himself in such a gathering? He would have risen to his feet, a noticeable act he would not have apologised for or disguised as she had done in stealth. He would have waited till they stopped their talk and looked at him, then said with a formal bow of good manners, You will excuse me. I must go and evacuate your company. No, he would have done better than that. He would have circumvented them altogether. Wise before the event, he would not have come. She closed her eyes and immersed herself in memory.

After half an hour, Mabon came to look for her and found her still in the dark. 'Are you well?'

'Yes, I'm fine. It was – those jokes.' For once she put her hand out for reassurance and, surprised, he held it.

'Can't you take it? You should hear them when they talk about what they've actually done. That is wild.' She shivered. Could she be the currency of such a dialogue? What was private? What was principled? 'Aren't you coming out again?'

'No. Tell them I'm cold if you want. If you want to stay.'

'I think they are going to move in here. The wind is chill. We won't be long.' He checked the time and worked out at what point it was seemly to leave. 'I'll start them on something else if you like. But they've drunk rather too much.'

'Thank you.'

When the group re-assembled indoors, the English girl came and sat beside her in a corner, out of the way. She was pretty in the way of English women, light and fluffy haired and it was a pleasure to watch her and hear the accent of home. Esme was tempted to ask if the spit and sawdust mentality prevailed in the Royal Air Force messes, but restrained herself from exposing too much strangeness.

However, the new arrival to the Saguenay had an equally thought-provoking comment for the other outsider. She glanced round the room where nothing had been done to make them feel special or wanted because they were the bienvenues, and said, 'Don't you think it's extraordinary how little effort the Canadians make to welcome newcomers? Well, you can see what they think of the French, and they're not any better disposed to foreigners.

They just don't want to know. The world stops at Prince Edward Island for all they care.'

Esme had not noticed this particular xenophobia, taking it for granted that she was peculiar and unlikeable. 'I can't blame them in my case. I'm a bit of a misfit, being married to a Canadian. They don't know what camp I'm in.'

'I have to compare it with the way we extend hospitality to people on exchange to the RAF. We do everything for them in the year they're with us. Here you can sink or swim. No one cares.'

They reached home about one in the morning and Mabon parked, as he always did, at the side of the house and they walked a few yards round the corner to their door at the bottom of the basement steps. The only car that stood in the street as they approached was Esme's. Her eyes fell on it in horror. In the middle of a mild night the car was covered with snow, gleaming pale in the high moonlight. The sight arrested both of them and involuntarily her heart lurched with fear and she took his arm. How could the heavens open and snow exclusively on her car? It was the worst omen, a praeternatural sign that she was singled out from other mortals for the special attention of the gods.

He walked up to the car, undaunted, and read on the windscreen the words 'Trick or treat'. Local children, frustrated by ringing at the darkened house and obtaining no reply, no candy or money which was their statutory due on Hallowe'en, had carried out their threat of retaliation and sprayed her car with mock snow from an aerosol can.

'It'll wash off easily enough,' he said.

For days there was a flotsam of white frothy grains along the roadway from which she averted her eyes every time she passed.

As the autumn developed she drove about the countryside alone, as if she were trying to lay by a store of memories and colour to last her through the forthcoming close season. She was a strange and solitary figure, sitting on a rocky promontory that gave a view downriver between the high-sided cliffs to where the sea might lie, out of sight. In the pools below her feet she could see fish swimming without hindrance. They moved freely, gliding, turning. Some might even steer into the current of the St Lawrence

461

and from there break out into the wide flow of the Atlantic. Salmon made the journey across the ocean regularly, swimming from salt to fresh water, back to their home breeding grounds. No one prevented them. They obeyed their natural instinct. She sighed that even the fish in the sea were free when she was not. True, they arrived exhausted, worn thin from lack of food through the stupendous effort of their navigation upriver, but wouldn't she do it at that price – wouldn't she? What weirs and waterfalls she would leap to reach the inland streams of her birthplace, impelled forever onwards by the outline of home, stamped on the retina, ingrained in the imagination so that every cell in her was moulded by it as emphatically as by gene and chromosome. Barred from that resource, those cells would die or distort, changed by the wasting sickness of nostalgia.

Another day, when she was probing the inland routes of the Laurentides, down the side roads that crossed the tracts of forest, she came across the deserted farmhouse again, though by a different road from the one she had taken the year before and passed by without recognising it. She stopped the car and reversed.

The same ghostly air pervaded the place. It was a film set gone to ruin, a place hard to associate with real on-going life. She parked the car off the road and got out. The intervening winter had finally demolished the house. The rafters were gone and the shingles of the roof splayed on the floor of the rooms below. The doors she touched apprehensively, battened on their hinges. Their nails and screws would last another month or two, then snap and allow the elements unimpeded access.

Birds had nested in the outhouses. The barn was filled with droppings while straw and twigs protruded from under the eaves. Some rodent made a colony under the floorboards of the porch, to judge by the gnawing of the wood surrounds, but she was too timid to look and see which animal hibernated there.

She walked further from the house into the paddock, crossing a stile in the perimeter fence which was made up of wooden poles, oddly intact, though it was mossy and wet underfoot. She discovered that there was an orchard behind the house. Nobody had picked it for many a year and the pendant branches dipped low. Fallen apples lay on the ground, worm-eaten and rotting. Huge globular apples that were ruddy on one side, silver pale on the other, some Johnny Appleseed variety she didn't recognise. There were a hundred pounds lying at her feet and gone to waste. She grieved for that loss, for she would much rather peel, core and stew the whole and unadulterated fruit than buy a can. But she couldn't salvage them. They were too heavy for her to carry, and apart from that the decay was too far gone.

She went a long way round the outside of the fence, pausing to rest at times from the unaccustomed pressure on her legs, or stopping to marvel at the sea of tree tops buoyant to the edge of the sky. Seedlings grew on the inner verge of the fence and she realised that in a very little time, five years perhaps, they would have enroached entirely on the homestead which would be invisible to the passer-by, a patch of fertile cultivated earth where the conifer would grow a little higher, a shade richer from the soil that vitalised it, but otherwise obliterated.

She was tired when she got back to the car, which was blissfully warm. The windows had concentrated the rays of the sun, though she had come to regard this as a hollow friend. She drew out Alexis' coat, too small to wear in the last stages of pregnancy, but a comforter still. She wrapped herself in it and lying along the front seat, out of sight, out of mind, she fell asleep.

It was dusk when she woke, uncomfortably stiff. She sat up at once to start the car and head for warmth and shelter. The sun had gone down and she shivered with the drop in temperature as she pushed the coat away. The engine under her hands whirred and went dead. She tried again. Nothing. A click and no roar of energy. The battery was flat and she recalled that Mabon had been warning her for days that she must use the block warmer again now that the nights were starting to freeze. The pathetic motor was susceptible to the first snap of cold. It was quite dead.

She sat and pondered this dilemma for some minutes, almost amused at herself, but not quite. And then she realised, by the seizure of pain that swept her lower abdomen, that her labour had started. Or was it a false alarm, brought on by this anxiety? She listened to the rhythm of pain which broke across her sporadically. These were contractions, surely, not spasms of fear, though she was aware of those as a marginal commentary on the first. She looked down the long tapering road into the distance, while as she watched night closed in completely and shut off her view. Ahead and behind it was empty. In the three or four hours since she parked the car not a single vehicle had passed in either direction. Whatever she planned to do, she must do it on her own.

She lay back again and wailed mentally at her solitude, her idiocy in coming out like this so near her delivery date, her stupid lack of sense. All the things that made her into herself, she bemoaned. Oh, shut up, Esme, and think. She tried to time the contractions and they seemed to her to be coming rather frequently. There was a sum she had to do to work out how long the birth would be when contractions were this close together, but she could not remember what either Cleophas or the textbook told her.

Walking to Chicoutimi seemed her only way out. But how could she accomplish it, lying down every few minutes to bear the pain? She panicked, feeling herself helpless. When she lay back there was relief, pulling up the coat like a counterpane and hiding from the facts that kept impinging on her consciousness. Mabon would kill her when he found out. And then the comedy of this thought struck her. She had rather more to fear from circumstance than from him. She had spent so many hours afraid of giving birth in a ditch at the roadside and here it was an imminent possibility. But there was no snow. The fuzzing was in her own brain. The clouding was of fear and unpreparedness. What would happen to her if she had to deliver the child herself? Would she or it survive a cold night? She remembered fleeting images of birth, blood, a cord to cut. Oh hell. What with? She had neither knife nor file. Such ignominy if it came down to dying like a dog in a ditch.

Then she recollected herself after the first bout of terror. She would survive. She was not going to die or even disgrace herself in some remote Canadian backwood. For goodness' sake, what stuff was she made of to be such a wilted flower in a crisis? Let Hannah with her clutch of children help her now. All those pioneer women had done it in preceding generations without anaesthetic, without medical help, alone in log cabins with a husband away hunting in the woods. This land was peopled by survivors and she would be one of them. If she could just think.

Turning on her side she saw in the half light the glimmer of metal. There were three canisters rolling on the floor at the back of the car. They were flares left over from the party at the lake.

Mabon had removed them from the sedan because he was tired of hearing their rattle, and it was easier to drop them in her car than take them indoors. At once she saw their potential and picked one up to peer at the instructions. There wasn't enough strength in the battery to light the bulb in the car interior. On closer inspection she saw they were different types of flare. Two were slow burning like the ones used to light the edge of the runway in the white-out. These might burn for an hour. The third was a distress signal, like a rocket, which would last a very few seconds and would have to be employed judiciously.

Another contraction blotted out her rational thought. They were definitely coming closer together, but she couldn't waste minutes timing the interval. She got out of the car and found the evening was raw and appreciably colder. It was sleeping that had let the car and battery chill over. Could she die of cold in November? She vaguely recalled the story of a man who was liable to freeze in the Andes. He had kept himself alive by walking round and round a rock, never allowing the pervasive lull of sleep to distract him. What a country this was. You could be eaten alive in summer by flies you could not see and freeze to death in winter in a cold you could not feel – all under a blue and laughing sky.

She walked twenty yards ahead of the vehicle and set off the first long burning flare. It spouted a cone of yellow light, a fountain rising and falling which enabled her to see while she repeated the action twenty yards behind the car. They were assurances, not perhaps of human presence but of the forces of light and civilisation in the face of encompassing night and the endless vacuity of the forest. Someone, somewhere, might see.

Her plan was that twenty minutes after she set off the flares she would try the rocket and if that brought no response in half an hour she would set out for Chicoutimi on foot. It was better to be on the move than to sit here a palpitating mass of nerves.

The flares burned without a reply and she realised their light was visible only from the air. That was their purpose, and they were almost useless at ground level. The trees of the Laurentides Park swallowed them up. In their glow she read the directions for the distress flare, and by now she was beginning to feel it was not wholly inappropriate. Two more spasms in rapid succession warned her she had possibly an hour or two to go, rather less than the time it would take for her to reach habitation.

The canister had a pull device like a can of beer and she set it on the ground, forewarned that there was a delay before firing of about ten seconds which gave her time to stand clear. With trepidation, as though she were pulling the pin on an explosive grenade, she tugged at the metal which unwound in one coil and then stood back. With a whoosh it went up before it arced over to the east. It took with it a trail of white that turned after some seconds into red stars which burst quite noticeably, and with a retort loud enough to raise the dead. Oh God, what a performance. No wonder Mabon grew exasperated that she could do nothing normally. She imagined what such a rocket would achieve in Edinburgh or Lochearn. All the emergency services would turn out, fire, police, ambulance and probably the bomb disposal experts as well. Here, she would be lucky if a farmer, bolting up his livestock for the night, saw a red light and wondered if it was a shooting star or a meteorite gone to earth.

She retired to the car again and waited. She thought she had taken the wrong course of action after all. She should have set out at once when she discovered the engine would not turn over. Dithering and panicking. Wasn't that just like her? Why couldn't she get a move on and accomplish what she had to do? What a fritterer. The pain welled again like a flood rising behind a dam, pressure, pressure, pressure, until it subsided unaccountably like the ebb of tide waters.

And then, faintly, came the drone of an engine. What engine she did not know but it was more companionable than her own heartbeat, more awe-inspiring than Man Friday's footprint on the deserted island. It meant the world was inhabited by someone other than herself.

A helicopter hove into sight, flew up the road and turned to come downwind again. It hovered over the surface of the road, then settled like a waterboatman on a pond. She queried whether the road were wide enough for any craft to land, but these men were trained to bring it down in a jungle, on aircraft carriers in the middle of an ocean or on the top of skyscrapers. She watched the rotary blades slow until from under them there appeared the pilot, a man they called Demoine, and with him, miraculously, was Tom Westwater, the best face she ever saw.

'Why, Mrs Caulderwood, what's happened here? Have you crashed?'

'No. I'm afraid the car wouldn't start. I thought of walking for help but, you see, I have started in labour.'

The navigator was stunned. She stood in front of him so calmly, even apologetically. He turned with her towards the rescue plane. A bachelor, he was almost as baffled by things maternal as Esme, but felt it should not be like this though he could not decide whether the lack of pampering was to her credit or not. By what criterion was he to judge the unique? He must treat her like a routine air sea rescue until the emergency was passed. He flicked off his reactions and flicked on competence. 'I think, then, ma'am, we'd better take you in the whirlybird straight to Dieu St Vallier. You are booked in there? I can radio for your doctor. We'll come back for your car in daylight.'

She insisted on walking to the helicopter by herself. 'Did you see all the flares?'

'We sure did. Lucky they were there.' He saw her settled in the rear of the craft, fussing gently so that after lonely anguish she was brought to the verge of tears by such simple manifestations of concern as he would have shown to any walking wounded. They lifted almost at once into the air. The car, the homestead, the trees, were distanced in seconds and she could see the lights of Chicoutimi and the northern suburbs were not so far away.

'What should I have done?'

'You did just fine.'

She wished she was confident that Mabon would echo this opinion. The machine wheeled and turned, a giddy spiral that distracted her from her internal gyrations.

'Part of the squadron is out on exercise, but I'll radio Mabon when I get back to Base.'

'No. Don't do that. Don't create a commotion. Just leave a message in his office.'

The city loomed below, divided by the chasm of the Saguenay. 'Visiting time should be over for the afternoon. I hope the car park's free. Do you know the layout, Tom? There isn't time to warn the ambulance bay, is there?'

'Oh, I'm not an ambulance case.'

All the same, when the landing was safely executed, she was

submitted to what she thought was undue fuss and was embarrassed further when Bob Findlay passed her on his way out of the hospital after a parochial visit.

He paused and turned. 'I like to see a woman who can arrive in style. What have you been doing to yourself now?'

'Oh, this is me on a quiet day. You should see me when I'm trying to be a nuisance.' She smiled thinly, too pressed to give much account of her activities.

While Tom saw her into medical care, Bob stood and spoke to Demoine who reckoned they were fortunate to have been flying over that patch. As the craft departed, rising vertically to report on its delayed return, Bob hesitated. It was a cold evening. He pulled the collar of his parka up and hurried to his car. Thoughts of the woman stayed with him. He had kept away deliberately, not through the moral disapproval to which Esme wrongly ascribed his absence, but because of an access of sadness that she should waste herself, and a private guilt that the pastoral role was clouded by the personal one. He liked her humanly. She was alone. She was having her first child in a strange land, parentless, husbandless, surrounded by doctors and nurses who spoke a foreign tongue. He swung on his heel and went to consult the receptionist as to her whereabouts.

She was already in the delivery room, dressed in a white gown while nuns and nurses worked round her according to their own logic.

'Hello. I thought you'd left.'

'I came back. Tom Westwater's your fan for life.'

'I didn't think he'd ever forget me.' She began to ramble, diverted by pain.

He took her hand. 'Shall I go? I'll stay if you want.'

'Stay till the doctor arrives. It's lonely, isn't it? And I don't understand what they're saying.'

She gripped his hand so tightly he thought his fingers would break. The matron saw the white knuckles and had pommels brought to affix to the side of the delivery bed, so that she might strain on those instead. They looked to Esme as primitive as the leather strap patients bit on before the days of Lister and Simpson. Still, it was her decision not to have the epidural injection in her spine. The pommels brought to mind an auto-datfé popular in the

Inquisition. The heretic was strapped a limb apiece to four wild horses who were released into an arena of spectators. She saw her body quartered before their eyes. Uncontrollable cries broke from her, and the matron asked Bob to move aside as the doctor entered the chamber, scrubbed and gowned.

'C'est le mari?' he inquired.

'Non, un ami.'

'Le père?'

'Un père de l'église.'

'Ce n'est pas normal.'

'Elle est toute seule.'

Esme broke through their staccato conversation in a long groan which finished in the words 'J'ai honte, vraiment.'

They laughed in spite of themselves, and so did she. She looked up into the face of her doctor, masked and strange. 'We wish, madame, to allow a group of students to be at the delivery. For their training, it is useful. If you would agree.'

She nodded. The room changed. Bob took her hand for the last time and left, promising to wait below. The chamber was dark, with a huge wall of glass and lights in a series of alcoves. She lay alone on a narrow bed. From a side entrance there was a quiet scuffling as maybe twenty young girls filed in, standing discreetly till they were called forward to watch. She rolled. She panted. She screamed. She was awful. She hoped she was not typical, for their sakes. The staff spoke in whispers, obscure in the foreign tongue. At her side a trolley was wheeled in bearing the instruments of torture: knives, callipers, forceps. A crucifix hung on the wall, a clock on another, but time was at a standstill and would never move on. She was so far down the road to mind-shattering pain she could not remember why it was familiar but knew that somewhere she had lived the moment before.

Cleophas looked out of the window and when the rending pains became too noisy he came to her bedside. 'Madame, are you still certain that you do not want an anaesthetic? It is only to make it easier for you and the child. There is no danger, no disgrace.'

She nodded. 'Il me manque le courage.' Perhaps the split in her was language as she attempted to convert her meaning into terms they understood. Perhaps the split in her was place.

Judging the birth was a mere five minutes or less away, he

administered a full anaesthetic so that she would be completely drugged and he could proceed with the delivery without the interference of her struggle away from pain, which was uncontrolled and unhelpful. She had very nearly made it on her own, had failed only by a last push of determination. But the liquid, pouring into her veins, made her head reel. She went down into the vortex of pain and oblivion saying, they were sure she had, 'Ce n'est pas moi, ce n'est pas moi, ce n'est pas moi.'

45

For once the orchard at Inchcombe obliged with a glut. The buds had not frosted in the spring, the hard apples did not perform their required drop in June, neither insect nor worm had attacked the full fruit and the result was that he was drowning in them. Mrs Galashan carried away a full pannier on her bicycle; the weavers and knitters and anyone else who called likewise; Graeme had refused recent offers. He might have to resort to leaving a box by the gate with a notice: Please help yourself.

Even so, he couldn't abuse them or see them rot. Now that he had picked the lower branches clean, he was having a job to reach the highest ones where ripe fruit gleamed enticingly out of range. There was no one to pass them to, no careful hands waiting to cradle them like eggs. An inadvertent bruise, unnoticed all winter, would contaminate the whole fruit and, worse, infect others. He picked them systematically with his right hand, the fruit so heavy it needed merely to be touched to fall, then transferred each to the left hand and deposited it in a trug hung at the top of the ladder. He went on journey after journey to the dairy where every shelf was swept and laid with clean paper on which, meticulously, the apples sat in ranks that did not at any point touch. Over-wintering, the apples grew a film of wax, changed shade from green to yellow, red to amber, the texture too mellowing with the flavour as the sweetness of the flesh developed out of its natural acidity. Two daily were his diet, morning and night, and they never failed to surprise and please him.

Mabon unpeeled the band. He might as well smoke one of his own cigars. He looked down into the box which at the start of the evening had held a hundred Havanas, packed tightly into their wooden crate. There were maybe a dozen left. Paternity gave him instant success. It was easier than flying his way to fame. Even the doubters gave the plaudit to his achievement.

The band came off easily. A pink band on which there appeared the names Sophie Maria, before he crumpled it in the ashtray. It was her choice. The tobacconist in Chicoutimi had done a good job, having them printed up in a matter of hours after his order, with lettering pale grey and restrained. He recalled that in the welter of congratulations that met him when he arrived at the Mess, some joker had commented, Good try. Better luck next time. It was true. He couldn't help registering a twinge of disappointment. A girl was second best and he felt, against all genetic reasoning, that his wife had not done her utmost by him. She might at least have taken up the male sperm.

He spoke to Dr Cleophas briefly after the delivery. The man raved about the child, for reasons he himself found hard to fathom, seeing nothing but a red faced and red haired mass squirming in a glass box. 'La belle blonde petite anglaise' was not how he would have described his daughter.

He removed the cellophane and cut the end off the cigar using a Swiss army knife he carried for emergencies, and sitting back in his lounger he gave himself up to the pleasanter thoughts that fitted with a passable dinner and familiar surroundings.

The birth had been announced twice. Once on the radio system that served the Base on a wave band anyone who wanted could tune into in the Saguenay. In England it would have gone discreetly into the *Telegraph*, the broadsheet of the services.

CAULDERWOOD, Flight Lieutenant Mabon and Mrs Esme (née Rosowicz) at L'Hôtel Dieu St Vallier, Chicoutimi, Quebec, Canada. 23rd November. A daughter. Sophie Maria. Mother and child well.

In this outpost, the insular community rejoiced more openly in its rising stock and the details were broadcast over the air in a way he knew she would consider blaring and obvious, feeding tittle-tattle.

He would not tell her about that little detail.

The other announcement was Tom's. He came back from his helicopter flight looking for Mabon, running backwards and forwards to the hangar as excitedly as if it actually concerned him, telling everyone he met about the flares and the fabulous Mrs Caulderwood, praising her to the skies. Mabon heard it all eventually from the breathless ruffled Tom, as he undid his flying suit in the office and folded it away. She had been strong, she had been brave, she had been resourceful. The pilot was sceptical. She wasn't any of these things as far as he knew. She had simply been desperate.

As he strolled back to the Mess with Tom he was overcome with feelings closer to anger than admiration that any woman should place herself in a position of jeopardy like that. Walking in the forest at the end of November was an eccentric enough occupation when you weren't near term, then letting the battery run down, falling asleep! The woman was absurd, lacking the most basic instinct for her own protection and unadaptable to the prevailing conditions, a creature doomed to extinction like the dodo or the dinosaur, a reminder of the grand scale that was no longer relevant, a passé style, the baroque manner outmoded in the halls of the modern. She did fail gloriously, but still she failed.

He saw the patently ridiculous scene with the flares as Tom described it to him. It was by the slenderest chance that they had been in the car, that she had noticed them and they had been seen burning by a wary crew. Those flares were set off seaward as a rule or in the area of an aircraft gone missing from the radar screen. No one watched the whole sky for a distress signal. One could not work on so low a percentage of survival. By his odds she or the child should have been a casualty of careless planning, as the conception was. He was not pleased with her.

Tom sensed the withdrawal of the other from his state of enthusiasm and, baffled, justified the incident and Esme by saying, 'She's had a hard time.'

Mabon cast a baleful eye on him. The man had gone sweet on her. The planes of his face jutted more forcibly. Hard time! Could that by any chance be Tom's assessment of his treatment of his wife? If so it was impertinent, for whether or not Esme might fear otherwise the personal was far outside the scope of their dialogue.

They did not tread on home ground. Or did he mean her labour which he shared in the early, slower phases? Mabon had listened while women swapped their own horror stories. He was tired of hearing them say how hard a time they had in childbirth. They all said it. That meant it could not be true. It was done to make the male feel guilty and to increase the female's importance in the functioning of life. If she said it was easy, then it mattered less. He wondered if parturition was any more difficult than night flying in a blizzard when one of your engines cut out. It was their biological function, after all.

He went to the Mess and enjoyed his hero's welcome. There was no point in going back to Arvida to an empty apartment and he gave himself up to bachelor ways. Every man who took a pink banded cigar offered to buy him a drink and he saw less reason than usual to refuse. He slipped towards relaxation, not inebriation which was impossible for him anyway. Alcohol poisoned his system after a while and, like a bird fed to gluttony, he could not down more. Loosened, warmed by male company, he felt good. Being back in the Mess was like going home. He was known, accepted and admired for what he did and the way he did it. He did not need to justify himself and that was a relief.

He talked to the other officers as they came and went, congregating and dispersing according to the patterns their evening projected. Demoine had a new mistress in Chicoutimi he was much taken up with. Mabon did not tell him she could be had for the price of a decent dinner but endured quietly while his wife's rescuer raved about the type, small, dark skinned, French, expressive hands, you know. He knew. Charles Cartier had a new automobile, a Chevrolet, two-tone, metallic finish. He got a special discount from the dealer. It had press-button windows and a smoke windscreen and reclining seats. Automatic locking doors. Slick. Didn't Mabon think so? Mabon thought so.

It was seven o'clock and time for him to go and put in his statutory appearance at father's hour at the hospital. But he was not the cooing type. The early evening was stretched out with alternatives. The bar was noisy and congenial. Cigar smoke hung in the air binding them all together. He didn't feel like going. He fished in his jacket pocket and found the keys. He put them ceremoniously on the side table as an incentive to himself to go.

He found it difficult to focus on them. His mind wandered away from the point. Looking out of the plate-glass window at his side into the raw November evening, flat and uneventful, he remembered it was a year ago that John Wilkes and the trainee pilot had been killed in their Voodoo. He recalled that Sunday precisely when he drove back from Montreal with Esme, the news of the crash he walked into, going over to Chicoutimi Nord to see Mary Wilkes afterwards. Perhaps some tiny adjustment of timing would have made the difference. Perhaps he should have married the widow. Perhaps he would have done if it had not been for Esme's counter-claims.

Mary Wilkes had many attractions. He reconstructed her in his mind's eye, a complaisant woman. She did not argue too much, was not too wilful. She knew the life and liked it, did it well. Since she moved back to Montreal and he saw her from time to time on his official visits there, indeed gave up paying hotel bills when he could stay in her house free, he had begun to appreciate how easy her company was. He came close. But there were two snags. She had been someone else's wife before his, and he did not reckon to be an afterthought. She also had a small daughter. He was not prepared to play the father and pick up the tab for someone else's child. He let it go.

He was ashamed of himself over the hesitation of regret. It was the first time he had heard in his thinking the hypothetical note caused by uncertainty. To him, not knowing what to do, or admitting to a wrong decision was the most grievous example of weakness. In the split second timing of his craft it was the conditional tense that killed. It killed John Wilkes because in the vision of sudden death, as the contraption of mortality rolled towards him without remorse, he did not even try to dodge it. His was the act of a hero but a dead hero. Mabon was astute enough to see that in the piloting of his own life it was Esme who created that danger. She disputed orders, she undermined his assertiveness and made him, by her insidious attacks, question his own validity. She came between him and the accomplishment of his mission. He did not intend to be impaled in his profession or in his aircraft because of the query of self-doubt which put the hand on the wrong control, made the wrong deduction from the dials.

He left the keys on the side table and when his Squadron Leader walked past, looking for someone to join, he called him over to the vacant seat.

Alexis read Rejean's letters with undiminished helplessness. They were too accurate a reflection of Esme's equivocal attitudes. Yes, she was well. Yes, the baby was healthy. No, she was unhappy. They were too selfconscious in their fairness and he ended with nothing concrete. Would he not have been the same talking to Rab about Rhona? What was natural in the exercise? He would have to wait for the anon to arrive in the fullness of time, but how slowly that fullness ripened.

He went to Prestwick to pick them up when they flew back in the first week of December. He stayed a day or two at Canonmills, which had reverted at last to the pied-à-terre he had always meant it to be before Aileen's six-year occupancy had made it a domestic alternative. But either his feet or the earth were slipping; he did not care for an austere bachelor pad any more. He was spoiled by Mrs Galashan's housekeeping and found he could not do for himself in a way that was commensurate with the tastes he had acquired. He got the kitchen in a midden. Sadly, freedom came at an age when one was past using it, so a man was habitually out of step with himself. He hovered at Inverleith getting underfoot wherever he settled, for Aileen engaged decorators the moment she got back to have the rooms ready for Christmas and the massive entertaining she planned. She had her guest list drawn up and issued invitations in good time for Boxing Day.

'Can't you paint your own walls?'

'You get a much better job done professionally. Imagine the mess Rejean would make of it. Besides, I want a really special effect in here.'

She stood in the sepulchral dining room someone had painted mauve, unpacking the parcels she brought back from Montreal. They had gone over the baggage allowance but so what? She needed these things at once for setting up house properly.

'What's this?' he asked. It weighed at least a couple of pounds.

'A cake tin.'

'Don't they have things like this in Jenners?'

'This is a particularly good American one. You can't get them over here.'

He browsed among her spoils while she went on methodically slipping off the paper, folding it for re-use, dusting the article before she put it in place. He was as intrigued as by the contents of a saleroom, strewn over chairs and table that had sat for twenty years in his house, not Chippendale but good. He looked at them with some remembrance but did not want them back. On top were percale sheet sets in different floral designs. They were cheaper, she said, they were better. But did anyone have to buy in dozens?

He came across a box of barbecue implements and admired her faith in providence that she was going to barbecue often enough to need them in Inverleith. Skewers, turners, brushes, spoons long handled in bamboo grips. On the side of the box he read that they had come from a shop in Chicoutimi.

'Have you been to see Esme?' he asked on a sharper rise than he intended.

'Hm. Didn't Rejean say? We went for the day and stayed for four. He was besotted by the baby.' She sighed her own sigh and carried on. 'So I went round the shops and did some stocking up. Mabon was at work so we didn't see much of him. It was pretty dull. I'd have had a better time if I'd stayed in Montreal but I haven't seen Esme at all this last year, so I felt I had to go.'

He cleared a chair of bric-à-brac for himself. 'And how are they?' he asked brightly.

'Rejean says she's beginning to be terribly homesick. I don't understand it but Rejean does apparently. They can talk for hours about it, which is odd when you think she is talking about here and he is talking about there. It's the disease without symptoms. It all sounds a bit feeble to me. I mean how can you miss pavements? She's having newspapers sent out. She says she doesn't know what's happening in the world because Canadian papers print nothing but Canadian news. Rejean has to agree with that. I suppose we're lucky. We have the best of both worlds.'

He listened, wishing there were not that glibness in his child, wishing there were the tremor of compassion. 'And does he understand?' He held his breath.

'Mabon? No, he's no idea. He's not her type, if that means anything. No, it doesn't. But I ask you, who could Esme have married?' she declaimed. 'I don't suppose there's a perfect mate for somebody you expect too much from.' This caused an unbearable degree of angst, wanting to hear and turn deaf simultaneously. 'She's still labouring under the fallacy of the ideal instead of getting on and making the best of what she's got. He's mannerly, astute and definite. That's important. It's what Esme lacks herself and needs in a partner. And he's quite unreasonably attractive.'

'You mean he's more right for you than for her?'

She was surprised at his comment and faced what she had been vaguely aware of since the beginning of their acquaintance. Certainly the only parts of her visit she enjoyed were in Mabon's company. 'You may be right. We talk more easily than they do. He's pretty sharp about business and thinks he'll start a flying school when he comes out of the RCAF. He is very inflexible, but I can tolerate that more than she can. I like them both but I don't have to live with either of them. They may sort it out. The baby is delightful, the best mistake Esme's made and she's made a few. She fell straight out of a Titian. Esme's funny, though. She said to Rejean, Thank goodness it was a girl. He'll let a daughter go. I don't know what to make of that.'

Alexis did. 'It sounds hopeless.'

'Yes, well, she does wear what I can only describe as a faraway look. Fey and wistful as though the present were not quite good enough and she had her eyes fixed firmly on eternity. It would infuriate me to be married to someone who was so other-worldly.' Then she bit her tongue. 'I confess my sympathies are all on his side. I think he has a lot to put up with. That's very wicked of me. Maybe I'm seeing too much, too soon. It wasn't the best time to see them together. And she doesn't confide in me. She may do in Rejean. I don't know about that. They're thicker friends than we are.'

Left alone while she went to instruct the painters on how to do their job, Alexis tried to disentangle her from this judgment, and the prejudice against one's own kind in matters matrimonial. It was very easy to forgive the faults of the opposite sex, assuming smugly I could succeed where you have failed.

He was not convinced of the truth of her opinion at the end. If only he could see and be satisfied for himself that things with her were one way or the other. How could he act on second-hand information, reported opinions? If he saw her, literally set eyes on her, he would know without her saying a word. She reflected her mental condition the way an animal did, in its coat. There was no lying with Esme, no dissimulation behind the screens most women erected. A glance would tell him if this lowness of spirits were a temporary recession, attributable to childbirth, the onset of winter frosts, a quarrel or whatever; or whether she was ready at a stroke to come away with him. But her unhappiness from any cause, however minimal, he could not endure. He believed Aileen to that extent. Esme was unhappy over something, but how at so many thousand miles remove was he to unravel and ameliorate her condition?

On what possible pretext could he appear in the wake of the year and imply by his attitude, Excuse me, sir, but are you mis-treating your wife? Well, why not? A skilful parent would do as much. Only he wasn't her parent and his interest could not be seen as so altruistic. To descend on them was to prejudice her chances of success as wife and mother, because he firmly believed that if he and she were together ever so virtuously, so high-mindedly, so abstractedly lost in a book, the other man, the mere aide, would be left out. Their minds were too married for it not to happen. The other might be sitting with them thinking, How very nice for Esme to have a safe, rather aged companion I need not worry about, but all the time, under cover, he would be filching the man's prerogatives. The husband might be the means, but his would be the motivating end, and in time she must do away with the vicarious.

And that was a wickedness, to wish her to fail, to anticipate failure in his own interests. His own cause was not so urgent, never so primary with him that he need press it. Let it wait; let it mellow; let it over-winter at least.

46

The Friday after Esme's confinement Bob Findlay went into his study to write the sermon for that week's service at the Protestant Chapel at which her child was to be christened.

He took as his text Corinthians I chapter 13, for no good reason other than that he had not used it before, and did not like it. 'Though I speak with the tongues of men and of angels and have not charity, I am become as a sounding brass or a tinkling cymbal.' He felt like a challenge that particular day and settled his mind to make something of the intractable passage.

The first problem he wrestled with was that word 'charity'. It did not refer, he was confident, to the eleemosynary instinct. Paul was not exhorting the disbeliever to alms as a means of salvation, for that reading was directly contradicted by the later sentence, 'though I bestow all my goods to feed the poor . . . and have not charity, it profiteth me nothing.' The two could not be synonymous. Charity here was 'caritas'. He came back to the ubiquitous and meaningless word 'love'.

For all that the language was richly endowed with substantives, he felt the lack of lexical range in that area of English. Latin did make a distinction between 'amor' and 'caritas', for which 'love' did joint service. French was worse still where 'aimer' was 'love' and 'like'. Was there some unknown tongue where the same word embraced like and hate conjointly, denoting all feeling amorphously? Certain things could not be said in such a language. Extraordinary to think there were concepts which could not be expressed, could not even be thought because the words were missing. One tended to assume twenty-one consonants and five vowels covered the whole phonetic vocabulary of the human vocal chords. Not so. Other mouths made other noises. One of his favourite records was Miriam Makeba singing in Xhosa, what the English call the 'Click Song' because they cannot say – the unpronounceable sound. He liked it because it reminded him of what he did not know and could not do. Similarly, the French 'r' and 'u', the German umlaut and guttural 'g', the Spanish tilde, these were variants of inflection which for all he knew might correspond to words, definitions, experience he had as little knowledge of as the maps drawn on the far side of the moon.

Love then spanned the galaxy, its limits stretched to breaking by what one expected of it. Pathetic over-used word. Why hadn't someone supplemented it with variants along the way? Would 'humanity' or 'philanthropy' do here? 'Philanthropy suffereth long and is kind.' Oh dear no. Better was Shakespeare's 'humankindness'. Well, he could hardly embark on his own glossary of the

New Testament or annotate his copy with personal emendations. The word as it was given not as he would wish it to be writ. He would have to stick with the hard and flinty 'charity'.

Part of the trouble he had with these verses was the trouble he had in general with Paul of Tarsus. When the apostle said 'though I speak with the tongues of men and of angels' he was caught in the act of patronising his fellow evangelists who were more accomplished preachers than himself, for though he wrote like an angel he was but poor Poll in speech. Bob thought this disingenuous of the missionary. He was a plain-faced man and knew it, but he did not decry others because they were more favourably endowed, and hoped he would feel the same if the gifts of nature were bountiful in reverse.

He suspected the convert, that was it at bottom, this Judas turned the other way. He did not see how the persecutor changed into the disciple in one blinding flash of inspiration. Like the early Christians, he feared the advocate might be a spy or an opportunist, although he became the greatest apostle of them all in time, Peter the rock of the Church, Paul the walls built upon it. But what credence could be given to dramatic reversions of faith? How could you trust a man's word when he said yea one minute and nay the next? All fluctuation cast doubt on constancy. Defections from a given stance could not be final for they implied a weakness of conviction in not choosing well at the outset, in not believing wisely. Any infiltrator could be a double agent. Hold fast was his motto, and he still stuck by that.

This was hypocrisy on his part, and he knew it. It was uncharitable; it was unChristian. If the sinner repented, he was more welcome than the Pharisee who upheld his own righteousness to the exclusion of the aberrant. Let him not be sanctimonious. Let him have a more embracing creed. If anyone could find forgiveness in his heart for the mistaken impulse it should be he, for what was he but a religion taster, hopping from one faith to another. The cup of Postum on his desk, caffeine free, reminded him of his own mixed heritage. Well, I only went between shades of grey, not from black to white, did not provide a whole excuse. It was the principle of forgiveness which was immutable even if men, in interpreting it, fell short of the ideal.

But he was a man and only a man. He knew he did not burn with the fire of the zealot and was therefore limited in his understanding of those who did. He was not an impassioned being. His were slow misgivings, slow thoughts he revolved day by day, word by word, and he felt almost resentful of the declamatory style which drew attention to itself and its sweeping recantations. For he was the unprodigal son who begrudged his father's division of the second portion in favour of the brother who had already given his away.

Ah, but it was not quantifiable, the love of the father. Dividing did not halve it. It was the steadily replenished source, however much one drew on it. It was endless. Could he not adhere to the concept of infinity, numberless stars, teeming space, life without end? Sometimes, watching the flow of the river or the expanse of pine to the horizon, each supported by a molecular structure so complex, an ecological connection so delicately poised between growth and destruction, that they defied independence from a creative, overseeing mind, he glimpsed eternity and was overwhelmed by the scale and by the balance. Let caritas prevail.

That same morning, Maurice opened the pages of the *Montreal Star* and found himself in it twice. He consulted the dealings in the shares market and found his own had risen. Over the previous twelve months, there had been a thirty-seven per cent increase in the value of shares in his company, and the rise continued. A few months earlier he had agreed, on Rejean's advice, backed by sound financial consultation, to sell off a further fifteen per cent of their joint holdings. They waived their veto and went for cooperation on the board instead. The sale was announced by a full page spread in the *Star* and had been over-subscribed fivefold.

These facts, and others, made up the gist of an article in the business section of the newspaper which appeared that Friday morning. A reporter had requested interviews with himself and Rejean, and anyone else who would speak to him, and Maurice gave them willingly, thinking it was promotion, it was publicity, and it was free. Like many persons interviewed, however, he was less than happy with the printed outcome. Claire read his brow over the breakfast table and made sure nothing was out of reach, spread his toast for him and stirred his coffee before he drank it.

He came across phrases like 'the revitalised company' and 'under the direction of the energetic new vice-chairman' and even

481

'the younger generation'. He was incensed. Had he said these things? He did not recognise himself, or his company, or his son. He had a good mind to call the editor, whom he knew, and accuse the journalist of putting words into his mouth, or of biased reporting. But biased against what and in favour of what? He perceived this would make him into a laughing stock. If he employed the media for his own gain, he became subservient to their standards. The power of veto had gone.

He folded the page around the article, pointedly, and passed it to Claire. 'I expect Rejean will want to see that when he gets back from Chicoutimi.'

When he arrived at the office complex, his manager passed him in the corridor commenting, 'Great coverage in the *Star*. Did you get a chance to read it? I left a copy on your desk in case you missed it.'

Maurice winced at the salt and for an hour, during his reading of letters, dictating of replies, shuffling of pieces of paper from one side to the other, minute acts which corresponded in fact to the moving of bulk orders of timber, raw, treated, jointed, from Ontario to British Columbia, east to west, north to south across the expansive continent, he steadfastly ignored the article. When his secretary disappeared, closing the door behind her, he took up the newsprint again as if he were facing up to a bout of aversion therapy and tried to read it through objectively.

His reactions were less extreme on second reading. He surely was responsible for 'the unquestionable solidity of management and product'. His was one of the 'remarkable successes of post-war marketing'. Against this backdrop. Rejean's ideas seemed less vivid, though they were all there. Greater compactness of organ-isation, selling of assets to provide capital for investment, new techniques, new technology. These notions were not pie in the sky after all. He had independent corroboration from two sources, the rising value of his stock and this journalist's hard-headed assess-ment of where the company was going and who was taking the lead.

He'd been upstaged, again. Out-thought, out-manoeuvred.

He watched his reactions curiously. Was he angry? Was he upset? No, he did not think he was. He was a realist and said to himself, If Rejean can add something, if that's what he's good at, let him do it. It would be foolish to refuse an injection of talent if it was on his doorstep.

He glanced at his watch and thought Rejean would have left the Manoir du Saguenay where he and Aileen were staying and would have gone on to Arvida to spend the day with Esme and the new arrival. He flicked on the intercom system.

'Get a line to Miss Rosowicz, will you, in Arvida? It may be under Mrs Caulderwood. I don't know if we've transferred the entry.'

He waited for her to find the code, planning the words he would use. He would say, 'Great coverage in the *Star*. Have you had a chance to read it? I'll keep a copy on your desk in case you missed it.'

Mabon said to Esme, 'It's a Ladies Night at the Mess. Are you interested?'

'Me? No. You'll have to make my excuses. I'm not up to that. Besides, there's Rejean and Aileen to be considered. We couldn't go off and leave them.'

'All four of us could go.'

'And what about the baby?'

He had forgotten about the baby. 'Madame will look after her.'

'I happen to know she's going to a party.'

'Or one of the girls.' He was incommoded by this oversight.

'One cannot presume. And I don't want to go. I've only been out of hospital three days.'

'Oh.'

She did not know whether he was exasperated by this fact or not. 'Why don't you take Aileen instead? She would enjoy seeing the Mess.'

'Do you think?'

'Yes, I'm sure she would.'

'And Rejean?'

'He wouldn't mind. I'll ask them when they come later today.'

She was right. There was no resistance to the suggestion. Aileen panicked a little, having brought nothing suitable in her luggage. She looked in Esme's wardrobe but found only one dress, which she discarded; she spent the day in Chicoutimi searching for the perfect garment, returning at five well pleased with the plunge-back dress she had bought.

The division seemed natural, the sociable and the private couple realigned. Rejean stayed home. Aileen went out. Neither of them thought they got short shrift by the exchange.

Rejean played happily with the things of childhood. He inspected the safety mechanism on the side of the cot, running the flap up and down its steel rods to watch while it clicked in place. He made sure it could not be undone by other than an adult. He jangled the toys that were strung across it. He found her fold-away pram and her sledge in the utility room as he poked about the apartment, while she got on quietly with the daily enormity of baby care. He asked her a hundred questions. Why no pillow? Why was the child sleeping in the other room and not by its mother?

'Mabon wouldn't have it. She woke up the first night and he was quite indignant.'

Why did she cover the baby's hands? Her hair fell over the child she was undressing on her lap, and she swept it back unconscious of the effect she made.

In the end she gave him her copy of Dr Spock with which she supplemented the ambiguous advice from Cleophas. He tested her on the arresting topics of mothercraft: wind, colic and digestion. He was stunned by her colossal ignorance of everything biological. She thought babies were not weaned till they were three years old.

'I've heard of nature healing, but don't you think nature mothering is taking the thing to extremes? Don't you know anything useful?'

'I don't know anything, useful or otherwise.'

She ran warm water in the kitchen sink, testing its temperature with the elbow under her rolled up sleeve. She held the infant and placed her in the minuscule bath. As she was immersed, the child flung out her arms in surprised reaction, causing him to cry out like the prophet at baptism, 'Hallelujah'. She took the bathed, powdered, wholly renewed baby on her lap and fed her.

It was a privilege to be with her. He was submerged by tenderness for the diverse forms of life, and especially for things that grew, for the new and unmoulded. He was alerted by the strength of the grasping fist as it closed over his finger, the power of the sucking jaw, the thing that claimed life and would not let it go.

Already, seven days old, she was an entity. Although she was baffled by light, noise, water and the elements of hard and soft, warm and dry in which she found herself, soon she would rationalise these in an intelligible sequence of response so that instinct would develop subtly into character and the capacity to choose. And, God forgive him, he had almost advised she terminate the life. His breathing stilled with guilt at the half suggestion. Had he incurred his own childlessness by it, the nemesis for his overweening confidence that procreation might rest in his control?

What surprised him almost as much as this assertiveness in the apparently helpless infant was the intuitive quality in Esme's mothering. Where had she learned it? If he asked, Who taught you to be a mother? would she still reply, Whoever taught me to read? She was wholly ignorant of the facts but in this or in anything he was not certain if the facts mattered. She groped her way to the answers, blindfold and indecisive, but coming up with the best impulses at each turn and twist of the maze. Esme would never know where she was going, though she carried on convinced it was somewhere, off her or anybody's map. Her instincts were right although she saw no further than this moment.

His development had been the reverse. He started out with the goal firmly fixed in his mind, this work, this marriage, these talents, and tried to fit people and circumstances around them. This deductive logic did not apply to life which refused to come out as though it were a soluble problem. People and circumstances did not mould themselves to his pre-arranged scheme, so that he was forced to acknowledge a shift both in his objectives, and in his power to realise them. He thought Esme's approach was more sound and more useful; what the day brings is enough.

Aileen encountered a different room from the one Esme stood in for the first time a year before. Aileen saw people and people only. Furnishings, atmosphere, whatever was sensory or emotive was lost on her. She saw a hundred and fifty men and women, on some of whom she was going to leave an impression. She hoped at the outset of the evening that some would be memorable, or would provide her with a few additions to her own stock of names, faces and anecdotes, carrying on a form of trade in the small change of society, so that she unconsciously looked for fellow barterers. This did lead to certain habits Mabon might have found irritating had he not shared them himself: a tendency to watch the door for the next person who came in, in case it was someone important, to circulate exclusively in one's own rank or that above it, to name-drop. Not vices, means to an end, the tools of those who are on the up and up.

Mabon's Squadron Leader passed them at the bar, and inspired by the friendly reception from the pilot a week earlier he asked cheerfully, 'Is Esme here this evening?'

'No. She stayed home.' But explanations for the absence of the wife gave way to an introduction to her cousin. Aileen came forward and Mabon noticed that when she moved the cloth of her dress hung away from her shoulder blades, allowing shafts of insight almost as far as her waist. She was perfectly poised in his milieu, abjuring on instinct a handshake as being too man and too French fashion for this setting. Besides, she was a woman and she was British. She was going to impose that on them whatever. She took the Squadron Leader in her stride.

'Yes, I'm visiting. I live in Edinburgh though I'm looking for a house in Montreal for next year, so I'll be permanently domiciled here for at least part of the time. I suppose I am what you might call an international commuter.'

'Ah, a jet-setter. I've always wanted to meet one.'

'Well, that's not a phrase I go for,' she reproved him. 'I do actually live in both places, not on board a plane.'

'Have you been to the Saguenay before?'

'No. I came this time to see Esme, but my husband has links with the region. I expect you know the name Maurice Simard.'

He was forced to admit he did. His own house in Quebec was a Simard blueprint and she knew exactly which model he had bought. Did he know there was a new module available which transformed that rather regular square into a hexagon? Then she would mail him a brochure.

Mabon, half in and out of the dialogue, admired her patter. She cut ice. The Squadron Leader hung on, finding that in the turn of her head to his questions she gave specific encouragement for more.

As they talked, Aileen noticed that wooden shields were hung round the panelling of the bar. They were conspicuous to an outsider, decorated with what looked like insignia and each was topped by the royal crest with a motto in a scroll underneath. There were too many for them to be a whim of interior design. They meant something. She asked the two men what they signified, not because she was interested in the answer but because it gave them an occasion to instruct and she felt she had done more of the talking than was the norm among their female companions. There were times when it behoved a newcomer to ask and be meek, so she played the novice for their benefit.

They turned to look at the shields they took for granted, for these were hung everywhere, so common Mabon did not make a display of his at home.

'They're targes for the different Air Force bases in Canada. Goose Bay, Trenton, they've all got one. Every man who's spent a tour of duty at a base is presented with the shield from that station when he leaves.'

'And this is the one for Bagotville?' She spotted it out from the rest. 'Défendez le Saguenay. What's the emblem?'

Mabon examined the crossed sticks, painted brown on a cream ground. 'Indian clubs.'

'And what are they? Religious or mystical? Or are they part of a game?' They did look like hockey sticks. She thought the use of heraldic symbol quite specious in this context, rather like an academic making up new words in a dead language, a farcical way of modernising antiquity. Translating *Winnie the Pooh* into Latin could not be anything more substantial than a joke. Of course, she did not say so in case it alienated her from the men she wanted to impress.

'Indian clubs? No, they're used for gymnastics today but the original clubs were for combat. They were used for hand to hand fighting.' She pondered. Strange motif.

As the room filled, Tom came across and not having expected to see Mabon, asked enthusiastically, 'Where have you put Esme this evening?'

'She's at home.' Mabon's brow began to furrow. 'It's only been a week,' and was chagrined that this sounded like a justification for her absence rather than a straight fact.

The navigator's cheerfulness dimmed a little. 'Oh? Too bad. I was looking forward to speaking to her.' Aileen looked him over, took in the cropped hair, the shirt too small, the rotund good nature and dismissed him as a genial nonentity. She turned her head back towards the Squadron Leader.

Over dinner, Charles Cartier and Aileen, who were skilfully placed together, discovered that they knew mutually several eminent Montreal personalities she had made it her business to meet over the preceding months. They talked politics and he found she knew the history of the Dominion better than most natives, how the Senate and the House of Commons were composed, in fact and in spirit, and even understood how the different provinces tended to align *en bloc* with their traditional allies for tactical voting. She spared a word of commendation for his uncle's ministry which he deprecated, gently, to indicate he acknowledged the flattery but could not share it. She grasped the political nuances of the day and held him in debate on why Diefenbaker had had so long a run of power, because in a country without polarities of rich and poor the stability of government counted for more than political ideals. He agreed, finding her incisive and informed. He was impressed and gave her full attention, thinking her sharper than her cousin.

Aileen also knew how not to make enemies. She listened rapt while Yvonne gave the authorised version on their house, not far from the Simards' own, and they notched up several more neighbours on the hill of Mont Royal whom they knew in common.

'I must say, having looked round most of the city this last month with estate agents, I've come to the conclusion that it is the ideal place to live. You're guaranteed there is going to be no more building when the park is as close as it is, and the real estate nearby has been developed, and very sensitively developed, already. The only danger is when residents sell off part of their plot for infill housing. That really is a shame. But still, it's not going to be caught up in urban sprawl exactly. And you're only five minutes from the freeway. It's got everything.' She sighed realistically. 'You wouldn't happen to be thinking of selling, would you? It would save me another round of the agents.'

'Is Esme well?' Charles asked with kind solicitude, leaning behind the back of his wife's chair to address Mabon, as the women reached to each other down the table, talking and laughing past him.

'Yes. Tired.' The terseness of the reply warned the older man to inquire no further.

Mabon thought he should have had a placard printed with the phrase 'Esme at home OK?' announced on it. He hadn't anticipated being embarrassed by his wife's absence like this, and couldn't imagine what she had done to deserve popularity which, at that juncture, eclipsed his. They asked about her even before they greeted him.

When the table at which they sat disbanded after dinner, and the musicians laid out their ensemble, he turned round and saw that Bob Findlay, who had dropped in late after another engagement, was standing in the doorway. The padre registered him without acknowledgment, hardly relieving the frown that was his normal expression towards the pilot. He dismissed the aeronaut from his view, though both men were aware that the formalities of congratulation were in order, and instead scanned the other tables for a glimpse of his wife. Had she been there, Mabon knew the padre would have spoken to her before anyone else in that room, irrespective of rank, and it grated on him. His eye came back to Mabon and hovered. He picked out the new face at his table but did not come forward to meet the woman beside him, though the pilot was on the verge of hailing him if only to make matters plain. Then he shrugged. Dammit, he could think what he liked. But a second or two later when Demoine and his woman joined them Mabon did not feel so impervious to the visible strictures of the Chaplain. Their obvious liaison seemed to rebound on him so that he felt awkward at the introductions, in case anyone bracketed the French girl and Aileen. He most earnestly hoped that discretion would be maintained.

He was uncomfortable without knowing precisely why. He had detailed her duties as Mess wife to Esme, but he had not gone all the way to applying the change in status to himself. It had not dawned on him that as a married man and a father he could not appear in mixed company without his wife or with another woman and avoid the obvious inferences. This was a social infringement he had overlooked. He felt it told against him and for a second he railed against the power of the public image which inhibited him from doing exactly what he wanted. Then he remembered that was Esme's complaint, too; in conforming to the accepted, she lost what she was naturally.

He turned to dance. Finding Aileen already bespoke, he went to Yvonne, dropping easily with her into the routines of long-standing coquetry. He did the round of arms, going from one to another without a break. The men might wonder why he was on the loose again; the women were simply glad. And sometimes Aileen, catching sight of him among the other dresses, smiled a signal smile.

The CO made to go towards eleven o'clock, which was his tactful indication that they had been good, on parade for long enough and could stand easy once he disappeared. Mabon happened to be standing nearby as he and his wife went to the swing doors. The pilot leaned forward to open one of them and allow the couple through. His wife murmured good night as she passed.

As he followed her, the CO regarded him more closely. 'Is Mrs Caulderwood not here this evening?'

'No, sir, still resting.'

'Ah yes, of course. I haven't congratulated you, have I, on the birth of your daughter?' He came back a pace or two and shook Mabon by the hand. The men were on the far side of the swing doors, in the comparative quiet of the hallway, while the lady waited patiently by the outer door.

The handshake went on a fraction longer than was normal. Mabon looked at his commanding officer and felt the man stood outside rank for once, searching for something personal to say. He was much respected, this commander, an ace pilot during the war and so one of the last of his era. He was a good administrator too, oversaw every communication personally, knew all his men by name. But was never casual. So in the deluding pause of intimacy Mabon could not find a reason for the protracted handshake or the appearance of genuine sincerity in his superior. 'Congratulations,' he repeated.

'Thank you, sir.'

The other withdrew. 'You will give my regards to Mrs Caulderwood? She'll do you proud.'

As the man and wife took their leave of the Mess, Mabon stood alone, riveted and incapable of going back to the noisy, communal dance room. These words were a revelation to him. The congratulations, the lengthy handshake, the phrasing of the commendation of Esme; at first he might imagine these related to the birth of the child which was their apparent target. He did not think that was all. The CO had said, She'll do you proud, which referred to a future state of achievement, not one that was past. The three details together, he felt certain with a blinding flash of conviction, were a hint about his forthcoming promotion. He was waiting for it. He calculated the odds on his own success as expertly as a gambler backing a favourite. He knew his elevation to Squadron Leader was a possibility that year, but a remote one. Not one of his training class had made it yet, so his appointment would put him ahead in the stakes. It must be! Why else would the man talk that way, dwell on the congratulations? Not for a child. Children were neither here nor there. His promotion had been recommended, must already have received official sanction at the appointments panel, and would be announced within the month on the New Year lists. The thing he had waited for since the beginning, to be ahead of the field, was imminent.

Aileen opened the door at his back and he spun round, so involved with his own thoughts that he was caught off guard by her interruption. 'I wondered where you were, you were gone so long.'

'Ah yes,' he said, allowing the moment to trail so that he could compose himself. 'I was detained. But I'm afraid there's a serious omission I've made this evening.'

'Oh?' She looked up inquiringly, thinking he would have to leave to remedy it, and disappointed that there would be a premature end to the evening.

He heard the regretful drop in her voice and enjoyed teasing her. He knew where he was. 'We haven't danced yet.'

She put her hand in his and allowed herself to be led away.

They stepped out on the floor. She danced in a manner that was so like Esme's it perturbed him, until he put it down to the way they had been taught rather than physical similarities. As with their voices, there seemed to be a borrowing between them so that you had to listen carefully to distinguish one from the other. He adjusted to her little by little and discovered the distinction. The likeness was superficial. They moved their feet in the same patterns, but they used their bodies differently. Esme stayed aloof. Aileen leaned into him. At first he found this comforting, that he could step as he pleased and she would follow his lead without query. Then, gradually, he was overtaken by a sense of ennui about her moves, as if he watched himself in a mirror. He had grown used, in the last year, to something more than his own self coming back. He was swept by nostalgia for his wife's nearness. It was not sexual, or not primarily so. It did not start in the genitals, but above, in the solar plexus or in the apparatus of his breathing or his heart.

He re-examined the CO's words, She'll do you proud. In the context of their professional distance, this was a most personal remark. The more he thought about it, the more it sounded like praise for someone who could go as far as himself up the ladder. But there was an underhang to the words. They seemed to imply that Mabon had not felt so, had denied that sentiment by bringing another partner that evening, and that the senior was forced into recommending his own wife to him.

He looked down at the woman who came easily to his arms. She was a special woman in her way, polished, elegant, with city airs even if they did not give off the warmth that appealed to him. There was no erratic element in her dress which let the person show through. A body not a being. Dancing with her, he was aware that she withheld nothing. The signs were there, the pressures, the winding of the fingers, the use of her hair against his cheek. He was certain that if he could find a venue at that hour Aileen would come.

For the first time, he felt a physical revulsion at the overt invitation. He had turned down offers before, but not of this calibre. Too easy, were the words that came to him. He glanced across the room at Yvonne and beyond her shoulder saw Demoine and his French woman, dipping and swooning together.

It came back to him that during his training programme there were certain tests he was expected to perform, aptitude skills by which his suitability for the craft of flying was gauged. These tests were rated according to their degree of difficulty and the stress was not in the straightforward pen and paper tasks but in the simulator, where actual flying techniques and speed of response were called for. He had prayed daily as a trainee pilot, Let me not crash this plane, even in theory. Let me do well on the most difficult things, whatever they give me.

He was suddenly homesick for the tussle with Esme. Yes, she

was a challenge, yes, life with her was hard going, but he was not the man to be satisfied with the problem that came undone in minutes. He needed an opposing force the way a satellite needed gravity to keep it in orbit. He fought against the power of the drag but it was precisely that power which kept him buoyant too.

Others recognised her quality. He should heed this independent corroboration, for he suspected there had been a minimal reproach in the CO's comment, She'll do you proud as you have not done her. It was much the same as Tom had implied when he said, She's had a hard time. It sounded as though there was a consensus of opinion among his colleagues that Flight Lieutenant Caulderwood was rough on his wife, or was this interpretation of innocent remarks due to the still voice of his own conscience? He remembered the evenings she had waited in vain for him to come to the hospital, the times he had browbeaten her with her shortcomings or ignored the quiet, undemonstrative pleas for justice and fair play. He would not have treated a man the way he treated her, or any woman he did not want to lose by negligence. He imagined because she was a wife he could not lose her but was overtaken with the alarm of foreboding that, in spite of every safety precaution and technical advance, marriages and planes did crash.

At the end of that dance he dropped Aileen's hand the way the CO had dropped his, terminating an interlude that could have gone on indefinitely. He left her in a group with the Cartiers, excusing himself. He walked away ignoring the question in her look. Why not? Down the corridor from the entrance hall there was a telephone from which it was possible to call out directly. It was a public phone, on a side table. He made a point of not using it because the spot was a thoroughfare and conversations could be overheard by anyone in the passageway, but on this occasion it would have to serve. He called home, shaky and nervous. He did not know why he was nervous. When Esme picked up the receiver at once, he found he didn't know why he had called or what he wanted to say. There was no sense in telephoning the woman you lived with, and would see again before midnight.

'Are you all right?' he asked eventually.

'Yes, of course I am.'

He struggled with the unfamiliar diction of his feelings. 'Everyone's been asking for you.'

'Oh? They must be short of entertainment this evening to think of me.' It was easy to rebuff the accusation that she hadn't done her duty. It was made so often she had a stock of replies as armoury.

'I wish that you had come this evening.'

'Well,' she sighed, leaving a long pause, 'how nice if that feeling were mutual.' In spite of her hard reply she was surprised. Wish. When did he favour her with his wishes except as disguised coercion? I wish you to do this or that. Now he seemed to wish as other men wished, for the unattainable and the past. But, no matter what, she would not put in another performance on those boards. They had come a long way. She did not specify that her decision not to be his social wife was final and he did not expostulate at the withdrawing silence. He was not angry when she backed off but tried to find something positive to say.

'I'll be back before twelve.'

He heard her thoughts ticking at the other end. 'Don't bother to hurry. I've no trouble filling my evenings.'

He said goodbye and rang off. He sat on for some seconds while his features worked in a way his colleagues would not have recognised, for it suggested he was in pain, either physical or mental, a circumstance which was new to him. He had not suffered a single disability in his life. Then he glanced down the corridor to his right and realised that the padre had been looking at the noticeboard and might well have overheard him make the call. In fact Bob had wanted to show himself as soon as he realised he was eavesdropping, but couldn't find the moment when their eyes would not have met in embarrassment, and hoped to go undetected. Mabon got up and walked away, ashamed at having revealed the tremble of emotion.

'What did he want?' asked Rejean.

'Goodness knows. Absolution, I think.'

He hesitated to ask more about the feelings that prompted the dismissive phrase, but it would be the last time he saw her till the returning spring. He was as aware as she was that Alexis waited for a report or a reply.

'Do you want me to give Alexis any message?'

She looked up from the knitting with which she kept the hours at bay. 'No, I don't think so, Rejean. I've thought about it all the time in hospital and how you said he'd take me back. Isn't it strange? It sounds as though I've been an unfaithful wife and with my own husband too.' She smiled drily. 'Let's be realistic. If I left Mabon, I might also lose custody of the baby. I have no grounds to leave him, or none that a court would uphold. I mean, what could I say conclusive? He doesn't beat me, or keep me short of money, or commit adultery as far as I know. His behaviour is not unreasonable, certainly not definably so. If anything, mine is. I'll have to wait and persuade him, somehow, to let me go. Perhaps I could persuade him to desert me instead of the other way round. Mixed marriages, you know, a great mistake.'

'Aren't these extreme passes? You could spare yourself this collision course, and with Mabon it will be a collision. I don't like to go away and leave you so vulnerable.'

'Then what do you suggest?'

'You could fly back with us next week and take your chance.'

'No, that's too soon.' She grimaced a little at the solution which had precipitated her towards the continent in the first instance. 'Does Aileen know? About Alexis?'

'No, I don't think so. She's never indicated.'

Esme lapsed back into silence, pushing away what was not of immediate concern. She was tired, too tired for change or even decision. The status quo would have to do till she was stronger. She felt her mind refuse to focus on anything outside the range of today. To cope with one thing extra was impossible. She was worried in case the baby would misbehave at the christening in the morning. Her first outing. Would she cry? A week was short notice for the Chaplain but if Rejean was to be godfather, as he emphatically wanted, it was better to chance it now than wait till the following year by which time anything could have happened.

Bob wondered on the same issue, crossing the compound on foot to go back home where his sermon awaited the finishing touches. But he was less interested in the behaviour of the infant than of the father. Mabon's call puzzled him, one-ended, and he would have given a good deal to hear Esme's replies. The protracted wait afterwards in gnawing thought made him suspect the replies were not favourable. His attitude to the situation which was evolving between the couple he had joined was ambiguous. A part of him would like to see them reconciled. They had such determination in their different ways, and it seemed a waste of human energy when it went to nothing better than cancelling each other's out. In spite of the plea in that voice, throbbing along the airways, the pilot had been met with silence and the vacuum of unlovingness. His just deserts? Bob was not sure. Certainly as a male he relished seeing the other man, who was so arrogant and pushy and cocksure, thwarted in what he had assumed he could inevitably command, but the pastor was more charitable. He reflected sadly that some conversions came too late, that human love was not divine love and that the very word covered areas of response he would not have denoted as love at all. The word was too catholic to be useful.

47

Esme retreated little by little. She started on companionship and withdrew that wifeliness. Wherever he went, he went alone. She made one exception to this social exclusiveness and agreed to spend three days over Christmas with Claire and Maurice in Montreal.

Even that was a mistake. She refused to go to the Communion service of Midnight Mass. She couldn't raise her spirits to be convivial. Sitting at the dinner table, she knew her coldness shocked them. The repetition of the scenes of the previous year haunted her, and nothing appealed to her directly but was felt through the transmuting element of the past; knowing she had done it before inhibited a fresh response. The span of time was an insistent reminder of the difference in herself, the millennium that separated her from the girl of last year, the virgin if not virginal. It was at this table, sitting in these places, that she gave him the scarf and received the ring in return. What mock exchanges! She should have packaged her good name and he his child and traded those instead. It was a false equation, like the other. Her gift was lost. His was a daily reminder she carried still, and would forever.

After dinner in the library, Mabon served brandy with the aplomb he had in making himself at home in everyone else's house.

'No, I won't, thank you,' she said.

He went on pouring it for Maurice and Claire.

'Can't I get you something, Esme?'

'What something?'

'To drink.'

'No,' she insisted. 'I've already said so.'

Claire shifted.

'Non-alcoholic?'

'No thank you.' She grew chill.

His hand was forced. 'You can't drink a toast in air.'

She submitted to orange juice, thinking, He's going to make some embarrassing and effusive speech of thanks, or wish them a happy season as if happiness were something to pull out of a cracker with a motto.

He came back. He sat down again, resting easily in front of the fire. He cosseted his great news, his overwhelming present to her. They watched him and waited. He did not hurry. He relished the frequent notice he was given which attested to and fed his vanity. He knew he was that very unusual man. He overshadowed every woman in sight, the way a haggard peregrine can outpower much finer feathers.

'My promotion has come through. It'll be in the New Year lists.' Seeing that there was no immediate response, none of the deafening clamour he had anticipated, he explained, 'I'm the first.'

'The first what?' asked Esme.

'The first of my year to make it.'

The moment was crowned in silence. The Simards courteously waited for the wife to rejoice first but, try as she might in the prolonged pause, she could not hit upon the phrase which would say what he wanted without going too far towards expressing the negatives of her response.

'I am so pleased. You have worked hard for it.' It was just. No more.

Words rose to the surface and fell again. A picture flashed through her mind of what Claire would have done in such circumstances. She would have bounced up from her chair and flung an arm around his neck, spontaneous and sincere, rejoicing in whatever he rejoiced in because he was her man. But she couldn't find the gesture or the words to repair the moment and make it less disappointing for him.

She let Claire's enthusiasm drown out hers, pinching his cheek, kissing him from side to side, in that wallow of Frenchness she shut her eyes to, looking away into the fire behind its mesh of curtains. Even at one remove, Claire could demonstrate more affection than she. Her own strangeness seemed more and more dismal.

The other couple heard the silence disconsolately, for they knew it of old. It meant the facts had not been discussed privately between those whom they concerned. Mabon was eliciting public interest to mask her secret indifference. They were slow to condemn or interfere, thinking their son's marriage had come right in the end after such a coolness, hadn't it? More profoundly, if this was the modern trend and a larger and larger proportion of men and women were finding out after the event that they had nothing in common and did not like each other, then they preferred to remain ignorant in the face of what made them helpless.

To relieve the tension of his worry Maurice poured more brandy and then went to his cellar and produced a vintage bottle and cigars. He busied himself and did not notice these were celebrations Esme could not share any more than the verbal ones.

Part of her difficulty was that she couldn't remember exactly which rank came after Flight Lieutenant. They sounded indistinguishable to her and she was tongue-tied between the various nomenclatures of Air Force, Navy and Army. He could be a Brigadier or a Commander for all she knew. She hoped it would crop up in conversation shortly. The other wives would know. Promotion was the sum of their existence. The best she could muster was, 'When did you hear?'

'The CO called yesterday afternoon.'

'It was good of him to let you know.'

'Yes, he knew I was going on leave. I think he was sincere in his congratulations.'

'Well, why shouldn't he be sincere? You've deserved it.'

'They have to say these things, but I think he means them more than most.' He frowned, reflecting on how Charles Cartier had rung through to the office with a follow-up which sounded effusive enough, but Mabon felt afterwards that the praise was couched in odd terms. He said, You have merited this kudos. He wasn't happy about the inflated phrase, thought it smacked of sham congratulation and wondered for a moment if Cartier's section had started on the pre-Christmas drinking which tipped the scale into excess.

He would not have cared about this nag of emptiness at the core of what he wanted so much if Esme had carried out the scene that was enacted in both their heads. The surge of joy, the arm flung round the shoulder, the recognition. It had not happened before and would not now. That was the major disappointment. She would not embrace him and diminish the pain which settled injuriously in the region of his solar plexus.

'And what will happen after this?' asked Maurice, swilling.

'I'll get a new posting in February or March.'

'Where to?' Esme wondered.

'I expect it will be Trenton on the training schedule for the new jets. We take delivery of three about then and they ought to be fully operational by Easter. I've already submitted a report on the programme I envisage, so I think I'll be in charge of one of the training units.' He was tentative but she knew he would not give an opinion that was unsound. What he projected was the way it would be.

'Where's Trenton again?'

'South of Montreal. In Ontario. Milder. You'll like it.'

She nodded in agreement. He might as well recommend Newfoundland or the Yukon, for her thoughts had taken a divergent path the moment he spoke. He was moving on and up. His life would be full, anointed by the success he wanted more than anything else and maybe that would be a diversion under cover of which she could slip away unnoticed. Like her cousin before her, she thought, No, I am not coming with you. I am not going to jump simply because you say so. Though, having less raw courage than Aileen, she wondered how she was going to tell him. Her pulse raced at the thought of broaching it, while the others did the planning and the arranging for her as she nodded and smiled distractedly, accepting their plans because her own were unmentionable.

Maurice, who over the past months of long-awaited domestic peace was in danger of turning into a Dickensian paterfamilias, projected some form of hybrid ménage, one set in Montreal, the other nearby in Trenton, each bringing up their family. She did not have the heart to disillusion him on the truth in either household, seeing that he felt his lineage was secure. She couldn't tackle it with him any more easily than with Mabon, when he had his solutions worked out pat and she kept coming along like the flaw in the pattern, spoiling everyone's assumptions.

She left them early, knowing the baby would be promptly awake at six, but delayed going to bed since she enjoyed the luxurious privacy of the bedroom in the Simard house. Her belongings took on a new aspect in the changed setting and it was pleasant to find time to straighten a cuff before the crease set in place and hang her skirt up, instead of rushing at things pell-mell.

She lay down and let sleep haze the room as well as the problem of what she was going to do. But before she managed to drop off, she heard Mabon's footsteps in the corridor and braced herself unconsciously. As he undressed in the half light, filtered by gauze and curtains, she could not stop her eyes from taking in his body which was, in the context, newly unfamiliar. That was something she'd forgotten, how his frame emerging from his clothes was made vulnerable, wholly naked whereas she felt redressed in nudity.

He came and sat on the edge of the bed beside her, knowing she was not asleep. She watched him warily. He ran his hand upwards from her shoulder to the nape of her neck, but she reacted away from it like a cat stroked backwards. Aileen spoke in her ear and told her not to be such a dreamer. For heaven's sake get *on* with it, Esme. Here was her marriage, waiting to be resumed. How long had it been, she asked herself, since they made love or touched? Months, literally months, flares and quarrels intervening. A lifetime ago, but the hiatus was to make no difference, it seemed.

He kissed her. After so long, she felt the sensation burst like an explosion, as shattering to her peace of mind as Rejean's first brushing kiss in Inverleith Botanics, a single volcanic fumarole which was out of proportion to the seismic power it registered. Why could she not stop the earth from quaking afterwards? The kiss itself was hesitant, not his kiss at all but a stranger's. It trembled with emotion like no other which had passed between them, demanding more than corporeal response. As a machine he always functioned; as a man he could lapse.

She moved her head away and for a long moment they looked at each other, admitting wordlessly the strength of mutual desire which was aroused not so much by attraction, which guesses at the unknown, as by physical knowledge. She remembered Bob's text at the christening. 'Charity suffereth long and is kind. Charity never faileth.' She wondered if the Chaplain shaped his sermon as a private treatise for her, a prompt towards the fact that her marriage vows were complex, and unlike her social duties were not to be discarded lightly.

That idea triggered off another memory, a phrase that made ripples for a while in sedate Edinburgh society, misquoted to make a lurid headline from the Reith Lectures. Charity before Chastity. That was her instinct too. She felt the urgency of basic need – a hungry traveller pitched up at her door, would she not feed him, warm him – and felt impelled to lessen that particular suffering of his, as well as hers. Making contact, being patient and being kind, seemed rather more important than the virtues of celibacy and monastic aloneness. She pitied him and raised her hand to stroke the back of his head as he lay against her, flesh to flesh, the mindless gesture everyone makes to an animal in welcome as it brushes against the legs. But it only acknowledged recognition. It didn't ask it.

She didn't ask it. She watched, admittedly mesmerised that she had so little control over her physique when she could ache – already and in spite of their differences – for the particular alchemy of his touch. If he kissed her, he could evoke the warmth of response and it was the only way he could. If he drew his fingertips along her pelvic girdle, and the new vacancy of her abdomen, he could arouse the primal desires. Le diable au corps. He had it. Frightening and indisputable. But the carnal was hardly worth having when, out of bed, they were and always would be at loggerheads. She couldn't learn to live with the facets of his personality even if the form, the externals, were pleasing to her, no man more so.

She couldn't plan her withdrawal and concurrently pretend they were to continue as normal. Being abstract mentally and involved physically, that was to perpetuate the dilemma she had been in with him from the start and she couldn't go on being such a liar. It was too much duplicity.

So she stroked his hair with the slowing rhythms that pacified

501

and hoped he would grow quiescent.

He waited, tense, for an embrace and remembered he had always waited. He had made the first moves towards what he thought was a reconciliation – the telephone call, the announcement, the kiss – and was determined she would make the next. What more could be expected of him? But she was like a drop of mercury – the more you tried to corner and compress it, the more it fragmented. He waited for her to uncoil and clasp him, but she slid away. He would not ask. She would not offer. Impasse.

He tried to recall when he had last been so angry, that is, helpless, and could not. Neither pain nor anger came within his compass. In the course of his work he quelled opposition by a form of sarcasm while privately the threat of his strength of character, and withdrawal of pleasure, was enough to give him the ascendancy. There were far too many women he might like, to waste time with those he didn't. He began too to loathe the male anatomy which declared his inclination and his dependence. Whatever erection she had, she hid and remained in control of. They lay like this for some time, technically together but in bitter antipathy.

Eventually, he moved apart and looked at her, willing her to make a decision. 'It's time.'

'No, I'm not ready.'

'But you are. You've had long enough.'

That was a blunder, for she was alarmed all over again that he knew so much about her. It was impossible to hide the smallest fact about her body from him, a map he glanced at to read. Every time he reduced the surface to a transparent parchment, she had to add another opaque layer to maintain her privacy and wholeness.

'No. Not yet.' She resorted to her most useful phrase. It covered almost every eventuality. She had said it so often over twenty years that it had become second nature.

He wouldn't humble himself to plead or argue further. He got up from her side and pulled on a dressing gown. Opening the window to the garden, he went outside. The temperature was a few degrees above freezing but he didn't mind. The sharp night air invigorated; it cleansed the pores, cleared the head. He tried to focus his attention on where he had gone wrong with Esme, on why his strategy had failed, making mental recriminations against her at various turns in his walk and then, halted on a path that looked through gloomy leafless trees to the winking city of his birth, he admitted apportioning blame did not alter the impulse towards her which grew more rather than less with her remoteness.

Maurice, locking up, heard a prowler in his grounds and went to investigate, both relieved and dismayed it was only his guest strolling through the shrubbery after midnight. The cause of such untimely perambulations was specific to him.

'Not cold?' he asked sharply, as if it were his son.

'No. Not too cold.' All the same, he folded up his lapels and turned towards the house.

Maurice fell into step beside him and wondered whether he should say something to ease the young man's perplexity and, if so, what? Words of comfort. Words of explanation. Such intimate words seemed inappropriate when they were only acquaintances by proxy. As they took the path that turned into steps and had to separate, Maurice felt the presence of the missing person who was the real bond between them, like a spectre at his elbow, summoned in thought. 'Boxing Day,' he said, and looking down river added, 'I wonder what they're doing on the other side.'

'The other side?'

'The UK. Scotland.'

'Oh. Rejean and Aileen.' His breath, exhaled from the warm interior of his mouth, condensed for a moment in a thin cloud and then evaporated in the night air.

'And Aileen's father.'

'Do they spend Christmas with him?'

'I think he was going to Edinburgh. Claire wanted to fly over but I told her it was too soon. They needed time to settle, by themselves.' He thought he should say something.

'Has he recovered?'

The question made Maurice look up. 'Recovered?'

'Didn't Aileen's father break a hand in the crash?'

'Yes. He's recovered fully from that, I believe. Quite fit.'

Esme heard their voices coming back up the slope towards her. Although she couldn't pick out their words, she was seized with apprehension about the subject of the dialogue. Alexis. The easiest thing for Maurice to say something tactful and explanatory. She panicked and the pulse which had calmed after Mabon's exit started to race again. Then she thought, What could be better? She

503

had prayed for someone to help her and here was the miraculous release from the responsibility of doing it for herself. Imagine if Mabon could come in through the French window and say, collected and in good humour, Maurice has explained and I think it would be best if you went back. Oh for simplicity.

Her ears ached with listening. After a time, her husband slid the panel back and closed it behind him again. No. There had been no saviour, no deus ex machina. She was going to have to be her own deliverer. He removed the dressing gown and lay down beside her, as a reminder that the act was only deferred.

In the New Year, Esme was surprised when mid-afternoon she heard footsteps along the garden path to the area steps and saw a man descend them. A visitor was so unexpected that for a second she confused the appearance with the only other casual caller she had had, Rejean, and thought it must be him, muffled in a parka and transported incongruously from Inverleith to Arvida without forewarning.

But it wasn't Rejean who emerged from the hood. It was Bob. It was what she had wanted, someone to drop in, but she was caught off guard although she jumped up to greet him.

'I was in Jonquière and thought I'd call. You don't mind?'

'Of course not. How could I mind? Let me take that. Sit down, do.'

'It's been such a long time since we saw you.'

She tried to dodge the accusation. 'Yes, I've been . . .' But knew there wasn't really any excuse for rudeness towards the people who had been kind to her.

'Running away?' he supplied jocularly.

Involuntarily, she glanced towards the table she had been sitting at, mulling over a pile of papers, and he followed her eye. A map. A newspaper. An envelope. What was in that to make her startle and look guilty?

'In a sense.' She smiled, making light of it. 'Escapism. Sit down. I'll make some tea. Oh sorry, something else?' She went and found him the apple juice he favoured, since with ice it actually looked like something harder. When she came back, she found him sitting by the table browsing through her newspaper, the *Sunday Times* which arrived by surface mail, three weeks after publication. She jarred, wishing she had had time to cover her trail.

He put the journal down. 'And how are you, in spite of hibernation? You look well.'

'Yes, I go out almost every day, somewhere in the car. Then walk. In case I forget how to do it.'

'No dead batteries?'

'No. I don't forget the block warmer now.'

'And where do you walk?'

'Oh, anywhere. I've been drawing,' she admitted tentatively. 'Pen and ink. I just go where there's something to draw.'

'I didn't know you drew.'

'I'm pretty bad, really.'

'Show me.'

'I didn't mean to show anyone. They were something to keep me busy, and remember the places by when I've gone.'

'To Trenton?'

She looked round from the drawer where she kept the folio. Did he mean that question as it sounded, sceptically? She pretended it was literal. 'It's definitely Trenton, then?' She straightened up and handed the sheaf to him.

'For Mabon, yes.' He thumbed through them attentively, like a model visitor who enjoys photographs and doesn't have to falsify his enthusiasm. 'This is the bridge from the hill outside Chicoutimi Nord. That was ingenious to get the cross in the foreground. And you've discovered that bay too, have you? You do get around.' She appreciated that he didn't make out they were any more than thumb-nail sketches, with merit other than as personal mementoes. 'Does Mabon like them?'

'Oh, I don't show him. They wouldn't stand up to such ridicule.'

He paused, slewing away from the topic she offered him. He wasn't ready yet. He picked up the newspaper. 'Port Alfred next, I see.'

A few days before, she had been intrigued to discover on the back page of advertisements, among other more exotic forms of travel, the fact that a cargo boat travelled a weekly route from Port Alfred to Avonmouth, near Bristol in England. It cheered her up to think there was a link from shore to shore, however tenuous. She studied its schedule as though her life depended on it. For all

505

she knew the boat might have brought her newspaper and so she was hopeful, thinking, That's my way out. If that's the way in, then it can be my escape route too. She ringed the advertisement and on that he put his finger, unerringly.

'You have your map out, too.' A route map of the province was unfolded and beside it the atlas lay open at the correct page for Avonmouth and the Bristol Channel. It was too purposeful to be an entertainment. She was evidently plotting something.

He wouldn't ease the silence but let her sit plumbing the depths of guilt. 'What are you planning to do, Esme?' Seeing that she still wouldn't answer, he prompted again, 'Does Mabon know you've sent off for a new passport in your married name and added the baby to it?' It jutted an inch from its envelope, under an Ottawa franking. Their eyes accused each other. 'No, I didn't look. I guessed.'

'No. He doesn't know.'

'How could you add the child without his signature?'

She folded up the sketches and returned them to their drawer. 'I forged it.'

'I wouldn't have thought you'd do something so unscrupulous.'

She was brazen now, remembering all the times he'd caught her out and felt she had no reputation to lose. 'I reflected that there were much worse forgeries than that.'

'That isn't for you to judge.'

'Or for you either. Remember I don't accept your religion or your apostleship.'

He sat forward, stung. 'No, I don't judge you, Esme. What I am saying is that it's an offence – a moral one, but we'll leave that. It's also a legal one. The permission of the father is a very sensible precaution against one parent in a marriage of mixed nationalities abducting a child. Now I presume that is what you are intending to do.'

'I don't know what I intend to do.'

'You wouldn't have gone this far if you didn't mean to put it into operation.'

The weight of guilt silenced her again.

'Have you talked to him about it?'

'Have you ever tried that? He's quite impervious to alternative points of view.'

He sighed, deriving the grim satisfaction of having been proved right. 'You can't disappear without an explanation, you know. It isn't fair. You can't run off by the most obscure route and leave him wondering what's happened.' She shook her head. 'Let me give you an instance. Your parents separated like this, but imagine if your mother simply never knew? Stefan Rosowicz disappears, walks out and she doesn't know if he's alive or dead. That not knowing is intolerable. It's so inhumane you can't inflict it on anyone. You've got to tell him, and you've got to tell him yourself. I can't condone an abduction.'

'I'm not asking you to condone it. Don't know about it.'

He tapped the fingers of one hand against those of the other. Which to choose between them; the woman he liked and the man he didn't. 'You put me in a very difficult position, Esme. I have some responsibility and if you go through with this I will have to act against you. I can't unknow what you've done. If you don't warn Mabon then I will have to, much against my inclination, as you know. Promise me you won't abscond without saying something. Give yourselves the chance to make amends or repair what you can of it.'

She thought about divulging more to him on the reasons for return which seemed to her imperative, but she anticipated beforehand how feeble they would sound to him compared with a legitimate marriage and a legitimate child, both of which he had solemnised. 'Those whom God hath joined together, let no man put asunder.' That was a fairly daunting clause. Personal inclination hardly counted against it or his absolute faith in its meaning. He had turned prelate on her after all.

'I will, then. I promise not to go without telling him.' Not because he asked, but because she remembered too clearly the state of not knowing herself.

But he knew he paid the ultimate penalty for trading on their friendship and forcing her to give an involuntary oath. When he closed the door of the apartment behind him, he suspected that the view he had of her holding her child behind the double glass and the mesh of a fly screen would be the last one. She lifted the child's hand to wave to him. She wouldn't lift her own. Whatever she did and wherever she went, he had lost her confidence. His sharp intake of breath was brought about less by the sudden drop in temperature as he hit the rush of outside air, which penetrated his clothes and his lungs in a second, than by the poignant regret that he could not wholly fuse the interests of man and God. Somewhere, as intermediary, he lost out. Neither God nor man thanked him for his moral intercession, so that he was left with the bleak companionship of duty done.

She drove out to Port Alfred the next day, almost in defiant mood.

The second winter in the Saguenay evolved differently from the first. Bitter days alternated with gentler ones. The deep penetrating frosts which hadn't relented the previous year abated and were softened by days at a stretch when the temperature rose above freezing, and in these benign moments it was quite warm behind a barricade or in the lee of a wall.

Tell him! That was what Rejean had said too, his final words as he backed out of the doorway. Easy for him to say. He had been rather less than successful on the same score. What trumpery advice friends gave. He couldn't impose his emotional state on those around him any more than she could, because he was too self-effacing. The marriage, the homesickness, his book, even his affection for her which he felt so unnecessarily ashamed of, were problems he kept to himself, penned in mute misery until a decision was forced on him by his illness, but to her mind that was hardly a path he had chosen out of courage. If nothing else, it brought a fragment of his make-up to the surface and made explanations easier. Was she as vacillating as that? Were the two of them as deferential as each other, not weak, precisely, but locked in for fear of endless repercussions, incommunicado? Was she in fact waiting, always waiting for something extraneous to happen which would absolve her from the crisis of choice?

Tell him, said Bob. One by one, they withdrew their support and left her with agonising decision. Even Alexis was silent, though that didn't puzzle her. She repeated to herself many times the letters he had written to her in her last month at the old house, learned by heart. He did not write again because the correspondence needed no addition. His offer stood. To have to repeat it was to trivialise its intention. And his silence declared something more powerful than words, and something about him. He wasn't going to get himself tangled up in the stupidities of how or why. He said to her: this is freedom, this is emancipation. You make your own choices. You deal with your own problems, otherwise you are not the woman I thought you were, or the one I want. It was the final statement, assuring her that only silence cannot be equivocal.

Courage. Where was courage? She looked back and told herself for maybe the hundredth time that she was a fool. Here she was driving along the same roads she drove along last year, without being paralysed by terror. Snow, the drifting wind, a piercing blue sky, but she survived. It was not so bad. Certainly the weather conditions were not incompatible with life, even if there was a violence in the winter season which was without parallel in the maritime climate. If she had known this before, she could have made a go of it. She could have made more of the experience instead of allowing the experience to dominate her. Whatever she wanted, she could accomplish if the will were strong enough, here or anywhere. Under the pressured newness of this last year she had forgotten it, forgotten herself and let determination slip out from her code. What an abject creature she had become, hidebound, malebound, weatherbound. She had submitted to an awesome loss of identity, deferred and prevaricated over and over again until she lost the initiative in her own life. Now she was in solitary possession of her body once again she might regain her other faculties.

She stopped and got out of the car. There was the jetty from which the packet sailed to England, under the boarding of Maurice Simard et Fils. She walked to the edge of the wooden causeway. As far as the eye could see, the Saguenay was frozen. Absurd, such disappointment that made the tears like points of ice standing in her eye. She had illogically thought the sea would be clear and afford her an immediate passage east. The vessel wouldn't sail for many a long week.

She looked out to sea and made up her mind to walk as far as the huts the fishermen erected. Wrapped in Alexis' coat, shod in sealskin, pulling her sledded infant, she was indistinguishable on the horizon from an esquimau mother, as homely on the frozen ice pack as a weathered boulder, grafted to the earth.

She wished, as she walked towards the mid-channel of the frozen water course, that the Saguenay and the Atlantic might freeze over completely and allow her to drive across, or walk, yes she would walk it if she had to. It could turn into a new Red Sea that didn't divide but solidified, allowing her to flee to the other side like the children of Israel released from captivity. But as she went further and further out she saw that the bondswoman would find no passage across this river.

The Saguenay had frozen over again, but in a strange way. The flow of water from upstream continued. The deeper channel of the river seemed to be constantly in motion, no matter how inert the surface was. The inevitable current from high to low, mountain to open sea went on, even though it was thwarted by the incidence of a frozen river. Opposite the wide banks of the Baie des Ha-Ha, in the turbulent areas mid-stream, the extremes of pressure between the two layers of the river, solid and liquid, together with the repeated thaw and freeze of this fluctuating season, had created an exaggerated rippling. Jagged splinters of ice were forced upwards into the air like trapped icebergs, sheets twenty foot high and a foot thick at an angle of forty-five degrees. She could not tackle those cliff faces, even fleeing from the chariots of a Pharaoh.

She shuddered at the violence of whatever gripped her. Madame told her it was a healthy place; it was too cold for bacteria. She could believe it. Nothing lived here. Embalmed at her feet were leaves, bits of bark stripped from the trees by gale-force winds, a dead bird or two, preserved whole in amber ice. The surface gleamed like marble, veined, whorled, crystalline and cold, patterned with the granular stuff of evolution. So cold that in polar storms the wind shredded pine needles into hair-like particles that coated the lungs of those who lived in such hostile territory. It was the antithesis of the air she needed to breathe. How could she imagine that this landscape would relent when she had seen it all before? It could not change. It was the might of the universe, unassuageable.

48

Esme gazed long and hard at her child. It was a fine specimen, vigorous and sound in limb, though she was not over-fond of the species child and rather wished it would hurry through these early, automatic phases of growth and speak to her instead of lying mutely content with things as they were provided. The face which she stared into remained an enigma however long she looked at it; it wasn't her face, it wasn't his face, it wasn't her mother's face though it did retain her mother's colouring, and these were the only faces she knew that might have influenced it. Mysterious child.

They looked into each other's eyes for hours and wondered who they were – simply a reflection of one another, a re-wrapped package with the same faults and tendencies and aspirations underneath the skin? The responsibility of reproducing herself like this shocked Esme from time to time. Who had the right, who really had the power to shape another human being? She didn't. She felt too young. There had been such a short interval from being someone's child to being someone's mother. She felt more than ever prone to error, for she had no one to show her how to do it, was convinced everything she did was wrong. She grew the antennae of concern for someone who was breathing or not breathing in the next room. She checked hourly.

Going on instinct she sang her to sleep, though Esme would have been the first to admit she did it with a notable lack of tunefulness. The flat notes she emitted put her off her stride. Still, the infant wasn't to know a good from a vile singing voice. Dr Spock confirmed that it was better to sing badly than not at all. Apparently these rhythms were as important as the rocking although she fell into them before he told her she should do it, or why. Experts propounded theories. Women were not experts. They just got on and did it. She avoided the doggerel of nursery rhythmes or nonsense verse which the majority crooned to their children and went instead for the oldest songs, the ballads which had better tunes and better words to keep her interested in the recital. So, sitting alone on winter evenings when the light was gone and a lamp illuminated the empty corners of the apartment, she sang whatever plangent lines came spontaneously to mind.

Yestreen the Queen had four Maries,
    The night she'll hae but three;
There was Marie Seaton and Marie Beaton,
    And Marie Carmichael, and me.

Then, reaching the end of the refrain, it struck her this was a strange lullaby to rock your child asleep to. She paused to ask herself for the first time, Why? What was going to happen to the fourth Marie that she could sing about it with such passive indifference? She hadn't heard the song performed whole, it was probably too long, and so she didn't know the end of the story. She would have to look it up.

That turned out to be difficult. She looked through her own books first, but couldn't find one with the ballad of Marie Hamilton. She resorted to the library at the Base, without much hope of success. The section for verse turned out to be twenty strong and partisanly favoured the North Americans. Someone had taken Ogden Nash out the previous month. Emily Dickinson hadn't had an airing for two years. Half of literature was missing. Where was it? Did no one want to read it? Milton, Keats, Wordsworth — were they all dead letters? She wanted to complain to someone, the librarian or the CO or an Ottawa department which allocated reading material suitable for servicemen and their dependants, though, going to the desk to ask if there was an interlibrary borrowing scheme, she realised this form of complaint was spurious. What she was aggrieved at was that she was so conspicuously the anachronism. It was she who was the odd man out.

She hovered at the counter while the librarian rebuffed every inquiry she made. No, she couldn't reserve what she wanted from another library. No, she didn't know the name of a Montreal bookseller. No, they didn't keep telephone directories for Quebec province, only the local one. Esme went outside into the cold wind. She felt deflated and half wondered about making her peace with Bob. He might well have a volume of Scottish ballads on his shelf. She would trade her hurt pride against a book of poetry at that moment, she was so frustrated at being kept ignorant of why Marie Hamilton spoke about herself in the past tense.

Driving home along the wind whipped roads, she knew at the back of her mind where she could find the answer. She saw herself walking over to the bookcase in Alexis' office, a six foot run which was built to house his collection of poetry, floor to ceiling. It was a strange and ramshackle collection in which every book of verse he'd ever laid his hand on found a place, without discrimination. There were his schoolboy texts so heavily annotated that the poem faded into the background, thinly compressed between margins of pencilled notes, saleroom bargains by the job lot, penny finds down alleyways and backstreet antiquarian stalls when he was a student, altogether the hoard of the committed rummager, the insatiably curious. She had thumbed through them often and often, guessing by what devious route they came to be counted among his property. She ran her hand along the backs and encountered the ridges of the spines. There was morocco and levant, tooled with palladian leaf and the motifs favoured by generations of book-binders, which alternated with Everyman editions in cloth covers and creasy paperbacks. They were arranged in his personal embellishment on the Dewey decimal system. He catalogued his library by subject material first, but after that was done broadly he went into a further segregation of colour blocks. He couldn't put a blue book next to a red one, or his father's and grandfather's first or rare editions in the proximity of a humbler minting, because he was an aesthete before he was an intellectual. She smiled when she told him this. Though he agreed, content that he was something of both. So she knew where to find his copy of Child's Ballads because she knew how he thought, observing logic primarily with taste as a cross-reference. It was here, on the top shelf, between Matthew Arnold and *Beowulf*. Her fingers stopped searching and closed round the very one.

Or, better still, she could look up from her table and say, 'Alexis, why was Marie Hamilton going to die?' and he would know the answer, surely. He might know it well enough from memory to chant the relevant verses the way they did in the ceilidh, minstrel fashion as in the days of their invention, without accompaniment, for he was more melodic than she was. He could actually hum a line so that it was recognisable, the right hand beating an erratic pulse of rhythm against the arm rest. Imagine being able to turn to that for reference.

But that was out of reach, a moment that had been real, could be real again but for the time being was consigned to a life in the imagination. In the end she had to order it by telephone from a bookseller in Quebec, whose name and address were printed on the Proust she had bought on her honeymoon. She looked on these purchases as a wicked self-indulgence which she hid from her husband. He would buy her a dress any time she wanted. He would not buy her a book.

When it did arrive, a day or two later, she was dismayed by the truth. Her heroine of song was the Queen's lady-in-waiting, as she had guessed, who had fallen from favour at court. She was also the King's mistress and bore him an illegitimate child in spite of his effort to 'scale the babe from her heart'. Marie tried to destroy the evidence of this illicit love by drowning the child. She

row'd it in her apron,
And set it on the sea
'Gae sink ye or swim ye, bonny babe,
  Ye'se get nae mair o' me'.

Esme pondered for a long time on the weakness of the King who could not protect her and the lack of resource in Marie herself. Then she called to mind the walls of Linlithgow, the incestuous confines of a mediaeval court and its retinue, and another discovery she had heard of – the skeleton of an infant a few days old, hidden in the wide embrasure of a wall in Edinburgh Castle. It was all too likely. There might be innumerable such births concealed. But it was the callous refusal to nurture the child which shocked Esme more than the other motives behind unnatural infanticide. That was the significant divide between herself and the woman she might have been five hundred years before. Yes, that was just about where she would come, below gentry but above the scullery maid, at best a Katherine Swynford, at worst an Alice Petters. She certainly wasn't Marie Hamilton and couldn't kill the child of her womb, though the crime real or imaginary made her suffer for the suffering that would make any woman murder her own future. Education made that difference. It was unthinkable to kill her other self, her lifelong companion to be. The child was the repository of her talent and she could not think of a worse future than to be deprived of seeing it grow.

She let the book slip from her knees. She stared into the face of potential being and wondered how it would shape. How would her child talk in the years to come? She tried to imagine the first words and realised, sadly, they wouldn't be spoken with her accent or her voice. Maybe the timbre would be preserved, in an inherited alignment of the vocal chords, but the tone – that would be North American.

She anticipated the kind of childhood she could give her off-spring. Like the child of other servicemen she would move from place to place every two years, and every one of them would be new to her and new in itself. Esme would choose by inclination to live in a house older than herself, but foresaw a lifetime condemned to inhabiting the modern, surrounded by an immature garden scratched from the tundra or the shield. A patch fitting into a grid pattern of regular squares. Raising a child in ugliness. Rented furniture. A life without belongings and, worse than that material lack, a life without belonging. These were deprivations it might not be possible to recover from, starvation of the eye and of the mind. How would her child be schooled? Not in Virgil or Catullus or any of the other missing poets, it seemed. What would she know of the subtle webs of kinship: aunt, uncle, cousin? These terms would mean nothing to the isolate child, reared outside a family.

It was hard for Esme to envisage a shaping force that was so unlike her own childhood. Would this girl do the things she had done, swing high over the top of an orchard on a home-made swing, pick blackcurrant bushes with stained hands, feed a loft full of throaty pigeons and let them off from their baskets on Calton or any other hill? She thought not. She could not translate the mores she grew up with into the social context of this new world. The thin line of her heritage, what she knew, what she understood, was going to die without real issue, as irrelevant to the next generation as the culture of Poland was to her. How could she educate her child in a vacuum, without support from language or history? She faced the fact that hers was a morganatic marriage. The children could not be the inheritors, and whatever was missing in their birthright in the way of title, beauty, poetry she had denied them in the terms of her marriage settlement.

Esme tried to be honest in her thinking and she did stop and challenge herself with the fact that she was using the child to justify her own wishes, that is to return home with a clear conscience. Mabon had asked her is she was certain she had the right to speak for his child. She wasn't – but if she didn't take on the role of a protectorate, who would? Not him. She recognised that the strength of this desire to hand down what she had received, and to reconstruct her own past, was exceptionally strong in her. She clung ferociously to the known because her adventures into the unknown, that is, the part of her that derived from her father's side, had turned out unproductively. Apart of course from the child, whose future life as well as whose birth she felt she must salvage from the mistakes of procreation. She had already discovered for herself that the pull of the fatherland was stronger than blood ties and was afraid that if she allowed the infant to grow up in this environment they would become strangers to each other. She didn't want a foreign child, an implant, a cuckoo who would turn round in time and oust her old world ways. Not to give her child the benefit of maximum fullness in growth and choice was as wicked a crime as Marie Hamilton's. She might as well have taken the life at its inception as murder its potential.

All reasoning brought her to the same conclusion. The most important thing she could do for her child was not implied in the obvious care of motherhood: nourish it, wash it, care for it, stop its crying. These were mechanical tasks any competent wet nurse could carry out. Her role was to provide the same educational base that had nurtured her. Esme realised that times had moved on. They probably didn't sit on flap-up seats in primary school any more, or write with a stylus on a wood-framed slate which was ruled in lines on one side for writing, left plain on the other for arithmetic, or dip their pen nibs in china inkwells recessed into the right-hand corner of the desk and protected from dust by a sliding trapdoor of brass. In these ways she was the last Victorian, a fifty year retrograde, balanced on the pivot of change. She couldn't reproduce that environment exactly, but she could go part way. For the daughter she most wanted, the one she projected most clearly on the retina of inner vision, was a gym-slipped, pigtailed simulacrum of herself. Was that regressive of her? Mabye, but it was more vital than progress when progress meant multiple choice, worksheets and all the other forms of mental conditioning. Accept them? No, she would not accept them as valid, open-ended systems of thinking. Then she remembered how she had fought her education latterly, and questioned its purpose, but with hindsight she felt she understood the significance of the struggle with her tutors and her books. The scheme of things had encouraged her in fighting and questioning. Inquiry was built into it. Every tenet she was given demanded that she prove it first. Freedom the goal, education the means. She was never made a slave by slavish copying.

She thought back over the preceding months and saw how she had changed. At its most basic, the child gave some purpose to what she did. She never had worked except to deadlines, and these were four hourly. She had to be quick to live a little in between. She could keep to a discipline when it was superimposed in this way. It could not ever be dodged, rewritten like her voluntary timetable for revision, extended or begged remission from. It was life. The schedule was implacable, but in meeting it she found herself enlarged, not limited. She did not leave the shopping behind now, for someone relied on her. She re-acquired the practical skills, knitting, sewing, cooking for the child's benefit. She put into her body what would nourish it, but most importantly she continued to educate herself as though she were storing up information, books, a whole culture to recycle for her progeny. She tutored herself in the way she would have done for a pupil to whom she would later transmit the information. The learning process was vicarious for Esme. She only fully understood what was transfused through the mind of another, needed to be told or needed to tell. She re-read the classics on her shelves, thinking, I am doing this so that these books won't be forgotten. I won't let them die with me. I am going to hand them on. She read everything that came to hand, almost compulsively. She pulped the *Sunday Times*, which took her a week until the next one came. She read every column, irrespective of whether she was interested or not, and assimilated more useless information than during her degree course. She knew the smash hits of the London stage, the latest cinema releases, and mugged up on the bestsellers as avidly as the dilettantes of the metropolis. Why, she didn't know. Few of these diversions would ever come her way and she grieved a little for the things that eluded her, moments that were taking place somewhere over the horizon. Perhaps she did it in case she forgot how to. Reading assumed an exaggerated significance in a life deprived of other stimulus or entertainment. In it she silently defied the sociable and the transient. It became the best excuse for not emerging into the tiresome everyday. It was a total escape.

Innocent though this seemed, the retrospect led into the seductive regions of nostalgia for what was missed, into dialogue with the past. Small things brought on the yearning, things which were unconnected and unpredictable, like the smell of newly sawn wood in a lumber yard she passed. There was a trestle on the foreshore at Lochearn which was used to support a fallen tree, and Alexis cut across it, patiently and mechanically sawing the wood into logs. Washed wool. The sight of a stone wall coming unexpectedly in the suburbs of wood and plaster, leapt out at her with a new realism. Tiny in themselves, they were nevertheless a meiosis of the huge.

But the strongest trigger was the written word. Reading to keep her mind in some kind of training fitness, to remind herself of the signposts to home and the man who was home, she laid herself open to the pining sickness for what is out of reach. She edited her own anthology of exile. 'If I should die, think only this of me.' 'Oh, to be in England.' Yes, a good many had been down this path before her, living out sad phases on foreign soil. Half of her countrymen had left their homeland on some errand, whether they were the soldier or the missionary or the herded evacuees. Living-stone, Stevenson, Liddell and many more had died away from their own shore, incubating the strange fevers of the exile. Why should one small country be so prodigal with her manpower? The Scots came second only to the Jews for their widespread dis-semination over the surface of the globe. They were a flock that had to migrate but at the same time looked backwards with un-accountable yearning and loyalty to the land of their birth. They had to leave, and had to regret it, two equal and compensatory forces. 'My heart's in the Highlands, my heart is not here.' 'Land of my sires, what mortal hand can e'er untie the filial band that knits me to thy rugged strand.' 'Will ye no come back again?' The loss of the image of home, aroused perhaps by the fluctuating fortunes of the national history, with raids, forays, sacked home-steads, had the most pervasive hold on the mind. She wondered if these men too kept a book of verse around them or listened to the songs of home which spoke the most directly. She herself could barely see the shape of the Canadian boat song on the page without giving way to choking spasms of longing. It might have been written for her. Blue mountains, heather clad. A city built of stone on seven hills. It was unreasonable that such trite images could make the tears flow, but they did. It was not the thing itself. It was

518

the enforced removal from it that tormented.

Dandling the child on her lap, the lines from her book –

Oh little did my mither ken
    The day she cradled me,
The lands I was to travel in
    Or the death I was to die.

– were heart-breaking. They carried endless layers of meaning for
her so that she could not escape their application. She experienced
the ultimate loss of her mother for she stepped up and took over the
place herself. Mother, the word she had overlooked in her unending search for the meaning of father. She foresaw at times that
lonely and uncommiserated death for herself sitting alone, endlessly alone, rocking her child into a passive state she admired but
never attained herself. They reminded her of the vagrancy of her
present life when no point in the universe seemed fixed, warning
her against the idleness of conjecture about her own or this child's
future. They brought back the fear, terrible and real, that she
might never see home again, like the lovely Marie Hamilton who
stepped up to the gallows of the Netherbow, in the shadow of
Edinburgh's castle, to enact the jealous Queen's revenge for being
too beloved by the King who neither knew of nor anticipated her
demise.

In these ballads it was the little words that undid her. Translate
the line into 'Oh little did my mother know' and the sense was lost,
the sense for her and the sense as it was intended. If she did not
attempt to hand them on, these words would wither away and die,
Gaelic, Erse, the Cornish dialect gone down to universal English.
They were the Scots infill in a larger English terminology, which
gave it strength, character, the indefinable something about the lie
of the land. They were the coping stones that held the dry-stane
dyke together and made it weatherproof. Without them she was
rubble.

When she arrived at this point, she knew she had made one of
the large transitions, from the dependent to the adult mind. She
would never be a child again. She knew what was ultimately
valuable, not from derivative sources of hearsay, from books or
from fashionable thought. She knew it for herself and by herself. It
was her own truth. The thing that mattered most wasn't any of the

objectives the people around her pursued so avidly, ambition or money or religious belief or human love. It was the surge behind all these drives which entailed but also superseded the individual. It didn't have a name, or not one that she knew. Maybe 'continuity' came nearest, or 'tradition'. Culture, in the sense of what grows between people rather than what was suggested by effete or exclusive mental zoning. Whatever was polite or civilised or cosmopolitan; born of society. Someone give her a word for it. Man's estate, the kingdom both mental and physical which he inherited, lived in for a while and then passed on. The estate of which he was the tenant but not the possessor. A holding-in-trust. Faith in the future.

She realised she had stumbled on the secret of happiness. Being not having. Though it was no secret at all. Everyone knew it who ever thought about it. Alexis did. By a long and rambling process, she had finally arrived at his starting place. But this sense of reaching the journey's end gave way rapidly to another and more anxious moment, when she thought that in the interregnum he had read and discovered and been what she might never know, and for a little while she despaired that she would forever be a lap behind.

49

In early March, Mabon went out on his last sortie before he left Bagotville. The squadron was detailed for an exercise which involved splitting up into pairs for a one-to-one practice interception, and as the wind whipped over the remnants of snow on either side of the runway he felt a keen relish for it. It might be a long time before he flew in the Voodoo again. He wanted to put everything he had into this encounter. The weather was ideal for it. Tom reeled out the altitude reading, together with the wind speed and direction. He rubbed his hands up and down his legs to warm them, for the cabin was cold and musty after a prolonged spell in the hangar when flying was suspended.

The sky over the Saguenay was clear of cloud. It would not take long to warm up. Already he felt an arc of light fall on the fuselage to his left, heating the metal till it was companionable. Visibility was perfect. When they took off a minute or two after the first jet from the squadron which it was his job to track, pinpoint and exterminate in theory, he climbed to his optimum altitude with absolute ease. This was one of the days when the plane flew itself. He had grown accustomed to its shape, which might have been ergonomically designed for him and nobody else. His measurements were so aligned with the cockpit's that his body and the craft were seamed together to fit, and he hardly needed to think to fly it. He did work. He went through the motions. But he did not have to tell himself to check and double-check the instruments or make the calculations on speed and direction. That came automatically and knowing it was the last time filled him with a kind of nostalgia for the plane which had served him so well. In the end, it was the best friend he had. It had its faults. It rolled and lumbered like an old bus at times, but he would miss it.

And the Saguenay too, shrinking below him as he distanced himself into the future. It had seen the largest changes in his life style and could not be divorced from them entirely. The feel of the valley was imprinted for him on the place which in most men is reserved for sentiment. But he felt, veering towards the area where Tom indicated the 'enemy' plane was sited, that he might never come back to Bagotville once this tour was over. It was an odd career, spending two or three years in a spot not of your own choosing and then moving on, according to the regulations of the RCAF, meeting the same handful of people on different parts of the circuit, like intersecting parabolas that crossed but couldn't run parallel. His career and his service record were unique.

He worried sometimes that, as he advanced towards forty and suspension from flying, he might be given more and more desk-bound jobs away from the operational bases. That would be a penance for him. He tried to guess what lay ahead, out of sight, but imagination failed. A flying school was a pleasant pipe dream. He thought he should buy a house sometime but only because it was a sound investment, not as a guarantee against rootlessness. He could not see himself balancing on top of a ladder to paint ceilings or clip a hedge. He grimaced a little at the emasculation of others, Charles Cartier and Rejean Simard, by the domestic goddess of the hearth. That was for men who were already elderly in spirit and

521

had abandoned themselves to womanishness. He did not think he would be joining them for a while.

Tom called his attention to their instructions. Yes, the matter in hand. Ground control signalled to them where their target might be flying and Tom transposed latitude and longitude onto his map reference and converted these into a change in their flight path. Though Mabon got there before him, to the annoyance of both men.

'Slowing up,' said the pilot.

There was no other answer than, 'Yea.'

They flew after the non-existent enemy, a speck they might never catch sight of, trusting to the technical adjuncts of their skill, radar and radio, that it was somewhere in the arc of the sky they traversed. Mabon remembered as a boy reading a story about a man in the south of England who showed films of wartime bomber raids, but projected them on the screen of the night sky, not realising that to passing craft the shadowy extinct planes were as good as real. He imagined the consternation of a pilot dodging collision with an imaginary, soundless plane that cut out suddenly in the air above him. Possible at night. Possible to become confused in the crowded traffic lanes of England, but in the free air space of northern Quebec and Newfoundland it was not likely that anyone would encounter a plane except by looking for it. No flights were chartered over these zones apart from military ones.

The skies were empty. Only himself and his navigator and the steady droning of the jets that kept them aloft. It was almost peacefully dull and hard to imagine that exactly these conditions would prevail in war when his mission was to kill. Did he have it in him, that battle hardiness? He could not guess. He thought of any aircraft as an expensive piece of equipment, and its pilot rarer still. When it came to manning the sights, these instincts to preserve what he respected, man and machine, might well predominate over the acquired training of the fighter pilot.

Then suddenly, about three miles away, the enemy craft was visible to the naked eye, a speck moving at this distance with lazy slowness like a drowsy bluebottle across his field of vision. They must have spotted him too, if they had their wits about them. They were joined. They circled. The object was to manoeuvre the jet so that you yourself remained out of range of the air-to-air missiles of

522

the opposing plane, but flew above and behind it, thereby forcing it into a position from which you could make the kill. His pulse quickened as he felt the drive to win, to make it stick on this one occasion because it was the last time. He didn't want to limp out.

All other conditions were equal. The two pilots had an identical fix on each other. Their craft were the same in dimension, range and performance. There was nothing to choose between them. As in all the best games, there was no element of chance to create an imbalance which could deprive the ultimate victor of his laurel. There was no cut, no die, no luck of the draw. Whoever won, won on pure skill.

'Who's flying?'

'It's the Yank.'

Mabon smiled. The man on exchange from the US Air Force was a very good pilot, resilient and ingenious. When he crashed in a light aircraft in the North-West Territories, they said he'd shot and eaten his pet dog to stay alive. There was no point in being soft-hearted about these things. Even civilised men would cannibalise when in such a plight and nobody could say for sure that he would not, before he was put to the test. A dog's life was less than a man's, and a trained pilot's was worth more than most men's. Mabon had lost against him before, and won, so the honours were even, but all the same it made it easier to want to defeat him when he was only a Yank and not his countryman.

The two planes flew at a consistent interval apart, like poles on a giant Ferris wheel, then without warning the American took the initiative and tumbled his aircraft in a roll which dropped him out of sight in seconds and Mabon was compelled to go after him, knowing the other could fly behind him and manoeuvre without challenge, then surface suddenly above and take him. He had to keep him in his sights or risk being surprised.

At moments like these, when stalking or hunting the quarry, the flying was instinctive. It had to be done on reaction, the two men, pilot and navigator, cooperating with each other as intimately as right and left hand of the same body. Pauses or fumbles were unthinkable.

But how could you hunt for another aircraft in an empty, cloud-free sky? There was nowhere to hide, or so it seemed. Speed was the screen. Speed and sound and light linked together to make a subtle mesh across the sky. The jet travelled so fast that it could vanish from view before the sluggish eye, however 20-20 perfect, appreciated the fact. It dipped apparently below the line of immediate vision, the horizontal to which the human was restricted while the shape of the cockpit made it impossible to see above, below or behind. There was every danger of losing the scent and wandering around aimlessly.

Mabon had watched the other man fly and had noted a tendency to favour a certain manoeuvre, the way an expert diver like Rejean Simard still returned to a particular execution to enter the water because it suited his technique, his body naturally falling into the swallow dive as the easiest way to go. He imitated this left-hand bank himself, listening to the altered pace of the jets as they dropped altitude. He must be here somewhere, but though Tom and he searched minutely, they could see nothing in the enormous void. The fear was that, though unseeing, they were themselves seen.

This creeping through the sky at more than three hundred miles an hour called for the acme of concentration. It was frustrating and exhilarating and dangerous. The mind hurt with the effort of keeping alert for the hostile engine, of keeping aloft, of keeping alive. There was nothing ahead, so he must be behind. He turned as sharply as he dared and found the Yank again, a dot in the quarter on port. In seconds they crossed the arena that separated them, two all-in wrestlers who opened their contest with mime and gesture but now dispensed with the feints of showmanship, and came to grips with each other. The circle within which they flew was maybe three miles in diameter, the limit of vision and the limit imposed by the Voodoo's turning power. Inside this boundary they fought as viciously as two men could who cannot touch each other. But the pugilistic skills were there, the roll, the ducking, the turns and passes as they struggled not exclusively with each other, but with the alien element and the limitations of the plane. They could not approach closer than three or four hundred yards, and this was the distance of a second or two, a span eroded further by the dangers of going into a stall or flying too near to the upper g force and blacking out if the pilot swerved suddenly to avoid encounter at close quarters. These clinches could be deathly, not from the skill of the opponent alone but from failure to accord due respect to the unforgiving nature of the sky. The aeroplane was both weapon and armour, but it could turn against its captain and wound him mortally too.

At the crux, the navigator became a redundant onlooker. The pilots were on their own. They had turned into a new breed, with craft and man fused in one, a terrifying bond of matter and mind, power and reason in control of it. The one thing more terrifying was power outside control. The two creatures fell like tumblers in the air, trapeze artists whose antics would make a watching crowd below gasp with fear and horror thinking at any moment their timing must fail, they must collide or crash.

When it became too hair-raising, either man could give the 'chicken' call on his radio and turn his back on the competition. Neither would resort to that here. Their national pride was at stake, as well as the undeclared wager on Mabon's last exercise which the Yank would fly half a g closer to death to spoil, being a madman himself.

They drew into a tighter and tighter ambit, each knowing they risked more than they ought and that they were on the outer edge of what they and their machinery could endure. Others of their squadron would have given up and gone home, content with halving the match, but they stuck it out though they were deafened by the roar of the jets and blinded by watching each other's moves. The blood in their veins had dispersed with the centrifugal force of the turns, then filtered back, but differently so that the jelloid mass of their cells and tissue felt strange for they had indeed flown through the barriers of self.

Tom said nothing for quarter of an hour, half afraid of the killer instinct he did not have himself, but occasionally muttered 'Jesus' under his breath when the turns were brain bursting. Mabon had long ago given up hope of out-flying his counterpart. His skill was not greater, but maybe his stamina was. He could wear him down, dog him, shadow his slightest move which frayed the nerves of endurance.

The two planes were locked together. They flew in close formation, or peeled off to reunite like a split image, the manoeuvre and its mirrored counterpart. Mabon would not let him go. He watched the other tire visibly as the Yank's turns became less precisely executed, his dodges repetitive. Imperceptibly, he gained the upper hand. Flying almost wingtip to tip, Mabon had a second of apprehension that the other man would turn into that predictable left-hand bank to shake him off, heard a millisecond of the changed rate in the engine beside him, and without thinking throttled back and went into the same move. If the Yank had not banked at the same moment, dipping below him, they would have touched, catastrophically. Mabon risked four lives and two aircraft in the swoop but that hardly seemed to occur to him. He achieved what he wanted. He was above and behind. He had the Yank fixed in the quarter on stern and knew with absolute jubilation that if he had the power of trigger on his missile button instead of the camera film which was the only corroboration of his victory, he would have pressed it. He could do it. He could kill.

And the American acknowledged as much by immediate capitulation. He dropped speed and altitude and turned for home.

Tom said nothing for congratulations were out of order, but felt it could be true that after a harrowing exercise some men removed their headgear and discovered they had gone white from shock. He left it to the Yank to say, as they descended from cockpit to tarmac, 'It's men like you who make widows. I don't reckon my wife wants to collect my pension just yet. You should be reported for that stunt.'

Mabon knew he was not seriously angry or shaken and replied, 'You could have chickened out at any time.'

'Some chance.'

'Then why grouch if you can take it?'

That was a good point. The Canuck had taught him something useful; don't go through the same move twice unless you want to be caught, and he was grateful for the lesson. Next time it might count. His face fell into the creases of a smile. The look was the unspoken admiration of vanquished for victor, for the comradeship in death that nothing could defile.

Elated with his exploits, Mabon came back to Arvida and found things were to his liking. The child was asleep, safely behind a closed door. The apartment was tidy. There were no books in the bathroom and Esme slid past him noiselessly serving tea.

He soaked for an hour to unwind. It was hard to come back down and re-enter the humdrum life of women and children, so he lay reflecting on the events of the day and gaining what solace he could from the fact that the other navigator told him it was the most brilliant piece of flying he had seen, unnecessary but brilliant. He lay vaguely wishing he smoked or drank with anything resembling pleasure, to relax the tensions of the first few hours after a long and arduous exercise. He did not fraternise so much at the bar since his promotion to a rank which was regarded as senior. There might be a time when he would have to discipline these junior officers.

He shut his eyes in the closest he came to stupor, and saw her pass by the open door of the bathroom.

She came and went, passing like a flicker in the light in front of his eyes. She had changed in the eighteen months he had known her, softer physically, harder mentally. She didn't ask him anything now but went her own way. He didn't know what she had done today or yesterday or the day before. To some extent, it surprised him that he wondered, but as she became sexually more elusive he was alerted to the fact that she was mentally untraceable as well, as though a radar screen had inexplicably gone blank and left him guessing where she was in the space around him. He looked at the bookshelves she had filled since her arrival. Did she live there? She didn't receive many letters from home or friends. She didn't see many people. As far as he knew, no women came to take coffee or afternoon tea in her company. The contents of the apartment were her whole sphere and he thought her almost grotesquely limited because of it. She did nothing, achieved nothing.

But she was beautiful and that made up for her inertia. Beauty was activity enough.

He called her imperiously. 'Esme, come here.'

She came and stood in the doorway. 'Yes?' She saw his eyes trail over her form and grew afraid.

'What have you done today?'

'Nothing.'

'Really nothing? You didn't go out or see anyone?'

'I went out but I didn't see anyone, no.'

'Where did you go?'

'I don't know. I just drove.'

'You shouldn't go off like that. Driving alone. You'll get lost again.' He could tell she resented this imputation, the standard jibe made at her that she didn't know where she was. She shrugged but it wasn't indifference that made her do it, but wilfulness.

'I wasn't lost. I always knew my way back.'

'Then you must have known where you were going.'

She was trapped by his remorseless questions. 'I went down the road to Malbaie, towards St Simeon. But it was too far and I had to turn back.'

'Why did you want to go there? There's nothing at St Simeon.'

'I wondered if the sea had melted.'

'Why? Are you going for a swim?' The facetious sat ill on him. Seeing that she did not respond to this question, he grew serious again. 'It's clear as far as Montreal. I could have told you that without you driving on those back roads. I don't want you to do that again – while I'm away.'

She compressed her lips. She didn't need to say, I'll do what I want whether you are here or not. Her face said it for her although she was sufficiently intrigued to ask what lay behind his injunction. 'What have you heard? Have they given you a date?'

'I've had my orders.' She still thought this sounded like a novitiate taking the cloth but suppressed a smile. 'The seventh of March. I've to report by then.'

She sat down on the wide ledge surrounding the bath. A week! Just a week to pack and go, or tell him she wasn't going. How precipitate. She didn't see how she could manage either way. 'That's very short notice.'

'Yes, I know. I'm not satisfied with the way it's been handled but you don't complain when you want the next job as much as I do. You've told Madame, have you?'

'Yes, at New Year. She's sorry we're going but absolutely dismayed that the baby's going too. "L'enfant des cieux".'

'These French. I think if you can manage it on your own it's best for you to stay till the end of the month and then come down. I'll have found accommodation by the beginning of April.'

'Yes, that seems . . .' She trailed her hand in the water distractedly. Why wouldn't the words speak themselves without having to be pushed out by her volition? She was thinking that there was a common element in their discussions. He pursued a fact that she was reluctant to give or agree to because it involved an emotional state she couldn't declare to him. This gave the shading to their dialogue, an apparent depth which arose from the things she withheld.

A ripple in the water told her he had submerged a fraction more. 'Wash me. I'm tired.' She looked about for an excuse to refuse the conspicuous invitation to touch his body, but there was none. There was no cry, no boiling over, no form of urgency for her time and her attention except his. It was a strange intimacy when, contrary to his normal independence, he allowed himself to appear helpless, to be helpless while she nursed and tended him. 'Wash my hair,' he said when she hesitated. 'It doesn't feel good. They should make those helmets lighter. Imagine if I go bald. A lot of pilots do.'

'There doesn't seem much danger of that.' She couldn't reasonably refuse and knelt by the side of the bath determined to separate the practical from the erotic. She drew fresh water and dampened his hair with it. Then into her left palm she poured a quantity of shampoo and transferred it to the hair. Her nails as she rubbed it in made contact with his scalp and each individual shaft of his hair encountered the groove of her fingerprints. He gave way to the massage as her arms lifted on either side of his head, while she scooped the lather before it dripped into his eyes, blotting out other sights and other sounds and other smells. His senses were filled by her action. The involuntary took over. Enveloped by the circle of her managing hands and arms, he found he couldn't avoid putting his lips to the vein that ran from her ear down the side of her neck and taking that pulse. It was the most natural place to rest. She didn't resist but dropped her head a little, apparently entrapping him though there was a slight hint of reluctance too, of concession, about the gesture. The pulse quickened against the sensory tissue of his mouth. It brought back memories of the shapes she drew, performed in semi sleep, triangles made with intersecting curves and all the paradoxes of union. A fusion of dissimilars. The impossible achieved.

In drooping her head as she did, Esme thought, In spite of what I decided, I can't carry it out. I cannot deny him or any man I have allowed to get into this state. I cannot do it. I am not a tease and I never will be. It was a moment of pure agony. She saw her principles descend, as they mostly did, into the dust. She was excellent at pegging herself to the level of perfection, and then was dismayed when she fell short. But like a sensible woman, having concluded it was not fair to work a man into excitation and then not satisfy him, she applied her will with equal force to destroying the hypothesis as she had in maintaining it before it proved unworkable. That was the source of what might be called illogical in her; empiricism.

She leaned further over the edge of the bath, dipping lower towards the water so that she could hold him securely with her left arm. His head was completely smothered by the arch of her neck and the canopy of her hair draping over him. He was submerged by the feminine and let himself be swept down that tide without inhibition. She caressed him with adroitness. Hadn't he taught her himself? The adaptable hand made rings and ridges, simulars of anatomy and could improve on the action of every other limb and organ, to flatten, knead, enclose in one. The exceptional combination of the hour which was neither afternoon nor evening, the venue both private and exposed, his elation from flying and longstanding abstinence gave to the encounter a special ambivalence. The tensions had almost nothing to do with the act compared with its setting in the sequence of withdrawal. To be with her and without her was not perhaps the way he would have chosen to resume relations but this dissolved under the flooding relief that they were resumed at all. To Esme, it did not seem inappropriate to commune through the medium of water. Only one more distortion.

She got up without a word. The shoulder of her blouse was damp where he had lain and she went to change it.

In the mirror she caught sight of herself and looked away. She did not like the hypocrite she saw behind her eyes. She knew she had started on the business of making artificial distinctions. We will not make any sexual communion, was where she began. This evolved into, I will gratify him provided he does not enter my body. Then, he may enter my body provided I do not enjoy it. And finally, he may enter my body provided I do not enjoy it much. Where, in fact, was she going to draw the line between these marginal gradations from the extremes of celibacy and wholesale indulgence? Was there any point in sexual abstinence? To be alive was to be bound up with the processes of life. She did not know how she could abstract herself from them.

Perhaps between the second and third. It was no more arbitrary than another division.

He discovered the weak spot in her choice the moment he joined her in the bedroom. She brushed her hair and while she was unguarded he bent and kissed underneath the parted hair, making her shiver. The weak spot was that her desire did not rest conveniently between the second and the third injunction.

'What do you want me to do?' he asked. No one was more scrupulous in sexual fairness than he was.

'Nothing. It doesn't matter. Get dressed and we will eat.'

But tonight when he undressed again and she did, and tomorrow night? A week of nights before he went away. What was she going to do then? Give in. Admit the third phase and the fourth and so on. Or face up to the worst form of self-abuse, allowing herself to be used. Unnatural sex was so much harder than natural, so she forecast untold feats of invention she would have to conjure up to keep him satisfied. When this was carried out without the affection that justified any physical embrace or activity between partners, it must lead to utter repugnance against self. Or lie. Why had she got to be so conscience-stricken about everything? It didn't matter. Lie. Most other women seemed to lie – to this one about what she did with that, pandering to man's love of exclusiveness. Nobody would know who she'd fornicated with or how, except herself. And her own eyes looking back at herself getting smaller and smaller and smaller as the only god she served, honesty, deserted her.

Why do it? Why put up with the actual physical pain of celibacy? To prove to herself that she could do it. To keep something intact from the garbled message of her intentions. To restore her self-respect. Most of all to restore herself. Sexual abstinence became a kind of churching which might allow her to return after childbirth to Alexis with one tiny corner preserved. She did not know if it was feasible even for one week. She thought back to the woman she despised in her lifetime as only half a woman, but marvelled in the circumstances at her aunt's fortitude. To resist for twenty years when she could barely stretch to six months! She asked Alexis if such self-denial were possible and he answered, Yes, if you were determined enough, if you were disinclined enough. Her personal irony was that she was not disinclined. Still they both believed in a principle, she and her aunt, and Esme prayed for some of that strength to stiffen her resolve. No adultery. She barricaded herself into the fortress of Thou shalt not, in which she found herself closeted invidiously with her aunt as company and example.

He dressed, putting on a red sweater he favoured. She went on brushing her hair. In the tilt of her head and the glance of her eye through him and past him, he found a renewal of invitation. So as not to stand between her and the mirror, he embraced her from behind, letting his arms drop in front of her until the contrary hand rested on each hip. His arms made a red cross over her torso, a form of cancellation. Restrained, she stopped brushing and looked in the glass straight into his face, above and behind hers. Their eyes held each other's through the reflecting medium until he dropped his head and found the vulnerable spot again at the nape of her neck.

'Why did you hold out on me for so long?'

Because I love someone else and have done since the day I met him, since the day he entered my consciousness?

She rocked the back of her head a little against his collar bone. There was no answer.

She turned to dreaming. At night, in bed, in the dark she knew the rich experience. The mind was released from its housing which left both free to wander outside their mutual restraints. She dreamed of the things she couldn't attain in reality: physical love because her thinking interfered with temporary gratification and the distant place, home, from which she was removed in body. The twin factors came and went below the surface sometimes separate, sometimes touching, to make the vital spark of the man who fused the two.

She hadn't known what lust was till she discovered it in her mind. At one time, being outside the sphere of a man's influence, that is being alone, gave her some immunity from the forces of sexual desire. That was gone. The demons were in her head, acting out a Bosch landscape of carnality, absurd and unpretty, Le Jardin des Délices come to life. Except that the scenario stayed flat; it was just two-dimensional. It did not go on to the third, however she bent and postured, whatever nameless man stood between her legs as she executed turns of such extraordinary athleticism that they reminded her of the girl troupers painted on the wall of the palace at Knossos, somersaulting over the horns of the Minoan bull, quite out of keeping with her ambulatory self. Could she really be like this if she extended herself? But no matter how she strove, she found that for a woman, anyway, orgasm was impossible in sleep. The titillation, the torments but not the release. She hurt. Her womb contracted but inevitably she awoke at the moment of impact, more frenetic than she had been when she lay down to rest.

The other dreams seemed kinder. They took place at dawn, a half light that softly illuminated the interstices between there and here, waking and sleeping, being in her mind and out of it. She walked. She took the low road and met some old friends along the way. Rabbie Burns was there, jogging to the excise on his horse with a sheaf of poems folded under the flap of his pocket in case he got a moment's peace to shine them up. He lifted his hat to the place her body occupied, but didn't speak. She found Chris Guthrie standing on the top of Kinraddie Mearns, among the monolithic stones. The peewits wheeled round her, mewing from hilltop to hilltop in their sad ancestral cry. But Chris didn't hail her either, so that they crossed without a greeting. Strathearn swam before her eyes as she hurried towards it on foot. It was calm and stately as she remembered it, mirrored in the waters of the loch, the valley of the mind, the place of repose; but as she passed the foot of the rocks that hid Inchcombe from the road, just at the moment when she could expect to catch a glimpse of Alexis and maybe Ian helping him, working late in the garden, going to take a last turn round the outhouses to make sure all was well before nightfall, or hear the familiar lilt of their voices going out into the evening air with a beckon, she woke and knew she was still imprisoned in the present.

Such frustrations as she tossed her way through, time after time. At last, she fell soundly asleep and heard the long promised thaw which she had been waiting for, to herald the end of winter, start in the night. Rain fell, a little at first, a pattering on the crust of snow, speckling it with craters which gradually widened through the night hours into shallow dishes full of rainwater and melted snow. It dripped from the wet branches of the trees around her room. It broke through the deadening layers of snow in patches, and showed up green, green, that living colour again. The fertile land was restored. It was the season of Demeter once more and Pluto's reign was ended. Though the torrent gushed loudly by her ear, interrupting sleep, she rejoiced. It was the signal for her release.

When she woke up and raised the blind, full of hope and expectation, she saw it was as desperate a dream as the others. The snow lay thickly, as ever. The sound was a trick of wind in this room, like the keening dead she heard in her first storm. The whipping against the wire of telegraph poles sounded like water drops. She was exhausted by torn nights, such long and tangled dreams.

Not yet. Not yet.

50

At Lochearn, the winter melted into puddles and then ran away down guttering. It was the tilt of the year when the light reached a fulcrum point and tipped over into a new phase. The days were drawing out again; clear varnished days of spring. The light was thin, the sun weak, as though it had travelled a long distance over the horizon and arrived faintly. The periods of twilight with pearlised dawns, slow colourless sunsets caught in the balance between night and day, were enormously extended at this time of year and particularly in this place where the sun dipped over the hills, leaving the valley a bowl of reflected light, borrowing from the upper atmosphere what was denied directly. He caught it, for a moment. It was the gloaming. No other word would do. This spring was unusually mild. The month of March had none of its characteristic bluster which inhibits one day what it has encouraged on the previous. It was a balmy, uniform season, providing conditions ideal for rejuvenation. The gardener could not have asked for better. Frost-free nights. Steady noons. Alexis was prompted to look for the summer visitors and scanned the skies with more hope than certainty. It might still be premature.

He too hovered between one state and another. Sitting down at his desk he went to turn the page on the calendar and realised that at the end of the month he would be forty-five. That was a sobering age. As his hands went methodically through the day's paperwork his mind was free to make a more agonising tally among the men he knew and admired, sorting them into those who had finished their main work before this elevation to seniority and those who had still to achieve their best. He hoped he fell into the latter category, for he abhorred the prospect of dwindling output and of having nothing more to discover himself. Decently obscure? He shunned the idea of impending mediocrity.

Distracted, his eye fell on a note which lay to one side of his work desk. It was penned hurriedly from Munich where two friends had mounted a successful exhibition which they were bringing back to Edinburgh in the autumn. Was he interested in making a third? Why Munich? he asked himself. There seemed to be yet another wave of Celtic revival. Scottish scenes, Scots faces were news again. If he could put Fingal's Cave or Ossian into paint, he'd lead a vogue. He would need a selection of about twenty to twenty-five canvases to make a representative showing. He was tempted. He counted back among the paintings he had in his possession. There were maybe fifteen fit for hanging in such company, but he knew he could borrow several more from private collections where his work had found its way. Some people bought him every year, so it was intriguing to wonder what crevices he had filtered into, where he was stored, where admired in private. The offer excited him. It had the right ring about it, falling into place without any agitation on his part. He liked their work, too. The triumvirate would sit well together. Duncan Pollock was one, and he felt it was an oblique form of reinstatement as well as acknowledgement that the work he had been presenting the last year or two at the Royal Scottish Academy was serious and professionally recognised. It conceded he was more than a Sunday painter. His mind moved ahead to a one-man show. Not immediately. A year or two. Some polishing. But it was possible and he wandered away down enchanting lanes of praise and fame, until he caught himself designing the catalogue for it, and stopped short.

Suppress it as he tried, he had begun to feel the urgency he recognised from past experience as the prelude to creative impulse. It was a strange and unsettling feeling. Working towards a peak you couldn't see, had lost sight of temporarily, because you were in a narrow defile of rocks or the sheerness of a precipice prevented you from looking upwards. But he felt a particular atmospheric pressure, almost a lightness of the head which warned him that in a little while he would break free from the difficult ground and would have to make his decision. Up or down. Attack or retreat. It was a watershed one way or the other, though he was alarmed by it and the challenge it would present him with. He didn't know if he had the resources to meet it, whatever it was, looming, threatening, tantamount to a menace out of sight.

He pushed away the dull inventory of commerce, a dozen bales, a gross of knitwear, itemised by eights, and looked at the calendar again, ticking off not days or months but years. It was almost two and a half years since he met Esme. Two and a half years of celibacy. That was another sobriety he hadn't reckoned on. It was so unprecedented in his adult life it warned him, if nothing else had done, that this involvement, which he hadn't looked for and didn't understand, was wholly exceptional. Was the cause age only, or another kind of circumspection? It had seldom struck him before that one woman was worth giving up another for and so he did find it ironic that the consummate passion of his maturity was a denial of everything that had gone before. He remembered Graeme saying, in the shadow of the yew trees, You will ruin her. What can there be for her after you? In the last two years he had tested the inverse and found that was more true. He was the one who was ruined, left in ruins, derelict. No other woman had deflected his misery with an easy transitory passage from chair to bed. Nor could he conjecture what woman might follow Esme in the long term. His mind drew a complete blank on that.

He called it the consummate passion of his maturity and yet it had no culmination. It was unfulfilled, compressed into a mental longing or abstraction, at odds with what he understood as normal. He began to dread the power of the relationship over him because it was associated in his mind with other symbols of his life's achievement and whatever was unrealised in it, the thing he pursued and did not capture, ever. He knew there were many areas of himself he had not utilised, languages he let slip like people he was once familiar with, and had cast off. Opportunities and potential gone astray. He still felt in touch directly with the brilliant boy he had been and could remember what it felt like to be dux, head boy, the captain of teams and winning ones, all the forms of juvenile attribute rolled into one. Oh, the shining talents he had possessed! There was nothing he could not do with these, practical or intellectual or physical – except apply them. Like Dr Johnson he could look back regretfully and say of his youth, What genius I had then. Genius, the in-breathing spirit. He certainly wouldn't lay claim to

536

having it now. All round him, persons of more meagre ability succeeded and were happy with their success. Were those narrower minds, uncluttered by the totality of being? If so, he envied them, for in his roundness he seemed to lose direction.

He had been too prolific, and maybe too promiscuous. They were one and the same, fecundity and its release; but then he did have to stop and ask himself, To what end? Profusion by itself was not something to boast of. Every old boar rutted his fill. Esme had done that for him, arrested the squandering and dissipation of himself in air. In loving one woman as opposed to loving women in general, he found the fixed point which had been missing in his focus up till then. She impressed on him the importance of a single objective, and that the highest. He recalled saying to her when they were sitting in the gallery that he didn't care for art enough to pursue it to the bitter end. Now he regretted voicing the sentence because of the paltry sentiment it contained. How right she was to turn on him for being content with the second rank of achieve-ment, but the more he distanced himself from the hollow core of the statement the more he was afraid that he had spoken an unwitting epitaph. His own words returned on him with a sagacity he hadn't meant at the time. And they were true. He took it all too easily. He rarely pushed himself to the point of pain, that refine-ment of patience, till the brain ached and the hand fell open in exhaustion. He'd worked hard, but only for acquisition, not for creation. What had he to show for a quarter of a century? One child, an occupation, a house, a contentious marriage. Hardly exceptional. Any middle-class banker had the same.

He looked at the note again and without further reflection put one word on a card and added his name. Yes. The affirmative. He would pursue it to the bitter end. He could make the conversion from failure to success even in his own terms, from the half to the whole-hearted if he wanted it enough. He was sure he was right. The last couple of years had been the penultimate phase, a clear-ance of old attitudes, a restocking of himself. Next was a huge push forward. Whatever it entailed, he did not think he was meant to accomplish it alone. He did not like living by himself and wanted more than the echo of his own footsteps down the corridor when he came indoors. Living in enmity was better than living alone. He was one of the men, cursed or blessed in it he wasn't certain, who needed woman. Woman was ingrained in his make-up as man was in Esme's. They were receptive to the other sex to an unusual degree. That was why they made an indelible imprint on each other, a stamp in fast dyes that would not fade or wear with time. She was vivid still. He felt the strongest need then to redeem this relationship, for itself, but also for the forward momentum it would bring. Other men at forty-five began again. Why not him? Pursue her then. If he wanted her as a companion he would have to go after her in person, instead of drawing back the way he did from participating in his own life. He calculated the days ahead and made himself a firm promise. If he hadn't heard by his birthday, he would go and intervene. He had to know, although he anticipated the shock his apparition would bring about on the far shore. Orpheus had done it, gone all the way to the Underworld to redeem his chosen woman. Charm the ferryman to transport him there and back, pacify Cerberus and the judges who sit in watch over the depths of Avernus. Plead with Pluto himself for redemption. But what talent did he have to persuade, like the power of Orpheus' lyre that 'made trees and mountain tops that freeze to bow themselves when he did sing', and even if he agreed, what condition might black Hades set on freedom? A child? A seasonal return to the winter solstice? Death would set a test. Looking backwards despondently to where she was, he had a premonition that, try his utmost, Eurydice might slip away for ever when he was on the point of reclaiming her from the shades of the dead and everlasting night.

The rooms were in chaos. One week to pack wasn't enough. The apartment seemed small until she started on the clearance, and discovered his belongings had made their way into every drawer and cupboard. Not that there were so many of them. He had acquired almost nothing personal in a year. He wore the same shoes, the same watch, and even these were issue. The main work was in his uniforms which had to be cleaned or pressed and in the complex retinue of shirts, winter, summer, dress shirts. Before she packed them she checked them over, sewing on buttons and mending tears with more diligence than she had exercised previously. He had to complain at least three times before anything was repaired and even then she often jettisoned it behind his back, thinking, He has plenty more or he can buy another from stores. What was the point in preserving something that had no value?

But his maps and papers and instruments seemed to have percolated into the oddest places because he didn't have his own work desk at home. She felt guilty about this in retrospect and said to herself, He must have a separate area for work in Trenton; and then looked up from her packing and sighed. What would he do? Not go back to living in the bachelor Mess, surely. And he wouldn't be eligible for a married quarter. So he would rent an apartment like this one and have rooms and rooms to spread himself without disturbance. There was so little, a trunk, a suitcase, some boxes crammed with papers, that it would all go into the sedan and didn't overflow into her supposed luggage for the follow up. This was the difficulty. Discreetly packing for herself, silently throwing away things neither of them would have use for unless they lived together. She couldn't use her record player in Britain because of different voltage and so she either had to go through very complex reasoning with him on why he should take it, or throw it out. She decided in the end to leave it behind when she did go, as a present to the Chantals' daughters.

Glancing round the mess she'd made she was dismayed that this was all it amounted to, sifting belongings. Packing up and moving on somewhere else. She was further depressed by the fact that there was no integration in their possessions. They held almost nothing conjointly so there wasn't a contest over ownership.

The only real winnowing came when she found the photographs of the wedding and christening. Mabon had commissioned the photographer most in demand at the Base. She'd had no say in it, didn't know they were being taken till the day and still felt surprised by their high gloss sheen and the way they'd been filed by someone else in chronological sequence in a white doeskin covered album, monogrammed with their initials and the boast, Our Wedding. The whole package appalled her. These moments she hadn't thought about for nearly a year, had effectively forgotten, perpetuated after all in the kind of self-adulation she had eschewed since she acquired sense. Pause by the door. The bride alone. The groom. The smile. Thank heavens they'd managed to avoid the kiss. What aberration of good taste had made the cameraman miss out on that? One in particular made her shudder. A close-up of their hands, newly joined with the ring in central focus. Some encircling wreath was made by flowers. This composition was a novelty to her and she assumed it was a local fad. It was horrific to see those two left hands overlaid in pseudo-union.

Well, there were some things about herself she still admired and could live with. She'd not once bared her teeth into that lens. She liked the grain of her suit and thought she'd done the right thing not making a bonbon from the outfit. But, oh dear – the day. What a mistake. What an unending, compromising mistake. After all this time she still looked for the missing faces. There was a layer behind the light sensitive paper which was capable of recording the surface only, and this remained unaffected by the immediate impression. She felt someone could highlight that layer, in the way infra-red rays were used to reveal the mutations of a painting before the artist changed his mind. The ghosts of what they might have been would show through, and did anyway to her eyes. The gestures they wished they'd made, faltering and so inevitably cancelled out by a stronger hand, made to conform to the overall design. Here and here, the cameraman said, I want you to stand just so. Please move over. I'd like you to close up that gap on the left. But underneath was the daguerreotype of pain, etched on the plate by long and slow exposure.

She turned to the more recent pictures of the christening. She wore the same suit and the same hat, though the ensemble was transformed by an apron of lace, the christening gown of the child in her arms, which fell about her like a double skirt. Her fears had been unfounded. Sophie was a model of infancy on the day. Like her father, she put on the best shows in public. Among all these, the most interesting faces belonged to the godfather and his wife. Esme tilted the emprints this way and that to the light, sitting back on her heels in the middle of the living room, which by now was strewn with crates and a heap of papers on their way into and out of boxes, according to some scheme he devised and she was to implement, by numbers. From whatever angle she viewed her cousin, Esme came to the same conclusion. Aileen had grown a veneer it was impossible to peel away. She looked identical in every one. A half smile like the Gioconda. The right foot placed to the instep of the left like a ballerina preparing for an intricate piece of toe work. So poised. So unnatural. Nothing could fracture her perfection. She remembered Aileen's more fragile moments, waiting for Rejean, making the first split, and felt she herself had done nothing to make them less brittle. She was a compounding factor in the hardness that began to set her cousin's features. In not

540

one of them was she standing beside her husband who looked, throughout, miserable and preoccupied. It was conspicuous at this distance that the pair who stood together, who came out of it looking confident were Aileen and Mabon. In fact in one of them, surely – no, the camera must lie.

Why did they seem unreal, making her reject them as false witness? When she got out the envelope with the old photographs her father sent they were strong and vital in comparison. Maybe there was a hasty, glamorising effect to colour whereas the monotint looked deep dyed and therefore unfading. She suspected she was dismissing them not for themselves, there was nothing intrinsically wrong with them or their subjects, but because of the antipathy she felt towards the two events they portrayed. Making a ceremony of it, too! When she looked at Rab's prints there was a rather plain and scrawny child but she was at least running, moving about, doing real things in real places not on stage settings. She might be wrong, of course. Maybe these make-up, mock-up collages would in time acquire the patina of truth. But she doubted it. Perhaps she was back at her contretemps between the modern and the old, but there was no way she wanted these as souvenirs.

Just one she rescued from the albums. One moment. Rejean and Bob caught in a background so takingly she had asked the photographer for a blow-up from the proofs he gave her to examine. A single flash as Bob hung down from the pegs of his shoulders and Rejean turned round to say something to him, deflecting the other's wit with a slanting smile. The two men, her friends, so patently amused each other, flipping words like coins to see how they would spin, that she had to keep a record. As for the rest, she never wanted to see them again and hurriedly rammed them underneath some of the other papers in his pile when she heard Mabon descend, two at a time, down the area steps.

'Nearly done?' He glanced around the conspicuous disarray.

'Not long to go.' Was that the time already? She was at the last tick of the clock again. Her heart seemed to implode, sending reverberations to her extremities when she realised he would drive off in an hour or two and she must have delivered her ultimatum by then. How was her mouth going to formulate the words? She knew she would stammer and become incoherent, lose ground in the argument because he had greater command of himself.

He leaned over her and picked up a photograph of his squadron, twenty men spaced out in a triangle on the tarmac with a Voodoo behind them closing the scene.

'Three of these pilots have been killed since that was taken,' he said without emotion. He tossed it negligently into the nearest box.

'I'm behindhand because the phone hasn't stopped ringing for you all afternoon.'

'Oh? Who was that?' In minutes he gathered up the boxes, stacked them to one side, and cleared the debris she had been labouring over all afternoon. That was why he was tidy. He kept the surface neat and didn't bother what was underneath.

'All sorts of people.'

'Esme, you really must get into the habit of making a note of who called. There is a pad and pencil there.'

'Yes, I know. I was busy with all this.' She detested the self-justification in her voice. He'd be better off with an answering machine. 'There was the accommodation officer at Trenton.'

'What did he say? I ought to be down for one of the MQs close to Base. You know the post is priority and we should have first call.'

'I didn't discuss it,' she prevaricated. Imagine living actually in a married quarter!

'And who else?'

'Oh, people. I don't know. All official. I told them you were at your presentation this afternoon and gave them the office number at Trenton. I said they could get you there from Monday. That's right, isn't it?' He nodded, mollified. 'I went up to see Madame for a while and didn't hear the phone once. It stopped just as I came back down.' He looked exasperated that she should waste his time with this pointless recital, and she concurred. He was making her nervous. 'How did the presentation go?'

He settled back, pleased with himself, and swivelled in the black chair. 'Oh, almost everyone came. Quite a turnout. I thought the speeches would never end. Everyone who was sober decided to get to his feet. They liked my speech of thanks.'

'Well, it should have been good. You worked on it all last week.'

'On and off.' He would much rather have given the impression that he delivered it off the cuff.

'You were a long time. Was there a lot of drinking?'

'Yes. More than usual. Being a Friday most people stayed later.'

'But you didn't? You've got to drive, you know.' His safety was not her real concern. Alcohol relaxed everything except the musculature of his loins. Not one more, she thought, not one more conjuring act.

'Well,' he grinned a little, 'a bit more than I should. I tell you what,' he added, changing tempo, 'Charles Cartier is leaving.'

'Where's he going?'

'The Ottawa job he was chasing. He'll be a defence chief before he's through.' He ground his teeth. 'Of course he had to announce it this afternoon.'

'When's that?' She went on laying the table, cooking the meal, thinking, Soon; soon I must say it.

'Next month.'

So they were beginning to move on, break up like an ice floe starting on its journey downriver. 'Is Yvonne pleased? I should think Ottawa is more her milieu.'

'I haven't seen Yvonne for months.' He paused. Spirits loosened him into confidentiality. 'I suspect she's having an affair with someone in Montreal. Bad, that, for the career. But at least he's not in the services.'

There was no adequate reply Esme could make so she let it pass. Yvonne was mortal after all!

He packed the car with his uniforms and the boxes until bit by bit the room returned to a normality which was hardly depleted by his removal. At the last he added the objects he had been presented with: a pewter tankard inscribed with his name and rank and the wooden shield which bore the emblem of the crossed Indian clubs. He was ready. There was nothing else.

They sat down to take their last dinner together by candlelight. Esme could barely steady her hand over her fork, not knowing which was the greater trap, to speak now or to be hounded later for not speaking. She could have deferred explanations even at this stage, excusing herself by saying she would write or phone – tomorrow; but she remembered that she promised Bob she would do it before he left and she would do it in person. He was the conscience prodding her thoughts. Mabon saw her jittery state and for once misread the prevailing wind.

He stretched out and stilled the left hand. 'Are you going to be OK on your own? You don't need to stay till the end of the month if you don't want to. I'll put pressure on for a quarter and you join me in a few days.'

She quaked so violently she had to put her glass down. It was clashing against her teeth. 'Would it matter to you? Would it matter if I didn't come to Trenton?'

He heard her in astonishment. 'But you've loathed living in the Saguenay. You must want a change.'

'Yes, I want a change. But not to Trenton.' She cupped and uncupped her hands. 'I don't want to stay here.'

He moved his hand to refill his glass. 'Let me get this straight. You're not staying in Arvida. You're not coming to Trenton. Where do you think you're going?'

She gestured loosely.

'Well, say it. Where?'

'I don't know yet.' If she said where she intended going, he might start on a reasoned attack on location, transport, access to the baby and it was better, she thought, to establish the principle of dereliction first rather than get herself tangled up with the small print of negotiations.

'I see. So heading somewhere specific matters less than not going where I'm going?' He heaved a sigh. 'Is this another one of your isolationist trends? Walking into the unknown? If so, I think we've had this conversation before. What do you think you're going to do in this place you haven't decided on?'

She took a mouthful of what was in her glass, but couldn't taste it. 'I'm going to live with someone else.'

'Ah. You won't come to Trenton because you think you're leaving me.' He was caught off balance, though he didn't show it. As a rule, he paid little attention to the shifts of a relationship; it was either on or off as far as he was concerned. He didn't believe her, but was diverted by the fact that she was sufficiently unhappy to make up a covering story for her disaffection. He was disappointed. He felt in their encounters there had been an improvement of late. Less open warring. He did not perceive this might imply more subterfuge. 'I must say I admire your timing. Or has cowardice prevailed until the last moment?'

She consented by silence.

'Tell me you're leaving me. Go on, say it. Tell me.'

'I'm leaving you.'

'But why?' When it was contorted by a question like this, his face became vulnerable. He forgot to make it handsome and therefore, in the way of human weakness, it became more sympathetic. That she caught the point of transition in his feelings alerted her to the fact that she did not hate him, could not hate anybody. She saw his point of view too clearly to exclude it from her reasoning. That was her trouble, really, and woman's. She saw and reflected everyone else's state of mind so deeply it inhibited the exercise of her own. She could not be single-minded. 'Have I mistreated you?' he persisted.

This was such an overwhelming question that no response would surface for some seconds. She struggled against tears and remorse, not wanting to inflict pain but appreciating the nuances of removal would be lost on him. 'No, I can't say that.'

'You came to my bed, you will recall.'

'Emphatically. How could I ever forget? It was the exercise of my free will.'

'Did I hesitate to marry you?'

'No,' she said dejectedly, forced to acknowledge that in the technical stages of their progress he had not been remiss. 'But perhaps you should have done. We are not alike. I can't say more.'

'We are not alike? Men and women generally are not alike.' She nodded vacantly in agreement. 'Who is alike?'

She could see this would lead into imponderables of whose union was successful and whose was not. 'Then we are too dissimilar. It would end in divorce sometime.'

Now she did infuriate him by handing out these abstract edicts as though they did not impinge on them personally. She managed to talk about them in the third person as if they weren't man and wife, sitting at the same table, working towards a decision which was implicitly, to his way of thinking, practical. Divorce. At one remove. Not as it touched them. He reflected bitterly on the account he would have to give to his new Commanding Officer of a separation, however temporary, until he could persuade Esme to change her mind. Persuade. Well, that was a big undertaking with Esme. He hadn't been too successful in persuading her to appear socially with him since the party at the lake, or in persuading her to his bed. It was she who changed tack. There was not one thing he could do to influence her acceptance or non-acceptance of him as a companion, or a lover, or a husband. He could appreciate how stern her independence of him was and knew his approach had been all wrong. 'Divorce! How can you talk about divorce when we haven't been married a year?'

'I know. I was persuaded against my better judgment. It really is my fault and I take all the blame.'

Once or twice she had seen him angry before, a spasm of rage against objects rather than people, which burned itself out almost immediately in some constructive action. But there was none to hand here. She couldn't be re-organised or re-scheduled or explained away. She was an indelible stain on his record, the flaw which it was impossible to hide.

'That makes it a whole lot easier, doesn't it? You try to keep the plane in the air, you know. You don't say whose fault it is when it crashes. We have a marriage. We have a child. You are destroying them.'

'Yes, I take that point. What I am doing is very destructive to you. But I can't go on living with you. That's too destructive to me.'

He moved ground, saying, 'You can't abduct the child. I'll stop you.'

This was the one area Esme was crisp on. She had worked out her argument in relation to the baby, although she instantly forgot what she was going to say under the pressures of the moment. But her emphasis remained. 'Oh Mabon, she doesn't even matter to you. In three months you haven't once gone into that room to pick her up or look at her. You aren't interested. Don't be so mean-hearted. What kind of man would say he'd use my child to restrain me and make me more unhappy still? It's failed. I'm sorry, I don't want to fail, but it has failed.'

His silence conceded that he had not shown due interest in paternity. He stood up, too resentful of the facts and their presentation to sit passively any longer. He walked backwards and forwards apparently attending to things, making coffee, putting his travel documents by his greatcoat, but performing them through the screen of her recalcitrance, her imperviousness to persuasion, physical or mental. If he could kiss her or take her to bed he could change her mind, though he began to know the particular feel of her obduracy when she opposed his will. She could defy him so secretly; even under compulsion doing what he wanted, she could defy him in a corner of her mind.

She did not understand the complications she threw him into. Every aspect of his service life was governed by the fact that he was married and supported a wife and child. His salary scales were adjusted accordingly. His travel arrangements and payment for removal of household effects, the very mileage allowance he was permitted to claim took account of her. This change in status, which was enormously complex to him, she imagined she could reverse idly, on a whim of homesickness or lovesickness.

Love. That too. He couldn't ignore it. There was the unaccountable pain of her withdrawal from him. Esme was skilled in the giving of pain as much as devastating pleasure. That blend must testify something to her power over him, but admitting it was like admitting weakness. To confide the secret to Delilah was giving away the source of his own strength, which was indifference. She could shear him at any time. The words, which he hadn't spoken to her or to any other woman before her, struggled up for expression; he couldn't help thinking they belittled him for they were the token of need and so the tone of voice that accompanied his utterance, full of loathing, denied its message.

'I love you. Does that matter?' He went up to her and tried to touch her, tried to reason with her using the most powerful argument he knew, the body.

She was aghast. The signs had not been awry. He cared, obliquely and hurtfully, but he cared. 'Don't mock me. How can you love me when you do not know me?'

'I do love you.' They were not so hard after all, could become a habit if one said them often enough.

She felt repelled by the statement and by the hand that made a caress, offered at this stage as a bribe she was meant to find irresistible. She flinched away from the responsibility they imposed. 'Don't use those words to me. They are not for you and I don't want to hear them from you. You are poaching. That is someone else's territory and you have no idea what they would mean if he said them.'

His face changed. He stood rejected. He! Rejected, and by the woman he had elevated first by marriage and then by the discovery that she mattered. It needed an adaptable mind to perceive that the reverse order might have been more useful. And who might speak the words with meaning? He wondered what eloquence the other man had that eluded him, feeling helpless in the sphere of words, but it was an impotence that enraged him because he did not respect the values of oratory. 'You mean it, then? There is someone else?'

Esme realised she had made a cardinal error. He had thought it was a blind, and she saw he would hound her until she told him a name he could then use as an instrument of torture. She should have lied.

'Who is it? Someone here, someone I know?' He racked his brain but she hadn't met anyone likely in the last few months. She had lived inside these walls and alone, with no visitors.

She was startled by the almost ludicrous assumption that she might have a fling with a fellow officer and shook her head.

'I will know. You're not going to make a fool of me by trailing after some guy and then crawling to be taken back.'

'You flatter yourself. After this evening, you will not see me again.'

He was even more offended by this cool persistence and pushed the remains of the table setting away. 'Who is it? I do have the right to know that.'

She sat dumbly miserable. Rights. Well, yes. Rights. She tended to give way on those. 'Someone I've known for a long time. No one here. Not in the Air Force.'

He stood by the door, for nothing more detained him. He saw the words 'Trenton, Ontario' on the top of his warrant and the pass which would give admittance to the Base. They were duplicates of two he had the year before, just at this time when he was away on the jet training course and Rejean was taken ill to L'Hôtel Dieu St Vallier in Chicoutimi. Why was the other so conveniently in Arvida when he was absent? He remembered all the other times Esme had been inexplicably busy at weekends before and after the night of the storm that closed the Base, and them in it. Aileen in Scotland. The field clear. He thought back to see if there was some special regard between them, his wife and his friend. His mind went further back than the hand-holding episode in the garden which he dismissed as puppy stuff.

Then it came back to him that Esme said on their first evening together that she had run away from someone but he followed her and would not go away. He took her literally. He remembered too that Rejean and Aileen were due back in Montreal in the next few days. Was there a coincidence in timing? Was that why she didn't know where she was going, because she would be continent-hopping with the migrant?

'Does Rejean know you intend to leave me?'

To Esme this came as a non-sequitur. Her brow contracted in what looked like guilt. 'He knows I've been mistaken in the marriage.'

Why did she say 'mistaken'? Wasn't the mistake in the baby which had propelled them into it? The marriage was the remedy for that ill, or were the two separable after all? And then he had it. The flash of inspiration. He had sensed it all along. He would have felt warmer to his own child. The cool nature of his response was corroborating proof. Rejean adulated the child. The man hadn't spent time acting as nursemaid for nothing. She was his. 'How unfortunate he was already provided with a wife and couldn't give his own name to the child.'

Esme opened her mouth to refute the lie and then was stilled. It could be her escape route. Blame the wrong man, make the wrong inference and she might get clear with less turmoil than if she tried to explain the nebulous. She saw how perfectly it fell into place and admiring the complex fusion of falsehood and reality was dumbfounded. She could not have invented a better alibi and five minutes earlier it had not entered her head. She was too bemused by the conflicting emotions of their argument to see that when she did lie, or allow a falsehood to stand, it was in the way likely to be most injurious to him. And to her.

He was driven to extremes by the pain of the deceit. He dipped back into some earlier time of certainty and the old word came to him. Cuckolded. Cheated in the age-old way and with a child foisted on him, too. The child did not matter to him indeed! How should she matter? He had been the fall guy, on whom Esme and Rejean carried out an elaborate deception they could not unfortunately sustain. He thought back to the congratulations he had received from his fellow officers, the cigars burned in honour of his quite fictitious fatherhood, and knew sickeningly how they would laugh at him behind his back when it came out. There was no means of hiding personal disaster, given the intimacy in which they lived and worked. Someone always knew someone else. He saw the jeering faces in the Mess, the snicker of sympathy. And he would have sneered at the predicament too – if it were someone else's. What explanations would be wrung from him and passed on all the rest of his working life, preceding him from station to station? He heard the variants they practised on his name to make a handy introduction for new members of his squadron. How could he order the men under his command when they had such knowledge of his weaknesses? Graffiti. Jokes, halted mid-air when he entered. He winced. He couldn't bear to be seen to lose at anything. He would never make it to the top now.

'And who was it decided on the restriction of intimacies, you or him?' His voice was steel and cut through her. Esme's blood ran cold. A degree of bravura would have stood her in good stead, but she did still regard the personal as intensely personal. She couldn't outface him and say, Yes, it was all done to calculations, but found equally inaccessible the expression of what was gentle and tender born in her regard for him. 'Who denoted which parts of you I can and cannot have? Just so much and no more. You servicing whore. Tell me what I've paid for so I make sure I get good value.'

'Such hard words you give me. I am not sure I deserve them. I have tried to be fair and I promise you,' she said, 'I have not cheated you.'

He did not hear her, did not care, was beyond reason. 'Those virginal ways you practised. I nearly came to believe in them.' He was bitter with self-delusion and spat out the words to rid himself of their taste.

Esme read his expression correctly. He would not be diverted from his revenge, no matter what she said. He was going to punish her one way or another. It was coming. He seized her from the chair where she had sat throughout the interview, and shook her by the shoulders till she was speechless and her head rattled and her spinal column creaked. Then, as she went limp, he pushed her away again disgustedly. In vertigo, she staggered back against the chair and prevented herself from falling by stretching out her hand on it to steady her balance. He hardly saw her. He took a step away, then turned back, thoughts furiously racing. His best man! Even on the day of the wedding they were tête-à-tête on the verandah, deep in some secrecy. He remembered her abjectness in Quebec in spite of all he did to entertain her. Yes, no doubt she wished herself elsewhere and in another embrace.

She did not know what she could do. Seeing his features blacken, she took the measure of his uncontrollable rage. She was reminded of Don Gesualdo, Prince of Venosa, whose killing of his wife and her lover was the most notorious crime of his generation. In cold blood he ordered their infant to be hung in a cradle from the palace ceiling and rocked violently until it 'rendered up its innocent soul to God'. Marie Hamilton's crime seemed more humane and more driven.

'Please, whatever you do,' she begged, 'please don't harm my child.' This sounded like permission to harm her. She had no resources. She was easy to kill, had no dodges, no power of escape. She could cower and hide from him, protecting her head from whatever blows he might rain, be kicked and scuffed under the furniture. But she wasn't going to do that, go like a badger down a hole, worried by dogs and brought out piecemeal, yelping. However he might assault her, he would look into her eyes while he did it. There weren't many of her countrymen at Flodden, Solway Moss or Culloden Moor who died with wounds behind. Pitchforks and ploughshares were no match against the cannon, but bravery might bridge the gap and make them heroes yet. She couldn't fight but she could die well.

She collected herself and stood up straight, although she jarred in every nerve. She told herself it didn't really matter if she lost her life. She was one quite inconsequential thread in the entire fabric, a step out of the dance, a single bird from the flock. The cycles would continue without her. She wished there was someone to call to her aid, but there was no one. Never was. Never would be.

'Tell me the truth,' he panted, and she was warned that he was running out of control.

'I don't know what kind of truth you would understand.'

His temper snapped when she could give no simple answers but tricked and eluded him with words. The beauty in her seemed a subtle cheat, a form of decoy below which a snare lurked ready to trap him. Being caught in it made him want to stamp on the device.

With the flat of his hand he struck her once across the face. His hundred and eighty pounds to her hundred and twenty told in his favour, heavy to featherweight. He had the pleasure of producing an instantaneous result. The marks of his fingers were imprinted like ridges, a kind of living fossil on her cheek. Again, before she had time to recover from this and stand up, he caught her a glancing blow on the rebound with the back of his hand which made his knuckles crack. Under the impact of this jolt below her jawline, she reeled and fell back. She didn't utter a sound. He wouldn't wring a single cry from her or a single tear to streak her face. Slipping and falling backwards, because she did nothing to save herself, she caught her head on the corner of the table. There was a rending pain. Her head split open and a fountain spurted from it. She heard something fall. And it was her. Before she reached the ground, in the half second between being conscious and unconscious, she recalled a thousand incidents the way people are said to do before they die. She remembered being told that pilots executing an air roll could catch their brain, which was no more than a soft jelly, in the curvature at the back of the skull. All the things they knew and all the things they might have known came to an end in one instant, for the head was quite weak after all in spite of its helmet of protection, when it was subjected to this violent internal collision.

But before she blacked out she gave a valedictory glance to all that was good. She remembered the important moments of conviction. She clung to them. They were all there was to go on. She remembered another man and another place, too fleetingly to specify, but winged her way to them extra-terrestrially.

51

Rejean came back and sat down again at the dinner table.

'Still no reply?' Claire asked.

'No, I can't understand it,' he said frowning. 'It's either engaged or there's no answer. Which is unreasonable. They must either be there or not there. When did you say they were moving?'

His mother held up her serving while she explained for the third time. 'My dear, all I know –'

'Claire, we know what you know. Now could we eat and Rejean can call again later.' Maurice noticed Aileen's edginess every time her husband went to the telephone and tried to divert what he was sure was the result of travel fatigue. 'Now, how's this house coming along? Tell me what improvements you've made this winter.'

Rejean sat impatiently through her catalogue of inefficiencies by other people, plumbers, paper-hangers, carpenters, impinging finally on his own that he wasn't a master craftsman as well as the man who just paid for it all. He'd had his opinion consulted and ignored so many times about swatches of wallpaper and curtaining that he was pervasively tired of property and the bonds of owner- ship and began to recant on his decision to add another millstone in Montreal. She threatened him with a whole week of estate agents.

Before dessert he excused himself and went away to the study. The number he knew by heart, and dialled rapidly. But it rang and rang and rang and he roundly cursed the invention when it wouldn't give back the reply he wanted. No babysitter, even. Where would all three have gone to at this hour? He put the receiver down and, pausing at the door, thought he couldn't face the trouble with the damp course at Inverleith just yet.

He opened the window and stepped out into the evening air. Patches of snow clung on in corners of the garden but it was a sheltered plot, south-facing on a hill and notable for the early flowering of its varieties, compared with gardens as little as half a mile away. He loved this garden more than any other because he'd had a hand in it. It gave unstinting welcome when he returned and was perhaps the one vital proof to him that the time he spent away was not completely lost. Things went on happening whether he was there or not. He was humble enough to find this a consoling feature. In his absence the leaves had dropped and formed their humus on the soil. He stooped and lifted it. Underneath the winter debris the shoots began again, bleached and sun-starved but full of vigour. He trusted that recurrence, patting the warm layer back into place again.

He walked down the slope, cut into by the stone steps. Spot- lights shone from the house above, illuminating his way so that the route of his perambulation was marked by choice, not by hesi- tancy. He stopped. He admired. He breathed in. The damp air was an inspiration, coating his lungs with the dew of home.

All round him the trees grew up. Some were established, dating from before the building of the house, but most of them he'd planted personally to see how they would take. He'd thrown them in without trying to adjust the soil, acid, alkaline, lime or peat, and miraculously they came up and repaid his effort a hundredfold. There was a carob tree from the Mediterranean, eucalyptus, palm, the miniature maples, magnolia grandiflora and more, grown for the interest of their bark or leaves. There were some casualties but the things he had experimented with when he was twenty came to fruition. Plants which were more tender than the climate allowed, according to standards of horticulture, seemed to thrive in this corner and passers-by in front of the house often slowed down or stopped to admire the novelty of his arrangement against the graduated hillside. He effected some strange pairings: a broad smooth leaf against one with fine dentation, blue on green foliage, horizontalis breaking the line of a columnar evergreen. In fifty years it would be a showpiece, an oasis of the exotic surrounded by the mundane.

Well, he thought, a garden. That's to my credit. He went on, wrapping himself warmly in recollection of the book, now lying ready crated in a warehouse for dispersal to the four winds. If he were to die tomorrow, he had those. One garden. One book. Who does more? Their progress had been very similar, negligently conceived, maybe even executed in haste – but revised, pruned, shaped time and time again, so that he had to acknowledge they invaded his other activities, more powerful as they grew and most important of all in retrospect. He turned on his heel and took in the whole view, trees, garden, street, city and river, muted as it was by dusk and the blue of artificial light.

In the middle of this benign aura of oneness with himself, thoughts of the woman rose unconsciously to mind, though they were quelled almost at once by anxiety that she did not answer his call, and the perverse annoyance that she was not where he expected her to be at that time, did not conform to his projections. He tried to feel out into space to guess at the spot she occupied, stood on damp stones and willed himself upwards and outwards through the filter of boughs into the unknown regions of the life she lived to herself. It was idiotic to feel she should suspend her activity on the off chance of talking along a telephone wire to him, but all the same he felt it and felt grieved that his impulse to communicate his arrival on home soil to her the moment he touched it was not reciprocated.

He walked down the steps to a dell of silver-leaved specimens which in a few weeks would be carpeted with the blue flowers, scyllae, the grape hyacinth and the open star shapes of anemone blandula. Why blandula? Pale and washed out, like animula vagula. Sad little flowers he found them, tinged with the AI of alas.

It wasn't much he asked, reverting to his prior interest, just to be acknowledged, to be thought about and anticipated. He thought of her, directly or indirectly, a dozen times a day. Not lustfully, although on odd occasions he found himself remembering the turn of her ankle, or how in reading she caught a piece of hair and twisted it into a loop. But these were only symbols by which he knew her. Where her foot tended, what her mind thought in perusal took him into the realm of conjecture – nothing more substantial.

He did sometimes wonder if being excluded from Esme's affection, or that share of it he once aspired to, gave him the most complete insight into her character. He had so little to go on that moments assumed monumental importance. He had to re-live details, projecting outwards from the part to the whole, and focus on such fragments of personality that he did feel he knew her better than anyone else. Not by familiarity but by concentration, the way an archaeologist who tries to reconstruct a vase from a square of pottery shard knows that vase more comprehensively than one that comes to him intact. Understanding involved hours of puzzlement. A vanity, was that, a sop to pride? No, he was convinced that their type of friendship was more knowing than love. Was that it? He corrected himself again. Love denied was a more complete form of knowledge than love gratified. It went on. It went on being; missing its objective it became perpetual.

The stars set, tracing an orbit over his head. He waited, wishing that the naked eye could see them actually move, but knew the wait was futile, like watching the hands of a clock – you always blinked at the point of transition and missed it. Thinking of Esme, he remembered that Dante said 'Possession is one with loss'. When you have something in your grasp, you lose it by making it commonplace. That seemed to be what he was driving towards himself, but he was not pleased with such tragic negativism that appeared to turn happiness to ashes and made man into a petulant child in quest of the new, never satisfied. If he turned it on its head, he found he was more nearly content with the statement, Loss is one with possession. Yes, that was more affirmative; it redeemed a little from hopelessness. He knew most intimately the states from which he was excluded: love of a peer, having a child, being beloved by one's father, reaching home. He dwelt on these quarterings of the global situation with a passionate intensity which the happy man could not bring to bear on fulfilment. Yearning carried to these lengths became almost its own consolation.

Though this contentment with the abstruse was denied as soon as he heard, reaching the top of the stone steps, the telephone ringing in the study and he hurried forward to the French window with an eagerness that belied any passive acceptance of what was meted out to him. He hoped, still, and knew his own logic was a lie.

Somewhere a child cried. Down a corridor. A long, long corridor. So far away that she could hardly hear it, a faint cry. Someone turned the volume up. It became imperative. A life cry. It was the cry of a human wanting succour, afraid that life was terminal. Her body responded to it, but oh so slowly. It was night. Or was it dark only in her head? She could see nothing and when she tried to move she realised she could feel nothing either. Her legs were a mile away from what controlled them. Her head, raised up from the floor, refused to make contact with the rest. She knew she had survived, but by how small a margin she could not guess. She moved a hand to steady herself as she sat up and it pulled damply on something sticky. She rubbed her fingers together. Blood. It was her own blood. She bowed her head and remembered, afraid that he was still here, waiting for her to come to. But his coat had gone from the doorway. He had left her to it.

The child went on crying and Esme was impelled to struggle to her feet. Its need was greater. She stood as a bear does, from all fours. She was afraid. She knew she was damaged. Spots, black spots, coloured flashes, a whole borealis of patterns rose and set before her eyes. She was too afraid to touch the wound and told herself she must go and attend to the child first. She would have to suspend herself for a little longer.

She dragged herself through to the bedroom. How much blood had she lost? How long had she been unconscious? She picked the baby up from the cot and was glad of the snuffling warmth, overheated by crying, for she herself was chilled to the bone. The crying might have gone on for hours. Madame must have wondered why. She was relieved that the woman had not come to investigate and found her slumped. She staggered back to the living room, her head swimming, but did not put the light on yet because it might reveal the depth of blackness in her head. She sat on the settee and fed the baby. All energy drained from her. Movement was exhausting. She seemed to hit on a vacant area in her brain every so often, a black hole of outer space, and lost contact with how long or where. Time had disappeard down the vortex. It was truly dark, she established with adjusted eyes, but it could have been the darkness of evening or the middle night. The impressions in her head reverberated without her being able to put them in order.

Tentatively she switched on the softest light in the apartment, that in the hall which gently illuminated all the rooms without further glaring addition. It did not cause too much pain to her dilating pupils, striking her as grey as if she saw it through an army blanket. With great labour she attended to the baby, who wriggled and gurgled and squirmed in a liveliness quite beyond her resources to restrain, far less enjoy. She did the same thing two or three times over, folding and unfolding, pinning and unpinning in a daze.

This done, she went to run herself a bath and was sickened at the sight of herself however dimly lit in the mirror. It took her back to the day of the vat dyeing when she had been stained and spattered with the shades that lived in Alexis' vials. This was the colour he had aimed at, a good blood red, spotting her face, her neck, her clothing almost to the waist. She touched her head fractionally and drew her hand away again, terrified of the gel that oozed from her. She trembled. Why should she not tremble when her life leaked from her? She dared not put her head in the water but sponged her hair on either side of it, grateful for its dense profusion that might have softened the impact of the table's edge.

Lying comforted by the hydrotherapy, she tried to recall the sequence of events since she came to. She had seen to the baby, but she thought she had phoned Montreal at one point, assessing her own need for help as critical. She had dismissed the much readier assistance Bob Findlay would supply because she did not want to implicate him in Mabon's offence, whether criminal or moral, or in her own.

She seemed to remember dialling instinctively, her SOS, and hearing a familiar voice in answer against a background of music and normality at the other end.

'Rejean? It's Esme. I didn't know for certain if you were back.'

'Yesterday. I've been phoning you during the day but you were always engaged. So I gave up and was going to try after dinner. How are you?'

'Alive. That's something to be going on with.'

'What's happened?' He grew tense.

'Can you come? I don't know what time it is but –'

'It's almost nine. I'll be there by midnight. Do you want Claire or Aileen to come with me?'

'No. Just you.'

'I'm leaving now.' And he put the receiver down.

Had she done it in reality, or was it like the imagined rain, a projection of what she wished to happen? She tried to test it, the way one tests a dream on waking, and decided it was truth not invention. It contained the concrete fact of his arrival the day before, and substantiation of the telephone being busy because it had indeed been ringing all day. She could not have invented such circumstantial detail in her present state.

So he would be here – soon. She must hurry to dress. And then she remembered the pool of blood by the table. She could not let him see that, far less clear it up. Groaning that demands of alacrity should be made on her, she dried herself and half dressed. With infinite labour she found a pail and filled it with water and carried it to the spot and knelt and washed and squeezed and washed and squeezed until she could do no more. It was nauseous to make contact with the stuff on her clean hands. And after all her scouring something remained. The wooden surface of the floor had absorbed a modicum of her, a trace element that a forensic scientist could collect and establish as her blood type. Tomorrow she would have to bleach it out; or would it be like the stain of Rizzio, a recurring offence? She might almost think so, going back into the bathroom, for she had forgotten in her haste to clear up one mess, to empty the bath water. Surely a Roman senator had slashed his wrists in it and let his life seep away out of his veins. She pulled the plug quickly, averting her eyes from the evidence of her own fragility caused by so much loss. How much of her remained? She could not tell.

Rejean came in, tumbling down the steps with as much anxiety as the evening of his first drive from Montreal when it was he who was ill. The scene he opened the door on, unannounced, was not worse than he had imagined second time around. He put the main light on and found the table laid for two, a meal of half-eaten food abandoned mid-course. The candles in their holders had burned down while she was unconscious and melted at the end, so that a pool of cold wax had set on the surface. The thing explained itself, a tableau on a stage where an assembly of props at the end of an act demonstrated the sweep of events, even though the actors themselves had gone into the wings.

He went through to the bedroom and found her curled up in a ball. They put their arms round each other. 'I can imagine. You don't need to tell me.'

'Oh, Rejean,' she rolled closer into the comforting body, 'don't I make a mess of everything. Other people have such clean and tidy lives.'

'Now none of that. Let me look at you. He's gone, has he?'

'Yes, you probably passed him at some point.'

He looked at the wound and looked away. 'How could he leave you like that?'

'I don't think he knew. I fell against the table and passed out.'

'That was very unlucky.'

She sat up and in all seriousness said, 'Don't you believe it. If I hadn't been unconscious, he'd have beaten me to death.'

He paled at the idea of physical violence. 'You don't mean that.'

'I do. He'd gone beyond the point of knowing his own strength. The disgrace my leaving him would bring was too unbearable and he'd rather have killed me and been tried. It was more manly than having your wife leave you for someone else. Falling and cutting my head was the luckiest thing that ever happened to me.'

'You know it'll need treatment?'

She lay back tired again after the effort of speaking. Words fluttered away from her tongue as she tried to capture them. She wanted to sleep. 'Tomorrow.' She closed her eyes.

'No. Now. I'll have to take you to the casualty department at Chicoutimi.'

'I don't want to move.'

'Are you feeling sluggish?'

'Wouldn't you?'

'You may need a transfusion. And the head needs sutures, I think.'

'Stitches? Not in the scalp, surely?'

'They have alternatives nowadays. But I can't take the responsibility because I don't know. You must see a professional. I'm not trying to alarm you. I want you to see that it's essential you come, now.'

She resigned herself and found her coat while he lifted the baby out of her sleep and wrapped her against the night air. 'We'll have to have a story,' she said in the car. 'Say I fainted and fell.'

'How cautious you are.'

'Oh, the first thing they'll ask is how I did it. Who are you going to be, by the way?'

'Not your husband. I might be cast in the role of wife beater and that doesn't agree with me very well.'

Night was almost indistinguishable from day in L'Hôtel Dieu. The sick and the dying did not choose social hours in which to be sick or die, so that the critical period between midnight and three in the morning had a transitory feel as the day brought life or death to a climax. They were almost the only out-patients, however, and this time Esme received the attention commensurate with her condition. Nuns walked beside her as she was pushed by an auxiliary in a wheelchair down vacant corridors to a nursing room where a young duty doctor examined her with suspicion. He obviously did not believe her story for a second since he felt her jaw, prodded its incipient bruises, touched down the length of her spine, looked at her teeth and the inside of her mouth.

He gave her several opportunities to come up with the truth but she resisted each time. Eventually he sent the nurse away on a pretext before saying, resting on the edge of his desk, 'You've been forcibly struck by a man considerably heavier than yourself. Whoever he is, you could bring charges of assault.'

She felt the screens of privacy being dragged away. 'No, I can't do that.'

'Your husband? Not the man who came with you.'

'No, not this man.'

He shrugged. Such domestic incidents were ugly, and fortunately rare in this area. But he had served his freshman's year in an American city known for the violence of its street life. He knew the score. He was impatient when women did not prosecute since he regarded rape and battery as primarily medical conditions of abuse, and overlooked the emotional trauma involved in giving evidence, of admitting oneself brutalised, especially by a man on whom the victim was dependent. Besides, it was a poor defending

560

counsel who did not try to prove she had asked for it.

'It's up to you. I will put my conclusions on record in case you change your mind.'

'It would be the end of his career.'

'That matters more than your life?'

The fact that she almost accepted the equation showed her how warped her values had become. 'To him, yes. I'm leaving. It's not important now.'

He hesitated. 'I'm letting you go home tonight because you have someone with you. But I want you back at nine o'clock tomorrow morning for an encephalograph and by then we will have the result of these tests. I want you to watch in particular for signs of excessive drowsiness for a period of time, up to a week from now.'

'Concussion?'

'Yes. I would prefer if you were not alone. Will your friend stay?'

'If I ask, yes.'

She was demoralised by his briskness, from which she inferred a professional annoyance that she could come cluttering up the neat corridors with her human mess.

In the morning, after some sleep on both sides, they were less restive with each other. He took considerable time to explain her X-rays, the straying pulse of her brain scan – was that the shape of thought then, after all no more exciting than a child's doodle? – and monitored the blood transfusion personally.

He did not see many English women here, and no Scots, so he found himself liking the way she spoke in strange inflexions, the wryness with which she put them both down laughingly, in spite of everything retaining humour. He was perilously close to straying beyond his brief and asking the outright question, Why? What kind of man would lift his hand to her, and in what circumstances? By default he spent some time with Rejean and got no further than finding him ascetic, maybe academic and not, he thought with the glib assumptions of the young, her type.

Intrigued by the possible combinations of man, woman and child together with the shadow of the external man, he took a chance and looked them up in the hospital's records. To some extent he was rewarded by finding Flight Lieutenant Caulderwood named as the father, though the man had no record of his own.

And yet how the other man, the asthma sufferer, accompanied to hospital the year before by the woman in exactly the way that he accompanied her now, how he cared for that child! Carried her everywhere with him, did not resign his commission to a nurse, invariably patient while she slept or woke. The baby treated him as a familiar, too, though she had come into the age of recognising strangers, and shrank from his own friendly gestures. How interested would he have been to discover there was a third name on file he could have consulted, the name of Stefan Roberval and the date of his admission, together with the date he died and the cause of death. Would his treatment of Esme have been any different if he had known this was her father? Might he have thought it a genetic lead he should follow up, and taken another test or added a rider? Possibly not.

The records carried him no deeper then, but rounded out his surmises. He never forgot them. Hearing their names again some time later, when their books came his way, he knew exactly who they were and plotted the chart of their progress from afar.

Rejean slept beside her. There seemed no point in preventing the basic comfort of companionship, so they didn't even discuss it. He was terrified that in the night she might slip away from him, as he had nearly done from her. He couldn't leave her alone.

'What did you tell them in Montreal before you came away?' she asked, curled into his side when they awoke. She began to connect again with the wider sphere and remembered there were other people who wanted to know what they were doing together.

'That there had been an accident. I phoned later on and said to Aileen it was complicated. Mabon had left and I would have to wait till you were better. Nothing more. They don't need to know if you would prefer it.'

She frowned. 'No, I'm not worried about that. Did you have to say he wasn't here?'

'There was no point in my being here otherwise.' Reluctantly he added, 'I'm supposed to be launching my book. It had to be a good reason to make me delay that.'

She was dismayed by her own self-absorption. 'Oh Rejean, you must think me so selfish. I use you all the time. I even used you against Mabon and now I'm afraid it'll make trouble for you in the future.'

'I've leaned on you in my time. It's your turn. But why do you think it'll make trouble?'

'When I told him I wanted to break away – oh, how I wish I hadn't told him but gone and done it. Fait accompli. Well, he knew it was for someone else and jumped to the conclusion it was you, and that you were Sophie's father. I know, it's hard to reason that away. I didn't hurry to disillusion him. But I think I may have done you a great disservice in letting the lie stand.'

'And yourself.'

'I know the truth. Aileen and the others don't. He could write, or harbour it.'

'I don't think it'll matter, unless you're going to see him again.'

'No. He's moved on and I won't see him again.'

'So what will you do?'

'Go back to Alexis, of course. That was always set, with or without Mabon, with or without Mairi.'

'You're sure?'

'Without a single doubt.'

Compelled himself to regard it as inevitable, he said, 'Alexis gave me an envelope for you. He didn't want to send anything in case it made matters difficult for you with Mabon. Shall I get it?' He went and found his wallet and brought it back to bed, letting a little more light in under the blind for her to read by.

It was a plain, sealed envelope which was an unnecessary precaution. Rejean would never have looked inside, and what he wrote was readable by anyone. A single sheet emerged on which he had written.

For lo! The winter is past
The rain is over and gone
The flowers appear on the earth
And the time of the singing of the birds has come.

She smiled at the gentle cliché. Her knowledge of the words went back into the twilight of unconsciousness. Was there ever a time when she had not known them? They were as old as thought. Intoned at Sunday School in the church hall opposite the house, dusty skirted on the floor, met again in Antonia Ridge's *Family Album* which Rhona read aloud to her at night before she fell asleep in the back bedroom where she made half love to Alexis, then analysed methodically for what they were in Religious Knowledge, spiritual love of the church. She would keep meeting them round the corners of her life. That was why he had chosen them, to reinforce the familiar: to couch the direct appeal of man to woman in what was indirectly irresistible between them, the language of poetry.

She passed it to Rejean. 'Was there ever a more two-handed invitation? What a reluctant lover I have. He always leaves it up to me.'

'How wise of him.' He hid his regret that such tactics had not worked for him. 'When will you go?'

'At once. I want you to do something for me tomorrow, if you're going to the Port Alfred office. There's a cargo boat sails from the quay there to Avonmouth, in England. I want you to ask if they'll take a passenger, as an exception if need be. Plead my case. I don't care how much it costs, or how unlavish the berth.'

'But you'd be so much better to fly.'

'I'll never sit in another plane as long as I live. I want to go home by sea. It matters to me, it really does. And I shall take the car and my books and the records and all the baby things.' She had a mental image of the sledge used for tobogganing on the slopes behind Inchcombe and hurried towards it, impatient of delay. 'Everything can be packed inside the car. Will you ask for me?'

'Of course.' He conceded that in spite of her nature, her lack of preparedness, she was learning something. Eccentric, always, but to a purpose.

'I want to go on the first boat out. Is the river thawing?'

'Yes. The ice-breakers have been up. It's been a short winter.'

The line operator was reluctant to take her, and the local agent insisted on telephoning to the head office in Montreal, where fortunately the manager was known to Maurice and very distantly to Rejean. He was more sympathetic and agreed to take her, provided she and the child were covered independently by an insurance policy, the safety of passengers being outwith the scope of their shipping contract.

Aileen was irritated by her husband's protracted attendance in the Saguenay and summoned him home; the fact that he refused, quite pleasantly, to do so or to give a full explanation about Esme and what she was doing was further evidence of the limitation of her

564

own influence over him. She put the phone down in the hall and walked over the echoing parquet to the study where Claire sat alone embroidering a hanging in petit point.

Aileen dropped neatly into a fireside chair but could not settle. She crossed and uncrossed her legs. She picked up a book and shut it again. 'Do you think it is quite – right – for them to be alone there together?'

Claire looked up from her needlework, surprised. 'My dear, they are brother and sister.'

'More like brother and sister-in-law, I would have said. There is a difference.'

Claire gave it her consideration, which was short-lived. It had not struck her as other than natural that her son and Esme were friends. Everyone liked Rejean. Why shouldn't she? But she admitted after all he might be a man as well as her son, that he might have a life beyond that which she ascribed to him, though to the anxious face she said calmly, 'Nonsense. You make these things happen by imagining them.'

Esme telegraphed to Alexis: COMING BY SEA. DO NOT LOOK FOR ME BEFORE I ARRIVE.

52

Rejean waited till the day of the sailing. The weather was propitious, and he saw her aboard unceremoniously within a week. The car was strapped to the deck to brave five days of Atlantic spray. Its removal was not a step he approved of unconditionally, foreseeing the problems more than she did, but he could run two cars, left and right-handed, one for each continent.

'You realise you'll be forever driving on the wrong side of the road?'

'Typical, isn't it? What am I going to do? Throw it overboard?'

He lounged over the rail, watching the break-up of the ice floe in the mid-stream waters which threaded a path below the buttress rocks of Eternité and Trinité to the open sea. It beckoned. It was a long time since he had been on the ocean, and flying over it five times in eighteen months gave not the slightest hint of the effect of being on it or in it and adrift. To fly was only to pass time; to sail was to experience.

'I wish I were coming with you.'

'You don't really. You're going back to all the business of the book launch and Montreal again, your friends and Aileen. Besides,' she added as he looked doubtful at this catalogue of pleasures, 'you've only just left the UK.'

He did not point out to her that the journey to and fro was not what he had meant. He wanted to go with her and her child. Or did she deliberately side-step the issue of his emotional interaction with her? Ignoring it made it less, in her eyes. If she said, Travel back with me, for fun, for devilment, just to be near, he would have wired to Montreal and gone. He was discovering the excitement of her waywardness. It had no boundaries. Everything she did was peculiar, and accepted as such by others. Under her influence, he found himself tempted to abandon more and more of the dicta of conformity as the appeal of 'do as you like' laid hold on him. There was a grain in his own make-up that responded to her oddity.

They were both rapidly becoming stateless persons, exiles, fugitives, those for whom the image of their own identity was overshadowed by a larger fear of losing it, or the effort of finding it. Whatever, they were not ready-made people. Travel, physical vulnerability, foreign-ness gave that impermanence to the mind.

She placed herself outside conventional marriage. He would not have had the fortitude to do it, not as a woman at any rate, and the times were not so advanced that they smiled on those who flouted order. As the century progressed in the liberality of its thinking in some quarters, equality in sex, race, religion, the access to democracy and freedom of speech, conversely in other ways these were limited or at any rate supervised by the mechanism of government, that is bureaucracy. How sympathetic would the Inland Revenue be to her status as a tax deductible asset? What status would she have in standing outside the law of her country? Still, she was fortunate. She operated under the shelter of the mother of parliaments. Any British consul anywhere in the world would see she got back to the mainland safely. What if she were a Turkish Muslim, a South African coloured, a Sikh woman of the northern provinces running away from her lawful husband? Unthinkable.

The fact that he thought these things on her behalf defined the difference between them. If they had occurred to her, she had dismissed them as irrelevant. He still hedged his bets. She was all or nothing.

He was impressed by the strange forms of courage that she had. She had the mental expansiveness of the free-roaming spirit. Although she might stay in one spot for the rest of her life, seldom moving outside the valley of Lochearn and then only to the Lothians, she could see as far as the horizon. She could see over it for the one reason that she wanted to know what lands were drawn on the other side. She felt intuitively the roundness of the world. She was aware of the contours of other people's landscape. She was the best person to travel the seas with.

How could he go back to the narrow and the circumscribed? Aileen, Montreal, his parents' house, the predictable entombed him. He was like a man on parole who thinks it might be worthwhile to make a break for it rather than go back to serve out his sentence. The sentence was interminable. It was life. One week on this unromantic boat with its rusty bulwarks, its paint-flaked prow, heading into the Atlantic breakers might make it bearable, one week in the cradle motion of its bows. It would be a pillow under his head for the duration, a private solace making the confined more tolerable.

She took both his hands. 'Don't ask it. Don't even think it. For, thinking it, I can read it. I owe you too enormous a debt not to feel obliged. My life, maybe. I don't know. If you asked me outright, I couldn't be so miserly as to say, No, go home and be sensible.'

'You would let me stay?'

'Yes.'

'And love you?'

'Yes.'

He drew a long breath and let his thoughts aspire to happiness. The first mate called to them that it would be only a few minutes till they cast off from the jetty. The hawsers were released. The gang plank wavered. Already the throb of the engines sent waves over the unfrozen water and as far as the boom of logs which bobbed up and down and creaked behind their restraining harness. His logs. His boom. Shortly to start on their own journey downriver to the industrial pulp mills of Ontario. They would be turned into houses, window frames, furniture, books. He saw the logic of their progression from seed to tree to book and knew himself to be an inherent part of it. He was not an escapist, or not in the physical sense. He had arrived at his own equilibrium and must not upset it. It was a fragile dam he built to shore his own life up.

He kissed both the hands that held his. 'That's enough. That you would.' He held her close. Strange. He had kissed her only once, and that was long before he knew how much she mattered.

He walked away down the connecting bridge. She stood near the helm, face to the sea, as stationary as the shape of a figurehead against the skyline. They didn't wave, but he watched until the boat pulled out of sight behind the rocks of the headland, diminished to the size of a white seagull skimming the black waters, before he walked away. He sat in his car and his heart sank for lost opportunities. This side he was too aware of Mabon's claim; on the other, Alexis'. The open sea might have been his territory in her. But he was overly guarded to seize the moment, too circumspect to live dangerously, and so the larger experiences passed him by. The next time he saw her she would have come under another form of guardianship than his. She would be on her own soil, and would not need him so urgently again as to say in those breathless and unequivocal words, 'Just you.'

There were a dozen men on board to ship the consignment of bauxite and aluminium to Avonmouth. And herself. She could understand why the company didn't take passengers. They couldn't possibly make a profit out of them. They fed her constantly. It seemed at two-hourly intervals there was a break for sustenance, liquid or solid, and usually both. A steward, an émigré cockney, brought her tea at seven in the morning and checked on her regularly after that if she hadn't been seen on deck, perhaps in case she had fallen overboard but mostly because he liked the change in routine and the feminine company. In the evenings she was always in demand, and the four officers refused to allow her to be tired and make a quiet withdrawal after dinner. They listened to the radio, which transmitted the BBC as though Shepherd's Bush were in the hold instead of a thousand miles away, and played canasta. With one officer on duty she was needed for the fourth hand, and learned to meld with the best of them. She never did establish who took her place on other voyages, or if they played three handed.

She grew stronger, possibly healthier than she had ever been. No, she had not died at his hands but at moments, finding a weak spot in her brain scan, wondered if she had started on the road to death. Alexis, handling the shuttle left to right, knew there was a twinge as ligament rubbed against ligament. The cells mended, the wound healed over but not entirely. There was a hairline crack or a flaw in the tissue which was mortality coming to nag them on the raw nerve, with a consciousness of their stress point and its breaking strain. Along that line would they fracture. But they did not say with Dunbar lamenting the makars, Timor Mortis conturbat me. No whingeing fear. They counted themselves among the strong to whom a contest is puissance. It provided a measure of their strength and so it fortified. They rejoiced to have got off so lightly and came back with an access of vigour frrom the brink of defeat. They knew it was a tournament with death they had to lose, but like true champions they would fight every round on points. No knock out result for them. They would go the distance.

She took the restorative waters of the voyage. Three times a day she walked the deck with the baby in her arms, for the weather was steady and kind. She was wind burned, her nails and eyes novel in their whiteness against a brown skin. On the finest days she would wrap herself in a blanket with the baby, and sit on the starboard side in the lee of the wind to take the benefit of the sun. Then the sea itself was a tireless companion, sending up spume and furling waves to dash spray on the deck. Shoals of fish surfaced and dived round the bows. Birds flew close to what they knew was a source of food and a resting place if they flagged. They kept pace day by day with the petrel and the porpoise.

They had one day of heavy swell off Ireland and her excitement began to ride high, too, passing land. 'Butting through the Channel in the mad March days' was more thrilling than to arrive by argosy in style.

'Friends waiting?' asked the steward, coming up to her as she leaned over the side and deciphered the coastline of the island.

'No. I've a long drive, to Lochearnhead in Scotland.'

'Tell the Captain to see Customs handle your car first off. Get away sharpish.'

'When will we berth?'

'Let's see.' He consulted his watch. 'Wednesday, fifteen hundred hours.'

'You mean three o'clock.'

'That's right. Three o'clock. Should dock Thursday early. You might be all clear by midday.'

'I can't drive all the way in one day?' She measured the journey against the equivalent distance from Chicoutimi to Montreal but found even mileage was differently calculated. Travel was double on this side, because there were so many places in the way of space.

'Not likely. Not with the kiddie. You take it easy. Stop over. Know the road?'

'No. I've never been in England before.'

'Go all the way to Canada and you've never been to England? Well, they've got new bits of motorway here and there. Go on those for speed.'

'I'd rather go on the old roads.'

'Nice route through Scotch Corner. Slow but nice if you've got a month to spend. Got a map?'

'No.'

'Didn't think you would have. Buy a map at a petrol station and follow this route.' He jotted down half a dozen names for her. 'Can't go wrong. Know your way from Edinburgh? They've opened the new road bridge.'

'Such changes!'

'Don't stand still, you know, just because you've been away.'

By the time he reached Montreal, Rejean still hadn't arrived at the best way to explain all this to Aileen. He wondered about concealing parts of Esme's story, exonerating Mabon, being less than specific about her going back to Inchcombe to live with Alexis, man and wife in everything but name, until it was time for their own sojourn when seeing them in fact might be less shocking to Aileen than being told about it. He thought it would be shocking, the further he drove through the environs of the city. He did not know why he worried about it so much. Indeed he could get away with saying nothing if he wanted to, but this was to build up trouble ahead when the time for explanations came, and like Esme he felt to let the thing explain itself was deceitful. Silence made his own protracted stay look all the more what it was, the voluntary rather than the necessary term which he could shape it by narrative. Should he speak to her privately or with Maurice and Claire to . . . to what? To prevent their being alone? He grew ashamed of his own circuitous duplicity in a plot where he was, in all respects, the onlooker. Let it happen, he told himself. Let it happen how it will.

But explanations were imminent. The pose was accusatory in all quarters, the arm laid too deliberately along the chair with an air of refusing to move until things had been settled. Rather than face the awesome hiatus of a mood, a coolness to be coped with and survived, he made a natural and immediate start on things.

'I'd like you both to come into the library while I explain to Aileen what's been happening.'

They came warily, Maurice making noises about his absence from the business for which he was being paid a salary after all, Claire concerned over the neglect of his book which he had so carefully nurtured in the preceding year, Aileen over her own abandonment and nothing else.

He wondered, pouring himself a drink from the cabinet, which of the three lines of his narrative would have most effect. Pausing to contemplate the forming of his tale, he saw graphically how Esme's story was dominated by the three men, husband, lover, friend; past, future, hypothetical; west, east and mid-Atlantic. He was the inbetween man, the one without a claim, yet he was sure that if he spelled out Mabon's conventional suspicions his part would supersede both the others, his role bring the loudest shout of disapproval from his waiting audience.

'The first thing to say is that Mabon and Esme have separated, definitively.'

This kept them busy amongst themselves with idle speculation and recrimination. Hadn't it been here that they had met? They recalled the evening and sought for premonitions. Didn't they bear some responsibility for not helping?

'How?' asked Aileen. 'How can you help?' And they silently concurred that there was no therapy that worked.

Then Maurice it was stopped to ask, Why? And he explained as shockingly as he could how he had found Esme and the traces she had not been able to wash away, in order to reinforce two things: how necessary it was for Esme to leave her husband and, equally, how imperative his own intervention was. Both aspects of his narrative apologised and prepared for the strands he was intending to develop later, when he had got his breath back.

'But that's not like Mabon,' objected the older man. 'Do you

571

think? You've known him a long time. In fact we all have, all three of us. He wouldn't act so out of character unless provocation were extreme.'

This brought down howls, while Rejean sat mutely thinking probably the provocation of Esme's stubborn refusal to say anything to the point was extreme.

'How can you think that?' said Claire. 'About Esme too. When I think of him leaving her unconscious. What can any woman do to provoke that?'

'It is inhuman,' agreed Aileen, forced into condemnation, though a voice in her head said, It wouldn't have happened to me. I'd have managed him better. 'You can't honestly mean she deserved it?'

'I would like to hear his side before I pass judgment. You'll admit he may have a point of view.' So they ranged against each other, men with men, women with women, while Rejean waited thankful that their attention had been diverted from the other consequent forms of why.

'Rejean,' Aileen called his mind to order. 'Is he a brute or not?'

'Oh, I think it was accidental, that episode, but the break-up was inevitable.'

'Why, was it always so bad?' asked Claire, anxious as ever that domestic harmony should be seen to be done, and disbelieving that other couples did not agree.

Rejean hesitated, anxious not to betray himself and his own marriage on its weaker points, but clear in his own view that he could hardly talk of the ill-founded suspicion without implicating himself.

'There was very little common ground.'

He wavered, sure that now was the instant to produce with a laugh and a shake of the head the absurd proposition that he was Esme's lover, Sophie's father, when they were baffled with other causes and other effects. But he could not laugh any more than he could wish it wholly absurd that the husband was jealous of the friend. He wished he had given grounds for the other to divorce on; that was the sum of it. Guilt of intention rather than guilt of deed silenced him. He watched the moment pass and couldn't redeem it when Claire interrupted.

'But what is Esme doing now? Why didn't you bring her back with you? You haven't left her in Arvida by herself?'

He got up and walked away from the fire they always burned, which seemed to consume the oxygen in the air. Allied to double glazing and central heating it made for a stifling atmosphere. He wanted to throw the French windows open and walk out, down to the edge of the garden where he saw from afar the jonquils were in bloom under the sheltering boughs of an Atlantic cedar, leaving them and explanations behind.

'She sailed for the UK this morning. I expect she'll be alongside Prince Edward Island by now.'

'Why, whatever!' exclaimed Aileen. 'How ridiculous. Where is she going to stay?' She looked round for some confirmation of her opinion that this exodus was the most extravagant of Esme's actions, cutting her off from the rights she might have enjoyed even as a divorcee. Aileen had already calculated a settlement and a new lifestyle for her cousin. Some part-time teaching in Montreal, life in one of the city's apartment blocks with no garden to keep up. She looked on the going back to Scotland as a spur of the moment decision, prompted by sentiment, like flying out to Canada in the first place to look for a quite hypothetical father. But finding no response in Claire or Maurice or Rejean, whose eyes were carefully averted from hers, she paused and re-thought. 'You're not surprised, any of you. What do you know that I do not?'

Maurice rose too, somehow vexed at having been proved conclusively wrong, vexed that Esme had not entrusted him with a measure of her confidence because she assumed he would disapprove and he did, still. All the same, he would have supported her in a resolute decision, as he supported Rejean belatedly. He did not understand why this offer of help, coming after the crisis, might be less than welcome, for he like his son had missed more opportunities than he had seized. He spoke to him directly, 'Things are as they were?'

'Of course. When do they change?'

'When did you find out?'

'Six months ago.' Rejean turned to Aileen, excluded from this dialogue but following it avidly. 'She has gone to live with Alexis.'

'Oh?!' She drew a breath and for a moment arranged the folds of her skirt so that the stripe in each lay parallel along the line to the knee. Quietly she folded them in order, as though they were the tartan of a kilt, meant to hang without fracturing the pattern of the weave. 'Live with him, or do you mean sleep with him?'

'Evidently they're going to live in the same house. Beyond that I hardly know. If I say yes, you'll censure them, and if I say no, you won't believe me.'

She turned away. They knew and she did not. That was the gall. That made her the imbecile, and she could not help feeling, isolated in her seat, that there had been some collusion on their part to keep her ignorant. On the part of all of them, the three here her relatives by marriage, but also by Esme and Alexis, her relatives by blood who hid more by being nearer. At this moment she too could have shaken Esme senseless. But why? Why did she feel such outrage? Was it only because she was the last to know when it concerned her most, or at the incongruous pairing itself?

She remembered Lochearn at its most typical for her, the time between tea and bed, when on many days of the year the idiosyncratic weather made that roll of cloud two-thirds of the way down the hillside. She saw the places she played in, the slip stream between their plot and their neighbour's she had tried to divert with hours of childish effort, the flat rocky cove she called 'the animals' combination place' because one evening walking back in the dark from the village she came across rutting stags, except that they were not. Behind a rock they were a man and woman pantingly engaged, so that she was afraid to come back again to that spot for a long time afterwards. But in these places now another walked instead of her, Esme or Esme's child or her own sibling, unknown, half way across the world. She shuddered at the change in which she had no part.

'You do realise I can never go home again?'

'Don't say what you don't mean,' he reasoned.

'I do mean it. I can never go to Lochearn while they are living in sin.'

He grimaced, perhaps injuriously. 'Didn't we?'

Maurice turned on his heel and walked to the window. He did not like such exposure and regretted the loss of simplicity in their affairs.

'That was different,' she objected, knowing he would pounce but having no other recourse.

'How?'

'I'm shocked. He's too old for her and she already has a husband and a baby. Besides, I can't see Esme as my step-mother, can you?'

'No more than I can see her as my mother-in-law but that's

beside the point. They do as suits them.'

But she was stunned and impervious to logic. She had reacted instinctively, and whatever he said to mitigate the shock she would have to go back to her initial response: she could never go home again. The world turned upside down for her, more than at Mairi's death because Alexis and Inchcombe had been constant through that, stanchions in her past. Now she saw the passions she dreaded as the most destructive elements in the human catalogue seep like damp rot into the foundations of her life, the places and the people of her childhood.

Discreetly they withdrew one by one and left her alone with her thoughts. She remembered many things: Mairi's warning that Esme created too much disturbance, Mabon once saying jokingly that the trouble with Esme was she invaded other people's air space. The force of what they meant came home to her now. She felt her portion had been divided and sub-divided. Another woman she would have welcomed in Alexis' affections, a sedate dowager she had envisaged for her father, not her own cousin. It was too much muddling. Esme was too near a contemporary for her not to feel ousted as a daughter. And then she felt the brunt of Alexis' own deceit, stretching back, oh, to the beginning. That close questioning on Esme's position, work, well being, husband, child, she had responded to in innocence and he had taken advantage of it without declaring his interest. The convoluted perfidies revolted her. What her heart perceived, her mind rejected. She could not be glad for him at the price of honesty.

And Esme too had cheated her. Such one-sided sharing had rebounded. Do not let me take from you, her cousin had said, in case I am too indebted. But all her generous giving had failed to elicit the most basic of decencies, truthfulness. She heard the footsteps on the landing at Lochearn, and the door close in the room overhead and knew, tardily, that they were Alexis' feet that had tended to her cousin's room. What embraces had it witnessed? She recalled the dinner, and the departures made from it, the dance with its own aberrations. What a fool to be so buoyed by her own events that she had no eyes to notice theirs. She remembered how Mabon had dropped her hand and wished she had not let it go, but had rectified the balance of accounts.

Had her mother known? Yes, and Graeme too. With hindsight, the strange tensions of the past became explicable. And all this had passed before her eyes and she not seeing. How could she be so gullible? They were open now. A part of her admitted secrecy was so unlike Alexis, not to share everything with her, that it was done from a desire to protect, to give her as smooth a send-off on her wedding day as was possible. But equally she felt the exclusion was because he confided elsewhere. The smaller had been absorbed in the larger, and she was superfluous.

Then her character rebelled at itself. How mean, how paltry to push her own importance so far as to deny them happiness if they could find it in each other. All relationships were one in the end, and it was greedy to section off so much territory in other people and say, This bit is mine, do not trespass. And to forbid trespass in others. You couldn't bring affection and sympathy to a point of law, though most people thought of their fellows in that way, as possessions or status symbols, but she had never hankered after that form of power before and was ashamed to find it in her repertoire.

Esme and Alexis. Shock, exclusion, but most of all envy, the selfish and unshareable reaction. Rab's favourite, and her father's, maybe Rejean's too. She could not hold herself aloof from noticing the ease with which Esme employed the human skills, nothing learned. She even produced effortlessly the baby her husband adored; would she ever have a child who mattered to Rejean as much as Esme's did?

Was that it, at bottom, the jealousy of the barren woman for the fertile one? She recalled the indignities of the clinic they had attended in Edinburgh over the winter, with no positive outcome. There was apparently no definable reason why she should not conceive, though that was little consolation for the barrage of tests she had had to undergo, the endless probing examinations undressed on a trolley which left her vacant, dazed, vulnerable to a hundred interpretations. All that she was became focused into one tiny urgent nucleus; failure. Failure to conceive, failure to be a mother, failure to be a wife, failure to be a woman. And the questions! Where, when, how, how often? To make love under the implicit assumption that the act was devoid of its essential aim, was to rob it of beauty or mystery or grace. Pleasure evaporated. Desperate to conceive she was as truly mechanical as any harlot.

Birds build – but not I build; no, but strain,
Time's eunuch, and not breed one work that wakes.

576

That hopeless negation she felt to the core. She remembered the pathetic Mary Tudor, swollen with dropsy but deceiving herself she was with child. She unloosed the cord of her gown hoping to distract her husband Philip, who had eyes only for her vital, carefree half-sister. In the human race, she would always be to Esme proxime accessit, the runner up.

Rejean found his mother in the kitchen, delaying a meal until she felt someone would be ready to eat it. He put his chin on her shoulder and muzzled like a spaniel. She stopped what she was doing and paid attention to him. 'Don't ask me what I think, Rejean. I think everything and I think nothing.'

'What did you feel when you first knew about Alexis and Esme?'

'That it was unfair on her, so young, and so defenceless and that I had to help her. But she has made up her mind a second time and it's not my business. I am a simple woman. I was very lucky and that means I can't understand people who haven't had my luck. I would always stay with my husband because that is easier. Esme is different. She has to do things the difficult way. Don't worry about Aileen. She'll get over it.' And she stirred on.

Going back to call her for dinner, Rejean was less certain. She sat with the radial pleats of her dress closed and folded in place, too prim and contained to understand the extravagant, the implacable gestures of her wayward cousin. She lifted a resentful and accusatory eye. He was charged on many counts, he felt, the greatest being the shirking of his narrative. Did Aileen guess? Would she guess sometime what Mabon's grounds were? He was indolent, he knew. He let the tares grow and seed themselves until they were endemic in the soil, and no amount of patience would root them out completely.

53

Esme stopped at a garage outside Bristol as the steward had suggested, and bought a map. There was a bookshop across the road which sold her a newspaper. Its print was vivid, its paper crisp. Black and white Britain. She was back. As she waited at the counter with the substantial coinage in her hand the headlines slotted into place like crossword clues, filling space with meaning but teasing her with something that was not quite resolved, not final. She read on for elucidation, hungry for news, for what was happening in the world at large. As she was going out she passed a rack of books by the door. One title leapt at her from the rest. Of course, it was out trans-Atlantically. *Deforestation and Its Consequences* by Rejean Simard. She couldn't ignore that. She dug deeper into her pocket to find some pound notes and paid again.

She went back to the car with her trio of reading materials. The map should come first, but she had to run her fingers over the pages of Rejean's book appreciatively. The dedication gave her pause. 'To my dear wife without whose help . . .' That had an ironical ring to it she did not care for. She wondered what was happening behind her in Montreal – another botch she'd run out on. She shut the book until she had time to read it thoroughly, and try to make sense of its compilation of statistics so that she could tell him what she thought of it in a way that would satisfy his questions.

The counties of England spread out in front of her. They were as colourful on the page as the wallchart on which she'd first read their names. She plotted them with her hand. There was Worcestershire where Piers Plowman had eaten fried collops on the Malvern Hills, six hundred years before. Then Warwickshire, Leicestershire, Lincolnshire, the counties streamed out in front of her probing fingers all the way to the Border country. The roads that strung them together and along which she chose her route were ancient. They had been paved by the invading Romans, Watling Street and the older Icknield Way, tramped by successive armies during the Jacobite and Civil wars and celebrated recently by the open-air poets, Masefield, Davies and Chesterton among them. The map, as she read it, turned it, was not a flat thing. It was as profound as an archaeological site, revealing layer upon layer of habitation, dense with relics among the strata. She knew the names, the way she knew Minos and Troy and Carthage, but these places along her route were still extant, not ruins of a dead civilisation. They lived on. She hurried to acquaint herself in person.

They were surprisingly beautiful. Reputation had turned the Midlands into an industrial wasteland, but her initial impulse was right and the old roads which she chose took her through largely unspoiled territory. She'd left behind the last vestiges of dirty snow in Quebec, where things were only beginning to be, and so this mild spring, lush, verdant, fully stated, was a revelation. Another season might have been less balmy, but this one was an exemplar against which other springs were measured. Verges of roadside grass were broken by the points of English spring flowers, crocus and daffodil spilling out from gardens. The complements of mauve and yellow were extremes of a chromatic scale which moved through tones and gradations rather than loudly or by contrast. Ornamental almond blossom whitened on boughs that overhung the road, a precursor of the fruit orchards which lay neat and cultivated on either side. The land was fertile, breaking out into innumerable forms of botanical architecture. She was moved by the fecundity of the garden of the world, as stunned as Columbus or Balboa who expected a wilderness and found another Eden, not in newly discovered land but in the old one, rediscovered. It ached with reminiscence. Everything wore the dust of antiquity, a fine chalk that filtered from the bones of the earth, crushed gently underfoot. The creaming surface of a meadow, the sun line on the backs of standing cattle, the pollinated catkins; these forms took on a temporary nimbus, a sun halo of blessedness that may well have been in her eye only, composed as it was of relief and gratitude for what was recognised, the internal light. Spaces, dimensions, definitions, she knew them at last, knew she was not wrong in feeling that their power was essential to her own growth, for what was she but a cell in the organic pattern of home?

Night drew on and she was still a long way short of her goal. She admitted reluctantly that she would have to stop over, although she hurried for an hour over the moorlands of Northumbria so that she could at least spend the night north of Hadrian's Wall, if not north of the border, for wherever she stravaiged and dallied on the way she was impelled forward by the certainty that all roads led to Lochearn.

She stayed in a wayside cottage which she chose because it looked like her destination and seemed to shorten her distance from it, compact, stone built, angle-on to the road. She slept and dreamed, then waking in the dark got up to look north, straining for distant lights. She was in a dwalm, fearful of the shifting mirages of her own imagination. She had told him not to look for her before she arrived, but she might have been wiser to ask for a confirming reply. What if he were away in Edinburgh, Perth, the

Hebrides? An absence, however temporary, would unsettle her. It prophesied indifference. She dreaded finding the house empty, dreaded arriving back late, in the dark, to cold rooms and dead fires. She might knock and knock like the Traveller on the moonlit door and receive no reply other than echoing emptiness. Was he real? Was he there? Was she the returning spirit who could make no contact because that generation had all gone, one by one, into the shades of the dead, or was she without knowing it a ghost coming to haunt the familiar place? She shivered with apprehension.

Daybreak reassured her. It was all right. She was on her way.

Once she was over the border the road turned into a switchback, rising and falling through the gentle glades of traditional sheep country with its tweed mills. There were signposts on either hand to the towns of Jedburgh, Melrose, Kelso, Galashiels, once powerful but decimated by Cromwell and the skirmishes of border war. All the time the road gave her tantalising glimpses north, of a hiatus in the scenery, of an impending city in the blue haze of the distance, of an Edinburgh.

When she came to it, she stopped the car and got out. It was impossible to go on and not acknowledge its hold over her, for it was as familiar and as personal as the hollow of her hand. The afternoon was misty, the mist which often hangs over the inlet and turns the streets into a sea, a grey wash from which the seven hills surfaced like islands, verdant landscapes floating past. From this vantage point it was not a city she knew. The suburban dwellings which were so imposing in town settled at the foot of the hills like a residue. The leonine hump of Arthur's Seat, Castle Rock, Calton, Braid and all the other hills re-asserted themselves in a remote perspective, resumed their true scale and soared above the human. Valleys and mounds which were obliterated by the domestic at ground level stood out at this distance, pockets of green in one long vista to the sea. The geological lie of the land was supreme after all, the setting which inspired the rest. It was hard to believe five miles outside its perimeter that it was a metropolis where half a million people rose and slept, and between times lived grubby lives under what was essentially a smoke pall. She knew this, but she did not believe it. The city was full of mystique, full of what is reconstructed in images that cannot be daunted by grimy reality. Those islands would eternally be the stuff of romance, a picturescape by

Watteau done in the pastoral style, an embarkation for Cythera.

She skirted it and took the old road north; hasten slowly, she told herself through the little townships and the drawing on of evening. She had driven for a day and a half, travelled for a week and a half and was fraught with the creeping lassitude of movement over the surface of the globe. Linlithgow, Stirling went by. She remembered the road well from Rejean's car window. She passed the spot of the accident south of Callander, and slowed her pace, both respectful and fearful, until in a repetition of those cyclic and frustrating dreams which haunted her in Quebec, when she awoke at the point of making contact, she came to the head of the loch as the sun went down. She turned right along the northern shore and drove quite unconscious of time or relative distance until she reached the tree-hung ledge which prevented an immediate view of the house from the roadway.

She trembled on the verge of change. Dreams did not convert well. The five-bar gate was fastened open, unusually, and she took this as a sign of hospitality. Someone was waiting. Someone expected her. She stopped the car in the drive and got out. There were no voices to accompany her arrival and no lights, indoors or out. Still, she told herself, it needed no lamps lit to welcome her. The solidity of the house and its courtyard, standing square, was an embrace in itself. She put her hand against the stones of the gateway and they gave back heat.

She lifted the baby in her arms and pushed open the door of the kitchen, unable to suppress the sickness of high tension at expecting to find him seated there. How was he really? They said he was well, but how well? The Aga was lit. It glowed in the corner comfortably, and on the table in the middle of the room was a place setting for one. Things were neat, attended to, although she couldn't guess whose hand was responsible for the almost tangible goodness of a lamb stew in an earthenware pot. She felt it might have been her own, for that was exactly what she would have cooked. But no footsteps and no voice.

She wandered through the dining room and into the parlour, rooms which had altered in her recollection, the way landforms do after a storm that brings down boulders and re-distributes soil, changing the water courses. Still she didn't find him. It was quiet, it was orderly, but it was empty. She went out by the main door which gave onto the oak tree and looked for him in the office. It too was vacant, though it was full of his employment which in itself diverted her attention. She sat down at his desk and looked over his papers unashamedly. Opened books, newspaper cuttings under a paperweight. She wondered what had taken his fancy. She picked one out and read his mind, an article on land reclamation which he had marked in the corner with the words 'For Rejean'. A new motto was pinned on the board between the two large windows to his right, among a hundred other squares of paper. 'Knowledge of all that is, is the supreme delight.' Underneath he added, 'Cicero, from the Greek.' She smiled at the trail of snippets.

On a calendar the days were marked off heavily, until today where he had added to the 21st of March, 'the vernal equinox'. The desk was partitioned the way he always had it. There was the rough draft of a pattern, a bundle of swatches from the machine, a pile of letters in a clip for answering, and her own telegram propped conspicuously in the foreground of his work. Perhaps she was substantial after all and not a figment of her own escapism, willing herself forwards, backwards, anywhere other than the present. But where was he? To see the paraphernalia of his routines was to whet her appetite for the man himself.

This was him. This was his room. This was his studio, his study, his life space. It seized her with unbearable excitement, as usual, the work place where if she sat for a hundred years she would not come to the end of all he could invent. It was different from her invention, but sympathetic. She did not want to do what he could do, could not accomplish it, but wanted to know how it was done all the same. She picked up one of the samples that took her eye. What had he being doing lately? She stretched it and found that it was double thickness. The motif was knitted in two colours, so that the pattern showed up as predominantly taupe on one side, white the other, and reversible. She puzzled over how this might have been achieved. Had he fused the skills of knitting and weaving as he had wanted, with some new technical advance; could he really weave in the round, knit garments without stitches?

He came back from the loch with a bundle of driftwood he had collected under his arm, sauntering as though to say to himself, Of course she will not come today. Don't expect it. He hadn't gone more than a quarter of a mile from the house since her message, but

582

knew too much sky-watching made the birds agonisingly slow to alight. He forced himself into a nonchalant appearance of normality, turned down invitations for the day and the foreseeable time ahead with careless indifference, on the excuse of work and business. No one knew what hope leapt in his heart every time a car slowed on the bend, or a foot fall was heard on the cobbles. He was wrung with the artificial stimulus of waiting. The close of each day was almost a relief, for he could cross it off the interminable list of days to come and say, Of course she will not come now. It is too late.

Rounding the corner of the boatshed he saw the foreign car and quickened his step. At that moment she came out of the door of the office and walked along the footpath by the wall of the house, holding her child with her back to him. He didn't recognise her. Or rather there was something about her he did not recognise but he knew the form of old. It was an eternal motif, mother and child. In ten seconds, as he walked towards her in the dying light, he painted a dozen images of the scene she gave him, as though there wasn't enough time to explore its message there and then. An altarpiece, a running frieze, a triptych composed of their time together and separately since, like wings that folded from the centre making one whole. He made a hundred notes for future reference.

She turned round at the sound of his feet and stopped. He came closer and they looked to see if they were indeed themselves. Easy to say they fell into each other's arms. They did not. In eighteen months anyone can become an object of strangeness to himself. They were awkward with each other not knowing whether to smile or to cry, for the tumbling emotions of their recognition prevented any one from predominating. Besides, though he might lay his bundle on the ground, she could not dispose of hers so readily.

He pushed open the door to the house and followed her inside. The foolish and the immediate rose to his lips but he quelled the impulse to fill the moment with a commonplace until she had laid the baby in the bield of an easy chair and stood facing him with her back to his fire, the humorous questions in her eyes. She still had those teasing looks. Well, here I am. And what do you think of me? they asked.

'You've turned into a pre-Raphaelite.' He touched the hair which fell around her shoulders in a shower. That was what he hadn't recognised about her, the long hair which grew into a luxuriant, unkempt abundance, like his garden only marginally controlled. It made the vagary of her nature complete, releasing the gypsy or peasant quality which had been latent in her appearance.

'I've grown it all the time I've been away. For warmth as much as anything. But you'll not chide me for being untamed when you've turned lion yourself?' Tentatively she put out a hand and felt the beard which by now had assumed its own form that borrowed as little from W.G. Grace as from Kaiser Wilhelm, but struck a likeness between the bohemian and the patrician that was his own.

'Yes, I forgot about that. Does it alarm you?'

'Only when I look at you.'

'Ah well. I must excuse you if you look away.' Which she did, but not from antipathy. After a moment, he reclaimed the head and brought it to rest on his shoulder. 'Something has happened to you that you haven't told me about.'

She straightened and looked at him. 'I will in time.'

He held her head between his hands to reach its elusive meanings, stroking and flattening the hair that bounded back irrepressibly. 'Is there time? You won't go back? Remember you haven't said and I've been in suspense thinking you're not here for good.'

She measured these words and the distress of uncertainty they laid open to her. She had inflicted that on him. When she replied, it was to be as positive as she could and not as a boast about immortality. 'I am here for all time, if you wish.'

'I wish.' As though she were expressing the surge of joy he couldn't voice because it might stifle in his throat, the baby sitting neglected in her chair gurgled instead. He turned round and noticed her and scooped her out of her chair in one. 'How rude and self-absorbed we are. Will she eat lamb stew?'

'If I mash it first,' she said, following him into the kitchen. He had found a chair in the loft when he was taking part in Mrs Galashan's ritual spring clean a week before, and brought it downstairs in readiness. It was a folding contraption that made into a high or low table for eating or for play, and into this he manoeuvred the infant, bending her legs under the tray with an

584

ease remembered from when his own daughter sat in it. 'Who cooked the stew?'

'Ian's mother. She's been here a long time now and I couldn't have managed without her. Goodness knows what she'll say in the morning shen she finds you here. Probably give me my cards. Maybe not. She's very indulgent with me. Sometimes lets me have my own way. A gentle bully.'

She had not thought there would be an addition to the household and foresaw the old difficulties of secrecy, guilt and blame. 'Seriously, is it . . .' She hesitated.

'Seriously,' he mocked her tone, 'it'll be easier now.'

'Except that I'm the married woman.'

'Tomorrow's the time for that.' He kissed the distracted cheek. 'Today I am here, I have you, there's a fire burning and a meal on the table. I want nothing more. Don't tell me you of all people have forgotten how to be simple.'

'Yes, perhaps. I have stopped being grateful for today.'

'Come, now,' he said to divert her, 'tell me about your journey. When did you leave?'

Though she tried to make her travels entertaining, to extract the frivolous and repeatable, her face clouded over with the recollection of what she couldn't bring herself to impart. Time and time again he saw the signal and distracted her. She was deeply tired, he saw, would tail off into an unhappy absence of mind and at such moments he too was overwhelmed by the enormity of the unspoken, by the other people they pushed into the corners to minimise their existence, by the sheer difficulty of beginning again.

She went to put the baby to sleep. Alexis sat on in the parlour, letting the light from the fire suffice. The dancing flames showed him an altered room. A chair was heaped with baby clothes. There was a trail of powder as far as the door. Esme left her bag on another chair and near it lay the objects she meant to put inside, but hadn't quite: a bundle of keys, a handkerchief, a photograph of Rejean with a minister. He would ask who and when later. There was nothing out of the ordinary, but when had the everyday held such glamour for him? This was the way it would be from now on, clutter, being busy to some purpose. He felt that the echo of his own steps was deadened and she was the layer that softened the impact of himself. Had he actually come to the end of loneliness and of waiting, for all the halves to turn into wholes? In a moment she would come down again, tidy the room a little, putting a bundle of things at the bottom of the stairs for economy of effort, to be lifted later, and he would watch her, tense until she decided where to sit among the many places that he offered her. Imagine, she might choose to share his. He couldn't quite believe it, and held back reticently from drawing up a catalogue for the future.

They unpacked the car together, making a dozen journeys back and forth until the hall was strewn with her belongings. In the boot he came across her coat, part garment, part blanket, but mostly a treasury of association, a touchstone to waft her back in time and place.

'No, don't tell me how much you paid for it. It'll upset me. That was the best bolt I turned out. It came off well in those colours. I'd almost finished experimenting by that stage and hadn't got bored with it. I'm glad some of it came your way.'

'Yes, it was unnerving to hear your praises sung in Chicoutimi High Street. The lady knew what she was talking about.' But thinking of that brought back the day of the purchase, and she vehemently pushed it away from her recollection. 'Rejean liked it too, though he didn't know it was yours. That reminds me.' She dived down behind the driving seat and produced the book. 'Have you seen this yet?'

'No. He promised to send me a copy which is probably on its way. It's a vile cover. They should have used a photograph for that. Infra-red. I wish he'd asked me first. How quick of you to spot it. In Bristol? Well, what strange places one finds one's friends.'

They sat up till midnight without realising it, reading each other paragraphs and arguing over what they meant.

'That's Aileen's syntax. Can't you tell?'

'No. How can you?'

'That's the way she'd phrase it. See how she ties it up, no quibbling, no ambiguity. A handsome sentence all the same, don't you agree?'

She propped her head on his arm to see it again and while he read on, restfully, her eyes closed. The fire fell deeper into the basket and she cast herself adrift on the hour. It was a while before he realised she had fallen asleep on him and although he was pinned down, unable to move without waking her, he felt like a thief enjoying furtively the warmth of her body, the relaxation of her face he could peruse at leisure. In the course of the evening he had re-acquainted himself with it, some of the features familiar, some surprising. Memory, however loving, faltered when it came to precise details. Her mouth, he saw as though he'd never seen it before, was sharply defined at its fullest, but a blur at the corners as though a painter had laid on its shape carefully, then thought, This is too hard, and smeared the edge a little with his thumb to soften it. This impression was general. Maturity blunted her but he found the fall from the brittle outlines of youth endearing. The careworn imperfection of a face made it more compassionate, more accessible. Her eyes still retained their wise innocence, the paradoxical combination of naivety and sophistication which had kept him wondering all along.

Thinking like this brought him round to something Hardy said of Tess, which he often pondered on. The creator decided, as his heroine walked across an upland pasture, that her face reversed its inner thoughts, and the more elevated her mood, the less elevated her aspect. When she thought she became plain, was the inference.

Alexis had never found this a satisfactory inversion. It implied vaguely that women should not think, or should not think troubled thoughts if they are not to impair their beauty. It implied that with her eyes closed Esme was as interesting as with her eyes open, or as lovely, and for him she certainly was not; once he had acclimatised to the form, he hardly noticed it. The essential quality in her face was the thinking, however anxious or unsettled. That was the thing he tried to trace. She was subtle. He did not find her predictable with the predictability of flesh. Most beautiful women held their clothes or their persons according to the dictates of beauty, and ultimately the fashion of the times, pleasing the eye only. Esme was outside that. She was original and unpractised, for she hadn't forced herself into the mould of today's image. She had no notion of why she attracted, did not care especially if she did or did not, for the appeal shaped her; she did not shape it. She couldn't see it. The vital moment, the action of the eyes encompassing ideas was something the mirror did not reflect. It was transient in the best sense. It moved between states of certainty, leaping like a current of energy across gaps in knowledge, and he watching it leapt too.

Her voice unnerved him. That was perhaps the first characteristic to be forgotten in an absence, the way sound cut through air, but how pervasive it was in reality. A wooing voice it was, its range captivating. At times it made a plunging descent into cavernous notes, deeper than those normally found in a woman's voice, at others it curled and looped up in a question mark that made him laugh by its intonation, whatever the purport. He had overlooked that. He had overlooked much. It was a rich seam he might never work out.

She opened her eyes and shifted drowsily so that he could put his arm round her more fully. 'What time is it?'

'After midnight. Time you went to bed.'

She thought and looked at him. 'Where?'

'Wherever you want.'

'I want to sleep with you, in your bed all night, and wake up in the morning to find you're not a dream. That I haven't imagined it.'

'You will.'

'But I'm afraid too.' She took his hand and passed it along her temples, her cheeks, her eye sockets, her first gesture revisited.

'Why afraid?'

'In case there's a quality in these things. I had no reserve before. It was easy. Everything we did was easy. Now I'm cautious.'

'The quality is yourself.'

'I thought so once.'

'There's no hurry. Sleep. Rest. For as long as you want.'

'You're so patient. Patiently waiting for me to grow up, grow wise. I may never catch you up.'

He kissed her into a passive form of quietude. These years! Would she ever recover? Could he ever make her whole again? 'Go on upstairs. I'll lock the doors.'

In the morning he was down before Mrs Galashan arrived. He said to her simply, as she went into the kitchen from the hall to start her daily round, 'Esme and the baby will be staying here from now on. I hope you won't find it too much extra work.'

She tied her pinny steadfastly behind her back. She had seen the car as she descended from her bicycle and put two and two together fine. He hadn't been in a fidget these ten days for nothing. The girl wouldn't make more work for her, indeed she would probably lessen the load, for she had washed up and tidied away, which was more than he got round to in an evening. She could tell at a glance the two of them could work alongside without getting in each other's road. It was a pretext he offered her, but she appreciated that he had supplied a convenient excuse any time she wanted to use it.

'We'll just go on as we are, shall we, and see how it shapes?'

Then the baby woke and feet stirred overhead. The man and woman waited below, knowing out of the store of their experience what she was doing upstairs, lifting and laying, and how it was commonplace, but the moment was tense with the anticipation of each other's reaction. Their terms of intimacy were to be defined in a minute or two and both hoped the third party would not strain their good accord.

A girl as scoured as the child she carried came downstairs. The strangers said good day but neither smiled. Mrs Galashan watched as she sat down at his side, so close they brushed their arms in reaching, not opposite and apart the way the other wife had done. The woman could not feel as dispassionate as she had hoped to do. It was what she had wanted for him, his home and heart to be replenished, but she had misgivings all the same. It was right in every aspect except that the bairn, whosoever it might be, was not his although he took it on his lap so that she was free to eat, as if that were the least of his concerns. There was more kinship in those three than in a hundred homes up and down the strath that morning. She bent her head and went out of the room, stricken with the flaws in happiness.

From an upper window, dusting, she could see the girl hurl a pram into the sunny corner of the yard and fasten her charge inside. Bending low, she caught her hair on a button and disentangled it, pausing to adjust the set of the hood against the glare. The baby made the noise of happiness and the mother bent impulsively to kiss. Her heart burst open like a flower that blooms once in a dozen years in memory of that moment with her own child, so long ago that even the recollection of such simplicity hurt. No wonder. Oh, no wonder.

They came upstairs behind her. She moved on in her cleaning but not before she heard the young woman say, 'You know Mr Scott wrote and told me that Mairi had left me some things. He didn't say what and I was intrigued. I understood you were looking after them for me.'

Mrs Galashan shut the door of the room she was in, so as not to hear more of their business.

He took her by the arm into the room next to theirs, and let her adjust to it.

He'd forgotten himself what it was like. He remembered removing the busy wallpaper that ruined the room's proportions, prompted by Oscar Wilde who also disliked pattern on the walls, for the eye needed repose if the mind were to think. He'd tried out various alternative finishes, stippling or making foliar shapes from rags dipped in paint, but settled after these false starts for an elaborate pointillism in colours of eggshell softness: magnolia, mother of pearl, the pink of eternelles. The room when he finished it was as colourless as a new page, where the strongest design was no more obtrusive than a watermark. He liked that effect, tones of neutrality, and took pleasure fitting the furniture in context against a hazy background. He reverted to precision in the effort to centre and align each, having enormous fun to himself by creating links and balance no one else would ever notice. That was the best of artistry, the indiscernible processes. There were half a dozen pieces of furniture like the escritoire, casual finds. Casual he might call them, but he'd spent all the previous winter searching for them, waiting for the irrefutable yes of rightness to make its appeal.

'This was the room. She left you all its contents.'

She sat down in the sunlight filtered by shutters he opened slightly to admit the view across the garden and the foreshore to the placid waters of the loch on a spring morning, barely ruffled.

She took them in one by one, a day bed, an oval table with an inset workbox, a screen with pleated silk curtains, a flute back club chair covered to match. Things reeded, inlaid, delicate with scrolls. It was a period piece he had reconstructed, not in all probability very different from the room where Josephine looked out onto her beloved garden at Malmaison, flanked by rose borders, cool and light and airy, or the chambers fitted out from Mrs Fitzherbert's furniture in the Pavilion at Brighton, full of the grace of Regency without a touch of Victorian heavy-handedness, the age of the feminine preceding the masculine.

She ran her hand along them, and wondered at their collective rarity, amassed in one place. Was this what her aunt was capable of choosing? How she had lived? Where were the functional items, bed and wardrobe and clothes chest? No, however carefully it had been assembled, she could see it had not been lived in. No one had been here before her. It awaited her occupancy and hers alone. The shelves stood empty till her books filled them, the desk was bare until her writing materials found their own niches, the walls her personal choice from among his pictures, either old or new or those still to be painted. It was a solar, a withdrawing room, a bower unmistakably and contrived with her taste and habits in mind. Not one item of it was a bequest.

She looked round at him where he leaned against the louvres of the shutter, striping him with radial bars. He assessed her reaction curiously.

'Why did you do this?'

'Why do men go on Crusade?' He came forward a step and put his hands on her shoulders, to feel the security of her presence but also to hide a little. 'An act of faith. I couldn't help myself. No one else realised but I had to believe you would come back and use it. A votive offering, if you like, an imprecation to the gods to be kind and restore you.'

They were so quiet they could hear the water lapping a hundred yards away. She spread her hands along the open surface of the bureau. 'You know me too well.'

'Only by guesswork.'

Graeme called unannounced late in the afternoon and could not fail to be taken aback at the turn of events, which he disguised as best he could when she walked into the office where he sat with the master who had not given a single word of prior warning, and enjoyed seeing his visitor flounder. She put her tray and her baby down and shook hands with him in a way he could not think was less than cordial. On such occasions the mildness of the season, the plumpness and good nature of a child, the quality of a scone can be gratefully indulged diversions.

She'd come back, then, husband or none, child or none. He was put out at such profligate dispersal but decided, whatever he thought, civility would rule their first meeting. So the searching questions he left alone, but the searching looks he could give under half closed lids. He saw that they burbled together like the confluence of waters, no longer an underground stream. He felt the idleness of his attempt to stem that flood. They would be inseparable henceforth as one element from its like. Folly to resist it.

All the same, when he took the road home at six o'clock with Mrs Galashan, it was with a heavy heart. His conscience would not give him an easy decision on whether it was right to acknowledge them or not.

The woman pushed her bicycle alongside him, keeking now and then into his averted features. She went no further than fifty yards before she said, 'You are troubled by what you see, Graeme Sutherland. I know you are wondering what you should do, whether to cast him off as your friend forever because he's taken a mistress, as you nearly did before. You needn't try to hide it from me. I've known you too long to be mistaken.' She sighed and looked back along the whitening road they had travelled. 'Yes, I know you better than any other being on earth, bar my own flesh, and that was maybe why I didn't choose you as my husband when you asked me. I thought we were not distant enough and took the dashing stranger instead. Don't think I haven't lived to regret it, though maybe I shouldn't say.' She glanced anxiously where once she was bold and the difference saddened her. He did not look her way or respond to her tone, but walked straight ahead. 'Maybe it is shocking to speak about it after a quarter of a century, but you know I wouldn't breathe a word of my troubles to another soul, and that maybe entitles me to unburden myself just once. If I caused you suffering, and I think I did, I have suffered too. I've upbraided myself in private for my mistake. What would I not give for my path this evening to lie alongside yours? I know you would have been a better father to my son than his own, and a better husband to me than the one I chose. He is an idler and I will go drudging to the end of my days. Believe me, I look over to my man at nightfall and wish another sat in his place.'

He made no reply, reviewing the old shock of his double loss, of the woman he did marry who died prematurely, and of the sweetheart who turned him down. Out of their futile courtship one moment rose to mind when he was a lad lying with his lass, and her hair undone spilled out mixing with the bracken and all his winding would not separate them. Its painful sweetness did not diminish but neither did it help him in his present dilemma. Self-indulgence in that sweetness seemed less important, on balance, than enduring rejection.

She went on, as they plodded the road under the quiet of

on-coming night which gave her the courage to say what she felt once and for all. 'Tell me, when was it ever so simple as one man and one woman? Not often. Not for us and not for them. Don't stand aloof from them. Take pity. Whatever you think, leave them be to find their own level. I am sure that man's affection was never given in vain, or any man's for that matter. What is wasted that gives life?'

She felt him start at what sounded to him like blatant suggestion. She knew he would see only the outrage of convention, ignoring the unwieldy force convention disciplines. It was like his religion. He observed the outward forms slavishly, but in pursuing his devotions forgot faith. She would have softened that intractability in him. She would have made him more compassionate. Sure enough, he said, 'And what of God's holy ordinance? Will no one keep the marriage vows? If we don't begin there, what becomes of us?'

'What a strange law it is that our nature won't enforce. Adhere to one, whatever. You may think you have found the answer in duty, but for myself I have found duty a cheerless bedfellow. You are a fortunate man, Graeme Sutherland, if you know for certain, for I have sought as hard as anyone and I have not found it. I have knocked and it has not been opened unto me.'

So she parted company from him where his path rose upwards and hers proceeded along the level road to St Fillans.

Below them, the couple in question strolled hand in hand along the shore, Alexis carrying the infant on his free shoulder, and the house left wide to all comers. Perhaps the presence of the third party, though mute, gave to their frequent embraces an air of respectability which they took advantage of. At any rate, their progress was slow for they stopped every few hundred yards not to admire the view but each other.

'Let's be serious, Esme,' he enjoined.

'Already? I've only been back a day.'

'We mustn't let it drift. Have you decided what you want to do? In the long run, what do you want?'

She wound herself under his arm again and encircled both him and the child he carried, impeding all progress for the moment. 'I want to have your son, with your consent.'

He looked down astonished. 'Well, that certainly wasn't the

reply I expected. When?'

'Soon. I think I shouldn't leave it too long.'

'Are you strong enough?'

'Yes, now I am here and with you, I am strong.'

'And how do we go about begetting a son specifically?' The humour she engendered got the better of them both.

'Oh, I'm not such an ingénue as I was. I'll do it the way I want next time.'

He had heard of the theory she propounded and thought it was feasible. A houseful of sons! That was the most seductive idea of all. Still, he did not allow himself to be carried away by the visions she unfolded. Something else came first. 'And what about Esme? What will she do?'

'She will take up her pen and write.'

'That's good. That's what I wanted. A book, a novel?'

'No, that takes too long. I'm too impatient. I will write poetry, at last.'

He moved them on but felt compelled to sound the cautionary note. 'I'll enjoy that, but you do realise this is the stuff that dreams are made of?'

'Oh, surely you're not asking me to become a realist at the eleventh hour?' and she laughed away the restrictions placed on them by chance or talent, or even time.

54

Dear Aileen,

You find us coping with an annus mirabilis. We have a drought in the strath, well it is widespread in the Highlands. Not a drop of rain has fallen in the four months since you left. They are harvesting already, and talk of putting in a second crop. Unheard of. The machines are going night and day, baling, and men are out hay-making as long as there's light. I went out and helped stack a barn at Balquhidder, though it wasn't Balquhidder at all but somewhere in Van Gogh, yellow bales on a yellow field against an impossibly blue sky, and there were huge swatches cut in the stubble where he'd just lifted his brush and left the marks raw.

Nothing exists but the next bale and the next forkful. The stuff is in your ears and your nostrils and your eyes, a vegetable pollen dust and bits of chaff find their way through your clothes, even through the eyelets of your shoes till you are saturated in it and start to identify with vegetable yourself. Quite magical, that smell. Green and golden, and you lie on top of the heap, cushioned by twenty feet of newly dried stems and think, Who wouldn't be a farmer, on harvesting days? Blissfully done in.

I went up to Inverness last week and don't ever remember the countryside looking so parched. There isn't a green hill in sight, all rolling dusty prairies. It could be California – without the sprinklers. We have water restrictions, so really it isn't amusing in the least. Livestock are beginning to suffer and the farmers are having to work overtime just to keep the animals watered. The level of the loch is lower than I have seen it and they say the hill streams have dried out completely – dry gulches. Quite threatening and hard to believe by the law of averages it will rain tomorrow, since by the same law it should be raining today.

We adopt foreign ways; take a siesta, crawl out of the heat of midday and work before and after the sun is fierce. The place takes on a kind of camaraderie as though we were under siege. Everyone has licence to stultify his neighbour with boredom about the state of his beans or the meagre brown bath he has to run. People who haven't addressed each other in twelve months suddenly find an abiding mutual interest in recalling the hottest summer they remember or the longest drought and air a fund of country saws and maxims in support of their claim. Middling stuff, but quite compulsive – how you feel caught up in the communal, and worry.

Enough of me. I am really writing this to ask how you are but as usual I am sidetracked into barbarous egotism. I checked on Inverleith when I was last down at the wool sales, everything seems in order. I left the keys with Mr Scott afterwards, as you'd instructed him. He will carry out the inspections from now on. I won't trespass again. Rejean said in his last letter you hadn't settled on anywhere suitable in Montreal and are still with Claire and Maurice. Is it presumptuous to think this means you'll be coming home all the sooner? I hope so, if I may be allowed to hope.

Well, let us come to the point, Aileen. You haven't written and you haven't phoned, and I presume this is a deliberate policy on your part – not answering – and that I am being ostracised. I don't know quite how to put my case, although I do appreciate I've had long enough to prepare one and that it's taken me a fair while to disembarrass myself of the facts. Esme is living here as my wife, let's be clear about that. Esme is my wife, would be so legally if it weren't for the mishaps of place and person. Do I produce that a little defensively? It's rather late in the day for conversions to monogamy, I grant you, but some of us remain surprised at the manifestions of faith, even human faith.

Here I am apparently well settled into geriatric widowerhood and then I go and misbehave yet again, only this time she's my daughter's cousin and contemporary, has a husband and a child and in spite of it all I mean to hang on to her. That's hard for you to take. Yes, there are changes here but I don't want you to feel they're exclusive. I certainly don't want to exclude you though this silence of yours, if it tells me anything, tells me you feel left out. I'm baffled by recent changes myself. There has been so much to and froing these last couple of years, so many trips to Prestwick to see off and uplift – how I hate departure lounges – that I dupe myself into thinking you've removed yourself physically, and then it strikes me cold that you are removed mentally as well. That you have gone away for all time.

I don't know why you should feel cut off like this. You are not. I'm not trying to cut you out or disinherit you. My house and my hearth are yours for as long as you want to share them. This is the house you grew up in, after all. It grew up with you and round you, and it can belong to no one else in quite the way it belongs to you because you had a hand in it. You saw it evolve. How can I convince you of that except by saying the door is always open? Walk in. Don't stand outside looking through windows. Come indoors. There is a welcome and a place for you, always.

We don't change by being together, you know. Esme is still the same person you liked so much when you called on her the day her mother died, admittedly at my asking. I shouldn't have to recommend her to you and your kind thoughts. I haven't materially altered either, except that I'm glad every minute of the day, and very nearly disbelieving that I have survived into the age of fulfilment. Should I be ashamed that each day is a triumph of the will and the senses? I am completely alive. How can I be sorry for that? I've waited a long time to release that potential in me. It won't be thwarted now.

This is made not hollow exactly, but ironic by your withdrawal. Why do I always have to lose one person to gain another? Is it really excessive to look for two relationships at once in life? I am beginning to feel there's something fundamental I've overlooked – is it that women do not like each other? I would not have believed it. I do not believe it. And yet everyone seems bent on proving that it is so. Maybe it's not women who are at cross-purposes. The claims of love may oust all others, of friendship, of children, of work even. I suspect one achieves very little substantial in this euphoria and other people avoid the sufferer until he has recovered, knowing not one sensible word or act will be produced until the fever ends. But I earnestly hope not to recover from this particular affliction, so don't depend on that acquittal.

Please don't snub us. This long silence hurts me and reminds me of so many other silences and so many other hurts. Your aunt cut off from her family by their action, not hers, waiting an eternity to hear from her husband. Will you send me a packet of photographs in twenty years' time without a letter inside, just to remind me that you once existed? And will I look at them and think, Oh yes I remember I used to have a daughter but I mislaid her somewhere along the way? It brings back your mother's stoic silences and I know so intimately how prejudice and antipathy can be made to flourish in that soil, a thorny cactus in a desert. Don't harbour grievances against me, I implore you, not only for my sake, though I would be immeasurably the loser, but for yours. Don't turn spiteful, Aileen, whatever you do. It isn't like you. It isn't a useful state of mind.

I settle down to the realisation that this is going to be my personal purgatory, waiting for the letter that doesn't arrive, a recurring nightmare I'm going to have to re-enact every morning of my life when I go downstairs and sort through the envelopes. I stand there like a fool who doesn't learn by experience, telling myself the blue sheets are missing because there's been a postal strike, it's a holiday or the woman I wait to hear from is too busy with her own life, though you can't imagine how I begrudge the occupations that distract her and sever her from me. What alchemy lies in distance that can make the loved one so unkind.

Waiting day by day like this to pick up an airmail letter with a Canadian stamp is a potent echo of the interminable time Esme was away, and how all that happened to her was unknown to me in the vacuum of her absence. I feared for her, and with justification. I fear doubly for you, because you are me. She is only like me. Out of sight is never out of mind. I wish it were; I could sleep through the dawn that way. I am anxious for you. I want to know how you are. I am not easy with myself if you are distanced. There is not a day passes when I do not think of you.

So, you'll come back in the autumn with Rejean. Is it feasible that you'll be in Inverleith and I'll be at Canonmills, a quarter of a mile away, and we'll never meet, that there will actually be a silent injunction on our meeting? I find that as hard to believe as you and Esme not crossing paths in ten years of education together. Edinburgh is a vast place after all when people can lose themselves in it so readily. Will we let these divisions harden? Surely not. What if we cross on the pavement? Will you cut me dead? Or you may drive past me in the car, but look the other way and pretend you haven't seen me. How? Why? I don't understand. I'll come and ring at your door, and if you send me away or refuse to answer I'll come back the next day, and the next, and you'll have to go on refusing to acknowledge me as your father a thousand times, and still I will not understand. I can't believe I'm going to be estranged from my longest-standing friend, who is only incidentally my daughter. Every day I wake up with the same refrain running through my head, a lament that never ceases to make me grieve. Alas for the sleight of life that makes us miss each other. Yes, think what that means. I come and you're not there. We pass each other somewhere, and miss making contact. I miss your being here. We are all missing persons.

Maybe you don't know what this means yet. You're not a parent. You won't understand the force of what I'm saying till you are one and have begun to live outside the boundaries we normally regard as identity. Parenthood is a new country that makes you forever an exile from yourself and from simple, unicellular thinking. You start to live in someone else. What I am trying to get over to you is that I am a divided person, a divided state, and I want to be united – just for once to be at peace with myself. I am asking you, begging you to come back to where I can reach you again.

55

Esme made some quietus with the local folk when she established it as her practice, on the first Sunday after her arrival, and on all subsequent Sundays, to walk with her pram along the highway to Lochearn village, sometime before the morning service was announced by a toll of bells. She went into the churchyard between the two portal yew trees and found Mairi's headstone, in the shadow of which she placed her spray of flowers, or when these were not available from the garden at Inchcombe a knot of evergreen. They could not guess, coming later for regulation prayers, what her motives were in doing this and ascribed to her action the superficial respect of niece to aunt, or the more righteous among them read it as an apology from the unhallowed woman to the sanctified one whose place she usurped. They might have been more impressed if she had adopted the old pew and sat through sermons, but she would slip out of the back gate before the minister Galbraith or anyone else of good intentions tried to persuade her inside. Pantheist, she worshipped outdoors. On her homeward journey, however, she could rejoice that formalised religion left some tangible evidence above ground which time or distance could not blur. She revered neither her aunt nor her predecessor specifically, but ancestry in general. Rab and Hannah, the scattered ashes from her mother's cremation, the remote cairn of her father, were beyond her reach and it was in memoriam for all of these that she laid her wreath.

Rejean flew back briefly at the end of the summer. He had been attending a conference in Geneva on forestry techniques, organised by the United Nations Agriculture and Fisheries Agency, and travelled over to visit them for two or three days when it was finished.

When he and Alexis arrived back from the airport they found Esme and the baby installed in the garden. Basket chairs were set in a circle in the shade of the oak tree, for the heat of the season continued cruelly into September, mixing summer and autumn incongruously. The leaves had started to colour earlier than normal, not so much from a premature nip in the air as from dehydration. Heavy dews at nightfall helped the surface rooting plants stay green, but Rejean noticed the dry rustling overhead, though the sky was permeated with the intense blue of mid-summer.

Rising out of her chair to greet him she was another anomaly. She was wearing a white linen dress to which he couldn't affix a specific date. It might well have been a nightgown belonging to Alexis' mother she'd shaken out of a press and thought, This is too good to lie unused. In it she appeared Edwardian; or Grecian if she tied fillets round the bodice, or Empire with her hair bound up; or a space-age maiden from the year 2000, stripped of ornament – and might be all of these women another day. He remembered Alexis telling him once, when they talked about spinning natural threads, that flax had the unique property of shedding a layer of its surface each time it was washed so that the fibre was constantly renewed and durable beyond anything that man could make. He felt it, feeling her in his arms again, clean, cool and simple.

Alexis receded a little into the shade with a pad and paper, and let them take the pleasure of each other's company unimpeded. As he went on with his jotting, outlining on the page the static movement of a hand or the detail of faggoting on the hem of her dress, he listened to them review names and places together, and thought, How animated she is with the young man. She doesn't see enough young people. She doesn't see enough people. But the savage jealousies he experienced the evening of the dance had burned themselves out. He did not worry. He did not think her fickle but was able to consider dispassionately the friends he ought to introduce her to, the men who'd talk to her and bring that light into her eye. He mustn't let her grow over-serious with herself.

The baby was a diversion. Rejean held her while she genially trampled him, but she wasn't one to be held for long. He put her back on the ground to let her range more freely, though even then the grass wasn't a large enough territory for her explorations. One or other of them had to keep rising in turn to prevent her crawling too far out of sight, although with inherent devilment she returned again and again to the fascinating, moveable water.

To try and keep her rooted for a little longer, Rejean went and fetched one of his cases from the hallway which he deposited in front of Esme.

'You've not been buying presents?' She was stern.

'You'd only tell me to take them away again, or insist on paying me afterwards. I bought for the person who can't refuse.'

She undid the straps of the case and found it contained more toys than the nursery upstairs. 'Oh, Rejean, how long did you spend buying these?'

'One afternoon. I did the toy shops of Geneva. But the things I wanted to buy were rather advanced. They'll have to wait for another time.'

'You'll ruin her, Rejean. You mustn't be so extravagant.'

'Why not? I like playing with them too. She's an excuse to indulge myself.'

Esme had to give ground on that, as she turned the pages of a cloth book, a replica of the one she had owned herself in infancy.

He lay along the rug and meted them out one at a time to the baby. She played for a few minutes with each, the picture-covered bricks, the hoop of bells, sitting sedately like a propped doll herself. Then, after an interval, realised these were an artifice compared with the real earth and the real grass and the real wet loch, and abandoned the substitute.

'Failed again,' he sighed and rolled over on his back, watching out of the corner of one eye the hunched shape of the infant as she made with determined enthusiasm for the margin of the shingle.

Mrs Galashan brought them out tea and he sat up again.

'I've had an invitation,' he said, spreading a pancake, which was part of the cook's repertoire of assorted teabread. 'Is this your jam, Esme?'

'Yes, it is. We went out and picked the raspberries last week in Comrie. It's been a bumper crop.'

'It's very good.' He was silent, eating and spreading in turns, while they waited for him to begin again. 'It's an invitation from the Department of Forestry at Edinburgh. They want me to give a series of seminars in the winter months. Maybe ten or twelve in all. I could fit them in before and after Christmas.'

'That's interesting,' said Alexis. 'And to be invited. Was that in Geneva?'

'I'd had a letter previously, sounding me out, but there was someone I knew at the conference who backed it up. It transpires I can do what I like in effect.'

'Will you take it up?' asked Esme.

'I don't know. What do you both think? It's an honour to be asked but it's a nuisance too. Just at the moment.'

'Why a nuisance?'

'I had hoped to start another book this winter.'

'So soon?'

'Yes. I think I shouldn't leave it too long. This may get in the way.'

Alexis foresaw some phenomenon – a mobbed lecture hall, filled with students who were not necessarily matriculated in that subject, coming to listen for the sake of listening to what was lucid in the form of new ideas that probed out to the perimeters of present knowledge. He could become a cult, Rejean Simard. And so he edged him towards it, gently. 'I think it's a good opening myself. You never know what may come of it. And it's quite compatible with writing, isn't it? You can't spend four months cooped up in Inverleith, day after day. Don't you think the teaching might help you focus some of the ideas for it? You could lecture around ten or twelve projected chapters and get double mileage out of the work you're putting in. And you'd have good facilities for your own research if you were attached to the department. Somebody might actually give you an idea. That's always welcome.'

Rejean and Esme smiled, not being deceived by this eagerness.

'Yes, I thought that would be useful. I may well do it.'

'What does Aileen say?'

'Oh, she doesn't know yet.'

'What were you thinking of for the next book?' asked Esme, to cover the silence which the last remark occasioned.

'The thing this conference seemed to come back to – how to give trees the best start. The latest idea in forestry is plant food. Have you seen the new sticks of food which you push into the soil?'

Alexis said he had but Esme shook her head.

'They're about this big,' he indicated the length of his thumb, 'and contain a year's supply, phosphates and nitrates. It's in a form that is released slowly to suit the take-up rate of the root system. The most common are for vegetables. What we're looking for is something similar for trees. But ideally it should incorporate protection for saplings from deer and other predators and bad weather. If you could build the mixture into an outer casing it would be perfect. But I'm not a chemist. Somebody else will have to come up with the answer, even though I know where the answer lies.'

'Take Esme over to the Forestry Commission office tomorrow. It's time she met the Green Man. He'd be interested in that. Last time I saw him he was planting on the far side of Ben Vorlich, and worried to death about the deer stripping the bark.'

Then the telephone rang in the office behind them, and Alexis left them for a few minutes to answer it.

Esme leaned forward to Rejean's chair. 'How is Aileen?' she asked when Alexis was out of earshot. 'He's so dismayed she hasn't written and answered his letters. Should I write to her? Would it make a difference?'

'I'm dismayed too. I can't make any impression on why she feels whatever it is she feels. We don't talk about it any more.'

'And you haven't heard from Mabon?' She produced the name as though she were exhuming it.

'No. Why, did you think I would? Have you?'

She shook her head. 'He doesn't know I'm here, does he? And I'm content to leave it like that. But I did wonder if he might ask you where I was. He must be telling people something about my non-appearance.'

'What will you do if you want a divorce?'

'Why should I bother with all that upheaval?'

'It would regularise things, for people like Aileen anyway.'

'Is that what it would take to bring her round? I'm afraid she may be disappointed in me yet again. Being a common law wife suits me well enough and it's not all that unusual round here. There are a good many housekeepers and companions in disguise. I did go to see Mr Scott about it when we were last in Edinburgh, with some trepidation. I feel he knows what I'm going to say before I start. He said he thought I might lose custody of the baby if it went through a Canadian court, since I was living with Alexis and the child is obviously not his. An immoral environment, as you see. If Mabon wanted to be awkward, that is, and he might well want to be awkward. Or it could open up the whole vexed question of paternity, which I wouldn't wish on you, or on Aileen. Of course I didn't tell the lawyer about that, or how we parted.'

'Does Alexis know?'

'Oh yes. He knows everything.'

'And what does he say – about divorce?'

'It's my decision.'

'Why did I ask?'

'For all that he tries to leave it to me, I think he might like to have it settled, especially –' She heard his footsteps, and looking round saw the subject coming from the office.

'Especially?' Rejean prompted. But their eyes caught each other's straight on and communicated what there was no time to say.

To cover his confusion at this outcome, though why should he be surprised when it was to be expected, he got up and went to retrieve the baby who was now at the limit of her wanderings. Every man created and procreated. Every man but him.

Sophie had crawled down to the edge of the grass and was hesitantly pawing the shingle, afraid that the change in colour hid a pitfall. She turned her head, hearing him come up behind her and Rejean stamped his feet on the ground as though he were chasing her. This brought about the striking effect of a deep throaty laugh which was quite out of keeping with the infantile lungs that produced it. Alexis and Esme looked down and smiled, while their guest's vanity was tickled that he had an instant success in extorting her first laugh.

'Can she paddle?' he called back towards where they sat.

'Yes,' the mother gave permission.

He held the child by the arms and swung her over the water, causing breathless intakes of air and further gasps of laughter. Esme too was enchanted at the figures on the shoreline, and laughed to see him cavort like this, forgetting himself and his own gravity.

'Are you happier when he is here?' asked Alexis studying her shaded face.

'Happier? Why should I be happier? You forget happy is already a superlative for me.'

'That's a good answer, Hapax.'

She put her hand out and he took it. 'What a precocious name you call me by. I do not care to be so precocious.'

'I like it.'

'Well then,' she conceded, 'to please you.'

He kissed the ends of the fingers which emerged from his and their heads lowered an inch or two towards each other as though suddenly weighted and insupportable.

Down by the water Rejean had dispensed with his own shoes and was wading deeper with rolled up trouser legs. 'It's time you taught this child to swim, you know. She's a water baby.'

'She can't walk yet,' called Esme.

'That doesn't matter. I'll teach her to swim next time I'm over. I'll make her into a cross-Channel swimmer before I've finished.'

Esme leaned back and watched. If there was one moment she might want to photograph and preserve it was now, with the only people who finally mattered to her together in one place and in one mood. A moment of rest, a pause before they each got up and went on with what was next. After dinner, when the sun had gone down and the baby was in bed, they would talk seriously, talk that meandered over many rooms and occupations, constantly shifting. They would get to grips with their achievement, severally, discussing Rejean's book, what it said and what it didn't. The two men would argue, even heatedly, because they liked to threaten the calm surface of equanimity with just a ripple, just enough to stop it being dull, about reclaiming land, moor, polder, tundra, desert. Whether one should or shouldn't. Whether one could. And she, being entirely ignorant of course, would wonder why the hypothetical gave them so much entertainment, but listen to the contrapuntal phrasing of the passage nevertheless, intrigued because she couldn't disentangle the various notes but heard all through the hidden harmonies.

Then, when he was good and ready, when he'd won whatever it was they were intent on winning, Alexis would slew round and tell the younger man about the exhibition. A first. His first, and like all births attenuated by the fear of emergence, a chrysalis anxiety. He might show him some of the newer canvases, propelling them both out to the workshop to try on him the angles Esme had already exhausted. He would detail the rooms they had at their disposal for the showing and make Rejean give answers to the unanswerable. Should they take a room each and not mix their styles, or was it better to make groups by subject matter or tone? They all had paintings of the Hebrides and segments of Edinburgh. What sort of title would cover everything without being bland – or should they leave it at names only? He could compel a response, and having tested various opinions would take none but his own as reference.

And then, when her turn came round and they said, Right, Esme, show us what you've done, what would she have to say for herself? Not yet – again? They wouldn't let her away with that, not these two. She might stall for time and say, like the mother of the Gracchi, My children are my treasure, my accomplishment. I may achieve the great happiness with one man and these are not inconsiderable.

They'd put their heads together before they answered, No, these are not inconsiderable. We'll take them as down-payment on the rest. But really you've had long enough. You've had the education. You've had the experience. You've got that room of your own – you've had as much as we have. Now get on with it. How long are you going to keep us waiting?

To which there was no reply unless she wanted to look feeble with excuses.

So in the morning when they had dispersed to their various pursuits, Alexis to the work sheds, Rejean to the telephone, she went back upstairs to the room that was waiting for her and sat down at the bureau. How very white the white page was. How very unwritten on. A dot on it looked insignificant though, as she ran her finger down the edge of the pad, she found there was some consolation in its thickness. It would take a good few dots to fill it, but each sheet gave the opportunity for correction. The first word need not be the last. So she stepped out and wrote, without too many pauses. She launched herself on the inland voyage that would occupy the rest of her days.

And down the page there flowed a line, a rhythm that was neither marked nor regular. A wave. A current of thought that moved and shifted following impulses that were sometimes towards sound, sometimes towards idea, but always at variance with the shape she might have liked to impose on them. The words went on writing themselves. Lines, half-lines, metres tumbled down the page quite undisciplined, with ragged margins that left a pattern like a tidemark. Impossible to control.

When she had finished she sat back and looked at the rough draft. It was a start. That was the content down, a hurried approximation to what she wanted to say, but it wasn't a poem. Oh no, it was a long way short of that finality. It was fun to conceive

he idea, but now the shaping started and the real work. This was
ust uncut diamond, worthless until she put the facets on it. Form.
That was what was needed. Free verse would not do, in fact there
was no such thing for the two words were mutually exclusive, 'free'
and 'verse', or maybe like free love it was too easy to count as a
ignificant example. Chaos in masquerade. Both had to conform to
some rule, though what that rule was she couldn't say for certain.
Not rhyming pairs, emphatically enforced. The language did not
care to be tricked out in jingles, and it fought against conspicuous
rhythm too. The swell of Anglo-Saxon stayed with the line in
poetry, stressing the internal sound. So she came back in a circle to
what was nearest prose, what was open and variable. Which, then,
tidy sonnets or the random lines in front of her? Who did she most
want to please? Whose standards really mattered, hers or the
poem's or the unknown reader's who looked over her shoulder and
was stricter than either? What would the men say? Probably tell
her to scrap it and begin again, undo it line by line however
painfully until she got it right. Her heart sank a little, for she knew
how many hours would go to make things straight. She wrote the
opening lines again as if they were an ode, the fluid regularities of
which she could adhere to. She went on bracketing and adding
words for some time, but by now the ink in her pen flowed
differently and the emendations stood out as if they were their own
commentary, or a new and separate poem. Admiring this, she
became lost in thought and in the end decided nothing substantial.
In the evening she would read it to the men, and together they
would decide on form.

The doors and windows stood open, creating a through draught.
The wind took the edge of the page and fluttered it, until she
weighted it with the half pebble. The yard was busy. A van was
being loaded. Men's voices gave and took instruction and it
seemed enough to know the business of the day unfolded. When
the engine roared, a sound she might never recover from, and
petered out through the gateway along the Perth road, it left a soft
vacuum other sounds did not hurry to fill. She heard footsteps
rising to her window, the clatter of looms she became used to day
after day, and then another sound she had not heard in this place
before, had not heard for such a long time she had to concentrate to
locate it. It was whistling, carefree, impudent whistling from
human lips. The cadence rose and fell and made her smile; a minor

skill, but why did it always carry the overture of joy? You could no
whistle with a hangdog expression. The muscles automatically
took on the form of happiness. They lifted and uplifted. Curiosity
drove her to the yard side and she leaned out into the eastern
sunshine which flooded the morning. Alexis went below. Why, he
was himself trilling mirthfully. She listened to the notes he let out
into the mellow day, and wondered what the air was, a jaunty
ballad. 'Whistle o'er the lave of it' maybe, or another Burns tune,
'Whistle and I'll come to you my lad', but whatever the burden of
the songs she was glad that they were Scots at heart.

He did not look up for he knew without confirmation that she
was at the window listening and watching. Days and nights were
strangely composed. It was the banality of their life together that
thrilled him, a man and a woman under the same roof, as natural
and as consequent as the rising and the setting of the sun. It was
divine normality. At any hour, standing in the dark well of his
house he could call out, Esme, are you there? And have her
echoing reply, Yes, I'm here. What do you want. She had given
him the nearest words to this in song,

Life is our work
Home is our children
Love is each other every day

and these lines, played on her record in the quiet evenings alone,
brought back the old and almost forgotten word, helpmeet. That
was more than husband and more than wife. She was his working
partner and he hers. There was no need to allocate tasks. They
shared. In a room together they worked wordlessly through what
had to be done. Or if he caught sight of her apart, in something as
simple as hanging out the washing in the courtyard, holding the
line down to her waist with her left hand and pinning the articles
with her right, he was inspired by the recurring platitudes of the
day to day. A woman with a billowing skirt outdoors. A woman
who came round the corner laughing, tousled, full of cold fresh air
and smothered you in her arms, warm and cool in harmony. If
there was more life, more joy, more colour to be had than this
sensual sunburst, he couldn't guess what it might be. He would
have to wait for heaven or other hereafters to reveal it.